I

II

The Whisperers
and the Guardians of the Veil

Book One

Of

The Nexus Chronicles

Bryce and Destiny McLaren

Λ

Forward

This book was never written to explain everything. Some ideas aren't meant to be defined—they're meant to be felt. To spark a memory. To stir something ancient. To whisper truths you already know but haven't yet said aloud.

At its heart, this is a story born from curiosity, synchronicity, and the kind of lived experience that can't be taught—only survived, questioned, and eventually transformed. While every chapter is fictional, it's also deeply personal. The lines blur in ways we can't fully explain. And maybe they're not supposed to.

One moment in particular shaped the direction of this book more than most: a conversation with someone who reminded us that the way we perceive the world doesn't have to fit any standard to be valid. They didn't need sight to see what others often missed—and that truth made its way into the character who ultimately carries this story. That spark of inspiration led us to reimagine our main character's journey through blindness—but it was the personal experience of living with limited vision that made it immersive, textured, and real in a way that might be difficult to fully understand unless you've lived it. Visibility, after all, isn't just about eyesight. It's about presence, power, and the courage to take up space in a world that often looks the other way.

This series began with a simple idea: to explore realities that exist just beyond what we've been taught to see. Because it is through experience—lived, felt, and sometimes hard-won—that we pull the unknown into our awareness and make it real. This story is our way of inviting others to step into that liminal space with us. To wonder. To question. To remember.

We did our best to honor the sacred threads woven through this narrative—traditions, beliefs, symbols, and systems that mean something to people. We approached them with care, knowing we could never represent them all perfectly, but we could at least do so with deep respect. This is our version. Our world. Our characters. And we loved bringing them to life. We hope that as you read, you feel that energy—not just in the story, but in the spaces between it. The parts that call you to question, remember, or dream a little differently than before. Enjoy the ride.

To the dreamers, the seekers, the ones who know there is more to the story and question why they're here in a world that often feels upside down— this story is for you.

You are not alone.

You were never meant to play by their rules.

You came here to rewrite them.

VIII

-Prologue

October 1931- Wellville, Colorado

The weather had already begun to turn from bad to worse just outside the small mining town of Wellville, up in the Rocky Mountains. It was early in the season for such inclement weather. Snow poured out of the heavens but not yet sticking to the ground. The altitude was more than a mile high and with night coming on and the ground cooling, there was a likelihood that the snow would be plentiful and sticky.

Technically outside it was still daytime, although the sun would not be shining through the thick cover of clouds on this miserable day. The temperature in the air was a chilling thirty-three degrees Fahrenheit. Despite the bitter weather, a team of miners, on a well-paid contract from a man who claimed to be an agent of the Federal government, calling himself Clovis Krott. He offered a more than satisfactory offer of financial compensation and a bonus structure based upon time of completion. The dark man's papers and affairs were all in order.

The request seemed odd to tap into a dead mine that had already been extracted of all its ore. The pay was too good to refuse. The mysterious man from Portland Oregon who had shown up out of nowhere had disappeared equally quickly once the deal had been made with the mineworkers leaving only a phone number to be reached at, on a black business card that said in golden letters Oregon Allied Securities. The caveat was that he did not want to be contacted unless it was the utmost dire of emergencies or when they achieved the goal they were hired for. The terms of this contract were mutually understood and agreed upon.

The five hired men struck hard at work deep within the heart of the Earth following the work of others down a mineshaft that had yet to wield any resulting ore of value. The mysterious Clovis Krott had informed the Chief, upon hiring, that he had good reason to believe that this unproductive and near abandoned mine shaft was still holding greater treasure within. Underground the bitter howl of the wind above was little more in sound than the whisper of a church mouse. Inside the shaft, the temperature kept slightly warmer allowing the five men to keep on working throughout the afternoon and into the early evening. Their body heat helped keep them going.

At the end of the longest tunnel, the "C" tunnel, into the side of the mountain, the men smoked cheap cigars while they talked about hitting the motherload of gold or silver and their dreams about what each man would do with his share.

One man said that he would buy his own ranch out in Wyoming to raise cattle. Another said that he would blow all his money at the saloon gambling and drinking. Two agreed that they'd buy more chickens and hogs for their lands, maybe even a few cows. The last man wasn't too sure what he would do with the money for the fact that he had never actually had that much money in his entire life. Hell, he barely ever had more than two nickels to rub together in his time on Earth. It mattered little to them, although they did find it odd that the dark-skinned man dressed in all black who hired them was more interested in what was below than any kind of mineral or precious metal rights.

The miners received half their pay upfront, so they had no cause to believe there was anything afoot or amiss about their job offer. The five men paused their labors and ate lunch of dried meats, fruits, and bread washed down by water or beer. After an extended break from digging, the five resumed their task. Another hour passed with nothing more to show than a couple of empty carts of rocks. That was until one of the men hit hard against the farthest wall. A split formed wide enough to see a hole in the rock the size of a grown man's fist.

"Hey, fellas!" The scruffy man with oil and dirt-stained clothes yelled back along the tunnel at the other four of his fellow miners. "Come check this out! I think I might have found something!"

The chief in charge was first over to check on the news. "Looks like we may have struck into a cavern or something." He looked again through the small hole. "This must be what the spooks in Washington are paying us a lot of money to find."

"Well, let's find out, chief." The scruffy man replied as he bent down to retrieve his pickaxe off the ground. "No time like the present and we aren't getting paid by the hour, right?"

The chief signaled to the two of the other miners who had stopped their pursuits elsewhere to join the party staring at the crack in the rock wall. All four of the miners, with pickaxes in hand, wielded merciless blows to the rock. The wall caved inward, indeed revealing a large and expansive underground cavern. Their lanterns did little to illuminate the vast expanse they had exposed. Inside the hole came a draft of wind filled with the musty aroma of a mausoleum. "What the fuck have we gotten into?" The boss asked aloud to no one in particular.

"Would you look at that?" The quietest in the bunch said with awe in his voice as he saw broken pottery painted with Native American designs on the ground inside the hole near the wall they had just broken through.

A light could be seen a short distance away from the hole in the mine shaft, down and into the wide mouth of the cave below. It was unbelievable what they could see, a source of illumination shining hues of pink and blue. One of the miners, the man named Kevin that found the opening in the first place, took it upon himself to step over the threshold and down into the cave.

"Kevin!" The Chief shouted. "Get your ass back here! This is above your pay grade!"

Still the man continued on, and the Chief had no choice but to follow the man in, about 10 to 12 feet behind him and advancing as the two approached this anomaly, this intrusion of energy into this cavern. "Kevin!" The Chief tried again, but his words were hitting deaf ears, the miner before him, in some kind of trance as he approached the anomaly.

The other three miners watched from the hole in their mine shaft, looking down from a perch into the cavern.

"You guys need to come back!" One of them shouted to the two below.

Nothing changed. Kevin was within arm's reach of the anomaly.

"Something is going on up here! We need you both to come back!" They shouted downward.

No sooner had the words been spoken from his mouth that the fifth man ran towards them from the opposite end of the tunnel from where they were standing with a panicked look on his face.   "What's the matter, boy?" The chief asked him, looking away from Kevin for a moment back up to the hole in the mine shaft above.

"I thought I heard something." He paused. "I guess I just got freaked out."

When he turned back around, he saw Kevin touch the anomaly and in a split second there was a flash of light, and the miner was there no more. The chief, scared out of his mind, ran as fast as his overweight body could take him back to the hole in the mine shaft.

"I'm scared, Chief." "What in God's name happened to Kevin?"

"What in the hell is going on here?"

"Shh… I think I heard something." The chief interrupted the three miners that were confused and trying to get answers from him.

In the "C" tunnel, everything became quiet as the miners tried listening intently to hear what their friend had heard. After maybe a minute of silence, nothing unusual could be heard.

"It wasn't anything, man. Just probably an echo of us talking here now." One of the other miners said, feeling slightly jumpy, but trying to play it off.

"No, I swear to God I heard something." The other insisted.

"Well? One of the other miners asked argumentatively. "What was it then? Chief, where is Kevin? Where did he go?"

"He touched the light and then was just gone. I was scared so I ran back and that's when I heard it?"

"What?" The miner asked. "What did you hear?"

"I don't know, it sounded like someone was talking really soft in my ear."

The chief was about to diagnose himself as a loon, sick with the claustrophobia from being in the mine too long, but the oil lamps above head in the tunnel began flickering. One by one, the other three men caught the ear of a humming noise coming from the distance. At first the men attempted to dismiss it as being one of the adjacent tunnels caving in. As the sound grew increasingly closer and closer, the men started changing their opinions about the nature and origins of the noise. The sound grew very close now; they were able to differentiate that the sound now resembled a loud whisper.

Each man, however superstitious he may have been, was sure that it wasn't at all a good noise, and it was somehow connected with this cavern and the anomaly within that took their friend and fellow miner Kevin, dead to the world. A breeze of cold air came blowing in from the mouth of the hole at the end of the tunnel, seemingly crashing toward them. Despite the howling sound it made, the whispering sounds could still be heard as they grew louder and louder. Again, the breeze from the cavern picked up causing all the oil lamps to flicker and go out all at once leaving it completely pitch black.

Left alone in the darkness, all the remaining men's phobias were set loose to wander freely and plague them with impending claustrophobia and fear-inducing whispering. They all considered themselves to be God-fearing Christians. All four miners were on the verge of nervous breakdowns, praying that the lord Jesus Christ would relieve them from this madness and forgive them of whatever sins they may have committed. From the distance, one of the miners spotted a glowing green light. As they focused their gaze it became clear that the light seemed to be coming in the miner's direction down the tunnel, straight toward them.

One of the men yelled out, "Help! We're down here!" Evidently, he was trying to spark the attention of whoever had wandered into the tunnel with the four miners.

The mysterious green light source crept closer and closer edging its way down the passage moving slowly towards them. The men soon realized it was a group of individual lights all close to one another that gave off the illusion of one constant light source. Perhaps, they thought, it was a search party sent by those who hired them to bring the five miners out safely. Despite the light source, the whispering began to take its toll on the miners. Maybe one of the other shafts did collapse after all. It was difficult to tell, and no one wanted to walk toward the menacing lights to find out.

They peered at the green illumination coming nearer. The light split and split again and stopped at eight sets of two lights side by side. By the time the miners realized that they were indeed eyes, it was already too late. The men became surrounded by the green-eyed entities. Nothing else could be seen in the blackness. Then there was an eerie silence as they were being circled for what felt like an eternity, though it only lasted about a minute or two in total.

The sound of cloth ripping tore into the empty air followed by the familiar sound as one of the men lit a match to a makeshift torch of his torn shirt sleeve onto the wooden handle of a shovel. It cannot be said as to whether the man who carried the makeshift torch suffered a heart attack at that exact moment, the narrow tunnel lit up around the man's face as he held out his torch, his attacker could be seen. Face to face, the miner was, if he were to be so blunt, with Satan's incarnation himself. He found himself allured by the hypnotic glow of those eyes, the same way mosquitoes and other flying insects are attracted like a moth to a flame. A humanoid form could be seen in the light, but somehow, he could see through the body.

XIII

He was shaking with fear and had difficulty keeping the light steady in an attempt to understand what he was seeing before his eyes. That moment would never come. At the sight of razor-sharp blades held to the throat of his friend a fraction of a second before the torch burned no more, he shrieked in horror. The quietest man only heard the other miners scream bloody murder as if they were being torn limb from limb. The shock being all too much, all the man could allow himself to do was curl up into a fetal position on the ground with his face down praying with all his heart that God would save his soul from Satan and his angels from Hell on this less than forgiving day.

As quickly as this plague came upon the men, there was a loud hum unlike the whispering sound made by the attackers. The tunnel filled with a bright white light and then nothing. The green-eyed whispering entities were gone. The lights were all gone out and replaced by an ear deafening silence and pitch blackness. The oil lamps were rekindled of what seemed of their own accord. The bodies of the man's fellow friends could not be found as he arose from the dirt. They all had completely vanished. All that remained of the incident were bloody scraps of clothing and the words of desperation written on the wall of the tunnel in blood.

Help us!

-Chapter 1-

Echoes of the Unseen

In southern Oregon, Scarlett turned down a private key-shaped driveway stretched long and winding up toward a roundabout at the end, lined with ancient oaks whose branches intertwined overhead like watchful sentinels. By the time Scarlett arrived, the sun was sinking low, casting golden rays that flickered through the trees. As she stepped out of the car, the earthy scent of the land filled her lungs. She paused, closed her eyes, and took a slow, deliberate breath. She whispered a quiet prayer, grounding herself before stepping onto the property.

The screen door creaked, and Teddy stepped onto the porch, drawn by the sound of her arrival. He leaned casually against the railing, his arms crossed, as he watched Scarlett with mild curiosity. She hadn't yet noticed him; her attention was focused on something near the edge of the trees. Teddy followed her gaze, but to him, it looked like nothing more than shifting shadows in the golden light.

Scarlett, however, stiffened. Her fingers brushed against the beaded pouch at her side, pulling it open to retrieve a small bundle of sage and a lighter. She crouched, striking the flame with practiced ease, and waved the smoldering sage in a purposefulmotion around herself. Softly, she chanted under her breath, the words rhythmic but indecipherable to Teddy.

From his vantage point, it looked like an old Native American superstition, but the sharp focus in Scarlett's eyes suggested otherwise. She stood, turning slowly to face the house, her movements deliberate and sure, as though sealing an unseen boundary.

On the porch, Teddy tilted his head, his curiosity deepening. "What did you see?" he called out, his voice light but edged with intrigue.

Scarlett's lips pressed into a thin line, and she met his gaze for the first time. "Not what. Who," she replied, her tone even, yet heavy with meaning.

Teddy straightened, his casual posture evaporating as his gaze flickered between Scarlett and the tree line. For the first time, he wondered if the stories about the property were more than just stories.

"Well, well," he said, grinning. "Look who finally decided to grace us with her presence. I was starting to think you'd chickened out."

Scarlett opened her eyes, her gaze sweeping the house before settling on him. "Flat tire, GPS failure, and what I can only describe as interference. Something really doesn't want me here."

Teddy's smirk faltered, and he stsssssssraightened. "Well, too bad for them. You're here now."

"So, this is the place, huh?" Scarlett said, eyeing the historic B&B Teddy had talked about endlessly. He'd told her all about how he and two friends had carefully saved for years, watching the market like hawks until this perfect property finally became available. It had everything they wanted— rustic charm, loads of character, prime location, and, of course, as with any truly too-good-to-be-true deal, it was haunted.

It had been several months since they'd moved in, and the supernatural activity had ramped up to an unsettling degree. The once-quaint home was now practically vibrating with unexplained phenomena, far beyond Teddy's usual expertise in documenting the paranormal. Scarlett and Teddy shared a long history of ghost-hunting adventures, making her the first person he thought of when he found himself and closest friends to be his next big case.

The screen door creaked again as Robyn stepped out onto the porch, her presence commanding without effort, tall and athletic. Her blonde hair shimmered in the last light of the day, glowing like a halo, though the lines of worry etched across her face betrayed her unease.

She crossed her arms, the silver charm bracelet on her wrist jingling softly. Robyn's sharp blue eyes landed on Scarlett, studying her for a moment before a flicker of recognition crossed her face. "You..." she said, her tone tinged with surprise. "I don't know if you remember, but we've met before—yes? That case, the one with big house, too many doors!" Robyn gestured broadly with her hands, as if to help the memory along.

Scarlett tilted her head, her brown eyes narrowing slightly. "Right... that one was a doozy."

Robyn gave a small smile, though it didn't quite reach her eyes. "You were so busy then... I hoped maybe, one day, we would meet again. But not like this." She waved a hand vaguely at the house, the dark trees pressing close around them.

"Well, I'm here now. Let's see what we're dealing with."

Robyn accepted the handshake, her lips curving into a faint smile. "Scarlett, yes... now I remember. You look different here."

Her eyes drifted down, catching sight of the beaded pouch at Scarlett's hip. The smile faded, replaced by something sharper. "That... where you get this?"

Scarlett's hand instinctively rested over it. "It was a gift from my grandmother. She taught me how to use it."

Robyn stepped closer, her gaze narrowing. She tapped the charm bracelet on her wrist. "Same. This is not just a decoration, this is talisman. Strong one. Protect us from what we cannot see... and sometimes what we can."

Scarlett nodded. "That's why I never leave without it."

Robyn hummed, almost approving, but muttered, "Hope they work." She turned toward the door, muttering in Ukrainian, "Ya bachyla bahato vs'akogo layna, ale nichoho podobnoho do tsoho..."

Teddy tilted his head, frowning. "Robyn's one of the toughest people I know, which makes it super comforting when she starts saying stuff none of us can understand."

A voice from beyond the screen door chimed in, "She said she's seen a lot of messed-up shit... but nothing like this."

Robyn smirked slightly. "Exactly."

Scarlett's hand brushed the pouch at her side. "These things... they work because of belief, because we care for them. Neglect them, they fade."

The door creaked open, and through it a small blind woman stepped out, her cane tapping lightly against the wood before finding the porch. Her dark curls framed a calm, curious face. Mid-twenties, unassuming—but grounded. She moved with a quiet confidence that she didn't need eyes to feel the space around her.

Robyn's face softened immediately. "There you are."

They did everything together—nearly inseparable. Though strictly BFFs, each called the other her "Wifey for Lifey." Both were, somehow, still single. Kiara was quietly hetero, Robyn unapologetically not, her past full of shadows she rarely spoke of. Kiara was the only one who knew.

The thick brown curls on Kiara's head shifted slightly, her face calm but curious.

"You done muttering ominous things out here?" she asked dryly, amusement tugging at her lips. "You're making it sound like I dragged you onto a horror movie set."

Robyn was at her side in an instant, guiding her elbow even though Kiara clearly didn't need it. "Maybe because it feels like one," Robyn muttered, her eyes darting toward the trees, tense.

Kiara sighed, tolerating Robyn's fussing with the patience of someone who had long since resigned herself to it. "It's fine. There's nothing here but creaky floors and some weird drafts." She paused, her lips curving into a small, knowing smile. "But I appreciate your concern. Really, I do."

Scarlett observed the interaction with quiet interest, noting the balance between Robyn's protective nature and Kiara's composed independence. There was something unspoken between them, a mix of trust and exasperation that only came with deep familiarity.

Teddy smirked from his spot on the railing. "Well, if it is a horror movie, at least we've got a solid team for it. Scarlett Littlehorn is the Spirit Talker. If anyone can sage the bad vibes away, it is her. Robyn can yell at the ghosts in Ukrainian, and Kiara—well, you'll probably just sass them into submission."

Kiara chuckled softly, shaking her head. "That sounds about right."

Scarlett nodded and followed them in. The air in the house was heavy, dense with energy that clung to the walls like cobwebs. It wasn't just one presence, it was many, layered upon each other, restless and watching. Kiara sat on the couch, her walking stick resting beside her. Her dark curls framed a face that was calm yet guarded. She turned her head slightly, her unseeing eyes following the sound of Scarlett's footsteps.

"Scarlett," she said with a faint smile. "It's nice to finally meet you."

"And you, Kiara," Scarlett replied, her voice steady and warm. She placed a hand briefly on her chest, a gesture of respect, before sitting across from her. "Robyn, Teddy," she added with a nod.

Robyn and Teddy sat on either side of Kiara, flanking her protectively. The air between them was thick with unspoken worry. Scarlett leaned forward, her tone measured but probing. "I need to ask you a few things, Kiara. And I need you to be honest."

Kiara tilted her head slightly, confused but cooperative. "Go ahead."

Scarlett set down a hand recording microphone in the middle of the table and pressed RECORD.

"Have you felt... unsettled here? Heard things? Sensed anything unusual?"

Kiara hesitated, her fingers curling around her walking stick. "Sometimes. Little noises—static, whispers, maybe the wind. I feel like I'm being watched sometimes, and things I know I put away always come up missing when I go to find them. But I doubt it is anything that can't be explained."

Scarlett's brow furrowed. "Static?" She turned toward Robyn and Teddy. "Have you had the property cleansed?"

Robyn sighed, her accent thickening. "We had it sprayed for bugs so many times, they stop charging us. Nothing to spray for, but they still come. Waste. We don't want that."

Teddy snickered. "Not unless you want us glowing in the dark."

Scarlett allowed a small smile, placing her palm lightly on the coffee table, eyes closing. "This land carries a lot of history," she murmured. "Everything leaves an imprint. Kiara, have you noticed if it's worse in some places?"

Kiara shifted. "Not really..." she started, but Robyn cut in, her voice sharper.

"Not true. You told me about bedroom. We never fight before, but since this house? Always tension, anger."

"You think that's because of this house?" Scarlett asked.

Robyn shook her head, frustrated. "We wanted warm home. Loving, safe. But this place? It is dark. Heavy. I feel it. All around. No wonder the place was so cheap."

Teddy grinned, raising a hand. "Robyn, no need for the thick accent— we get it. Everyone's just a little spooked."

Robyn narrowed her eyes at him, her lips twitching into a mischievous smirk. Without warning, she gave his arm a playful smack. "You think this is funny, yes?" she said, mock-stern, her voice carrying the exaggerated lilt of her accent.

Teddy laughed, dodging another half-hearted swipe. "Oh, come on, you know I love it when you get all feisty. Adds character. RAWRRR" Playfully, Kiara groaned, shaking her head with a small smile. "Trust me, I've seen weirder." She gave a small shrug. "This? This just feels like home."

Scarlett chuckled softly, watching the scene unfold. "Honestly, it's good you're so close. And that you can still joke around. This place is definitely... heavy." Her smile faded slightly as she glanced toward the walls, her gaze lingering as if she could see the energy pressing against her. "Feels like it's weighing down on me already."

The playfulness between Robyn and Teddy paused, both of them exchanging a glance that seemed to acknowledge Scarlett's words. Teddy has a tender heart and a pleasant demeanor, rarely getting upset or insisting on having his way, conceding to his friend. Totally NOT a diva. Kiara and Robyn could tell right away upon meeting him that he was very much a mama's boy. Beyond his two friends whom he adored spending time with, Teddy found enjoyment in cooking, partying, and drinking; Ever the entertainer, he was exceedingly good at all, with a quick wit that never let the opportunity for a good time go to waste. They all knew that he was often the life of the party. Like Robyn, he is extroverted and actively takes a role in pulling Kiara, sometimes kicking and screaming out of her indoor nest that she had decorated so homely and intricately.

"A bird needs to fly." He had told her on several separate occasions. He knew that Kiara always appreciated it in the end, but getting from A to B was sometimes a difficult challenge. "Fly, little bird, fly."

Scarlett broke the silence with a question. "So, where are the bedrooms?"

Teddy gestured over his shoulder. "Mine is downstairs, right off the den. Robyn and Kiara are up on the top floor."

Scarlett raised an eyebrow. "You let the blind woman sleep on the top floor?"

Kiara laughed, a dry chuckle. "I count steps. I can go anywhere on this property safely... okay, maybe not past the maintenance shed. But upstairs? Feels safer. And I don't exactly need handrails to know where I'm going." Her smile was easy, practiced.

Robyn grinned, ruffling her hair. "She's stubborn, like I say. Tell her 'don't do'? She does."

"Damn right," Kiara shot back. "I don't break that easy."

Teddy tilted his head. "So... that stuff about talking to animals—is that real?"

Kiara shrugged, almost amused. "Not like Disney-princess real." She tapped her cane lightly. "It started after my accident. I think I just... learned to listen, I had to. When you listen, you notice the subtle things.

The way something moves, the feel of the air. Sometimes I get these flashes, or a vibe, I guess. I don't know. It's not like I sit around having conversations with squirrels."

Teddy looked half-impressed, half-lost. "But it happens?"

"Sometimes." She gave him a sideways smile. "It's just one of those weird things. I don't overthink it."

Robyn nudged her again. "She say it different first time."

Kiara groaned. "Nope, not doing that." She shook her head, still smiling.

Scarlett, silent until now, watched them closely. Her eyes lingered on Kiara, thoughtful. The way she spoke about it—so casual, like it was nothing—but it wasn't nothing. There was more to her. Something deeper, something just out of sight.

Robyn grinned, nudging Kiara. "You should hear how she talks about it. First time she told me, she was like, 'It's no big deal... just thug life.'" She laughed, shaking her head. "Sounded like my babushka, if babushka had attitude."

Kiara chuckled. "She did not say 'thug life.'"

"Not exactly." Robyn winked.

Teddy waved his hands. "Okay, okay, let me hear the real story. You've got animals lining up to chill with you? How does that even happen?"

Robyn lit up. "Few months ago, I find her down by the lake—just sitting there, quiet, still. And around her? Deer, birds, squirrels... all just hanging out. Like some enchanted forest crap." She shook her head, smiling. "Weirdest thing I've ever seen—but beautiful too."

Teddy raised an eyebrow, half teasing. "What, you casting spells down there, Kiara?"

Kiara shrugged, brushing it off. "Nah. I was just... sitting. Thinking. They came over, that's all."

Robyn added, softer now. "She was making these sounds—gentle, like singing but not words. They stayed until she noticed me. Then, poof, gone."

Teddy looked between them, amused but curious. "And what'd you say after all that?"

Kiara smiled. "I told her they just wanted to meet us. I dunno, I got the vibe they thought we were the ones living in the creepy house."

Robyn laughed, the memory hitting. "I forgot about that! Can you believe it? Even the animals think our house is scary." Scarlett smiled at the exchange, feeling a small sense of relief in the warmth between the three of them. But the weight of the house still loomed, pulling her attention back to the task at hand. Her smile faded, replaced by a look of quiet determination. "Let's take a closer look around."

They moved from the sitting room into the grand foyer, which was the first thing to draw Scarlett's eye. The chandelier overhead sparkled faintly, its crystals catching the late afternoon light streaming through the tall windows. It was an elegant, almost otherworldly centerpiece, but there was something about the way it hung—heavy, commanding, as though it had watched over the house for centuries.

"That's original, isn't it?" Scarlett asked, nodding toward the chandelier.

Robyn smiled faintly, her fingers brushing over the banister of the staircase. "Yes. One of the few things we didn't have to restore. Everything else—" she gestured toward the polished wood of the staircase— "well, let's just say time was not kind."

"Or fire," Teddy chimed in from behind them. He pointed to a section of the staircase railing where the grain of the wood didn't quite match. "The stairs had to be rebuilt after a fire in the early 1900s. They did their best to salvage parts, but, you know..." He shrugged. "Not everything could be saved."

Scarlett ran her hand lightly along the banister, feeling the coolness of the wood. Her gaze drifted upward, following the staircase as it curved to the second floor and disappeared toward the top floor. "What about the rooms above? Were they damaged too?"

"Not all of them," Teddy said, hesitating. "But the... uh, larger suite on the second floor and the one directly above it had to be gutted. The fire started there, apparently."

Robyn folded her arms, her lips pressing into a thin line. "It's a miracle the chandelier didn't come crashing down with everything else. Maybe it's a sign of good luck."

Scarlett tilted her head, her gaze lingering on the chandelier. "Or resilience," she murmured, her fingers brushing over the banister again.

As they continued their walk through the house, Scarlett's attention flicked to the details others might overlook—the faint scorch marks on the ceiling near the grand staircase, the way the floor creaked more loudly in certain places as though the wood carried the weight of what it had endured.

When they reached the second floor, Scarlett slowed her steps, letting the group move ahead while she lingered. The hallway stretched long before her, lined with several doors on either side. She paused near one, the frame slightly warped, as though it had been replaced or re-settled more recently than the others.

"This one here," Scarlett asked, her voice even, her eyes narrowing slightly. "It's one of the rooms that was rebuilt?"

"That's right." Robyn nodded without looking back. "It's... bigger than the others. Used to be the main bedroom, I think."

Scarlett touched the door lightly, her fingers brushing the smooth wood. As she pushed it open, the air seemed to shift, growing heavier and thicker. Her gaze moved upward, landing on the faint patchwork of newer plaster on the ceiling. The room felt still, but not empty.

She stepped inside slowly, her movements deliberate, trailing her fingers along the smooth wood of the bed frame. Something about her posture changed—alert yet distant—as she paused near the center of the room. Robyn watched her from the hallway, her brow furrowed. "Scarlett?" she prompted, her voice uneasy.

The spirit talker did not respond right away. Her head tilted slightly, her attention caught by a faint chill that seemed to radiate from above. Her fingers grazed the wall nearest the bed, lingering on the cool surface before turning back toward the hallway. "Let's go," she said softly, her tone firm but distracted. "I need to see what's upstairs."

Without waiting for a response, she moved past Teddy, her steps quick but measured, as though guided by an unseen force. The others exchanged uneasy glances but followed her up the staircase.

This time, Scarlett led the way, her hand brushing lightly against the banister. The third floor greeted them with a quieter energy—serene, almost peaceful—but to Scarlett, it felt like the calm before a storm. Her unease deepened as they reached the landing, her steps slowing as her gaze locked onto the suite at the end of the hall. Kiara remembered Robyn closing that door, as she had always done, in a very meticulous manner so many times before.

Scarlett stopped in front of the door, her fingers hovering near the doorknob. For a moment, she stood still, her breath shallow, as though she were listening for something just beyond the threshold. "This one," she said finally, her voice low and steady. "I need to see this room."

Robyn gestured with a small flourish. "This one is ours," she said, her tone proud but thoughtful, her accent rounding the vowels. The suite was spacious, with two small adjoining bedrooms, a sitting area, and a single bathroom. It felt warm and inviting, but Scarlett couldn't shake the feeling that something was missing—or hidden.

Teddy trailed behind them, laughing nervously at the intensity on Robyn's face. "Glad I chose a room on the main floor."

"Kiara is right—it feels safest up here, yes," Robyn said, nodding firmly. "But sometimes, it sounds like… a parade is marching through."

Scarlett raised an eyebrow. "A parade?"

Robyn shrugged, giving an exasperated smile. "Footsteps. Pacing. Sometimes soft, sometimes heavy—like someone moves furniture around. But when we check, there is nothing. Just the old house making noises, no?" Her words were light, but Scarlett noticed the tension in her jaw and the way her hands fidgeted at her sides.

Scarlett stepped into the room, her gaze sweeping across the space. The warm lighting and carefully chosen decor gave it an inviting feel, but the air carried an undercurrent of tension she couldn't ignore. "I've seen the videos and pictures Teddy sent me," she said, her voice calm but measured. "The scratches, bruises… and the sounds." She looked at Robyn, her expression serious. "It makes sense now, strange as it sounds."

Robyn frowned, tilting her head. "Does it make sense? How?"

Scarlett took a deep breath, choosing her words carefully. "It seems like… something's trying to grab her. Not to hurt her, but to get her attention. Almost like it's desperate to be noticed."

Robyn's eyes widened slightly, her lips parting as if to respond, but she hesitated. Instead, her gaze shifted to Kiara's neatly made bed in the corner, then back to Scarlett. "You think it is dangerous?"

Scarlett hesitated, her fingers brushing over the beaded pouch at her hip. "Not yet," she said, her voice low. "But whatever it is, it's not going to let her ignore it."

Her attention shifted suddenly to the window. "What about the out-buildings?" she asked. "Specifically on the northwest corner of the property?"

Robyn frowned, tilting her head. "There is nothing there. You mean the northeast corner—by the shops, yes?"

Scarlett's gaze didn't waver. "Show me," she said firmly.

The group stepped outside, Scarlett leading the way with a deliberate, almost measured pace. Every few steps, she paused, her head tilting slightly, as though listening or watching something unseen. Her fingers occasionally twitched, brushing against the air as if waiting for a nudge, a sign.

They approached a weathered structure—one of the outbuildings Teddy had mentioned before. It stood crooked, almost surrendered to the creeping vines and moss that wrapped around it like nature's slow claim.

Scarlett stopped, eyes narrowing.

"This one's old, but it's not what I'm looking for," she murmured, more to herself than to them.

Teddy tilted his head. "This was the servant's quarters, right?"

Scarlett stepped forward, brushing her hand against the doorframe. "It's quieter here. Residual, not active. They lived, worked, even found joy... but it wasn't without fear, at least in the end."

Robyn hovered near Kiara, who was unnaturally still. "How do you know that?"

Kiara shook her head slowly, but her shoulders tensed. "It's... muted. Like something's holding its breath."

Scarlett's brow furrowed. She inhaled deeply, eyes closing for a moment. "They're telling me this isn't where it happened. Not the worst of it."

She turned, stepping back from the building, then looked toward the thick brush beyond.

"My guides are leading us this way…" she directed the group. "They want me to go further," she said quietly, her voice tinged with something more than certainty. She glanced sideways at Kiara. "Not just mine. Yours, too."

Kiara blinked. "Mine?"

Scarlett's lips twitched, almost a smile, but not quite. "You're helping. Even if you don't know how."

Without waiting, Scarlett moved off the path, her steps guided by something unseen. The undergrowth seemed to part around her as she cut through the brush.

"Scarlett?" Teddy called. "The shops are the other way."

"Not there," she replied, her tone distant, but sure. "This way."

They followed her through the dense foliage until a structure emerged—half-swallowed by the forest, sagging, its shape barely discernible beneath moss and decay.

Scarlett stopped abruptly. "This is it."

She stepped closer, her hand grazing the wood. The air grew thick, heavy, like the ground itself was remembering.

"It was meant to be hidden," she murmured. "And forgotten."

Teddy lingered a few steps back, eyeing the place warily. "Okay, but this definitely feels like tetanus territory."

Robyn rolled her eyes. "Really?"

Scarlett turned back, more focused now. "It's safe. For now. Our guides—yours and mine—say it's okay to go on. But it won't be easy."

Kiara hesitated. "I don't want to hold everyone back."

"You're not," Scarlett said, reaching for her. "You help me see more clearly. Let me guide you."

Scarlett's hand met Kiara's, her touch steady, grounding. Kiara flinched slightly, breath catching, but didn't pull away.

"You feel it, don't you?" Scarlett asked softly. "When I met you, I knew. There's more to you than you let on. They're showing me... we're supposed to do this together."

Robyn watched, wide-eyed, as Scarlett's gaze drifted—unfocused but intense. For a moment, the moonlight seemed to catch something in Scarlett's eyes, casting them in a strange blue glow. Or was it something more?

Robyn swallowed, unsure. Something was happening, but she couldn't explain it.

Kiara didn't answer, but her grip tightened.

They circled the building, Scarlett's steps purposeful, despite the tangle of weeds clutching at their legs. On the far side, a crooked door hung open on rusted hinges. Scarlett nudged it, revealing a narrow staircase descending into darkness. She turned back, her eyes sharp, but kind.

"You don't have to come."

Teddy scoffed, crossing his arms. "And miss all the creepy fun? Nah. I'll just, you know... not touch anything."

Scarlett gave him a faint smirk and led the way down. The air shifted as they descended—cooler, damper, thick with the scent of rot and earth left untouched for decades.

The basement felt frozen in time—rows of cots lined the walls, rusted lanterns dangled precariously, and forgotten relics lay scattered, their edges dulled by layers of dust.

Scarlett ran her fingers over one of the cots, her voice low and reverent. "This was where they lived. Before."

Kiara took a tentative step forward, her breath catching in her throat. Her hand brushed lightly over the back of a chair, but her focus had already drifted beyond.

"I can hear them..." Her voice trembled. "Crying. Laughing. Yelling. All at once."

Robyn moved to her side, alarmed. "Kiara?"

"I'm fine," she whispered, but her eyes glistened with unshed tears.

Scarlett placed a hand gently on her shoulder. "You're hearing their echoes. They've been waiting a long time."

Kiara nodded, barely breathing. "And the fear."

Scarlett's gaze deepened. "Yes. The fear."

Kiara's steps pulled her further into the room, almost without thought. Her head turned slightly, drawn toward an old furnace tucked into the far wall. Her hand reached out, fingertips hovering near the cold metal. "I've been here," she murmured, eyes wide. "I've seen this."

Scarlett moved closer, silent, watching her.

"I think... these were her kids," Kiara murmured, her voice far away. "They're the ones who come to me. They look... nicer dressed than the others." She paused, hand drifting toward the furnace again.

"They weren't supposed to be here. But they were hiding, laughing, running around. And then..." Kiara's fingers recoiled, her breath catching. "One of them knocked something over. A lamp? No—something already burning. They tried to stop it, but it spread. Too fast."

Scarlett's voice was barely a whisper, but steady. "It must've been the furnace. Someone's dress—or something—caught fire. It probably just went up too fast. They didn't know what to do. Next thing they knew... they were trapped."

Kiara's breath shuddered. "The staff's kids too. All of them. They tried to hide it, tried to stop it—but they couldn't."

The silence was thick, clinging like smoke in their lungs.

Scarlett turned slowly, her eyes lingering on the crumbling walls. "There were two buildings," she said softly. "Now I see why they wanted this one forgotten."

Teddy crossed his arms, glancing uneasily between Scarlett and the shadows. "Brett and Sydney Chase didn't mention any of this. I mean, seriously—this place? Not exactly your average fixer upper."

Robyn gave him a sidelong glance. "And you are just figuring this out now?"

Scarlett ignored the exchange, her focus sharp as her gaze swept the area. "The fire didn't just destroy the building—it left its mark on everyone tied to it." Her voice dropped, as though she were speaking more to herself than to the others. "But this… this goes deeper. The fire wasn't the start. Something was already here, long before the first stone was laid. Something that fed into what happened."

Back at the house, Scarlett's fingers trailed along the edge of a charred beam, its polished surface doing little to hide the deep, ancient scars beneath.

"This place doesn't just hold pain—it cultivates it. Twists it. What started as healing... turned into something else. Something that fed on suffering."

Robyn's voice was tight, the air around them growing heavier. "You mean... the fire?"

Scarlett shook her head slowly. "There were two. The first took the children. The second—her. But neither was the beginning. That was just where it all snapped."

Teddy glanced around nervously. "Snapped how?"

Scarlett stepped back, eyes scanning the walls, like she could still see the shadows of what happened. "This was supposed to be a sanctuary. A retreat. But it became a prison. Starvation passed off as cleansing. Pain, called purification."

Robyn's face went pale. "They let people die?"

"They didn't believe they were dying," Scarlett said, voice low. "They thought they were purging... ascending. But when Adelaide—when she tried to stop it, when she got too close to seeing what it really was—the staff turned on her."

Kiara's breath hitched. "They killed her."

Scarlett nodded. "Locked her in. Maybe for the keys, maybe just to shut her up. Whatever the reason, something caught fire. Maybe it was desperation. Maybe revenge. But the house didn't stop burning after her. Her grief... her betrayal... it tore open something worse. It's been feeding on it ever since."

The air seemed to press in tighter.

"She's still here. Burned, broken—but clinging to the belief that she was right. That what she did was justified. And the thing that grew from her pain—it lashes out. Whenever it senses fear, anger... it feeds."

A plate hurled itself off the counter, smashing into jagged pieces on the floor.

Robyn gasped, pulling Kiara back instinctively. "This has to stop!"

Scarlett's voice cut through the tension, calm but sharp. "You can't fight it with force. And you can't feed it with fear. If we're going to help her—help any of them—we have to stay calm. Stay clear. Or it'll turn on us, just like it turned on them."

Kiara stood firm, her face pale but set. "She's hurting. I can feel it."

Scarlett nodded slowly. "And her children—they think you can help her. That's why they come to you. They're warning you, because you can feel what she felt."

She took a step closer, her voice dropping, intense. "But you can't let it in. Not for a second. That's how elementals work. They're not born good or evil. They feed on the land, on energy—like fear and pain, those are powerful surges. It draws them, twists them. And this one? It's already twisted."

Robyn's arms tightened around herself, her earlier skepticism replaced with unease. "So, all the sounds, the bruises... that is them? Trying to—what? Shake her awake?"

Scarlett nodded. "In the only way they know how. It's not aggression—it's desperation. They sense that Kiara can help. That's why it happens there, in the room she honors. It's the only place they feel safe enough to reach out."

Kiara leaned forward, her hands clasped tightly. "But how am I supposed to help them? I don't even know what I'm doing."

"You do not need to know everything right now," Scarlett said gently. "But the fact that they're reaching out to you means you've already started. Tonight, we'll focus on the house. On clearing the energy and giving them space to communicate. Once we understand what they need, we can guide them—and their mother—toward moving on."

Teddy exhaled loudly, running a hand through his hair. "So, just to recap—we've got a houseful of stuck spirits, a grieving mother that appears like a zombie corpse, and a bunch of kids trying to send us dream messages. Totally normal weekend."

Scarlett gave him a wry smile. "This isn't normal, Teddy. But it's manageable—if we work together."

Robyn glanced at Kiara, her expression softening. "Are you sure about this? I mean, we can find another way if it is too much for you."

Kiara shook her head, her voice steady despite the weight of the situation. "No. If they're trying to reach me, I can't just ignore them. We'll do it tonight."

Robyn leaned forward, her voice trembling. "Maybe it is time to sell to that developer guy who came by?"

"No," Kiara said, her voice resolute. "This house can be redeemed. I'm not leaving."

Scarlett nodded. "It's going to be more than just tonight, but in that case, you'll need to work with me. No wandering off alone, and you must learn to control your gift. If you stay, you'll have to face what's here."

Kiara agreed, determination shining through her fear. "Deal. I promise."

-Chapter 2-

The Cleansing

A couple of hours later, Robyn cleared away the last of the takeout containers from the coffee table, leaving the carefully placed camera positioned opposite the couch where Kiara had reluctantly agreed to sit. The meal had provided a welcome reprieve from the day's tension, but now, with the sun dipping below the horizon, the atmosphere thickened with expectation.

Scarlett stood by the fireplace, the warm glow casting flickering shadows across her face. "All right," she said, clapping her hands softly. "We've gone over the plan, but let's do a quick recap for the camera before we get started."Kiara sat cross-legged on the chaise lounge, running her fingers over the cool surface of the crystal pendant Scarlett had given her earlier. Robyn perched beside her, hand resting protectively on Kiara's knee, while Teddy leaned against the wall, camera in hand, ready to roll.

"Now that we know this place is active," Scarlett said, "tonight is about clearing the energy and restoring balance."Kiara gave a nervous laugh.

Scarlett kept her tone light, but Teddy caught the flicker of uncertainty in her eyes.

"I'll start outside, with Teddy following me with the camera," she continued. "Once we finish the perimeter, we'll move through each room while I perform the cleansing. Kiara, you'll stay here with Robyn and the main camera."

"Don't worry," Robyn said with a crooked grin.

"I'll keep an eye on you, KeeKee. If anything tries to sneak up on us, at least we'll have footage of our murders for posterity."

Scarlett arched a brow and handed Kiara a pair of noise-canceling headphones. "As we discussed, these will help block out external distractions so you can better hear any EVPs. Just say whatever you hear or feel—don't analyze it. The less you filter, the clearer the messages."

Kiara adjusted the headphones, drew in a steadying breath, and nodded. "Got it. Listen, don't think."

"Exactly." Scarlett squeezed her shoulder. "And if anything feels off, let me know immediately. We'll stop."

Teddy slung the camera bag over his shoulder and smirked. "Let's go cleanse some ghouls and boys."

Scarlett groaned, pinching the bridge of her nose. "That was… I'm not even going to dignify that with a response." She shook her head and straightened. "Okay, let's do this."

Scarlett gave a final nod to Kiara and Robyn before heading to the front door with Teddy trailing behind her, camera already recording. The heavy oak door creaked as it opened, releasing the warmth of the parlor into the cool night air. Outside, shadows stretched long across the frost-dappled grass beneath the pale moonlight.

Teddy adjusted the night vision settings on the camera. "Anything you're already picking up on?"Scarlett's brow furrowed. "The usual discomfort...but there's something else. Older. Like the land's holding its breath."They began a clockwise sweep around the property's perimeter, Scarlett whispering a rhythmic chant as she walked. The sage crackled, releasing a thick, earthy smoke into the cold night air.

About halfway around the house, Teddy hissed and stumbled.

"What the hell?" He twisted around, lifting the camera like a shield as though expecting someone to be behind him.

Scarlett halted mid-chant. "What happened?""Something...touched me," Teddy said, voice tight. He rubbed his shoulder, the skin beneath his jacket prickled with goosebumps. "Like cold fingers. Right here."Scarlett's gaze swept their surroundings. The hair on her arms stood despite the sage's warmth. The night was still—no wind, no sound save for their breathing and the soft crunch of leaves beneath their feet.

Then, faint as a breath on glass, a voice drifted through the air.

Teddy's eyes widened. "Did you hear that?"Scarlett gave a tight nod.

"Mark the timestamp," she said.

"Got it. Ten twenty-seven p.m.," Teddy narrated for the camera. "Unexplained whisper. Possible EVP."They took a few more cautious steps when a soft, high-pitched giggle broke through the night.

Teddy froze mid-step. "Did you—""Keep moving," Scarlett said, voice sharp.

"Noted." Teddy forced himself to step forward, angling the camera toward the sound. "Ten twenty-eight p.m. Unidentified giggling. Childlike. Will review later."Inside, Kiara shifted on the chaise. The steady hum of static offered little comfort as it blended with the crackle of the fire. The warmth of the room grew stifling, pressing down on her chest.

"You're all right," Robyn whispered. "Breathe."Kiara tried, but the static warped into something more distinct—a soft, eerie giggle that sent a chill down her spine.

Her breath caught. "Robyn... I hear giggling. Creepy ass giggling."

Robyn blinked, unsettled. "Giggling?"

Kiara nodded, gripping the cord tightly. "Yeah, and... there's something else. A voice. It said... 'Come find us.'"

Robyn's mouth went dry. She glanced nervously at the camera. "Okay...okay. Maybe Scarlett stirred something up outside. Let's... let's mark the time."

She checked the clock for Kiara. "Ten thirty-two p.m.," she whispered.

The static crackled again, and beneath it came a faint, bell-like sound. Laughter—light, airy, and close.

"They're playing," Kiara whispered, voice taking on a detached, far-away quality. "Playing hide and seek."

Robyn's breath caught. "With who?"

Kiara didn't answer. Her head slowly turned toward the fireplace. Outside, Teddy's camera caught movement along the tree line.

"Movement," he whispered. "Timestamp: ten thirty-two p.m. Could be shadow play, but—"A child's giggle cackled right beside them.

Teddy cursed under his breath and spun toward the sound.

Scarlett's chant faltered, then resumed, louder now.

"Jesus," Teddy muttered. "That was right next to me."Scarlett's jaw tightened. "It's feeding on the energy we're putting out. We need to keep going."Inside, Kiara felt restless yet anchored in her seat, as though she was exactly where she was needed, despite how uncomfortable it felt in that moment. The steady hum of static blended uneasily with the crackle of the fire. The warmth of the room grew stifling, pressing down on her chest.

"You are all right," Robyn whispered gently, her accent softening the edges of her words. "Just breathe." Kiara drew in a shaky breath, trying to focus, but the static morphed into something else—a distant, airy giggle, then another. She flinched.

"Did you hear that?" she whispered.

Robyn leaned in, "What do you hear?" she asked, lifting up one of the earphones.

"Children..." Kiara's voice trembled. "Laughing...playing... but they—" She froze, her head tilting as if straining to catch a sound only she could hear. "They're scared."

Robyn swallowed hard. "Scared? Of what?"

The static cracked, followed by a faint, fragile voice. "Please...help us..."

Kiara gasped, whispering, "They want help... they're trapped."

Robyn's expression hardened, but her voice stayed calm. "We help. Yes? We will help."

The tapping started next—a soft, uneven rhythm against glass. Robyn turned sharply toward the fireplace mirror, her breath hitching as she clutched the camera tighter.

"Kiara?" Robyn's voice wavered. "What is—"

Kiara's lips parted, her voice distant and airy. "They were hiding..." she whispered, then paused as if listening. Her tone shifted higher, fragile and childlike. "We want to go home... but... someone's coming..."

Robyn's heart pounded. "Kiara, that's not funny," she whispered harshly, stepping closer. "Who's coming?"

Kiara's head tilted slightly, and her voice trembled, mimicking the children's. "Mama's coming... she's lost... help her... please help her..."

"Kiara..." Robyn's voice cracked, panic creeping in. She knelt beside Kiara, gently shaking her shoulder. "It's me, babe. Come back."

Kiara's breath quickened, her voice dipping into something deeper, almost pleading. "She doesn't want to be like this... but the pain... it's too much..."

Robyn's stomach clenched. "Nope. Nope. Not okay." She reached for the headset, fingers brushing the padded earpiece. "We're done. I'm pulling you out."

As her hand grazed the headphones, Kiara's hand shot up, startlingly precise despite her blindness. She slapped Robyn's hand away, her grip unrelenting as she clutched the headphones tighter. Robyn gasped, stumbling back.

"Kiara?" Robyn whispered, voice trembling. "How did you...?"

Kiara's head jerked back slightly as a low, guttural whisper crawled from her lips. "She broke... we broke... we all burn... we burn..."

Robyn's eyes widened in panic. "Kiara, stop. You're scaring me. Please."

Her free hand fumbled for the radio. "Scarlett! Get in here! Now!"

Outside, Scarlett's chant faltered, sensing the shift in energy. She exchanged a worried glance with Teddy.

"Did you feel that?" he whispered, adjusting the camera toward the woods.

Scarlett nodded, voice tight. "Something's stirring... and it's close."

Robyn's stomach flipped. "Kiara?" she prompted, voice careful.

Kiara didn't respond. Her eyes had lost focus, pupils dilated as though looking through the room rather than at it, unfocused and glassy, as if staring into a void that no one else could see.

Robyn inhaled sharply and returned her attention to the camera feed. The mirror above the fireplace reflected Kiara's slack expression, the flames below casting her face in shadow.

Kiara's voice softened again, taking on a childlike timbre, barely above a whisper. "We hid when the bad came..." Her lips curled into the ghost of a smile. "We used to play in the woods... before the ground shook. Before it came."

Robyn's fingers clenched around the camera. "Before what came?" she whispered, dread curling in her stomach.

Outside, Scarlett's chant faltered again. She met Teddy's eyes. "They're talking through her," she murmured.

Teddy's grip tightened on the camera. "I thought kids' laughter was creepy," he muttered. "This is worse.""Mark it," Scarlett instructed, her voice strained but steady.

"Timestamp: 10:37 p.m. Subject vocalizing in childlike voice. Reference: 'bad came' and 'ground shook.'"Scarlett resumed her chant, voice sharper now, as if trying to slice through the thickening tension. They reached the back porch steps when the wind shifted, carrying with it the acrid scent of scorched earth.

Teddy coughed and wiped his sleeve across his nose. "That's not from your sage, is it?""No," Scarlett said, voice tight. "That's coming from the ground."Inside, Kiara's breathing quickened, shallow and uneven. Her head jerked toward the mirror as if drawn by an unseen force.

"Robyn," Kiara whispered, but the voice that came out wasn't hers. It was older, brittle with fear, each word cracking under the weight of anguish.

Robyn's heart raced. "Kiara? Who's speaking?" she asked, forcing calm into her voice despite the panic clawing at her chest.

The muscles in Kiara's neck twitched violently, her head lolling to one side, eyes still unfocused. When she spoke again, her voice was stronger, cold, and weighted with unfamiliar authority.

"I tried to warn them…" Kiara said, the words ragged as though dragged from deep within. "The land was never ours to claim."

Robyn's gaze flicked toward the mirror, and her breath caught in her throat. Behind Kiara's reflection stood the faint outline of a woman in a long dress, her face pale and drawn, eyes hollow but intense.

"Scarlett," Robyn hissed into the radio, panic making her accent thicker. "You might want to get in here. Now."

Scarlett's voice crackled in response, tight with urgency. "We're finishing the outer perimeter."

"Forget it," Robyn shot back, voice rising. "Kiara's channeling someone named Adeline. And she's talking about the land."

Scarlett's chant faltered for the third time. She looked at Teddy, eyes wide. "We need to move."

Inside, Kiara's voice dropped to a hoarse whisper, the sound sending chills down Robyn's spine.

"It woke when the earth shook," she rasped, each word jagged and raw. "It does not forgive. Does not forget."

The flames in the fireplace roared higher, licking at the stone mantel like angry tongues, casting erratic shadows across the room.

Robyn stood frozen, torn between staying with Kiara and fleeing the room. The crack in the mirror spiderwebbed outward, the woman's reflection growing sharper with each fracture, her eyes locked on Robyn.

"Scarlett!" Robyn shouted into the radio, voice cracking. "It's here!"

Robyn stood, torn between staying with Kiara and fleeing the room. The crack in the mirror spiderwebbed outward, the woman's reflection growing sharper with each fracture.

"Scarlett!" Robyn shouted into the radio. "It's here!"Kiara's body tensed, her head tilting as a low, distorted voice oozed from her lips. "It was never hers... the land remembers... and so do I."Robyn's heart pounded. "Who are you?"Kiara's voice flickered between two tones—one fraught with anguish, the other cold and ancient. "She returned... twisted by her grief... but what she brought with her... defiles me."The flames flared violently, casting elongated shadows that seemed to reach for them.

"She fed the land with blood," Kiara whispered, her eyes glassy. "Her sorrow... her madness... soaked into the roots, the stone, the air."Robyn swallowed hard, her voice cracking. "Adeline?"A guttural laugh rattled from Kiara's throat. "Adeline is lost... hollowed by her choices... bound by them. But I am not bound by her."Robyn's hands trembled as she clutched the camera tighter. "What do you want?"Kiara's mouth twisted into a grim, detached smile. "I am older than your kind... indifferent to your suffering. But her stain... it corrupts me. She must be bound... to where she was burned alive...."The temperature in the room plummeted as Kiara's body convulsed, her head snapping toward Robyn with eerie precision.

"Only the soul that walks in darkness and light can cross her over. Outside, Scarlett and Teddy raced toward the front door, their breaths visible in the chilling air.

Inside, Robyn lunged forward, trying to pull the headphones from Kiara's head, but Kiara swatted her away, unseeing eyes locked on the fireplace. Her voice softened to a broken whisper.

"Help her...... only then will the land forgive.""The mirror cracked further, a deep, haunting hum resonating from within.

Scarlett burst through the door, chanting fervently, but Kiara's voice overpowered her for a moment, guttural and raw. Scarlett dropped to her knees beside Kiara, chanting louder, her voice shaking the walls.

Teddy flung salt along the doorways as Kiara's lips formed one final whisper.

"The vessel's soul... must guide her... or I will cleanse it all, I will sanctify the land... with fire."With a final pulse of energy, the shadows surged toward the floor beneath them, retreating into the master suite below.

Kiara gasped, her body going limp and starting to convulse as Robyn caught her.

Scarlett exhaled shakily. "We need to finish this."Kiara's ragged breathing filled the room as Robyn cradled her, whispering soothing words that trembled with her own fear. Scarlett pressed her hand firmly to Kiara's chest, grounding her with steady energy as she continued her incantation.

The air thickened, the shadows in the corners of the room pulsing like a slow heartbeat. Teddy circled the perimeter, scattering more salt, his hands shaking as the camera hung forgotten around his neck.

Kiara's eyelids fluttered, and a final, raspy whisper escaped her lips. "She's waiting..."

The words hung in the air as the flickering fire settled into a low, steady burn. The mirror, now shattered into jagged shards, vibrated once more before falling silent.

Scarlett's voice softened as she finished the cleansing, her body sagging with relief and exhaustion. She met Robyn's wide eyes. "We have to seal her in that room. Tonight."

Robyn nodded, holding Kiara close. "How? She's barely hanging on."

"We'll help her," Scarlett replied firmly. "We have no choice."

Suddenly, Kiara gasped, clutching Robyn's hand. Her voice, barely audible, murmured, "The land... it forgives... but it's watching."

A chill crawled down Scarlett's spine. She turned to Teddy. "Grab the gear. We're going upstairs."

Teddy's voice cracked. "Tonight?"

Scarlett's eyes were hard. "Is that a joke or a question?"

"I don't want to go up there!" Teddy retorted, glancing toward the dark staircase leading to the upper floors.

"Neither do I," Scarlett admitted, her voice steady despite the tremor in her chest. "But if we don't... none of us are leaving this place."

Robyn helped Kiara to her feet, whispering, "We've got you, Kee-Kee."

As they approached the grand staircase, the old wooden steps groaned beneath their weight, each creak amplifying the thick silence around them. The air grew heavier, laced with the faint, unmistakable scent of smoke and charred wood.

"Not an option," Scarlett whispered back.

They ascended; the soft thud of their footsteps lost in the deafening quiet. Shadows danced along the walls, stretched and distorted by the flickering light. Kiara, leaning on Robyn, whispered under her breath—words not meant for the living.

"Adeline... waiting... she knows." Kiara's breath hitched as she froze once again. She clutched Robyn's arm with surprising urgency. "Go back," she whispered softly, her voice barely audible. "Back to the nursery... it's safe there."

Scarlett froze mid-step, her eyes narrowing. "Who are you talking to?"

Kiara's head tilted slightly, as though listening to something no one else could hear. "The children... I'm telling them to go back... to the nursery."

Robyn's brows knitted together. She felt her pulse quicken as the realization crept over her. The nursery... upstairs...

Her mind flicked back to their first night in the house, how Kiara had instinctively chosen the east wing of the third floor. She couldn't see. She had no way of knowing. Yet that was exactly where the nursery had been—a space meant to protect, to nurture.

Robyn's throat tightened, her Ukrainian accent thickening as she whispered, "Bozhe moy... Of course. That is why you chose it, Kiara... navit koly ne bachaesh, even when you cannot see... you feel them."

Kiara's voice softened, distant and fragile. "They're waiting for us there."

Teddy swallowed hard, his flashlight beam flickering along the staircase. "I swear, if one more ghost kid giggles, I'm fucking out."

At the top of the stairs, the narrow hallway loomed, its faded wallpaper peeling like ancient skin. The door to the nursery, slightly ajar, creaked on its hinges.

Scarlett raised a hand, signaling silence. Before their eyes, the door to the master suite at the end of the hall slammed shut with a deafening thud.

Teddy's breath hitched. "Okay...that's not good."

Scarlett's eyes narrowed. "She's trying to stop us."

The hallway stretched endlessly before them, each step a hollow echo. The faded wallpaper seemed to peel further as they advanced, curling away from the walls like dead skin. The temperature plummeted with every footfall, their breath visible in the dim light.

Scarlett clenched her jaw, quickening her pace. The closer they got, the heavier the air became, pressing down on them like an invisible weight. As they reached halfway down the hall, a sudden gust of icy wind shot through, extinguishing the last flickering candle on the wall.

Then, without warning, Adeline appeared—no longer just a flickering shade but fully formed, her face contorted with rage and hollow torment, eyes wide with malice. Her spectral hands clawed at the air, lunging directly at Scarlett.

Scarlett gasped, staggering back, her arms thrown up in defense as a blood-curdling scream tore from her throat. She could feel icy claws grazing her skin, the weight of something unseen pressing against her.

But Teddy kept walking, completely unaware of Adeline's assault. He turned around at Scarlett's scream, brows furrowed. "What's—?"

Scarlett's breath hitched as she realized—there was nothing there. Or was there? She trembled, lowering her arms, but the sensation lingered. She felt raw, exposed, and a sting along her forearms burned where her hands had shielded her face.

"Scarlett?" Teddy asked, confused.

Her eyes darted to the master suite door just as it slammed shut again, the resounding thud vibrating through the narrow hallway.

"Grab the door!" she shouted, panic sharp in her voice.

Teddy, startled, lunged forward, catching the handle just in time. The unseen force fought against him, trying to push the door closed, but he gritted his teeth, muscles straining. "I swear... this house... hates me!" he grunted through clenched teeth.

Scarlett bolted forward, slipping through the barely open door as Teddy held it with all his strength. The moment she was inside, she felt the weight of the room's energy pressing down on her—suffocating, hot, and furious.

Adeline's distorted figure flickered in the far corner, twisted and monstrous, her jagged mouth stretched into an unnatural snarl. The room seemed to pulse with her rage, every shadow lengthening, reaching.

Scarlett's heart pounded, but she steeled herself, whispering fiercely under her breath as she reached into her bag for the salt.

"I need... I need to do the whole room," she muttered, realizing with dread that she'd have to walk every inch of the space.

Teddy's voice, strained from the hallway, called out, "Make it fast!"

Scarlett poured a steady line of salt along the doorframe first, then began her slow, deliberate path around the room, chanting under her breath as she moved. Each step brought her closer to Adeline's corner, where the twisted figure watched with dark, unblinking eyes.

As Scarlett approached the windows, her hands shook. She reached into her pouch for the consecrated ash, pressing symbols against the glass with trembling fingers, whispering prayers and incantations.

Adeline's mouth opened wide in a silent scream, her form flickering violently as if the light from Scarlett's markings burned her.

"You are bound to where you burned," Scarlett hissed through clenched teeth, voice growing stronger with each word. "Until you're ready to cross, you cannot leave!"

Adeline lunged again, flickering out of sight just before reaching Scarlett, but the door shuddered violently as she tried to trap Scarlett inside. Teddy groaned, pushing back harder, sweat dripping down his temples.

"Scarlett!" Robyn's voice called from the hall, frantic. "Hurry!"

Scarlett traced the last symbol on the final window, completing the barrier. She turned sharply, eyes blazing. "Adeline, you are done!"

The spectral figure reappeared, but this time she was crawling—her twisted form scaling the ceiling with unnatural speed, joints bending at impossible angles. Her eyes gleamed with malice as she scuttled silently above Scarlett, waiting.

Scarlett, breathless and focused, emerged from one of the suite's side bedrooms, the final symbol traced onto its window. She turned toward the door—but froze. She felt it before she saw it. A shift in the air, a shadow moving where it shouldn't.

Her eyes darted upward.

Adeline's contorted face hovered inches from hers, mouth stretched wide in a soundless scream. Scarlett's heart stopped, then lurched into a frantic rhythm.

"Shit," she whispered.

Adeline lunged.

Scarlett bolted for the door, her boots skidding against the wooden floor as she sprinted. Teddy, still bracing the door open, yelled, "Scarlett, MOVE!"

She dove through the narrow gap just as Adeline's clawed hand swiped at the space where she had been. Teddy threw his weight against the door, slamming it shut with a loud crack. The lock clicked, trapping Adeline inside.

From behind the door, a furious, blood-curdling shriek reverberated through the hallway, the sound vibrating through their bones.

Scarlett stumbled back, gasping, clutching her arms where unseen claws had left burning scratches. Teddy stood rigid, his breath ragged, as the screams turned into a guttural wail of defeat.

Footsteps pounded up the stairs. Robyn and Kiara appeared at the end of the hall, eyes wide with alarm.

"What the hell was that?!" Robyn shouted, her accent thick with panic.

Scarlett, still catching her breath, leaned against the wall. "She's... locked in," she whispered, voice trembling. "For now."

Kiara, her sightless eyes narrowing, tilted her head as if listening. "She's furious," she whispered. "She knows she can't leave... but she's still... there."

A final, agonized scream echoed from inside the master suite, then silence.

The house groaned softly, as if reluctantly surrendering to their presence.

Teddy let out a nervous chuckle, still leaning against the door. "Nope. Nope. Not doing this again. That room? Dead to me. Doesn't exist. Scarlett, I think your stones might actually be bigger than mine."

Scarlett, still catching her breath, shot him a tired smirk. "We'll have to deal with it eventually."

Robyn snorted softly, shaking her head. "Not if we pretend it doesn't exist. Like the thirteenth floor. It's gone. Poof."

Teddy nodded vigorously. "Exactly. As far as I'm concerned, this hallway ends right here."

Kiara's voice, soft but clear, broke through the moment. "She's waiting... and watching."

Scarlett's eyes darkened as she whispered, "Then we'll be ready."

The hallway stood eerily still, the air heavy with the promise that this wasn't over.

-Chapter 3-   An Unlikely ReunionThe following morning, sunlight streamed through the trees, painting the forest in shades of amber and gold. A group of old friends was meeting nearby, the quiet hum of the woods broken only by the crunch of tires on a dirt road.

Aron O'Keenan navigated the familiar path, his dusty truck rumbling along with practiced ease. As he rounded a bend, his sharp eyes caught sight of a car and camper parked in a small clearing near the trailhead. Pulling up next to a Jeep, Aron spotted two familiar figures leaning against it, with two others sitting in the back seat waiting. The vehicle bore the logo Oregon Allied Securities, LLC—one of many fronts run by the Order of the Ancient Serpent, all conveniently sharing the OAS acronym. It was a convenient way to have a legitimate business front while covertly operating their agenda outside of the watchful eyes of others. Aron knew this, but for the sake of his friendships with Marcus and Cesaro, he kept his mouth shut. For now.

Marcus, his easy grin and relaxed posture unmistakable, waved as his old friend Aron stepped out of his truck. Beside him stood Cesaro, exuding his usual restless energy and cocky smirk. All three were friends from about a decade ago when they all played college football together at Southwest Washington State University before the world split them apart. Now, they were back together, and it felt like the best of times with three old friends. Cesaro and Marcus had spent the entire drive coming down here reminiscing on their memories and glory days together in the past. Plus, Aron worked in the field of fish and wildlife preservation, among other side hustles. His knowledge of the forest, Marcus believed, could be invaluable.

All five men got out of the vehicles and posted up by the back of the van that had been driven by the Doctors.

"Aron, you made it!" Marcus greeted him, clapping him on the shoulder.

"Didn't think I'd miss seeing you lot again," Aron replied, his thick accent—a hybrid of Irish and Australian—tinged with skepticism. His eyes flicked between them. "I've been on so many treks around the world and back home to Ireland, and I just seem to keep coming back to the American Pacific Northwest. Tell me again why Ogma's letting strangers crash his party? He's not exactly... inclusive."

Marcus laughed, pushing off the Jeep. "Not sure about any rave, but come on—you missed me. Admit it."

Aron smirked. "Missed you? Sure. But him?" He nodded toward Cesaro. "That's debatable."

Cesaro's grin didn't falter. "Don't worry, I missed me enough for both of us."

Aron shook his head with a snort, pulling his pack from the truck. "So, what's this about, then? You show up after all this time and want a tour of the weirdest place in the state?"

"Not exactly," Marcus said, his grin fading. "Kane set this up. We're supposed to meet Ogma."

Aron's brows lifted. "Ogma, now? And he agreed?"

"Apparently," Marcus replied, shrugging. "Told us you'd take us."

Aron exhaled, glancing out toward the tree line, thinking. "Ogma's throwin' a festival right now. Figured that'd mean no visitors." He paused. "But if he's expectin' ya, then we go."

Cesaro raised an eyebrow. "So, he's fine with... everyone? This isn't exactly what I pictured."

Aron adjusted the strap on his shoulder. "He doesn't do 'fine.' If you're here, it's 'cause he wants ya here—or at least, he's lettin' it happen. That's how it works with him."

Marcus frowned slightly. "And that doesn't bother you?"

Aron shrugged. "Used to. Not anymore. You stop fightin' what makes no sense, it gets easier." He gave Marcus a half-smile. "We've both seen stranger."

They started moving toward the trailhead, packs on, boots crunching over gravel. As they walked, Aron spotted a car parked off to the side.

"That one's new," he said, nodding toward it.

"Randoms?" Cesaro asked.

"Could be," Aron replied. "Doesn't matter. If they're meant to find the place, they will. But we don't talk to 'em unless we have to. It's...

better that way."

"Ogma's orders?" Marcus asked.

"Not exactly. More like... experience." Aron's tone was quiet, but firm. "You don't always know who you're dealin' with out here."

The trail narrowed, winding into deeper woods. Sunlight flickered through the canopy above, shadows moving like something alive.

"You ever think he planned this?" Marcus asked, more to himself.

Aron glanced back, a flicker of something in his eyes. "He doesn't do anything without a reason. I've stopped tryin' to guess what Ogma plans are, just easier that way..."

It was almost midday, many hours until sunset and the hike inland would take up a smaller portion of that time. According to the instructions from Kane, they would go to the location and stake out the coming and going of the guardian of the forest Ogma the magical satyr. Next, they would follow Ogma back to his hidden lair and force him to reveal one particular location of passage to the hidden tunnels that lead to the Hollow Earth within the planet's core. Sounded simple enough, except Marcus and Doctor Patel had to explain to Cesaro what exactly a satyr was. Juan was not familiar with all the creatures of mythology.

"What the fuck is a satyr?" Cesaro asked his companions, confused.

Aron opened his mouth to begin explaining the origins of this mythical creature, but got waved off by Doctor Moses"This particular satyr, Ogma, that we are looking for is about 6 feet in height, rather tall for his species having the hindquarters, legs, and horns of a goat, but the body and face of a human." Doctor Moses explained. "He is recognized as basically a god of the wilderness. He offers his companions of the forest a sanctuary for the nymphs, fauns, and other magical creatures."

"He is NOT El Diablo, despite how he may appear to you." Aron helpfully added in, to which Cesaro laughed. "Maybe he could introduce me?" he quipped, in response. Though neither would ever admit it, they enjoyed each other's company almost as much as they enjoyed it with Marcus, so they all relaxed a bit in the fun atmosphere, helping clear the tension that had previously been felt by everyone.

Regardless, he was ready to proceed with the mission and so were the other four.

"The Boys Are Back In Town" by Thin Lizzie played on the Marcus

Kydd soundtrack.

It took just under an hour for the five men to near their destination, following Kane's unusually specific instructions. They didn't know exactly what to expect—just that it involved a long hike, dense forest, and enough gear for a few days off-grid: tents, sleeping bags, survival equipment, food and water. The word "camp" had been thrown around loosely, but only Aron seemed to know where they were actually headed.

"How much longer?" Dr. Patel asked, his tone laced with impatience. "We better not be hiking past a perfectly good road just for the ambiance."

Aron smirked but didn't slow his pace. "We're not far. There's a lake up ahead. We'll need to cross it to get where we're going."

"A lake?" Marcus asked, raising an eyebrow. "Don't tell me we're swimming."

Aron shook his head. "Relax. There's a boathouse with a couple of motorboats. It's faster than hiking the long way—and I need to patrol the lake anyway."

"You patrol the lake?" Cesaro asked, skeptical. His brow arched, but his tone held a trace of curiosity beneath the sarcasm.

Aron ignored Cesaro's grumbling, his focus shifting to the growing shimmer of water visible through the trees. Moments later, they arrived at the edge of the lake, where an old wooden boathouse stood partially hidden by tall reeds. Aron walked up to it and unlocked the door, revealing two motorboats inside.

"Hop in," he said, stepping into the nearest boat. "We'll take the faster route."

In the first boat, Aron manned the wheel, focused on keeping them steady as they cut across the shimmering lake. His eyes stayed locked ahead, scanning the horizon like it was his second nature—which, out here, it was. Beside him, Dr. Moses clutched his gear awkwardly, clearly not the outdoorsy type.

In the second boat, Marcus handled the controls with careful focus, more comfortable in a lab coat than behind an outboard motor but doing his best to keep things steady. Cesaro, stretched out near the front like he was on vacation, cracked open a beer and leaned back to enjoy the ride. Dr. Patel sat uneasily beside Marcus, gripping the side rails tighter than necessary.

The engine's hum made conversation more like shouting matches. Dr. Moses tried anyway, calling over the noise, "Favorite movie, anyone?!"

Marcus shot Aron a look. Aron didn't bother responding. He was busy with his binoculars, the leather strap tight in his grip as he zeroed in on something far off near the opposite bank.

"Hold this course," Aron said, raising his voice just enough for Marcus to catch it. "There's something I need to check."

Marcus nodded, steering the boat in the direction Aron had motioned. No need to ask questions—when Aron went into Guardian mode, you just did what he said.

In the lead boat, Aron was at the wheel, steering with the ease of someone who practically belonged to these woods and waters. His eyes stayed locked ahead, scanning the tree line, while Dr. Moses sat stiffly behind him, clutching a GPS unit like it might somehow keep him dry.

In the second boat, Marcus guided the vessel a short distance behind. Dr. Patel still looked like he'd rather be anywhere else, while Cesaro sprawled near the bow with his beer now sloshing onto his jeans, looked like he was about to declare this the best camping trip ever—until the boat bounced over a wave.

The lake air was brisk, and the boat engines were loud enough to make casual conversation pointless. Every now and then, Marcus tried yelling something over the motor to Patel or Cesaro, but between the noise and the wind, it was just head shakes and shrugs.

In the lead boat, Aron barely glanced back. He raised the binoculars, scanning the water's edge. "Keep pace, Marcus," he muttered, knowing full well they couldn't hear him. The Guardian's instincts were prickling—something was off.

Dr. Moses cleared his throat. "So... Aron, any wildlife out here we should be worried about? Bears? Wolves? Maybe a rogue satyr?"

Aron didn't answer, too focused. His hand tightened on the throttle as they neared a bend in the lake.

Meanwhile, Marcus fumbled for the walkie, finally giving up on shouting. "Second boat to first—anything up there?" he called into the radio.

Aron's voice crackled back, low but firm. "Just keep close. We're not alone out here."

Cesaro perked up, tossing his empty beer can into a bag. "Alone, huh? This getting interesting?"

Marcus just shook his head, eyes narrowing as he followed Aron's line of sight. "It's Aron's turf, man. If he's twitchy, we should be too."

Aron lowered the binoculars slightly; his gaze still locked on the paddle boats drifting near the far bank. He shifted his stance, thoughtful, briefly scanning the shoreline and the scattered figures along the water's edge.

Marcus noticed the change. "You spotting something?"

Aron didn't blink. "Maybe. That lot in the boats... they're off. Either not locals or just green, yeah?"

Marcus followed his line of sight, squinting. "Weird time for tourists."

Aron gave a slight shake of his head. "Tourists're fine. I'm more interested in them," he said, nodding toward the lake. "Ease it in slower."

Marcus nodded and eased back on the throttle. The engine softened to a low hum, and the boat glided silently across the calm water.

Ahead, the paddle boats rocked in quiet disarray. Their passengers moved awkwardly, out of sync with the rhythm of the lake, like they weren't used to being out here—or weren't expecting to be seen.

In the lead boat, Scarlett sat near the bow, her eyes scanning the tree line. Her posture was relaxed but alert. Beside her, Kiara gripped the edge of the boat tightly, knuckles pale.

"You're fine," Scarlett said calmly. "Just breathe."

Kiara let out a shaky laugh. "Easy for you to say. You're not trusting a paddleboat and blind faith."

A few yards away, Robyn and Teddy floated in their own boat. The water slapped gently at the sides as they drifted.

"It's your turn to paddle," Robyn said, narrowing her eyes at him.

Teddy stretched back, hands behind his head. "Let the lake guide us. Maybe it knows something we don't."

Robyn rolled her eyes but relented, resting the oar on the side. "Fine. But if we drift into reeds, you getting us out."

Nobody noticed the approaching hum of a motorboat until it was nearly on them. Aron's boat cut across the lake with speed and precision, his face unreadable but sharp with focus.

"Looks like we've got company," Teddy said, shielding his eyes. "Did we paddle into a restricted area?"

Before anyone could answer, Kiara and Scarlett's paddleboat rocked violently. Kiara, already tense, lost her balance and slipped into the water with a sharp gasp.

"Kiara!" Scarlett yelled, leaning over the edge.

Robyn and Teddy paddled hard toward her as Kiara's head dipped beneath the surface. Aron was already in motion, diving cleanly into the lake and swimming with forceful, practiced strokes.

Scarlett leapt in just after him, but Aron reached Kiara first, wrapping an arm around her waist and pulling her upward.

"Easy now, I've got ya," he said, his voice steady but firm, his accent cuttin' through the chaos like a tether.

Kiara sputtered, coughing as he guided her toward the motorboat. Scarlett swam alongside them, swift and focused. Aron hauled Kiara aboard, laying her gently on the floor. She coughed hard, water spilling from her lips until her breathing began to steady. Her face was pale, curls plastered to her cheeks in dark, wet tangles.

"Alright then, love, y'still with me?" he asked, the familiar tone of his accent softenin' the edge in his words.

Kiara blinked up toward him, dazed but smiling. "Aron? Is that you?"

Aron froze, leaning closer. "Kiara?" he asked, his tone a mix of disbelief and familiarity.

"It's me," she managed amidst coughing, her voice still rough but steadying. "I'd recognize that voice anywhere. I can't believe it's really you."

"Sorry if I gave ya a scare," he said, pullin' her upright.

Kiara tried to laugh but it made her cough again. "You didn't scare me so much as causing waves that knocked me over. New job?"

Aron chuckled, brushing the wet hair from her face. "Leave it to you to find the most reckless crew on the lake."

Kiara grinned, breathless but steady. "What can I say? We like to keep things interesting."

Aron shook his head, a fond smirk tugging at his lips. "Some things never change." He hesitated for a moment, then pulled her into a brief, steady hug, more grounding than playful. "It really is good to see you again."

Kiara let out a soft laugh, leaning into the familiar warmth of it. "You too. It's been awhile."

"Marcus?" Scarlett shouted. "And Cesaro, is that you?"

"Scarlett!" Cesaro shouted, having immediately figured out where he remembered her voice from. "What are you doing out here in the woods?"

She came over to his boat and gave him a big hug.

"I know these guys! Guys, these are my best friends Kiara, Teddy, and Robyn."

"Nice to meet you, I was hoping to thank you one day for saving Scarlett's life. ...so, thank you!" Robyn said kindly to Marcus.

Marcus eased the second motorboat closer, cutting the engine as he scanned the scene. His eyes narrowed at the sight of Kiara, drenched and still catching her breath, but before he could say anything, Scarlett turned, waving him down.

"We're good here," she called out, voice carrying over the water. "Just a little excitement."

Her gaze shifted past Marcus—and landed on Cesaro. Her face lit up.

"Cesaro?" she said, half in disbelief, standing to get a better look. "What the hell? Is that really you?"

Cesaro stood, his grin wide and genuine. "Scarlett Littlehorn. Thought I recognized that voice."

She laughed, already climbing aboard Marcus's boat. "You've got some nerve showing up out of nowhere."

"Missed me, huh?" he teased, arms open.

Scarlett didn't hesitate—she pulled him into a hug, hard. "Damn right I did."

Pulling back, she gave him a once-over. "Where've you been hiding?"

Cesaro smirked, eyes glinting. "Everywhere. Long story."

Her attention flicked to Marcus, a spark of recognition. "And you... we've crossed paths before, haven't we?"

Marcus nodded, stepping forward. "Yeah, back at the San Juan site. Briefly."

"Right," she said, piecing it together. Then her eyes narrowed slightly, curious now. "So, what brings you lot out here? This can't just be a coincidence."

Cesaro chuckled, scratching the back of his neck. "Funny... we could ask you the same."

Scarlett tilted her head, smirking. "Fair enough. But let's say I'm a little more used to strange crossings these days."

Robyn, hovering close, stepped in, her brow knitted. "Wait... you know these men? Tak? Who are they, Scarlett?"

Scarlett glanced down at Kiara, brushing damp curls from her face with gentle fingers. "We need to get her to shore first," she said, her voice firm, already slipping into leadership mode. "I'll explain once we're on solid ground."

Aron didn't argue. He swung the boat around and steered them toward the nearest bank, back where the paddleboats had been secured. The silence was filled only by the hum of the engine and the soft slap of water against the hull.

As Kiara stepped off, still dripping, Robyn rushed forward, wrapping a towel around her shoulders, muttering softly in Ukrainian. "Tobi ne treba buty z nimi... we do not need to be with them..."

"I'm fine," Kiara said, voice unsteady but determined. "Just... give me a minute."

Scarlett helped her to sit, then turned to the others. "Stay close. We're not done yet."

The rest of the group followed Scarlett's lead, their feet crunching on damp earth as they moved inland slightly, gathering near the trees for privacy.

Teddy shook his head; arms folded tightly across his chest. "This feels like one of those setups. Like... you just happened to run into old friends while we're stuck in this mess?"

Dr. Patel laughed, shrugging. "Call it fate, or bad planning. Either way, we're in it now."

Teddy rolled his eyes but gave in, drifting toward the doctors, drawn to the calmer energy they gave off.

Aron stood with one boot planted on the muddy bank, arms crossed as he surveyed the group. His sharp gaze lingered on Marcus, Scarlett, and

Cesaro in turn, the forest quiet around them except for the faint crunch of damp earth beneath shifting feet.

"So..." he said slowly, a wry grin tugging at the corner of his mouth. "Didn't expect a reunion today."

Marcus adjusted his pack, glancing between them. "You could say that." he replied, his tone light, but the curiosity in his eyes didn't waver.

Scarlett stepped forward, boots sinking slightly into the soft ground. Her stance was firm, but her face gave nothing away. "We need to talk. All of us."

Aron's brow furrowed, his arms tightening across his chest. "Seriously. What is going on here?"

Scarlett met Aron's gaze, her voice cool but edged. "Good question. I've been trying to get a hold of Cesaro for months. And now, out of nowhere, he's standing here in the middle of the forest with you and Marcus."

Marcus shifted, rubbing the back of his neck. "Hey, I'm sure he wasn't hiding from you. We've just been... busy."

"Busy?" Scarlett raised an eyebrow. "With what, exactly?"

Cesaro gave his usual grin, easy but hollow. "Football, mostly. Business here and there. You know me—can't stay in one place."

Scarlett wasn't buying it, her lips tight, but before she could press, Teddy laughed. "You guys have the weirdest family reunions."

Robyn muttered, low and sharp, "Vona kazhe, tse povna mayachnya."

Kiara, almost offhand, replied, "Mozhlivo, tse dolya."

"HEY!" Teddy cut in, eyes wide. "Share with the rest of the class!"

Kiara shrugged, dry. "She says this is total bullshit."

Robyn spun to her, grinning. "And she say maybe is fate. But I think she just happy guy who knock her into lake turn out to be hot Aron from college."

Kiara flushed. "Robyn!"

Teddy doubled over laughing. "Ohhh, it's like that now, huh?"

"I can't even see him!" Kiara's face went red.

Teddy hooted. "How does that work for blind people when you're into someone?"

"Ya tebe poshlyu do chorta..." Kiara muttered, shaking her head.

Robyn just laughed. "You did. You said, 'Mozhlivo, tse vsesvit.' You can't take it back now."

Kiara rolled her eyes but didn't argue. "I said maybe. That's all."

Scarlett stepped in smoothly, like she'd been buffering this kind of thing her whole life. "Teddy, don't be nosy. Let the girl have her mystery."

"But was it fate?" Teddy pushed, grinning like a kid with a new toy.

Kiara offered a soft smile. "Honestly, the water probably did me a favor. I needed the jolt."

Aron chuckled under his breath, but before he could say anything—Cesaro leaned in, grinning. "Hey, that's your specialty, right—"

WHUMP. Aron's elbow landed sharp in Cesaro's side, cutting him off mid-sentence.

"Shit, man!" Cesaro twisted, half laughing, half wincing. "What was that for?"

Marcus didn't even blink. "Don't."

Aron, already a step ahead, shot Cesaro a final warning look. Cesaro held up his hands, mock surrender in his eyes, though he rubbed his ribs. "Alright, alright. No need to short-circuit over it."

Kiara tilted her head, catching the shift. "Wait... what was that about?"

Marcus waved it off quickly. "Old jokes. Cesaro's got a way of running his mouth—especially when he shouldn't."

Robyn, watching the tension closely, snorted. "Some things never change."

Teddy, trying to smooth it over, clapped Cesaro on the back. "Maybe stick to paddleboats, huh? Keep it safe for everyone."

Scarlett crossed her arms, cutting through the tension. "So... what now?"

Marcus stepped forward. "Actually, we're headin' somewhere not far from here." he turned toward Scarlett. "Kane sent us."

Scarlett raised a brow. "For what?"

Marcus nodded. "Can't say. We're meetin' Ogma later, but we've got time. If there's a party already going on, you lot should come."

Aron gave Kiara a quick look, then glanced at Robyn and Teddy. "Like he said—there's a festival on. Local thing, bit wild. Music, drinkin', folk off their heads on shrooms and whatnot. Won't be quiet, but you're welcome to join us as my guests."

Teddy's face lit up. "Finally, someone's speakin' my language! I'm in!"

Kiara turned toward Scarlett, tilting her head. "You going?"

Scarlett's gaze slid between Marcus and Cesaro. "You're serious?"

Marcus shrugged, that half-grin of his back. "What've we got to lose? Come on—it'll be fun."

Robyn folded her arms tight across her chest. "We do not come for party. We come to rest."

Kiara leaned toward her, playful. "Maybe rest is there."

Robyn narrowed her eyes. "You say that now, but you think it's sign, tak? Universe wants us to go?"

Scarlett stepped in, voice low but steady. "It's not just a party, Robyn. Something's pulling at me too. Come, one hour. If it's no good—we go."

Robyn clicked her tongue, thinking, then threw her hands up. "Fine. But someone brings mushrooms—I leave."

Teddy snorted, slinging his bag over one shoulder. "Hand 'em to me first, darlin'."

Scarlett laughed softly. "Deal."

Aron, watching them with a crooked smile, chimed in. "Right then, we best get movin'. Don't want Ogma thinkin' we've bailed."

It didn't take long to gather up their things. Aron and Marcus led the way, with Dr. Patel tracking the route on GPS. About ten minutes into the hike, the caravan came to a sudden halt—not because of the trail, but because Kiara had stopped mid-step.

"Wait," she said softly, crouching down with one hand outstretched in front of her.

Aron turned, stepping back toward her. "What is it?"

"A ladybug," she murmured, fingers hovering, then gently closing around something so small no one else had noticed it. She walked a few steps off the path, carefully setting it onto a leaf. "She landed on my arm."

"You could feel her?" Aron asked, eyes narrowing with interest.

Kiara stood, brushing off her hands, her head tilted slightly as if still listening to the space around her. "It's not just feeling... it's the way they move. Ladybugs? They're light—really light—and quick. Ants aren't as light, but they're faster, like they've got somewhere to be. Beetles? Heavy. Slow. Like they land and stay there, real solid. Spiders feel rough—light, but fast, like they know exactly where they want to go. Flies? Annoying. Erratic, like they're everywhere at once."

She swatted at her neck with a loud smack, a small grin pulling at her lips. "Mosquitoes? Worst of them all. I've tried to reason with them, but they have boundary issues."

Teddy cracked up. "Sweet and savage, spoken like a true princess."

"She's like princess from forest," Robyn said, deadpan.

Kiara laughed. "Better than letting them bite me."

Aron, walking a step behind, glanced over with a raised brow. "Not many people can feel all that... You must be pretty tuned in'."

She shrugged, modest but not dismissive. "Once you have to rely on it, you notice more. Bugs, trees, even the air... it's all different if you're paying attention."

Aron hesitated for a second, then offered, "I get it. I mean... not because I have to, but... bein' out here enough, you start to feel it too. There's a rhythm. Most people don't take the time."

Kiara turned toward his voice, intrigued. "You live out here?"

"Mostly. I work these woods, kind of a ranger, kind of..." he trailed off. "It's complicated."

They walked on, her cane tapping lightly against the dirt path. The group was starting to spread out as the trees thinned, sunlight spilling in through the branches, warm on their faces. Kiara paused for a second, feeling the shift in the ground beneath her feet.

"Here," Aron said softly, and without fanfare, he offered his arm, sliding into step beside her. His hand didn't grab, didn't guide—just there, steady, giving her the option.

Kiara hesitated, then slipped her fingers lightly around his forearm. No one made a comment, and that was what she liked about it.

Chapter 4

Threads of the Unseen

As they moved forward, Aron pointed out things as they continued on—Describing lesser-known creatures he had spotted in the area, weaving in little bits of lore or his experiences with each sighting. Or the way moss grows on the north sides of older trees, how the air shifts when a storm's coming long before clouds gather.

Kiara listened with intrigue, her hand still resting lightly on his arm, the subtle weight of his presence grounding but not intrusive.

Teddy leaned toward Robyn, whispering just loud enough. "He's good at this... Look at 'em."

Robyn gave him a sideways glance, not smiling, but not arguing either.

Scarlett, walking a few paces behind, caught the exchange and raised her voice just enough. "You know, you all might have more in common than you think."

Teddy grinned. "What, you mean with these guys? We don't exactly scream 'rugged forest type.'"

"No," Scarlett said, her tone light, "but weird shit follows us around. Them too."

Robyn raised an eyebrow. "Tak? Like what?"

Scarlett gestured around. "This. All of it. Ogma's festivals aren't exactly on tourist maps, Robyn."

Teddy snorted. "Yeah, but we're used to weird. Haunted forests, creepy hotels... remember that one where you swore the mirror blinked?"

Robyn shuddered. "That mirror was cursed."

Scarlett laughed softly. "And still, you came."

Teddy nodded. "Hell yeah, still waiting for a Sasquatch. Got my camera."

"Best stuff you caught wasn't in the woods," Scarlett reminded him. "It was inside the B&B."

Robyn crossed her arms, but her voice softened. "Because Kiara is magnet for this. Always was."

Scarlett glanced at Kiara, then back to Robyn. "Exactly. That's why I was there so late last night. Helping her figure things out. She's not just a magnet—she's... something more."

Teddy's eyes widened. "You mean the channeling thing?"

Scarlett nodded. "Elementals. Spirits. She's walked a line most people never get near."

Robyn, still protective, didn't argue. But she didn't relax either.

Teddy, rubbing his chin, looked over at Cesaro. "You know... I swear I've seen you somewhere before."

Cesaro's brow twitched. "Football, probably."

Teddy shook his head. "No... like, not on TV. Something else..."

He trailed off, the memory just out of reach.

Robyn's eyes snapped to him, sharp. "Wait—you recognize him?"

Teddy hesitated. "Maybe?"

Robyn didn't wait. She pulled out her phone, tapping quickly. "I know where."

Cesaro's face went pale. "Don't."

But Robyn was already playing the video, holding it out for everyone to see.

The Jeep. The transformation. The blood.

The woods felt colder for a moment, even with the sun.

Cesaro turned away, hands clenched, jaw locked.

"Is that you?" Robyn asked, not unkind—but direct.

Scarlett stepped in, voice low. "Robyn. It's not what you think."

Kiara, quiet till now, stepped closer to Aron, her voice barely above the breeze. "He's hurting."

Aron nodded, his jaw tight. "I know."

Scarlett stepped in, her voice calm but firm. "That was before. It's not like that anymore."

Teddy blinked, stunned. "Holy shit... that's where I saw you. I did not see that coming!"

Cesaro's voice was low, rough. "Most people know me from pro football. Wish that damn video would disappear already."

Robyn, arms crossed tight, didn't let up. "So... you killed people? Or just eat their faces?"

"No." His head shook, jaw clenched. "Not anymore. I didn't want any of that... it's complicated."

Marcus stepped forward, firm. "Whatever you think you know, it's deeper. He's not that anymore."

Robyn didn't say anything else, but she didn't put her phone away either.

Scarlett touched Cesaro's arm. "I give him shit, but he's like a brother. That's why he bailed—why he kept avoiding me. And let's be honest," she glanced around, "he's not the only one here with shit we wish we could undo."

Kiara's voice cut through, soft but steady. "But you choose now?"

Cesaro looked toward her, locking on the direction of her voice. "Yeah. I do."

Aron, tense but measured, nodded slowly. "Then that's what matters."

Scarlett turned to the others, scanning Kiara, Teddy, and Robyn. "I met Teddy at the bookstore—we clicked. He's followed me into more haunted places than I can count. Forests, abandoned buildings... hoping for Sasquatch out here."

Teddy raised a hand. "Still am. Got my camera right here." He patted the rainbow sparkle fanny pack on his hip.

Scarlett gave him a look but smiled faintly. "Best stuff he's caught? Inside their B&B. Shit's been ramping up since they started renovations."

Marcus shook his head. "You mess with a house, the house messes with you. That's how it works."

"Exactly," Scarlett said. "But this wasn't just any haunting. There's an elemental on the property. That's why I was out there last night—and stayed, because of Kiara."

Robyn's eyes flicked to Kiara, protective.

"She's got abilities," Scarlett added, softer now. "She channeled the elemental—and at least one ghost. Back and forth. At the same time. It was insane."

Aron turned fully to Kiara now, brows furrowed. "She did what?"

Kiara shifted, standing firm. "It wasn't on purpose. It just... happened."

Marcus straightened, eyes sharp. "You're sure?"

Scarlett nodded. "She practically started walking on the ceiling. That's why we're grounding her, working on boundaries, perception, all of it."

"If anyone can teach her, it's you…" Marcus nodded in agreement.

Cesaro finally turned, still pale, but more guarded. "And she's just out here like it's nothing?" His voice rough—somewhere between admiration and fear. "Damn. Pretty tough."

Robyn shook her head, stepping closer to Kiara. "She strong but stubborn. Says it's not real. But if it happens, and we're not there…?"

Scarlett didn't flinch. "That's why we're all here. Whether we meant to be or not."

She nodded at Marcus, Cesaro, and Aron. "These guys? They've seen worse. If shit hit the fan, this is who I'd call."

Teddy raised an eyebrow. "You're making them sound like meta-physical special ops."

Scarlett gave a small laugh. "Close enough."

The group stood in thick silence for a beat, forest humming around them.

Teddy nudged Robyn. "So, we trust 'em, or what?"

Robyn didn't answer right away. Her gaze locked on Scarlett, then Cesaro, then back to Kiara. Finally, she exhaled through her nose. "Maybe. Maybe not. But I watch."

Scarlett nodded, respectful. "Fair enough."

The two doctors looked intrigued, clearly picking up every word despite the low tones. Cesaro, though, looked annoyed. "So that makes you what—the mediator?" he asked, condescending.

Scarlett arched a brow. "I can't imagine why they wouldn't trust you…"

She leaned toward Marcus, pulling him back toward her. "Something feels different about the space right now, it's almost like it's enchanted or something magical is happening in these woods this evening, I can feel this energy building. I wish we had Clarice here."

"It does feel a bit different; I just figured it was all the clean air…" Marcus joked. "I wish she were here too, but she is on a mission in Puerto

Vallarta right now. We're supposed to meet up with her and her team in a few days."

"All I know is that I was definitely pulled here. For whatever reason, I'm supposed to be here to be part of it." She explained.

"How fortuitous for us then." Doctor Moses replied casually, as though he had been part of the conversation, stepping forward in front of the team. "We will have plenty of time to catch up and hear more along the way to 'big event'. Shall we?" He insisted, pointing toward the direction they needed to go.

"What 'big event'?" Kiara nervously asked, wondering if they would be able to come along. She looked around first, from Doctor Moses to Scarlett, then from Marcus to Aron.

The men looked back and forth, not knowing if they should divulge the information, but just like Scarlett's friends had trusted her, Cesaro as the leader of the team gave the nod to disseminate the information.

"We can't tell you everything, but know that we are working for some very important people." Cesaro explained. "What we can tell you," Marcus began. "Is that…"

"It's a festival!" Dr. Patel blurted out, a little too eager, before Dr. Moses jumped in to smooth the delivery.

"Yes, a private one," Moses added, giving Patel a look. "Something of a… local tradition."

The two exchanged a glance, filling in just enough details to keep things comfortable, but everyone could feel they weren't telling the whole story. The rest of the group, especially Marcus and Cesaro, knew better than to correct them.

The information was enough, though—Scarlett, Kiara, and Robyn didn't press. There was something about it that felt familiar, even if it didn't make total sense yet.

"Let's put it this way," Aron said, stepping up beside Kiara, his voice lower, that soft Irish-Aussie lilt giving the words a calm weight. "An old fella owns these woods—bit of a recluse, but he watches over it. We've all worked with him, helped him out now and then."

Kiara tilted her head, listening.

Aron continued, "He's protective, doesn't like just anyone wander-in' in, so they—" he nodded at Marcus and Cesaro, "asked me to guide them. Know the trails better than most, and it's not the kind of place you just stumble on. That said…" he gave a small shrug, "I was headed there anyway."

Robyn's brows knit, still uneasy. She turned to Scarlett, her voice quiet, but firm. "You sure they want outsiders? We do not go far if we're not welcome."

Scarlett looked between Aron and Marcus, then back at Robyn. "We're not crashing anything, trust me. If they didn't want us, we wouldn't have even made it this far."

Aron gave a half-smile, glancing toward Robyn now. "Aye, no one gets in unless they're meant to. And if you're here… well, maybe you're meant to."

Robyn still didn't look sold, but she didn't argue either.

They had been walking for a good while, long enough that the trail behind them felt like a different world—thicker, heavier somehow. But as they pressed on, the woods began to open up, the air thinning, lighter, almost charged with something... old. Then they saw it.

Another lake, tucked away beyond the pines, stretched out before them. The water shimmered like glass, so clear they could see straight to the bottom, where smooth stones and flashes of light played tricks on the eyes. It was too perfect, too still—too beautiful to be real.

Cesaro stopped in his tracks, eyebrows raised. "Now that's more like it."

Marcus let out a low whistle. "No one mentioned this."

"It's not on any maps," Aron said quietly, a faint smile tugging at his lips, though his eyes stayed on the water. "You only find it if it wants to be found."

Scarlett turned slowly, taking it in. "We're in, aren't we?"

"Aye," Aron replied. "We've crossed."

Since there was still time before sundown, Cesaro shrugged off his pack, rolling his shoulders. "I'm taking a swim," he announced, glancing back toward the group. "Took us long enough to get here—might as well enjoy it."

"You sure about that?" Marcus asked, half-joking, half-wary.

Cesaro grinned, already moving. "Come on, look at this place. You can see all the way to the bottom. Can't fake that."

Scarlett watched him go, her gaze flicking to Aron. "This lake... it's safe?"

"As safe as anything here ever is," Aron replied, but there was no warning in his tone—just respect, like someone stepping into a church.

Teddy let out a low whistle. "Okay, now this? This is worth the hike."

Cesaro was already pulling off his shirt, stretching his arms wide. "Twenty bucks says I'm in first."

"No one's bettin' you," Marcus laughed, dropping his pack.

The group settled near the shore, dropping their things, shaking out limbs tired from the trail. Robyn stripped down to her tank and shorts, her long legs catching Cesaro's eye.

He grinned, wading toward her. "You're lookin' like the queen of this lake, I gotta say."

Robyn raised a brow, smirking. "Oh? Too bad for you, I like queens more than kings."

Cesaro paused, caught off-guard. "Wait, what?"

Scarlett, grinning, tossed her shirt onto a rock. "Welcome to the club."

Teddy leaned in, voice full of pride. "And I'm gay too, babe. Triple threat."

Cesaro blinked, taking it all in, then turned toward Kiara, who was standing near the edge, barefoot, just listening.

"Well, what about you, darlin'?" Cesaro started.

Before he could say another word, Aron stepped in. No sound, no warning—just a quiet shake of his head, brow arched, a smirk tugging at the edge of his lips.

Cesaro froze, caught it immediately. "Alright, alright. I see how it is."

Marcus gave Aron a sideways glance, eyebrows up. "Damn... that's rare."

"Didn't even get a shot off," Cesaro muttered, hands up.

"Didn't need to," Aron said, calm as ever, stepping beside Kiara.

Teddy, floating on his back, laughed loud enough for the trees to hear. "Oooohh, someone's got claims."

Kiara tilted her head, sensing that subtle pause again. A knowing smile teased at her lips. "What just happened?"

"Ah, nothin'," Aron replied smoothly, stepping closer, water swirling around his ankles. His arm brushed lightly against hers, offering steady support. "Just enjoyin' the view, that's all."

She slid her fingers around his forearm, grounding herself. "Mm-hmm," she murmured, unconvinced but amused.

Robyn, distracted from undressing, pointed suddenly, eyes narrowing at Aron. "You! Where you from? This voice—drives me crazy. Aussie? But... not only Aussie. Irish?"

Aron chuckled, wading in a bit deeper. "Dead on, love. Grew up in Ireland, but me folks worked in Oz. Picked up a bit o' both."

Kiara grinned. "I knew it wasn't just one. It's nice though... familiar."

Robyn crossed her arms. "No Britain?"

Aron laughed, shaking his head. "Nah, none o' that. Maybe me grand-dad, but I never lived there."

Scarlett, already knee-deep in water, smirked. "Told you you'd figure it out."

Marcus called from behind, "Didn't you go back to Ireland a couple years ago?"

"Aye," Aron replied, water now brushing his knees. "Couple months… but that was almost a decade ago. Got this gig when I got back—reckon I've been watchin' over these woods for near six years now."

Marcus raised a brow. "Back for good?"

Aron shrugged, glancing at Kiara. "It's complicated, mate. Y'know how it is…"

Ever the observer, Marcus found himself lost in thought as he watched the others. Seeing Aron again pulled at something deeper than he'd expected—reminding him not only of how much he'd missed his friend but stirring a strange feeling, like there was something he wasn't saying. Aron had grown up, no doubt. The wild streak was still there but muted somehow. Back in college, Aron had always been the guy to scale cliffs during hikes, the one who made four hundred bucks at a bonfire party by betting he could leap clear over the flames. He chased adrenaline like it owed him something.

After discovering their abilities together, Marcus had assumed the worst—that Aron, out here in the middle of nowhere, would be restless, maybe even lost without the constant thrill of the world. He used to live for that. The traveling, the chaos, the good times. The wingman, the party-starter. The man's man.

But now? Now, there was a shift in him. Calmer. Grounded. And yet—Marcus could still see it—that familiar spark, alive and well in his eyes. Just...different.

He watched Aron now, subtly flirting with Kiara, trying not to overdo it, while also keeping an eye on Cesaro, who was clearly noticing her too.

Marcus tilted his head slightly, curious. She wasn't any more beautiful than the women who'd thrown themselves at Aron before, but something about her—something—was different. Special. He could feel it. Like it was stitched into the air around her.

Aron had already asked a string of questions, drawing Kiara and her friends into conversation about the bed and breakfast they were renovating nearby. Robyn did most of the talking—her English thick with her Ukrainian accent, sometimes skipping words, but clear enough. She called her friend "Kiki," though with her accent it came out sounding like "Kee Kee." Marcus found himself grinning at the thought of Clarice hearing that—she'd love it. His smile faded as his eyes drifted back to Kiara.

Aside from mentioning the recent progress on their B&B, Kiara hadn't said much. She wasn't exactly shy, but she didn't fill space with unnecessary words either. There was a quietness to her—one born of living more in her head than in the world, shaped by a life where vision loss kept her from diving into the unknown like most people did. The world felt exciting to her, yes—but also heavy. Fragile.

Marcus wondered if that was how she kept the world from feeling too big, too unpredictable. Maybe, for someone who couldn't see it, downplaying things made it more manageable—more grounded, but also more distant.

Still, she'd found something in the paranormal that pulled her in—a space where the limits were different, softer. A space she didn't have to see to understand. Robyn was her anchor in that world, the first and only one who'd truly believed her when she spoke about those strange moments, the ones most people shrugged off. They'd met by chance, but whatever had sparked between them ran deeper than coincidence.

Kiara had helped Robyn, too—especially during those early years after she'd immigrated, struggling to find her place in a world that didn't quite fit. Together, they'd stepped into the unknown, into things that defied logic and explanation. That bond only deepened when they moved into their current home.

The group was interrupted suddenly, as music pulsed through the trees—low, rhythmic, like it had always been there. Then laughter—carefree, wild. They all turned as a group of hikers appeared, stepping right through the water farther down, splashing each other as they moved toward the other side.

Bright colors, beads, and tie-dye lit them up like human kaleidoscopes. A guy with spiky hair and glitter across his chest raised a hand as he passed.

"DJ Yeti's already spinnin'! Don't be late!" he called, water dripping from his sleeves.

Teddy blinked, then grinned wide. "This is some Narnia ass shit."

Another hiker, catching Teddy's look, winked and waved as he skipped past. Teddy gleefully jumped out of the water and began getting dressed, screeching as he ran. "Oh, he noticed me."

Robyn looked around, treading water. "Did they just… come out of nowhere?"

"They do that," Aron replied, pushing his wet hair back. "It's normal… for here."

Kiara turned her head toward the sound, smiling faintly. "It feels... different."

"You got no idea," Aron said, quieter now.

-Chapter 5-

Hidden Realms

As they made their way out of the lake, dripping and buzzing from the strange encounter with the hikers, the forest seemed to hum differently—like it was waiting. They dried off quickly, pulled on what clothes they could, and followed Aron deeper into the trees. The trail stretched longer than any of them expected, winding through thickets and uneven ground. After nearly twenty more minutes of walking, the terrain shifted subtly beneath their feet.

The forest, once wild and dense, began to thin in patches. Broken stone peeked out from under moss and leaves, like a forgotten roadbed swallowed by time. Cesaro paused, nudging a chunk of cracked asphalt with his boot. "Was this... a road?"

Aron nodded, brushing a hand over a nearby tree trunk, as if greeting an old friend. "Aye. Used to be. This was the path to the park—closed off years ago. Nature took it back."

Robyn's eyes narrowed, scanning the ground. As they weaved through the overgrowth, her eyes caught the faint outline of something carved into a crumbling stone slab, half-buried at the edge of what looked like a long-forgotten parking lot. At first, it seemed harmless—a smiling face, childlike, painted in faded pastel. Then another. And another.

Dozens, half-hidden in moss and dirt, all grinning with eyes too wide, watching. She shook it off, chalking it up to old park decorations, relics from a simpler time. But the deeper they walked, the trees thinning around a twisted metal archway, her stomach dropped.

"I can see why nobody would come looking for this place..." she groaned.

"You just don't," Aron replied with a crooked smile. "Unless Ogma wants you to."

As they moved further, the remnants of what might've once been a parking lot came into view—half-swallowed by creeping vines, with only the faintest outlines of painted lines and rotted signs left to hint at its past.

Then the trees parted, opening up to a vast clearing, ringed by the towering forest before them. Twilight bathed it in soft, golden light, making it look almost surreal. The ruins of what had once been a theme park stood scattered—faded archways, moss-covered statues of fairy tale figures, and weathered signs pointing toward long-forgotten attractions. But this place wasn't abandoned.

Tents and canopies were strung between the skeletal remains of old rides, colorful lanterns floating lazily in the air, glowing with an inner light. Music throbbed, pulsing from speakers hidden among the trees—low, hypnotic, and layered with the hum of something ancient beneath it.

Scarlett's breath caught. "It's like... a dream."

"No," Aron said softly beside her. "It's Ogma's realm."

Teddy spun slowly, eyes wide, practically glowing. "This is insane. Like stepping into a storybook—one that got left behind... and maybe shouldn't have been."

Robyn shivered, but not from the cold. The arch ahead loomed like a gate to another world, rusted and twisted but refusing to fall. Painted figures danced along its frame—twisted fairy tales, their features warped, almost mocking. A wolf with human teeth, a girl in red with hollow eyes, a crooked house on legs.

She froze, eyes wide. "De kuty—what is this place?!" Her breath caught, panic rising as she spun on her heel, glaring at the group. "WHERE THE HELL ARE YOU PEOPLE TAKING ME?!"

Kiara, still holding onto Aron's arm, tilted her head, blissfully unaware of the horror etched on Robyn's face. She let the strange harmony wash over her. "I like it here," she smiled.

Another group appeared, seemingly out of nowhere—laughing, splashing barefoot through a shallow stream cutting across the entrance. Their clothes were a clash of eras: rave gear, fantasy garb, tribal accents.

At the front, a tall, barefoot figure with wild hair and a grin that caught the light. He glanced at them, winked, and melted into the crowd.

"Who the hell was that?" Cesaro muttered, brow raised.

"That," Aron exhaled, "is Joshua. DJ Yeti's right-hand."

As more figures weaved around them, the ruins alive with music and strange revelry, the group followed, every step like a threshold—into something older, enchanted, just now pulling back its curtain.

The music swelled, wrapping around them. The air buzzed—not just sound, but something living.

"Anyone else smell that?" Kiara asked, grinning.

"You get used to it…" Aron said with a chuckle.

"I smell it too." Cesaro glanced at Marcus—both catching the pungent trail of cannabis wafting through the clearing.

Robyn perked up, "I need joint now." sniffing at the hazy cloud hanging in the canopy above them. Strobe lights pulsed; bubbles floated skyward from somewhere in the crowd.

The clearing was alive—lanterns strung across the canopies and between trees, casting a surreal glow. At the entrance, a table piled with snacks and a punch bowl that shimmered unnaturally.

Aron stopped abruptly, arms crossed. "Well, this is... somethin', innit?"

Cesaro squinted at the lights, rubbing his temples. "This place reminds me of one of those TV warnings. 'If you've got epilepsy, look away.'"

The group proceeded slowly, stopping when the music suddenly paused.

Teddy's eyes lit up as he approached the table. "Snacks and punch? Don't mind if I—"

Aron caught Teddy's arm just as he reached for a cup of glowing punch. "I wouldn't, mate—'less you're into psychedelics."

Teddy's grin widened, eyes sparkling with mischief. "A little adventure never hurt anyone," he said, pouring himself a generous cup anyway.

The others watched as Teddy took a long, deliberate sip, swaying slightly as the music wrapped around him.

Kiara tilted her head toward Aron; curiosity laced through her voice. "Is it always like this out here?"

"Not even close," Aron muttered, his gaze scanning the surreal crowd. He reached past a stack of odd, fruit-infused drinks to grab a small bundle of herbs, stuffing them into his pocket. "That's what's got me worried."

"Shit- guess I'm passing out somewhere on the ground out here, cause I am NOT gonna walk home after this shit!" Teddy declared.

Kiara's fingers brushed the rim of a cup, hesitating.

Robyn's voice cut in sharp. "Ni. Tse ne dlya tebe."

Kiara raised an eyebrow, grinning. "Come on, Mom. Let me live a little!"

Robyn frowned, crossing her arms. "Is not good idea."

Kiara turned toward Teddy, playful but firm. "What do you think?"

Teddy beamed. "As long as we can find some ground to crash on, I've got you, babe!"

Aron stepped closer, voice low but sure. "We've got extra tents... but you might not feel the same in an hour. Ogma's brew's a... special blend."

"Then I'll only have one cup!" Kiara shot back, lifting it halfway. "But I'm not drinking alone."

A slow grin tugged at Aron's lips, amused—and maybe a bit impressed. "Aye, I'm in. But how about we share that one?" He leaned in slightly, eyes warm. "Then maybe just a few ales after, yeah?"

Teddy whooped, spinning in place as the beat kicked up. "Now we're talkin'!"

Robyn sighed, arms crossed, but there was a flicker of a grin she couldn't quite fight. "No trips for me... but I still want joint." She sniffed the air again, eyes sharp.

"I got you," Scarlett laughed, slipping her hand into Robyn's and pulling her toward the crowd. "Let's find you a doobie."

Kiara smiled as she brought the cup to her lips, taking a small sip. The brew was strange—sweet but earthy, like something that wasn't meant to be made but just... grew. A strange hum moved through her chest, and she passed the cup to Aron. He met her eyes for a moment, then drank slowly, watching her reaction with something unreadable behind his gaze.

"Look..." Marcus pointed up into the canopy.

A hush rolled over the crowd as a large figure rose in a vine-wrapped booth at the center of it all. The lights shifted, beams cutting through the trees, revealing musicians seated below, their instruments ancient and alien. A cello-like instrument thrummed, joined by flutes and deep drums, weaving an otherworldly sound.

From the branches above, towering women appeared—seven or eight feet tall, moving like whispers wrapped in silk. One tossed a hoop high into the air, caught mid-swing by another, their limbs curling around the branches like dancers born from the trees themselves. Gasps and scattered applause followed as they struck a final pose, still as statues, shimmering in the soft glow.

The large figure in the booth settled back, fingers working a strange console, blending the ancient song into a pulsing modern hook. The bass dropped, deep and hypnotic, and the forest seemed to breathe with it.

Robyn, caught in the moment, pulled out her phone and raised it toward the performers.

Scarlett and Aron both shook their heads sharply in unison. Robyn grumbled but tucked it away without protest.

Further ahead, past the shifting lights and moving bodies, an open field stretched into a dreamscape of carnival rides. A slow-turning Ferris wheel loomed in the distance, its lights flickering in odd patterns, while a carousel spun lazily, its painted horses worn but still dancing.

The group couldn't help but move with the rhythm, the music pulling them deeper in. Even the doctors loosened up, their feet tapping along to the relentless beat, the forest's strange pulse sinking into their bones.

Marcus swore under his breath, eyes scanning the crowd. "Alright, time to move. We split—two teams. Now."

He glanced at Aron. "You good?"

Aron's jaw tightened. "Not really. Looks like it's gonna be a long night."

"Yo," Cesaro chimed in, a smirk tugging at his lips, "this party's off the hoof."

Doctor Patel cut in, voice firm. "Radios on. Regroup here in twenty."

Aron turned to Kiara, guiding her toward Teddy. "Gotta check on somethin'. Watch over this lot for me, yeah? I'll be back before things get sparkly."

Kiara nodded, offering him their shared cup. "Here. I only had a few sips."

"Smart girl." He downed the rest with a grin and disappeared into the crowd.

The team split—Marcus, Aron, and Moses peeling left, slipping into the sea of bodies and light. Cesaro and Patel veered right, swallowed by the pulsing haze and sound.

"D-D-D-D-DJ YETI!!!" The massive, wooly cryptid behind the booth let out a roar into the mic, his voice rolling like thunder. His hands flew across turntables, spinning records, twisting knobs, remixing hits into something raw and primal. The bass dropped—and the ground shook.

The crowd exploded—hands, feet, paws, claws, and other less definable limbs thrown skyward, bodies lost in the hypnotic pulse of sound and light.

The bass thumped so hard it felt alive, vibrating through their bones. Speakers lined the entire U-shaped clearing, pumping sound in every direction. Bubbles shot into the air from somewhere unseen, catching the strobe lights, creating a dizzying wall of iridescence that made it nearly impossible to see. Both teams—Marcus's and Cesaro's—pushed forward, eyes scanning the crowd, searching for one thing: the unmistakable horns.

Ogma's horns.

There were plenty of satyrs in the chaos, weaving through dancers, but none like him. Most were shorter, the usual five-foot, playful creatures with wild grins and manes like horses, tails flicking behind them. But Ogma—he was something else. A progenitor. Bigger. Older. Different.

Where others had equine features, Ogma was more goatish—his horns thick and curled black, legs covered in reddish-black fur, hooves striking the earth in time with the beat. His chest and face, though human-like, were tanned, almost glowing in the shifting lights.

All of them—Marcus, Cesaro, Aron, and the doctors—converged near the stage, the music so loud it seemed to drown thought itself. And there he was, Ogma, dancing behind DJ Yeti.

The cryptid at the booth was a sight himself—a towering figure covered in shaggy white fur, his pointed ears poking through dreadlocks that spilled from beneath a skullcap. His thick eyebrows gave him a naturally intense look, but now he was beaming, arms pumping the air, hyping the crowd with every rise and drop of the sound.

Marcus felt the pull—the raw Vril energy here was thick, like wading through liquid sound. His whole body buzzed with it, vibrating from the inside out. He found himself fighting the urge to just give in, to move with the crowd, to feel whatever this place was offering.

Were they still in the forest? He wasn't sure anymore.

The trees loomed taller here—ancient, gnarled, their branches arching like the ribs of some forgotten beast. This wasn't the same forest they'd pushed through before. And that carnival? It hadn't been there, but now it stretched beyond the dance floor, lit in flickers of gold and violet, spinning rides casting warped shadows.

Marcus scanned the crowd, eyes narrowing.

Creatures mingled freely—elves, pixies, fauns, even sasquatches moving with uncanny rhythm. Near the edge of the clearing, something massive—horned—stood just beyond the light before melting into the shadows. It was unreal. And somehow, it all made sense.

This place throbbed with energy, alive in ways that shouldn't be possible.

Scarlett and Robyn spun near the back, laughing, tangled in the rhythm. Kiara danced with them for a while, her body in motion, but her mind elsewhere. Then something shifted. Robyn noticed first—the way Kiara's eyes drifted, unfocused, like she was tracking something invisible.

A bubble floated by and popped right in front of her. Kiara flinched, breath catching.

Scarlett's voice came low, steady. "Don't freak out… Let her have this."

Everything shimmered.

Waves of light and color pulsed with the beat—blues and golds dancing in time with the bass, ribbons of green trailing behind every note. It wasn't just music—it was a symphony of light, alive, wrapping around her, through her.

Bubbles floated nearby, no longer just flickers of reflection, but threads—connections. Each one burst with a flash of sound and light, as if they sang when they popped.

"Do you see this?" she murmured, almost to herself.

Robyn laughed, oblivious. "What do you see?" She popped another bubble.

Kiara's fingers hovered, catching one as it spiraled close. It burst with a soft violet ripple, a hum that lingered in the air. Her heart raced—not with fear, but with wonder. Something inside her was changing.

Scarlett tugged her hand, drawing her back into motion. "Don't think too hard about it—trust me, or that's all you'll do for the rest of the night."

But Kiara couldn't let it go. The world had shifted. And it was beautiful. At that moment, somewhere in the crowd, Aron searched—his senses on edge, not knowing that she was already slipping into something deeper.

Marcus's mind flicked to Clarice. She'd be wondering where he was by now. No phones, no way to check in—this place was cut off. It had been days since they'd last spoken, and the silence was getting to him.

The music cut out, and the crowd roared with applause. Above, strange lights flickered—Marcus wasn't sure if they were from DJ Yeti's setup or something more... alien.

From opposite ends of the stage, Marcus's team tried to approach but were blocked by towering sasquatch bouncers, wearing oversized tees with DJ Yeti striking a pose like a cryptid DJ god. Ogma leaned in, whispering something to Yeti, who turned back to the crowd, mic in hand.

"Yo! We got some humie guests tonight!" DJ Yeti's voice boomed. "Give it up!"

Silence.

No one clapped. No one smiled. The lights turned cold, washing the crowd in white. The tension cut through the music like a blade.

Marcus, Aron, Cesaro, and the doctors moved cautiously onto the stage, the bouncers finally stepping aside.

DJ Yeti grinned, but there was no warmth in it. "You lot got balls, crashin' a party like this. But you don't want this smoke."

Ogma's eyes narrowed. "Say no more. I know what Kane wants. But this isn't the time—or the place."

Cesaro bristled, the familiar edge of rage curling in his gut. "Give us what we came for, or this won't end well."

Ogma didn't flinch. "You've no idea who you're messin' with, boy."

Cesaro snapped.

In a flash, his form shifted—spines ripping through his back, limbs contorting, eyes burning yellow. The Chupacabra stood, snarling, towering over the stunned crowd. Marcus stepped in without thinking. Cesaro lunged, claws slashing. Marcus caught the hit, blood streaking down his face as he slammed Cesaro to the stage.

"This is NOT how we do things!" Marcus roared, standing between the beast and Ogma.

Cesaro writhed, furious, until Ogma lifted a small pan flute to his lips. A haunting tune filled the air, carried by the speakers. The crowd calmed. The beast stilled.

Cesaro collapsed, gasping, human again—and naked, covering himself under the sudden glare of a spotlight. Moses tossed him a coat.

"ENOUGH!" Ogma bellowed.

He grabbed Marcus by the collar, lifting him, eyes scanning his bleeding face.

"You stopped him," Ogma said, releasing him. "For that, I offer you one wish. Not now—but tomorrow. Stay. Enjoy. Prove you're more than what I've seen."

Marcus nodded, breathless. "We'll stay."

Ogma turned to the crowd. "Get this man some clothes."

A sasquatch tossed Cesaro an enormous DJ Yeti shirt, signed in marker. It swallowed him like a tent, the crowd laughing as DJ Yeti hyped them up again. The music resumed, louder than before.

Ogma led the squad backstage, where the thrum of bass softened behind them, replaced by the hum of magic that seemed to live in the walls. The satyr gestured casually toward a table covered in ground herbal blends—swirls of blue, green, and earthy brown powders laid out like a feast.

The group exchanged uncertain glances, no one was quite sure how to proceed. Marcus's eyes drifted past the table, catching sight of a fawn-legged woman laughing as a man sprinkled the shimmering dust across her bare chest, inhaling deeply before pulling her into a slow, heated embrace. A nearby forest elf reached into Ogma's robes, drawing out a curved vial, her grin wicked.

"Gentlemen," Ogma interrupted smoothly, as if this were all perfectly normal.

Marcus cleared his throat, stepping back, every instinct telling him to get out of there. "Right. Thank you—for not killing us."

Ogma grinned, all charm. "Not my style. But a little fun? That's encouraged." He handed each of them a fresh cup filled with a sparkling liquid that seemed to hum with light. "Drink, relax. The night's still young."

They took the cups, hesitating only briefly before following Ogma's lead as he vanished into the trees with his entourage, leaving them at the edge of the trail that looped back to the rave.

Cesaro sniffed his cup, then took a swig. "En fuego," he muttered, eyes already brightening.

Whatever was in the punch, it hit fast. The moment they stepped back into the clearing, the world exploded into color and motion. Bubbles floated from unseen places, catching the lights and bending them into prisms. The beat dropped, and suddenly, none of it mattered—fears, doubts, the mission—they were gone. They danced, unrestrained, lost in waves of sound and light.

The punch and the Vril energy twisted together, opening something inside them all. The veil between worlds thinned, and they felt it—the pulse of something ancient, loving, infinite. Here, time didn't tick forward. It stretched, curved, and shimmered. They weren't just in a forest. They were somewhere else entirely, a pocket of existence where Ogma bent the rules to his will.

As the rave faded, the carnival lights flared brightly. Laughter echoed from the games, the rides spinning lazily under the starlit sky. Many drifted away, but plenty stayed, drawn deeper into the surreal night.

Marcus couldn't tell what time it was. Here, it didn't matter. Time felt… optional.

Aron moved through the crowd, the energy thrumming beneath his skin, each step syncing with the deep pulse of the music. The air felt thicker here, charged—but not heavy. It was alive. And something about it, about her, pulled him forward.

He spotted Kiara near the edge of the dance floor, her face lifted, smiling at nothing—and everything. Bubbles floated around her, catching the colored lights, refracting them in bursts of pink and gold. One drifted close, hovering near her cheek before bursting in a shimmer of light, and she laughed—soft, genuine, like it had whispered something just for her.

Aron paused, breath caught somewhere in his throat. His whole life had been edged with control, with keeping the static in check. But now? Now, he felt it bending—melting—in her presence. The buzzing that usually clawed at him, demanding restraint, softened. Around her, he didn't need to hold back.

She turned slightly, like she sensed him, like the air between them shifted. Her energy—it wasn't just around her, it reached, wrapped, welcomed. He could feel it brushing his skin, light and electric, like the bubbles bursting all around them.

One floated between them, catching the light in a perfect sphere, and Aron couldn't help but grin. He reached out, gently tapping it with a finger. It popped, sending a ripple of sound, like a tiny bell, through the air.

"Where them girls at?" someone shouted from deeper in the crowd, and the DJ cranked the beat higher, matching the burst of joy that rippled through the dancers. Kiara laughed again, turning her face toward Aron, even if she couldn't see the way he looked at her—completely, utterly captivated.

He stepped closer, just enough. Close enough to feel her, not just through the music, but in the air itself. The pulsing beat faded, not because it stopped, but because everything else did.

Kiara turned, sensing him there. Her lips parted, a question maybe, but she didn't speak. She didn't have to. The bubbles rose around them like tiny worlds, each one catching fragments of light—blues, golds, violets—and when they popped, they left whispers of color in the air. Aron could feel them too now, not see them exactly, but something in him recognized it. Her energy—her wonder—it pulled at him like a tide. His hand lifted, almost of its own accord, fingers brushing a stray curl from her face, lingering just long enough to make her breath catch.

"I see you," he murmured, voice low, raw.

A slow smile spread across her lips. "I think... I see you too."

There was no hesitation. No second-guessing. He leaned in, his forehead gently resting against hers for the briefest moment—like asking permission without words. Her hand found his chest, steady, sure. Their lips met, soft and certain. A kiss that didn't demand but promised.

Around them, the forest swayed, the music deepened, and the world— just for now—was nothing but them. The static between them wasn't something to control anymore—it was something to share.

Marcus found Aron with the women, all of them now under the spell of the enchanted punch. Sweet, tangy, and earthy—it went down easy, but its effects were just starting to ripple.

The carnival felt like something out of a dream—tents glowing under strings of lanterns, vendors calling out in lilting voices, offering food, trinkets, odd little souvenirs. Games of chance buzzed with laughter, and the air shimmered with fireflies, their glow mingling with the warm torchlight below.

Robyn and Scarlett darted off toward the Ferris wheel, laughing as they ran. Kiara and Aron followed, slowly, caught in something quieter between them, waiting for their own turn on the ride.

Alone, Marcus wandered, falling in step with Cesaro, who threw him a look, half-grin, half-defensive. "Come on," Cesaro muttered. "Let's win somethin'."

In one of the cages of the Ferris wheel, fueled up by the punch they had drank, Scarlett and Robyn began passionately kissing and fondling one another. The light of the fireflies gave a little illumination into the cage that now hung high in the air but had not yet reached the top. Scarlett lifted up Robyn's shirt and played with her breasts, licking and suckling gently on the nipples. Excited and aggressive, Robyn pushed Scarlett back against the seat and spread her legs. She was already wearing a skirt, making it easier for Robyn to pull off her panties in one expertly fell swoop.

Scarlett squirmed and moaned as Robyn kissed the insides of her thighs, moving gently in a forward movement. She breathed heavily in that spot. Her thighs quivered. Robyn used her tongue in a circular motion across the clitoris, using her fingers to separate the velvety skin of the vulva so her tongue could provide the pleasure of cunnilingus to this beautiful brown skinned woman Scarlett. The skirt hid most of what was going on, but in order for Scarlett not to scream out in pleasure, Robyn put Scarlett's own wadded up panties in her mouth to muffle the noise as she continued the oral pleasure. The woman's eyes were rolling into the back of her head as she shook from the carnal act she was partaking in.

As they waited their turn, Kiara stood close beside Aron, her fingers brushing his arm, feeling the subtle shifts in his stance. The air around them buzzed with music and laughter, but she was tuned into him—the steady thrum of his presence, grounding in the swirl of sound.

The next pod rolled up, and Aron stepped forward instinctively—only to freeze mid-step. Robyn and Scarlett were tangled together inside, oblivious, lost in their own world as the ride eased past. Aron blinked, then smirked, casting a glance at the Ferris wheel operator, who grinned knowingly. "Looks like they're enjoyin' the view, we'll take the next one." he muttered, backing up beside Kiara. She didn't ask—she didn't have to, the grin in his voice and the giggles that followed from above, told her everything. He guided her into the next pod, his hand gentle at her back, steady as she settled into the seat beside him. The wheel creaked, lifting them slowly, and the noise below faded into a softer hum. Just their breaths now, just the sway of the cage.

She reached for him, fingers tracing the line of his jaw. The kiss was soft at first, tasting faintly of that strange, sweet punch. Then it deepened—the air thickening, alive. Kiara felt it before anything else—tiny pops on her skin, like sparks skipping across her arms, her throat, her lips. She gasped, pulling back, her hand flying to her chest. "What was that?"

Aron froze, hands hovering, breath caught. "Shite... I'm sorry." His voice cracked, the words tumbling out faster now. "It's me—I can't always stop it. It's—ah—it's kinda why my friends can't tell you everything about us."

She tilted her head, skin still tingling, but not afraid. "What do you mean?"

He took a deep breath. "Alright... so this'll sound mad—but we're not just regular people. Marcus, Cesaro, me... we've got these abilities. Vrill-Enhanced, touched, or however you wanna call it. Nexus stuff. Power." He paused, swallowing. "Mine's electric. Been like that since I was a kid. I pull it from everywhere, charge it—sometimes if I can't ground it, it builds too much."

Her brows lifted slightly, but she stayed close. Listening.

"You didn't see it, but Cesaro? Back there on stage? He... changes. It's ugly, and not his fault, but he's strong. That's why we all work together. It's not just missions or whatever—it's survivin' what we are while protecting others from the things they don't want to know about and protecting them from the rest of the world."

He glanced down, his voice softer now, threaded with something raw and uncertain. "And I've never met anyone who didn't flinch... until you."

Kiara's fingers tightened gently around his, steady and deliberate, grounding both of them in the moment. "Why would I flinch?" she asked, her voice low but sure. "It doesn't hurt... it's not something I'm afraid of."

Aron shook his head slightly, the tension still lingering in his frame. "No, it doesn't seem to, but you felt it though, didn't you? That pull... that charge between us. Most people feel it and they pull away. You didn't."

Her smile deepened, faint but genuine, her head tilting just enough to catch the shift in his tone. "I did feel it," she admitted, her fingers brushing against his hand again. "But it wasn't painful—it felt... familiar in a way I can't explain."

Relief flickered across his face, softening the lines of worry that had crept in. For a moment, he just let himself feel the quiet between them, the way she didn't shy away, how her presence seemed to ease something inside him he didn't even realize he was holding so tightly.

"I think I'm different too," Kiara added, her voice thoughtful now, as if she was only just starting to put the pieces together herself.

He looked at her with quiet curiosity, his voice gentle, coaxing. "Different how?"

There was a pause, not of hesitation, but of reflection, the kind that comes from deciding whether to finally share something long kept inside. "Scarlett and Robyn love to tease me about how I used to talk to animals," she began, her tone carrying the weight of old memories mixed with a wry sort of affection. "They make it sound like I'm some kind of forest witch, whispering to trees and birds like it's some parlor trick."

A soft laugh escaped him, but he didn't interrupt, sensing there was more behind her words.

"I never corrected them, but I don't admit it either," she continued, "because... it doesn't happen the way they imagine or make it out to sound. Not anymore, anyway…I wish it did." Her fingers rested lightly against his, as if drawing strength from the simple contact. "When I was a kid, it was real. I used to hear animals, plants... sometimes even the wind. They spoke to me in ways I could feel, not just words, but something deeper. I didn't question it—I just accepted it as part of my world."

Her voice softened further, a memory surfacing like the gentle ripple of water. "There were voices too, ones I couldn't see. They came in dreams, or when I was alone, and I would wake up knowing things—things that no one else could understand. When I tried to talk about it, people dismissed it. Said it was my imagination, that I was too sensitive or just making things up. Except Robyn, she believed me, she always has."

Aron stayed silent, but his presence was unwavering, listening in a way that didn't demand explanation, only offering understanding.

"I had this... presence with me," she said quietly, almost as if afraid to disturb the memory. "It wasn't human, and it didn't need to be. It was just... there. I could feel it, hear it, like it was watching over me. I thought it left when I got older. Maybe I stopped listening. Maybe it stopped speaking. I don't know. But now, standing here with you, feeling what I've felt since we met... I wonder if I've just been waiting to feel something like this again."

The air between them seemed to hum with a quiet energy, not the sharp sparks from earlier, but something deeper, a resonance neither of them fully understood.

"You haven't figured it all out yet," Aron said, his voice laced with something close to awe, "but you will. I can feel it."

Her hand brushed his chest, and they both felt it again—that subtle pulse, like the earth itself was breathing through them. She didn't flinch, didn't retreat. Instead, she leaned in, her forehead resting lightly against his, the closeness anchoring them both.

"Maybe we figure it out together," she whispered, her voice steady, but tinged with wonder.

A slow smile spread across his face, the tension that had gripped him now giving way to something warmer, more certain. "Aye... I'd like that."

Their lips met again, slower this time, savoring. The sparks came, soft and rhythmic, like the pulse of the earth beneath them. Her hands moved up his back, pulling him closer, every touch igniting more of that strange, shared current between them.

He pulled back just enough to speak, voice low and hoarse. "You're sure? Because I can't always—"

"I'm sure," she whispered, cutting him off with another kiss. "I want this."

They stayed wrapped in each other, exploring that edge, that pull, letting it hum between them—intense, but not overwhelming. Just enough to lose themselves, just enough to know this was real, and they'd both crossed into something neither of them expected.

-Chapter 6-

The Calm Before the Storm

Sunlight streamed through thin curtains, painting soft patterns across the wooden floor of Kiara's room. The air was still, touched with lavender and something warmer—her.

Aron stirred, heavy-limbed, his mind swimming in half-formed memories, blurred edges of a night that didn't feel quite real. He blinked, eyes adjusting, trying to make sense of the unfamiliar space—the room's quiet charm, the scent, the warmth beside him.

He turned.

Kiara lay there, curls spilling like ink over the pillow, her breath slow, steady. Her eyes were closed, but her lips curved faintly, like she'd caught a piece of a dream she didn't want to let go.

"Good mornin'," Aron murmured, his accent soft, curling around her like a secret.

Her lashes fluttered, head tilting toward his voice. "Good morning," she whispered back, her tone curious, amused. "How did we get here?"

The door creaked open just enough for Teddy's grinning face to pop through, eyes immediately narrowing at the scene before him.

"Well, well, well... Look who couldn't keep their hands to themselves," he teased, leaning against the doorframe like he owned the place. "Mornin', lovebirds. You missed one hell of a party... but looks like you found your own."

The door creaked open just enough for Teddy's grinning face to pop through, eyes immediately narrowing at the scene before him.

"Well, well, well... Look who couldn't keep their hands to themselves," he teased, leaning against the doorframe. "Mornin', lovebirds. You missed one hell of a party... but looks like you made your own fun."

Aron raised an eyebrow, deadpan. "You peekin', or just jealous?"

Kiara laughed softly, tugging the blanket up lazily. "Teddy, you're too loud for this early."

Teddy marched in like he owned the place. "Loud? Bitch, please... I had to listen to your asses all night!" He crossed his arms with mock offense. "Meanwhile, yours truly woke up in bed with... wait for it... no one. Nada. Zilch." He threw his hands up. "Do you know how traumatic that is?"

Aron chuckled, shaking his head. "Really?"

Teddy clutched his chest dramatically. "I'm fragile!"

"It's actually my fault," Teddy went on, flopping onto a nearby chair. "I kept drinking the punch—don't judge me, it was delicious."

"That tracks. I'm sorry, though," Aron smirked, sitting up. "I tried to warn ya... Ogma's brew is not for the faint of heart. But if it helps, I think you're a nice-lookin' guy, and I'm pretty sure you would've gotten very laid last night."

Teddy gasped, beaming. "Aw, you're too sweet!" He sighed. "It's okay, I had a blast—right up until I passed out! "But don't worry, I made therapy pancakes. That's why I came to wake y'all up."

A short while later, Aron stood in Kiara's kitchen, leaning casually against the counter as he watched her move with ease...

"You get around here like someone who's been doin' this their whole life," Aron remarked, his tone light but curious.

Kiara paused, turning slightly in his direction, a small smile tugging at her lips. "It's been almost a decade. You figure it out, or you let it stop you. And I've never been much for stopping."

Aron chuckled softly. "Aye, I can see that. Still, you make it look effortless."

Her smile widened as she placed a mug of coffee in front of him. "Let's just say I've had some practice—and Robyn's learned not to mess with my system. She rearranged the kitchen once. Never dared again."

He laughed, shaking his head. "Best not mess with you, got it!"

"Cream or sugar?" Kiara asked, her tone casual as she moved toward the counter.

"Sure," Aron replied, still watching her.

He couldn't help but notice the way she tilted her head—not just listening but feeling the room in a way he couldn't quite explain. Then the cabinet door beside her creaked open, slow and deliberate.

Aron stiffened, the coffee halfway to his lips. "Did you...?"

"Nope," Kiara said casually, pouring herself a cup.

Before he could ask again, a spoon slid across the counter and hit the floor with a sharp clink.

Aron blinked, lowering the cup. "Right... your spoon just-"

Kiara just bent to pick it up. "I told you—it's the house."

"The haunted house?" he asked, brow raised, half-laughing but still very much on edge. He had faced a lot of creatures in his time, but none he couldn't see.

She nodded, totally unbothered. "One's bound upstairs. Scarlett trapped it. The others are still... around. At least until she clears them."

Just then, a soft knock echoed from somewhere down the hall—three quick taps, then silence.

Aron paused, the coffee now back in his hands, but forgotten. "And you live here?"

She grinned, taking a long sip. "Yep. Welcome to my world."

He wandered toward the window, peering out at the well-manicured yard. The sunlight was bright, but the air seemed heavier than it should have been, like the stillness before a storm. He shook the feeling off, turning back to find Kiara setting two mugs on the table.

"You get used to it," Kiara said as she took a seat, wrapping her hands around her mug. "The noises. The energy. It's just... part of the house. It's not as bad as it was yesterday, this is a lot calmer."

Aron sat across from her, studying her carefully. "That doesn't bother you? Especially after everything Scarlett said?"

Kiara tilted her head slightly, her lips curving into a faint smile. "It did at first," she admitted. "But now? No. It's like the house has a personality, you know? It's not just wood and stone—it's alive in a way."

He leaned forward, his tone quiet but insistent. "And you're okay with that? Knowing what was once tied to it?"

"I've learned to be." Her smile widened, but it didn't quite reach her eyes. "It doesn't feel... bad. More like something that's been holding its breath for too long. Like it's restless—waiting—but it doesn't know how to say why."

She sipped her coffee, thoughtful. "Scarlett's right. It's waiting. For something, or someone."

Aron watched her, the weight of her words pressing in. His unease warred with something else—something quieter. A pull. He took a slow sip, letting the warmth settle him.

"You're braver than most," he said finally, voice low, a mix of admiration and disbelief.

Kiara gave a soft laugh, shaking her head. "Don't give me too much credit. I just started admitting any of this yesterday. But I can't fix a problem I won't admit exists, right?"

He nodded, eyes steady on her. "Like how you can't understand what you are until you trust it's real."

She stilled for a beat, eyes narrowing slightly, as if the memory hadn't caught up yet.

"You told me," Aron reminded her gently. "About when you were a kid. The voices, the dreams. Robyn believing you when no one else did. That's why you both wanted the inn—with Teddy. So, you'd have a place, something to build."

She looked at him then, expression unreadable.

"I think Scarlett's the perfect person to help," he added, meaning every word. "She knows what she's doing."

Kiara nodded, her voice carefully neutral. "She does."

Aron offered a faint smile, but his mind was racing.

Nine days later, it was just another ordinary morning. The kind where the house felt still, but not in an unsettling way—just the calm that came with routine.

Kiara sat at her desk, fingers gliding over the keyboard, the soft hum of her adaptive equipment blending with the low chatter from her headset. The voices of distant coworkers droned on about reports and tasks, none of it urgent, none of it strange. She took a slow sip from her coffee, savoring the last warmth from the cup, and let her hand drift along the familiar edge of her desk. Every surface, every sound in this space belonged to her, worn in by countless mornings just like this one.

Life had slipped into something resembling normalcy. That surreal night under the trees, wrapped in music and impossible creatures, had faded into something that felt almost dreamlike—kept real only by the steady presence of Aron and Scarlett. Without them, Kiara, Teddy, and Robyn might have questioned their memories entirely.

But they were real. They were here. And despite everything, Kiara couldn't help but feel grateful and enjoyed their new version of normal.

Things were busy, sometimes too much so to dwell on the lingering questions that tugged at the back of her mind. She was just happy to see Aron when she could, even if it was only for a few hours after work.

Today felt like every other day—until she heard the faint rumble of his truck engine, familiar now, reaching her ears earlier than expected. She paused, head tilting, listening. The crunch of gravel followed, tires biting into the roundabout, then silence as the engine cut out.

Her lips curved into a smile as the steady rhythm of his boots hit the porch steps, followed by the knock—two firm taps, then one softer, just like always.

"Come in," she called, her voice carrying across the quiet room.

The door creaked open, and from the hallway, Robyn's voice rang out, unmistakably amused, her accent thicker now, unfiltered.

"He has coffee in one hand, tools in other...maybe he come to fix house, tak?"

Aron chuckled, holding up an extra cup as he stepped further in. "Here you go, one for you too."

Robyn took it with a satisfied grin. "I approve, Kiki—smart man, this one."

Kiara laughed softly, listening from her office behind what was eventually going to be the front desk, as Aron stepped toward her, the cool air following him like a cloak. She didn't need to see him to know he was standing there with that easy smile and looking at her, not realizing he'd come to work.

Running a hand through her curls, she became suddenly aware of the soft lounge pants and oversized hoodie she'd thrown on that morning. "Sorry, I didn't expect you so early. I'm in full comfy mode."

Aron paused for a beat, eyes taking her in—more intrigued than anything else. "You're apologizin'?" His lips curved into a slow grin. "You look cute. I'd kiss you, but you got a lot goin' on there."

He stepped in closer, nodding toward the sleek headset resting above her ears. "What's that?" Genuine curiosity lit his voice. "Never seen one like it."

Kiara touched it lightly, her fingers brushing the band. "It's bone conduction. I can hear my screen reader without blocking everything else out. Keeps me... connected."

Aron nodded, impressed. "Smart. Never seen anything like it before." His gaze lingered, softer now. "You really are full of surprises, aren't ya?"

"You've no idea," she said, slipping off the headset and reaching for him.

He leaned in, brushing a gentle kiss to her lips before pulling her into a warm hug.

"Ogma sent me home early," he said, shrugging out of his jacket, draping it over a nearby chair. "Said there's a storm on the way. No weather app agrees, but you can never tell with that cryptic old goat. Thought I'd help you batten things down... maybe knock out a few projects."

"Who am I to argue?" she teased, grinning. "We'll take all the help we can get."

Aron set his coffee down, glancing toward the pile of tools and supplies stacked in the corner. "So, what's top of the list today? Porch steps? Gutter? Or is something else ready to fall apart?"

Kiara leaned against the doorframe, thoughtful. "Porch steps are probably the best place to start. Just in case Ogma's right about the weather."

"Right then, I'll take a look." He grabbed his tool bag and turned for the door.

Robyn wandered in, cradling her coffee, a knowing smirk on her lips. "You know, this house's held up better than most... but if you hear voices later, don't say I didn't warn you."

Kiara rolled her at. "Robyn..."

"What? That one upstairs has been loud still."

Aron raised an eyebrow, pausing. "The one in Adeline's old room?"

"She's stuck there," Kiara said, brushing it off with a small wave. "It's fine."

"Right..." He wasn't fully convinced, but he let it go, pushing open the door and stepping into the crisp morning air.

Scarlett arrived a few hours later, breezing through the entryway and tossing her bag onto the front desk. She hugged Kiara from behind, her voice low with amusement. "I brought grounding crystals, sage, and if that doesn't work—we burn it all and start over."

Kiara laughed. "Hopefully, we don't have to go that far. Other than Adeline, it's been pretty quiet."

Scarlett's eyes flicked upward. "Calm's always relative."

Outside, Aron wiped the sweat from his brow, the freshly repaired porch steps firm beneath his boots. He stretched, rolling his shoulders, then glanced toward the open window where laughter and voices drifted out into the cool air.

Teddy leaned out, a grin tugging at his lips. "She says thanks for the manual labor."

"Tell her I'll send the bill," Aron shot back, his own smile widening.

Teddy cocked his head, mischief glinting in his eyes. "You ever do tai chi with her? She was askin' about it."

Aron blinked, caught off guard. "She was?"

"Yeah. I told her you probably do it shirtless. Said we'd narrate for her."

Aron laughed, shaking his head. "Sorry, Teddy... private show. Invitation only. Speakin' of which, is she off yet?"

Yep, looks like the ladies are headin' upstairs to the balcony—Scarlett's got Kiara workin' on that field thing."

Aron paused, wiping his hands on a rag. "Field thing?"

This is a really solid start! It strikes a great balance between real conversation and deeper emotional undercurrents. Here's a refined version with slight tweaks for flow, clarity, and natural rhythm—while keeping all of your great points intact:Teddy nodded, leaning casually on the windowsill. "You know, grounding, energy, all that. Said Kiara's gettin' better at feelin' her own space, so now they're movin' on to boundaries and perception. Probably a lot of breathing and floaty hand stuff."

Aron chuckled under his breath, eyes flicking toward the house. "Pretty sure that's not how it works, mate."

Teddy shrugged, watching him for a moment. "Didn't think you'd be back so much, but... you keep showing up. You really like her, don't you?"

Aron paused, caught slightly off guard by the directness, but nodded. "Aye, I do. Are we havin' that talk now? Where you tell me to treat her right?"

Teddy didn't laugh this time. "Most guys don't even make it to day five. And the ones who stick around? They act like she's some full-time job. She's not. I mean—she is a pain in the ass, but that's a totally different issue."

There was no hesitation in Aron's voice. "I think I get what you mean already…real independent, that one. I know blokes who'd bail just for that—even if she weren't blind. I don't mind though. I quite like when she lets me lead her and narratin' the world. She always listens. And I love hearin' how she notices things I don't even catch. Gives us loads to talk about."

Teddy seemed to weigh that, then gave a small nod of approval as Aron grabbed the ladder, heading around the side of the house to return it to the maintenance shed.

Inside, Kiara stretched out her legs before standing, her muscles grateful to move after the long day. She heard Scarlett's soft steps at the bottom of the stairs, her voice low but full of that usual excitement.

"Today we're working on boundaries—how your energy feels when it's yours, and when it's not. We'll use breath and movement to help you notice the shifts, remember?"

Kiara nodded, brushing her hands down her hoodie. "Right. And try not to overthink it."

Scarlett smiled. "Exactly."

Scarlett met Kiara near the stairs, her voice warm but focused. "Alright, we're stepping it up today," she said, holding out a small cloth bundle. "You've got the grounding down—breath, posture, even the floor work last time. So now, we start working with your edges."

Kiara tilted her head, curious. "Edges?"

"Your field," Scarlett clarified, guiding her toward the balcony. "You've been sensing inside—now it's time to feel what's outside, what's yours and what's not."

Robyn followed, carrying a bowl, a soft feather, and a pouch of smooth stones.

Scarlett set them down with care. "We used breath before, right? To center you. But this" she picked up the feather and lightly brushed the air near Kiara's arm. "This helps you feel the edge of your energy. Where you stop and everything else begins."

Kiara shivered, feeling the subtle shift. "It's... different."

Scarlett smiled. "Exactly. And these stones?" She placed one in Kiara's hand. "We'll use them to mark your boundary points. You'll place them when you feel your field meet the space. It's about claiming your space, holding it."

"Is like when you push against wall, tak? Only you do not see wall—you feel it inside."

Kiara, intrigued: "What's the bowl for?"

Scarlett chuckled. "Just in case. Water brings you back if it gets too much—it clears the static, helps reset."

They stepped into the afternoon light, the gentle hum of the woods settling around them like a familiar blanket. Scarlett guided Kiara to the center of the balcony, her hands steady on Kiara's shoulders, helping her stand tall—feet grounded, spine long.

"Alright," Scarlett murmured, "close your eyes. Just feel for a minute. Notice where you end... and the world begins."

Kiara exhaled slowly, her chest rising with the rhythm of her breath. Her awareness stretched outward, soft and tentative at first, then fuller as Scarlett circled her slowly.

"Good," Scarlett whispered, moving around her. "Can you feel where I stop? Where you keep going?"

Below, Aron caught a flicker of movement out of the corner of his eye. He paused, wiping his hands on his jeans as he looked up. The sight caught him off guard—not because it was strange, but because of how natural she looked. Standing there, focused, present, like she belonged to the world around her in a way few ever did.

He watched, something tightening in his chest, not out of worry—but pride. She was growing right before his eyes.

As if sensing him, Kiara tilted her head, cheeks flushing. "He's watching, isn't he?" she asked, her voice playful, a smile tugging at her lips.

Scarlett chuckled. "He is. And apparently, you're doing just fine."

Before either could say more, Aron appeared at the top of the steps, tool bag forgotten. "Didn't mean to interrupt," he said, stepping closer, voice calm. "Just wanted to see."

Scarlett raised a brow, handing him a small crystal. "Then help. Hold this near her shoulder. Let's see if she notices."

Aron moved beside Kiara, his hand steady. "Alright, love. Let's give it a go."

Kiara stilled, breathing deep. Almost instantly, she could feel the shift—like pressure, subtle, but there. "That's you," she whispered, reaching up toward where his hand hovered.

He grinned. "Not bad, but you're bit stiff. It always flows easier when you're relaxed."

Scarlett nodded, stepping back. "She's getting it, she's just nervous because you're here."

"Nothin' to be nervous about, love. I'd say you're a natural," Aron murmured, lowering the crystal.

Kiara turned toward him, her head tilted. "You really did this before?"

"Yeah." His voice softened. "Tai chi, breathwork… My parents made sure I knew how to handle energy, not just my own, but what comes at me."

Scarlett stepped in, handing Kiara the crystal now. "Maybe you should try it with him."

Aron smiled, meeting her hands. "Go on, see what you feel."

Dinner was light, casual—one of those effortless meals that didn't feel planned but somehow came together perfectly. Teddy, Robyn, and Kiara had thrown a hearty soup together with whatever was in the pantry. One of the wooden tables, sitting in a dining room big enough to easily host at least 50 people, groaned under mismatched plates and laughter, the kind that rolled naturally between bites and half-finished stories.

Kiara sat beside Aron, their shoulders brushing now and then, neither pulling away.

"You've got a nice setup here," Aron said, slicing into his food. "Cozy. Feels like home."

"It's getting there," Kiara replied, smiling. "Still a few ghosts to deal with."

Robyn snorted. "Is understatement. But yes... almost home."

Scarlett raised her glass. "To homes, haunted or not."

They clinked their glasses, and for a while, everything just... was. Easy.

As dusk turned to night, the group thinned out. Scarlett yawned, declaring she'd had enough ghosts for one day, and Robyn followed with a promise to lock the top floor.

Teddy lingered a bit longer, then stood, stretching. "Alright, I'm out.

Got editing to do."

He leaned in toward Kiara, stage-whispering, "Don't stay up too late." With a wink, he was gone. The house exhaled into quiet, soft and familiar. Aron leaned back in his chair, eyes flicking toward the window, then back to her.

"Doesn't look like that storm ever showed up," he said, a small smirk playing at his lips. "From what I can tell, skies are still clear."

Kiara tilted her head, smiling softly. "Seems like Ogma just wanted you out of his hair."

"Maybe," Aron mused, swirling his drink. "But... I was thinkin' I might stay tonight. Just in case that storm changes its mind."

Her heart skipped, but she didn't hesitate. "I was hoping you'd say that."

He reached for her, his hand warm and sure. "Good."

For the first time, he didn't leave for the night. He stayed through the quiet, through the flickering lights, through the strange, low hum that settled over the house.

They headed upstairs, where the room quickly fell quiet, the soft hum of crickets outside filling the air. Kiara's breathing slowed as she drifted off, her head resting near Aron's shoulder. Aron lay awake for a while longer, the peace of the moment settling over him like a warm blanket. It didn't last.

<h1 style="text-align:center">-Chapter 7-</h1>

The Pulse

The quiet of the night was shattered by a loud banging on the bedroom door. Aron stirred first, his heart pounding as he sat upright. Beside him, Kiara groaned, her hand flying to her head. The sound of hurried footsteps and Robyn's frantic voice came from the hallway.

"Aron! Kiara! Get up! Something's wrong—really wrong!"

Aron scrambled out of bed, pulling on his shirt. "What the hell is going on?" he muttered, his accent thick with sleep and alarm.

The door burst open, and Scarlett rushed in, her face pale and her eyes wide with panic. "They're here!" she yelled, pointing toward the window. "The ghosts—the ones I told you about—they're outside, walking. Crawling. They're... missing pieces."

"What?" Aron asked, his brow furrowing as he moved to the window. "What are you talking about?"

Kiara sat up slowly, clutching her head. "What's that noise?" she asked, her voice trembling. "It's screeching, scratching—it's everywhere."

Robyn appeared behind Scarlett, her expression just as frightened. "She's not imagining it. I saw them too. They're coming closer."

Scarlett's voice cracked. "I wasn't just seeing glimpses before. This is real."

Aron yanked the curtain back, his body tensing at the sight outside. In the moonlight, shadowy figures emerged from the tree line. Some limped, others crawled, their forms twisted and unnatural. The sight froze him in place; his breath caught in his throat.

"What... the hell?" he whispered, his voice barely audible.

Then, as his gaze lifted, the blood drained from his face. A jagged crack stretched across the sky, glowing faintly like fractured glass. It pulsed with an eerie light, flickering in and out, casting strange shadows over the yard.

"What the fuck is that?" Scarlett demanded, her voice sharp with fear. "The sky—it's breaking."

"I see it," Aron said, his tone low and filled with dread. "But how the fuck would I know?"

Kiara moaned softly, her hands clutching her head tighter. "I can't... I can't focus. Everything's too loud. It's like the house is screaming."

Scarlett crouched beside her, gripping her shoulders. "We need to leave. Now."

Aron tore his gaze away from the window, turning to Kiara. "Can you walk?" he asked, his voice steady but urgent.

Kiara nodded, though her face was pale. "I'll be fine."

"We are most definitely not fine!" Aron shot back, grabbing his phone and remembering he had turned it off earlier. His jaw clenched. "Of course."

"What's happening to the sky?" Robyn whispered, her voice trembling. "Why does it look like that?"

"I don't know," Scarlett said, her voice trembling but firm. "But we're not staying here to find out."

The group exchanged a brief, tense glance before Aron moved toward Kiara, helping her to her feet. "Come on," he said. "We'll figure this out later. Right now, we just need to get the hell out of here."

It was clear talking was becoming difficult for her. "Where would we even go?"

"That place in the woods..." he was interrupted by his phone ringing.

"WHERE THE FUCK HAVE YOU BEEN?" he heard his sister screeching the instant he accepted her call.

The air inside the room was unnaturally cold, and the metallic tang in the air sent a chill down Aron's spine. As his eyes adjusted, he spotted the source of the tapping.

"Something's... at the window," he murmured, narrating for Kiara—and Rose, still on the line. "It looks like spider legs. They're... moving."

Rose's voice cut in sharply. "Aron? Are you still there?" Their connection going in and out.

"I'm here," he said, stepping back with Kiara as the spindly limbs twitched erratically against the glass, then vanished into the shadows outside.

"It's gone," he said, his chest tightening as he pulled Kiara close.

"Aron, you need to move!" Rose snapped. "Whatever's out there—get out of its way!"

Without hesitation, he grabbed Kiara's hand and bolted down the hallway toward the stairs.

"Rose—"

"Something big went wrong," she interrupted, her voice barely audible through the static. "Mallah says Marcus, Cesaro, Clarice—there was an accident."

"What kind of accident?" Aron demanded as they leapt down the first few stairs.

"She doesn't know yet," Rose replied. "But you need to—"

The line went dead as they reached the second flight of stairs.

"Rose?" Aron's voice echoed sharply, but the phone was silent.

"Aron!" Scarlett called from the base of the stairs, her voice panicked. Rose smacked her hand on her steering wheel in frustration. "Great. Line's dead. Again. Aron, if you can hear me, I'm calling Mallah to let her know I got through. Maybe she can get one of her techies to ping your location. Just don't die, okay?"

He didn't hear her. Shoving the phone into his pocket, Aron gripped Kiara's hand tighter as they raced toward the exit.

His breath came in shallow bursts, a leaden fatigue seeping into his limbs. Every step was heavier, his vision blurring as the room tilted slightly. He staggered, catching himself on the back of a chair.

Scarlett, gripping the window frame, turned toward him sharply. "It's not just you, is it?" she asked, voice wavering. "Something's pulling at all of us."

Teddy stumbled back from the web-covered door, his phone slipping from shaking hands. "Yeah. It's like... like the air's pressing down, trying to crush me."

Aron clenched his fists, forcing himself upright. "We can't give in," he growled. He crouched beside Kiara, brushing a damp curl from her face. "Kiara, wake up. Focus on my voice."

Scarlett's eyes darted to the window again, her voice lower now, less certain, like she was trying to make sense of something too big to name. "This... this isn't just ghosts. The air's wrong—it's like something's ripped open."

Aron's breath came shallow, chest tight. He shook his head, jaw clenched. "I've never seen anything like this—not even close."

Kiara winced, pressing her palms hard against her temples. "It's not just here. I can feel it—something's shifted. Everywhere. Like everything's... off."

Scarlett turned to Aron, desperation creeping in. "Could this be Marcus? Or Cesaro? Maybe something went wrong—maybe they triggered—"

"How the hell would I know?" Aron snapped, pacing, hands running through his hair. "If it was them—they'd have told me. This is somethin' else. Bigger."

Robyn's voice wavered, barely above a whisper. "Whatever it is... it's bigger than this house."

Scarlett bit her lip, eyes flicking to the jagged tear in the sky, glowing faintly, pulsing. "Then we're not safe anywhere."

Aron's voice cut through, rough but certain, like a plan starting to form. "Ogma sent me here."

Scarlett blinked. "What?"

"When he told me there was a storm comin'." Aron's eyes narrowed, staring at the fractured sky. "Knew that old goat was up to somethin'. Didn't make sense then—no one else saw it. But he knew. Not like this, but... he knew somethin' was comin'. He knew I'd come here—might as well have sent me himself."

"To protect her?" Scarlett asked, glancing at Kiara.

Aron nodded slowly. "Seems that way now, doesn't it? Either way, we need to get to him. Whatever's happenin'—he'll know what to do."

Kiara stirred, her voice faint. "We... can't... stay here."

Scarlett glanced between the door and window, jaw tight. "I'm down to leave, but that web's got the front locked."

"There's another way," Teddy gasped. "The cellar—it's got a hatch out back."

Aron nodded. "Then how do we get to it?"

Scarlett moved deliberately, as if wading through water. "We have to go now. This thing's getting stronger."

Without hesitation, Aron scooped Kiara into his arms. "Teddy, lead the way. Scarlett—stay on me."

Teddy bolted toward the kitchen. Scarlett shot one last look at the grotesque forms outside, then followed. The scraping at the windows grew frantic, desperate.

"Stay with me, Kiara," Aron whispered. "We're getting out."

But every step weighed more. The air thickened like tar. Aron stumbled.

"Aron!" Scarlett dropped beside him, shaking his shoulder. "You need a plan. We can't muscle through this."

Vision swimming, Aron smirked weakly. "Tell that... to the web."

Teddy reappeared, dragging a bucket of ash from the fireplace. "What if we smother it? Starve it out?"

Scarlett eyed the ash, then the lighter in her hand. "It's worth a shot. Fast."

Aron rose with Scarlett's help. "Do it," he rasped. "Better than waiting to be eaten."

Teddy spread ash on the web near the door. Scarlett flicked the lighter, bringing the flame close. The strands recoiled, quivering as an acrid stench filled the air. The webbing thinned—but didn't break.

"It's working!" Scarlett cried. "But we need more."

Teddy dashed back to the fireplace. Aron knelt by Kiara again, catching her faint whisper.

"They're... inside."

His blood ran cold.

A shadow shifted in the hallway. A low, guttural clicking echoed, followed by claws on wood.

"They've breached," Aron said, voice flat. "Teddy! Scarlett! Forget the web. Barricade the doors!"

Scarlett bolted to the kitchen. Teddy froze.

"What about her?"

"She's with me," Aron snapped, gripping the fire poker.

The clicking grew louder, the scuttling legs closer. Aron braced himself, standing between Kiara and the dark.

Scarlett reappeared with a knife and a skillet. "Let them come," she growled.

They exchanged a look—no fear left, just resolve.

But Aron's knees buckled. The poker clattered to the floor.

Kiara reached for him, her lips moving silently.

The heaviness wasn't just fear. It was in the air, creeping under their skin. The webbing wasn't just binding the house—it was inside them now, laced with something thicker than dread. Aron's limbs felt heavy, like lead. His breath came in short bursts, eyes struggling to focus.

Scarlett swayed, grabbing the wall. "It's... in the web. It's in us."

Teddy stumbled, wiping sweat from his brow, eyes glassy. "Why can't I—breathe...?"

Aron clenched his fists, forcing himself upright, fighting the pull. "No... we don't sleep. Stay... up."

Kiara's voice cracked. "I... feel it... sinking."

Scarlett's knife slipped from her fingers, clattering beside the skillet. She hit the ground next, her breathing shallow, her limbs refusing to respond. The silence was deafening, broken only by the chittering of spiders and the scrape of legs as darkness closed in.

Rose gritted her teeth as the Jeep bounced hard, the suspension groaning in protest. She'd driven these roads more times than she could count, but tonight? Tonight, it felt like nature was staging a full-on revolt.

Branches littered the path like broken bones, and the rain had turned the dirt into slick, treacherous sludge. Her wipers fought a losing battle against the downpour, smearing more than clearing, and the sky above pulsed with that same fractured light she'd glimpsed before.

"Ogma, if you're listening, I swear to God, this storm better be part of the plan," she muttered, yanking the wheel as she swerved around what might've been a fallen tree—or something worse.

Her phone buzzed in the cup holder, Rose snatching it up with one hand, eyes flicking between the road and the flickering screen.

It was the Emergency Broadcast System.

"All travelers are advised to stay off secondary roads due to increased reports of wildlife migration and unexplained seismic activity in the following regions—"

The voice cut out, static filling the Jeep as a flash of movement caught her eye. Something large and fast darted across the road ahead, vanishing into the trees.

Rose cursed under her breath. "Great. Now we've got cryptids everywhere playing Frogger."

She hit the gas, tires spitting mud, engine roaring. Every second wasted was one more Aron didn't have. Lightning forked across the sky, illuminating a cluster of deer—not running, but standing dead still—eyes glassy, turned toward something in the distance.

As much as she wanted to, she couldn't stop to see what it was they were staring at. She forced the Jeep forward, hands tight on the wheel, knuckles white. The roads were closing in, the storm tightening its grip, and every instinct in her screamed move faster.

-Chapter 8–

The Elder Council

Halfway across the world, a crystalline chamber thrummed with a deep, ancient pulse, the kind that resonated not just through the walls but through the bones of all who entered. Intricate designs, etched by hands long gone, shimmered faintly along the curved surfaces, alive with quiet energy. Each pulse of light seemed to echo with the weight of centuries.

Mallah stood in the center of the chamber, her posture straight, hands clasped tightly behind her back. She'd faced these elders a hundred times before, but today the air felt heavier—like the Veil itself was watching.

Around her, the elders of Witchaven sat in a crescent, their faces lined with wisdom and weariness, eyes like still waters reflecting storms. No one spoke. Not yet.

Finally, Mallah broke the silence.

"The crew we recovered from Agartha is stable," she began, voice even but carrying an undercurrent of urgency. "Though most remain unconscious."

She paused, letting the words settle.

"Marcus Kydd, Clarice Murphy, and Juan Cesaro are among the injured. Clarice has regained consciousness, but she is... fragile. Her focus is entirely on Marcus. His condition remains critical—his energy is... disrupted."

A flicker of concern passed over the face of Elder Nael, the youngest of the circle. His fingers tapped the armrest of his seat, restless. "Disrupted how?"

Mallah's jaw tightened. "I believe the Hollow Earth has marked him, not just physically. His metaphysical core is... fragmented. If he wakes, he may not be who he was."

A murmur swept through the chamber, hushed but sharp.

"Skyler," she continued, "a videographer who accompanied them, has offered footage of their journey in exchange for limited access to Witchaven."

At once, the elder at the center, Elyon, leaned forward. His voice cut cleanly through the hum. "We do not trade our sanctity for information,

Mallah. You know this."

Mallah met his gaze, unwavering. "I do. But the footage is not a bribe—it is a key. We need to understand what happened in Agartha. And more importantly, what Kane did."

A pause. The air seemed to tighten.

"The footage will be reviewed under veil-lock. Skyler's access will be restricted. No knowledge of this place will leave with him."

Elyon considered, eyes narrowing. "And what of Kane?"

Mallah's breath caught, just for a second. "Clarice claims Ivyg manipulated the events. The patterns fit—deception, chaos, exploiting wounds we thought healed. If that's true, then Kane was a pawn."

A voice to her right, Elder Sarin, spoke, his tone skeptical. "Or a willing participant."

"Perhaps," Mallah admitted. "But I knew him. Before all this. He's not reckless. He doesn't move without purpose."

"Purpose can change," Sarin replied coldly. "Especially when twisted by Ivyg."

The elder to Mallah's left, Vara, spoke now, her voice low and tinged with unease. "Ivyg has always been dangerous, but this? Orchestrating the collapse of the Veil itself? This is more than power—it's madness."

Mallah nodded. "The Veil isn't collapsing. It's... shifting. Cracks have appeared across multiple regions—Agartha, the Pacific, even near the Northern Reaches. Creatures are slipping through. Shadows of what's coming."

She paused, eyes scanning the elders. "If we do nothing, these cracks will become rifts. Entire realms could merge."

Nael looked up sharply. "You speak of it as if we have no choice."

"We don't," Mallah said quietly. "The Pulse has begun. It cannot be stopped."

Silence fell, heavier this time.

Elyon's voice was grave. "Then we stand at the edge of the end."

"No," Mallah said. "The end of what was. The beginning of what must be. The Veil was never meant to last forever. It was a cocoon, not a prison."

The chamber dimmed slightly, the light from the walls pulsing slower, deeper.

Elder Vara leaned forward. "And Marcus? Does he hold answers?"

"I don't know," Mallah admitted. "He's silent, caught between worlds. Clarice speaks to him as if he hears—but I feel nothing from him. Yet... something lingers."

"And Cesaro?" Sarin pressed.

"Unconscious. His energy is... volatile."

The elders exchanged uneasy glances.

"We stand on the precipice," Elyon intoned. "If Ivyg is behind this, it is not just realms at risk—it is balance itself. This is not merely a breach. This is war."

Mallah lifted her chin. "No. This is evolution. War is a choice. This... is inevitable."

Sarin's eyes narrowed. "And if Kane stands in the way?"

"Then he will be removed," Mallah said, though her voice lacked conviction.

Nael caught the hesitation. "You believe he can still be saved."

Mallah didn't respond immediately. "I believe he still serves a purpose."

A long pause.

Elyon stood, the first to rise. "Prepare Lemuria. Witchaven will hold as long as it can, but its sanctity is already compromised."

The word Lemuria hung in the air, ancient and alive.

Vara's voice was a whisper. "We had hoped to avoid it."

"So had I," Mallah murmured. "But Lemuria is not a retreat—it is the next step. If we falter, it will rise."

Elyon nodded. "Proceed. And Skyler's footage—bring it to us. If it confirms Ivyg's involvement, we move."

"And Kane?" Vara asked softly.

Elyon's gaze darkened. "Find him. Watch him. But do not strike... yet."

As she stepped into the open corridor beyond the chamber. Her assistant approached, tablet in hand, expression tight.

"Ma'am, we've located Aron. He's under attack. His sister Rose is en route with reinforcements."

Mallah's heart lurched, but she kept her face still. "Good. Coordinate with her. Keep Lemuria's readiness at priority one. If Witchaven falls, there will be no warning."

The assistant nodded, hurrying off. Mallah lingered, her eyes drawn to the distant horizon, where the Veil shimmered—beautiful, fragile, dying. She closed her eyes, feeling the hum of the Pulse beneath her skin.

"One sanctuary at a time," she whispered.

But even as she spoke, she knew sanctuaries could only hold for so long.

-Chapter 9-

Awakening

Denver Colorado

Kathleen O'Brian's sleep was restless; her mind caught in a vivid dream that felt more like a memory than a figment of her imagination. The sounds of rain drumming against canvas filled her ears, a torrent that seemed endless. She saw herself—or someone who felt like her—seated among a group of women, their faces illuminated by the flickering glow of a campfire. The damp air was heavy with the scent of wet earth and smoke.

Her name was Elewisa, and she was a Holy Knight, her armor polished but scuffed from countless battles. The campfire crackled as the women around her laughed and drank, trading tales to break the monotony of the rain-soaked journey.

When it was Elewisa's turn to speak, the firelight danced on her face, and she hesitated. Her heartbeat faster, though not from fear—rather, it was the weight of the story she was about to share. Taking a swig from her tin cup, she began.

She spoke of her homeland; a trading town nestled near a sacred lake. The peace of the town had been shattered by a monstrous troll, Jabir, who extorted travelers and disrupted the trade routes. A bounty had been posted, and Elewisa had led a ragtag group to confront the creature.

The scene shifted, and Kathleen felt herself step into Elewisa's boots, gripping the hilt of her sword tightly as she approached the fallen tree bridge where Jabir lurked. The troll's lanky, bark-like limbs and cold yellow eyes sent a chill through her—through Kathleen.

"Judgment has come, Jabir!" Elewisa shouted, her voice firm and unwavering.

Laughter rumbled from beneath the bridge as the massive troll emerged, towering over her. Its voice was deep and mocking. "You have no power here, little knight. Leave, or I'll crush you like the others!"

The confrontation was a blur of arrows and blades; the air filled with the troll's enraged bellows. Kathleen could feel Elewisa's determination, the adrenaline surging through her veins. She felt the thrill of dodging a massive foot, the weight of her sword as she leapt onto Jabir's back, and the satisfaction of the final strike as the blade severed the creature's head.

Victory brought relief but also something unexpected—a connection. Vulen, the elf archer who had fought alongside her, stood close, his pale features softening as he smiled. His admiration was clear, and as he reached for her, Elewisa—Kathleen—felt her heart race again, though for a different reason.

In the dream, their embrace was electric. She felt the warmth of his kiss and the bittersweet ache of knowing their union could not last. Vulen's duty to his people—his arranged marriage to an elven princess— loomed between them. Still, their brief love affair was perfect, a stolen moment of joy in a life of duty and war.

The firelight dimmed, and Elewisa's voice carried through the camp. "I was meant to live the life of a warrior, not a trader's wife. Right here, with you women, is exactly where I'm supposed to be."

The women cheered, their laughter and camaraderie filling the night.

But the dream began to dissolve. Kathleen felt herself pulled away, her perspective shifting, as if watching from above. She saw Elewisa smiling beside the fire, her image blurring, morphing into Kathleen's reflection.

Kathleen woke with a start, her breath catching as though she'd been running. Her heart pounded in her chest, her mind scrambling to make sense of what she'd just experienced. Blinking against the early morning light spilling into the room, she stared blankly at the ceiling. The dream felt too vivid, too layered with emotion to dismiss outright.

Elewisa. The name clung to her mind like a whisper, along with the images of rain-soaked camps, crackling fires, and that final, fierce battle against the troll. She could still feel the weight of the sword in her hand, the sharp chill of the alpine air.

Her gaze drifted to the Jack Daniels bottle on her nightstand, three-quarters empty, standing as a silent witness to the previous night. The throbbing ache behind her temples reminded her of her indulgence, and she groaned, muttering, "Never again." But even as she tried to blame the dream on whiskey and fatigue, a nagging thought lingered—it wasn't just a dream.

The alarm blared, relentless, until Kathleen slammed her fist down on the Winnie the Pooh clock. With a groan, she swung her legs over the edge of the bed, her fuzzy puppy slippers waiting faithfully on the floor.

Staggering into the kitchen wearing nothing but a camisole and panties, Kathleen felt as though she were wading through a fog—not just of the hangover, but of questions. She needed caffeine, something strong enough to cut through the haze.

Her fancy espresso machine hummed to life as she measured the beans with precision, tamping them down and watching the liquid gold pour into her metal cup. The sharp aroma began to steady her nerves, but it did little to settle the memory of Elewisa's voice or the visceral clarity of that battle.

Was it just her imagination? Kathleen frothed oat milk with the steam wand, her motions slow and deliberate as she mulled over the idea. Maybe it was inspiration—an idea for her next book. It wasn't unusual for her to dream up characters or plotlines. Still, there was something different about this.

She poured the milk carefully into her mug, finishing with two pumps of vanilla syrup and a drizzle of caramel. Taking her first sip, she leaned against the counter and sighed. "Just a dream," she told herself aloud. "Or maybe a story idea."

But the thought didn't sit right. It felt too personal, too rooted in something deeper. She shook her head, brushing the feeling aside. It didn't matter—not now.

What mattered was Wellville.

Her laptop sat waiting on the kitchen table, where she'd spent hours combing through the information she'd gathered. Strange reports about odd noises, disappearing hikers, and the feeling of the woods "being alive" all tugged at her curiosity. She still hadn't pieced it together, but something about Wellville felt charged, as though the town itself was holding its breath.

Kathleen carried her latte to the table, setting it down beside her notes. She'd jot down the dream later, maybe even start drafting a few scenes. For now, though, her focus needed to be on the here and now—on what was happening in Wellville and what it might mean for her.

As she opened her laptop and took another sip, she couldn't help but glance at her hands, half expecting to see them clutching Elewisa's sword instead of her mug. The dream lingered, tantalizingly out of reach but undeniably real.

"Later," she murmured to herself, forcing her attention back to the screen. Whatever Elewisa's story was, it could wait. Wellville couldn't.

Since her divorce several years ago from her now ex-husband Arthur Davis, a well-known doctor in the community, Kathleen had devoted herself full time to writing. To stay focused and not drift off into loneliness, she bought herself a cat to keep her company. She called the black and white tuxedo fuzzball Spooky.

Now that she had finished the promotional tour for her book and was back home, she had decided it was time to start working on her next book project.

Across the house in her study, which she had turned into her computer room after Arthur left, she made her way toward the desk. Pulling up a seat to the computer console, carefully sipping her latte as the computer began booting up. Sure enough, hitting her with just the right kick, the caffeine was exactly what she needed to wake up. The monitor showed message notifications with a flashing icon. Clicking it open, she found a message from her editor congratulating her on her third week in the number one spot on the best seller chart.

Feeling slightly embarrassed, Kathleen blushed and smiled. She still wasn't used to getting this much attention, even from when she had been married. Touring around to promote her book, she felt like a butterfly emerging from its cocoon.

On the computer screen, she closed the window for her emails and opened the file icon on her desktop titled "The X Factor". This was the title of her new book. She had been laboring on this new one intensely for about twelve months and was moving into the final several chapters, close to completion. She had planned to do with this book the same as she had done with her previous two books and that was to travel to her favorite mountain retreat of Wellville Colorado and finish there alone, without the distractions of the city she lived in, including her agentKathleen thought the cool, crisp mountain air might do her some good. She decided then and there to put her plans on hold for a short while and make the trip to Wellville. It wasn't just about her writing—though that was the excuse she used when she told herself this was a rational decision.

She'd been avoiding Wellville ever since the incident three months ago, a night that still haunted her in flashes of memory she couldn't quite piece together. Something had happened, something she couldn't explain. The drive back to Denver afterward was a blur, her nerves too frayed to think clearly.

Since then, Kathleen had been digging. She'd poured over maps, local legends, and forums where others shared stories that seemed eerily similar to her own. Strange disappearances. Whispered tales of ancient energy buried in the mountains. None of it made sense, but it felt connected.

Two weeks ago, a package arrived on her doorstep. There was no return address, only her name scrawled in tight, angular handwriting. Inside, she found an old, leather-bound journal filled with cryptic symbols, fragmented sketches of something that looked like a map, and a note written in the same sharp script:She'd read those words over and over, trying to decipher their meaning, wondering who had sent it and why. She wanted to dismiss it as a prank, but she couldn't shake the feeling that it was meant for her—that whoever had sent it somehow knew about her night in Wellville and the questions she'd been chasing ever since.

The package unnerved her, but it also reignited her curiosity. Maybe this was the missing piece she needed. Maybe Wellville held answers to questions she hadn't even known to ask yet.

For years, she'd been spontaneous about little things—picking a destination for a weekend getaway, trying a new café, taking a different route on a walk—but returning to Wellville felt bigger, heavier. During her marriage to Arthur, decisions like this would have been impossible. He'd planned every detail of their lives down to the minute, leaving no room for the unexpected. Now, after years of being free from his control, Kathleen reveled in the ability to follow her instincts, even when they led her back to places she'd sworn to avoid.

The mountains had always been her haven. Growing up, she'd vacationed across the country with her family, finding inspiration in places like the Blue Ridge Parkway, Yellowstone, and the Sierra Nevadas. Colorado's mountains had always been her favorite, though, and Wellville was the most convenient retreat when she needed solitude.

The little town had felt so unassuming at first, nestled among the peaks like something out of a postcard. But the more time Kathleen spent there, the more she realized there was an undercurrent of strangeness she couldn't ignore.

She wasn't heading back just to finish her book. She needed answers, and whether or not the journal and its cryptic note were part of some elaborate hoax, Kathleen knew one thing for sure: she couldn't ignore the pull to return.

Her laptop chimed softly, pulling her back to the present. She glanced at her notes, her thoughts flitting between the novel she'd been working on and the mystery she was chasing. For a moment, she considered setting the dream she'd had earlier aside as inspiration for a story. But even as she opened a fresh document to jot down her ideas, her fingers hesitated on the keys.

The dream felt... different. Real. Like a message she hadn't yet decoded.

Shaking her head, she saved the draft and closed her laptop. Whatever was waiting for her in Wellville would have to take precedence. The dream, Elewisa, and the strange memories it stirred—those were threads she could pull later.

For now, the mountains were calling.

Looking for her document icon, she peered into the usual area on her screen when she was suddenly distracted by a surge of energy that ran through her like a wave, tingling as though her leg had just fallen asleep…only throughout her entire body, causing her to look down at her hands and feet. Kathleen's heart raced as she felt this new kind of vibration inside herself. She stood up to get some circulation going, since it was not uncommon for her to experience the sensation…at least in her extremities…and usually after at least a few hours of sitting. While trying to shake it off, she heard a ruffling sound behind her, causing her to spin around to see where it was coming from. To her surprise, the very same papers she had heard were swirling around in the air in a cyclone before crashing down to the ground. "What the hell just happened," she wondered to herself.

She waited to see if it would happen again and nothing. Was this just a hallucination? The scattered papers across the desk and floor indicated that she did indeed see what she saw, not a delusion of her hungover mind. The only other rational explanation is that it was her that made that happen. She didn't know how though. She tried to make it happen, concentrating her mind, but again nothing. Kathleen tried to put it out of her mind, but she couldn't. It was the itch she couldn't scratch, filled with the urge to get to Wellville. It all was going to be revealed in Wellville. Something big was going to happen in Wellville. This snapped her back from what felt like a daydream. She knew that she had important things to do.

After turning the computer off, she bent down and found her laptop in the second desk drawer and carried it with her into her bedroom. Out of her dresser, Kathleen got out some of her clothes and set them out on the bed. Half an hour later, after an invigorating hot shower, Kathleen felt refreshed and ready to go, though she continued to feel pieces of the energy she felt before. She pushed though the waves that created some mild nausea. In only a matter of minutes her suitcases were packed with everything she would need: t-shirts, bras, underwear, socks, sweaters, jeans, and of course makeup and shoes. Picking up the two bags off the bed, she headed down the main hallway of her house toward the garage. Before leaving, she kept feeling like she was forgetting something. The solution eluded her and eventually she pushed the thought to the back of her mind and finished getting ready to leave.

Her favorite cold weather coat already lay over the back of her kitchen chair as she grabbed it under one arm and opened the garage door. The time was 12:30; she could easily make it there in an hour and a half, but she gauged approximately 2 hours for herself to make sure it covered a couple of stops she would eventually make upon the way for food, gas, and bathroom breaks. Upon her arrival in Wellville, she would check into the Mountain View Motel first thing and be well on her way to finishing her book by this evening. After double-checking to make sure her laptop was in her bag, she got into her SUV and backed out of the garage.

The drive was uneventful at first, the familiar route winding through stretches of highway and the foothills she had come to know so well. But as she drew closer to Wellville, things began to feel... off. The sky, an overcast gray when she left, seemed strangely tinged with a faint reddish hue near the horizon. Small groups of birds circled in odd, tight patterns overhead, their movements almost mechanical. Kathleen tried to shrug it off, but a chill ran down her spine when she passed a gas station with a broken sign that flickered erratically, the only car in the lot seemingly abandoned with its driver's door left ajar.

"Just your imagination," she muttered to herself, gripping the steering wheel tighter. But the unease lingered, an itch she couldn't scratch.

By the time she reached the Mountain View Motel, the familiar rustic building with its weathered sign was a welcome sight. The motel had always been simple but charming, with flower boxes hanging from the windows and the faint smell of pine lingering in the air. Kathleen parked in her usual spot near the entrance and stepped inside, eager to get settled.

The clerk at the front desk, a middle-aged woman with a kind but tired face, greeted her with a polite smile. "Welcome back, Ms. O'Brian. Glad to see you again." She paused, her brow furrowing slightly. "I hope your trip up was safe?"

Kathleen blinked at the question, taken aback by the note of concern in the woman's voice. "It was fine," she said, hesitating for a moment. "Though... I did see some strange things on the way in. A car left open at the gas station, flocks of birds acting... weird." She laughed nervously, shaking her head. "Probably just me overthinking it. Long drive and all."

The clerk gave a knowing nod, her smile tightening. "You're not the only one who's mentioned odd things this morning," she said, her voice dropping slightly. "A few hours ago, someone called about the streetlights flickering on Main—said it was like they were all blinking in sync, even though it's broad daylight. And there was a report from the Ridgeway trailhead—something about how the river sounds... wrong. Like it's echoing when it shouldn't be."

Kathleen raised an eyebrow. "Echoing? That's strange."

"It gets stranger," the clerk said, leaning in slightly. "People have been saying the Ridgeway trail feels off. Warmer than it should be for this time of year. And don't even get me started on the missing people."

Kathleen stiffened. "Missing people?"

The clerk seemed to realize she had overstepped but sighed and continued anyway. "Three in the last month. All locals. It's got the whole town on edge, especially since no one knows if it's tied to... you know." She glanced around as though someone might overhear. "The Pulse."

Kathleen's stomach flipped, the tension in the room became suddenly heavier. "Do they think it's connected?" she asked carefully.

"Who knows? The official word is 'no evidence of foul play,' but you know how small towns are. Folks can't help but talk." The clerk leaned back, brushing a strand of hair from her face. "But let's be honest, this town's always been strange. The Pulse just made it worse."

Kathleen tilted her head, curiosity sparking despite her unease. "What do you mean, always been strange?"

The clerk chuckled dryly, crossing her arms. "Oh, Wellville's always had its share of oddities. People swear the woods are alive, that they move when no one's looking. There are old legends about lights in the forest leading folks astray—folks who were never seen again. And then there's the Ridgeway river."

"Interesting," Kathleen said, though her mind was already turning over the possibilities. The clerk hesitated for a moment, then leaned in conspiratorially. "And then there's the creature," she said, lowering her voice. "A few people claim to have seen something up near the old logging trail real early this morning—a creature like nothing anyone's ever seen before. I heard it's tall, with glowing eyes and some kind of shimmering fur or skin that changes in the light. The hunters around here have been trying to track it all morning, but no one's even gotten close. No tracks, no scat, nothing. Just... gone, like it's part of the forest."

Kathleen blinked, her eyebrows rising. "And people are taking this seriously?"

"Folks out near the trail won't let their kids play in the yard, and the hunters who've gone after it? They come back shaken. Say it's like the woods are working against them. Whatever it is, it's freaking people out."

Her writer's instinct couldn't help but latch onto the mystery. She forced a smile, trying to lighten the mood. "Sounds like a goldmine for inspiration."

The clerk gave her a faint smile, sliding the room key across the counter. "Your usual room's ready for you. If you need anything—or if anything strange happens—you know where to find me."

"Thanks," Kathleen said, taking the key. The chill of the metal felt sharper than usual against her hand, and as she walked down the hallway, she couldn't help glancing over her shoulder.

The motel felt different this time—too quiet, the air too thick, as if the walls themselves were holding their breath. She shook off the feeling as she unlocked the door and stepped inside her room.

The space was as she remembered: a cozy queen-sized bed with a patchwork quilt, a small writing desk by the window, and the faint scent of pine lingering in the air. She set her bags down near the dresser and perched on the edge of the bed, staring at the plain, unassuming room.

After a few moments of stillness, Kathleen opened her bag and pulled out the package that had been haunting her thoughts for weeks. Its edges were worn from handling, but the envelope remained sealed, the same sharp handwriting on its face:"For your eyes only."

She took a deep breath before carefully breaking the seal, her hands steady despite the flicker of unease curling in her chest. Inside was a stack of documents stamped with the words CLASSIFIED – DO NOT

DISTRIBUTE in bold red letters. Her stomach twisted as she skimmed the first page, a typed report dated five years ago.

The words were clinical and detached, but the story they told was anything but:"Incident #237-A. Subject reported seeing shadowy figures in the woods near Ridgeway trail. Subject claimed to hear voices that grew louder as they approached. Subject disappeared for three days, found in a disoriented state by local authorities. No recollection of time lost. Physical exam revealed extensive scarring resembling symbols of unknown origin."

Kathleen swallowed hard, her pulse quickening. She flipped to the next page, a hand-drawn map of Wellville with several locations circled in red ink—Ridgeway trail, the abandoned logging camp, and a few unnamed spots deeper in the woods.

More reports followed. Stories of strange lights, sudden disappearances, and people who returned… changed. One file described an entire family vanishing from their home, their belongings left untouched. Another detailed a group of hikers who emerged from the forest days later with no memory of their trip but identical marks on their arms.

The final document was a photo, grainy and overexposed, of what looked like an orb of light hovering above a clearing. In the margins, someone had scrawled a single word: "Unstable."

Kathleen set the papers down, her mind racing. The package offered no context, no explanation of who had sent it or why. But the stories it contained were too vivid, too detailed to ignore.

She leaned back against the headboard, staring at the documents spread across the bedspread. The note that had come with the package had told her to come here today, but it offered no further guidance.

Why now? Why a week after the world had been shaken—literally— by an event no one could explain?

Kathleen let out a shaky breath, her gaze drifting to the window. The room felt too small, the walls pressing in on her as questions swirled in her mind. Why had someone sent her this? Why did they want her here? And what, if anything, did the Pulse have to do with the strange occurrences cataloged in those files?

She glanced at the photo of the glowing orb again, its faint, otherworldly light almost mesmerizing. The words scrawled beside it seemed to echo in her mind:"Unstable."

Kathleen's hands curled into fists, the faint tremor of nerves overtaken by a surge of determination. She didn't know what was happening here or why she had been drawn into it, but one thing was certain: she had to find out.

The answers weren't going to come to her. She would have to go looking for them, and Wellville was as good a place as any to start.

The thought sent a shiver down her spine.

-Chapter 10-

Redhead to the Rescue

It was no secret that Rose was furious about getting pulled away from the elusive cryptid she had spent days tracking, but as she sang along to one of her favorite songs for the eleventh time that morning, she was more than feeling that sentiment as she belted it out for a twelfth time that seven armies could not hold her back, upon being told that morning about how her brother had gone missing. Despite wishing she had the same connections he had, like Ogma, who could create portals and pocket dimensions, she actually had to spend the time driving up from the northeastern corner of the California green triangle, deep into Oregon to get to him and whomever the girl was that he was with. Not only was this an alarming occurrence, due to the fact that her brother was usually the one rescuing her. After all, he was the tactician and knew the Pacific Northwest like the back of his hand, after working with Ogma for so long to help protect the creatures who roamed the area. His specialty was working with the ones even the locals rarely knew about, which was what Ogma had hired him to do. Having grown up among a variety of them, Aron and Rose knew how to track, handle, and transport a vast number of species that would be a danger to human population, or in danger of them.

She was making great time but becoming a bit nervous she would run out of fuel before finding a gas station, now wishing she would have stopped at one of the ones just off the highway. Technically, she had pulled off and into a location, before immediately pulling right back out upon seeing how busy it was all the way around, since there was no time to wait in line for twenty minutes. Coasting into one she had run into nearly an hour later, Rose quickly paid the attendant before making her way inside to get a drink while he filled her tank. Hoping she could get a better signal upon seeing a few buildings nearby, she pulled out her phone to refresh her navigation screen since it had crashed and stopped working about twenty minutes back.

Saoirse Rose O'Keenan went by her middle name Rose because she felt like Saoirse sounded like an old lady's name. Her parents thought it refined and had passed it down from her mother's side for generations. Her brother Aron got a normal name, after all, it was much more fitting to Her character as a person was much better suited to the name Rose anyway. It could have been her long, curly red hair that gave her the likeness—bouncing and flowing like petals in the wind.

"This had better be worth it," she muttered under her breath as she pulled open the door. The bell above her head jingled, and all eyes within the business turned toward the Irish woman who was clearly out of place in this rural setting. The mounted deer horns on the walls, neon beer signs, and men in red plaid flannel shirts and jeans screamed lumberjack country.

She made her way to the back coolers and selected a drink from the tap. She poured herself a smaller cup, skipping the ice. The habit had stuck ever since watching a reality show where her favorite British celebrity chef tore into the unsanitary practices of restaurants and their ice machines. The thought made her smirk as she imagined his voice in her head, dropping f-bombs and snarky one-liners about the state of some poor kitchen.

Like her famous chef idol, Rose had a penchant for using the f-word freely, much to the discomfort of strangers. She also had a knack for causing awkward silences with her unfiltered truths about the cosmos, the nature of human behavior, and whatever other deep or obscure topic happened to cross her mind. These weren't exactly the kinds of conversations most Americans were used to, but Rose didn't care. She'd always been a bit of a rebel, with her affinity for Gothic and medieval styles, and she had no trouble finding people who appreciated her uniqueness.

Mallah had helped her tap into that individuality, unlocking her Vril power and teaching her to channel it into helping the unseen world—the realms most people either ignored or couldn't perceive. Though Rose's abilities in this life differed from those she'd wielded in past incarnations, she'd adapted to them like a fish to water. Now, at 29, she was confident in her power to manipulate reality with psychic energy, even if the visions that plagued her mind still left scars she couldn't entirely ignore.

As Rose moved down one of the aisles toward the counter, a man stepped out in front of her, blocking her path. She stopped abruptly, her green eyes narrowing. His grin was slow and predatory. She didn't need to look over her shoulder to know someone else was behind her. Still, she did—a quick glance confirmed another man, just as broad and rough-looking, standing at the other end of the aisle.

Her pulse quickened, but her face remained neutral. These were the same men she'd noticed earlier, sitting in the corner with their buddies, hooting and hollering as she walked in. She'd ignored their crude comments then, but now they weren't giving her a choice.

"Hey there, red," the man in front of her drawled, his gaze dragging over her like she was something on a menu. "In a hurry?"

Rose's fingers twitched at her sides. Her instincts screamed for action—the faint hum of her Vril energy buzzed at the edge of her awareness, begging to be used. A single push would send them stumbling back and give her enough space to slip by. But no—not here. Not unless she had no other choice. She exhaled slowly, letting the tension settle in her shoulders instead of her hands.

"Outta my way," she said evenly, her tone carrying more steel than she felt. She shifted her weight, ready to move if they didn't step aside. "Mate, you've got no idea."

"Aw, no need to be like that," the man behind her said, his voice dripping with mock sweetness. "We're just being friendly."

Rose's eyes flicked to the mounted deer horns on the wall behind them. Their sharp points seemed to mirror the sharp tension rising in the air. The neon beer signs glowed faintly, reflecting off calloused hands and worn plaid flannel. She sighed inwardly. Backwater lumberjacks with less charm than a dead trout. Just her bloody luck. At least it wasn't a cryptid.

She remembered Mallah's words, calm and grounding in moments like these: "Keep your focus sharp and let the world bend around you." Rose tilted her head slightly, her gaze steady and unyielding as she looked the first man square in the eye.

"And where d'you think you're goin'?" he asked, reaching back to grab her arm and spin her toward him.

Rose scoffed, pulling her drink closer to her lips, savoring the fizzy sting of the soda as she cleared her throat dramatically. "Oi, I'm tryin' real hard to stay civil here…" She tilted her head, her eyes narrowing as she leaned in. "So why don't you and yer mate over there take a hike, eh? Before I lose me patience."

"Bobby, you leave that woman alone!" the older lady behind the register yelled at him.

Grumbling under his breath, Bobby finally backed off and joined his party at a table near the register, but not without a lingering glare that made Rose's skin crawl. She shot him a pointed look, her jaw tightening.

After paying the woman behind the counter for her drink, Rose glanced down at her phone, waiting impatiently for a signal. She could feel Bobby's gaze still drilling into her, the weight of his anger and bruised ego palpable. Ignoring him, she grabbed her change, nodded at the cashier, and walked briskly toward the door.

She hadn't even made it halfway to her car when Bobby's voice cut through the air like a blade.

"Good thing you're pretty, 'cause you're a real BITCH!"

Rose stopped mid-step, her hand on the car door. Slowly, she turned back to him, a slow smirk curling her lips. A flicker of crimson flashed across her irises, almost imperceptible but unmistakable to anyone paying close attention. Bobby froze, his cocky expression faltering.

"Careful now," Rose murmured, her voice low and laced with venom, "yer mouth's gonna get you in more trouble than yer tiny brain can handle."

Before Bobby could respond, the sound of fabric ripping caught his attention. His belt snapped clean in two, sending his pants tumbling to his knees, exposing his sad excuse for underwear. His face flushed crimson as the other patrons burst into laughter, their jeers following him as he scrambled to fix himself.

Rose chuckled under her breath, turning back to her car.

As she reached for the handle, the distant rumble of an "AFTER-SHOCK!" from just outside the store made her pause. She turned, watching the men retreat into the safety of the gas station, crouching behind their table.

The sky above rippled with light, arcs of energy illuminating the horizon like a surreal aurora borealis. The brilliance swallowed the rising sun, casting everything in a dazzling glow so intense Rose had to shield her eyes.

She fumbled for her key fob and quickly reached in to grab a vinyl eyeglass case with the words 'Omnispects' written across it, standing up just in time to get a good look at the creature that had just stepped in from wherever it had entered this dimension. Caught a little off-guard, Rose was having trouble maintaining her own inner balance, her body flooded with Vril energy, her fight or flight response kicked in and her body glowed with a red hue as she moved the power around with her hands in the air.

Having noticed this, Bobby and his friends stepped back outside, enamored at the sight of Rose, who knew it was no aftershock they had been running from, but a tear in the Veil opening up right there in the middle of the parking lot like a zipper in space and time. To her surprise, something she never would have imagined had entered into our world, a creature Rose only ever believed to be a myth.

"Black Annis." She said as she saw the eight-foot-tall blue skinned hag monster with iron claws that had a taste for human meat. "Didn't see that coming…" she said, tilting her head as she assessed it.

The creature dove right in on feeding itself on the flesh of the redneck loggers, ripping the head right off of the one who had called out to the others, drinking up the blood with smacked lips and a crimson mask. Rose ducked out of the way as Bobby was snatched up by the hideous hag that turned its victims into leather to make clothes to cover its body. The Black Annis had already broken his leg leaving him unable to defend himself or run away. It looked ravenous as it licked its lips, circling its prey, preparing to feast. Rose thought about how Bobby, albeit an idiot, didn't deserve to die like this, even if he was a misogynist douchebag, Rose didn't have it in her to let another person die at the hands of this foul wretched creature. Using her telekinetic Vril powers Rose created a temporary shield over Bobby, who used that moment to crawl under her vehicle. Black Annis was angered by this and turned its attention toward Rose, who, unlike the men, did not back down from the creature. It may have haunted a few of her dreams as a child when she and Aron still lived in Ireland. That was before their time living in Australia as teens; before their Vril powers manifested, before meeting Mallah, and before ever hearing about Witchaven. The nasty creature slashed at Rose with her sharp, hooked iron claws, tearing a hole in her dress. This really pissed the spicy Irish redhead off. "This is my favorite dress, you fucking bitch!"

Black Annis shrieked back at her. "ARRRRRHHHHHH!" in response.

"That is enough of this nonsense…" Rose scowled.

Using her telekinesis, she pulled one of the chainsaws from the logger's truck. She pulled the cord, and it revved up to life with a familiar noise. When the hideous hag came to attack again, Rose fended off the claws with the chainsaw. Another swing from the hag tore her dress again.

"Fuck!" Rose screamed, her voice sharp with fury. "Yer really bloody pissin' me off now!"

The hag tried to strike again, but Rose caught its arms in an energy field. Crimson light glowed around her hands as she spread the creature's limbs wide, pulling hard until its body strained against the force. With a determined yell, she brought the chainsaw down, slicing clean through the hag. Blood splattered across the ground as the bisected corpse crumpled into a twitching heap. She released the red Vril power, and the limp bifurcated corpse plummeted to the ground with a splat.

The lady behind the counter inside the shop came out to see what had happened and was shocked to see Rose, covered in blood, helping Bobby back inside the gas station, laying his body down on the floor. Rose ran to grab supplies, returning with some ice, alcohol, paper towels, baby wipes, and a blow torch she managed to find in the back end of the store.

The shopkeeper followed Rose's prompts to help hold him still. Covered in blood but calm, Rose was focused, moving quickly as the injured man groaned in pain.

Rose grabbed a bottle of alcohol and flashed a crooked grin as she pulled a crisp hundred-dollar bill from her pocket. "This is gonna hurt, darlin'," she said, her tone laced with dry humor.

As Bobby stared at her, confused and wary, a bright crimson glow began to radiate from Rose, bathing the small shop in an eerie light. She knelt in front of him, placing her hands on his mangled legs. The shopkeeper, still in shock, hurried to Bobby's side, gripping his hands tightly.

"Here," Rose said, holding out the bottle of alcohol.

Bobby hesitated, his wide eyes darting between Rose and the shopkeeper. Rose arched a brow. "Go on, lad. Crack it open. You're gonna need it."

The sound of the bottle opening filled the silence, followed by gulps as Bobby chugged desperately. Rose's hands glowed brighter as she pressed them firmly against his legs. The intense heat from her Vril energy sizzled against his skin, the smell of burning flesh rising faintly in the air.

"Emergency services aren't comin', mate," she said sharply, her tone leaving no room for argument. "They've got their hands full out there, and even if you are a huge douche-waffle, I'm not about to let ye bleed out all over this floor. I like the shopkeeper too much for that!"

Bobby screamed, his body arching as the searing waves of energy coursed through him. His grip tightened on the bottle, the alcohol spilling down his chin as he took another desperate swig.

"Good lad," Rose muttered, her voice steady despite the chaos. "You'll live, but ye might not thank me for it tomorrow."

The glow around her hands began to fade, leaving behind cauterized wounds that no longer bled. Bobby gasped for air, his chest heaving as the pain slowly subsided into a dull throb.

A few moments later, Rose stood and wiped sweat and blood from her brow. She noticed her change sitting on the counter and smirked as she stuffed it into the shop's tip jar.

"Keep the change," she said, winking at the shopkeeper.

Grabbing a baby wipe from the pack, she cleaned her face, adjusted her sunglasses, and headed for the door. "Now, if ye'll excuse me," she called over her shoulder, her tone casual despite the carnage, "I've a brother to find."

With that, she was gone, leaving the shopkeeper and Bobby in stunned silence.

-Chapter 11-

Connections

The opulent chamber brimmed with quiet luxury, a blend of classical elegance and cutting-edge technology that could only be afforded by those accustomed to the highest echelons of privilege. Ivyg, the ever-gracious host, moved through the room with a practiced ease, his tailored suit pristine and his smile as smooth as the amber liquid swirling in his glass. Around him, his guests—politicians, tycoons, and a few other well-connected elites—laughed and toasted as if the world beyond their enclave hadn't shifted on its axis.

"The wine is exquisite," one of them remarked, raising a crystal goblet.

"Only the finest for my esteemed guests," Ivyg replied smoothly, his tone warm and measured. "I wouldn't dream of offering anything less."

He let them bask in the illusion of camaraderie as the orchestra in the adjoining room played a soft, haunting melody. But as the laughter and conversation continued, Ivyg excused himself with an apologetic nod and disappeared behind a gilded door into the private observation chamber.

Inside, the mood was colder, the air crackling with tension. The room was bathed in the glow of holographic displays, each one pulsing with data streams and energy maps. The observation chamber buzzed with low voices and the hum of data streams as Ivyg strode in, his presence instantly silencing the room. His tailored suit was immaculate, his expression sharp and unreadable. He scanned the gathered group of aides, analysts, and operatives before fixing his gaze on the holographic display dominating the room.

"Begin," he said, his tone brooking no delay.

One of the analysts stepped forward, their hands moving swiftly over a control panel to expand the projection of a large, shimmering landmass. The outline was unmistakable—Atlantis.

"Initial teams landed shortly after sunrise," the analyst began. "The structure remains intact. Early reports indicate the area is stable, with no signs of residual seismic activity. The survey teams have confirmed access points and secured the perimeter. It appears uninhabited."

Ivyg nodded once, his attention fixed on the rotating hologram. "And the energy fields?”

“Minimal interference so far,” the analyst continued. “We’re detecting faint ley line activity, but nothing that poses an immediate threat.”

“Good,” Ivyg said. “I want updates every hour. Ensure the area remains secure. Send word to the C.O.O.—he’ll be on-site by tomorrow evening. Brief him fully before departure.”

“Yes, sir,” the analyst replied, their voice steady.

Ivyg turned his gaze to another projection, this one a smaller landmass with jagged coastlines and a strange, flickering glow. The energy radiating from it was far more erratic, almost sentient. The room seemed to grow heavier as his eyes narrowed.

“Lemuria,” one of the operatives muttered, breaking the silence.

Ivyg’s head snapped toward them, his voice cutting through the air like a whip. “We don’t call it that.”

The operative stiffened, swallowing hard. “Of course, sir. The South Pacific anomaly.”

Ivyg turned back to the hologram, his expression darkening. “What’s the latest?”

Another aide stepped forward hesitantly. “There was... an incident. One of our private pilots attempted to land on the island early this morning.”

Ivyg’s jaw tightened. “And?”

“We lost contact with him shortly after. No distress signal, no trace of the aircraft. It’s as if he vanished.”

A tense silence fell over the room. Ivyg exhaled slowly, his tone dangerously calm. “There’s a reason I didn’t order anyone to approach the island. It’s protected. Any unauthorized incursion is a death sentence, as your pilot has now demonstrated.”

The aide’s face paled. “Should we... send a retrieval team?”

“No,” Ivyg said flatly. “The man was a fool, and he isn’t worth the risk. Inform his superiors that his death was the result of insubordination. Let it serve as a warning.”

He leaned closer to the hologram, his fingers brushing the edge of the console. “We’ll proceed as planned. Deploy a team from Hawaii, but no ships will disembark directly onto the island. The waters surrounding it are too volatile. We'll need to establish an entry point from an existing, modern city nearby."

The aides nodded, taking notes as they prepared to execute his orders. Ivyg straightened, his gaze sweeping over the room. "I want reconnaissance teams ready within twenty-four hours. No mistakes this time. If I find anyone else acting outside of protocol, the consequences will be... final."

He turned to the woman standing at the edge of the group, her striking presence commanding attention despite her silence. Her dark eyes met his, unflinching but guarded.

"Callista," he said, the name rolling off his tongue like a mockery. "Ensure my directives are followed to the letter. No improvisation. You've already failed me once—I won't tolerate it again."

Callista inclined her head, her movements precise and deliberate. "Understood."

Her voice was calm, but Ivyg caught the faint tension in her posture. He smiled faintly, enjoying her discomfort. As she turned to leave, he called after her, his tone cutting.

Ivyg's gaze lingered on the projection, the faint shimmer of ley lines converging over the South Pacific anomaly. His voice cut through the hum of the room like steel slicing velvet. "Oh, and Callista?"

She paused at the door; her silhouette framed in the soft glow of the holograms. "Yes, sir?"

"Remind the team in Hawaii that I don't care how long it takes," he said, his tone cool and deliberate. "The islands won't yield to force, but they will to patience. No ships disembark, no unnecessary risks. I won't lose more resources to amateur mistakes."

She nodded in agreement, not because she actually did, but to convey her compliance. "Understood." The quiet click of her heels faded as she exited the room.

Ivyg turned back to the display, but his attention shifted to another section of the map—three faintly glowing points, scattered like breadcrumbs across the Atlantic and Pacific. His jaw tightened, and he gestured sharply to the nearest aide.

"Expand these locations," he ordered, his voice low but commanding.

The display shifted, magnifying the areas he indicated. Each anomaly pulsed faintly, their energy erratic and unstable. His eyes narrowed as he studied them, the wheels in his mind spinning faster than the swirling projections.

"Could it be Witchaven?" he murmured, more to himself than anyone else.

From the corner of his eye, he noticed Callista lingering just beyond the threshold, her return quiet and hesitant. Her presence piqued his suspicion. He straightened, his expression hardening. "Callista," he said, his tone sharp. "You seem... reluctant. Is there something you wish to tell me?"

Her hesitation was slight but enough to draw his full attention. She stepped back into the room, her heels clicking softly against the marble as she approached. "I don't know," she said carefully. "These anomalies... they match some of the descriptions, but I can't confirm. Witchaven has always been cloaked, beyond even our best efforts to find it. If the Pulse revealed it, it could be one of these—or none."

Ivyg's eyes narrowed, and he stepped closer, his towering frame casting a shadow over her. "You don't know?" he repeated, his voice dripping with condescension. "You've spent years overseeing this search. Are you telling me you've learned nothing?"

Callista held her ground, her dark eyes meeting his with quiet defiance. "The Pulse changed the rules," she said evenly. "What was once hidden may not stay that way. But if this is Witchaven, it's not a place we can simply walk into. You know that."

His hand shot out, gripping her chin in a sudden, calculated motion. The movement was swift but not violent—just enough to assert dominance. "Let me be clear," he said, his voice dangerously soft. "If I find out you've been withholding anything, there will be consequences. Do you understand?"

She didn't flinch, though her jaw tightened beneath his grip. "I understand," she replied evenly.

He released her, stepping back as if the exchange had never happened. "Good," he said, his tone returning to icy composure. "Prepare reconnaissance for each of these sites. I want them thoroughly examined, no details overlooked."

Callista hesitated for a fraction of a second before nodding. "Of course, sir."

"And one more thing," he added, his gaze returning to the glowing map. "If you value your position, Callista, find out which of these is Witchaven. I don't tolerate inefficiency."

She inclined her head and left the room, the tension lingering like a shadow in her absence. As the door clicked shut behind her, Ivyg turned back to the display, his fingers steepling as he studied the flickering anomalies.

"Witchaven," he murmured to himself, the word heavy with both fascination and hunger.

-Chapter 12-

Dystopia

"Where are we?" Kane gasped, his breath ragged as he struggled to sit up. His head throbbed, his vision swam, and the faint metallic tang of blood lingered in the back of his throat.

"I was really hoping you could tell me," came the familiar voice of his friend and colleague, Dr. Sanjay Patel. Sanjay crouched beside him, offering a hand to help him up, but immediately winced and gestured to Kane's arm. "You're going to want to use the other... well, hand."

Kane followed Sanjay's gaze to the crude bandage wrapped around his stump. His breath hitched, his stomach turning as he stared at the bloody nub where his right hand used to be. "What the—?!" he stammered, panic overtaking him as he instinctively reached for his injured arm.

"Yeah, I wouldn't touch that if I were you," Sanjay interjected, his tone dry and tinged with sarcasm—an exaggerated edge that cut through his normally thick Indian accent. "Trust me, it's not going to make you feel better."

"What the hell happened?!" Kane demanded, his voice rising with a mixture of fear and anger.

"I don't know!" Sanjay shot back, throwing his hands in the air. "One minute we were stabilizing the portal, the next thing I know, Marcus sabotages us, and then... this!" He gestured to the eerie, desolate surroundings.

For the first time, Kane took in the landscape. The street was empty—no wind, no birds, no animals. Not even the faint buzz of insects. It was as if life itself had abandoned this place. Across the way, the crumbling ruins of an abandoned building loomed like a specter.

"See that creepy-looking place over there?" Sanjay asked, pointing to the dilapidated structure. "We need to get there. Now."

"Do you think this is funny?" Kane snapped, glaring at him.

"Funny?!" Sanjay scoffed. "No. Necessary? Yes. Unless you think I can carry your stubborn ass with this." He gestured to the needle protruding from the middle of his own chest, the metal glinting faintly in the dim light. "So, unless you've got a better idea... move!"

Kane clenched his jaw, biting back a retort. With Sanjay's help, he rose unsteadily to his feet. Pain radiated from his arm as he leaned heavily on his friend, the two of them hobbling toward the ominous building.

Each step was agonizing, but Kane forced himself to keep moving, his eyes scanning their surroundings. There was no sign of life anywhere—no movement, no sound. It was as if they had stepped into a void where the rules of the natural world no longer applied. The silence was oppressive, pressing down on them like a physical weight.

Once inside the building, Kane collapsed onto a dusty chair, sweat dripping from his brow. The air was thick and stale, the faint scent of mildew and decay clinging to every surface. He pulled back the dressing on his stump, staring in disbelief at the smoldering, charred edges of his wound.

"How did you cauterize this?" he asked, his voice hoarse. "We didn't have the gear for this. Hell, we didn't even have time."

Sanjay rummaged through the remnants of the front desk, pulling out a dusty first-aid kit and a set of keys. "I didn't," he said bluntly. "The portal—or whatever the hell that was—did it for you when it sliced your hand off. Very efficient, actually. Convenient, even. Just not exactly gentle."

Kane grimaced, his lips pulling into a bitter smile. "Pride comes before the fall, right?"

"Yeah, well, you can freak out about your fall later," Sanjay quipped, grabbing some gauze and disinfectant. "Clock's ticking. I need to get you somewhere safe before you pass out again." He held up the keys, shaking them with a wry grin. "Lucky for us, this shithole used to be a hotel. Rooms for rent, no reservations required."

Sanjay helped Kane to his feet again, guiding him through the dilapidated hallway toward the nearest intact room. The carpet was stained and damp, the wallpaper peeling in jagged strips. A faint, metallic creak echoed from somewhere above, but neither man had the energy to investigate.

Once inside, Sanjay cleared debris off a sagging mattress and motioned for Kane to lie down. Kane hesitated, eyeing the bed with visible disgust.

"What?" Sanjay asked, his tone incredulous. "Don't be picky. We've both slept in worse."

Kane sighed, muttering something under his breath as he lowered himself onto the mattress. The springs groaned beneath his weight, but it held. For now.

Sanjay knelt beside him, carefully unwrapping the crude bandage around his stump to inspect the wound. "You're lucky, you know," he said, his voice softer now. "A little higher, and you wouldn't have just lost a hand. You'd be dead."

"Yeah," Kane muttered, his eyes fluttering closed. "Lucky."

The room fell silent, save for the faint sound of Sanjay's rummaging as he prepared to patch Kane up properly. But the unease lingered, heavy and unspoken. Whatever had brought them here, it wasn't done with them yet.

Kane gritted his teeth, using what strength he had left to stand again. His legs wobbled beneath him before giving out, sending him crashing back onto the floor. He watched Sanjay stow the medical supplies they'd scavenged, his friend's movements brisk and efficient despite the weight of the situation.

"I can't believe Kydd turned on me…" Kane muttered, his voice low, shaking his head as he stared blankly ahead. The betrayal gnawed at him, mingling with the ache of his severed hand.

"Sulk later," Sanjay said sharply, without even looking up. He knelt to retrieve a roll of gauze, his tone as dry as ever. "You're no good to me half-dead. Let it out, pass out, and let me handle things."

Kane groaned, his pride warring with his exhaustion. He couldn't stop his mind from replaying everything that had gone wrong, dissecting the events over and over. The visions, the foresight of the Oracles—everything had set him on this path since the fall of Atlantis. That event had shattered the perfect timeline. His perfect timeline. He wasn't even mad at Marcus, not really. Deep down, he believed everything was happening for a reason, even if that reason was elusive in this moment. Had he pushed the young man too hard? No matter. The pain from his right arm was real enough, but not as sharp as the sting of his wounded pride.

Sanjay interrupted his thoughts. "So, where are we anyway?" he asked, straightening and glancing around the decrepit room.

Kane scowled, irritation flaring. "What?" he snapped. "I thought you wanted me to pass out?"

"Obviously, you refuse to allow yourself to!" Sanjay retorted, exasperation creeping into his voice. "And you're not the only one with a lot on their mind, you know!"

Kane exhaled, his anger dissipating slightly. "For the first time in a long time, I can honestly say I don't know. But what I do know is this place looks like a post-apocalyptic wasteland." He gestured vaguely at their surroundings. "And since we know alternate dimensions exist in the same space—"

"We do?" Sanjay interrupted, raising a skeptical eyebrow.

"Yes," Kane snapped. "It means we've either caused this timeline to collapse in our own time or..." He trailed off, shaking his head.

"Or?" Sanjay pressed.

"Or we've jumped into a different timeline," Kane finished reluctantly, his voice heavy with resignation. "But I don't want to speculate yet."

The two fell into silence, the weight of Kane's words lingering in the stale air. Kane rolled onto his side, trying to get comfortable on the creaking mattress. A few moments passed before Sanjay spoke again, almost as an afterthought.

"Haven't seen any sign of Batticus or Green... in case you were wondering."

Kane grimaced but said nothing. He had completely forgotten about them and didn't want to admit it aloud. The two men had served their purpose in getting him this far—nothing more. He wasn't concerned with their fates, but he couldn't say so outright, not to Sanjay.

"Wherever we are," Kane said instead, his tone curt, "we need to assume other living beings are nearby. It won't take long before our presence is noticed. I need to rest, but we move at first light."

Sanjay nodded, already in agreement. "Fine. I'll see what provisions I can find, but don't go anywhere without me."

Kane smirked faintly. "I'm not going anywhere."

Sanjay left the room, heading back into the motel lobby and office area. The silence outside was unsettling, broken only by occasional rustling sounds. Through the grimy windows, he peered out into the haze but saw nothing. A faint breeze swirled the dust, but the world beyond remained eerily still.

He rifled through the remnants of the front desk, opening cupboards and drawers until he found a handgun stashed beneath the counter, along with a few loose bills in the register. He stuffed the cash and the weapon into his bag before venturing into what must have been the manager's living quarters. There, he found a backpack, canned food, a can opener, and other odds and ends—towels, socks, and a pack of playing cards.

As he moved back toward the lobby, the scuffling sounds outside returned, louder this time. His hand instinctively went to the gun tucked into the back of his waistband. He stepped outside cautiously, but again, there was nothing visible in the darkness. Just the haze, swirling lazily under the faintest glow of moonlight.

Then, in the distance, headlights pierced through the gloom. Sanjay froze, watching as the vehicle's beams grew brighter, accompanied by the faint rumble of an engine and the unmistakable riffs of heavy metal blaring through the air. He waved his arms overhead, stepping into the road to flag the driver down. Relief surged in him—someone who might help.

But before the vehicle could reach him, Sanjay was tackled to the ground by a large figure that emerged from the shadows. The impact knocked the wind out of him, and he hit the pavement hard, the music and engine noise fading as the car sped past without stopping.

"What the fuck, bro?!" Sanjay shouted, struggling to push the man off.

"Those people weren't going to help you," the man growled, his voice low and gravelly. "They would've killed you or taken you straight to Him. I just saved your life."

Sanjay blinked, his confusion evident. "Thank you, I guess? Who the hell is Him?"

"The self-proclaimed God King," the man replied. "And trust me, it's not safe out here. Call me Nova. I saw you and your friend come through that portal. I was planning to check you out in the morning, but then I saw you waving your arms around like you're begging to get caught."

Sanjay stood, brushing himself off. "Fair enough. Let's get off the road."

Together, they returned to the motel. Kane stirred awake as they entered, his eyes narrowing suspiciously at the stranger.

"It's fine," Sanjay reassured him quickly. "This is Nova. He may be able to help us."

"Is that true?" Kane asked, his tone skeptical.

Nova crossed his arms. "I might. Depends on what you're looking for."

"What is today's date and what the hell happened here?" Kane asked.

"Let's start there."

"November 22nd, 2049." Nova answered flatly. "And what do you mean what happened here?"

"That portal you saw us come through brought us from the same day nearly twenty-five years ago…" Kane informed him in a very matter-of-fact tone.

Nova stared briefly, reflecting on his words. "Right, so you missed a lot then…the HADES Virus, wars, famine, fallen governments now run by the Order of the Ancient Serpent and the self-proclaimed 'God King', who isn't just the richest and most powerful soul on the planet but also the closest thing to what used to be considered the 'the antichrist', though nobody really believes in the existence of any God now. No God could allow what has happened, all that pain, all that suffering…" he trailed off.

Kane straightened, his voice firm. "We need to meet the God King."

Nova raised an eyebrow, his expression incredulous. "Why the hell would you want that?"

"To right the wrongs that led us here," Kane answered simply.

Nova hesitated, then nodded slowly. "What is that supposed to mean? Are you saying you caused this?

Sanjay turned toward Kane, waiting to see what his response would be.

Kane carefully considered his next words, buying time as he shifted his weight.

"Did you fuck with something in your time?" Nova pressed.

"I didn't fuck with it," Kane snapped, his voice sharp as he turned back toward the bed and sank onto the edge with a wince. "I helped build it. I knew exactly what I was doing. I was sabotaged."

Sanjay flinched at the venom in Kane's tone but pressed on. "Well, the virus and then the Great War happened right after that... so what if—whatever happened—set all of this into motion?"

"Three steps ahead of you, kid," Kane interrupted, cutting him off with a glare.

Patel's shoulders slumped, his mind spinning. "Did we do this?" he whispered, his voice trembling as he sat down on the broken bed next to Kane's.

"No," Kane said, his tone icy. "Ivyg did this. That prick. This whole mess has his name written all over it."

Nova, who had been leaning against the wall, straightened at the name. "You know the God King?" he asked, his voice tinged with disbelief.

Kane turned to face him, his expression unreadable. "He's my brother," he said flatly.

The room fell silent. Patel and Nova exchanged stunned looks, the weight of Kane's words sinking in. Nova opened his mouth as if to speak, then thought better of it, his gaze lingering on Kane with a mix of curiosity and suspicion.

Kane leaned back slowly, grimacing as he tried to find a comfortable position. His trembling hand clutched at his injured arm, the pain evident in his pale face. Patel moved instinctively to his side, helping to prop him up with makeshift padding from the remnants of the bed.

"Time to get some rest," Patel said firmly, his tone leaving no room for argument.

"I live in an underground refuge nearby," Nova said, breaking the tense silence. "It's safe for me but bringing you there would be too dangerous."

Kane nodded faintly, his eyes half-closed. "It's fine. Completely understandable."

Nova crossed his arms, his expression thoughtful. "I don't know the whole truth behind your little story, but something tells me it's no coincidence you landed here—now."

"Agreed," Kane murmured, his voice soft but resolute. His eyes closed completely, the lines on his face easing slightly as he leaned back against the headboard.

"So..." Nova said, a hint of determination creeping into his tone. "I'm gonna help you. I think you might be our best chance at fixing things."

Kane let out a weak chuckle, cracking one eye open. "I hope so. That's my plan, anyway."

"Plan?" Patel interjected, raising an eyebrow. "You have a plan? Since when?"

"Still working on it," Kane admitted. "But you know me—I'll come up with something soon. First, I need to rest. Fix my arm. Then, figure out a way to get us back to our own timeline."

Nova reached into his pocket and pulled out a small foil-wrapped pill, holding it out to Kane. "Food's scarce, so we mostly live on these. I always keep one handy, just in case."

Kane smirked faintly as he took the pill. "Don't suppose you've got water in your other pocket, do you?"

Before Nova could reply, Patel dug into his bag and pulled out a collapsible water pouch, holding it out. "Here. This one's yours. Mine's almost full."

Kane sat up with their help, his movements slow and stiff. He swallowed the pill with a sip of water, then sank back down with a sigh. Patel and Nova exchanged a look—silent but heavy with understanding. Whatever lay ahead, it was clear they were both responsible for keeping Kane alive.

"I'll be back in the morning," Nova said, heading toward the door. "See what I can scrounge up."

Patel nodded, his gaze following Nova as he left. Once the door shut, he turned back to Kane, his brow furrowing in thought. Kane's eyes were closed, but Patel knew he wasn't asleep. The lines of concentration on his face were unmistakable.

Though Patel didn't voice it aloud, he couldn't shake the unease gnawing at him. The Nexus had been a calculated risk; one he'd believed they could control. But something had gone horribly wrong—not just with the Nexus itself, but with him.

In the silence, Patel's mind drifted back to Agartha. He thought of his other half—the twin he'd absorbed in utero, Alibi, who had remained a consciousness within him for most of his life. Rarely did Patel separate into two beings, but during their time in Agartha, it had been a necessary deception. Now, however, he was painfully aware that he was split from his other half, likely left behind in their timeline. Patel wasn't even sure if his current self was the original or the copy—an unsettling thought that made his skin crawl.

Kane, though wracked with pain, seemed to sense Patel's distress. "You're overthinking again," he muttered without opening his eyes.

Patel flinched but said nothing. He turned his attention to the task of organizing their sparse supplies, hoping the monotony would drown out his racing thoughts.

Nova's words lingered in the back of his mind: "I think you might be our best chance at fixing things."

Patel just hoped they were right.

<h1 align="center">-Chapter 13-</h1>

Rose versus the spiders

Rose squinted at the road signs, carefully scanning for the one she needed to turn onto. Her fingers tapped absently on the steering wheel as she tuned into yet another radio station. The host's voice crackled through the speakers, recounting the latest attack or sighting of strange creatures—a phenomenon that had been flooding news outlets and social media since moments after what people were now calling "The Pulse."

Everyone had felt it. The inexplicable energy that rippled across the planet had sent shockwaves through every corner of the world, especially along ley lines. The reports were eerily consistent: unexplained vibrations, flashes of light, and, of course, the sudden appearance of bizarre and often dangerous creatures. Rose's jaw tightened as the radio host rambled on. She didn't need their theories to connect the dots—whatever had caused the Pulse was directly tied to her brother's disappearance.

Her thoughts fractured as something darted across her line of sight and slammed into her windshield with a wet thud. She screamed and slammed on the brakes, her SUV skidding to a stop in the middle of the deserted road. Her heart hammered as she gripped the steering wheel, her eyes darting around to locate the source of the impact.

Nothing. Just the rustle of nearby bushes, shaking violently as though something was hiding—or retreating.

"Nope," Rose muttered, her voice shaking. "Not today." She floored the accelerator, sending the SUV roaring down the road. Whatever that thing was, she had no intention of sticking around to find out. With her luck, it was something that could tear through metal.

The sun had fully risen now, bathing the forest in golden light. Unfortunately, the daylight didn't bring comfort—it only made the bizarre creatures easier to spot. The remainder of the drive felt like a surreal fever dream. Rose's mouth hung open as she took in the parade of absurdities scattered through the trees and occasionally across the road.

There was what appeared to be a bunny rabbit—except it had a disturbingly human face. A group of goblin-like creatures crouched in the shadow of a mossy tree, their glowing eyes tracking her vehicle as it sped past. And high above the treetops, she caught glimpses of something massive and reptilian gliding through the sky. She blinked hard, certain

122

she was seeing things, but the leathery wings and the long, sinuous tail were unmistakable.

"I swear," she muttered, gripping the wheel tighter, "people would pay good money and take a cocktail of hallucinogens to see half this shit. And I'm out here stone cold sober."

Her stomach churned with a mix of nerves and adrenaline as she pressed onward, her eyes scanning the road and treetops with equal intensity. Just when she thought nothing else could surprise her, she spotted the familiar street name from her navigation before it had glitched out earlier. Relief washed over her—briefly.

Nearly missing her turn, Rose yanked the wheel hard to the left, her tires squealing in protest as she skidded onto the gravel driveway. She let out a long breath, steadying herself before looking up at the property. Her relief was replaced with confusion.

At the end of the drive was what she could only describe as... a house-shaped cocoon. The entire structure appeared to be encased in something—silvery, translucent, and pulsating faintly, like it was alive. Rose's eyes narrowed as she pulled into the roundabout and parked in front of a weathered sign that read, Valet Parking Only.

She sat in her SUV for a moment, staring at the shimmering cocoon. "Well," she said aloud, her tone dry, "this is either the weirdest bed and breakfast I've ever seen, or I'm officially losing it."

With a deep breath, Rose grabbed her bag and stepped out, the gravel crunching beneath her boots. She scanned the property warily, half-expecting one of the creatures she'd seen earlier to leap out from the shadows. Whatever was happening here, it was unlike anything she'd ever encountered—and considering her life, that was saying something.

After confirming there was no immediate threat, Rose grabbed her bag from the passenger seat and cautiously approached the front of the building, her eyes narrowing as she tried to make sense of the strange encasement. With a soft click, she shut the car door and took a moment to scan the yard. Animals of all kinds were scattered around—too still for comfort.

As she walked by a cat lying limp in front of the porch steps, she knelt down to check if it was still alive. Its collar read "Felix", and its sides rose and fell in shallow, uneven breaths. Rose frowned, her fingers twitching instinctively toward the creature before she stopped herself. Whatever was happening here, she wasn't about to risk contact without protection.

The yard buzzed faintly with the sound of life, but it was disjointed. Birds flitted nervously in the trees, small creatures rustled in the underbrush, and insects buzzed in erratic patterns overhead. The closer she got to the house, the more it seemed like everything within proximity had been subdued—paralyzed or worse. Her stomach tightened as she reached into the satchel slung across her shoulders, pulling out a bulky mask and securing it over her face. Her next move was to fish for gloves, her hands brushing past various tools until her fingers found the familiar texture of thick, industrial-grade rubber.

With her gaze momentarily downward, a cloudy puddle near her foot caught her attention. A faint ripple spread across its surface as a drop splashed into it from above. Rose froze, her heart thudding in her chest. Slowly, she traced the path of the droplets upward, her eyes widening as she saw the splatter marks climbing the wall. The trail led to a corner of the awning where a massive, winged creature dangled grotesquely, cocooned in translucent webbing.

Biting back a shriek, she stepped off the stoop and moved carefully toward the side of the house. Turning the corner, she gasped quietly. The underside of the awning was lined with cocoons—large, pulsating sacks, some of which twitched faintly as if their occupants weren't entirely dead. Her gloved hand clenched instinctively as she counted at least five before retreating back toward the front of the house. She didn't need to see more. Her priority now was to get in, get what she needed, and leave undetected.

But fate, it seemed, had other plans.

Out of the corner of her eye, one of the cocoons twitched violently. She turned just in time to see it split open, spindly legs forcing their way out as a massive spider-like creature began to emerge.

"So much for undetected," Rose muttered, the familiar crimson glow sparking to life in her hands. She broke into a sprint toward her rental vehicle, each step punctuated by the rhythmic thud of her boots against the gravel. Just as she neared the car, a section of webbing tore open at the roof of the house, revealing another spider dragging a fresh cocoon from inside.

"Oh, no you don't," she hissed, hurling a fireball toward the creature as she dove for cover behind her vehicle. The ball of flame hit its mark, incinerating the webbing and forcing the spider back with an angry screech.

Rose barely had time to catch her breath before a sticky glob of silk splattered against the passenger side of her car, obstructing her view. She glanced over her shoulder, her heart pounding as she saw a slightly smaller arachnid scuttling down from the roof on the opposite side.

"Great, now they're flanking," she muttered, standing and firing another energy beam toward the advancing spider. It fell back with a sickening crunch, but she barely had time to process the victory before another glob of webbing shot toward her.

"Fine! Plan B!" she quipped, her voice sharp with frustration. Her glowing hands sliced through the webbing with ease, but the third spider used the distraction to leap from the roof. Its weight knocked her flat on her back, the force driving the air from her lungs.

The spider's mandibles snapped inches from her face, its claws piercing her skin as it pinned her down. Rose clenched her teeth, breathing deeply as the heat inside her began to build. Her entire body glowed crimson, the spider screeching and recoiling as if sensing the danger.

"Oh, now you're scared?" she spat, her voice trembling with fury. The spider leapt backward, retreating to the first-floor balcony, but it was too late.

Rose's energy reached a critical mass, her body a furnace of molten rage. She unleashed a wave of raw heat and light, the explosion sending the spider hurtling into the air before it disintegrated into ash. The blast left scorch marks across the ground and the front of the house, the encasement trembling as if in response.

Panting heavily, Rose pushed herself to her feet, brushing ash from her gloves. "Well, that was fun," she muttered, glancing warily at the remaining cocoons. She had bought herself a little time, but she knew more would come. And she wasn't sticking around to find out what else was lurking in the shadows.

The first and largest of the spiders had managed to escape, scurrying over the farthest corner with two of its legs ablaze as it scrambled away.

"Ughhh..." Rose sneered, waving a hand in front of her face, nauseous from the pungent smell of burning spider flesh.

She glanced up at the entryway, where entrails dangled grotesquely from the remaining upper half of the spider she'd obliterated. The second spider lay dead on the ground, and the blast seemed to have incinerated the thick webbing that had previously sealed the doorway. The path was clear.

Cautiously, Rose made her way inside, where she found Scarlett, Robyn, Teddy, Kiara, and Aron sprawled unconscious on the living room floor. Her chest tightened, but she pushed down the surge of panic and knelt by her brother, shaking his shoulder.

"Aron!" she hissed.

He groaned, blinking groggily as he turned over and instinctively reached for Kiara, who stirred beside him. Both struggled to regain consciousness.

"Rose?" Scarlett's voice came from across the room, faint but familiar. Scarlett's gaze settled on her, and recognition lit her features. "What's going on? What happened?"

"It was the spiders," Aron interjected, sitting up and rubbing his temples. "Their webs are venomous. The stuff becomes airborne as it hardens. I bet they had the whole bottom story wrapped up before we even hit the stairs."

"You must be Kiara Kross," Rose said, crouching beside the blind woman, her tone tinged with curiosity.

Kiara nodded groggily, but before she could speak, Aron checked his watch and sighed. "Seven hours. We've been out for seven hours."

His words drew the attention of everyone in the room. Scarlett, Robyn, and Teddy exchanged uneasy glances as the reality of their shared memories began to sink in—fragments of past lives, glimpses of a destiny none of them had fully understood until now. "What the hell happened to you?" Aron asked, finally taking in his sister's torn clothes, bloodied arms, and the mix of spider guts streaked across her face. Despite it all, Rose grinned at him.

"Mallah called me," she replied casually, brushing her curls back from her face. "I got held up, though... it's been kinda cray-cray outside."

Aron groaned, shaking his head as he sat up, still feeling the effects of the venomous trance. "Ogma was worried this might happen," he muttered, looking around the room. Scarlett, Robyn, and Kiara were slowly regaining their senses, but their expressions carried the weight of something unspoken.

"I had... the weirdest dream," Robyn began hesitantly, breaking the silence. She rubbed her temples and glanced around at the others. "It felt so real, like we were all there. Together."

Scarlett tilted her head, her brows knitting together. "Wait—were there women sitting around a fire telling stories of their past lives?" Her voice trembled slightly. Teddy's eyes widened. "Yes, and we all fought together!" Kiara sat up straighter, her face pale but intent. As the pieces began falling into place, they looked at each other in stunned silence. Each of them described their experiences, filling in the gaps from one another's perspectives. Aron leaned forward, his voice steady but urgent. "It wasn't just a dream. We were there. I don't know how or why, but we were all living through the same memories."

The realization sent a shiver through the room, the weight of their shared experience settling heavily over them. It wasn't just coincidence—it was a thread connecting them to something much larger than themselves.

Rose, who had been leaning against the wall with her arms crossed, finally broke the tension with a loud sigh. "Alright, alright," she said, stepping forward and clapping her hands. "Group therapy is officially over, folks. We've got bigger problems to deal with, like not getting eaten alive by spiders or, I don't know, finding some weapons."

Her words snapped them back to the present, the tension breaking just enough for the group to exchange uneasy but slightly amused glances.

Before anyone could respond, a faint buzzing broke the silence. Aron dug into his pocket, his expression tense, and pulled out his phone. A raw, gritty guitar riff echoed in the room—the opening to a Sabaton track. He flushed slightly when Kiara tilted her head toward the sound, nodding in quiet approval.

Aron answered the call quickly, glancing at the others as he listened. His expression shifted to something more serious. "Yeah. We got her," he said into the phone, his gaze flicking briefly to Kiara. "Any chance we can arrange a pickup?"

A muffled voice responded on the other end, unintelligible to the others. Aron's jaw tightened, and he exhaled sharply. "Understood."

He ended the call, his face grim. The weight of whatever he'd just heard was evident in the set of his shoulders. All eyes turned toward him, the room thick with anticipation.

"Who was it?" Kiara asked, her voice soft but steady.

"Mallah," Aron said, his tone low. "Who apparently knows my girlfriend by name."

Rose raised an eyebrow, her arms crossing. "Your what? Since when do you have a girlfriend?"

Scarlett, who had been watching him closely, furrowed her brows. "Wait... where have I heard that name before? Mallah?"

"How the hell would I know?" Rose snapped, her tone sharp. "It's Mallah. She probably knows everything—but that's not what matters right now. Aron, what's going on? You've got that look."

Rose knew her brother well enough to recognize the shadow of worry in his features. Whatever Mallah had said, it was serious, and it wasn't just about Kiara.

The scramble to leave was chaotic but efficient. Rose, still annoyed about the sudden expansion of her mission, stalked around the living room with a faint scowl, taking inventory of anything remotely useful. She'd brought her own weapons, but if Aron was insisting they take the others along, they'd need to be armed, too—or they'd all be sitting ducks.

"So," she said sharply, scanning the group, "what's the deal? You lot have anything worth taking, or are we doing this the hard way?"

Robyn straightened, her Ukrainian accent cutting through the din. "In safe. Upstairs. Pistol. Clips. Basement has blunt weapons."

"Blunt weapons?" Rose scoffed. "Brilliant. You can bonk the monsters on the head while they eat you."

"Not all of us are packing like soldiers, da?" Robyn shot back, folding her arms.

Aron's green eyes flashed as he stepped between them. "Rose," he said firmly, his tone brooking no argument. "They'll manage. You're not going to scare them into being better prepared."

"Fine," Rose muttered, rolling her eyes. "But don't blame me if we get overrun." She turned to Robyn. "Where's this safe?"

"Follow," Robyn said curtly, motioning for Rose to follow her upstairs.

As the two disappeared, Aron turned his attention to Kiara, who lingered near the couch. "You alright?" he asked softly.

Kiara nodded, clutching her bag. "I think so. Just... ready to go."

"Good," Aron said, his tone steady. "Stay close to me."

By the time Robyn and Rose returned, armed with the pistol and a bag of makeshift weapons, the group was assembled and ready to move. Aron stood by the door, his commanding presence unmistakable. His green eyes swept over them all, assessing quickly.

"Alright," he said, his Irish-Aussie accent firm but calm. "Stick together. No heroics. We'll take two vehicles—Rose's SUV and my truck. Let's move."

Teddy hung back near Rose's SUV as the others climbed into the vehicles, his sharp eyes flicking between her and Aron's truck. His grin was faint but knowing as he leaned casually against the side of the car.

"You're staring," he said quietly, his tone light but pointed.

Rose blinked, caught off guard. "I am not staring," she protested, crossing her arms.

Teddy arched an eyebrow. "Oh, please. You've been eyeballing her like she's hiding something."

Rose shifted uncomfortably, glancing at Kiara, who was seated in Aron's truck, her hand lightly brushing his arm as they talked. "I'm just trying to figure out... What's the deal, y'know? She doesn't seem like the kind of person my brother'd..." She trailed off, searching for the right word. "... take under his wing."

Teddy chuckled softly, shaking his head. "That's because you don't know her yet. Look, in case it hasn't clicked, she's blind."

Rose blinked, her skepticism doubling. "Blind? You're havin' a laugh."

"I'm serious," Teddy replied, lowering his voice and leaning closer. "But don't mistake that for weakness. She's sharper than half the people I've met with twenty-twenty vision. She's got this freaky sixth sense for where everything and everyone is. She knows this house better than any of us, and she's holding onto Aron because it's faster to follow his lead, not because she doesn't know where she's going."

Rose frowned, glancing back at Kiara, who seemed calm and composed even amidst the chaos. "Huh," she muttered, genuinely surprised. "Alright, fair play."

Teddy smirked, his tone growing firmer. "And just so we're clear—Robyn and I don't hesitate when it comes to protecting her. I might be gay," he said, his voice laced with subtle steel, "but that doesn't mean

I won't throw down if I have to. And Robyn? Trust me, you don't want to see her pissed off."

Rose's lips twitched, caught between amusement and admiration. "Gay, eh?" she said, her Irish-Aussie accent thickening as her tone softened. "Well, I'll be damned. Thought I had you pegged for one of those stylish metro lads who keep all the ladies swoonin'. Looks like my gaydar's busted." She gave him a quick once-over, taking in his tall frame, his semi-muscular build, and his dark features. "Gotta say, though, you're a fine-lookin' lad. If we'd met under better circumstances, I might've fancied my chances."

Teddy snorted, shaking his head but clearly amused. "Good thing we didn't, then. Would've broken your heart."

Rose grinned, raising her hands in mock surrender. "Fair enough. You're loyal—can't knock that. Just make sure that loyalty works both ways, yeah?"

Teddy straightened, his smirk fading into a more serious expression. "We're trusting you and Aron with a lot right now. Don't make us regret it."

Rose nodded, the grin slipping from her face as she absorbed the weight of his words. "You've got my word," she said sincerely. "I won't let anything happen to her—or any of you."

Teddy gave her a nod of acknowledgment before turning and heading toward the truck. Rose watched him go, her mind racing with questions and a grudging respect for the man who had so calmly and clearly laid out the stakes.

-Chapter 14-

Future shock

Nova paced the dusty floor of the dilapidated safe house, his black combat boots scuffing against the worn tiles, leaving faint tracks in the grime. The cracked windows let in shafts of pale, sickly light, catching on the swirling dust as if the air itself was tired of standing still. Though he barely knew Kane and Patel, their plan to deliberately surrender themselves to the so-called "God King" grated on every survival instinct Nova had honed over years of clawing his way through this hellscape. To him, it wasn't a strategy—it was suicide dressed up in ambition.

He couldn't believe he was even entertaining this.

"You're insane," Nova snapped, stopping mid-pace, fists clenched at his sides. His glare drilled into Kane like he could force sense into him with sheer will. "I've watched too many people go to that city and never come back. They vanish—like ghosts. And the ones who do return? They're broken. You know what they say? They whisper about gladiator games fought to the death, Kane. To the death. You refuse to pledge allegiance to HIM—your 'God King'—and you don't get a second chance. You end up as a smear in the sand while they cheer like it's entertainment."

Kane didn't flinch. He sat calmly at a rickety table, methodically rewrapping the bandages on his damaged arm. His fingers worked with practiced precision, like this was just another day, another plan, another war. His face betrayed no doubt, only the cold calculation of someone who had weighed the odds and didn't care what they cost anyone else. Nova hated that look—because it wasn't reckless. It was controlled.

Patel stood nearby, arms crossed over his chest, leaning against the wall with his usual mask of calm observation. He was watching both of them now, but still hadn't stepped in.

"I understand the risks," Kane said, voice low, like it didn't need to rise to be heard. "But there's no other way to get close enough. If we're captured, they'll take us directly to him. The games are a test, yes. But they're also an opportunity."

Nova barked a bitter laugh, taking a step closer, his voice rising. "Opportunity? For what? To die in front of a bloodthirsty crowd while that lunatic calls himself a god and plays puppeteer with the last scraps of humanity? Even if—if—you survive, do you honestly think he'll hand over the keys to whatever you're looking for? He's a tyrant, Kane. People like him don't share power. They don't rewrite history to make themselves weaker."

Kane paused, tying off the bandage. He set down the roll, his movements smooth, deliberate. Then he lifted his gaze, locking eyes with Nova—sharp, cold, and unyielding.

"You don't know what he's capable of," Kane said, almost too calmly. "What I know. This isn't about surviving the games. This is about getting close enough to take what we need. He has the technology, Nova. Time travel. The kind that doesn't just bend the rules—it shatters them. I can undo this. I can rewrite it."

Nova shook his head, stepping back like he needed distance just to process how insane this sounded. "You're banking everything—everything—on a fairy tale. What makes you so sure this 'God King' would let you tamper with the past? What if he sees you for what you are and buries you right there, in front of everyone?"

Kane leaned forward now, hands braced on the table, the light catching the edge of his grim smile. "Because I've seen the plans. Long before the Pulse, there were programs—hidden from the public. Joint operations between the Order, the military, and private corporations. Underground facilities, experimental vehicles, manipulations of time and space. All under the banner of progress, but every piece—every damn piece—funneling through the Order of the Ancient Sun. Their fingerprints are on everything, Nova. If they survived—and they did—then so did their tech. And now, he has it."

Nova paced again, hands raking through his hair. "You don't even know if he knows how to use it. What if he's just sitting on it? What if you never even see it?"

"Then I make him show me," Kane said, flat.

"Even if that's true," Nova countered, spinning around, "you think this maniac will let you just use it because you asked nicely? You think you'll get to him before he breaks you? You're walking into a trap, Kane. And you're dragging Patel with you!"

Patel finally pushed off the wall, exhaling sharply. "Look, Nova, I get it. You're scared. Hell, I'm scared too. But Kane has a point. If the Order's remnants are out there—and the Nexus wasn't just some random fluke—then the God King might have the means to send us back. Or fix this one."

Nova whirled on him. "Back to what, Patel? Huh? To repeat the same damn mistakes that led us here in the first place? Even if you succeed, Kane, what makes you think changing the past won't just create something worse?"

Kane's jaw clenched, but there was no hesitation in his eyes. "Because I know where it went wrong," he said quietly. "I know who set this in motion. The Pulse wasn't some cosmic accident. It was betrayal. Sabotage. And shortsighted fools who didn't understand the consequences. I can fix it. I have to."

Kane's jaw tightened, his eyes narrowing. "Because I know where it went wrong. Maybe the Pulse was inevitable—but what followed wasn't. The chaos, the collapse, the rise of tyrants—that was the result of betrayal, sabotage, and shortsightedness. I can't stop the Pulse, but I can fix what came after. I can steer it back to what it was meant to be. And unlike you, I'm not content to sit in the ashes of what's left, and hope things get better."

"Hope?" Nova's laugh was bitter, almost feral. "I gave up on hope the day the skies cracked, and the Veil fell. I've seen what's out there, Kane—creatures that defy logic, humans twisted into monsters, and factions tearing each other apart for scraps of power. You think you can waltz into the God King's court and make him an ally? He doesn't negotiate. He dominates. That's what tyrants do."

The room fell into tense silence, the weight of Nova's words hanging in the air like smoke from a dying fire. Kane didn't blink.

"Then I'll dominate him," he said, his voice quiet but cold as steel.

Nova stared at him, a mixture of frustration and reluctant admiration flickering across his face. "You're a stubborn bastard; I'll give you that. But if you're wrong—if you get captured and he kills you in those damn games—what happens to Patel? To the rest of us? What's your backup plan, Kane?"

Kane's lips curled into a faint smirk. "Backup plans are for people who plan to fail. I don't."

Patel groaned, rubbing his temples. "For what it's worth, Nova, I don't like it either. But Kane's right about one thing—sitting here isn't going to solve anything. If there's even a chance that this God King has the technology we need, then it's a chance we have to take."

Nova exhaled sharply, shaking his head. "Fine. But if you're doing this, you'd better be damn sure. I'm not watching another group of fools throw their lives away for a pipe dream."

"Then don't watch," Kane said coolly, rising to his feet, his silhouette sharp against the flickering light. "But if you're coming with us, be ready. This isn't just about survival. It's about taking back control of our fate."

Nova muttered a curse under his breath, but his shoulders slumped in reluctant acceptance. "For the record, I still think this is insane. But I'll come. Someone's got to keep you two alive."

Kane nodded, his smirk returning, though it didn't quite reach his eyes. "Good. We leave at dawn."

-Chapter 15-

Ogma's Realm

"Where are you taking us?" Scarlett asked, her tone cautious as Rose maneuvered the car out of the driveway.

"Not far," Rose replied, her accent adding a lilt to her words. "They didn't have enough hands for a proper extraction, so we're meeting up just up the road. Aron knows the area better than me, though."

"Ogma's?" Scarlett interrupted, her curiosity piqued.

Rose's head whipped around, her green eyes narrowing slightly as recognition dawned. "I knew you looked familiar! You're one of Kane's people, aren't you?"

"Not anymore," Scarlett said with a small smile, leaning back in her seat.

Rose raised an eyebrow. "They let you out?"

Scarlett sighed, her smile fading into something more wry. "Technically, I still work for the Order. I run a bookstore as a consultant... it's complicated."

Robyn, sitting quietly in the back, glanced between them. She could sense the weight behind their words but chose not to interrupt, unsure if drawing attention to herself would cause them to clam up. Instead, her focus drifted to Aron, keeping track of the road markers and landmarks he seemed to follow effortlessly. If she ever needed to retrace this route, she wanted to be ready.

"So, how'd you lot end up knowing Ogma anyway?" Rose asked, her tone shifting to curiosity. "Aron's worked with him for years, and he's always been weird about outsiders—he didn't even let me in at first! And speaking of weird, what's the deal with my brother and the blind girl? Is he, like, protecting her for someone?"

Robyn felt Scarlett's hand land lightly on her shoulder. She turned to see her friend smiling, as if to reassure her.

"It's a long story," Scarlett said, her voice carrying a hint of amusement. "But it started with Teddy. He called me a couple weeks ago—been friends with him for years. He tells me about these two women he's working with on paranormal cases. I'd heard about them, but we'd never actually met."

135

Robyn decided to chime in, her Ukrainian accent adding a melodic weight to her words. "It was our house," she said. "We had... unusual activity, so Teddy came to help. Scarlett, too."

Rose chuckled, steering the car through a sharp right turn. "I didn't pick up on anything crazy when we got there—maybe some residual energy, but that's everywhere."

"That's because Kiara deals with it," Scarlett explained. "She's been tapping into things since she was a kid. Just never thought it was anything out of the ordinary until now."

Rose shot a quick glance at Robyn in the rearview mirror. "Was she born blind?"

"No," Robyn said, shaking her head. "She had an accident as a teenager. It nearly killed her."

Rose didn't respond immediately, her focus returning to the road. After a moment, she muttered, almost to herself, "That explains a lot."

Scarlett picked up where Robyn had left off, her voice light but purposeful. "Anyway, we were out in the woods practicing one day, and we just happened to run into Aron, Marcus, Cesaro, and the rest of the crew."

Rose glanced at Scarlett sharply, her skepticism plain. "You're telling me that just happened by chance? Seriously?"

Scarlett grinned. "DJ Yeti was hosting a rave."

Rose slammed on the brakes, laughing incredulously. "A rave? Are you bloody kidding me? I can't even get near Ogma's without an escort, and they're out there hosting raves?"

"Tell me about it," Scarlett said with a laugh. "Anyway, Aron and Kiara hit it off. It was actually kind of cute, I guess they'd crossed paths before, though none of us got the full story. Next thing we know, they hook up, things get awkward, and then he shows up again, staying the night." She paused, her voice taking on a more serious tone. "And we all wake up to cracks in the sky... and dead people crawling all over the place."

Rose's grin faded, her expression sharpening as she caught Scarlett's eyes in the rearview mirror. "What did you just say? Cracks in the sky and dead people? Crawling?"

"Yeah," Scarlett replied matter-of-factly. "It wasn't just the cracks. There were bodies—so many of them. But I didn't just see them that night.

I'd caught glimpses before, here and there, usually faint, like echoes. But that night? They were everywhere, moving, crawling. It was... different."

"Different?" Rose echoed, her tone disbelieving. "And you didn't think to tell anyone this before?"

Teddy leaned forward abruptly, his face a mix of disbelief and offense. "Yeah, Scarlett, why the hell didn't you mention you were seeing dead people crawling around the place? That feels like something we might've wanted to know!"

Scarlett turned to him, her expression calm but firm. "Because, Teddy," she said evenly, "telling people things like that tends to freak them out. You didn't even want to know what their mother looks like now."

Teddy opened his mouth to reply but froze, his expression twisting with a mix of curiosity and horror. "Wait. Their mother? What... what does she look like now?"

Scarlett raised an eyebrow, her lips twitching into a faint, wry smile. "Trust me. You don't want me to answer that."

Teddy sat back, handsomely dumbstruck, his jaw tightening as if bracing against the urge to press further. "Right. Got it. No need for a visual, thanks."

Rose glanced at him in the rearview mirror, an amused smirk tugging at her lips. "Careful, Teddy. You're looking awfully pale back there. Might make people think you're the one seeing ghosts."

He shot her a sharp look but said nothing, clearly still processing Scarlett's words.

Scarlett exhaled, her tone softening as she continued. "Look, it's not like I didn't want to say something. It's just... most people don't want to know those things. And besides, I told you they were there, the fact that they were walking and crawling around wasn't even relevant until that night. By then, we were all too busy trying not to die."

Rose nodded slowly, her green eyes flicking back to the road as she adjusted her grip on the wheel. "Fair enough," she muttered, her voice tinged with grudging respect. "But next time, Scarlett, maybe don't leave out the part where the house is crawling with actual dead people. That seems like a detail worth mentioning."

Scarlett shrugged. "Noted."

The car settled into a brief silence, the weight of the conversation pressing down on everyone. Teddy, still stunned, leaned back in his seat, his dark features creased in thought as he stole a glance at Scarlett.

"Well, one thing's for sure," he muttered to himself. "You lot are a whole new kind of messed up."

Scarlett shot him a sidelong glance, her expression unreadable. "Welcome to the club."

"Still doesn't sound like my brother though…," Rose said finally, her tone carefully neutral. "Not at all."

The car fell into a brief silence, the hum of the engine the only sound as they closed the distance to their meeting point.

"She was hearing them, the ghosts." Scarlett pointed out. "Turns out, Kiara has been tapping into all that and more but just ignoring it since she was a kid…"

"Do you know if she was born blind?" Rose asked, turning toward Robyn, to which she shook her head in response.

"Some accident that almost killed her as a teenager." Robyn answered, trying to seem nonchalant but still more interested in where they were going. She tried to make a mental note of surrounding markers or something that seemed familiar from walks around the area.

The three exchanged glances before getting out of the car. Aron immediately took charge, his voice low but firm. "Stay together, no wandering off. If you see anything, keep calm and stay out of the way. We'll explain everything once we're safe. There's an entrance about a hundred meters ahead—but we need to hurry."

"What is it?" Robyn asked, turning toward Kiara, whose expression had turned apprehensive.

"I hear something," Kiara said, her brow furrowed. "I don't know… strange. Not like anything I…" She trailed off, clearly flustered as she searched for the right words.

The group collectively froze, their senses heightened as they strained to hear what she was describing. Around them, the forest was alive with subtle sounds—rustling leaves, faint chirps, and something deeper, almost like a low hum that seemed to pulse through the air.

"I can still hear it," Kiara whispered, her head tilting slightly as though following the sound. "It's slow, but it's getting louder."

"What the FUCK is that?" Teddy exclaimed, pointing past where

Aron was standing.

The others scrambled to see what had caught his attention, their gazes darting around the area. They searched the treetops, the underbrush, and finally the ground. Unable to spot anything unusual, they turned back to him with a mix of frustration and confusion.

Teddy rolled his eyes and strode past them, his long strides bringing him to the trunk of a massive tree. He pointed with exaggerated clarity. "There," he said, gesturing at a strange, undulating form clinging to the bark.

The group collectively exhaled in a mix of awe and unease. "Ahhh," they murmured, almost in unison—except for Kiara, who stood still, her expression expectant as she awaited an explanation.

"It's like a fuzzy snake," Robyn ventured.

"Or a giant caterpillar," Scarlett added, squinting as though trying to make sense of its bizarre features.

"No, no," Teddy interrupted, his tone dripping with self-assured authority. "That's not a caterpillar. It's some kind of tree-dwelling… uh… thing." He flexed his knowledge from various nature documentaries, though his specificity trailed off under the weight of the creature's sheer weirdness.

"Fascinating," Aron muttered, his accent sharp with impatience. "And completely irrelevant. Let's move."

The group fell into a tense silence as they pressed deeper into the woods. The air seemed to thicken with an otherworldly energy, the dim light filtering through the canopy casting shifting patterns that played tricks on the eye. Strange noises echoed around them—the soft chatter of unseen creatures, the flutter of massive wings, and a deep, resonant hum that seemed to come from nowhere and everywhere at once.

Aron broke the silence, his voice unexpectedly soft. "You know, these woods aren't like any other place on Earth," he said, his words directed at Kiara as she clutched his arm. "This whole region's famous for it, actually. Locals call it enchanted, and it's not hard to see why—if you're paying attention."

"Enchanted?" Robyn asked, her voice tinged with curiosity.

"Yeah," Aron continued, his green eyes gleaming as he glanced back at her. "Ever heard of the old theme park up this way? The Enchanted

Forest? Place looked like something out of Grimm's fairy tales—only slightly less terrifying. Turns out, it wasn't just clever marketing. This land's always had a pull, a sort of... hidden magic, if you will. Enough to inspire more than a few stories."

Kiara tightened her grip on his arm, a soft smile forming on her lips. "I can feel it," she said quietly, her head tilting toward the sound of massive wings overhead.

As if summoned by her words, a giant butterfly with iridescent wings floated into view, its colors shifting in the dappled light like liquid rainbows. Aron smiled as he described it to her, his voice laced with wonder. "There's a butterfly, Kiara. Massive. Wings like stained glass, all shimmering blues and purples. It's... breathtaking."

Kiara beamed, her face lighting up with joy as she leaned into him. "I love butterflies," she murmured.

Rose, who had been quietly observing the exchange, shot Aron a confused look. The tender moment between her brother and Kiara seemed so out of character that she couldn't help but feel a twinge of suspicion. Teddy, ever watchful, caught her expression and responded with a disgruntled glance toward Robyn, as if to say, Are you seeing this too?

The group pressed on, the forest around them growing denser and more surreal with each step. The last few minutes were marked by an almost reverent silence, broken only by the occasional exclamations as they encountered more strange and otherworldly creatures.

Suddenly, Kiara halted, her body tense. "Wait," she said, her voice barely above a whisper. "Something's wrong."

The group stopped, exchanging uneasy glances. "What is it?" Robyn asked.

Kiara turned her head slowly, her sightless eyes seeming to scan the woods. "I don't know," she said, her tone flustered. "But it's close."

Before anyone could respond, a loud snapping sound echoed from behind them, followed by a guttural growl. Aron's command was sharp and immediate. "RUN!"

The group bolted forward, feet pounding against the uneven forest floor. The air around them seemed alive with tension, the eerie sounds of snapping branches and low growls growing louder with each step.

"What the fuck is that?" Teddy shouted, his voice breathless as he risked a glance over his shoulder. The action nearly caused him to trip, and it only made it harder for him to keep pace.

A massive shadow loomed behind them, flickering in and out of the patches of light filtering through the trees. Whatever it was, it was fast, gaining ground with terrifying ease. No one had time to look back again as Aron led them toward the jagged opening of a cave.

"In here!" he yelled, grabbing Kiara's arm to guide her inside.

One by one, they scrambled into the cave, tripping over each other in their haste to escape. The space narrowed quickly, forcing them to crouch as they moved deeper into the passage. The faint echoes of the growl followed them, reverberating through the stone walls.

The group slowed only when they reached a small chamber where the cave opened slightly. Aron paused, catching his breath, and turned to face the others. He gently maneuvered Kiara behind him, shielding her with his body.

"Everyone okay?" Aron asked, his voice low but steady.

Teddy leaned against the wall, clutching at a stitch in his side. "Define 'okay.'"

Robyn nodded, her eyes wide with adrenaline but otherwise unharmed. Scarlett placed a reassuring hand on her shoulder as they both turned to Kiara, who seemed calm despite her blindness.

"Stay here," Aron instructed, his voice firm. "I'll show you how to get through—"

Before he could finish, Kiara reached her hand out, feeling the air in front of her. She stepped forward, disappearing through what appeared to be a solid stone wall. The group froze in stunned silence, watching as only her right arm and leg remained visible, protruding awkwardly from the rock face.

"What just happened?" Scarlett whispered, her voice tinged with awe.

"She walked right through it," Rose muttered, shaking her head in disbelief. "Alright, that's bloody impressive—but not surprising. The tricks in these parts are clever, I'll give them that."

On the other side of the wall, Kiara's voice called out, calm and confused. "What's going on? Why's everyone so quiet?"

The silence broke, and the group erupted in laughter, the tension of their escape momentarily forgotten. Aron pinched the bridge of his nose, trying to suppress his own grin.

"I was planning to wow you all with a bit of magic," Aron said, turning around to reveal a grin. He stepped forward and gestured toward the wall, "but someone decided to steal the spotlight by skipping ahead instead of sticking to the script." Kiara tilted her head, clearly puzzled, but didn't miss a beat. "Stealing your spotlight? I didn't realize this was a magic show," she quipped, crossing her arms. "Next time, send me the program so I know where to stand."

Rose smirked, her gaze shifting to Aron with a flicker of amusement and something close to approval. Her lips quirked slightly, as if she were beginning to understand the dynamic between him and Kiara, though she kept her thoughts to herself.

Kiara poked her head back through the wall, her expression bewildered. "Is somebody going to tell me what the hell is going on, or do I just keep guessing?"

Rose smirked and crossed her arms. "Best to stay close, love. Trust me, you'll thank your lucky stars we're not at Mount Shasta right now. If this place is a quirky little indie film, Shasta's the full-blown sci-fi blockbuster with a budget to match. Makes this look like a quiet Sunday stroll."

Aron chuckled, shaking his head as he waved the others forward. "Alright, let's go. Stay close, and for the love of all that's holy, let me lead this time."

The group moved forward, each person hesitating slightly before stepping through the illusionary wall. On the other side, the narrow passage opened into a larger corridor, its smooth walls glimmering faintly in the dim light.

Rose ran her hand along the stone, her expression sharpening with curiosity. "I've been here before, but it's humming differently. There's a lot more energy coursing through now."

Aron nodded, his tone calm but serious. "The Pulse changed everything. Places like this are more alive than ever—it's like the energy is running hotter, faster."

Behind them, Teddy cast a wary glance back at the entrance. "She just walked through like it was no big deal," he muttered, shaking his head.

"That's Kiara," Robyn said with a small grin. "She's great at making the impossible seem normal."

Aron's green eyes scanned the path ahead, sharp and watchful. Though he appeared relaxed, there was an unmistakable edge to his movements, his protective nature clearly heightened.

"It's like the whole place is buzzing," Rose murmured, catching up to walk alongside Aron. "More alive than I've ever felt it."

Aron gave a brief smile. "Ogma and his crew have always maintained this space, but since the Pulse, it's like the whole system's gone into overdrive."

The passage widened into a breathtaking hub. Water cascaded down a series of steps, pooling in the chamber below where the clear liquid was illuminated in intricate patterns, forming a glowing symbol at the bottom.

The group stopped in awe, their eyes scanning the magnificent sight. Kiara, however, was already exploring, her hands gliding over the walls with intent. She paused where symbols glowed faintly, tracing their intricate shapes with her fingertips.

"Kiara," Robyn began, stepping toward her, "there's—"

Before she could finish, a deep, resonant voice boomed behind them. "Welcome, my esteemed guests!"

Teddy and Robyn froze, their eyes wide as they turned toward the towering figure striding into the room, an enchanted, magical satyr. His horns curved gracefully, and his robe swayed with his steps, revealing glimpses of hooves beneath. His presence filled the space effortlessly, a mixture of elegance and power. Aron, on the other hand, seemed entirely at ease. "Ogma," he said with a respectful nod, his tone warm but tinged with urgency. "Didn't expect you to greet us personally."

Ogma's lips quirked into a knowing smile as his sharp eyes landed on Aron. "You've brought interesting company, as always."

"That's one way to put it," Aron replied, his gaze briefly flicking to Kiara, softening for just a moment before returning to Ogma. "I was trying to keep her—and her friends—safe."

Ogma's eyes followed Aron's gaze to Kiara, and his smile grew slightly. "Ah, yes. She was always meant to be here. As for her companions..." He glanced at the rest of the group, his expression turning mildly amused. "A delightful surprise."

Teddy shifted uncomfortably, whispering to Robyn, "Did he just call us a surprise? Like we're some kind of backup dancers?"

Robyn elbowed him lightly to hush him, though her lips twitched in a suppressed smile.

Ogma's sharp hearing didn't miss the comment. "Not backup, dear boy," he corrected smoothly, glancing at Teddy with a faint smile that was somehow both reassuring and unsettling. "Every thread in the tapestry has its purpose."

Kiara, who had been quietly listening, tilted her head in Ogma's direction. "What does that mean?" she asked softly, her voice steady despite her unease.

Ogma's tone softened as his gaze settled on her. "It means, my dear, that the paths we take may not have consciously been chosen by us, but it is always part of a greater design." His expression turned contemplative as he added, "The reasons always become clear over time."

The cryptic response left the group quiet, each person processing his words in their own way. Aron, however, broke the tension with a faint grin. "Always with the riddles, Ogma?"

Ogma chuckled, gesturing for the group to follow. "And you're still questioning them. Come, there's much to discuss."

Teddy, still visibly unnerved, muttered under his breath. "Sure, no reason to freak out when the giant goat-man says we're fine."

Ogma's sharp ears caught the comment, and he turned to Teddy with a glint of amusement in his eyes. "Satyr, actually," he corrected smoothly, "though I'll admit the confusion is understandable."

Rose chuckled, clearly enjoying Teddy's unease. "Relax, mate. If Aron trusts him, we're in good hands."

"Better than good," Aron added with a smirk. "He's the reason this place still exists."

Ogma's gaze shifted from the group to Kiara, who hadn't moved from her spot by the wall. Her fingers trailed over the symbols; her brow furrowed in deep concentration. It was as if the rest of the room had faded away, and she was entirely absorbed in deciphering the strange, glowing script.

The others exchanged glances, unsure whether to call her back or let her be. Ogma's towering figure moved silently toward her, his large hooves making surprisingly little sound on the stone floor. The satyr knelt beside her, his presence casting a long shadow that enveloped her small frame.

"You seem quite captivated," he said gently, his deep voice almost a whisper.

Startled, Kiara turned her face toward him, though her fingers remained on the wall. "I wasn't sure if it was real," she admitted, her tone both awestruck and uncertain.

Ogma's smile softened as he inclined his head. "I assure you, it is very real, as am I. My apologies for the... prolonged mystery," he said, his words measured and kind. "It was necessary to wait until now to explain everything."

The others, watching from a respectful distance, couldn't help but feel the gravity of the moment. Aron crossed his arms, a faint smile tugging at his lips as he watched Kiara and Ogma interact. Rose, on the other hand, muttered under her breath with a smirk, "Looks like she's got a new pen pal."

Teddy leaned toward Robyn. "Do you think he's always this dramatic, or does he save it for special guests?"

Robyn elbowed him lightly, her eyes still on Kiara. "Hush. This feels... important."

Meanwhile, Ogma gently gestured toward the symbols Kiara had been tracing. "These markings have waited for someone with your gift to truly feel their meaning. Do you sense their story?"

Kiara's fingers paused on a particularly intricate symbol, and she nodded faintly. "They feel... old. Like they've been waiting a long time."

Ogma's smile deepened. "Indeed. And so have I."

The moment lingered, charged with an unspoken understanding, as the group looked on in quiet awe. Ogma's towering figure stood silently for a moment before he moved with unexpected grace, lowering himself onto one knee beside Kiara. His eyes, warm and inquisitive, met hers even though he knew she couldn't see them.

Kiara's attention remained fixed on the wall's symbols, her fingers tracing their smooth, glowing edges. Slowly, as if sensing his proximity, she turned toward Ogma. Her hand extended, brushing the air before making contact with the fur on his forehead. A collective intake of breath rippled through the group.

"Kiara..." Aron's voice was cautious, his green eyes narrowing as he shifted his weight forward. Rose tensed beside him, and even Teddy's usual bravado faltered as he stared, wide-eyed.

Ogma, however, remained perfectly still, his expression calm and understanding. "It's alright," he said softly, his voice soothing as Kiara's hand moved over the ridge between his horns. "For one who relies on touch and sensation to navigate the world, this is simply another way of knowing."

Her hand paused on the inside of his left horn, her brow furrowing slightly as she traced a faint groove in the surface. "What happened to you?" she asked, her tone calm but filled with curiosity.

Ogma's lips quivered into a faint smile. "A long story, and one that matters little now," he replied gently. "More importantly, how are you feeling? Things must seem very strange to you at this time, yes?"

Kiara tilted her head slightly, as if weighing his words, before nodding. Her attention drifted back to the wall, her fingers resuming their exploration of the glowing writing. "It feels much smoother than the stone," she murmured, more to herself than anyone else. "What is it? What does it say?"

Ogma rose to his full height, his movements fluid and unhurried, though his gaze remained fondly on Kiara. "Quartz crystal," he explained, "interwoven with intention and ancient knowledge. These markings have been waiting for someone like you to understand their meaning."

Before he could elaborate further, Ogma's attention shifted to Teddy, who was still hovering near the back of the group, his expression a mix of awe and trepidation. "I believe you are the only one here I have not had the pleasure of meeting," Ogma said, inclining his head slightly. "Allow me to welcome you to my home. Though I cannot yet explain everything, suffice it to say, your presence is not by accident. Your world is experiencing a profoundly significant paradigm shift—in more ways than one."

Teddy blinked, clearly caught off guard but quickly recovering. "Then I'm honored to be here," he replied, his voice steady but quieter than usual. His unexpected formality drew a surprised glance from Robyn, who smiled and followed his lead, bowing her head briefly.

"To answer your question..." He said, looking back down at Kiara. "This is a nexus point that exists outside of but parallel to your dimension, just outside of your time and space. It serves many purposes but think of it as an interdimensional refuge and gateway to other nexus points."

He explained before reaching his hand down to point at the spot Kiara had asked about.

"What you are feeling is quartz crystal and while many things have been written here over the millennia, this section translates to "Only love may dwell here.", placed right there so it would be the first thing or last thing one would see, depending on which way they read."

Kiara smiled in response, continuing her fingers onto the next set of symbols, where she stopped briefly before continuing onto the ones after that.. "Will you translate this one too?" she asked.. "I recognize that one, feels like someone blowing one of those long horns that sit on the ground…but I can't make the other parts out…"

"Among the eldest of your ancestors, dating back to the previous age of man. Here, they are depicted in one of their ceremonial traditions, honoring their guests, since most tribes would take turns hosting and visiting others for a period, bringing with them gifts in exchange for seasonally grown items in each region. Dance was not simply for entertainment either, it is how they passed down their stories from one generation to the next."

"They must have learned to adapt to anything…" Kiara muttered, still feeling around the bumpy edges of the image.

"Indeed, since the beginning they have considered themselves to be part of the lands they inhabit. Food and resources were shared, with all members contributingThe group was silent, listening intently as he spoke.

"I actually have a very old didgeridoo if you would like to see it?"

Ogma led the way to his collection of encased artifacts in a nearby room. The others described it to Kiara, who smiled gracefully, while, unbeknownst to her, Ogma was fumbling to find the rarely used key, allowing her to feel its ornate carvings as she ran her hand downward and back up again. Another object that caught their eyes was a mask that looked like a bird, used in funeral ceremonies by the Dogon of Africa, so they were told.

"They believed the masks help allow the souls of the dead to pass over to the other side after the end of their mourning period had concluded." Ogma informed them with reverence in his voice. "Similar traditions can be found in cultures all around the world, even places that humans usually aren't allowed to go, like Antarctica. All cultures stemmed from the same source, the motherland of Mu. I will tell you more about this in due time."

He was sounding much like a librarian or museum curator as he walked them by exhibit after exhibit, pausing each time to tell a short story about how and where he got that item, at least until finally interrupted by a cloaked man as he entered the room. "Is it time already?" Ogma asked him, to which he nodded in response before turning around and leaving as quickly as he had entered. "Time to go!" the satyr announced, leading the group out of the room and down a set of stairs that surrounded the waterfall that cascaded down a series of rocks as they passed by. "This way…" he directed them, pointing toward another room nearby.

The group filed in ahead of Ogma, confused as he shut the door behind him, causing the room to go dark. Kiara commented on feeling something strange as he proceeded past them, opening yet another door that he directed them toward. "Almost there…" he assured them.

As he opened the door once again, a bright light filled the room followed by blue sky, much to everyone's surprise.

"Almost where?" Teddy asked in a condescending tone, pausing briefly before he finally relented and followed the others…upon hearing Robyn and Scarlett gasp in amazement. "What is…?" He started to ask, only to see for himself that they were now standing on a dock surrounded by ocean on all sides except for directly in front of them, where an ornately carved sign stood at the entrance to what appeared to be a trolley station. Aron, leading Kiara while assuring he would explain momentarily, and Rose quickly proceeded toward the mainland while Scarlett cautiously followed behind, waving Robyn and Teddy on, signaling for them to follow her.

The two looked back at Ogma, who had just finished closing the door behind him, nodding.

"I need to sit down," Kiara insisted, pulling on Aron's arm as they stepped off the pier. He turned to see her eyes were tightly shut, and the rest of her looked a bit queasy and unsteady.

"She gets seasick!" Robyn exclaimed as she approached from behind. "She is very sensitive to the swaying from the choppy water…"

"And the brightness…" Kiara interjected.

"I thought she was blind…?" Rose asked, suspiciously.

She can see light, dark, and even colors," Robyn explained softly, her tone measured. "But shifting from shadow to brightness like this—it's overwhelming for her, especially with everything else going on."

She paused, tilting her head slightly before turning back toward Aron, still holding onto his arm. "Are those seagulls?" she asked, her question prompted by the sound.

<h1 style="text-align:center">-Chapter 16-</h1>

Witchaven

"Welcome to Witchaven!" Ogma's booming voice could be heard over the waves crashing onto the beach around them.

"Not unlike my domain, this place is one of the best-kept secrets in the world…not even visible by outsiders. As we like to joke, you might say it's 'very exclusive'!" He laughed as though expecting others to as well. Rose shook her head, her tone playful. "Doesn't work on outsiders, Ogma. They've got no idea what the bloody punchline is."

All the while, Robyn and Aron watched Kiara as they guided her toward a small train awaiting them. It appeared as though she was trying to see something, pausing as she entered, turning her head several times, as if trying to place the direction of a sound.

"Are you okay?" Aron asked from in front of her, his Irish-Aussie accent carrying a note of concern. Kiara looked back down once again and nodded, proceeding on inside.

The group sat down inside the simple wooden caboose, Rose sitting furthest away.

Ogma picked up right where he had left off, starting first with letting them know that the train would leave momentarily, leaving the newcomers curious as to who was going to be operating it since nobody but them were aboard. He continued talking as it began moving.

"You will find a number of technologies here that you will not have seen anywhere else," he said as he pressed a button near the door and the train slowly started to move.

"As well as a number of other creatures unbeknownst to the rest of the world," he continued, noticing Kiara staring out of her window, which caused the others to turn their attention outward as well.

It wasn't long before gasps could be heard from nearly everyone.

"What are those?" Robyn asked, her voice tinged with awe as her gaze lingered on the jagged formations streaking across the sky. The patterns shimmered faintly, refracting light in unnatural hues, like the sky had been fractured and the cracks mended with molten glass.

"They started when the Pulse happened," Rose explained, her tone measured but uneasy as her eyes flicked upward. "And they haven't

150

gone away."

Aron frowned, his green eyes narrowing. "Why haven't they faded? What's holding them in place?" He turned toward Ogma, his expression both curious and guarded.

Ogma's gaze followed theirs to the sky, his expression unreadable. "They are scars," he said simply, his deep voice resonating in the stillness. "Wounds in the fabric of your reality. Left untreated, they grow deeper… and more unpredictable."

Teddy took a step closer to Robyn, his confidence wavering. "And what's 'treating' them supposed to look like?"

"I suspect that's a question you're meant to help answer," Ogma replied, his tone grave yet layered with subtle intrigue. "The Pulse may have been the spark, but the fire had been smoldering long before. These cracks were already there, hidden in plain sight. The real question is: what set them alight?"

Robyn glanced between Ogma and Aron, her brow furrowing. "So, this isn't just about the Veil, is it?"

Ogma's lips made a faint, knowing smile. "You are perceptive. No, this reaches far beyond the Veil. The boundaries between dimensions, between realities themselves, are fraying. If left unchecked, the consequences will ripple far beyond your world."

Aron crossed his arms, his voice hardening. "And yet, we're the ones left to clean up the mess?"

"To understand your role in this," Ogma said, his tone firm but patient, "You must first understand the nature of the Pulse. The Veil is both a shield and a mirror. It reflects the consciousness of those it was designed to protect. But as consciousness evolves—or fractures—so too does the Veil. The cracks above are merely reflections of what lies beneath."

A heavy silence fell over the group, Ogma's words weighing on them like an invisible force. Even Rose, who could usually be counted on for a sharp retort, seemed uncharacteristically subdued.

Aron exhaled sharply, breaking the tension. "Well, that's comforting," he said, his sarcasm barely masking the frustration in his voice. "Any other cheerful insights we should brace ourselves for?"

Ogma's smile returned, calm but resolute. "Many. But for now, let us continue. There is much more for you to see."

With that, the satyr turned and motioned for the group to board the train. As they filed inside, he leaned close to a tall, thin woman dressed in elegant robes, his voice dropping low.

"I trust these prospects are in good hands," he murmured, his tone carrying both confidence and gravity.

The woman nodded, her expression serious but tinged with a hint of anticipation. "If the reports are true, then yes—we've arrived just in time." She embraced him briefly before stepping back, allowing the train to begin its slow, deliberate movement. Ogma jumped off gracefully, disappearing into a nearby building with a wave. "Be well, my friend," she called after him.

Inside the train, Mallah seemed especially focused on Kiara. Though she spent much of the ride debriefing Aron and Rose, her gaze frequently returned to the younger woman. Kiara appeared oblivious, her own attention divided between the shifting sounds around her and the faint vibrations of the train beneath her fingertips.

Mallah's questions were incisive, aimed at untangling the threads of recent events. She pressed Aron about Morton Kane, Marcus Kydd, and even Marcus's fiancée, Clarice Murphy. Aron answered in his usual forthright manner, though Mallah's occasional sidelong glances suggested she already knew more than she let on.

Robyn, meanwhile, stayed close to Kiara, her protective instincts quietly surfacing. After all, the young woman had been unusually quiet since their arrival, and Robyn couldn't shake the feeling that Kiara was processing more than she let on. Every so often, Kiara would tilt her head as though listening to something only she could hear, her fingers lightly tracing the edges of the wooden bench beside her.

The rhythmic chug of the train provided a momentary reprieve, the group settling into a wary but tentative calm as the mysterious journey continued. At the city square stop, the women had their first up-close view of the thriving Witchaven community. The energy of the bustling town square was palpable. Artisans displayed their intricate crafts, bakers and restaurateurs filled the air with mouthwatering scents, cobblers and blacksmiths hammered away at their trades, and merchants hawked goods from colorful stalls.

It was a mosaic of life teeming with purpose and harmony. Humans, many of whom were witches and pagans practicing ancient traditions, worked seamlessly alongside supernatural beings—Hokuten, fairies, giants, pookas, leprechauns, and even ghostly spirits.

Robyn and Scarlett were captivated, unabashedly drinking in the sights, sounds, and smells. They longed to get off the train and explore the shops, imagining themselves enjoying an outdoor coffee and a pastry on such a fair, calm day. It was picturesque—almost too perfect to be real.

The train slowed briefly at the station, allowing a young Hokuten girl to board. Her sleek black fur contrasted with the soft blue of her dress, and a golden brooch on her neckline held a vibrant emerald that caught the sunlight as she moved. Her brilliant blue eyes, flecked with gold around the edges, shone with curiosity as she scanned the passengers. She asked politely to sit beside Kiara, Robyn, and Scarlett, her voice melodic and warm.

The Hokuten girl was chatty, her enthusiasm infectious as she peppered them with questions about themselves and their journey. Her energy was so genuine that even Kiara, usually reserved, found herself smiling. When the girl finally paused, she began telling a story passed down by the elders of her tribe—those who still remembered their home world of Praxis.

Praxis, she explained, was a distant planet in another part of the Milky Way galaxy. Half of it was a lush, forested paradise, while the other half was an icy tundra bathed only in the faint glow of distant starlight. Though she had never seen it herself, being too young when her people were displaced, she described it with vivid reverence, painting a beautiful yet bittersweet picture.

Her tale turned somber as she recounted how ancient magic had been used against her people by invaders from Earth. In their efforts to defend themselves, many Hokuten were scattered through space and time, becoming refugees on unfamiliar worlds. Mallah and the council had offered Witchaven as a sanctuary for the remnants of their kind, in exchange for their contributions to the island and occasional insights into their technology. Despite this refuge, the Hokuten, who were still in a medieval stage of development on Praxis, longed for their ancestral home.

"Though we are thankful for the generosity of those here in Witchaven, our people yearn for Praxis," the Hokuten girl said, her voice heavy with longing. As the train approached the village of Frostpaw, she brightened. "It was nice meeting you all. Unlike some in my tribe, I enjoy meeting new people, especially humans. Very fascinating you all are."

Kiara leaned forward slightly. "I'd love to talk with you more sometime. But… we don't even know your name."

"Nor I yours," the Hokuten girl replied with a coy smile.

"Kiara," she offered.

"Robyn," followed the second.

"Scarlett," came the third.

The Hokuten girl bowed her head slightly, her smile widening. "Kiara, Robyn, and Scarlett, it has been a pleasure. My name is Esme. I hope we meet again. You can teach me more about your people, and I can teach you about ours. My father says the key to coexistence is an open line of communication."

"He sounds very wise," Scarlett said warmly.

Esme nodded. "My father is the leader of our people. I hope to see you again soon."

The bell for the trolley train rang twice, and Esme disembarked gracefully as the train moved toward its final destination: the castle of Witchaven. The women watched the feline Hokuten girl disappear into the bustling village teeming with her kind, unique and majestic. Her presence lingered in their thoughts throughout the day.

As the train picked up speed, Robyn leaned back with a contemplative expression. "This place… it's like a dream."

"Don't get too comfortable," Rose said with a wry smile, breaking the moment. "You haven't met the council yet."

As the train chugged steadily along the tracks, the mist rolling off the surrounding cliffs gave the impression of a place suspended in time. Mallah stepped gracefully from the adjacent car into theirs, her presence commanding yet approachable. The rhythmic clatter of the train's wheels softened as she began to speak.

"Good afternoon," she said, her voice calm yet resonant. "My name is Mallah. Some of you I have met before, and for those I have not, it is a pleasure to make your acquaintance." She bowed her head slightly, her movements deliberate, conveying both authority and grace.

"As the steward here in Witchaven, I welcome you to this sanctuary."

The group exchanged curious glances, though they remained silent. Mallah's piercing gaze lingered on each of them briefly before continuing.

"You have many questions, and I do not like to repeat myself," she said, her tone kind but firm. "So, I ask that you hold them until I have finished. You may have noticed, during your journey here, that there are creatures roaming about which you likely do not recognize. Some may seem vaguely familiar, as though plucked from the myths and legends passed down through your cultures. And in a way, they are."

Mallah's sharp eyes flicked toward Kiara, who was leaning slightly against Aron, her head tilted as though trying to discern some distant sound. Mallah's expression softened before she resumed.

"The Veil," she continued, "was created as a temporary measure to protect all species involved. It was designed to keep the worlds of man and the unseen separate, ensuring the survival of both. But as with all temporary things, it was never meant to last indefinitely."

Her tone darkened slightly, and the group leaned in instinctively, drawn by the gravity of her words. "Yesterday, that veil was torn. For the first time in over ten thousand years, the boundaries between our worlds have unraveled. Creatures long hidden from humanity—many of whom have also forgotten humans exist—are now part of your reality once more."

Robyn, enraptured by the view outside, barely registered the weight of Mallah's words. Scarlett nudged her gently, nodding toward Mallah in silent encouragement. Mallah noticed the exchange and offered a small, understanding smile before continuing.

"The reason we call Witchaven a sanctuary is simple: the Veil does not exist here. This place has been used as a sanctuary because it lies outside of your time and space," she explained. "When the messengers and students of the mystics faced persecution, we set this land aside as a refuge. It remained nameless for centuries until it became affectionately known as Witchaven."

Mallah paused, her gaze once again drawn to Kiara, who appeared entirely absorbed in her own sensory world. The small woman tilted her head upward, her expression shifting between curiosity and discomfort as she tried to process everything.

"This is a place of safety," Mallah continued, addressing the group but clearly attuned to Kiara. "But it is also a place of profound responsibility. What has been hidden here is now part of a larger truth—a truth you are all connected to in ways you have yet to understand."

The group sat in contemplative silence, the clatter of the train's wheels underscoring the weight of her statement. Mallah let the moment linger, her gaze resting on each of them before continuing softly.

"We have much to discuss. But for now, let us focus on getting you acclimated to what lies ahead. We still have a way to go."

Mallah moved toward Kiara as she resumed speaking, her tone gentle but commanding. "As we speak, your closest friends and family are among the first people to witness these creatures, as well as entities that only a rare person has been able to perceive in a very long time." She leaned in slightly, observing Kiara's distracted, panic-stricken expression.

Raising her hand, Mallah signaled for everyone to stay still. She knelt beside Kiara and calmly placed a reassuring hand on her shoulder.

"Do not be afraid. I understand how overwhelming this must be, but I brought you here so that we can help each other," Mallah said, her voice steady yet soothing. With a final glance at Kiara, she turned to address the group again.

"What's wrong?" Robyn interjected, her voice edged with concern as she leaned toward Kiara.

Kiara's eyes, wide and searching, seemed fixed on something invisible to everyone else. Without responding, she rose from her seat, her movements deliberate and curious. She reached out with one hand to grasp the nearest pole for balance, while her other hand stretched cautiously upward.

Carefully, Kiara tapped her toes lightly in front of her with each step, inching closer to her unseen destination. The group exchanged confused glances, murmuring quietly as they tried to follow her trajectory. Mallah, however, remained calm, a knowing smile on her face.

"I knew you would notice her," Mallah said softly, her expression brightening as she moved gracefully to Kiara's side. "Go ahead, reach out your hand."

Gently, Mallah guided Kiara's hand, adjusting her fingers so that one pointed outward. With a soft laugh, she removed Kiara's tight grip from the pole and steadied her wrist instead. "He's much heavier than he looks," Mallah added quietly, her tone full of reassurance as she coaxed the invisible creature closer.

Kiara lifted her arm higher, and the others watched in astonishment as dimples appeared along her sleeve, trailing up toward her shoulder.

"That's very good," Mallah praised as she supported Kiara's arm, helping balance the unseen weight.

The group stared in awe; their excitement mixed with unease. Rose, however, crossed her arms, her expression a mix of confusion and irritation as she shot a questioning look toward Aron, who had stepped forward to assist Kiara.

"What is it?" Kiara asked, her voice quiet but filled with wonder as she stroked the invisible creature. Her hand followed the contours of something soft and pliable, the dimples shifting along her arm.

Mallah smiled, her voice encouraging. "Your turn. Since we're both treading new ground here, tell me what it looks like to you."

Kiara tilted her head, her brow furrowing as she studied the space just above her arm. "It's like... a snake had a baby with a bird," she murmured, stroking it tentatively. "But it's so soft... almost like fur."

"I thought you were blind!" Rose exclaimed, standing abruptly from her seat.

"Me too!" Teddy chimed in, stepping between them with a smirk. "I'm sure there's a perfectly logical explanation... right?" he added, glancing at Kiara with mock curiosity.

Aron, standing on Kiara's opposite side, raised a hand to calm the commotion. "She's not looking at Mallah, or at anything. She's perceiving it in her own way."

"What's happening to me?" Kiara asked, her voice unsteady as she handed the creature back to Mallah, who carefully coaxed it toward its perch.

Mallah turned to face Kiara fully, her expression both compassionate and thoughtful. "From what Ogma has told me, you've been able to perceive unseen things for some time—certainly since you moved into your new home," she explained. Gracefully, she extended her arm, allowing the creature to climb back onto its unseen perch.

"Was he watching me?" Kiara snapped, her tone edged with suspicion. Robyn gasped softly from behind her.

Mallah's voice remained calm but firm as she responded. "Ogma watches everything in and around those woods—for the protection of all who dwell within and near his sanctuary. It was he who told us about you, which is why we had always intended to bring you here when the time was right. You could be very helpful to us, once we teach you to fully use your abilities—abilities I suspect have been amplified by the breaking down of the Veil."

"Shit, that actually makes sense," Teddy muttered, his voice breaking the tension. He and Robyn stepped forward, each offering Kiara an arm to help her back to her seat.

"You knew about me?" Kiara asked, turning toward Aron, her voice softer now but still probing.

"That was a surprise to us all," Mallah interjected before Aron could answer, her gaze shifting to him with a stern authority. "But Aron and Rose grew up here. Aron has been working for Ogma for quite some time, while Rose oversees the neighboring region in Northern California. As Guardians of the Veil, they patrol their territories and know those woods intimately. Aron happened to be escorting a dear friend to a meeting with Ogma when they encountered your party."

"Who was that?" Rose asked, her confusion evident.

"Marcus and his crew," Aron replied, his voice steady but tinged with something deeper as his gaze fell on Kiara. She turned away, staring at the floor, her expression unreadable. From the corner of his eye, Aron caught Teddy making a ridiculous snarling face at Robyn and Scarlett, who stifled their laughter behind raised hands.

"Time is short, as we are about to arrive at our destination," Mallah interjected smoothly, her tone quelling the momentary levity. "That dear friend is now lying in a coma, his frantic fiancée anxiously awaiting the arrival of his best friend."

Aron's head snapped toward her. "What happened?" he demanded, his voice sharper now.

"There was a plan, but it went awry," Mallah admitted, her tone heavy. "They were all betrayed—Marcus, Kane, and others. We found Kane's hand at the center of the Nexus, not far from where Marcus was discovered."

"The Nexus?" Aron pressed, his eyes narrowing.

Mallah raised a hand to forestall further questioning. "I didn't say it was a good plan," she quipped lightly, though her smile was brief. She knelt before Kiara again, her demeanor softening as she glanced at Teddy and Robyn flanking her like protective sentinels. Teddy relaxed slightly, giving Robyn a subtle nod to do the same.

"Time is not on our side," Mallah continued, her voice low but resolute. "My typical apprentice trains with me for at least ten years before we even begin the work I need to teach you how to do. But with everything unraveling, we don't have ten years—or even one. I'll need you to trust me, Kiara, as well as those who brought you here. Your role in this is more important than you can yet understand."

Do, so I will need you to trust me in order to get you there, but I will if you let me, I promise…and once you are, you will not only be able to protect yourself, but your friends as well!"

Her eyebrow wrinkled upon hearing her words, appearing intrigued but skeptical and curious all at the same time. She stared down in her direction briefly, before nodding as she closed her eyes.

"It's too much, it hurts…" she said, shaking her head, to which her friends immediately tried to help. At which time, it was revealed Kiara had not gotten a chance to grab her earbuds, to which Teddy remarked how glad he was to have disobeyed Aron when he dashed off to grab some things. "I almost didn't grab them, I thought for sure you would have had yours!" he said, shoveling through the large bag he had brought with him. "Here!" he exclaimed, placing a small red case in her hand.

"I thought these were long gone!" she shouted with glee, to which Teddy revealed she had already gotten new ones, so he waited to surprise her.

"I have those extra ones too…" Robyn added in an annoyed voice, slapping Teddy's shoulder and joking that she was going to say something, joking about how much louder he is than everyone else.

"What can I say?!" he snapped back. "I like to be the center of attention!"

As the two bantered, Aron knelt down as Kiara was placing her earpieces. "Can I help or get you anything else?" he whispered near her ear.

She leaned in and closed her eyes, shaking her head no as he gently brushed his cheek to hers. The others watched as he whispered something else, to which she nodded before placing her second earpiece in her left ear..

"We have arrived!" Mallah interrupted, instructing them to follow the people awaiting them when they stepped out shortly, waiting to show them to their rooms. Still embracing her, Aron gently pulled Kiara upward, indicating for her to follow him, to which she did. Teddy and

Robyn stepped out of the way, glancing in surprise toward one another before following them and Mallah out of the trolley and onto another platform. Robyn looked back toward Scarlett, who was standing just behind her, noticing Rose staring at her brother as if confused by their interactions.

The group filed out to see the city most of them hadn't noticed as they arrived.

After Mallah pointed Aron to which rooms his friends were staying in, he darted in that direction, along with Rose who followed behind him.

"What's up?" Aron asked, maintaining his forward gaze.

"You tell me…" she chuckled.

"About?" he queried.

"So let me guess, you met this chick on your way to Ogma…who just happened to be throwing a week-long orgy, you guys drank the punch, then you fucked her til her tits fell off?"

"It was a festival!" He insisted, smiling back at her..

"WOW!" She exclaimed"What?" He asked"You don't feel a little weird about hooking up with a handicapped person?"

Aron stopped and shrugged, insisting he had at first but had not been able to get her out of his mind. To which his sister laughed off, as he reached for the door behind him that led to his friend. Rose approached quickly and had almost breached the threshold, before Aron reached out his arm to block her path.

"Are you kidding me? You look like a serial killer…er you ya forgotten?" He snapped, accentuating his accent. Rose had nearly forgotten she was wearing bloody clothing, relenting before turning around to head in the opposite direction.

"We aren't finished here…" she warned as she walked away.

"Oh, me thinks we are…!" he responded as soon as the door shut behind him.

-Chapter 17-

Echoes of the Past

Insisting she had somewhere to be but would check back in with them shortly, Mallah handed Kiara and her housemates over to a woman awaiting their arrival. The woman led them deeper into what Teddy and Robyn enthusiastically described as a castle carved into a mountainside.

Once inside, Kiara noticed only the endless hallways and countless steps. Meanwhile, Teddy admired the ornate carvings along banisters, archways, and molding, as well as the ancient artifacts and artwork that decorated the space. He marveled at how everything seemed to coordinate perfectly, pointing out details to anyone within earshot. Robyn humored him with playful banter, knowing how much Teddy loved to talk and how upset he would be if no one acknowledged his observations. Yet, her focus remained on Kiara, who moved differently from the others. Kiara's eyes were closed as she ran her hands along walls, banisters, and archways, quietly counting each step and committing the layout to memory. It was her way of understanding a new space, a skill she had relied on since they first moved in together back home. Back then, their dream project—a house with a few too many eerie occupants—had required some effort to claim as their own. Even now, Robyn felt a pang of protectiveness watching her best friend explore in her unique way, preferring to hug the walls rather than accept a guiding hand.

Though it had been only ten hours since Aron had awakened them in the middle of the night, followed by the strange event they were now calling "the Pulse," it felt like days had passed. Exhaustion was setting in, both physically and emotionally. When Kiara was finally shown to her modest room, she insisted on some time alone to settle in. She wasn't particularly tired but felt overstimulated and confused. Lying down on the bed, she closed her eyes, hoping to soothe her frayed nerves and piece together everything that had happened. As she listened to the muffled hum of activity beyond the door, she let herself drift inward, trying to make sense of it all—or at least as much as she could.

The first thing Kiara thought of as she lay in her room was Aron's mention of Kane, a name she hadn't heard in a very long time. The memory transported her back to Christmas 2009; a night etched into her mind forever. She had been eight years old, spending an evening with her mother, Natalie, in Portland's Old Chinatown.

Disappointment lingered in the air that evening. Her father, Oliver Kross, a renowned bioengineer, was once again working late, trying to wrap up his projects before taking time off for a much-anticipated family trip. The trip was meant to celebrate a monumental accomplishment—a reveal he had promised would change everything.

Despite her father's absence, Kiara found herself enthralled by the festive streets. Strings of lights illuminated the trees and lamp posts, and the window displays in the shops were filled with toys and gifts that captivated her young imagination. Her favorite part of downtown was Powell's Bookstore, a magical place where she felt at home among the towering shelves.

Kiara was already an avid reader, well ahead of her peers. Her love for books was a family trait, and Christmas always brought a new addition to her collection. That evening, she and her mother wandered the aisles, choosing a gift for Oliver. Kiara giggled as she held up a book with a goofy cover featuring a green ball with its tongue sticking out.

"This one!" she exclaimed, her voice echoing through the store.

"Shhh," Natalie whispered, smiling. "Not so loud, sweetie. Why this one?"

"It says, 'Don't Panic,' and look at this guy!" Kiara laughed, pointing to the illustration.

Natalie bemusedly picked up the book, holding it as they explored the store. Kiara's excitement was contagious as she darted between displays, making up stories based on the covers. Her mother eventually lured her out of the store with a promise of donuts from the iconic Voodoo Donuts, adorned in its signature pink.

As they walked to the bakery, Natalie tightened her grip on Kiara's hand. Groups of homeless people huddled in doorways, a sight that made her uneasy. She quickened their pace, glancing back occasionally. A man broke away from one group and began following them. His movements were erratic, and his slurred speech made it clear he wasn't in his right mind. Relief washed over Natalie when they reached the bakery, blending into the lively crowd.

Inside, Kiara pressed her face to the glass display, reciting everyone's favorite flavors as Natalie ordered a dozen donuts. The familiar routine brought comfort, and for a moment, they forgot about the lurking stranger. But as they left the shop and took a shortcut to meet Oliver, the man reappeared.

"Hey, you got a cigarette, lady?" he called out, his voice sharp in the quiet street.

"No," Natalie replied firmly, clutching Kiara's hand. "I don't smoke."

As she tried to walk away, the click of a gun's hammer froze her in place. She turned to face the man; his wild eyes and trembling hand aimed directly at her.

"Turns out, I don't smoke either, lady." He then demanded. "Now, give me your purse and jewelry."

Tears welled up in Natalie's eyes as she fumbled with her wallet. The man grew more agitated, barking for her jewelry. When she hesitated, he struck her with the butt of the gun, leaving a gash on her cheek.

"NO!" Kiara screamed, stepping in front of her mother. "Don't hurt my mom, you bad man!"

The man pointed the gun at Kiara. Before Natalie could react, a bald man emerged from the shadows. Without hesitation, he tackled the assailant, a flurry of punches landing as they struggled for the weapon. A gunshot rang out, and the would-be mugger collapsed.

The stranger stood over him, blood dripping from a cut on his head. Calmly, he picked up Natalie's scattered belongings, handing them back except for her phone. He dialed 911, reporting the incident before turning to Natalie and Kiara.

"You two should go now," he said in a low, steady voice.

"Who are you?" Natalie asked, her voice trembling.

"I'm the ghost of Christmas future," he replied, winking at Kiara before disappearing into the night.

Natalie clutched Kiara tightly as they hurried away. They slowed only once they were several blocks from the scene.

"Mommy, who was that man?"

"I don't know, honey," Natalie whispered. "I don't know."

Lying on her bed in the present, Kiara replayed the memory, recalling her first encounter with Morton Kane. She couldn't shake the feeling that his role in her life was far from over. If fate had brought him into her path that night, perhaps now it was her turn to save him.

Kiara reflected on Mallah's explanation about what she could see that others could not. Her thoughts were interrupted by a high-pitched frequency, faint at first but sharp enough to draw her attention. Sitting up, she strained to locate the sound's source, but it faded as quickly as it had appeared. She lay back down, trying to get comfortable, only to hear something else—a muffled crying from the next room.

The sobs trailed off briefly, then resumed louder, making it impossible for Kiara to focus. It was clear someone was having a far worse day than she was. The frequency noise rang in her ears again, piquing her curiosity. This was the fourth time in the past week she'd heard it.

Unable to ignore the sounds, Kiara moved toward her door and opened it, listening carefully. At first, there was only silence, but then the wailing resumed. Hugging the wall, she made her way toward the source—a door to the left of hers.

Standing outside the door, she hesitated. The crying had grown louder, accompanied by the sound of crashing objects. Kiara second-guessed herself, unsure whether to knock. Whoever was inside seemed to be in the midst of a breakdown, and she didn't want to intrude.

Before she could decide, Teddy's door flew open. "What's with all the racket?" he asked loudly, his voice breaking the tension. Moments later, Robyn appeared, followed by Scarlett, who suggested she should knock, claiming she recognized the voice.

But before Scarlett could act, the door flung open, and Kiara stumbled back, briefly losing her balance.

"I just wanted to see if you were okay!" Kiara blurted, her face flushing. She hoped to clear up any confusion and dispel the idea that she'd been eavesdropping.

To her surprise, the humming noise intensified. As Kiara turned her head, she was astonished to see the woman standing in the doorway. Her outline shimmered with radiant colors—distinct and clear, unlike the chaotic, flying blobs she'd witnessed on the train ride up from the pier. This vision was steady, vibrant, and undeniably real.

"Who are you?" the woman asked, her voice hoarse from crying.

"She's with me!" Scarlett answered quickly, stepping forward and gently pushing Kiara aside. Scarlett wrapped the woman in a warm hug, murmuring something soothing as the woman broke down on her shoulder.

"Aron and Rose are here too," Scarlett added softly. "I think Aron's with Marcus, and Rose…" She trailed off, smirking.

"Looks like a nuclear tampon, so hopefully in the shower!" Teddy interjected, breaking the tension with his irreverent humor as he joined the hug, wrapping his arms around both women.

Despite the absurdity of Teddy's comment, Kiara couldn't help but smile. The raw emotion, the laughter, and the strange hum of the unknown made the moment feel surreal. The outline of colors surrounding the woman lingered in her vision, a reminder that her senses were awakening to something far beyond what she'd ever known.

Clarice let herself cry, surrounded by some friends and some strangers, before inviting them into her room.

"You don't look so good yourself. What happened?" Scarlett pressed gently as they stepped inside.

Clarice sighed, visibly exhausted, and explained. She was worried sick about her fiancé, Marcus, who had been unconscious since the explosion at the Nexus—the event everyone was now calling The Pulse. Despite the burns scarring the left side of his face, Marcus was otherwise in peak physical condition according to the doctors. Yet, nothing explained his prolonged unconsciousness.

"I'm losing my shit!" Clarice exclaimed, stripping down in front of everyone as she prepared to step into the shower.

Kiara caught Teddy whispering to Robyn, "I did not expect the carpet to match those drapes," a sly reference to the bright pink strands woven through Clarice's hair. Robyn stifled a giggle before explaining the joke, causing Kiara to laugh softly despite the tension in the room.

"Where does that door lead?" Kiara asked, pausing briefly before opening it.

"Yep, that'd be your room," Scarlett confirmed with a quick peek inside.

After a quick shower, Clarice rejoined the group, leading them all down to the medical center. The air grew heavy as they entered, finding two men lying on gurneys with a curtain separating them. From the far side, a tall figure appeared. Aron's distinctive mix of red, brown, and blonde hair popped up above the curtain.

"SPARKY!" Clarice shouted, running full-speed toward him.

Aron caught her mid-sprint, lifting her off the ground and holding her tightly. She wept into his shoulder, letting the floodgates open as he whispered reassurances, promising everything would be okay. It was clear they shared a close bond. Even after the initial embrace, she clung to his arm, still overwhelmed.

"We just met, actually," Clarice said with a tearful laugh, wiping her face.

Kiara remained quiet, her focus fixed on the beds before her. She could hear Clarice talking to Aron, expressing her surprise but happiness that Marcus had found someone like Kiara.

"They're talking about you," Teddy whispered.

Kiara smiled faintly. She was already aware, and though she appreciated Teddy's protectiveness, she was too distracted to reply. Her head was pounding again, and the ringing in her ears had returned, louder than ever. She winced, shutting her eyes and concentrating on her breathing.

"What's up with you?" Teddy asked, noticing her discomfort.

Before she could answer, Aron stepped closer, his voice laced with concern. "You okay?" he asked, lightly touching her arm to guide her a few steps away from the others.

Teddy followed. "I just asked that," he said, shooting Aron a look.

Kiara tried to respond, but the pain was overwhelming. She reached up and removed an earbud, the pressure worsening her headache. Stuffing it into her pocket, she steadied herself, focusing on slow, deliberate breaths.

Teddy suddenly darted toward a nearby rubbish bin. "Uh-oh…" he muttered, but it was too late.

Aron turned back toward Kiara just in time for her to vomit on him, her face pale and eyes glassy.

Despite the mess, Aron managed to kneel and catch her as she collapsed. "Has this happened before?" he asked, looking up at Teddy, who was now positioning the bin next to them.

"No, but I can always tell when someone's about to puke," Teddy replied, kneeling beside them.

Kiara began seizing, her body convulsing uncontrollably. Aron's confusion turned to alarm as the others rushed over. A man stepped out from behind the curtain, drawing Aron's attention.

"Dr. Patel?" Aron asked, his tone a mixture of skepticism and surprise.

Dr. Patel didn't acknowledge Aron's disbelief, instead issuing quick instructions to stabilize Kiara. Aron followed his lead, helping carry her to a nearby bed once the episode subsided.

After ensuring Kiara was safe, Aron settled into a chair and stool beside her, staring at the ceiling as the events of the day replayed in his mind. Everything felt surreal—the Pulse, the strange convergence of people, and Kiara's sudden collapse. Even now, the lingering sense of interconnectedness gnawed at him, as though the pieces of a puzzle were falling into place, but he couldn't yet see the full picture.

The room was silent except for the faint rustle of the wind outside. Exhaustion weighed on him, yet his mind refused to settle. How was all of this connected? Was it mere coincidence, or had they been drawn together for a purpose far greater than any of them realized? As these thoughts swirled, Aron felt his eyelids grow heavy, until sleep finally claimed him.

The dream began abruptly, as though Aron had been thrust into someone else's life—or perhaps his own, in a distant past. It felt real, too real, like he was living the memory rather than observing it. Yet here he found himself in this place. It felt so real, it made him wonder who was to say what was real. If he were given the powers of the gods, then who could convince him that this wasn't just another step on his path to redemption. Except he was her, yet still him at the same time.

He felt confused for a moment before it dawned on him what was happening. It was similar to he and Rose's experiences with the walkabout, spending time among the aboriginal tribes of Australia during their time in the land down under. Then he discovered his past history of being the King of the Champions, the almighty Zeus. That had been a tough pill to swallow, but no more or less so than this concurrent life expression he now was living, fully engrossed in the experience.

The spring air was crisp as Athanasia stood at the edge of her family's estate, her heart pounding with a mix of fear and excitement. Her plan to join Godfrey of Bouillon's crusade was risky, but she was determined. The vision she'd received—the being of pure white light—had left her no doubt. She was destined for something greater than the life her father had planned for her.

The estate was alive with activity. Guests had arrived earlier in the afternoon, and the evening's dinner promised to be a grand affair. Among them was Bastian, a charming and clever suitor who seemed to understand Athanasia's plight better than anyone else ever had. Over tea in the garden, he had laid out a bold plan: he would propose marriage that evening, creating a perfect pretense for her father to grant her permission to join the crusade. It was a calculated gamble, but one that Athanasia believed might work.

Aron felt himself slipping deeper into the memory, experiencing every moment as if it were his own. He could feel the weight of Athanasia's anxiety, the resolve in her heart as she prepared for the dinner that would change her life. The faces of her sisters blurred into the background, their disapproving whispers drowned out by her determination. She would not be caged.

The dinner unfolded just as Bastian had planned. His proposal, delivered with eloquence and charm, left the guests in awe. No doubt it was the gossip on everyone's lips that night and many more. Athanasia's father, though initially hesitant, softened under the weight of Bastian's arguments and the presence of Godfrey himself, who spoke highly of her potential contributions to the crusade. By the end of the night, the arrangement had been made: Athanasia would join Godfrey's Knights of the Valley, leading a group of skilled women on a mission to support the holy endeavor.

The dream shifted, fast-forwarding to the journey. Aron felt the ache of days spent on horseback, the chill of nights under the stars, and the weight of Athanasia's doubts as she witnessed the destruction left in the wake of the People's Crusade. The trail of burned villages, murdered families, and senseless cruelty sickened her. She questioned everything—the purpose of their mission, the righteousness of their cause, and her own role in it all.

"How do we recognize the enemy if they look the same as us?" she wondered aloud one night, her voice heavy with despair.

Her companions—Malie, Elewisa, Tetty, and Jivete—offered their support in the only way they could: through shared stories, laughter, and moments of humanity that reminded her why she had joined in the first place. Together, they formed a bond that transcended their mission, becoming a family forged in the crucible of war.

Aron felt himself pulled deeper into the dream as the group reached Constantinople. The city's grandeur was overwhelming, its streets bustling with life and the promise of new challenges. Athanasia's resolve hardened. She had come this far, and she would see her mission through, no matter the cost.

But the dream began to fragment, slipping away like sand through his fingers. Aron woke with a start, his heart racing as the last image burned into his mind: Athanasia, standing at the head of a battlefield, her sword raised high, her voice ringing out in defiance as the armies clashed around her.

Back in the infirmary, Aron sat up, running a hand through his hair. The dream had felt more like a memory—vivid, tangible, and hauntingly real. And the strangest part? It hadn't felt like it was just his memory. He could sense the presence of others, as though they had been there with him, experiencing the same moments.

His thoughts drifted to the others: Kiara, Clarice, Marcus, Scarlett, Teddy, and Robyn. Was it possible they had shared the dream? The idea seemed absurd, yet it lingered, refusing to be dismissed.

As Aron lay back down, his mind raced with questions. Who had Athanasia been? Why had he felt so connected to her story? And what did it all mean for the strange path they now found themselves on?

Sleep eluded him for the rest of the night, leaving him staring at the ceiling, searching for answers in the darkness.

Opening the door slightly, Clarice was surprised to see Dr. Patel standing there, looking disheveled and deeply troubled.

"Give me just one minute," she said quickly, closing the door before he could respond. She hadn't intended to be rude, but there was no way she was having a conversation with him half-naked. Throwing on a robe, she reopened the door and gestured for him to come in.

"What's up, Doc?" she said with a chuckle, realizing how childish the phrase sounded. "Come on in."

Dr. Patel managed a weak smile as he stepped inside and closed the door behind him. "I'm sorry for disturbing you so late, but I had no one else to talk to. Not about this."

Clarice took in his pale complexion and the tremor in his hands. "You look terrible, professor," she said bluntly, though her tone was gentle. "Can I get you a drink?"

"That would be great," he admitted with a shaky nod.

Clarice poured him a scotch, neat. Ice was nowhere to be found on the island, so the drink would have to suffice. Judging by Patel's state, she doubted he cared much about the details. Handing him the glass, she motioned for him to sit.

"I think we're all a little overwhelmed right now," she said, breaking the silence.

Patel sighed heavily, his eyes fixed on the amber liquid in his glass. "The Order will come looking for us," he began. "I feel terrible, Clarice. I had no idea what was going to happen when we got to the Hollow Earth. Hell, I didn't fully believe it was real in the first place. My brother was always convinced. I'm more convinced that Ivyg and Kane had been in his head for far too long. Perhaps it made him forget where we came from, why we joined the Order. We wanted to be a part of something. Something beyond ourselves. Something that we could believe in. We were going to change the world."

Clarice poured herself a drink and sat down across from him. "We were all sold the same buy-in story, and we all knew the stakes going in," she said, shaking her head. "But we couldn't have seen this coming. Betrayed by our own… of all the fucked-up…" Her voice broke as tears welled up, and she quickly wiped them away.

"Don't do that to yourself," Patel said firmly. "None of us were meant to know. You know how they operate—this time it was us. We were expendable."

"NO!" Clarice cried out, slamming her glass down on the table. "We CANNOT let them win!"

Patel leaned forward, lowering his voice. "I think we can trust Mallah. She says we're safe here, though I can tell there's a lot we don't know about this place."

Clarice nodded slowly, calming herself. "She might be right. I remember Kane mentioning her once when they met for something. They seemed… familiar, but it was all business."

"There's more to that story, clearly." Patel's voice softened. "Which reminds me—have you had anything strange happen since The Pulse?"

Clarice chuckled dryly. "Stranger than everything leading up to it?"

Patel took a sip of his scotch before answering. "While I was unconscious, I had these dreams… strange dreams where I was someone else. But it felt like me." He paused, gauging her reaction.

Clarice tilted her head, curious. "Like what?"

"In one dream, I was a blacksmith—the greatest in the world—making weapons unlike anything I've ever seen. The technology… it was beyond what we have now, but it felt like it was in the past. It was the craziest thing." He shook his head, as though trying to clear the memory.

"You okay?" Clarice asked gently.

Patel stared into his glass, his voice distant. "I've lived in fear for so long, I don't know how else to live. But in that dream… it felt right. I knew exactly what side I was on, and how important the fight was. It was… amazing. Part of me feels guilty for feeling this way, especially being separated from my brother for so long. Yet here I am, and I want to feel amazing like that. I'd give anything to feel that way again."

Clarice placed a hand on his arm. "You will," she said, her voice steady. "We both will."

Their eyes met, and an unspoken pact passed between them. Whatever they faced, they would face it together.

"They didn't win, Clarice," Patel said firmly. "Whatever they were trying to do, I think part of the plan was for us to die. To keep us out of the way."

Clarice smiled faintly. "Well, they didn't succeed. They won't keep me from my happy fucking ending."

"Have you talked to Juan?" Patel asked after a moment.

"No," she admitted. "He just woke up, but he was still pretty out of it the last time I checked. I want us all to be together when we talk things out."

"Just Marcus left, then. Don't worry… I believe he's in good hands." Patel hesitated before adding, "Sanjay's still in denial. Losing his other half to Kane's portal… he's shattered. That's why I came to you."

Clarice nodded, understanding. "We're all in this together. I promise you that." She stood, tightening the belt on her robe. "Let me get dressed. We'll go down and talk to Juan, see what he remembers."

At the infirmary, the atmosphere was charged with anticipation. Everyone had gathered to welcome Juan Cesaro back. Clarice spotted him immediately. Their eyes met across the room, and for a brief moment, everything else fell away. Without hesitation, they rushed toward each other, colliding in a tight embrace.

It lasted just long enough for Clarice to catch a whiff of his clothes, still rank from the Hollow Earth journey. She pulled back, wrinkling her nose and making an exaggerated choking sound. "God, Juan, you smell like a sweaty jockstrap," she teased, attempting to lighten the mood.

Juan chuckled, running a hand through his unruly hair. "Yeah, well, showering wasn't exactly on my to-do list after everything we've been through."

Clarice's smile softened, and her voice wavered slightly. "I'm so glad you're okay."

"So am I," Juan replied, his expression serious. "And I'm sorry, Clarice. For what I did—to you and to Marcus. I swear, I have the worst luck picking sides. Seems like I'm always stuck on the wrong one when the shit hits the fan."

Clarice nodded, her throat tightening as she fought back the urge to cry. "Me too," she admitted, her voice barely above a whisper.

Juan stepped back, his gaze unwavering as he looked her straight in the eye. "I'm fucking tired of being used by the Order. If you and Marcus want out, I'm right there with you."

Clarice inhaled deeply, her resolve hardening. She held his gaze, her voice clear and firm. "I don't just want out," she said, her tone sharp with determination. "I want to take out the Order."

Juan's eyes widened slightly, but after a beat, he grinned—a small, knowing smile that hinted at a shared understanding. "Then let's make it happen," he said, his voice low and resolute.

In that moment, the air between them shifted. It was no longer just about survival or escaping the chaos that had ensnared them. It was about fighting back, reclaiming their agency, and dismantling the forces that had controlled their lives for far too long.

Clarice glanced around the room, her expression a mix of weariness and defiance. The battle ahead would be brutal, but for the first time in a long while, she felt a spark of hope.

"Me three," Scarlett said as she entered the room with Robyn trailing behind her. "When we all passed out yesterday morning, I had this crazy dream—and then I spoke with my spirit guides. The room was bathed in a soft glow from the lanterns hanging on the walls, their flickering light casting long shadows that danced across the floor. The air was thick with an almost electric tension; every sound muffled as though the space itself held its breath. Marcus and Kiara lay on low cots, positioned directly across from one another, their stillness unnerving in its quiet contrast to the anxious movements of those gathered around them.

Mallah stood at the foot of Marcus's cot, her calm, commanding presence a steady anchor amidst the rising uncertainty. She gestured for the group to gather close. "Everyone, please, sit. Form a circle around them." Her voice was calm but resolute, carrying an unspoken urgency.

Scarlett hesitated, glancing at Robyn. For a moment, she considered suggesting they wait until the ceremony was over to discuss what they'd experienced—but the intensity in Mallah's gaze left no room for delay. Whatever was about to happen demanded all of them, united and focused.

Robyn's usual humor faltered as she moved to take her place in the circle. Scarlett followed, settling beside her, and as hands joined, a subtle shift in energy swept through the room. Scarlett felt the familiar warmth of connection, a reminder of the unseen forces binding them together. Mallah's expression softened as she looked around the circle.

"Each of you here is here for a reason," she began, her voice steady and low. "You've all faced challenges, losses, and doubts, but you are still standing. That resilience is why you were chosen. Tonight, we bridge the Veil not just to wake Marcus and Kiara, but to understand what they've seen. This is a path only they can guide us on, but they need our help to return."

The group exchanged glances, some wary, others resolute. Aron broke the tension with a quip, his voice light despite the weight of the moment. "Well, I didn't sign up for just tea and biscuits, did I?"

Laughter rippled briefly through the circle, but Mallah quickly brought them back to focus. "This isn't just about them," she said. "What we do here tonight sets the stage for what comes next. Everything we've done, every choice we've made, has led to this point."

Dr. Patel, seated to Mallah's left, fidgeted with his hands, his guilt and grief palpable. Scarlett noticed and reached over to squeeze his arm gently, offering silent reassurance. Mallah gave a small nod of approval before closing her eyes and beginning to chant.

The words were unfamiliar, a language ancient and melodic, but their meaning resonated on a deeper level. Scarlett felt the vibration of the chant move through her, aligning her breath with its rhythm. Around the circle, others' faces shifted as the energy built, a tangible current passing between them.

The first sensation was warmth, a spreading heat that started at Scarlett's hands and flowed inward, pooling in her chest. Her mind drifted unbidden to the shared dream from the night before, flashes of images and feelings surfacing like whispers of a forgotten memory. She pushed the thoughts aside, focusing instead on the task at hand.

As Mallah's chant reached its crescendo, a sudden stillness fell over the room. The air grew heavy, the glow of the lanterns dimming slightly as if the room itself was drawing inward. Then, a soft hum—barely audible at first—began to resonate from the center of the circle, where Marcus and Kiara lay.

Scarlett opened her eyes, glancing at Marcus. His chest rose and fell steadily, but his expression was strained, his brow furrowing as if caught in a deep struggle. Across from him, Kiara's face was calm, almost serene, but her hands twitched slightly, fingers curling and uncurling in an unconscious rhythm.

"It's working," Mallah murmured, her voice tinged with quiet relief. "Stay focused."

Robyn's grip on Scarlett's hand tightened, grounding her as the hum grew louder. Scarlett felt herself being pulled, not physically but energetically, as if the boundaries of her own awareness were dissolving. For a moment, she thought she saw shapes flickering in the dim light—shadowy figures moving just beyond the edge of her perception. She closed her eyes again, trusting the process.

-Chapter 18-

The hum reached a peak, resonating so deeply it seemed to shake the very fabric of their beings, and then it stopped. A silence heavier than sound enveloped them, pressing against their ears, their senses, their thoughts. Scarlett felt a lurch, as though pulled from her physical body, and when she opened her eyes, the room was gone.

She stood, unsteady, in a place that felt like nowhere and everywhere all at once. The soft glow of a campfire illuminated the faces of the others around her. They sat in a loose circle, the fire casting flickering shadows that danced across their features. The air was warm, the sky above a tapestry of unfamiliar stars, and yet, there was a surreal stillness to the scene, as though time itself had paused to let them linger here.

"Where are we?" Scarlett asked, her voice barely above a whisper.

"This isn't the room," Robyn muttered, her wide eyes reflecting the flames. "What's going on?"

"It's a shared dream," Mallah said, stepping into the light of the fire as if she'd been there all along. Her voice was calm, yet it carried an unyielding weight. "Or, more precisely, a space of shared memory and connection. This is where we can reach Marcus."

"And Kiara?" Scarlett asked, her eyes darting to the empty seats.

Mallah hesitated, then shook her head slightly. "Kiara's path in this moment is different. She's... elsewhere, with Marcus, but not here. Trust that she is exactly where she needs to be."

The group exchanged uneasy glances, the weight of Mallah's words settling over them like a heavy fog. Scarlett noticed Aron fiddling with a twig he'd picked up from the ground, his usual smirk absent.

"What are we supposed to do here?" Clarice asked, her voice tinged with impatience.

Mallah gestured toward the fire. "We call upon him. Marcus has always been tied to all of you in some way. Your memories, your connections, past lives, they are the thread we use to reach him. Speak of him, remember him, and through your words, he will find his way back."

The group fell silent, the crackling fire filling the void. Scarlett's chest tightened. The idea of sharing memories, exposing fragments of herself, felt vulnerable in a way she hadn't anticipated.

"I'll go first," Rose offered, her voice soft but steady. "Marcus once told me that fear isn't something to be ashamed of. It's a tool, he said. Something you can use to push forward when everything else fails. I've thought about that every time things get hard."

Scarlett's gaze dropped to her hands. The firelight danced across her fingers as if daring her to speak. "He's always been... steady," she said finally. "Like no matter how bad things get, you can count on him to keep his head straight. Even when he's struggling, he makes you feel like you can handle it."

Robyn nodded, her lips curving into a faint smile. "He's got that way about him, doesn't he? Like he's carrying something heavy, but he doesn't let it crush him. He just... keeps going."

Aron chuckled dryly. "He's a stubborn bastard; I'll give him that. But it's not just that. He makes you feel like you're part of something bigger. Like you're not just wandering around aimlessly."

As the others began to add their voices, Scarlett noticed a subtle shift in the air. The fire seemed to grow brighter, its warmth wrapping around them like a living thing. The more they spoke, the more the space seemed to hum with an energy she couldn't describe.

Unbeknownst to them, in another place entirely, Kiara stood on the floor of a small, rustic farmhouse. More startling than the location was the fact that she could see—clearly. No blobs of color, no haze. Her surroundings came into sharp focus, a luxury she hadn't experienced in a decade. Her heart raced as she took in the room, the warm wood tones, the faint smell of something earthy, and the sunlight streaming through a window. This wasn't like her usual dreams, filled with fragmented memories and the perspective of a ten-year-old child. This felt different—tangible, deliberate.

She stepped carefully toward the hallway, her bare feet creaking against the floorboards, and moved down a set of stairs that beckoned her. Her hand trailed along the smooth banister as she descended, each step deliberate and measured. Reaching the bottom, she peered around the corner, aware that she was in some place of significance from Marcus' childhood memories. Kiara heard the sound of giggling as a young boy ran down the stairs and past her and out the kitchen door. She was going to follow him, even getting as far as the door when her instinct urged her to turn around. There, at a modest wooden table, sat the adult version of Marcus Kydd, casually pouring tea from a kettle. The window was open, and Kiara could see a body of water with fishing boats moored to the docks nearby. The smell of saltwater and fish permeated the air in a place that was rustic and old, but quaint and homely.

"It is lovely, isn't it?" he said, his tone warm and inviting, as if they were old friends.

Kiara hesitated, caught off guard. "Marcus? Is that you? I've never actually seen you before. Where are we?" she asked, stepping cautiously into the room.

He gestured to the bowl of apples and pears sitting on the table's center, then to the steaming cup of tea across from him. "This is the Nexus Consciousness," he explained. "Where I'm currently entangled. And yes, it is me. I've been waiting for you."

"For me?" Kiara asked, taking a tentative seat. "You barely know me."

Marcus smiled softly. "In this lifetime, perhaps. But we've been well acquainted many times before. Fought and died side by side. You've done me the same favor in the past, and now, I'm repaying the debt."

Kiara sipped her tea, letting the words settle. It was too much to process at once, so she chose not to respond, focusing instead on the flavors of lemon and honey infused with her drink, the comforting warmth of the tea in her hands.

"You've been brought here to learn to defend yourself," Marcus continued. "A necessary step. You'll need to create muscle memory to compensate for your visual impairments."

"Where is everyone else?" Kiara asked, to which Marcus nodded.

"They are already here," he replied. "They were sent to retrieve us. To them, almost no time will pass between their arrival and when we all awaken. But here in the Nexus consciousness? We're outside of time and space."

The room seemed endless yet intimate, its dimensions shifting subtly in the corners of her vision. She sat, gripping the edges of the table to ground herself. "How did I get here?"

Marcus poured himself another cup of tea with deliberate ease. "As I explained, you were brought here," he said, meeting her gaze. "And though it may feel like a coincidence, I assure you, it is not. My presence here and your arrival are connected."

Kiara frowned, her thoughts racing. "You mean you've been waiting for me?"

He nodded, sipping his tea. "In a sense, yes. You see, Kiara, we've known each other for a very long time. Lifetimes, in fact. We've fought together, died together, and always found our way back to the same purpose." He paused, his expression softening. "You've done the same for me before, and now I am repaying the debt."

She stared at him, bewildered. "I don't understand."

"You will," Marcus replied. "In time. For now, all you need to know is that this place—this moment—was carved out for you. It exists to prepare you for what's ahead."

Kiara looked down at the tea, the fragrant steam curling into delicate spirals. Her hands trembled slightly as she wrapped them around the cup. "Prepare me? For what?"

"For the trials you will face," he said simply. "You've been brought here to learn—how to focus, how to defend yourself, and how to harness what's inside you. And you'll have the time to do it."

She looked up sharply. "How much time?"

Marcus set his cup down and leaned forward slightly, his expression growing more serious. "This place," he began, gesturing around them, "is not just a refuge. It is a construct—a space where time bends to our will, allowing us to do what would otherwise be impossible. But it will not be easy."

Kiara looked at him, her brows furrowed in confusion. "I don't understand. If this place is outside of time, can't we just… skip to the part where I'm ready?"

Marcus shook his head, a faint smile tugging at the corners of his lips. "No, Kiara. The goal isn't to bypass the effort but to simulate it in a way that aligns with your reality. Growth, strength, resilience—these things cannot be conjured. They must be learned. And more importantly earned."

He paused, his gaze steady. "You and I will draw upon lifetimes of experience; memories etched into the fabric of our souls. But they are only threads. To weave them into something useful, you'll need to incorporate them into your current matrix—your physical self. That will take effort, discipline, and no small amount of trust."

Kiara frowned, her fingers tightening around the warm teacup. "So, what you're saying is… I have to relive it all? The pain, the struggle, the work?"

"Yes," Marcus replied, his tone firm yet gentle. "But think of it not as starting over but as remembering who you are—who you've always been. Everything you need is already within you. My role is simply to help you access it."

For a moment, silence stretched between them, broken only by the faint hum of the Nexus consciousness around them, permeating every fiber of their beings. Kiara exhaled slowly, the weight of his words sinking in. "And what happens if I fail?"

Marcus's expression softened, and he reached across the table to place a reassuring hand over hers. "You won't. Not here. Not now. This moment has been carved out of existence itself because it is necessary. You are necessary. And together, we'll make sure you're ready."

"Even if that takes an eternity.

Marcus smiled faintly. "So, that's the answer to your question, as long as it takes. To the others, only moments will pass. But for us, it will feel much longer. Do not focus on that, for it means little and will only distract you from what you came here to learn."

Kiara stared into her tea, the steam curling upward like tendrils reaching into the endless expanse of the Nexus. She was still processing Marcus's words, the weight of their meaning settling into her chest. The concept of being here—outside of time—was too vast to fully grasp. But his calm presence, his unwavering confidence in her, kept her from feeling entirely adrift.

"What now?" she asked quietly, setting the cup down. "How do we even begin?"

"I will help you learn to harness the powers of your mind, body, and spirit." Marcus stood and gestured for her to follow him. "But first, we start where we must always start, with the mind."

Kiara hesitated, then rose to her feet, her movements uncertain. The disorientation of seeing for the first time lingered, and every step felt exaggerated, as though the ground beneath her might shift at any moment. Marcus noticed her hesitation.

"It will pass," he said gently. "In time, your senses will adapt. But for now, focus on what you feel, not what you see."

He led her to a clearing that seemed to materialize from the shifting expanse of the Nexus. The air felt different here—denser, alive with a faint hum that resonated in her chest. A soft mat appeared beneath her feet as Marcus motioned for her to sit.

Kiara crossed her legs, settling into a seated lotus position as Marcus took his place across from her. The ground beneath her felt cool and solid, grounding her in a space that otherwise felt infinite.

"Close your eyes," Marcus instructed. "Breathe deeply and let the air fill your lungs. Release it slowly."

She complied, though her breaths came unevenly at first, her mind a whirlwind of thoughts and sensations. The effort to focus felt monumental.

"Your thoughts will come," Marcus said, as though reading her mind. "Let them. Do not fight them, but do not follow them, either. Observe. Breathe. Allow them to flow through you like the movement of water."

Kiara tried, but each time she found a moment of quiet, another thought intruded—a memory, a question, a flicker of anxiety. She opened her eyes in frustration. "I can't. It's too much."

"You can," Marcus replied evenly. "But it will take time. Quieting the mind is like taming a wild horse. It takes patience, persistence, and trust."

With a sigh, she closed her eyes again, returning to her breath. The cycle repeated—failure, frustration, and Marcus's steady guidance. But slowly, over what felt like days, she began to find moments of clarity. They were fleeting at first, but each success brought a flicker of confidence.

One day, as Kiara sat in rare, still silence, Marcus spoke again, breaking the rhythm of their practice. "You've done well," he said. "Now we must prepare you for a different kind of noise."

She opened her eyes, her focus sharpening. "What do you mean?"

"Ivyg's voice will be your greatest challenge," Marcus explained. "It is not merely a sound—it's a force. It will press against your mind, twist your thoughts, and unravel your will. Few have resisted it."

Kiara's stomach tightened, but she nodded. "And you think I can?"

"I know you can," Marcus said firmly. "But it will take effort."

He raised his hand, and the air around them shifted. A low, melodic hum filled the space, subtle at first but growing in intensity. It was hypnotic, tugging at Kiara's thoughts with an almost physical presence. She felt her focus slipping, her mind growing hazy.

"Anchor yourself," Marcus said sharply. "Find the center. Focus."

The hum grew louder, more insistent, filling every corner of her mind. She tried to fight it, but her focus faltered, the sound consuming her thoughts. When it faded, she opened her eyes, her heart pounding.

"I failed," she said.

"You began," Marcus corrected. "And you will learn from this and come back and try again. And again, until you succeed."

The exercise became a daily ritual, the hum returning each time with greater intensity. Kiara's progress was slow; each attempt a battle of will. But over time, she learned to anchor herself, to filter the noise and hold onto her own thoughts. When she finally resisted the voice completely, Marcus nodded with quiet pride. As her mental focus sharpened, Marcus introduced physical training, demonstrating a series of movements—fluid, deliberate, and efficient—and guided her through them step by step. His focus and determination, the way he taught her, reminded her of a movie she saw as a child, something her father had shown her about a bullied teen being mentored in martial arts, fighting against the odds to be a winner. Marcus snapped his fingers to awaken her from a daydream memory and focus on the here and now.

"Your body must remember what your eyes cannot see," he explained. "Muscle memory will be your greatest ally. When you leave this place you will once again be without your eyesight. Know this. Trust my words now when I tell you that if you give me your faith and know that I will not lead you astray, nothing will be able to stop you when you awaken."

She trusted in him like he asked her to do. Even though the drills were repetitive and exhausting, she kept going, never giving up, never surrendering to weakness. She even liked the saying from Marcus' college football coach, "pain is just weakness leaving the body.". Each motion felt awkward at first, her body uncooperative and unfamiliar with the demands placed upon it. But Marcus was patient, correcting her stance, adjusting her movements, and pushing her to repeat each sequence until it became second nature.

"Again," he would say, his tone calm but unyielding.

Kiara lived for the moments when he told her that her performance was good even though her muscles ached, her frustration waning with each success, building upon one after another. As the days stretched into weeks, her movements grew fluid, her confidence building with every repetition. Finally, Marcus brought her to a quiet glade within the Nexus, where the air shimmered with a faint, golden glow.

"This is the Vril," he said, his voice reverent. "The life force that flows through all things. You will learn to harness it."

"I can feel it, even before you brought me here."

"All your life, no doubt."

"Never like it is here. Never like it is now.

Kiara extended her hand, her fingers brushing the energy that pulsed in the air. It felt warm and alive, but wild and untamed. Channeling it into a focused form was another matter entirely. It swirled around and through her and she watched as it moved like something that was alive.

"Control requires focus," Marcus said. "The Vril is not yours to command—it is yours to align with. When you are in harmony, it becomes in harmony with you. Not before. Not safely."

Her attempts were clumsy at first, the energy slipping through her grasp like water through her fingers. But with practice and patience, she began to feel its rhythm, its flow. When she finally held a small, glowing orb of energy in her hands, Marcus smiled.

"Good," he said. "Now again."

As Kiara adjusted to the rhythm of her training, she began to notice subtleties she hadn't before. The energy of the Nexus wasn't just around her—it was within her, flowing through her in ways she couldn't fully articulate. During one particularly grueling session, Marcus paused, his gaze sharpening as he observed her.

"You feel it, don't you?" he asked.

Kiara frowned, catching her breath as she lowered her hands, the faint glow of the Vril fading. "What do you mean?"

Marcus stepped closer, his tone measured but probing. "The connection. It's not just sensory. You're drawing on something deeper—something intrinsic to who you are."

Kiara hesitated, unsure how to respond. "I don't know… It feels like I'm just… interpreting things. Like sensing vibrations, understanding patterns."

Marcus smiled faintly, his expression unreadable. "That's part of it.

But it's not the whole picture."

Before she could press him further, he motioned for her to continue the exercise, leaving her with a lingering sense of unease. The rest of the training session passed in silence, but his words stayed with her, gnawing at the edges of her understanding. Later, Kiara lay on the mat, staring into the endless expanse above her. Though the Nexus had no true sky, the faint light that filtered through the space dimmed each time she rested, and after a while, it would brighten again, simulating the rise of the sun. It was Marcus's doing, she suspected, a gesture meant to give her some semblance of structure in a place otherwise free from the rhythms of time.

The sun rose the same way each time, its light spilling slowly over the horizonless expanse. There were no clouds, no shifts in weather, and no seasons to mark its passage—only the unchanging cycle of day and night. It felt as though she were trapped in the same day, repeating endlessly, her progress marked only by the growing ease with which she completed her tasks.

At first, the repetition was comforting, a steady rhythm in the chaos of the Nexus. But over time, it began to gnaw at her, the monotony pressing against her mind. She missed the unpredictability of real life—the changing of the seasons, the subtle differences in each sunrise, and the sense of moving forward.

After each sunrise, Kiara began the day anew with Marcus, though the routine felt increasingly familiar, as if the repetition itself was becoming a kind of anchor.

"Why do you bother with the sun?" she asked one morning as they sat cross-legged, preparing for their meditation exercises.

Marcus tilted his head slightly, his expression thoughtful. "Would you prefer eternal twilight?"

Kiara frowned, glancing at the soft, golden light spilling into the space. "No… but it's strange. It feels like the same day, over and over."

Marcus's lips quirked in a faint smile. "Perhaps that's the point. It's not the day that changes, Kiara—it's you."

She considered his words, her frustration softening. The same day, yes—but not the same Kiara.

As she worked, Kiara couldn't help but notice the odd comfort the sun brought her, even if it was artificial. It marked the beginning and end of her training, a rhythm that steadied her amidst the timelessness of the

Nexus. Yet, it left her with lingering questions. Was she truly resting? Was there even a need for sleep here, or was the act simply a remnant of her mortal instincts?

When she slept, if it could be called that, her dreams carried echoes of her life outside the Nexus—Robyn, Teddy, and Aron's voices swimming around her mind, the feel of her home, the subtle joy of a changing sky. And when she woke to the rising sun, it felt as though no time had passed, yet everything was different.

-Chapter 19-

Fealty and Fire

Kane, Patel, and Nova talked a bit as they rested for several weeks before the long journey to what remained of Kansas City after the apocalypse. Kane told his companions of the fate they thought they had suffered in the "Neververse," though the two were confused when Kane and Patel had landed here. There were similarities between that place and this timeline—dark, apocalyptic, lack of hope, disgruntled beings that had once been trapped behind the veil, now freely running around trying to kill you. Kansas City had become the new hub of civilization in the United States, now ruled by the self-proclaimed living God-King, Ivyg Semagial Wistroc, known by many other names throughout history. What he had once feared had now come to pass. No longer content to merely oversee the Order—a sprawling network of powerful corporations that had masqueraded as independent entities while secretly acting in unison under his influence—Ivyg had consolidated his rule into something far greater. With the help of a small group of elites, seated well above the supposed power of the world's great leaders, he had controlled the narrative for generations, shaping reality to fit his own design.

As it turned out, the political figures and governments that the masses believed held authority were little more than puppets, their strings pulled by a select few. These families, with their immense resources and unyielding ambition, had earned Ivyg's favor—and he theirs. Over time, many of them perished, unable to keep pace with the relentless demands of survival in Ivyg's shadow. Those who remained were no longer his allies but his subordinates, serving him as dutifully as the rest of the world he now ruled. What had begun as an invisible grip on capitalism and global influence had evolved into total dominion that had started with the release of the infamous Hades virus. That was so long ago, now Ivyg no longer hid behind veils of secrecy or the thrones of world leaders. Instead, he stood openly as the master of a world reshaped in his image—a god in his own mind, ruling over a humanity that had unwittingly ceded its freedom to him long ago.

It was said that he enjoyed spending his time in what was formerly known as the United States because of the hedonism and debauchery of the humans that survived the Great War, willing to do nearly anything to survive in the wasteland that once was a great and prosperous nation.

There were some regions that prospered but everywhere was generally fucked from the radiation clouds and ash from the bombs that killed all the crops and slowly killed most of the humans and animals as well. Though two-thirds of humans had perished, nature had survived in the end and had taken back much of what it had lost in the previous century to rampant capitalism that had led to the collapse of society after an engineered virus had created a pandemic that killed about twenty percent of the population.

These and other continued threats ultimately led to the Great War as nations no longer trusted one another or abided by the previously signed treaties and accords. Somehow Kansas City had fared well, and life sustained despite the harsh conditions of a global nuclear winter that lasted many decades and led to dust bowl-like conditions across many parts of the world. Green parts of nature were in patches, slowly at first, but then ever growing and advancing as they took back what was once theirs in the first place—a living, breathing Earth that continued to survive despite the damage done by humans and the Watchers and Nephilim, among others that sought to control the fate of this planet.

Patel kept the only copy of a map that the group carried in his back pocket, bringing it out only on occasion to make sure that they were still going in the right direction. The passing hours in their journey soon turned into days. Nova told jokes as they traversed toward their destination. His humor kept the mood of their camp bright, despite their inability to light fires as it could draw the wrong kind of attention to their location. Along the way, they were able to find food at abandoned gas stations and restaurants—canned meats and vegetables, stale chips, and Twinkies. Little of it truly satiated their hunger. What Kane wouldn't give for a steak dinner with all the fixings. He, Nova, and Patel all talked about food as they approached Springfield, hungry and looking for more substantial supplies.

Nova spoke to Kane and Patel about a small tribe of people he was in intermittent contact with up in Denver, west in Colorado. The tribe had established a sanctuary in the mountains, offering safety and protection for those willing to brave the journey. Nova explained how the isolation of the region, combined with the tribe's ability to blend into the rugged terrain, made it a rare safe haven. The offer was genuine, and Patel's curiosity was piqued, but Kane declined without hesitation. Protection was the opposite of what he sought at this time.

"No chance of getting a ride, is there?" Kane asked semi-sarcastically to Nova. Despite his semi-sociopathic temperament, Alibi Patel was usually chatty and ADHD, but the somberness of the upcoming journey surrounded him with a dark cloud. He was tapped of energy and felt lost without his other half in the past timeline that he and Kane were separated from and needed to get back to, still mind-fucked from all the time he spent with Ivyg and the OAS. He could feel the distance between him and his brother, almost as if Sanjay never existed in the first place. For the first time in his life, he felt alone. Alone, yet not alone. No longer half of a man, but entirely yet his own man, still trying to figure that part out for himself. Patel knew that they couldn't return to their own timeline without the help of Ivyg, which was a scary scenario considering the post-apocalyptic environment Ivyg ruled over. Patel took the lead in leaving the motel that was conveniently right off Interstate 55, which they would be following for a long distance.

Kane's goal was singular and consuming. He wanted to be caught, deliberately drawing attention to himself so he could reunite with his estranged sociopathic brother. Their reunion, however, was not for reconciliation. Kane had been planning this confrontation for years, determined to end his brother's life once and for all. The plan wasn't overly elaborate, Kane had to admit, but he appreciated its stark simplicity. It suited him. The directness left little room for unnecessary distractions. Nova's support was unwavering, and though the plan had many unknown variables, he admired Kane's resolve. Nova also recognized a shift in Kane. Over the years, Kane had become so accustomed to teaching others that he had inadvertently closed himself off from learning—an irony he had only recently begun to acknowledge. Marcus had helped him see this. Marcus, ever the optimist, had likened life to an ocean: "We either learn to swim, or we drown under the waves."

Kane had always admired Marcus' go-with-the-flow, can-do attitude. Marcus had a way of drawing brilliance toward him, surrounding himself with people who were as inspiring as they were capable. Of all his students and collaborators over the years, Marcus was Kane's favorite protégé,. He would never admit it aloud, though. Marcus already faced more than his share of jealousy and resentment from others during their decade-long association. Kane's own pride wouldn't let him give voice to such favoritism, even if it were true.

A glance down at the bandaged stump of his right arm reminded Kane of his hubris. The power of the gods had once been quite literally in his hands, only to be undone by the very man he had considered his eventual successor. The irony wasn't lost on him. The pain and loss had forced introspection, stripping away layers of his arrogance. Eventually he would find a way to forgive his favorite student. Ever since arriving in this desolate place, Kane had been fixated on how he might replace his missing arm. He had a gnawing feeling that Kansas City held some of the answers he sought, though he suspected not all of them would be answers he liked.

Nova had warned them previously about the possible perils of going into an occupied city for food and supplies, which they currently needed to do. This particular small city was overrun by a gang calling themselves the Zuum's. They were not known for being friendly to outsiders, the opposite. None of Ivyg's people were there in this city that was run in a rather feudalistic manner, but with all the sin and debauchery of gambling, prostitution, drugs, and crime. All legal thanks to the leader of the Zuum's, a man referred to ironically as Gem, though pronounced like the name Jim. This warlord was known for having many fuel-driven vehicles at his disposal, having taken over an oil refinery years before, modifying cars, trucks, and motorcycles to drive on a special blend of fuel.

Gem didn't specifically go out looking for trouble but had his people on constant watch to protect and defend their fief from intruders and outsiders. Patrols searched around the perimeter of the city off the major highway intersections, driving back and forth. The cost of this fief for Gem was to turn over captured outcasts to the men who worked for the God King. For this, they were rewarded with independence, only having to pledge allegiance to the God King himself in an act of fealty. At this point, it was all quite common and well-known. There were few rules, and the only laws in effect were followed to the death. The humans that had survived only wanted to keep doing so, living in fear of the God King and his living Titan warriors, whom he made into Judges to rule over the humans in his stead as he ruled over other parts of the world and beyond. By this point, most of the Champions and other vril enhanced individuals had been killed in the Great War or hunted down by the Titan Judges at Ivyg's behest. Few remained and those that did tried their best to stay hidden, well under the radar of the overlords.

Ivyg's true throne was in Atla, as all knew, but his rule extended far beyond the ancient city. He had long since decided that those who remained after the Great War would not be permitted to live in isolation as they had before its catastrophic end. Atla's people had once fled, sensing the inevitability of its demise, a decision that haunted Ivyg and drove his resolve to use technology as a weapon against them. In his eyes, their retreat was a betrayal of his vision for unity and control, a rebellion that justified his merciless actions. Yet it was this very use of advanced technology that nearly destroyed the Earth itself, requiring even greater technological intervention to prevent the planet's complete annihilation. The devastation left scars that the natural world still struggled to heal, even decades later.

Now, under Ivyg's iron-fisted rule, humanity was forced into sprawling, walled mega-cities. These urban centers served as hubs of control, allowing the Titans to monitor and manage the remaining population more efficiently. Meanwhile, the wilderness—a shadow of its former self—attempted to recover from the apocalyptic wars that had ravaged it, as well as the preceding century of unchecked capitalism and greed. Life in this future was tenacious, finding ways to survive in the cracks and corners of a world reshaped by conflict and exploitation.

Most of the remaining humans become subservient to Ivyg's will, accepting his dominion as the price of survival. He provided them with shelter, food, and purpose, cultivating a twisted form of loyalty through dependence. They revered him as the God King, even though he was a ruthless, cold-blooded tyrant who would not hesitate to kill anyone who threatened his power. His reign was one of terror and tyranny, a legacy built on the corpses of those who dared to oppose him. The title of God King was not inherited—it was seized through unrelenting brutality and a single-minded determination to bend the Earth and its people to his will.

who resisted the suffocating grip of his rule—freedom fighters determined to reclaim their autonomy from the so-called God King. Nova had spent years quietly connecting with a network of these insurgents, learning their methods and motives. They operated in shadows and whispers, hiding their movements from the omnipresent eyes of the Titans and their enforcers. Denver had become a focal point for their rebellion, a hub of resistance where plans were forged and courage was tested. Though fractured and outgunned, these freedom fighters represented a spark of hope that had yet to be extinguished.

This knowledge would prove invaluable, though Nova couldn't have anticipated how soon it would come into play. Kane, with his calculated demeanor and cryptic motives, seemed oddly unconcerned about the danger they faced. In fact, he almost seemed to welcome it. He wanted to be caught. Whatever his reasons, it didn't take long for the patrol vehicles to take notice. One spotted them first, its headlights piercing the dim haze like predatory eyes. Then another appeared. And another.

Within moments, the three found themselves surrounded by armored trucks bristling with weapons. Men clad in dark uniforms emerged, carrying rifles and handguns—loyal servants of their King, their faces set in expressions of grim determination. The air grew tense, the weight of inevitability pressing down on them. Nova's pulse quickened as she calculated their options, but escape seemed impossible. From behind, the sharp crack of gunfire shattered the silence. It was an ambush. Nova, Patel, and Kane instinctively dropped to the ground, their bodies hitting the cold, hard surface in unison. Motionless, they appeared lifeless, as though the shots had found their marks. Around them, the soldiers advanced cautiously, weapons raised, their eyes scanning for any signs of movement.

The stillness was almost unbearable, but Nova's mind raced. This was not the end—it couldn't be. The resistance, Denver, the freedom fighters—it all meant something. Yet, in that moment, all she could do was trust the plan, trust Kane's inscrutable confidence, and pray that whatever came next would tilt the balance back in their favor.

-Chapter 20- Champion.exe

Back in the Nexus consciousness, where time seemed to stretch and blur, days flowed one into the next with no clear beginning or end. It was a place untethered from the rhythms of the outside world, leaving Kiara with only the golden light and the constant hum of energy to mark the passage of time.

One day, as the golden light poured across the space, Kiara felt an unfamiliar heaviness settle over her. It wasn't exhaustion, nor was it the ache of her muscles from the repetitive drills. This was different—an unease that prickled at the edges of her awareness, like a distant storm on the horizon. It began subtly at first, during her morning meditation. A flicker of an image—a shadowed figure with piercing eyes and an aura of malevolence. The vision came and went so quickly that Kiara dismissed it as a stray thought, her mind wandering as it often did during the stillness. But as the day progressed, the flickers became sharper, more insistent. By evening, as she sat by the fire Marcus had conjured for their rest, she couldn't shake the feeling that something—or someone—was watching her. She stared into the flames, the swirling embers taking on shapes her mind couldn't quite comprehend.

"Who is Ivyg?" she asked suddenly, her voice cutting through the silence.

Marcus looked up from his tea, his expression unreadable. "What have you seen?"

Kiara hesitated. "I don't know… shadows, maybe. A man—or something like a man, but more like a dragon. It's not clear, it's all fuzzy. Something feels… wrong. Dangerous."

Marcus leaned back, his gaze steady. "Ivyg is many things to many people. A figure of fear, power, and destruction. To you, he will be a test of your strength; everything from this life and all your former past lives."

"That serious?"

"Yeah, that's serious."

That night, as she lay on her mat, sleep came uneasily. She had just begun to drift off when the vision struck—a vivid, searing flash of Ivyg. He loomed above her, his face twisted with malice, his hand outstretched as if to strike. She could feel his presence, heavy and suffocating, and for the first time, she felt real fear. Kiara bolted upright, her breath coming in ragged gasps. The Nexus was silent, its calm at odds with the chaos of her mind. She turned to Marcus, who was seated nearby, his eyes already on her.

"What do I do?" she demanded, her voice trembling. "How do I stop him?"

Marcus regarded her for a long moment before standing. "You're asking the right question at last."

Marcus stepped away from the fire, his form beginning to shift. The calm and composed figure Kiara had come to know gave way to something far more imposing. Light radiated from him, golden and brilliant, spilling across the Nexus in waves. He grew taller, his features sharper, more regal. His entire being seemed to hum with power, the Vril energy coursing through him in radiant currents.

Kiara stumbled back, shielding her eyes from the blinding glow. "What… what are you?"

"This," Marcus said, his voice reverberating with a depth that seemed to echo through the very fabric of the Nexus, "is who I once was. A god of the sun, worshipped and feared. But I am no longer that person. I've learned, evolved, and moved beyond that lifetime. What you see now is a fragment—a lesson I've carried forward to my higher self."

He lowered himself slightly, his brilliant form towering over Kiara but not diminishing her. "You, too, are many things, Kiara. More than you can imagine. If you want to face Ivyg, to call upon the other aspects of yourself who have already fought and defeated him, to become one of the Champions, you must let go of the way you see time."

Kiara blinked, her mind racing to keep up. "I don't understand."

"You think of time as a line," Marcus explained, his voice softening. "A past, a present, a future. But in the Nexus, all of it exists at once. Past lives, future selves, parallel versions of you—they are all here, waiting. To access them, you must let go of your linear thinking."

Kiara's brow furrowed. "But how? Is there something I say or do to make it happen?"

Marcus smiled faintly, his radiant form still glowing. "It isn't about saying or doing. It's about being. Let go of your need to understand and simply allow yourself to connect. When you're ready, they will come."

Kiara sat back on her mat, her thoughts churning. The vision of Ivyg still lingered, his shadow burned into her mind. But alongside it was the radiant presence of Marcus, a reminder of the power that lay within her reach.

As she closed her eyes to meditate, she tried to release her thoughts, her fears, her need to control. Somewhere in the vastness of the Nexus, the many versions of herself waited. And for the first time, she felt the stirrings of their presence—faint but undeniable. The battle with Ivyg would come. But in this moment, she began to understand that she was not alone. She never had been.

Kiara's meditation deepened, the quiet hum of the Nexus fading into a vast silence. Then, slowly, an image emerged—a figure cloaked in shadow and fire. As the vision clarified, Kiara saw a woman standing tall, her stance unyielding yet graceful, her presence commanding. Prometheus.

The name rose in Kiara's mind like a whisper, carried by the echoes of a thousand lives. She knew this woman, not from myths or stories but from somewhere deeper. Prometheus, a Titan, her strength immense and her wisdom unmatched, but it was her compassion that defined her.

The scene shifted. Prometheus stood before a council of imposing figures, their faces obscured by smoke and shadow. Her voice rang out, steady and resolute. "They are not beneath us," she said, her tone a mix of defiance and pleading. "They are our children, our kin. They deserve the fire."

The council's response was a cacophony of anger and dismissal, but Prometheus did not falter. When they forbade her from interfering, she acted anyway, descending to the world of humanity with the gift of fire in her hands. She knelt as she offered it, her eyes filled with quiet determination as the flames caught and spread.

Then came the punishment. The council turned on her, their judgment swift and cruel. She was stripped of her place among the Titans, her compassion seen as betrayal. They bound her in chains, her body left exposed to the elements, but her spirit never wavered.

Prometheus's voice echoed in Kiara's mind, steady and strong. "To love is to suffer. To give is to lose. But without these, there is no creation, no growth. I would do it all again."

As Kiara watched the vision of Prometheus chained and punished by her fellow Titans, the image shifted. Time passed, though it was impossible to say how much. The fiery defiance in Prometheus's eyes dulled, replaced by exhaustion and pain. But even as the elements tore at her body and the chains held her fast, she endured.

Then, one day, they broke her chains.

Prometheus fell to the earth, her once-mighty form diminished. The Titans left her there, cast out and forgotten, her immortality stripped away. Her body ached, mortal and frail, but her spirit burned as fiercely as ever. The punishment was meant to humble her, to teach her the futility of her love for humanity. But as she staggered to her feet, bloody and battered, she vowed they would never succeed.

She walked the earth for what felt like years, her strength waning but her will unbroken. In flashes, Kiara saw Prometheus sheltering in caves, scavenging for food, and tending to her wounds. She was alone, abandoned by those she had once stood among, left to face the world she had fought to protect.

Then the vision shifted again.

A shadow fell over Prometheus as she lay beneath a dying tree, her body too weak to continue. Kiara could feel the weight of her despair, the fire within her reduced to a flicker. Yet, she still refused to succumb.

The shadow moved, and a figure stepped into the light—tall, imposing, and wreathed in power. His gaze was sharp, assessing, and as Kiara saw him, she realized who he was.

Aron.

No, not Aron—not yet. This was Zeus, the rising god who had turned against the Titans. His presence was both commanding and magnetic, and as he looked down at Prometheus, his expression was unreadable.

"You…are Prometheus," he said, his tone equal parts confusion, curiosity, and accusation.

Prometheus, too weak to rise, met his gaze with the remnants of her fire. "Ever the observer."

Zeus's lips twitched, not quite a smile. "I have been hunting you, not expecting a female."

She laughed, a hoarse and bitter sound. "Congratulations. You've found me. Are you going to kill me now?"

Zeus stepped closer, his eyes narrowing. "That depends. You're the one who tricked the Titans, aren't you? Stole their fire and gave it to mortals."

Prometheus's smirk was faint but defiant. "I am."

For a moment, he said nothing, studying her. Then, to Kiara's astonishment, he crouched beside her, pulling a waterskin from his side and offering it to her. Prometheus hesitated but took it, drinking deeply.

"I like your style," Zeus said, his voice low and amused. "Cunning. Defiant. Stupid, but impressive."

Prometheus chuckled weakly. "And you're what? Their executioner?"

"Hardly," he said, rising to his full height. "I'm the one who's going to end them."

Prometheus blinked, her mind racing despite her exhaustion. "You're… against them?"

Zeus extended a hand to her, his expression unreadable. "Get up. You're not dying here."

The vision faded, leaving Kiara gasping in the Nexus. Her heart raced, the intensity of what she'd seen leaving her shaken. It wasn't just the memory of Prometheus's strength or her perseverance—it was the face of the man who had saved her. She couldn't ignore the familiarity of his features, nor the strange pull she felt as his voice echoed in her mind.

"It was him," she whispered, her voice trembling. "Aron."

Marcus nodded, his expression calm but knowing. "You're starting to see."

As the memory of Prometheus faded, Kiara felt the warmth of fire replaced by the cool, rhythmic crash of waves. The air thickened with salt and mist, and she found herself standing on the edge of a vast ocean. The water stretched endlessly before her, shimmering under a silver moon.

A figure emerged from the mist—tall and statuesque, her presence commanding yet serene. Her hair moved as if caught in an eternal current, her eyes reflecting the depths of the sea. Kiara knew her instantly.

"Malie," she whispered, her voice trembling.

The figure inclined her head, her expression unreadable but somehow familiar. "You remember," Malie said, her voice low and melodic. It wasn't a question.

Kiara was no longer herself. She was Malie, standing at the helm of a great ship, her hand raised against a raging storm. She recalled seeing this lifetime from when she had passed out before coming to Witchaven.

The waves roared and swelled, but Malie's will was unshakable. Her connection to the water was absolute, an extension of her very being. She whispered to the storm, coaxing it into calm submission, her voice a lullaby for the raging sea.

The scene shifted, and Kiara saw Malie standing before a council of leaders. They begged for her intervention, their lands ravaged by drought and their rivers running dry. Malie listened with quiet intensity before rising, her gaze steady.

"The balance has been broken," she said. "It must be restored. But you will not like the cost."

The leaders pleaded for a solution that would not harm them, but Malie shook her head. "The sea does not care for your comfort," she said. "It cares only for what is right."

Kiara saw Malie unleash the ocean's fury, flooding the lands to bring life back to the rivers. The destruction was immense, but from it came renewal. Malie bore the weight of their anger and grief, but she never wavered. She understood the necessity of her actions, even as others cursed her name.

The vision shifted again, and Kiara stood on a rocky shore. Malie knelt beside a dying fish stranded by the tide. With a gentle hand, she lifted it and placed it back into the water, her touch light but purposeful.

"You are like me," Malie said, her voice soft but firm. "You understand balance, even when it is painful. You see what others cannot, hear what they refuse to listen to."

Kiara felt tears prick her eyes. "But I'm not strong enough. Not like you."

Malie turned to her, her gaze piercing. "Strength is not about force. It is about endurance. About knowing when to yield and when to stand firm. You carry that strength, Kiara. It flows through you, just as the tides flow through me."

Kiara saw glimpses of Malie's life—guiding sailors across treacherous waters, calming tempests, and punishing those who sought to exploit the sea's bounty without respect. Malie was a protector, but the role was isolating. Few understood her, and fewer still appreciated the sacrifices she made to keep the balance.

In one vision, Malie stood against a towering adversary, their form shrouded in shadow. The clash was fierce, the ocean itself roaring in

Malie's defense. Though she triumphed, it was clear the victory came at great cost. Her power was immense, but it required constant vigilance, and Malie bore the burden of that responsibility alone.

As the visions faded, Malie stepped closer to Kiara, her presence as vast and unyielding as the ocean itself.

"You are more than you know," she said. "You have carried me, just as I carried those before me. My strength is your strength. My balance is your balance."

Kiara hesitated, the weight of Malie's words pressing on her. "What if I fail?"

Malie reached out, placing a hand over Kiara's heart. "You won't. You are the tide, Kiara. Relentless. Enduring. Always moving forward."

When Kiara opened her eyes, she was back in the Nexus. Her heart raced, her mind filled with the weight of what she had seen. Marcus was watching her, his expression calm but knowing.

"You saw her," he said.

Kiara nodded. "Malie… She was incredible."

"She was you," Marcus corrected gently. "Her strength, her understanding—they're not just memories, Kiara. They are part of you."

Kiara looked down at her hands, as if searching for the power she had felt in the visions. "She carried so much," she said quietly. "It was lonely."

Marcus inclined his head. "Strength often is. But you don't have to carry it alone."

The words settled over Kiara like the calming tide, her connection to Malie a reminder of the balance she could find within herself. Though the path ahead was uncertain, she felt the ocean's rhythm echoing in her heart—a quiet assurance that she was never truly alone.

Kiara sat cross-legged on the Nexus floor, her mind racing with the fragments of memories and lessons she had been absorbing. The hum of the space around her seemed to grow louder, a rhythmic pulse that resonated deep within her chest. Marcus, seated nearby, regarded her with a calm but knowing gaze.

"You interacted with Mallah before," Kiara began, her voice steady despite the weight of her thoughts. "She taught you many things. What lessons would you say are the most important for you to pass on to me? I have to face Ivyg himself one day soon, and I need all the help I can get."

Marcus's expression softened, a flicker of something akin to pride in his eyes. "You will need more help than I alone can provide," he said. "So, I'm going to cut a step here in your training and retrieve the others to help explain this to you."

"Others?" Kiara asked, tilting her head. "Like my other lives too?"

Before Marcus could answer, the answer revealed itself. Kiara felt a shift in the Nexus, the air vibrating with energy. One by one, figures began to appear around her—a dozen, then dozens more. Each figure bore a resemblance to Kiara, their features reflecting different times, cultures, and experiences. The room buzzed with her own essence, amplified and multiplied until it was almost too much to bear.

The room quieted, and the selves began to organize themselves, stepping forward one by one to offer their insights.

"His influence was great," said Prometheus, stepping forward. Her voice was steady, her expression fierce. "He whispered lies into the ear of our king, poisoning his mind and turning him against us. His reckoning is coming, take great caution. Ivyg is the deceiver, and his tactics range from parlor tricks to deadly assaults. He misses little, and his attention spans far. Do not underestimate him."

Malie stepped forward next, her presence like the calm before a storm. "He will kill anyone to get what he wants," she said bluntly. "In my time, I saw him attack the white dragon Mallah. His rage was unrelenting, his desire for control insatiable. Do not wait for him to strike. Find him first and finish it before he finishes you."

A woman in vibrant South American attire spoke next, her voice rich and melodic. "He will stop at nothing to destroy you and Quetzalcoatl—the man you now know as Kane. Their bond is karmic, two sides of the same coin, intertwined for thousands of years. Trust in Kane's plan and believe in yourself. You will need both."

"Watch your back," warned a Viking man, his broad shoulders imposing. "He has spies everywhere and will continue to kill the Champions to keep us from uniting. But that is the key—unity. Alone, we are vulnerable. Together, we are strong enough to defeat him."

A smaller woman in dark robes stepped forward last, her eyes sharp with intensity. "Keep love in your heart," she said. "The deceiver thrives on fear and hate, but love will unravel his power. He stopped us once in Salem, turning the people against us as witches. He is a master manipulator, but his time is running out. The awakening has already begun."

The messages continued, the figures stepping forward in turn to offer advice and warnings. Kiara listened intently, but the sheer volume of information began to blur together, leaving her overwhelmed. There were glimpses of other lifetimes—her role in ancient battles, her struggles to unite the Guardians, her failures and triumphs. The collective knowledge of her past selves was vast, and the responsibility it carried weighed heavily on her.

"Enough," Marcus said finally, his voice cutting through the buzz of overlapping voices. The figures began to dissipate, their forms fading one by one into the infinite expanse of the Nexus. The silence was deafening, yet Kiara felt the echoes of her other lives lingering in the air—a presence that was both comforting and overwhelming.

As the last figure vanished, Kiara's gaze lingered on a detail that had eluded her before. "Wait," she said, frowning. "Many of them… they were wearing the same amulet."

Marcus's expression shifted, his usual calm taking on a deeper weight. "You noticed."

"What does it mean?" Kiara asked, her voice edged with urgency. "What's so special about them?"

Marcus stepped closer, his voice low but steady. "The amulet is more than a symbol. It is what ties the Guardians of the Veil together, a mark of what they have earned as Champions, tied to the fate of Lemuria. It is a conduit—a bridge to the knowledge and power of those who came before, and to those who will come after. Without it, they are vulnerable. With it, they are dangerous."

Kiara's breath hitched. "Lemuria? How?"

"Because of the vast knowledge stored within them," Marcus said simply. "Lifetimes of wisdom. They are the keys to the first kingdoms of old. These amulets were designed to provide those who chose to incarnate into the earthly realm with the memories and insights of their previous lifetimes. They remind us of who we are, where we come from, and our birthright as stewards of this planet—protectors of humankind."

He paused, his voice growing heavier. "Long after the age of humanity living alongside their ancestors was reduced to mere legends, these amulets carried the truth, passed down through the ages."

The weight of his words settled in the air. Kiara stared at him, her mind racing. "But why? What makes the amulet so important to him?"

Marcus's gaze grew distant, his voice taking on a reflective tone. "Because he abandoned his post for self-serving purposes, seeking to level the playing field by destroying others with the same level of wisdom as he possessed. That is, until someone managed to take his."

The Nexus seemed to hum in response to his words, and a new vision unfolded before Kiara's eyes. She saw a figure—cloaked and swift, moving through shadows. The figure lunged, their hand gripping an ornate amulet wreathed in dark energy. The object pulsed with power, and a roar of rage echoed through the scene as Ivyg emerged, his face twisted with fury.

The figure fled, clutching the amulet, but Ivyg's wrath was unrelenting. He tore through obstacles, his movements driven by a terrifying mix of vengeance and desperation. Kiara could feel his rage, his sheer need to reclaim what had been taken.

The vision blurred and shifted. She saw Ivyg in the aftermath—his eyes wild, his voice a venomous hiss as he vowed to destroy anyone who stood between him and his stolen amulet. His obsession with finding it became a hunt that spanned lifetimes, his hatred of the Champions growing with every failed attempt. Kiara gasped as the vision faded, her pulse racing.

"He's hunting us to get it back," she said, her voice trembling. "He knows how formidable you are." Marcus agreed. "He has not lost his memories, for him it is but a key, but for the rest of you…this creates a grave disadvantage for him. This is why he's gone to such lengths to stop the Guardians from reuniting. "He thinks we have his amulet." Kiara looked up at him in horror.

Marcus nodded. "It is another reason why your amulet is so important. With it, you will not only consciously remember who you were—you will know who you need to be. And you will have the power to challenge him."

Kiara clenched her fists, the weight of the revelations pressing down on her. "If he gets his amulet back…"

"He won't, it has long since chosen another." Marcus interrupted, his tone firm. Kiara took a deep breath, the path ahead crystallizing in her mind. She thought of the Champions she had met, their warnings, their sacrifices. She thought of the amulet waiting for her in El Dorado and the power it represented—not just for herself but for everyone who had fought and died to protect the Veil.

"It's the key, isn't it?" she asked, her voice steady despite the storm inside her. "The amulet—it's how we win."

Marcus gave a faint smile, his eyes reflecting a mix of pride and solemnity. "It's how you begin."

The understanding between them was unspoken but profound. The training was complete, but Kiara knew her true journey was only just beginning. She straightened her shoulders, determination hardening in her chest. She would go to El Dorado. She would reclaim her amulet. And she would face Ivyg—not as a single self, but as the culmination of every life she had ever lived.

"Does this mean our time here is complete?" Kiara asked as Marcus transitioned from his godly form back to the wise man she had come to know.

"Nearly," Marcus said, his voice calm and steady. "There's one last thing: bringing our interactions full circle. You've mentioned several times my relationship with Clarice and how much it meant to her. It's time we address that."

Kiara tilted her head. "Does that mean you're going to come back too? Your body is still there, and there are a lot of people who care about you. You shouldn't take that for granted. They love you. They need you."

Marcus gave her a wistful smile. "Marcus fulfilled what he came to Earth to do in his lifetime. The Pulse—what you call the Nexus event—was his exit point. I accepted my fate."

"So, you're not going to help us, then?" Kiara pressed, her tone tinged with frustration.

"I didn't say that" Marcus replied. "I've seen every timeline many times since I came here. If there were a further role I could play in this game I've repeated over countless lifetimes, I'd know it. Yet, this time-line—this life—is among the most significant I've witnessed. That means a great deal to me."

Kiara regarded him curiously. "Which was your favorite, then?"

"The one you just saw," Marcus said, his tone softening. "People knew me as a Sun God. I didn't have to be anything else but that. I worked hard to become him, but after that, none of us were allowed to take godly forms again. That's what makes this time so significant."

"How so?" Kiara pressed.

Marcus smiled faintly. "You'll find out soon enough."

"So… that's a yes?" she asked pointedly.

Marcus's smile widened. "Clarice was a love story not yet finished. Even if the rest of the world were to fall, I would have returned to stand by her side and watch it happen."

"Rebuilding it could be fun, though, right?" Kiara offered.

"Not as fun as you might think," he replied with a dry chuckle. "But you'll remember all of that again soon. We all will."

"What's that supposed to mean?" Kiara asked, but Marcus merely nodded toward something behind her.

Kiara turned and found herself suddenly outside, standing near the camp circle Marcus had spoken of. Figures sat around the fire, frozen mid-laughter and conversation. Her attention was drawn to two men who looked strikingly alike—one seemingly out of place. The incongruity was palpable.

"Who is that?" she asked, turning back to Marcus.

"Interesting," he murmured, stepping closer. "That appears to be Dr. Sanjay Patel. Or it could be his twin"

Kiara frowned. "Were you expecting him?"

"I was not. It was my belief that you knew him… though apparently, that is not the case."

"Actually," Kiara began, recognition dawning, "I do know that name. He's the professor who wrote that audiobook I listened to in college—the one about alternate realities, time travel, and extraterrestrial intelligences."

Marcus nodded knowingly. "And now that you've been here, his theories no longer sound so far-fetched, do they?"

Kiara hesitated, her gaze shifting back to the man who seemed utterly fascinated by the unmoving group before him. With a nudge from Marcus, she approached him.

"Dr. Patel?" Kiara called politely, her voice breaking his focus.

The man jumped, startled. "Who—? What is this?" he stammered, his eyes darting around. "Where am I?"

"You're safe," Kiara reassured him. "Are you okay?"

"I don't even know where I am or how I got here," he admitted, rubbing his temple.

Before Kiara could respond, Marcus joined them, addressing the man with familiarity. "Sanjay," he said evenly, "or perhaps I should say, Rajneel. Is it not?"

The man's posture stiffened. "I haven't been called that name in years," he said. "How do you know it?"

"Because this is the Nexus," Marcus replied. "And while you may not recognize it, you've played a role in bringing me here, just as I now play a role in your being here."

Rajneel frowned, his confusion deepening. "I don't understand. The timelines—"

"Have shifted," Marcus interrupted gently. "What you perceive now is outside the flow of ordinary time. Only those connected to the Nexus can observe such changes. The others remain unaffected."

Rajneel opened his mouth to question further, but Marcus cut him off. "I'm sorry but now is not the time. We'll meet again soon."

With a wave of Marcus's hand, Rajneel faded from view, leaving Kiara and Marcus alone once more.

Kiara turned to Marcus, her brow furrowed. "What happens now?"

Marcus's expression grew serious. "The Tower of Destiny awaits you. Find your amulet in El Dorado. It's the key to unlocking the past, and it will prepare you for what's to come."

Kiara took a deep breath, determination hardening her resolve. The journey ahead was daunting, but the path was clear. With one last look at Marcus, she nodded. "Then I'll go."

Marcus gave her a faint smile, the unspoken understanding between them echoing louder than words. The training was over, but her story was only beginning.

She wished she could spend her life looking at him, the beautiful man who had stolen her heart the night they met and then came back for her, protected her, and most assuredly was somewhere near to her, on the outside, at that very moment.

Her chest tightened as she considered how strange it would be, knowing she would never again lay her eyes upon him in this way. If not for that fateful night, would she have trusted him enough to follow him and her friends into the woods, into the depths of that cave? She wasn't sure, but she knew now that there was a reason for all of it—a reason greater than herself, or any of them.

The thought struck her that even his absence after their brief, but powerful connection had been part of the plan. Perhaps it was Ogma, orchestrating events from the shadows as Mallah had hinted. Still, her heart ached at the idea that she might lose this moment. She leaned in slightly, her voice barely above a whisper.

"I missed you," she said, her voice trembling with emotion.

Aron didn't answer, but the way he looked at her said everything. Kiara felt a pang of sadness mixed with a flicker of hope. She longed to feel his arms around her, to hold him close and forget the weight of the journey ahead, even if just for a moment.

"There is one more thing we must do before we go," Marcus's voice cut through the quiet moment, steady and deliberate. "It is time to learn the last bit of what you came here to learn."

Kiara turned toward him reluctantly, her gaze lingering on Aron for a fraction longer. Her heart ached at the thought of letting go of this moment. She had never seen him before, yet she recognized him as if her soul had known his forever. She didn't want this to end—not the way he looked at her, not the way his presence made her feel whole.

Marcus's voice softened, as though sensing her hesitation. "Tell me, Kiara. If you could choose, would you rather stand here forever, just staring at him, feeling the pull of a love that might remain unspoken? Or would you rather be with him—beside him, sharing the journey, even if it means facing the trials ahead?"

The weight of the question hit her like a wave. It wasn't just about Aron—it was about her path, her choices, and the life she wanted to live. Staring at Aron forever felt like safety, like solace. But being with him, truly standing by his side, meant facing the unknown, with all its risks and rewards.

She glanced back at Aron, her hand brushing his once more. "I want to stand by his side," she said, her voice firm despite the tremor in her chest. "I want to feel what it's like to face the world together."

Marcus gave a small, knowing smile. "Then it's time to finish what you came here to learn."

Kiara turned toward him, her brows knitting together. "What more is there? I've trained, I've learned, I've endured all of this," she said, gesturing toward the Nexus around her. "What could possibly be left?"

Marcus's expression didn't waver. "Do you remember what caused you to lose consciousness?"

Kiara frowned, the memory just out of reach. "I remember… there was this high-pitched sound. It was unbearable—I couldn't think straight."

"Go on," Marcus urged, his tone calm but firm.

Closing her eyes, Kiara concentrated. "I was seeing… strange things," she said hesitantly. "Flashes, images I couldn't make sense of. And my head—it hurt so badly. I tried to ask for help, but…" She paused, her eyes snapping open. "Oh, shit… I think I threw up on Aron!"

The realization hit her like a bolt, and she groaned, her face scrunching with embarrassment. "Ugh, that's so mortifying!"

Marcus smirked faintly. "Precisely," he said, ignoring her discomfort. "Focus not on the sickness, but on what caused it."

Kiara gave him a wary look. "Yeah, let's NOT replay that, okay?" she said, rolling her eyes. But as Marcus continued to stare at her expectantly, she sighed and closed her eyes again, pushing past the embarrassment to focus on the memory.

The sound, the flashes, the overwhelming pressure—it all began to come back to her, piece by piece. Something about it felt important, as if those chaotic moments were the key to unlocking a deeper truth. She concentrated harder, determined to make sense of what had happened.

"No, we would not want a repeat of that," Marcus said, a faint smile playing on his lips. "However, the expulsion of your stomach's contents is the least of your concerns. The real question is: why did it happen in the first place? What caused the headaches?"

Kiara wrinkled her nose at the memory, shaking her head. "It was… those weird, I don't even know what they were. Shapes? Flashes? And the sounds—makes my head hurt just thinking about it!"

"What you were seeing were, in fact, sounds," Marcus explained, his tone patient. "Your senses, already heightened, rewired your visual center. When 'The Pulse' occurred, it amplified these abilities tremendously, awakening dormant ones as well."

Kiara blinked, her brows furrowing. "I see sound? That's a thing?

How can I possibly control that?" Her voice wavered between confusion and skepticism.

Marcus nodded. "It is a thing, as you say. But control comes with practice—and practice cannot be gained here. I have prepared you to defend yourself, but that knowledge will mean little if you cannot perceive your attackers. Many visually impaired people have learned to use their senses in extraordinary ways, adapting in ways others rarely imagine. Now, as we enter a new age, it's time to remember just how adaptable the human body was designed to be."

Kiara crossed her arms, her lips pressing into a thin line. "You're going to tell me to center and focus, aren't you?" she asked flatly, recalling how often he had given her that instruction during their training.

Marcus smiled in response, his silence confirming her suspicion.

"When we return," Marcus began, his voice softer now, "I will not remember this conversation—or any other memories we've shared here. This moment exists outside of time, and only fragments will remain for me. The knowledge you've gained here is what matters most."

Kiara tilted her head, confusion flickering across her face. "Why won't you remember? And why me?"

Marcus's expression grew thoughtful. "Because we are kindred spirits, I agreed to aid you in this moment. My presence here is what you might call the 'sum of all my parts.' The Marcus you know is but one aspect of a greater whole. The connection you've felt to him—our shared understanding—is why I was able to guide you. Trust that everything you've experienced here will lead you where you need to go."

Kiara's eyes widened as the weight of his words sank in. "So, you're here… because my higher self asked you?"

He nodded. "Your higher self asked for my assistance in preparing you for the endeavor you are about to undertake."

Kiara took a deep breath, bowing deeply. "Thank you," she said, her voice thick with emotion.

Marcus offered her a small, encouraging smile. "When you awaken, there will be clarity. Trust yourself, Kiara. You already have what you need."

With a snap of Marcus's fingers, the frozen group reanimated as though no time had passed. The hum of the Nexus dissolved, and Kiara's awareness shifted. Her fingers brushed against the cold, uneven surface of stone, grounding her as she emerged from the trance.

Her senses were overwhelmed—faint shuffles echoed in her ears, coming from all around her, the scent of burning sage mingled with the earthy coolness of the infirmary, and the steady rhythm of her breath felt louder than ever. Yet beneath it all, something had changed.

Kiara placed a hand over her chest, feeling the energy thrumming within her. The connection she had felt—the strength, the clarity—was still there, though quieter now, like an ember waiting to reignite.

Guided by his oversoul, Kiara had learned to hear with precision, to filter the cacophony of sounds and emotions around her until they became crisp and clear. The haze of her blindness had lifted, replaced by a vivid awareness of the world vibrating and pulsing with life. She had moved with a power and understanding she had never known, as though the entire universe was laid bare before her.

She had seen—truly seen—Aron's face. The memory of his warm, gentle smile lingered like a fleeting dream, a beacon of comfort and connection. And then, it was gone. The darkness had returned, swallowing the light and leaving her disoriented and raw.

Her breath hitched, and the weight of the loss crashed over her like a tidal wave. "Aron?" she called out, her voice trembling as she reached into the familiar void. Tears streamed down her face, hot and heavy, as she fumbled blindly for the one anchor she knew would be there.

And he was. His strong hand covered hers, warm and reassuring. She clung to him desperately, the sobs wracking her chest as she let herself feel the full weight of her emotions.

"I'm here," Aron said softly, his voice steady and comforting. She could hear the concern in his tone, the gentle question behind his words. "I'm right here."

"I saw you," Kiara choked out, her voice breaking between sobs. "I saw you, Aron. And now… now it's gone."

Aron's hand squeezed hers gently, grounding her. "We're all here," he said, his tone soothing. She could tell he didn't fully understand what she meant, but his presence was enough. The clarity she'd experienced, the vivid sights, and the power—it was slipping away, already fading like a distant memory. But she wasn't alone.

Her stomach growled suddenly, a sharp reminder of the physical world, and she let out a breathy laugh, pressing a hand to her belly. The tension broke, the moment softening. She couldn't remember the last time she'd felt this ravenously hungry.

Aron chuckled softly, his hand brushing hers one last time before letting go. "I'll get you something to eat," he promised, his voice warm. She felt his presence withdraw as he and Teddy left the room, their footsteps fading against the ancient stone walls.

Clarice's voice cut through the lingering haze, sharp and tight with worry. "Marcus, are you okay?" Her movements were restless, her presence electric with tension. Kiara could hear her hovering near Marcus, practically glued to his side. The relief in her tone was palpable, but so was the fear.

Kiara turned her head slightly, listening to the room as her senses slowly recalibrated. The scent of burning sage mingled with the cool dampness of the stone walls, the echo of footsteps fading into the distance. Every sound, every scent, felt magnified, almost overwhelming.

A gentle hand rested on her shoulder, steady and reassuring. "Let me help you to your room," Robyn offered, her voice warm but firm. Kiara hesitated, wanting to stand on her own, to push through the disorientation, but she nodded reluctantly, accepting Robyn's assistance.

"Food," Kiara managed to whisper as Robyn guided her carefully to her feet. Her voice felt small, but the physical need was undeniable.

Robyn chuckled softly. "We'll take care of you," she said gently.

Kiara let herself lean on Robyn as they left the room, her mind racing with everything she had experienced. The connection to Marcus, the overwhelming presence of Aron, the vivid sensations of the Nexus—all of it weighed heavily on her, yet somewhere beneath it all was a flicker of hope. She didn't have to carry this burden alone. Not anymore.

Chapter 21

Echoes of Empire

The helicopter blades cut through the salty ocean air as Stan Wheeler leaned back in his seat, reviewing the latest updates on his tablet. The glossy screen displayed detailed reports, geological scans, and projections for the new settlement on Atlantis—Ivyg's grand vision finally coming to life. He swiped the tablet away with a flick of his wrist, tossing it onto the empty seat beside him. He didn't need another set of charts or figures to tell him what he already knew: this was a gold mine, and he intended to claim his share.

As the helicopter descended, Atlantis stretched out below him like an unfinished canvas. Makeshift tents and prefabricated structures dotted the landscape, a stark contrast to the ancient ruins being carefully unearthed in the distance. Teams of workers and scientists scurried around like ants; their voices barely audible over the roar of the rotors. A cluster of unfinished stonework—likely part of Ivyg's plan to rebuild the temples or tombs—stood as a testament to the company's ambitions, though it wasn't nearly complete enough to impress Stan.

The helicopter landed with a soft thud, and a small entourage greeted him immediately. "Mr. Wheeler, welcome," said a man in a pressed suit who was clearly out of place amidst the dust and chaos. "We've prepared a temporary living area for you while the main facilities are under construction. If you'll follow me, we can go over—"

Stan waved him off, stepping out of the helicopter and adjusting his sunglasses against the harsh sunlight. "I don't need a tour," he said brusquely, scanning the site with a practiced eye. "Just point me to the command center and get me the latest updates."

"Of course," the man stammered, motioning toward a large white tent flanked by security personnel. "Right this way."

Inside the tent, the air was cooler but no less tense. Staff members hovered around a large table strewn with maps, blueprints, and hastily scribbled notes. A young woman with a clipboard stepped forward nervously. "Mr. Wheeler, we've made significant progress on excavating the western quadrant. We believe we've uncovered what could be a ceremonial chamber. The symbolism aligns with—"

Stan held up a hand, silencing her mid-sentence. "Save it for Ivyg," he said sharply. "I'm here to make sure this place runs like a machine. Chamber doors and dusty relics don't mean squat until we're set up to operate."

The woman flushed, stepping back as another staffer jumped in. "We've also identified potential partnerships with local and international investors. If we can market this as a cultural and technological break-through—" "Now you're speaking my language," Stan interrupted, a thin smile curling at the edges of his lips. "Partnerships. Deals. Money on the table. That's what I'm here for."

He strode toward the large digital display at the far end of the tent, gesturing for someone to pull up the data he'd requested. As the screen flickered to life, the projection of revenues, logistical costs, and potential market expansion filled the air. Stan's eyes gleamed as he studied the figures.

"And Ivyg's priorities?" A voice asked pointedly from the corner.

Stan turned slowly to face the speaker: a man standing just out of the light, his posture rigid and his expression unreadable. It was Nicholas Varrick, a name that carried weight within the organization. Varrick's unwavering loyalty to Ivyg was well-known, and his presence here was no coincidence.

"Of course, Ivyg's priorities are always front and center," Stan said smoothly, though his dismissive tone betrayed him. "But let's be honest here—what's good for the bottom line is good for Ivyg. And this,"—he gestured to the display "is what's going to keep all of us on top."

Varrick's gaze lingered, his expression hardening as he observed Stan's barely veiled self-interest. "Ivyg was clear about the necessity of prioritizing the restoration," he said, his voice cold. "This isn't just about profits."

Stan shrugged, turning back to the screen. "I hear you," he said, though his attention had already shifted back to the numbers. "But the restoration will be meaningless if we don't have the resources to fund it. Don't worry—I've got it all under control."

Varrick's jaw tightened as he took mental note of Stan's arrogance. Ivyg would not be pleased. Stan, however, seemed blissfully unaware of the man's silent judgment.

As the meeting dispersed, the young woman with the clipboard ap-proached Stan hesitantly. He glanced down at her, his expression softening into a practiced charm. "Listen, you clearly know your stuff," he said, his voice dropping to a more casual, almost conspiratorial tone. "Why don't you walk me through the finer details? I could use someone who knows what they're talking about."

Her cheeks flushed, and she offered a small, bashful smile. "I'd be happy to, Mr. Wheeler."

Stan grinned, gesturing toward the exit. "Perfect. Let's talk outside."

As they stepped into the sunlight, Stan's body language shifted. He leaned in slightly, his tone becoming more playful. Whatever "details" he planned to discuss were clearly not about ceremonial chambers. Her giggle confirmed as much.

On the way, he caught sight of another staff member—a harried-looking assistant carrying a tablet. "Hey, you!" Stan called out, stopping the man in his tracks. "I need you to look over my notes and whip up a polished speech. I'm going live in less than an hour, and it better knock their socks off."

The assistant nodded quickly, fumbling with his tablet. "Of course, sir. Right away."

Stan smirked as he walked off with the clipboard-wielding woman, her laughter following them into the distance. For him, everything was falling perfectly into place. Little did he know, cracks were already forming beneath the polished veneer of his control.

The room was vast, cold, and dark, lit only by a faint, pulsating blue glow emanating from the crystalline console in the center. Ivyg stood alone, his imposing silhouette framed by the jagged window that overlooked the ruins of Atlantis. The expedition team below scurried like ants, their movements frenetic as they began excavating what was left of the ancient city.

Ivyg's sharp, pale features remained impassive as he observed the activity. His mind churned with calculations and possibilities. He pressed a slender finger to the console, activating a holographic display that floated before him, detailing the excavation zones. Symbols and coordinates blinked across the screen, overlaying the map of the city. One by one, he dismissed irrelevant sectors, narrowing the focus to a single subterranean chamber deep beneath the ruins.

"This is where it begins," He murmured to himself, his voice low and resonant.

A faint knock echoed through the chamber. Without turning, Ivyg called out, "Enter."

A tall, wiry man in a pristine black uniform stepped into the room, bowing slightly before speaking. "My lord, the initial excavations have begun. Our teams are reporting progress, but the outer chambers appear heavily deteriorated. No significant artifacts have been recovered yet."

Ivyg's lips curled into a faint smile, though his eyes remained cold. "They are looking in the wrong places, as expected. That is of no concern."

The man hesitated before continuing. "The press conference was well-received. Public opinion is rallying behind our efforts, and the governments have agreed to expand our funding for these expeditions. They're calling it a 'new era of exploration.'"

"Fools," Ivyg said softly, finally turning to face the man. "Let them bask in their illusions of progress. The world is so easily blinded by the promise of discovery, even when it walks them directly into my hands."

The officer nodded, unsure how to respond. Ivyg's gaze drifted back to the map, his fingers tracing invisible lines across the air.

"And the device?" The Grand Emissary asked abruptly.

The officer straightened. "The Vril interface is operational, my lord. The energy readings confirm this site has residual signatures consistent with… the artifact."

For a brief moment, something flickered in Ivyg's expression—anticipation, perhaps, or hunger. He concealed it quickly, his voice sharp and commanding. "Good. Ensure the readings are precise. If there is even a hint of instability, remove the operator and replace them. I will not tolerate incompetence."

"Yes, my lord."

Ivyg dismissed the man with a flick of his hand. As the door hissed shut, he allowed himself a moment of solitude. His hand rested on the console, the faint hum of the Vril energy coursing through the device vibrating beneath his fingertips.

"They think this land belongs to them," he muttered. "But Atlantis has always been mine. And soon, they will remember why."

-Chapter 22-

Quantum Entanglement

Kiara turned her attention to the room around her, feeling the shift in the air—a subtle disruption. Sanjay's breathing had changed, rapid and uneven with another, presumably the man she had met moments before. She caught a familiar scent, a mix of earth and iron, like dried blood. It looked like Sanjay... but not. The realization sent a shiver down her spine, and she focused in on him, trying to understand what was happening.

Before she could ask, Mallah's voice broke the moment. "I will handle this," she said calmly, her footsteps moving toward Sanjay. "I need to speak with the two of you... alone." Her voice was firm but reassuring. "I'll be back shortly to discuss everything." Kiara could sense the weight of Mallah's words, the unspoken promise hanging in the air as she led Sanjay away.

"We have a room, can you walk?" Clarice asked, climbing off of him, to which Marcus arose without issue. Without saying a word to anyone else, the two scurried away with Clarice following behind him, holding his gown closed as Marcus waved briefly. This behavior was fairly common and something their previous team was used to, watching them look at one another as though nobody else had been in the room.

The infirmary emptied slowly. Clarice was practically tugging Marcus out of the room, their footsteps moving quickly down the corridor. Kiara cringed, knowing their room was right next to hers. Robyn must have sensed her discomfort because she let out a soft laugh, taking Kiara's arm gently.

"They'll be... occupied for a while," Robyn said, her voice teasing but kind.

Kiara rolled her eyes. "Lucky me," she muttered dryly. "I'll try not to hear it."

Robyn chuckled, leading her down the winding hallways toward her room. Kiara followed the familiar sounds—the distant drip of water, the uneven texture of the ancient castle's floor beneath her feet, the soft swish of Robyn's clothes as she moved. They stopped at her door, and Kiara let out a breath she hadn't realized she was holding.

Mallah accompanied Dr. Sanjay and Rajneel to a quaint room with balcony doors opened up to a small balcony garden outside. The pair took a seat and watched her grab a very old water can, before stepping outside and sprinkling its contents around as she began asking them questions.

"I can't place your accent…" she began, delicately lifting a vine hanging over the ledge to get water underneath.

"America, Ma'am!" she heard them both answer simultaneously.

"Interesting…" she replied, smiling. "You must have learned it from your parents then?"

Again, the two confirmed in unison.

"You must be very close, almost like the same mind…I have known many twins that could finish each other's sentences."

"We are not identical twins!" Sanjay insisted, clearly knowing where her line of questions were headed.

"No shit!" she replied sharply, turning her head toward Rajneel. "Aside from the fact that you had told me everything, your mannerisms were also exactly the same…which would not be common among twins, not like that." she insisted, setting her canister back into its place as she took a seat across from them. "I thought you said his name was 'Alibi', a name you made up for whenever you would lose time when you turned into him?"

She was staring at Rajneel as Sanjay answered her, confirming that he must have changed his name, clearly watching to gauge his response. "Where did you go? And how long were you there?" Mallah interrupted him, knowing full well he had been eagerly awaiting his turn to explain.

"I changed my name because I never expected to return here, The God King forced me, he sent me back. For what we did in the Hollow Earth, I thought it was my fate to suffer in a world much worse than this."

"By back, I assume you are referring to having been moved forward? Is that where you went?"

"Yes!" Rajneel answered.

"How far? And why did he send you back?"

"We woke up eleven years from now and stayed there for several months. He said I was of no use to him." "But Kane is still there?"

"Yes, he had a plan of some kind…he said he was going to try to change things, but I think he was first focused on killing the God King. I don't know how he would manage that though after getting us intentionally captured!" Rajneel insisted, sounding annoyed.

"And yet he is there and you are here…" She smiled, shifting her focus back toward Sanjay. "Tell me about your other half here, should I be concerned?"

"I just want to live!" Rajneel snapped, standing up. "My whole life I was always there but never in control except when he wanted to use me as an excuse to do nefarious things…why do you think he called me 'His Alibi?'Mallah sat back and nodded toward his seat, nodding once again after he had sat back down. "You have nothing to fear from me, and I can assure you that no harm will come to you here."

Rajneel nodded politely "Thank you." he replied.

"What do we know about this 'God King' and what things did Kane want to change?"

"He was Ivyg and much of the world had been destroyed because of him. Kane lost half his arm to Marcus' explosion, and we had to scavenge supplies for days to build him a new one that would get him by until a professional replacement could be custom made. Most cities of that timeline are wastelands, and most people live in hidden villages underground or in the mountains."

As if withdrawing from the conversation, Mallah shrunk down into her chair for several seconds before calling out to someone outside. "Thank you, please escort Sanjay back to his room and see to it that our friend Rajneel is given a room of his own." She requested before turning back toward them as the tall man patiently awaited them smiled as he put his arms behind his back as if standing in military formation as Mallah walked around toward where Rajneel was sitting, looking down at him from the front of her desk.

"In this timeline, the same event that caused you to be hurled through the nexus into the future caused the veil protecting this dimension to be severely damaged, revealing a great number of places, things and beings that have created global chaos and panic in the aftermath.

Until I have a better handle on the situation and what to do with the both of you, it is in everyone's best interest that you stay here with us. There is no way to leave this island, and any communications go through me, so I would suggest taking this opportunity to have a bath, eat, and get some rest. Feel free to roam around all you would like, perhaps get to know some people…" Mallah smiled.

Rajneel stood as she walked back around her desk, waiting for her to face him once again before bowing and thanking her politely. "Since everybody I know knows me as him, I suppose I will have to start anew." he said as he walked away, looking back and smiling reassuringly at her- Not far away, Scarlett sat cross-legged on the small cot, her hands resting on her knees as she stared at the flickering flame of a single candle. The room was quiet except for the faint hum of activity outside. Her companions were elsewhere, preparing themselves for whatever came next, but Scarlett found herself trapped in a loop of indecision and uncertainty.

The dream—if it could even be called that—clung to her like a second skin. Shared past lives, fragmented memories, and cryptic truths had surfaced, threading together an experience that was as profound as it was disorienting. She wanted to speak about it, to process its meaning alongside the others, but the absence of Robyn left her hesitant. It wasn't just Robyn's absence, though—that would have been too easy an excuse. Scarlett didn't want to face the possibility of confirming what she already suspected: that Robyn wouldn't be around long enough for it to matter. Not in the same way, not in the long run. And the thought of excluding her now, even unintentionally, felt wrong.

Scarlett exhaled a slow breath, lowering her gaze to the small stone she had been absentmindedly rolling between her fingers, giving her thoughts of her native ancestors and their connection with nature and its energy. That same energy could be felt around her, even now, the spirits whispering to her, guiding her. The stone in her hand was smooth and cool, grounding her in the present. But her mind still raced, questions spiraling endlessly: What was the purpose of the dream? How much of it should they act on immediately, and how much was meant to be held back, simmering in the background until the time was right?

The answers seemed elusive, shrouded in the same hazy energy that had enveloped the dream itself. She closed her eyes and allowed the weight of her thoughts to press down, forcing herself into stillness. "What now?" she whispered, her voice almost inaudible. Scarlett rarely sought guidance through meditation—it wasn't her instinctive way of connecting. But in this moment, she needed clarity from a source beyond herself. She needed help from her guides.

The air around her seemed to shift, a subtle change that tingled against her skin. Scarlett breathed deeply, reaching out with her consciousness, seeking the familiar presence of her spiritual team. Her inner world quieted as she sank deeper into the meditative state. Images and feelings began to coalesce—nothing concrete, nothing definitive, but fragments that carried a soothing weight.

"You are exactly where you need to be," a voice whispered through her mind. It wasn't hers, and yet it wasn't entirely separate. It felt like an echo of something both ancient and eternal. "Trust the process. Have faith."Scarlett's brow furrowed. She wanted more —more answers, more certainty. "But what about Robyn? What about what we saw?" The question was met with silence at first, but then a wave of warmth enveloped her, like an embrace without form.

"It will unfold as it should. All of it. Your path is interwoven with theirs. Trust in that."Scarlett opened her eyes, the candle's flame steady and unwavering before her. The frustration of not receiving direct answers remained, but so did the comforting reassurance of the message. Her guides had been vague, yes, but they had also reminded her of what she already knew deep down: that not everything needed to be solved at this moment.

The pieces would come together when they were meant to. The dream, the past lives, the questions—they all weighed heavily, but Scarlett felt just a fraction lighter as she rose from the cot. She glanced toward the closed door, knowing that eventually, she'd have to face the others and decide what to share. For now, though, she focused on the present, grounding herself in the simple act of breathing. Whatever came next, they would face it together. That much, she could believe.

Mallah had returned Rajneel's gesture with a faint smile, her eyes following him and the others as they exited. Only when the door closed behind them did she exhale softly and raise her hand, summoning Ogma with a deliberate gesture. While she waited, her gaze drifted to the flickering candlelight on her desk, her expression unreadable.

Mallah's thoughts turned, unbidden, to their last meeting before the Pulse. Morton Kane. A name spoken with equal parts respect and suspicion, though neither encompassed the truth of him. She had known Kane for lifetimes, across epochs, under countless names and guises. Sometimes allies, sometimes adversaries, and once—briefly, foolishly—worshiped as gods by mortals who had no idea the price of such reverence.

But that was eons ago, and Mallah had learned to live in the present. Here and now, she had responsibilities far greater than the ghosts of shared histories. Witchaven demanded all of her focus. Hidden off the Irish coast, its very existence was a precarious balance of secrecy and sanctuary. It was more than her base of operations; it was a refuge, a haven for the forgotten and the feared—those who had no place in a world that would rather erase them.

Witchaven's inhabitants were as varied as the myths they inspired: humans, elementals, and beings thought long extinct. They worked alongside each other, not as equals by strength or stature, but in shared purpose. The island thrived not on wealth or power, but on its people— each contributing their skills, their care, their resilience. Here, the laws of nature held sway, and the harmony between its residents and the land was unbroken.

Yet Mallah knew harmony was fragile. Even a sanctuary as carefully tended as Witchaven was not immune to cracks. There were fights, fueled by drink and pride, though these rarely lasted beyond the next sea shanty sung in drunken camaraderie. Such scuffles were a reminder that even the most utopian dreams required vigilance. Witchaven was no pirate's den, but its people were the Guardians of the Veil, protectors of a world that would never know their sacrifices.

Mallah shifted her weight gracefully as she moved through her yoga practice. Her body bent into fluid shapes; each pose a balance between meditation and recalibration of mind and spirit. The motions steadied her, but her thoughts remained sharp, honed on the tensions simmering beyond the island. The Order of the Ancient Serpent—the OAS—loomed like a storm on the horizon, its reach insidious, its motives as poisonous as its leader.

Ivyg. Even the name carried venom. He was what humanity might call "the Devil," though Mallah would never dignify him with such power. He was a being of destruction, representing a single race from the Alpha Draconis system, whose hunger for domination knew no bounds. His influence stretched into the deepest veins of modern society, corrupting all it touched.

Mallah had no tolerance for war or violence, but she knew too well that those were Ivyg's tools of choice. Her priority was Witchaven's safety and all those who lived on the island of Hy-Brasil, but she could feel the winds shifting. Something was coming. The threads of fate were weaving a pattern she could not yet decipher, and it unsettled her, reminding her of the last conversation she had with Kane.

It had been quiet in her office, the stillness broken only by the soft crackle of a low fire. She was seated at her desk, reviewing the endless minutiae that accompanied governance, when it happened. The energy shift was so sudden it made her stand instinctively, the air vibrating with a force she hadn't felt in centuries. Across the room, a portal shimmered into existence, its edges glowing with a muted intensity. From its center stepped Morton Kane.

He looked… different. Older, perhaps, though not in the way mortals aged. His presence was sharp, his expression distant yet defined, as though he were seeing past the room entirely. The portal remained open behind him, a subtle hum of energy resonating through the space. Mallah's hands, resting calmly at her sides, concealed the tension she felt in her core.

"Kane." She said evenly, her tone giving nothing away. "It's been some time."

"Not as much as you'd think," he replied, a shadow of a smile crossing his lips. His gaze swept the room before landing on her. "You haven't changed."

"Neither have you," Mallah returned smoothly. She stepped out from behind her desk, her movements precise, deliberate. "And yet, here you are. From a portal, no less. I don't recall you ever being so theatrical. Or had that kind of power from the Vril."

Kane tilted his head slightly, as though debating how much to say. "I came because I had no other choice."

Mallah arched a brow, her expression cool but curious. "I doubt that."

"You'll understand soon enough," he said, his voice quiet but weighted. "Something's coming, Mallah. Something that will shake the foundations of everything you've built here."

She studied him in silence, her mind a whirlwind of calculations. Kane was no stranger to half-truths and veiled intentions, but his presence here was no coincidence.

"And you're here to warn me?" she asked, her tone betraying a hint of skepticism.

"To warn you," he confirmed, stepping closer, "and to ask for your help."

Mallah laughed softly, the sound devoid of warmth. "Help?!? That's rich, coming from you."

His expression darkened, the weight of something unspoken pressing between them. "This isn't about me," he said firmly. "It's about what's coming. The re-emergence of what the kids are calling Atlantis and Lemuria these days, the war that will follow, and the chaos Ivyg will unleash if he claims them first."

Mallah arched an eyebrow. "What the kids are calling them? You've been out of time too long."

"You could say that" Kane replied with a wry smirk, but his tone quickly sobered. "If Ivyg gets what he's after, none of this—Witchaven, the Champions, the Veil, any of it—will survive."

She folded her arms, letting his words settle before speaking. "You seem so sure of that."

"I've crunched the probabilities," Kane said, his voice heavy with conviction. "Countless iterations. The results are always the same."

"Interesting," Mallah said, her tone unreadable. "And yet, here you are, disrupting my evening with dire warnings. And you're too late, something the kids are calling 'The Pulse' just happened and Atlantis and Lemuria are visible once again. All after your trip with Marcus Kydd into the Hollow Earth, am I right?"

"I can explain…" Kane began to reply, but Mallah cut him off. "And Kiara Kross is here too."

Kane froze, his expression sharpening. "What?"

"She arrived recently," Mallah continued, watching him closely. "An intriguing character in this strange story unfolding before us. A recent interest of Ogma's… and now Aron's."

Kane's jaw tightened, his expression unreadable. "The Pulse…"

"Yes, the Pulse," Mallah said, her voice steady. "It's already set things in motion, Kane. Kiara has become a significant part of it. Marcus too. Even their friends. It's all coming together, the prophecy handed down to you by the Oracles, Izeci and Zok Grosz."

He opened his mouth to ask more, but the portal behind him pulsed, its edges flickering. Kane glanced back, a flicker of tension crossing his face. "Not enough time for details," he muttered. "Fine. We'll revisit this later."

He turned back to Mallah, his tone firm. "You'll need to perform the ritual. It's not just about me. Bring me back into my body—but also Marcus into his. When Marcus awakens, hand him the information I've compiled. He'll know what to do with it."

"And after that?" Mallah asked, her voice careful.

Kane hesitated, the weight of his words visible in his expression. "Send him to Wellville. There are two women—Linda Williams and Kathleen O'Brian. They've been poking around, uncovering fragments of the truth. Separately, they're unwitting resources. Together, they hold pieces Marcus will need. He'll understand when the time is right."

The portal flickered again, its hum growing louder. Kane stepped back, his gaze meeting Mallah's. "I can't stay, Mallah. I have to remain here, until everything is fixed."

Her brows furrowed. "And will you know when that happens?"

"I don't know," Kane admitted, his voice quieter now. "That's why it has to be Marcus. He'll see it through."

As the portal began to pull him back, he hesitated one last time, his gaze softening. "Keep her safe, Mallah. Kiara's more important than you realize."

And with that, he was gone, leaving Mallah alone in the flickering candlelight. For a long moment, she stood still, the echo of his presence lingering in the room. Finally, she moved to her desk, picking up a pen and writing down everything Kane had said. Her hand trembled slightly as she wrote, but her resolve remained steady.

The door to her side opened moments later, its familiar energy humming through the room as Ogma stepped through, his tall frame relaxed but alert. The door shut behind him with a soft thud.

"You called, my dear Mallah," Ogma said lightly, his grin already forming. "Dare I hope it's for something more entertaining than the last emergency?"

Mallah raised a brow, though her tone remained measured. "If by 'entertaining,' you mean complicated and mildly infuriating, then yes."

Ogma leaned casually against her desk, his arms crossed as he studied her. "What now?"

"Kane," Mallah said simply, her tone betraying nothing. "He was just here."

"Just here right now?"

"A few minutes ago." She confirmed.

Ogma straightened, his grin fading as his expression grew serious. "Well, that's interesting. I thought he was dead—or at least out of the picture."

"He should be," Mallah replied evenly. "And yet he stood here not moments ago, warning me of what's to come. We don't fully understand yet what happened to him and the others down in the Hollow Earth. Several people are still missing and presumed dead, specifically two military guys, Batticus and Greene."

"Never heard of 'em" Ogma folded his arms, his curiosity piqued. "What's Kane's angle this time?"

Mallah hesitated, her gaze thoughtful. "That's what makes this more believable. Kane didn't seem to know the exact sequence of events happening now. He spoke in generalities, referencing Kiara, Marcus, and what he called the re-emergence of Lemuria and Atlantis. He claimed the timeline could fracture beyond repair if they don't succeed."

Ogma tilted his head, considering this. "Kane? Speaking in generalities? That's not his style. He usually likes to gloat about knowing more than anyone else."

"Exactly," Mallah said, her voice sharpening. "It's as though he's acting on incomplete information—like he's stuck in a box and can only glimpse fragments of the outside."

Ogma's grin returned, faint but intrigued. "That does make it more believable. If he were spinning lies, he'd have filled in the gaps with flair. Instead, he's left the burden of choice on us."

"And that's what troubles me," Mallah said, pacing to the window. "He's convinced we must ensure Marcus survives to aid Kiara, that she's the key to holding the timeline together. But he offered no certainty—only probabilities."

"Probabilities?" Ogma echoed, his tone sharp with interest.

Ogma rubbed his chin thoughtfully. "It sounds messy, which, knowing Kane, means it's also true. So, what's his solution?"

Mallah took a breath, her expression hardening. "He suggested we prepare for the worst. If the Champions fail, Witchaven cannot remain here. We'll have to relocate—to Lemuria."

Ogma let out a low whistle, his usual humor fading. "Lemuria, huh? That's a bold move. I assume he's expecting fallout from Ivyg."

"Of course," Mallah said. "He didn't say it outright, but the implication was clear. If Ivyg regains control, Witchaven and everyone in it will be targets. We need to buy ourselves time—and relocating to Lemuria may be our only option."

Ogma shook his head, a faint smirk playing on his lips. "So, let me get this straight. Kane comes back from the future, doesn't know the details of what's happening now, and tells you to prepare for a worst-case scenario that might not even come to pass. And we're supposed to gamble everything on that?"

"It's not just his warning," Mallah said firmly. "Kiara's presence here, the Pulse, Marcus's awakening—it's all converging too perfectly to ignore. Kane's lack of specifics only strengthens his case. He's reacting to forces he can't fully control, and that's... unusual for him."

Ogma considered this, his expression thoughtful. "And what's your take on Kiara?"

"She's more than she seems," Mallah admitted. "Ogma, you were right to take an interest in her. She has the potential to be extraordinary—though I doubt even she realizes it yet."

Ogma chuckled softly, though his eyes remained serious. "I didn't intend for Aron to get involved with her, but it does add an interesting layer to her story."

"Interesting or not," Mallah said, her tone sharpening, "her role is vital. And if Kane's right, we don't have the luxury of waiting for her to figure it out on her own. Ogma's brow furrowed. "You think he's in the Nexus?"

"It's likely," Mallah said. "Kane didn't say it explicitly, but the signs point there. You know the Nexus better than anyone else on Earth. What's your insight?"

Ogma's grin returned faintly. "If Marcus was in the Nexus, pulling him out will require more than just a ritual—she must have had some kind of connection to him. The Nexus responds to bonds, especially those tied to soul contracts and quantum entanglement. If she was the one meant to bring him back, it's no wonder they are tied together on this."

Mallah nodded, her expression resolute. "Then he'll need to head to Wellville."

Ogma raised a brow. "Wellville? What's in Wellville?"

"The usual—a big government fiasco and cover-up... and two women, Linda Williams and Kathleen O'Brian," Mallah explained. "Kane believes they've each stumbled onto fragments of the truth. Separately, they're just curious investigators poking around in the wrong places. Together, though, they could become invaluable resources for Marcus."

Ogma chuckled, his grin tinged with irony. "Or Kane delivered one of those mysterious packets to each of them as well. He always did have a knack for recruiting unwitting pawns."

Mallah sighed, shaking her head. "Perhaps, but either way, they're now part of this. Marcus will need to connect with them once he's briefed on everything."

Ogma smirked, leaning back slightly. "So, just to recap: we're relocating Witchaven, preparing Kiara for a key future role, and sending Marcus to Wellville to wrangle a couple of civilian sleuths. Anything else on this cosmic to-do list?"

Mallah's lips curved into a faint smile. "Only to ensure we survive long enough to see it through."

Ogma's gaze turned serious, though his grin lingered. "Then let's get to work. If Lemuria is the fallback, I'll start bridging the realms. But Mallah—if this doesn't work, we may be betting on borrowed time."

Mallah's tone softened, though her resolve remained unshaken. "We always have been, Ogma. This is just the first time we're admitting it."

Ogma leaned back, his expression speculative. "So, we're dealing with whispers of the past, echoes of the future, and a girl who's a puzzle piece none of us fully understand yet. Sounds like a typical Tuesday. And what about Sanjay and Rajneel?"

Mallah's smirk returned, cold and calculated. "Rajneel, the former 'Alibi' for Sanjay, was his darker side…in that case, he will likely do what he always does—play both sides as soon as he gets a chance. But we'll ensure the side he serves most is ours- for as long as possible anyway."

Ogma nodded, his grin returning faintly. "Spoken like someone who's already five moves ahead."

Mallah turned toward the window, her gaze distant. "When you've been at this as long as I have, Ogma, you learn to anticipate the patterns. Even the ones no one else sees."

Ogma chuckled, though his expression quickly turned serious. "And what does this have to do with me?"

Mallah stepped closer, her hands clasped loosely behind her back. "I need your thoughts on how this all ties to the broader picture. If Rajneel's presence is part of the same game that placed Kiara within your realm, then we're dealing with something far larger than even Kane's warning suggests."

Ogma straightened slightly, his demeanor shifting from casual to focused. "You think Rajneel's involvement is tied to Kiara?"

"I think it's all connected," Mallah replied. "Everything is connected. Kane's sudden appearance, Rajneel's return, Kiara's placement—it feels as though every piece has been moved deliberately. Not by us, but by forces beyond even the Council's influence."

Ogma nodded slowly, his gaze thoughtful. "Higher agendas. Karmic debts. The usual suspects."

"Perhaps," Mallah said softly. "Or perhaps something more personal. Something we haven't yet seen."

Ogma rubbed his chin, his expression distant for a moment. Then his grin returned, tinged with irony. "Well, one thing's for sure—Kiara didn't end up in that house by chance."

Mallah arched an eyebrow. "No? Then how do you think it happened?"

Ogma shrugged lightly, his tone laced with curiosity. "If I didn't know better, I'd say it was one of those… cosmic nudges. The powers that be—or karma, if you prefer—setting the stage for what was to come. That house wasn't exactly the warmest welcome to my realm, but it was… fitting, wasn't it?"

"Fitting," Mallah repeated, her voice thoughtful.

Ogma's grin widened, and he gestured broadly. "Picture this: a husband lost to war, a family destroyed, and a woman driven mad by grief. She cursed the very land, and her death sealed the house in darkness. The haunting left the place in shambles, and the energy was so toxic it scarred the earth itself. By the time Kiara showed up, it wasn't just a bad place—it was a crucible."

Mallah's expression tightened slightly. "A crucible?"

"It forced her to adapt," Ogma explained. "To confront things most people would never dare face. And it wasn't just her—it pushed Scarlett too. That house forced them to grow, to awaken parts of themselves they wouldn't have otherwise. It was a setup—whether karmic or cosmic, who's to say?"

Mallah exhaled slowly, her gaze distant as she processed the revelation. "It wasn't just about the haunting," she murmured. "It was about preparing her for the Pulse."

Ogma nodded. "Exactly. It wasn't ideal, but it worked. She's stronger because of it—and so is Scarlett."

Mallah's brow furrowed slightly. "And you didn't think to clean up the land after all that tragedy?"

Ogma chuckled, his tone playful. "Clean it up? You know the rules, Mallah. Damage caused by humans isn't my responsibility to fix. It's up to them to clean up their own messes."

Mallah tilted her head, giving him a dry look. "Convenient."

"It's the truth," Ogma replied with a shrug. "Scarlett's already started the process, but there's still work to be done. If anything, it proves that even the worst places can be redeemed—with enough effort."

Mallah sighed, her lips curving faintly. "I'll make a note to provide assistance with the restoration—assuming we survive all this."

Ogma grinned. "Well, aren't you the charitable one?"

Mallah shot him a pointed look. "Don't push your luck."

Ogma smirked, leaning casually against her desk. "It's hard to ignore how perfectly timed Scarlett's presence was too. That paranormal investigator showing up just when Kiara needed her? Too convenient to be random."

"Convenient, yes," Mallah admitted, folding her arms. "But far from coincidence. Scarlett's connection to Teddy, Marcus, Aron, and her history with the Order made her a useful ally, even if it complicates matters."

Ogma nodded, his expression turning serious. "If we're being honest, it's all too perfect. Kiara, Aron, Scarlett, even the house itself—it all feels orchestrated. The stage was set long before we realized we were players in the drama and none of the actors had read the script."

Mallah's lips curved into a faint smile. "Karmic symmetry, then. Kiara didn't just stumble into her role; she was placed there by her guides—prepared, molded, whether she realizes it or not."

"Now she's here, center stage. I suppose it's a good thing she's a fast learner." Ogma chuckled, smirking. "And the bookstore? Don't forget that little detail. Having it as a front for the Order made everything much easier. It's as if they were bound to cross paths, one way or the other."

Mallah allowed a faint smile. "For once, your improvisation proved effective. But it doesn't change the fact that every step we've taken feels... accounted for."

"By whom?" Ogma asked, his tone lighter than the weight of the question warranted. "The Council? Or something higher? Kane? Ivyg and the Order."

Mallah's gaze met his, steady and unyielding. "All. None. It hardly matters. What does matter is that we stay ahead of it—or at least try."

Ogma leaned back against the desk again, his grin returning. "Well, here's hoping Rajneel keeps his head down long enough to make himself useful. And that Kiara doesn't hold a grudge about the house."

"If she does," Mallah said dryly, "she's not the person we need her to be."

Ogma laughed, his voice breaking the tension just enough. "Touché. So, what's next?"

Mallah's tone shifted, her words measured as though weighing every syllable. "Kiara passed out before the ceremony," she began, her gaze distant, as if replaying the memory. "I've yet to debrief her since she awoke, but something changed. Her energy feels... different. Altered, somehow."

Ogma raised a brow, intrigued. "Altered how?"

Mallah hesitated, her tone softening, though her focus remained sharp. "I'm not entirely sure yet. It's subtle, but even her physical form has started to change. There's something about her presence now, something I can't quite place."

Ogma tilted his head, watching her carefully. "And you're thinking this transformation has to do with the ceremony?"

"It's not a coincidence," Mallah said simply. "The ritual wasn't just about grounding her energy. It was designed to call Marcus back. I knew her energy would be the catalyst, but this—whatever this is—I hadn't anticipated."

Ogma chuckled softly, though his tone carried an edge of seriousness. "So, you used her."

"I leveraged her potential," Mallah corrected, her voice calm but firm. "She was the only one who could do it, even if she didn't realize it at the time. And now that she has, she's not the same."

Ogma nodded slowly, his expression thoughtful. "Transformation has a way of doing that. So, what's your next move?"

"First, I need to understand what's happened to her," Mallah said, her tone resolute. "Whatever she experienced during that time was more than a simple passing out. She's undergone something profound, and until I know what that is, I can't risk proceeding blindly."

Ogma rubbed his chin, a flicker of amusement crossing his face. "And here I thought you always had a plan."

"I do," Mallah said sharply, though her lips curved into a faint smile. "It's simply evolving."

Ogma chuckled again, leaning back slightly. "Speaking of evolving, I assume this means we're finally addressing what the kids are calling 'Lemuria' these days?"

Mallah arched her brow, her tone dry. "The kids? That's what Kane just said…I seem to recall it being called Dilmun the last time you referenced it."

"Dilmun, Tamil, Mu, Lemuria—it's all the same," Ogma said with a wave of his hand. "Different names for the same place, depending on who was doing the naming."

Mallah allowed herself a faint smirk. "Whatever you want to call it, it's time we started transitioning. Your realms are no longer invisible, Ogma. It's only a matter of time before they're discovered."

Ogma's grin faded, replaced by a thoughtful expression. "You know I'm not going anywhere. My place is right where I've always been."

"And if others in your realm want to leave?" Mallah asked, her tone probing.

"Then I'll let them," Ogma said simply. "I'll even help facilitate it. Just say the word, and I'll bridge the two realms. But don't expect me to set up shop in Lemuria."

"Of course not," Mallah replied, a hint of amusement in her voice. "But your cooperation in the migration will be essential. If Witchaven and your realm can't transition smoothly, the risks are too great."

Ogma nodded, his expression turning serious. "I'll handle the logistics. Just let me know when."

Mallah's tone grew more resolute, her words carrying the weight of the moment. "What's next is we prepare. Kane's warning, the importance of Marcus and Clarice, Rajneel's return, Kiara's transformation, the re-emergence of Lemuria and Atlantis... it's all accelerating. There's no room for error."

-Chapter 23-

Reckoning and Ruins

The room remained vast and cold, illuminated only by the faint, pulsating blue glow from the crystalline console. Ivyg's sharp features were highlighted by the ambient light as he gazed out at the ruins of Atlantis. Below, the expedition team moved frantically, their small figures mere specks against the backdrop of ancient stones.

The soft chime of an incoming communication interrupted the quiet hum of the console. With a flick of his fingers, Ivyg activated the interface. A holographic projection materialized, revealing a man in a black suit, his face tight with unease.

"My lord," the man began, bowing slightly. "There is a matter I believe requires your attention."

"Speak," Ivyg replied, his tone cold and impassive.

The loyalist hesitated, glancing over his shoulder before continuing. "It concerns Wheeler. He has been... less receptive to your directives than anticipated. I fear his ambitions may exceed his loyalty."

Ivyg's lips curled into a faint, humorless smile. "Stan Wheeler. A pretty face for our empire. And like all pretty faces, easily replaced."

The loyalist swallowed hard, his discomfort visible even through the hologram. "Shall I... take measures to remind him of his place?"

"No," Ivyg said sharply, though his voice remained calm. "Let him continue his charade. The press conference serves its purpose, and his usefulness has not yet expired. But make no mistake—should he falter, there are countless others willing to don his mask."

The loyalist nodded quickly. "Understood, my lord."

Ivyg leaned forward slightly, his piercing gaze fixed on the man who lingered, visibly reluctant to continue. "What else?"

"There are whispers, my lord," the man said, his voice lowering. "Among the upper ranks. Some question whether the timing of your plans is premature."

A low chuckle escaped Ivyg's lips, devoid of humor. "Let them whisper. It is the nature of the weak to doubt what they cannot comprehend."

"My apologies, my lord," the man said hastily. "I only wished to—"

"You wished to warn me," Ivyg interrupted smoothly, his tone edged with menace. "And for that, you have my gratitude. But do not mistake my indulgence for tolerance. The timing of my plans is perfect. Remind those who question it of their insignificance."

"Of course, my lord," the loyalist said quickly. "I will handle it."

"Excellent." Ivyg's voice dropped further, cold and commanding. "Now listen carefully. I am initiating an early departure tomorrow morning. You are to prepare for my arrival quietly. No one is to know, do I make myself clear?"

"Perfectly, my lord," the loyalist said, bowing deeply.

Ivyg's gaze lingered for a beat longer. "One more thing—keep a close watch on Landis. He is eager, but ambition without discipline can be... problematic."

The loyalist nodded, though something flickered in his eyes—a hesitation, quickly masked. "As you command."

With a flick of his hand, Ivyg dismissed the projection, the hologram dissolving into the blue glow of the console.

From the corner of the room, a shadow moved. His son, Landis Nash, stepped forward into the light, his youthful face a near-perfect reflection of his father's sharp features. He crossed his arms, his posture relaxed but his eyes calculating.

"You're leaving, father?" Landis asked, his voice carrying a cool detachment that mirrored his father's.

"Yes," Ivyg replied without turning, his tone indifferent.

"And you didn't think to tell me?" Landis pressed, though his voice remained calm. Beneath the surface, there was a hint of something more—a quiet challenge, a need for validation.

"There are things you are not yet ready to understand," Ivyg said, finally turning to face his son. "Your role will come in time. Do not be impatient."

Landis's gaze narrowed slightly, his tone measured. "You mean I'm not ready, or you don't think I'm capable?"

Ivyg's lips twitched into the faintest smile. "You will prove your capabilities when the time is right."

"And Wheeler?" Landis asked, shifting the focus. "He's a liability."

Ivyg tilted his head, studying his son. "He is irrelevant. If he becomes a problem, he will be dealt with. There are always others to take his place."

Landis's expression darkened momentarily before smoothing into a mask of indifference. "Perhaps I could deal with him," he suggested, his tone casual but calculated. "It would give me an opportunity to... clean up the mess."

A flicker of interest crossed Ivyg's eyes, but his tone remained neutral. "Ambitious. But unnecessary. Wheeler still serves his purpose, for now."

Landis straightened, his jaw tightening imperceptibly. "And if he doesn't?"

"Then you will have your chance," Ivyg replied, his voice cold and final. "But until then, remember your place. By my side and doing the things I tell you are important."

Back in the control room, Ivyg stood before the console, the pulsating blue light casting long shadows across his face. He closed his eyes, resting his hand on the cold crystal surface. The Vril responded at once, its familiar hum vibrating through his bones, filling him with the ancient energy he had long since mastered.

But this time, something felt wrong.

The rhythm faltered—a subtle hitch in the flow, like a breath caught in the throat of the universe. His brow furrowed, and a flicker of alien energy surged through the console, forcing an image into his mind. Symbols—Lemurian, old and unwelcome—rose in sharp relief, burning behind his eyes.

His eyes snapped open, the air around him colder, thinner, as if the chamber itself recoiled from what had just passed. The console continued to hum, steady and indifferent, but Ivyg felt the shift deep within—the unease that clawed at his core. The glyphs he had thought buried, erased from time, had returned. Not by his hand.

The symbols burned in his mind, ancient and precise, a language he had long since mastered, now speaking without his command.

"Who dares," he whispered, his voice low and sharp, slicing through the stillness. It was not a question, but a warning—to whatever unseen force had stirred.

Ivyg stepped back, the memory of the glyph burning in his thoughts.

He had anticipated resistance, yes—but not this soon. The threads he had spun were meant to hold until the final pieces were set. Yet something was stirring, pulling at the edges of his control.

He turned toward the window, his gaze sweeping over the ruins of Atlantis, where jagged stone and time-worn spires rose stubbornly from the earth. The city stretched below him, a fractured monument to an age long buried, yet still pulsing with secrets that refused to be forgotten. He had come here to reclaim what was rightfully his, to awaken the power that slumbered beneath the surface, but already he could feel the past stirring against him—restless, unwilling to yield.

His jaw tightened, the weight of centuries pressing in. This wasn't how it was meant to unfold. The timing was wrong, the currents shifting beyond his design. And still, he could not turn away.

The words sat like iron on his tongue, bitter and unspoken. Not yet. His fist clenched, the Vril's hum mocking him with its silence. He would find the source of this disturbance. And when he did, he would crush it.

-Chapter 24-

Wheel of Fate

Kane awoke in the back of a pickup truck and could see the dart that made them all pass out was still in his thigh. Looking around he could see Patel and Nova, but they were still unconscious from the sedatives inside the darts. Kane listened to what he could hear, which was very little. He could hear tidbits of voices here intermittently coming from the cab of the truck, voices of their captors.

Aside from the unexpected tranquilizing darts, everything was pretty much going according to Kane's plan. It took about another hour for Nova and Patel to awaken. Occasionally one of the goons in the cab would look through the back window to check on the captives. To Kane he looked just like any stereotypical goonish oaf, large, stupid, and knowing nothing but to follow orders. A useful idiot.

The drive to Kansas City was long, taking just over 5 hours, as the useful idiots had to stop several times to urinate along the way. Thankfully they had allowed their captives to take a bathroom break as well. Patel looked like he was going to cry at one point, as he attempted not to piss on himself.

Thankfully they had stopped, and he had not. It had been nighttime when they had been captured and now it was morning, and light had emerged from the horizon. Gem was so proud of having captured Kane that he decided to drive him, personally, to Kansas City to deliver to his God King Ivyg. Gem indeed knew who Kane was and it took a while before he figured it out. Gem had once been known as…"Graz Lax?" Kane asked loud enough for those in the cab to hear.

"That's a name that hasn't been spoken in years. Kane." The man laughed. "Neither has yours, for that matter. Where have you been man?"

"Oh, you know, here and there." Kane responded sarcastically. "When did you start going byGem instead of Graz Lax? Last time I checked you were the Grand Emissary for 10th Coven of the OAS in Dubai, oh how the mighty have fallen."

"Still a smartass, that's for sure." Gem replied. "That's ancient history. There are nosmall Covens any longer. They all merged together after the God King released the Titans, his final act in taking control of Earth. Ivyg is the one and only ruler over these lands now. We pay a small price and offer fealty, and he leaves our little city alone for me to rule over. The benefits could be better but who am I to complain?"

"What's the price?" Rajneel asked, speaking up out of nowhere.

"You, sunshine." Gem said as he burst out into laughter while jamming on his brakes sendingthose in the back flying forward. "We're here!"

The heavy air around the arena was thick with the mingling scents of sweat, blood, and something acrid that burned at the back of Kane's throat. The once-grand football stadium now bore the unmistakable scars of time and neglect. Rusted beams groaned overhead; their metallic complaints nearly drowned out by the distant roar of an unruly crowd. Kane shifted uncomfortably; his legs cramped from the hours spent confined in the back of the truck. His captors had been silent for most of the drive, saved for their occasional crude jokes and the shuffle of snacks being unwrapped in the cab.

He could still feel the dart lodging in his thigh, its sedative long worn off but leaving an ache that made his leg throb. Patel, trembling beside him, looked pale, beads of sweat glistening on his forehead even as the morning air cooled. Nova, stoic as ever, remained quiet, his eyes scanning their surroundings for any opportunity. They had finally arrived.

The truck screeched to a halt in front of the stadium, jostling its passengers forward. Kane caught Patel just as the younger man nearly toppled out of the open truck bed, his eyes darting in panic at the brutish men who approached with smug grins and drawn weapons.

Gem was pretty jovial for a maniac that had his hands still stained from his involvement in the apocalyptic destruction of life on this planet decades ago. It was disturbing that this man kept laughing all the way to take his captives into what once was a famous professional football stadium, now in a state of disrepair without the constant upkeep.

There was a dispute about pay between Gem and those who were in processing captured objectors. He felt like he should get more money for bringing the one and only Morton Kane, a highly valued target, who had been sought by Ivyg for decades now.

"Well, well, the famous Morton Kane," one of them jeered. He was a hulking man with a belly that strained against his tattered jacket. His voice carried the gleeful malice of someone enjoying his temporary power. "Gem was right. You don't look like much."

Kane smirked, rolling his shoulders as they hauled him down. "And you look like you skipped leg day."

The brute snarled but held his tongue, leading the three captives toward the stadium gates, where a decrepit sign swung on rusty chains. The once-proud lettering proclaiming the home team was now barely legible beneath layers of grime and graffiti. The arena loomed above them like a decaying beast, its maw wide open to swallow them whole. Inside, the air was damp and carried the sickly-sweet stench of rot. The distant roar of the crowd echoed through the hollow corridors, punctuated by laughter and the occasional scream. Kane's boots crunched against debris-strewn floors as they were ushered into a dimly lit tunnel.

Gem, their captor and self-proclaimed ruler of this twisted operation, strutted ahead, his voice booming as he bragged about his prize. "The one and only Morton Kane! Ivyg's been looking for you for decades, and now here you are. I think this deserves a bonus, don't you?"

"Give the man what he wants." A familiar voice spoke up upon entering the room.

"I'll be damned."

"You know this man?" Nova wondered.

"Clovis Krott." Kane scoffed, spitting on the ground. "One of my brother's most loyal stooges in the OAS. A public face for programs that were often in the grey area of legality."

"I'm surprised to see you as well, my old friend." The man said kindly but then changed his demeanor. "I'm sorry for what you've gone through to get here, but now you have to come with me, all three of you."

Clovis Krott, a wiry man in an ill-fitting suit, emerged from the shadows, his face a mask of bemusement. "Oh, Gem. Always angling for more. I'd say bringing in Kane earns you... my gratitude."

"Asshole."

Gem scowled but didn't press the issue, shoving Kane and the others forward. "Just get them ready for the Wheel."

Clovis's expression twisted into a smug smile, but there was an unmistakable flicker of tension in his eyes as he watched Kane. He adjusted his tie, a nervous tic that didn't go unnoticed by Kane, who raised an eyebrow but said nothing. Their history was unspoken in this moment, but it hung between them like a palpable weight.

"You know, Kane," Clovis began, his voice oozing with false camaraderie, "I never thought I'd see the day you'd end up here. It's almost poetic, really. A man like you—always so sure, so... untouchable. And now? Here you are, bound by the same fate as everyone else. To test your luck at the Wheel."

Kane's expression remained impassive, but there was a glint of something dangerous in his eyes. "Funny, I remember you being a lot quieter back in the day, Clovis. Or maybe that was just the fear talking."

Clovis's smile faltered for a fraction of a second before he regained his composure. "Fear? Please. I'm not the one stepping up to the Wheel of Fate; But I'll admit, you always had a way of making people... nervous. That's why I made sure to emphasize to our good Titan Judge just how unpredictable you can be. Wouldn't want any... accidents before you get your turn."

Kane chuckled softly, the sound low and menacing. "Careful, Clovis. That almost sounded like respect."

"Respect?" Clovis shot back, his tone sharp. "Don't flatter yourself. I've just learned to appreciate the value of caution when dealing with... wildcards like you. But don't worry, Kane. The Wheel will take care of that unpredictability soon enough. And I'll be watching every second."

Kane took a step closer, forcing Clovis to tilt his head back to meet his gaze. "Make sure you watch closely, Clovis. You wouldn't want to miss the moment when it all goes wrong—for you."

For a moment, the arena seemed to fall away, leaving just the two of them locked in a silent battle of wills. Clovis broke first, clearing his throat and stepping back, his grip tightening on his scepter. "Get them to the Wheel," he barked at the guards, his voice snapping with authority.

The guards moved in, shoving Kane, Nova, and Patel toward the looming structure. Clovis watched them go, his face a mask of satisfaction, but the faint tremor in his hand as he clutched his scepter betrayed his unease. For all his bravado, he couldn't shake the feeling that Kane wasn't a man to be underestimated—even now, standing on the edge of his fate. The suited man then led them out through the tunnel and onto the sports field. There were people in the stadium seats shouting as the captives were led into the middle of the field where a stage had been built.

"This is the home to the infamous Wheel of Fate, my friends." Clovis said loudly so all three could hear. "Here, chance will decide your fate. Come now." Kane had heard rumors of it in whispered conversations among the downtrodden and desperate. It was said to be the ultimate arbiter in Ivyg's dystopian empire, a grotesque game of chance that decided the fates of dissenters and rebels. The Wheel of Fate. Now, standing in the middle of the arena, he finally saw it for himself. Towering over the field, the wheel was a grotesque marvel. Its massive spokes creaked as it spun, adorned with symbols and illustrations depicting each potential doom. The crowd, seated in the crumbling stands, erupted into cheers and jeers as the wheel slowed to a stop for the poor soul currently at its mercy.

The unlucky man's fate: shark-infested waters.

A platform rose from the ground, and he was thrust into a glass enclosure rapidly filling with seawater. Kane didn't flinch as the man's screams filled the air, his fate sealed as fins began circling in the murky water.

Nova leaned closer, his voice low. "This is... worse than I imagined."

Kane's gaze didn't waver. "Worse than I planned for, but not worse than I'm ready for."

Patel shivered beside them, his hands wringing the hem of his shirt. "I can't do this. I can't spin that thing."

"You won't have a choice," Kane said, his voice even. "But remember this—panic will get you killed faster than the wheel itself."

"It's time to spin the Wheel of Fate!" An AI robotic symbiotic humanoid came up and He led them to a small line of people who had also been captured. Most of them looked rugged and malnourished, their only crime being dissent towards being enslaved by Ivyg and his nefarious forces of evil, forcing further cruelty upon survivors of the apocalypse. A Titan named Astraeus was presiding as Judge over these proceedings. Of the perhaps twenty captives in this line, only one was let go, but given a whipping for being somewhere they weren't supposed to go, everyone else was forced to step up in line.

The AI symbiotic being spoke loudly, introducing itself in an annoyingly upbeat tone. "Hi! I'm Murrin. Congratulations on surviving the apocalypse. As you are no doubt aware, life for humanity is not going so well at this time in history and the God King wants you to know that he doesn't give a shit about you or your plight. Your existence is only allowed by the will of HE alone and it is his will for you to die. Fortune has it for you, that you get to decide how you die."

"That sucks." Patel groaned.

"Things may or may not be going the way you had hoped?" Murrin asked condescendingly. "I would tell you that you should be grateful for being alive, but that might not be the case for long. Step right up and seal your fate. Remember, anyone that completes and lives through their challenge will be granted one wish from the God King. Failure equals death. Now get in line behind the rest. The games will begin shortly."

Kane wasn't really listening to Murrin. Nova had delivered them with accurate enough information to postulate a semi-predictable outcome. There would be no escaping their fate. Kane, Nova, and Patel would all have to spin the Wheel of Fate and hope the fates shine upon them. Before the wheel could spin, he was able to see some of the vile fates that could potentially be gruesome. Some of the calmer ones were endless falling, gladiator obstacle course, and the guillotine. Buried alive, robot assassins, drawn and quartered, shark infested waters, crushed to death, giant fighting, and woodchipper were some of the darker ones.

The Titan judge already seemed bored with the proceedings and urged Clovis and Murrin to speed up the pace, though he did get excited when it was time to spin the wheel. When the first unfortunate contestant stepped up and spun the wheel, it didn't even make it all the way around in a full circle before landing on beheading with an axe. Clovis used some kind of scepter, imbued with Vril powered technology and touched it to the forehead of the man facing his judgment.

The man was immediately teleported to the middle of the field where his head was chopped clean from his neck with a shiny blade of an axe. For the Titan, it was always his option to choose if he would save the defendant from a worse fate, like the man before whom he allowed to be whipped in punishment rather than face death for his crimes.

He triumphed as a noble judge, fair of mind and heart. Today after the first few deaths he was feeling a bit generous. The Titan god of stars and planets could not help himself to be captivated and mesmerized by the clear night sky. Despite some of the stadium lights being on, the acute eye could still gather a glimpse of the Milky Way galaxy. After a few more gruesome fates and a clear boredom of what was going on, it came time for Kane, Patel, and Nova to be in line.

"These three." The Titan growled in a low deep voice that sounded like thunder in the wind, visibly shaking Patel who clearly didn't know what to think at this moment besides fear.

"Yes, Judge?" Murrin answered back.

"These three came in together." The Titan bellowed. "Their fates will be the same as one another.

Kane noticed now what he hadn't noticed before. Behind the Titan, cleverly perched in what once were the viewing boxes for celebrities and powerful people to watch American football games. Clovis kept looking up in that direction where Kane eventually caught sight of the twin Oracles Izeci and Zok Grosz. He once held them in high esteem, holding on to their visions as above nearly all else. He looked upon them now with nothing but pity. Kane wondered now in this dystopian future how much they helped Ivyg to take over and dominate the surviving remnants of humanity ruling over this war-ravaged planet. They both looked down at Kane, amused by his presence after being missing for fifty years. They were equally amused by Kane's continued defiance of Ivyg's will. He could see it in their smirks—so familiar yet now twisted by time and compromise. What had turned them into this? Perhaps it was the apocalypse itself, or perhaps their knack for survival had always stemmed from blind loyalty. Deep down, Kane knew their fate was bound not just to each other, but to the one man who demanded the world call him God King. Their allegiance wasn't to Ivyg—it was to survival, no matter the cost. "Spin!" The Titan Judge demanded.

"Spin the Wheel of Fate." Clovis Krott laughed. "I'm looking forward to seeing your death, my old friend."

"I'll be gentle and swift when I kill you." Kane told him back.

"I thought you were the god of the seas and oceans, not god of over-confidence."

The wheel was much larger now that they were up next to it, with over 100 different fates of torture and despair. Missing his arm, Kane defaulted on the spinning of the wheel to the much larger statured Nova whose muscular tone gave a mightily impressive yank to get it going, eager to discover their fate of chance. The Judge smiled eagerly as the wheel spun round and round, having not seen such a forceful spin in a long time, since the time of purging the Champions.

The Oracles were on the edge of their seats. Patel and Nova were on edge. Kane looked cool as a cucumber, unphased in his demeanor. The Wheel of Fate began to slow passing fates like suffocation, hungry lions and just when it looked like they were going to be stuck on alien combat, it ticked over one more notch on the wheel.

"The famed Minotaur's Labyrinth!" Murrin exclaimed. "What a treat! What a joy! Many would be heroes, so-called 'Champions', and Vril

Enhanced Individuals tried to fight against the will of our God King only to meet their fate within the maze of the Beast. This truly will be a challenge for the ages. Best of luck to you all…and remember… it's all just a show! Keep your hands and feet inside the vehicle at all times and don't forget to enjoy the ride!"

The Wheel of Fate had spoken. Now, their survival depended on their wits, their strength, and their ability to outmaneuver the labyrinth's deadly guardian. The three men were led over to a metal platform. Clovis Krott used the God-King's scepter to open a portal behind the three men, who without hesitation stepped through the portal that closed right after them.

Neither Clovis nor Murrin were used to that kind of expedience. Most of the time they had to throw people through the portal kicking and screaming. Yet the crowd was enthralled with the lead up to this massive event. It was like Kane, Nova, and Patel were never there in the first place. Gone. The small crowd inside the stadium and the Titan Judge all cheered with excitement as they looked up at the jumbo screen to see what happened next.

<h1 align="center">-Chapter 25-</h1>

Gravity Wells

Finally, alone with a short moment of free time, Clarice pushed Marcus backwards onto the bed, climbed on top of him and shagged him rotten, needing to feel his intimacy. She had been fearful that he wouldn't awaken from his coma, and she could no longer hold back the emotions as she ripped his hospital gown from his muscular body as she kissed and nibbled at his sexy nakedness as she climbed atop and straddled him. Her blonde and pink hair waved with the motion as she bounced up and down on his manhood, her creamy white thighs forcefully pushing down to aid in maximum penetration. At first, Marcus looked lost for words and unsure what to do, but he felt the warmth from his partner, his lover, his soon-to-be wife, and he reciprocated her affections back, enjoying her large breasts bouncing in his face while laying on bottom, beneath her straddled legs. Flipping her over, he rolled on top of her and finished inside, filling her with his love, his seed, what hoped time and again would soon be their future child. Clarice giggled aloud as the two climaxed together, in a fit of romantic, yet carnal pleasure.

After making love, Marcus and Clarice got back up and took a quick sexy shower taking turns soaping the other up, spreading the lather over each other's naked bodies. This led to more sex as Marcus lifted her up, sliding her down onto his penis. She held on tightly as she climaxed again for a second time. She had to clean up again before drying off and getting dressed in a fresh set of clean clothes. Though they were physically done having sex, they didn't hesitate to keep eye-fucking one another the entire time they were putting on their clothes.

Marcus loved how she looked naked. and her eyes revealed the same in return. His eyes were slightly different now, she noticed, glimmering like the stars of the galaxy against a black sky of night, mesmerizing in a way that she could not help smiling from ear to ear, just about. She was happily in love with this man, through and through, with zero doubt in her heart that he had come back from the Nexus consciousness primarily for her, and to a lesser extent his newly discovered brothers that they were set to go meet.

In the quiet sanctuary of her room, Robyn guided Kiara to a chair, helping her out of her rumpled clothes. The echo of the shower's spray filled the space as she felt the warm water against her skin, soothing away

242

the remnants of the trance. She leaned into Robyn's touch as her friend carefully brushed out her tangled hair, the rhythmic motion calming her scattered thoughts.

"You're doing great, Kiara," Robyn said gently, her voice close to Kiara's ear. "One step at a time."

Kiara swallowed, nodding, not trusting herself to speak. She could still feel the weight of whatever she'd experienced in the trance, the world of the nexus consciousness, perceived through the mind of Marcus Kydd, hanging heavily in her chest. She knew she was stronger now, more in control of the world she couldn't see, but the return to darkness felt sharper, more painful. It was a loss she couldn't quite put into words—a reminder of what she'd glimpsed and what had slipped away again. At first it was painful, but in time she would remember and adapt, being stronger for it in the end.

Meanwhile, Rose was busy helping Cesaro. He leaned heavily against her as they walked through the castle, his familiar scent—like cedarwood and fresh linen—reassuring. "Can you take me to my room?" he asked, a hint of his usual flirtatious charm creeping back into his voice.

Rose smiled, a bit awkwardly. "Alright, but you're getting your own food," she teased, half-joking.

Cesaro chuckled, his voice warm. "Fair deal, as long as you come with me."

Rose hesitated, then nodded. "Okay," she said quietly, guiding him down the corridor.

Back in Kiara's room, she was finally dressed in fresh clothes, her hair neatly brushed. She felt more like herself—steady, even if still rattled. Mallah returned shortly after, her footsteps soft but deliberate. She sat beside Kiara, her presence gentle and comforting.

"What did you feel?" Mallah asked, her voice tender. "What did you experience?"

Kiara took a deep breath, her heart racing. She knew this moment was coming, but finding the words was harder than she'd expected. She had to rely on feelings, sounds, and impressions, painting a picture with the pieces she could grasp.

Mallah was mid-sentence, her tone gentle but urgent, when Kiara raised a hand to stop her. Her voice was steady, though her expression betrayed a mix of determination and weariness.

"I know you mean well but I need to say this to everyone," Kiara said firmly. "If I try to explain it over and over, it'll lose its meaning—and I made a promise to someone, and I know that time is precious."Mallah studied her for a moment, her eyes narrowing slightly in thought before a faint smile touched her lips. There was a hint of pride there, though she quickly masked it. "Wise beyond your years," she said softly. "You're right. Everyone needs to hear this, and it's a good time to reground and plan. I'll—"The sound of footsteps interrupted her, accompanied by a familiar voice. "Hope I'm not crashing the party."Both women turned—or, in Kiara's case, tilted her head toward the sound—as Aron emerged from the doorway, balancing a tray of food with casual ease, as if a waiter in a high-class restaurant. He looked tired but alert, his sharp eyes flicking between them.

"What did I walk in on?" he asked, setting the tray down on a nearby table.

Mallah arched an eyebrow. "You have impeccable timing.""Always," Aron quipped, though his tone softened when he caught Kiara's expression. "Seriously, though, what's going on?"Kiara took a breath, her hands fidgeting briefly before she stilled them. "I've got... messages. Things I was told to pass on. It's too much to repeat, and it's too important to just say to one or two people."Aron nodded, already catching the gravity in her voice.

Without hesitation, he straightened and reached for the door. "Then let me gather everyone. If this is as big as it sounds, you shouldn't have to explain it more than once. Besides," he added with a faint grin, "I've got extra food as a bribe to get them here faster."Kiara let out a soft laugh despite herself, grateful for his practicality.

Mallah gave him a nod of approval. "Do it. And tell them this isn't just a meal—it's a meeting. We have things to discuss and decisions to make."

Aron shot her a salute before disappearing down the hallway, his voice already carrying as he called out to others.

The room fell silent for a moment after his departure. Mallah stepped closer to Kiara, her presence grounding and steady. "You're handling this well," she said quietly. "Trust yourself, and the rest will follow. Soon, the others will look to you for advice, your leadership."Kiara swallowed, her nerves threatening to rise again. "I hope you are right. This feels... big. Bigger than me. Bigger than you. Bigger than all of us. All of this."

"It is." Mallah placed a hand on her shoulder, firm but reassuring.

"But that's why you're here."As the sounds of approaching footsteps filled the air, the hum of energy seemed to grow, vibrating in Kiara's chest. She couldn't see the faces that would soon surround her, but she felt their weight, their anticipation. She listened as Mallah talked with Ogma, who she had not realized had been lingering in the hall, before directing everyone else to a nearby room.

Kiara stood and reached for Robyn to assist her, taking a deep breath. She knew, in her heart, that whatever was to come, this was only the beginning, and she needed to be ready.

Nearby, Teddy sat alone in the quiet alcove of the castle library, his shoulders hunched over a steaming mug of tea. His mind replayed the shared dream experience—the moment he had become Tekla. The memory of her strength, her decisiveness, and the sheer clarity of her purpose clashed against his own feelings of inadequacy. How could he, the guy whose life revolved around documenting shadows and cold spots, live up to someone like her?

He traced a finger along the edge of the mug, his mind drifting back to the moment he had felt her presence, as though a thread of his own consciousness had been pulled taut and rewoven into another form. Tekla wasn't just a version of himself; she had her own cadence, her own will. She was him, but not him. And in that dream space, she had felt stronger, freer, bolder than he had ever imagined himself to be.

It had been disorienting at first, like stepping into a room where all the furniture was familiar but rearranged just enough to make him stumble. Yet Tekla had moved with purpose, her every step a deliberate stride toward a goal that Teddy couldn't fully comprehend. She had spoken words he didn't know he knew, wielded powers that felt as ancient as the stars themselves. And through it all, he had watched, half-immersed, half-adrift, as if he were both the vessel and the witness.

He exhaled slowly, pressing the heel of his hand against his temple. The headache that had lingered since waking wasn't just physical—it was emotional, too. Tekla had shown him things, felt things that he hadn't allowed himself to confront. Her fierce determination had been like a flame, illuminating corners of his soul he'd long left in shadow.

What am I supposed to do with this? he thought, frustration curling around the edges of his mind. He wasn't a hero. He wasn't a leader. And yet, Tekla had been all those things and more. The memory of her echoed in his chest, like a heartbeat that wasn't entirely his own. He let out a slow sigh, the tea's warmth doing little to ease the weight in his chest. The sound of hesitant footsteps in the corridor pulled him from his thoughts. A moment later, a dark-haired man poked his head into the room.

"Uh, hey," the man said, his voice tinged with awkwardness. "Sorry to interrupt. I think I might be lost. This place is like a never-ending escape room."

Teddy blinked, the tension in his shoulders easing slightly. "Where are you trying to go?"

"The living quarters," the man replied, stepping fully into the room. He looked around with a curious but wary expression. "I woke up here yesterday and thought I would have a look around, but I guess I zigged when I should've zagged."

Teddy stood, gesturing for him to come closer. "You're not far off. I can show you. Are you new here?"

"Yeah, sort of," the man said, offering a sheepish grin. "I'm Skyler. Skyler Holden"

"Teddy," he replied, shaking Skyler's outstretched hand. "What do you do?"

"Videographer," Skyler said quickly, his gaze darting away. "I, uh... mostly documentary stuff."

Teddy raised an eyebrow, catching the hesitation in Skyler's tone. "Documentary stuff, huh? For whom?"

Skyler's grin turned awkward, and he rubbed the back of his neck. "Uh, you know... groups. Organizations. People who need things filmed. Usually for posterity, I assume, I don't really ask"

Teddy chuckled softly, crossing his arms. "Let me guess. The Order?"

Skyler froze for a beat, his eyes widening slightly before he gave a nervous laugh. "How'd you know?"

Teddy smirked, tapping the device in Skyler's hand. "I keep hearing about them. If I were to guess, we were working with opposing factions that seem to somehow be merging, disbanding, I'm honestly not sure. Either way, I'm a Paranormal investigator. I think we're basically co-workers at this point."

Skyler let out a relieved breath, the tension in his posture easing. "Oh, thank god. I thought I'd already screwed up."

"Nah, you're good," Teddy said, chuckling. "But word of advice?

Maybe work on the whole 'secret agent' act."

Skyler laughed, the sound light and genuine. "Noted. So, paranormal investigator, huh? That sounds... interesting."

"It's a lot of late nights and unexplained noises," Teddy replied with a shrug. "But it has its moments. What about you? What's it like working behind the camera?"

Skyler's grin widened. "Mostly editing out people tripping over their own feet and pretending they know what they're doing. But every now and then, you get something real, and it makes all the hours worth it." He hesitated for a beat. "I'm not supposed to talk about my latest trip. To the Hollow Earth."

Teddy blinked, then gave an impressed nod, his respect for Skyler growing. "Yeah. I heard something about that. Pretty wild."

Skyler chuckled. "Wild doesn't begin to cover it. It's like being dropped into a conspiracy theorist's fever dream—only to find out they were right about half of it."

"That's comforting," Teddy said dryly. "Did you at least get good footage?"

"Some," Skyler admitted. "But most of it was corrupted by the time we surfaced. The energy down there does something to tech. Still, I got enough to make the trip worth the effort. Which is saying A LOT."

They turned down a corridor, their steps echoing in the quiet space. Skyler glanced sideways. "So, what were you doing in there? You seemed pretty deep in thought." Teddy hesitated, unsure how much to share. "Just... processing some stuff. Hard to explain."

Skyler didn't push. "Fair enough. Sometimes it's easier to focus on the weird stuff outside of us than the weird stuff inside."

Teddy smiled faintly, appreciating the sentiment. "You've got that right."

"Comes from years of pretending I'm not in over my head," Skyler said with a grin. "I figure if I keep the camera steady and act like I know what I'm doing, maybe the universe will believe me."

Teddy let out a real laugh at that. "I've been using that same strategy with EMF detectors."

Skyler chuckled. "Weirdly comforting to meet someone else whose job involves faking confidence around high-stakes supernatural events."

They shared a knowing look, an easy kind of understanding that didn't need a lot of words. "You know," Skyler added after a moment, "if we survive all this, we should collaborate. Paranormal docuseries. You hunt ghosts, I make you look good."

Teddy's smirk grew. "If you can keep my hair from looking like I got hit by a static charge, I'm in."

"That's extra," Skyler said, deadpan. "But I'll consider a friends and family discount."

Their conversation was interrupted as they turned a corner and spotted a familiar figure ahead. Scarlett stood with her arms crossed, her sharp eyes narrowing as they approached.

"There you are," she said, her tone brisk. "Everyone's getting ready to meet. We don't want to get left out of this one, trust me." She pointed out as she walked away.

Skyler raised an eyebrow, glancing at Teddy. "Is she always this friendly?"

"Pretty much," Teddy replied, smirking. "Come on, let's not keep them waiting."

As the three of them made their way toward the meeting room, Teddy felt a little of the weight in his chest lift. Skyler's easygoing nature was a welcome distraction—and possibly, something more. For the first time in hours, he didn't feel so alone. Maybe, he thought, this wasn't just about Tekla or himself. Maybe it was about the people he'd meet along the way—and the connections that would make all the difference.

-Chapter 25-

Convergence Point

Once everyone was assembled, Mallah stood at the head of the room, her gaze sweeping over the group. "Before we dive in, let's make sure everyone knows who's here."

She began with a nod toward the broad-shouldered man seated beside Marcus. "This is Pavel Borisovich. He and Marcus go way back to their time spent together working for the Order. They are with us now, so, let's hope their reunion doesn't bring the kind of chaos they were infamous for."

Pavel let out a booming laugh, clapping Marcus on the shoulder. "Chaos? No, no—I'm the picture of innocence. Marcus, though, is always the troublemaker."

Marcus shot back with a smirk.

"Next, we have Chef Cheng Wei," Mallah continued, motioning to a stoic man seated near the edge of the table. Chef gave a polite bow, his sharp eyes scanning the room.

"Just Chef," he said firmly. "And yes, Marcus, I'm here to make sure you don't ruin anything else."

Marcus held up his hands. "I'm on my best behavior this time, I swear."

Mallah gestured toward a sharp-eyed woman with an easygoing smile. "And finally, we have Robyn Kostyantynivna," she announced.

Robyn leaned back in her chair, a grin spreading across her face. "Good luck with that one," she quipped. "Kost-Yan-tye-niv-na. Don't worry, nobody gets it right on the first try. Or the second. Honestly, just stick with Robyn."

Pavel let out a booming laugh, slapping his knee. "Kostyantynivna? That's nothing! In my village, we had names so long they needed a second breath to finish!"

"Not helping, Pavel," Robyn said, rolling her eyes but chuckling along with the group.

Kiara tilted her head slightly, her voice curious. "So, what does it mean?"

"Something about being 'daughter of the steadfast one.'" Robyn replied, waving a hand dismissively. "At least that's what my mom used to say. My dad just called it a mouthful."

Teddy raised an eyebrow, smirking. "I think I'll just stick with Robyn."

"Smart choice," she shot back, grinning, but still sounding somewhat serious. "None of your silly nicknames either."

"I would never." He joked back.

"Robyn's been instrumental in keeping the group... cohesive." Mallah began again, regaining control of the conversation.

Robyn grinned. "Which is just a nice way of saying I keep Scarlett and Teddy from killing each other."

"Scarlett Littlehorn," Mallah continued with a nod toward the calm yet confident woman. "A spirit-talker and healer."

Scarlett gave a warm smile. "I prefer 'spirit wrangler,' but close enough."

"And Teddy Larson," Mallah said, glancing at the towering man sitting beside Scarlett. "Our resident muscle and—"

"And paranormal enthusiast," Teddy interjected with a broad smile, his gaze flicking briefly to Skyler. "Also, a videographer, in case anyone needs proof of the ghosts we'll be encountering."

Mallah's lips twitched in amusement but didn't comment on the exchange. Instead, she turned to the young man with short, groomed hair seated across from Teddy. "Skyler Holden. Who has graciously allowed access to videos from the trip to the Hollow Earth and the events leading up to the pulse."

Skyler gave a brief nod, his demeanor guarded but professional. Teddy's gaze lingered for a moment longer than necessary, though he quickly looked away when Scarlett nudged him under the table.

Mallah's gaze landed on the man sitting near the edge of the table, his imposing presence impossible to ignore. "Next, Juan Cesaro," she said with deliberate calm. "Many of you may likely know him from his days playing American professional football on television. He is another of Marcus and Aron's old friends, a former OAS member, and like them, a key player in this increasingly tangled tale."

Cesaro dipped his head in acknowledgment, his broad shoulders relaxed but his gaze sharp. "Fulfilling my obligations," he said simply, his deep voice carrying the weight of both regret and resolve. "Doing what I should have been doing all along. Trying to help—for real this time."

Aron, who had been quietly listening, cracked a small smile. "Cesaro here used to make defenses have really bad days for fun back in college. Cesaro played quarterback, Marcus was tight end, and I was his favorite wide receiver. Those were the good old days, so to speak—until we all went our separate ways after college; until things changed with the cursed ring that he discovered down in Mexico. Turns out it made him actually turn into a monster."

"Football to Chupacabra… that's a hell of a career pivot," Teddy added, unable to resist a quip. "Bet the scouts didn't see that coming."

A ripple of uneasy laughter spread through the room, broken only by Pavel's booming voice. "And yet, still terrifying on the field—or off it." He clapped Cesaro on the shoulder, though his tone carried genuine warmth. "Good to have you back on our side."

"A lot has happened since then. A lot has changed."

"You can surely say that again, da."

Cesaro met Marcus's gaze across the table, the lingering tension of past mistakes hanging unspoken between them. Marcus nodded slightly, the smallest gesture of reconciliation. "We're here now. That's what matters. I'm sorry for trying to kill you in the Hollow Earth."

"Me too. I feel like I was in a dream for some time, living but not alone in my head."

"Ivyg." Marcus reminded him. "He gets in your head and screws things up in there; controls you like his own puppet."

"Yeah, I don't need to be reminded. All I need you to know is that if you have my back, then I have yours. Okay?"

"Yeah, man. That's definitely okay with me."

Mallah's gaze flickered between them before settling on the group at large. "Ivyg may have turned him once, but Cesaro turned away from the Order to make things right. His abilities—and his experience—are an asset we'll need."

"Experience?" Robyn teased lightly. "You mean fighting against your friends in the Hollow Earth?"

Cesaro's lips quivered into a rare, dry smile. "Consider it practice. A warmup for a greater danger that is yet to come."

Robyn scowled, but she knew it was a moot issue to argue about, with much greater threats on the horizon.

"Next, Kiara Kross," Mallah said, her tone softening as she gestured toward the woman seated next to Aron. "She's—well, let's just say she's been keeping everyone on their toes since she arrived."

Kiara tilted her head, a faint smile tugging at her lips. "Happy to help," she said dryly, her tone carrying a hint of amusement.

"And finally, Aron and Rose O'Keenan," Mallah announced. "Both of them work for me. They spent time growing up here, traveling between Australia, Ireland, and Witchaven itself. Their college years in the United States connected them to many of the key players in this increasingly complicated story."

Aron gave a small nod, his expression serious. "Just trying to make myself useful."

"You've proven yourself many times. We could only ask that you continue to help in our cause. Everyone is here by choice. No one is forced to be here. That is a decision that all must make here and there is no judgment for those who have chosen to decline our offer. And now Rose."

Rose added with a smirk, "I'm mostly here to make sure Aron stays in line."

Everyone laughed at her jest. Aron never took things like that personally, he too laughed, but mostly because he knew it was true. And she had seen the eyes and the way that her brother and Kiara acted around one another. Very protective from an 8-minute older twin, one might think.

Ogma, who had been leaning casually against the wall, straightened with a grin. "And, of course, yours truly. Ogma the magical satyr—keeper of secrets, builder of realms, and occasional babysitter for this lot. Yes, yes, clap your hands. I do love the applause."

The room filled with quiet chuckles before Mallah raised her hand for silence. "Now that everyone's acquainted, let's focus. We have a lot to discuss, and time isn't on our side."

Mallah folded her hands in front of her. "Now that everyone knows who's who, let's get to work. Marcus, you'll have a chance to catch up with Pavel and Chef shortly. But for now, we need to focus on the bigger picture."

The gratitude for their reunion was palpable, adding warmth to the room's otherwise heavy atmosphere. Once the initial greetings settled, Mallah raised her hand slightly, commanding the room's attention. "Before we dive in, I have an update that impacts all of us," she said, her voice steady but weighted. "Kane has been located—sort of. Based on the information he provided, it appears he's somehow, through the Hollow Earth nexus portal, found himself and Dr. Patel's brother flung in the future. This file," she held up a thick folder, "was sent back with a message specifically for you, Marcus."

Marcus's brow furrowed as she passed him the folder, his fingers tightening around it. Clarice rubbed her hands on him for reassurance and support.

"The future?" She said, sounding unsure if it was a question or a statement, her tone a mixture of skepticism and dread. "How is that even possible?"

Mallah offered a faint, knowing smile. "If there's one thing we've learned, Clarice, it's that time is far less linear than we once thought. Your fiancé knows firsthand from his time spent inside of the nexus consciousness. Kane's presence in the future may hold the key to understanding—and potentially averting the chaos Ivyg is preparing to unleash."

Aron leaned back in his chair, arms crossed. "So, what's in the folder? More surprises?"

Marcus hesitated, his hand hovering over the seal. "Guess I'm about to find out."

Before he could open it, Mallah's gaze shifted to Skyler. "Skyler, I've granted you permission to record sensitive aspects of Witchaven for posterity, as agreed for the access to your footage from your recent journey. Let's further discuss how this will go, and then you are free to begin after the meeting."

Skyler nodded, his expression turning serious. "Understood."

Mallah turned her attention to Kiara, her tone softening noticeably. "Now, Kiara. Are you ready to share what you experienced?"

Kiara straightened in her seat, her expression unreadable as she gathered her thoughts. "Yes," she said, her voice steady but laced with anticipation. "But I need everyone here to understand—this isn't just about me. It's about all of us, and what's coming."

The room fell silent, all eyes on her as the weight of her words hung in the air. All eyes turned toward Kiara, who fidgeted slightly under the weight of their attention. Marcus, seated across from her, raised an eyebrow, clearly caught off guard. "Wait, what's this about?"

Kiara exhaled deeply, clasping her hands tightly in her lap. "It's... a lot," she admitted. "But yes, I think I'm ready."

She glanced briefly at Marcus before addressing the room. "Something happened when I passed out—or maybe it was during the ritual. I'm not entirely sure. But it wasn't just a blackout. I was... somewhere else. A dream space, I think. Except it felt real."

She paused, gathering her thoughts. "Marcus, I saw you there—or maybe it was your higher self, or an oversoul. You didn't recognize me, but you said that didn't matter. What mattered was the work we were about to do."

"Me?" Marcus leaned forward, his expression a mix of confusion and intrigue. "That sounds like something I would say, something familiar. Go on..."

Kiara nodded, her voice steadying as she continued. "It felt like months, even years. Every day, you trained me. Physically, mentally, emotionally. You pushed me harder than I thought I could handle, but I kept going. I didn't have a choice. And for the entire time I was there... I could see."

"Not to derail the moment, but does anyone else think she looks skinnier?" Clarice added. "Like, Nexus workouts really pay off, huh? Get it girl."

Mallah blinked and stepped back slightly, tilting her head as she looked Kiara over. "Now that you mention it..." she muttered, as if genuinely assessing.

Aron, clearly caught off guard, ran a hand through his hair before shrugging. "I mean… she did feel bonier when I hugged her earlier, but I wasn't sure. Now that I'm looking, yeah, she might be thinner."

Kiara sighed, her tone dripping with dry humor. "Glad to know my near-death experiences have a silver lining."

Teddy chuckled, holding up his hands. "Hey, just trying to lighten the mood, but it looks like the Nexus gave you more than clarity—it gave you cheekbones."

The room's tension eased slightly as a ripple of laughter broke out.

Mallah allowed herself a small smile. "Well, Kiara, if nothing else, you've proved you can handle pressure—and unwanted comments—with grace. Now, back to the matter at hand."

Her voice faltered, and she looked down briefly before pressing on. "The craziest part of all was that I saw everything. Including you, Aron."

Aron, seated beside her, straightened, surprise flickering across his face. "Me? I was there? What was I doing?"

"No, I mean yes—sort of," Kiara said, her brow furrowing. "You all were. But you weren't moving. You were frozen, sitting around a campfire. It was... strange. It felt like you were waiting for something—or someone. I don't really know what was going on there."

She paused, her fingers tracing the edge of the table as the weight of her words settled over the group. "And then, just before I came back, Rajneel showed up. Marcus talked to him and then sent him back here. Then he, or you, said... he was helping me as a favor for something I did—or will do—for him."

Her voice softened, trembling slightly. "When I woke up, I cried. Not just because I lost my sight again, but because of everything I'd learned. Everything I'd seen. I'm not the same person I was before."

Kiara looked up, her expression thoughtful. "He said I need to go to El Dorado to find my amulet. That I was…meant to go. Whatever comes next, that's where it starts."

Mallah glanced over toward Ogma, who looked toward her in the same instant.

The room fell silent, and Kiara could feel the unspoken tension hanging thick in the air. Her heightened senses caught the faintest shift—Mallah's posture stiffening, a sharp but quickly muted intake of breath, and a pause that seemed deliberate. Though Mallah said nothing, she knew full well that her subtle cues were enough for Kiara to know: Mallah understood exactly what the amulet was.

Kiara turned slightly toward Mallah, her own brow furrowing as she picked up on the silent exchange. She couldn't see Mallah's face, but the slight weight of her gaze seemed to settle on Kiara, a presence that spoke volumes without a word. It wasn't judgment or alarm—it was knowing. Mallah's next words, when they came, were calm and measured, but Kiara heard the layers beneath them.

"It's all coming together now." She said, looking up toward Ogma, who immediately returned her gaze. You've always been drawn to things beyond what you understand, child," Mallah said. "And what you've described aligns with what we already know. The amulet is a crucial piece of the puzzle. Its importance cannot be overstated."

Kiara nodded slowly, sensing the gravity in Mallah's voice. "He said I need to go to El Dorado. Whatever comes next, I know that's where I have to start."

Marcus leaned back in his chair, exhaling deeply. "I don't remember any of this," he admitted, his voice low. "But what you're saying... It feels right. Like a part of me remembers within, even if I don't recall it consciously."

He met Kiara's gaze, his tone softening. "I hope I honored you as much as you make it sound like."

"You did," Kiara replied with a faint smile, her voice tightening with emotion. "You pushed me harder than I thought I could go... but you never broke me."

Marcus nodded, something unspoken passing between them. Then he turned to Aron, his expression serious. "Look, if I promised her I'd help, I will. But you need to promise me something too."

Aron raised an eyebrow, his smirk returning. "What's that?"

"Don't underestimate her," Marcus said firmly. "I've got a feeling we haven't seen half of what she's capable of yet."

Aron held his gaze for a moment before nodding. "Noted." His smirk softened into something more genuine. "I'll try to keep up."

Kiara let out a soft laugh, the tension in her chest loosening slightly. She shifted her ears, focusing them toward Mallah again, still feeling the weight of her unspoken understanding. Whatever Mallah knew about the amulet—and her role in this—it was clear she wasn't going to reveal everything just yet.

Mallah stood, her commanding presence filling the room. "El Dorado may be where this begins," she said, her tone deliberate. "But it is not where it will end. This journey will test all of us. Every step forward brings us closer to the truth—but it also brings us closer to the forces that would see us fail. Make no mistake: there is no room for error."

The room remained quiet for a moment longer, the enormity of Kiara's revelation sinking in. Then Mallah stood, her presence commanding but warm. "Very well," she said. "If El Dorado is where you must go, then let's prepare. That said, we have much more to cover."

Without further explanation, Mallah turned toward the corner of the room, activating an old television set that looked like it hadn't been used in decades. The static hummed to life, filling the silence with a faint crackle.

"Hard pass!" Clarice interjected sharply, her voice cutting through the room like a whip. "I'm not ready to relive any of that."

"I've already seen what I needed to from the footage," Mallah replied evenly, her eyes not leaving the screen. "I only let you all in on that fact so that you know in case you're curious why a film crew will be following me after this meeting."

Clarice crossed her arms, clearly unamused, but said nothing further. Mallah flipped through several channels, her expression sharpening as she stopped on a live news broadcast. Across the bottom of the screen, a scrolling banner read: "Up next: 'Stan Wheeler, CEO, makes announcement at O.A.S. press conference.'"

"Wheeler," Marcus muttered under his breath. "That guy's like a cockroach. He always shows up when there's trouble."

Kiara wiped her eyes, still composed but clearly shaken, as she listened to the anchor finish a segment about a strange creature captured in a suburban neighborhood.

"Again, officials are warning residents not to approach these animals. Instead, call the number below," the anchor advised, her tone grave.

Clarice scoffed, shaking her head. "Approach? They make them all out to be predators."

"They'll study them—or sell them to the highest bidder," Aron said, his voice laced with disdain. His words carried the weight of experience, and the room seemed to shift under the truth of them.

The anchor moved on. "In other news," she continued, "we now go live to Trish Strong, who is attending the press conference called by Stan Wheeler, CEO of Oregon Allied Securities. Mr. Wheeler is expected to take the stage momentarily."

Mallah's eyes remained fixed on the screen, her expression unreadable. The tension in the room thickened as Clarice, Marcus, Cesaro, and the Patels exchanged uneasy glances. Scarlett leaned slightly toward

Skyler, whispering something Kiara couldn't catch.

On the television, the camera panned to the podium, where Stan Wheeler stepped forward, adjusting his tie with practiced ease. His polished demeanor and charming smile seemed almost too perfect, his calculated charisma filling the screen, his presence attracting of attention.

Stan's voice rang out confidently. "We at O.A.S. have long been known for our fearless innovation in the face of adversity. And while we know these are strange times to be living in, we are more committed than ever to securing the safety of our clients, employees, their families, and the global community."

The crowd erupted into applause, the camera cutting briefly to rows of smiling attendees.

Mallah's expression darkened as Stan continued. "In light of recent events," he said, "and the surprise re-emergence of unknown landmasses in the Atlantic and Pacific Oceans, we are pleased to announce that we are working closely with global leaders to explore and secure these new frontiers. Starting with what we are lovingly referring to as 'Atlantis,' we are moments away from setting foot there—possibly for the first time in modern history."

The live feed cut to footage of an expedition team approaching the shoreline. Their movements were confident, their equipment glinting in the sunlight as the waves lapped at the edges of the newly emerged landmass. The sight was both awe-inspiring and unsettling.

"We wanted to share this historic moment with you all," Stan's voice continued, growing more fervent. "And reaffirm our commitment to your safety and well-being. As the global leader in science, healthcare, and technology, it is our mission to establish the first colony, in partnership with scientists and ambassadors worldwide. Our hope is to uncover answers, find common ground, and—who knows? —perhaps even open these lands for future colonization, rewrite the pages of history. Maybe even change the world?"

The logo for OAS passed up on the screen with their slogan "Changing the World, one step at a time."

The room remained silent as applause thundered through the screen once more. Marcus, Cesaro, Pavel, and Scarlett all shook their heads, finally free from the propaganda of the Order. They were disgusted by this blatant spectacle of an event that seemed designed to drown out any critical thought, and for a moment, even the air in the room felt stifling.

Mallah clicked the television off with a sharp flick of her wrist. The sudden silence was almost jarring. "I smell a rat," she muttered, turning back to face the group. "I bet they arrived within hours and that this was all just staged!"

Clarice was the first to speak, her voice heavy with skepticism. "You mean besides the walking PR stunt? This whole thing reeks."

"I tried to stop Kane's machine that he built around the Nexus portal in the Hollow Earth. I didn't know that all of this would happen."

"It's more than that, Marcus." Mallah said, her tone grim. "What Wheeler said was scripted to perfection—but he revealed more than he intended. Their focus on Atlantis is a diversion, though I suspect even he doesn't realize it. All of this was seemingly meant to happen, the excursion to the Hollow Earth, the Pulse, and now this moment here and now where all of you are together at one time. It hasn't happened in centuries. With all that I've seen recently, I'm now believing that all of these things had to occur in order to bring you all here together like this. I'm sure of it."

"So, what are they really after?" Marcus asked, his brow furrowed. "Us?"

"Perhaps yes. Perhaps no. Ivyg has spent centuries planning his ultimate takeover of this planet. We are just pieces on the other side of the chessboard to him, and he is waiting his turn to strike. It's all just a game for him; haven't you all figured it out? The same thing he's always been after," Mallah replied, her eyes narrowing. "Among Ivyg's personal effects… he seeks control. Knowledge. Power. And above all else, leverage."

Kiara shifted slightly in her seat, her voice quiet but firm. "If Atlantis is the diversion, what does that mean for El Dorado?"

"It means we don't have much time," Mallah said, her voice taking on a sharper edge. "Wheeler is a pawn, but the forces behind him are playing a larger game. We need to stay ahead of them—and that begins with retrieving the amulet."

Aron smirked faintly. "And here I thought this was going to be a simple treasure hunt."

Mallah's gaze hardened, her tone leaving no room for misinterpretation. "Nothing about this is simple. We've entered the endgame, and the stakes couldn't be higher. If we fail, the consequences will ripple far beyond this room."

The gravity of her words settled over the group, uniting them in their shared determination. Whatever awaited them, they knew the path forward would be anything but easy.

"This is all Kane's fault," Marcus growled, shaking his head. His fist clenched on the table, the frustration in his voice sharp and unyielding.

"It would be easy to assume that" Mallah replied, her tone measured, "but I assure you there's more at play."

"With all that's happened, something feels off," Clarice said, glancing at Marcus. "Those goons work for Ivyg. Obviously, they're trying to stake their claim."

"Exactly," Mallah confirmed, her hands clasped behind her back, her voice taking on a hard edge. "Without going into detail, Kane and I go back a long way. While we rarely saw eye to eye, this 'Pulse' has Ivyg and The Order written all over it. This wasn't an accident—nor was their rapid response team swooping in to 'save the day.' The only reason they haven't attempted this on the other landmass is because of a treaty even Ivyg knows better than to break."

Her words hung in the air, heavy with implication. Then she straightened and continued, her tone shifting slightly. "This leads me to the reason I brought you all here."

She gestured toward a monitor as a map of Cairo appeared on the screen. "The Citadel of Saladin in Cairo, Egypt was destroyed this morning," she said gravely. "We have no clues as to who did it or why. It was another home of historical documents and artifacts, many of which appear to have been heavily burned or destroyed by the bomb blast. The only video evidence came from an ATM camera across the street, capturing three individuals seemingly walking into a lamp post and vanishing. The camera angle wasn't ideal, and their features are difficult to make out, but the flash of light as they disappeared was unmistakable."

Mallah's gaze lingered on the screen, her tone sharpening. "It's Vril energy. Someone who knows how to tap into it. A dangerous set of individuals, indeed."

The weight of her words was amplified by the sudden arrival of two men. One carried a small device, which he placed on the table before activating it. The other sat beside Mallah, opening a laptop and syncing the device to the screen. An image of the National Library of India in Alipore, Kolkata, appeared next.

"That was the largest library in India," Mallah continued, her voice cracking slightly as emotion broke through her usual composure. "Formerly the Imperial Library. One of my favorites left standing. It was home to profound works—national treasures. It was destroyed in another terrorist attack this morning. A terrible loss of life and knowledge."

Kiara, seated nearby, stood and instinctively reached out, offering a comforting embrace. Mallah, momentarily vulnerable, accepted the gesture with grace before turning back to the group.

"The epicenter," Mallah said, motioning to the image on the screen, "was here." "Should we be worried?" Kiara, still seated, broke the silence with the question, her voice steady but laced with concern.

Robyn, visibly shaken, crossed her arms tightly. Having grown up in Ukraine, she had seen more than her share of violence, and this hit far too close to home. Fighting back her emotions, she rewound the footage on the screen for Pavel and his group to analyze.

Pavel leaned forward, his expression grim. After a moment, he gave a curt nod. "Teleportation," he said with the clipped precision of his native Russian roots. "And I know the man responsible."

Everyone turned toward him, startled by his certainty. Pavel reached for his satellite phone, dialing with practiced efficiency. Three calls later, he set the device down with a heavy sigh.

"He goes by the alias 'Chet'," he continued, his accent becoming slightly thicker as he slipped into the weight of old memories. "Like me, he is man... displaced in time. Another product of Russian Army's cold war madness—experiments meant to advance science, da, but left men broken."

He paused, his voice hardening. "When I arrived here, far from war, I wanted peace. Chet, he went back to what he knew. Could not break programming. These time-travel projects—they were abandoned in record, but many scientists from Russia... from Germany... they ran to Americas. Operation Paperclip. I have lived through both wars—the Cold one and the one they pretend is not still happening."

His eyes darkened as he leaned forward. "War is stupidity. What they did to us? It was wrong. But without it—I would not be here. And now I am warning you: Chet is aiding terrorists. OAS—these people you think legitimate? They are only front. A shiny face. Below... they work in shadows. Energy, politics, markets, even charities. All corrupted. Always mask. Always manipulation."

Robyn's voice cut through the room like a whip, her native Ukrainian accent stronger than usual as her emotions flared. "Your friends told me you worked with the Order. You sure this isn't same game... just new players?"

Pavel turned to her, eyes sharp. He responded in Russian—testing her. "Ты веришь в эту историю, которую они тебе рассказывают?"

(Ty verish' v etu istoriyu, kotoruyu oni tebe rasskazyvayut?)Do you believe this story they're telling you?

"I do," she replied in Russian, her voice calm but resolute. "Я делаю."

(Ya delayu.)Pavel tilted his head, his voice dropping just slightly, almost amused. "Без обид... но ты, кажется, не тот тип."

(Bez obid... no ty, kazhetsya, ne tot tip.)No offense... but you don't seem the type.

"I'm not soldier," she shot back in English, her tone sharp and accented, "but I will fight for what is right."

Pavel's voice softened a notch, though his words were still edged with warning. "Never fight not knowing your cause. Never fight not knowing who you fight for. And always get paid."

Robyn narrowed her eyes, switching back to English with a hiss. "So, you're nothing but mercenary. Freelance. Who goes to highest bidder?"

The room fell still. Even Scarlett and Kiara exchanged glances—they'd never heard this side of Robyn before.

Pavel smirked faintly. "Don't be so pish-posh, lady," he muttered, reverting to his usual tone. "I am here now, yes? That says something. I defected. Like your friends. The Order will hunt me until I die. But better that than serve them."

"You choose freedom now," Robyn replied, her voice quieter but no less firm. "I hope you mean it."

Pavel held her gaze a moment longer, then nodded. "Freedom is all I have left."

"I do. (ya delayu)"

"No offense, but you don't seem the type. (bez obid, no ty, kazhetsya, ne tot tip)"

"I'm not a soldier, but I will fight for what is right. (YA ne soldat, no ya budu borot'sya za to, chto pravil'no)"

"Never fight without knowing your cause, never fight without knowing who you are fighting for, and always get paid. (nikogda ne srazhaytes', ne znaya svoyego dela, nikogda ne srazhaytes', ne znaya, za kogo vy srazhaytes', i vsegda poluchayte oplatu)"

Without missing a beat, Robyn replied in kind, her voice cold, speaking English. "So, you are nothing more than a mercenary. A freelancer for hire to the highest bidder?"

The room fell silent, the tension palpable. They had never seen Robyn like this before—sharp, commanding, and entirely unyielding, a fire in her eye.

Pavel smirked slightly, but there was no humor in his expression. "Oh, don't be all pish-posh about it, lady," he said, his tone light but his eyes wary. "I'm here now, aren't I? Does that not mean something? I defected, just like your friends did, from the Order. The Grand Emissary and his acolytes will no doubt search for us until the day we die. I have no other choice. Enemy of my enemy is now my friend. That is life."

"We all see where your loyalties lie," Robyn replied, her tone icy as she leaned back, arms still crossed.

"Freedom is where my loyalty lies." He said curtly back, feeling no need to pursue it further, waving her off with his hand in frustration. "You of all people should know about the struggle of freedom."

Robyn moved like she was about to launch her modelesque body at him, curled up like a serpent ready to pounce on its prey.

"Enough!" Mallah, who had been observing the exchange in silence, finally spoke, her voice cutting through the tension like a blade. "There are larger forces at play here, and we don't have the luxury of in-fighting. Pavel, your insights are valuable, but let me be clear: trust is earned, not given freely."

Pavel nodded solemnly, the weight of her words settling over him. "Understood."

Mallah turned to the group, her expression resolute. "We are in the midst of a 5D chess game, and every move matters. Prepare yourselves— this is only the beginning."

"What do we know?" Rose asked.

"As of now…" Mallah interrupted, her tone commanding. "Six people have been confirmed dead and dozens injured, some severely, during the blast. The explosion destroyed a large portion of one wing of the building. No official suspects have been identified yet, though officials are following up on all leads. If anyone has information…"

"You suspect Ivyg has something to do with this, don't you?" Kiara asked, her voice quiet but steady. "Or someone working for him in the OAS?"

"It is highly likely," Mallah replied, her gaze unwavering. "His heart is full of contempt, jealousy, and vengeance. I do not know what his intentions for this are, but I suspect no good will come of it. And if what I've been told is beginning to come true—if the threads are converging as I think they are—then we are indeed in for some trouble. This is only just getting started."

The room tensed at her words, the gravity of the situation settling over everyone. Marcus whispered to Clarice, perhaps words of comfort. She laid her head on his arm.

"Ivyg is not one to make idle threats," Mallah continued, her voice lowering. "And while his actions often appear calculated, his true motives are rarely obvious. What is unusual is his desire for anonymity. If this attack was his doing, we need to uncover his intentions."

"Sounds to me like he wants to take over the world!" Kiara joked, though her nervous laughter did little to lighten the mood.

"That's our concern as well. The time of the prophecy has come upon us."

A moment later, the device on the table emitted a soft chime, and a holographic image flickered to life once again in the center of the room. It displayed a map of a vast landmass surrounded by shimmering blue waters.

"Known by many names throughout history," Mallah began, "Dilmun, Tamil, Mu, and in modern times, Lemuria. Once operational, this continent is entirely self-sustained. It has been inhabited for over 200,000 years and consists of 113 islands surrounding the mainland. In total, it is nearly twice the size of Atlantis and is actually ready for colonization."

Marcus leaned forward, studying the map intently. "How many people are living there already? If it's that old, I'd expect it to be pretty crowded."

Mallah shook her head. "Aside from the occasional drifter who stumbles upon one of the outlying islands—those that remained above sea level—almost no humans have occupied these lands in over 10,000 years. Currently, there are a few refugees who were lost at sea, now occupying the ancient ruins left by the last generation of mankind. And, of course, there are other intelligent beings who call this place home."

"Other beings?" Cesaro asked, his curiosity piqued.

"Creatures that have evolved alongside humans," Mallah replied. "Some you might recognize from myth. Others… you wouldn't."

Kiara tilted her head, her brow furrowed. "What happened to them? What happened to Lemuria?"

Mallah's expression softened, her voice taking on a wistful tone. "Most left before the embargo. Of those who remained, many evolved beyond the need for physical form long ago."

Kiara's lips parted, surprise flickering across her face. "Yet they choose to call someone a 'Queen'?" she asked, the disbelief in her voice apparent.

Mallah smiled faintly. "That was never what they actually termed or thought of your role as. The point of the title was to use a word that would resonate with our descendants, our neighbors—those less enlightened. In many periods, such a title was the closest equivalent to 'Ambassador' or 'Representative.' Without a title of high status, you would not have been able to forge the relationships and alliances necessary to aid them."

Kiara frowned, processing Mallah's explanation but clearly unconvinced. Around the room, subtle glances were exchanged. Pavel raised an eyebrow at Marcus, who tilted his head slightly as if to say, Are you hearing this too? Scarlett leaned closer to Robyn, whispering something inaudible but clearly curious. Teddy, on the other hand, looked intrigued, mouthing the word Ambassador to himself like it carried weight he couldn't quite place.

The atmosphere grew heavier as the implications settled, though some appeared more confused than others. Aron's gaze flickered toward Kiara, a faint smirk tugging at the corner of his mouth as though he was the only one unfazed by the layered meaning in Mallah's words.

"This might be a stupid question," Cesaro interjected suddenly, breaking the tension, "but… what's an embargo?"

Mallah's smile returned, this time warmer. "It's an official ban—

placed on coming or going somewhere," she explained gently.

"Why was it banned?" Kiara asked, her curiosity rekindled.

"It wasn't specifically banned, not on its own," Mallah replied, her tone growing somber. "But after what you would call 'The War of the Gods,' the Titanomachy, the entire planet was placed under restriction. The Council deemed it critical to preserve certain areas—places of immense historical and spiritual importance—for future generations. These lands were hidden away, to be rediscovered when humanity was humbled enough to be trusted with technology and ready to remember its origins."

"Like Antarctica?" Aron guessed.

"And let me guess," Scarlett added dryly. "Atlantis?"

Mallah's gaze shifted to Scarlett, her expression softening. "Good to hear from you. But alas, no. Atlantis was a twice-failed experiment. It wanted to be its own nation and might have succeeded had its leaders respected the laws of nature as they were reminded to, time and again. Though it is still a home to a great amount of energy from the planet, and that's what makes it dangerous."

"Dangerous?" Clarice asked. "How is it dangerous?"

"If Ivyg and the OAS make Atlantis their home base, they will be able to enact his final plans of world domination, unleashing the Titans from their banishment in the pits of Tartarus, under the ice sheet of Antarctica." She paused, a trace of bitterness creeping into her voice. "Ever hear the expression 'nuke and pave'? That's what happened. All that remains of Atlantis is a barren wasteland, a layer of dust covering ruins and fragments of deconstructed technology buried in underground tombs."

The room fell silent, the weight of Mallah's words pressing down on everyone. For a moment, the only sound was the faint hum of the device on the table.

"So," Marcus said finally, his voice quiet but steady, "what are they looking for there now?"

"Desperation breeds delusion," Mallah said simply. "They're chasing ghosts, but they don't realize it yet. The energy is still there, but the technology is long gone and forgotten to time. What concerns me isn't what they hope to find in Atlantis—it's what they'll do when they fail."

Kiara's voice cut through the silence, soft but firm. "Then we have to make sure we don't fail first."

Mallah nodded, her expression one of quiet determination. "Precisely."

"That's their play then?" Clarice confirmed, perking up as though she had figured everything out.

"Yes and no, there is nothing there for them, but they don't know that…which is precisely why The Order have assured they were the first to arrive. Let them dig all they want; there is nothing left to find."

"So, what are we doing here? If Atlantis has nothing for them and they know better than to invade Lemuria, why do we care what they do?" Marcus asserted.

"Letting them pick through the bones buys us some time, but not long." Mallah explained, her tone measured but laced with urgency. "Once it is discovered that what they are looking for is no longer there, they will move to Plan B. The primary concern is that Witchaven has also been made visible. I strongly suspect it will be discovered soon, if it hasn't already. That puts us—everyone and everything we've built here—at risk. We cannot wait for that to happen."

A ripple of unease passed through the room. Even those who had known Witchaven's secrets for years seemed to feel the weight of Mallah's words.

"Our priority," she said, her voice steady but resolute, " is to transport our residents to Lemuria, the only safe haven left on this planet. Ogma and I have met and agreed to begin evacuations as soon as I return from scouting potential settlement areas, however, we face challenges. With everything happening, there hasn't been time to finalize a plan for where we will establish ourselves. And once we arrive, there will be no power beyond our generators until the key is recovered and we figure out where it goes."

Mallah's gaze landed squarely on Kiara. She extended a hand toward her, her tone softening. " That is where you come in, Kiara."Kiara blinked, caught off guard. "Why me?" she asked, her voice tinged with surprise and apprehension.

Mallah took a step closer, her expression both gentle and commanding. "Your destiny awaits in El Dorado," she said simply. Her words carried a weight that made the air seem heavier.

"The amulet you were told to seek out," Mallah continued, "is no ordinary trinket. It is a very specific and highly significant, sophisticated jewel, once belonging to a Priestess who miraculously obtained it as a child. She went on to provide counsel to the ruler of El Dorado until the city was buried and abandoned. As Conquistadors closed in, the residents destroyed the only known entrance to their ancient home to protect it from discovery." Mallah paused, letting the gravity of her words settle over the room.

Kiara frowned, her mind racing. "But how are we supposed to get in?" she asked, her voice laced with both curiosity and doubt.

Mallah's lips curled into a faint smile, a rare glimmer of humor breaking through her otherwise solemn demeanor. "Through an entrance only accessible from the Hollow Earth," she replied, her tone almost playful.

The room erupted with murmurs of disbelief and questions. Kiara, however, remained quiet, her thoughts swirling. Mallah's attention lingered on her for a moment longer, her piercing gaze seeming to see far beyond what was visible. There was a brief flicker of something—an understanding, an unspoken connection—that passed between them. It was subtle but unmistakable, even to Kiara, who couldn't see Mallah's expression but could feel the shift in her energy.

This wasn't just about the amulet, Kiara realized. Mallah knew something more—something she wasn't saying, at least not yet. The weight of that unspoken knowledge settled heavily in Kiara's chest, adding to the enormity of what was being asked of her.

"Kiara," Mallah said softly, her tone reassuring despite the gravity of the moment, "we'll speak more about this later. For now, know that you are the key to ensuring we have a future. Trust yourself, and trust that you were chosen for a reason."Kiara nodded slowly, her hands tightening around the edge of her chair. She didn't have the words to respond, but the determined set of her jaw spoke volumes.

Mallah turned her attention back to the group, her commanding presence returning. "We don't have time to waste. Preparations must begin immediately. Ogma and I will oversee the logistics of the migration, but the success of this mission rests on all of us."The room fell into a tense silence, the enormity of the task ahead looming over them. For Kiara, the path forward was clearer than ever—however daunting it might be.

"FUUUCK THAT!" Clarice shouted, springing to her feet, her voice reverberating through the room.

Mallah's sharp gaze turned to her, unflinching. "Bold of you to assum you were even invited," she snapped back, her tone cool yet commanding. With a pointed gesture, she insisted, "Sit down, Clarice. You, Marcus, and Cesaro will be heading to Wellville immediately.

Your task is to connect with Linda Williams and Katherine O'Brien. Kane believes they've each uncovered fragments of the truth about the Whisperers and other anomalies tied to Ivyg. Together, they could provide invaluable insights into what we're dealing with."

Ogma stepped forward, his tone calm but firm. "I'll take you back with me, from there you will head to the Portland airport, where you will fly to Colorado. From there, you'll drive to Wellville and begin your investigation. Mallah will arrange for accommodations and ensure you have what you need to follow the trail. You leave tonight."

Clarice plopped back into her seat with a huff, muttering something under her breath, though the words were lost to the room.

"What is it, Rose?" Mallah asked, her tone softening slightly as the redhead raised her hand to interject.

Rose tilted her head, her vibrant hair catching the light as she spoke. "I know the area well and have extensive experience with creatures from the Veil. Considering how crazy it is out there; I'd like to assist the team." Her words were confident, though her expression held a touch of mischief.

Mallah's eyebrows lifted in surprise as she glanced between Rose and the others, gauging their reactions. None seemed opposed, though Kiara offered a slight nod, and Marcus looked thoughtful.

"Plus," Rose added with a grin, "I know where we parked."

The room broke into a ripple of soft laughter, even Mallah's lips twitching into a brief, almost imperceptible smile. "Granted," she said briskly, acknowledging Rose with a nod before continuing.

"Since Pavel can teleport," Mallah went on, "he will escort Aron and Kiara to Peru, where they'll meet up with Zenobia, who will act as their guide. The rest of you will assist Ogma with the migration efforts—both for Witchaven and Ogma's realm in Oregon."

The room quieted as her words sank in. Mallah's eyes scanned the gathered group, her expression firm. "Does that answer everyone's questions?"

Ogma looked around to notice Marcus reviewing the file before him, responding strangely to her prompt, as if debating on whether or not to speak. As if feeling the weight of his stare, Marcus looked up at him briefly, before returning his gaze back toward the information

All heads nodded except Cesaro's. He sat back in his chair, his brows furrowed, a shadow of disappointment crossing his features.

Rose noticed and turned to him with a curious glance. "What's wrong?" she asked gently.

Cesaro hesitated, his shoulders sagging slightly before he sighed. "Nothing. I'll help wherever I'm needed," he said, though his tone lacked its usual energy.

Before anyone else could respond, one of the tech-savvy men who had entered earlier cleared his throat from across the room. "Actually, Mallah," he said, glancing up from his laptop, "we've been monitoring activity near Wellville as you requested. Something caught our attention."

The second man spun his chair around, an amused grin on his face as he added, "A motel outside Wellville has had… anomalies. Strange guests, inexplicable power surges, and a very particular energy signature that matches Marcus's and Kiara's recent, let's call them, adventures."

Mallah's brow arched, a rare flicker of surprise crossing her usually composed features. "Go on."

The first man gestured to the screen in front of him, clearly enjoying his moment in the spotlight. "We've booked rooms for Marcus, Cesaro, and Rose at the same location to investigate. The tickets were updated, and flights are all set."

Marcus blinked. "That fast? I'm a tech guy myself and even I'm impressed."

The second techie shrugged nonchalantly, leaning back in his chair. "You have your job. This is what we do."

Mallah let out a soft, almost incredulous laugh, shaking her head. "Well, I suppose I shouldn't be surprised, but..." She trailed off, a wry smile tugging at her lips. "You two are dangerously efficient. Remind me to double-check what else you're researching."

"Only the good stuff, ma'am," one of them quipped, grinning.

"Right," Mallah said dryly, though the glimmer of pride in her eyes betrayed her tone. She turned back to the group. "Well, it seems your accommodations and travel plans are already set. Efficient as that was,

I'll admit this whole online booking business still mystifies me."

"I'll show you sometime." Marcus told her.

"Either way," she said, gesturing toward him, "you've got everything you need. No excuses."

Pavel clapped Marcus on the shoulder with a grin. "No pressure. Just saving the world instead of breaking it. Easy, yes?"

Mallah's lips twitched into a smile again as the room relaxed briefly, even under the weight of their task.

Marcus shrugged on his jacket and put the envelope into his inside pocket for safekeeping, its contents from a private investigator contacting him about brothers from another mother, as ironic as that sounded. The door swung open to reveal Rose and Cesaro. She immediately wrinkled her nose in exaggerated disgust. "Wow, this room smells like sweaty sex," she teased, her voice dripping with mock disapproval.

Marcus raised an eyebrow, but before he could respond, Rose smirked. "You know, the stork is the bird that brings the baby, but a swallow is the one to prevent it."

Cesaro, mid-sip from his travel mug, choked, coughing violently as he fought to keep from spitting out his drink. Rose laughed, patting his back as he wheezed, his face turning an impressive shade of beet red.

"You're gonna kill me one day," Cesaro managed between coughs, still laughing.

"Just keeping things lively," Rose replied with a wink, earning an exasperated shake of the head from Marcus and a smirk from Clarice.

Once Cesaro had composed himself, Ogma appeared, his familiar set of magical keys in hand. With a deft turn of the ornate silver key, he reopened Marcus and Clarice's room into a shimmering portal leading to his pocket universe. As the portal shimmered open, Ogma glanced at Marcus, his sharp eyes narrowing slightly.

"You've been looking at that envelope like it's about to jump out of your hands," Ogma remarked, his tone light but curious. "Anything in there you'd like to share?"

Marcus hesitated, gripping the folder a little tighter. "Not yet. I need more time to process it."

Ogma shrugged, a knowing smirk tugging at the corners of his mouth. "Suit yourself, but don't wait too long. The clock's ticking, and answers have a way of slipping through your fingers if you let them."

Without further comment, Marcus followed the group as they stepped through the portal door, emerging on the other side in the same Witchaven antechamber they had used earlier. Rose, now familiar with the layout, led them through the tunnels and back to the parked vehicle waiting outside.

Rose's SUV hummed steadily as the group headed toward the Interstate, Portland-bound to catch their flight to Colorado. Clarice sat in the backseat, half-asleep, while Rose chatted idly with Cesaro, who was driving. Marcus sat in the passenger seat, his eyes scanning the road ahead.

Suddenly, his gaze sharpened, and he sat up straighter. "Hey, slow down," he said, tapping Cesaro's arm. "Those vans up there. I recognize them."

Cesaro leaned forward, squinting. "The hippie mobiles? Aren't those the ones we passed in the woods, on our way to see Ogma?"

Marcus nodded. "Yeah. Same vans, same paint jobs…except that pickup."

As they drew closer, the situation came into focus. The brightly colored vehicles were parked in a chaotic line along the side of the road, the pickup not far ahead. A group of people stood near the tree line, their raised voices carrying over the sound of the van's engine. In the center of the commotion was a small, frightened creature tangled in a net.

"Pull over," Clarice said sharply, now fully awake. Her tone left no room for debate.

Cesaro obliged, easing the van onto the shoulder. Clarice and Rose were out before the engine had fully stopped, striding toward the group with determined expressions. Marcus followed close behind.

"What's going on here?" Clarice demanded, her voice cutting through the arguing.

A wall of people stood between the creature and the man aiming a rifle toward them.

"This thing attacked us," he said, gesturing to the creature in the net.

"It looks terrified, not aggressive," Rose shot back, stepping closer. "Let it go."

The man sneered. "Not a chance. We don't know what it is. Could be dangerous."

Clarice's eyes narrowed as her right hand started to turn blue. She took another step forward. "Put. The gun. Down."

The tension thickened as the man's grip on the rifle tightened. Before he could say anything else, a low growl rumbled behind the group. Heads turned as Cesaro approached, his normally easy-going demeanor replaced by something far more primal. His eyes glowed faintly red, and his limbs began to elongate, claws emerging from his fingertips. Within moments, his body shifted into a monstrous form. The burly man froze, his face going pale. The rifle slipped from his hands and hit the ground with a thud.

Marcus stepped in, his tone calm but firm. "I suggest you leave. Now."

The man and his companions didn't need to be told twice. They scrambled to their vehicles and sped off, leaving behind the net, the creature, and an air of stunned silence.

Cesaro exhaled deeply, his form shifting back to normal. He ran a hand through his hair, his breathing heavy. "I hate doing that," he muttered.

"But it worked," Rose said, giving him a pat on the shoulder.

Clarice crouched by the net, carefully freeing the small creature. "You're safe now," she said softly. The creature chirped once before darting into the woods.

Additional friends of the people protecting the creature began pouring out of the vans, who had watched the entire scene from a distance, hesitantly approached. Their leader, a young man with a tie-dye gaiter around his neck, raised his hands in a gesture of peace. "Thank you."

"You're welcome" Clarice said, glancing back toward Cesaro, who was already making his way back to the car, her tone firm but measured. "And you're going to keep what you saw here a secret. Understand?"

The hippies nodded fervently. "We promise."

"Good," Marcus said. "Now get going."

As the hippies piled back into their vans and drove off, Rose turned to Cesaro. "I've got to admit, that was impressive."

Cesaro shrugged, looking uncomfortable. "Desperate times."

Clarice smirked. "Well, you've definitely got a talent for scaring people. But maybe next time, warn us before you go full cryptid."

The group laughed as they returned to the van. As Rose started the engine, Marcus glanced at the road ahead, his expression thoughtful.

"We've got a long drive," he said. "Let's hope it's less eventful from here."

"Don't jinx it," Rose muttered, leaning back in her seat.

The van pulled back onto the highway, the group settling into a tense but hopeful silence as they continued toward their destination.

A few hours later, the team arrived at Portland International Airport, where they would park in the garage next, follow down an escalator to the ticket counters, and check in for the next flight out to Colorado, giving them just enough time to get through TSA and even have a bite on the concourse before their flight would depart in just about an hour.

As they sat down at their gate, Marcus turned toward Rose, curious about why she had decided to join them. He had known her since they were teenagers, yet had never spent time around her without her brother being present, begging the question as to why she chose to go with them. After finishing the last bite of a burrito she had grabbed along the way, Rose explained that while she was coming around to the idea of Kiara, she was still feeling a bit protective of her brother and surprised that he was so keen on someone so quickly. She went on to explain how obvious it had become that the feeling was mutual, and that anyone in their presence would be subjected to the inevitable affections between the two, of which she was not remotely interested in observing.

"I'm glad some people get to find people they love, but that has not exactly been my experience…so I would already be grossed out, the fact that it's my brother makes it an extra hard pass!" She insisted, to which Cesaro related as he nodded his head in agreement.

"What's with the dark sunglasses and shit?" she asked him.

"Don't worry about it…" he answered, winking back at her.

"How long has it been since you played pro ball?" Marcus asked, reminding Rose.

"Too long!" Cesaro smiled back.

"I think it's cute that Sparky found someone so amazing!." Clarice said in a slightly pointed tone aimed at Rose, sounding particularly British in the process.

"Must be special in more ways than one, eh?!?" Cesaro grinned, shoulder checking Marcus while making a joke about Aron.

Rose rolled her eyes in response, chuckling as she looked away.

Cesaro felt bad for trying to kill his friend within the Hollow Earth, previously, and sought to make amends by atoning for his misdeeds. What neither Marcus nor Clarice knew was the deprograming that had taken place for the former professional football star who had been under the psychic influence of Ivyg, known for his ability to use people like puppets that he could bend until they broke at his will.

Clarice had hardly seen him since they had been brought back to the surface and when she did see him, it came at the price of a slap across his face, followed by a huge hug. This may have seemed like contradictory signals, but even she knew how close Marcus and he had been for so many years. It wasn't like Juan to act like that. He looked guilty, knowing why she was still harboring some resentment. He had no excuses for his behavior and didn't bother to insult her intelligence with a bunch of made-up nonsense.

The only thing he could offer the two of them was a vow to do his best to never fall under the influence of that evil Draconian man ever again and to do everything he could to stop him from hurting others on his path to world domination.

-Chapter 27-   Elysium

Morning came too quickly for Aron, who hadn't slept a wink. While most of the group had found at least periods or moments of rest, he'd spent the night meticulously sorting through equipment and supplies. It wasn't just about being prepared; it was about making sure they were ready for anything.

"I packed enough essentials for a week," Aron said, his voice slightly hoarse as he adjusted the strap on one of the sturdy backpacks now lined up neatly on the dock. "Light enough to carry, but with everything we might need: water filtration, medical kits, rations, and tools."

Kiara, standing beside him, tilted her head slightly in his direction. "You didn't sleep, did you?" she asked, her tone somewhere between amused and concerned.

"I figured you needed it more," Aron replied with a shrug, glancing at her. "And someone had to make sure we weren't walking into the unknown unprepared."

Kiara offered him a faint smile, grateful for his effort. She had slept, though it had been restless and punctuated by fragments of dreams she couldn't quite recall. Still, it had been enough to recharge her for what lay ahead.

Pavel strolled up, his usual casual demeanor intact, though his sharp eyes took in every detail of the packs Aron had assembled. "Efficient," he said with a nod, pulling the strap of his own pack tighter across his chest. "I approve."

"I wasn't exactly looking for approval," Aron muttered, though a small, tired grin tugged at the corner of his mouth.

"Good thing you got it anyway," Pavel quipped, raising a hand, gesturing for them to gather close. "All right, kids, time to make magic happen. Everyone ready?"

Kiara took a deep breath, her hands gripping the straps of her pack. "As ready as I'll ever be," she said softly.

Pavel nodded, tapping at the device on his wrist. "Zen's dock it is. She'll know we're coming."

"You're sure about that?" Aron asked.

Pavel gave him a sly grin. "Zen and I go way back. She'll know."

The shimmering air of Witchaven began to dissolve around them, replaced by the humid embrace of salty, sunlit air. Kiara blinked against the brightness, her senses adjusting to the sudden shift. The dock beneath her feet swayed gently with the movement of the water, and in the distance, a sleek ivory structure jutted out of the mountainside, gleaming against the emerald jungle.

The air around them shimmered briefly as Pavel's teleportation dissolved the dense foliage of Witchaven into a humid, salty breeze. Aron and Kiara blinked against the sudden brightness of the sun, now high above the glittering waters of the Pacific. They stood on a narrow dock stretching out from an island. In the distance, a sleek, ivory structure rose out of the mountainside like a crown, its polished surfaces gleaming against the rich green jungle.

"Welcome to Zenobia's domain," Pavel said with a smirk, his thick accent coloring his words. "We are currently off the Atlantic coast of Honduras and Nicaragua, in international waters. It's very beautiful here. She has a way of making an impression, no? This little island of sin."

Kiara tilted her head, feeling the warmth of the sun on her skin and the faint vibration of life all around her. Though her blindness rendered her unable to see the grandeur of the place, the energy it radiated was palpable—luxurious, alluring, almost intoxicating.

"She calls this her retreat," Aron muttered, crossing his arms. "Looks more like a billionaire's dream mansion."

"She is... particular," Pavel replied, his smirk widening. "and her clientele are elite. Follow me."

The path from the dock was winding, bordered by flowering vines and the occasional marble statue, until it led them to a grand veranda perched high above the ocean. A helicopter idled on a helipad to one side, its blades silent but ready. The air smelled faintly of hibiscus, incense, and something richer—like molten chocolate and crushed berries.

Zenobia appeared at the top of the wide staircase leading down to greet them. She was stunning, her tall frame draped in a flowing gown that shimmered like liquid gold. Her dark hair tumbled in loose waves over her shoulders, and her lips curled into a smile that seemed both welcoming and knowing.

"Pavel," she called out, her voice low and melodic, "you've brought me new guests. Delightful."

Kiara felt a shift in the energy as Zenobia descended. It wasn't just the elegance of her presence—there was something else, a subtle pull in the air, as if the life force of the space itself was bending toward her.

Zenobia embraced Pavel first, holding him close as she whispered something Kiara nor the others could hear. As they parted, Kiara felt a faint ripple, like a thread of energy flowing from Pavel to Zenobia. It was so quick, so practiced, she almost doubted it had happened.

When Zenobia turned her attention to Aron, her smile widened. "Aron," she said, extending her hands. Aron hesitated for half a beat before stepping forward, his usual composure slipping under her gaze. She pulled him into a brief hug, and again, Kiara felt the faint ripple, the absorption of something unseen.

Finally, Zenobia approached Kiara, her steps slow and deliberate. "And you must be Kiara," she said, her voice soft but commanding. She took Kiara's hands, her grip warm and firm. "You're as remarkable as they said."

Kiara tensed as Zenobia embraced her. This time, the pull was undeniable—a gentle but deliberate siphoning of energy that left her chest faintly hollow. As they parted, Zenobia brushed Kiara's cheek with her fingertips. "You'll do just fine," she said enigmatically.

Pavel cleared his throat, breaking the moment. "Zen, we'll need the helicopter."

"Of course," Zenobia replied breezily, gesturing toward the helipad. "But first, let's talk inside. You've come a long way, and there's much to prepare for."

Zenobia's opulent palace radiated decadence, a labyrinth of gleaming marble floors and statues, intricate gold accents, and towering glass walls that framed panoramic views of the ocean. The moment they stepped inside, the air seemed to shift, filled with the mingling scents of mango, coconut, and a faintly floral undertone that lingered like a whisper. It was almost intoxicating.

Kiara inhaled deeply, tilting her head. "It smells like a department store... but, you know, one with better taste. Mango, coconut, and money."

Aron stifled a laugh, but Zen grinned widely. "You flatter me, darling. Elysium prides itself on an immersive experience."

The grand foyer buzzed with quiet energy as staff moved gracefully between tasks—polishing surfaces, arranging exotic flowers, and delivering drinks on silver trays. Kiara couldn't see their faces, but the hum of their energetic signatures intrigued her. Most felt human, but here and there, faint flares of something different—aura patterns more intricate and layered—hinted at beings far older and more powerful than they appeared.

Pavel, taking in the scene, leaned closer to Aron and muttered, "This place could use a reality show. 'Paradise for Sale.' Or maybe... 'Zenobia's Den.'" His smirk was wicked, earning an eye-roll from Aron.

Zen turned toward him with a playful glare. "Pavel, you rascal, as much as I'd love the drama, my business runs on professionalism. Every staff member here—housekeepers, landscapers, chefs, entertainers, even the escorts—is highly vetted, well-compensated, and fully insured. They get competitive salaries, benefits, and stock options. We're an O.A.S. subsidiary, after all. Ethical luxury is my brand."

Kiara raised an eyebrow. "You're telling me Elysium has a 401(k) plan?"

"Absolutely," Zen said with a wink. "Even my personal assistant owns a share of the business. A sense of ownership gives one a sense of pride and makes employees happy. And happy employees make the best first impressions."

Pavel chuckled, his smirk as sharp as ever. "That's an interesting approach. Back in my day, keeping employees in line was much simpler. Threaten their lives—or the lives of their loved ones—and voilà! Instant compliance."

Zen arched a perfectly sculpted brow, her lips curving into a sly smile. "And how's that working for you in this day and age, Pavel? It's not the cold war any longer."

He sighed dramatically, shrugging. "It's not what it used to be. Too many laws, too many witnesses, too many feelings. Perhaps I should take a page from your book. Stock options, you say?"

"Welcome to the modern world," Zen quipped, her tone light but cutting. "If you ever decide to leave the dark ages, I might have a consulting gig for you."

Zen's lips curved into a smile, but before she could issue further instructions, the door opened, and a young staff member entered, holding a leather satchel. "Lady Callista," the girl began, her voice trembling slightly, "your supplies are ready for the journey."

The room went still. Zen's smile disappeared as though wiped clean. She straightened, the warmth draining from her expression. "What did you just call me?" she asked, her voice icily calm, though it carried the weight of an impending storm.

The girl's face turned beet red, her hands trembling as she clutched the satchel. "I—I'm so sorry! I didn't mean any offense. I thought—well, Lord Ivyg—he always…" Her voice trailed off as her eyes darted nervously to the floor.

Zen stepped forward, her golden gown sweeping across the room like liquid fire. "Let me make this very clear," she said, her tone as sharp and deliberate as a blade. "My name is Zenobia. That other name"—she gestured dismissively with her hand. "is not to be spoken here. It belongs to a narrative I reject and a man whose control over me is nothing but an illusion. Do I make myself understood?"

The girl nodded fervently, her hands clenching the satchel as if it were a lifeline. "Yes, Lady Zenobia. I won't make that mistake again. I'm so sorry."

Zen's hard gaze softened just a fraction, enough to let the girl off the hook without further humiliation. "See that you don't," she said coolly, turning back toward the group. "You're dismissed."

The girl fled, and the door closed with a quiet click. Zen took a moment to compose herself, drawing in a deep breath. She met Kiara's unseeing gaze and offered a faint smile, though the tension in her jaw remained. "Apologies for that unpleasantness. A reminder that even in the most progressive places, the past has a way of creeping in when you least expect it."

Kiara tilted her head slightly, her tone gentle but curious. "Callista. Was it something significant?"

Zen hesitated, her lips pressing into a thin line. "Let's just say it's a pet name Ivyg used to keep me under his thumb, never even my real name, or what I was once called by others. A different life ago when he bound my soul to his own, his little Persephone. A symbol of his attempts to strip me of my identity and make me a tool in his empire. It's not who I am, who I want to be, and it's certainly not who I'll ever be again."

Aron spoke up, his voice tinged with respect. "You handled that with a lot more grace than I would have."

Zen smirked faintly, the tension in her shoulders easing. "Grace, darling, is simply anger wrapped in patience." "I'll have to remember that one." Kiara told her.

Zen straightened, her commanding presence restored. "Now, where were we? The entire reason Mallah sent you here to me. Ah, yes—the amulets."

Aron picked up the thread seamlessly, lifting his own amulet from the table. "Like I was saying, it doesn't do much. Or at least, that's what I'd like to think. I mean, obviously, I'm already perfect, right?" He grinned, his attempt at humor cutting through the lingering tension. Zen rolled her eyes with exaggerated flair. "Perfectly insufferable, perhaps." She crossed her arms, her expression softening with a glimmer of amusement. "Your arrogance reminds me of someone I once knew—someone who also thought himself flawless. But in truth, Aron, the amulet doesn't show you anything because you already embody what it was designed to enhance. Your strength, agility, keen awareness, logic, and reasoning—they're not just traits; they're amplified abilities from past lives and experiences."

Aron's grin faded slightly, replaced by a thoughtful look. "So, it's not just some fancy piece of jewelry?"

"Far from it," Zen confirmed. "It's a conduit—a way of bridging your present self with the wisdom and skills of your past. And if you're already exceptional in those areas, the amulet won't show you what you already know. It'll wait until you need something new."

Kiara listened intently, her fingers brushing over the edge of the table. "So, it's like a key... but also a guide."

Zen nodded. "Precisely. Which is why your amulet, Kiara, will be pivotal to everything ahead of us."

With that, Zen turned on her heel, her commanding energy reinvigorated. "Now, enough delays. We leave immediately."

-Chapter 28-

While Marcus and the team were somewhere over the Rockies, the small town of Wellville was anything but still. Once the kind of place where little ever happened—save for the occasional community bake sale or neighborhood barbecue—the atmosphere now buzzed with a tension that had not touched its city limits in decades.

The air was thick with the acrid scent of smoke, and the rising sun cast long, jagged shadows over the rows of tightly packed houses. Police tape fluttered in the breeze. "Where the hell are the detectives?" Phillip muttered under his breath, glancing over his shoulder at the house. The oppressive air of fear seemed to bleed through its walls, clinging to everything.

Detective Philip Hurst stood at the edge of the scene, his broad shoulders hunched as he vomited perfectly timed with the arrival of a light blue Lincoln that pulled up to the curb across the street, catching Phillip's attention. A tall man stepped out, his long gray trench coat brushing against the hem of his polished shoes. He adjusted the brim of his black suede fedora, his movements deliberate. His presence alone seemed to silence the murmuring crowd.

Philip had seen his share of crime scenes over the years, but this one was different. It wasn't just the destruction that unnerved him—it was the unexplainable details. The kind that no training could prepare you for. His partner, Officer Nadine Flores, approached Dexter Simmons, leaving Hurst to compose himself, her expression grim. She held up a tablet displaying grainy footage from a nearby security camera.

"This was taken about an hour before the first call came in," she said, tapping the screen. The video showed a figure—tall, cloaked, and moving with inhuman speed—darting across the frame. The image flickered, and suddenly the figure was gone, replaced by a flash of light and a soundless burst of energy that blew out the camera's feed.

Dexter rubbed his temples, the beginnings of a headache forming. "Any witnesses?"

"None who saw much," Nadine replied. "The neighbors reported screams and the sound of something... tearing. By the time anyone worked up the courage to look, this is what they found." She gestured toward the blood splatter inside that could be seen from the open door.

Nadine hesitated, glancing over her shoulder toward the forensics team. "You're going to want to see this for yourself."

He followed her lead, stepping carefully. The house had been hastily cordoned off with yellow police tape, the local officers visibly overwhelmed by the sheer brutality of the scene. It was clear Hurst wasn't alone, that they were not prepared for this. Inside, there was blood everywhere. Splattered on the walls, pooling in the sink, even in the bathtub—everywhere. On the wall above the mantle hung a stuffed deer head. Obviously, it had been put there for show purposes and no doubt it had been killed in these very woods outside of this small mountain town.

'Savages' Dexter thought to himself as he inspected furniture bearing long shred marks in multiple areas. He spoke into his pocket-sized recorder. "Slashes in the furniture, possibly from a murder weapon, likely some sort of non-serrated knife or blade." At his feet, he noticed the television still on but had been knocked off of its stand onto its side. Blurring static of nonstop white and black snow sparked its way into view as the detective carefully turned it back right-side up from where it lay in an awkwardly dormant position, coaxial cable ripped clean out from the wall. Having repositioned the television, Dexter could now clearly read a bloody message that had been written by finger on the screen. He read the message aloud as two officers approached to investigate what the detective had found.

"They are back… Save yourself… the chosen ones will be…" The message ended with illegiblescribbles.

"Get a bag big enough for this TV and set it aside for evidence. Make sure it gets checked for fingerprints." The detective ordered the two officers.

"What do you make of the message, Sir?" One of the officers asked him.

Dexter ignored him as he mumbled into his pocket-recorder. Passing into the kitchen, everything appeared to be in perfect order. The dining room table had been set up for a luncheon for eight people. Nothing seemed wrong with the appearance of the setting. Silverware, glasses, everything was normal. He made a few comments about the dining room scene into his recorder before turning back toward the officer closest to him.

"All right, son. I'm ready to see the mess. How many are there this time?"

"Twelve, sir." The young man replied, pulling a handkerchief out of his pocket and wrapping it around his fingers, looking as if he were going to vomit as he smiled up at him.

"Between all the bodies that have gone missing or found dead, that brings our total to 37."

"Sir, are you trying to say there is a serial killer and that these deaths and missing people are all somehow connected?" The young officer asked. "No, son, not officially, we never say anything, certainly not until we have a better handle on things." He explained, turning toward an all too familiar face. "Speaking of which, tell that damn reporter to get his ass out of here. He's going to compromise the integrity of my crime scene."

The young officer shouted as he ran up the stairs ahead of Dexter, who took his time looking around to be sure he hadn't missed anything before beginning his ascension. Dexter could hear the young officer yell something at the reporter and as the detective nearly reached the top of the stairs, the reporter followed by the officer passed him on their way down. Dexter got a dirty look from the reporter, as he shouted about the public's right to know what was going on, but didn't appear concerned about it whatsoever. He could see the flash of the coroner's camera coming from one of the rooms at the top and to the right.

The sight he was greeted with at the top of the steps made his skin crawl and the hairs on the back of his neck stood straight up. Detective Simmons had been to Vietnam with the ARMY and had seen and done a fair number of bad things but couldn't recollect ever having seen ANYTHING quite like this or ever having been this bothered by a crime scene. Even though Dexter would never show his fear publicly, this time he was scared, and he was glad that no one could see the look on his face. As he looked to his left, a single bedroom with the lights out seemed of no particular interest at the moment.

The solid wood floor underfoot creaked softly as he walked causing him to look down. On the floor, he could see scratches in the wood that looked eerily like fingernail scratches. He noted this in his pocket recorder. It appeared as if multiple people were dragged across the floor and forced into the room that Dexter now stood in front of with a cracked door.

"Multiple sets of fingernail tracks suggest multiple accomplices or killers." Looking up from the floor as he pushed open the door to what once had been the master bedroom, he saw a horrific sight. The coroner paused taking pictures of the bodies to speak to the detective. "What do you think we've got here, Dex? Could it really be a serial killer?"

"I suppose so, Ray. This one just doesn't make a whole lot of sense to me. So far not a single fingerprint aside from the victims has been found. And did you see the message written in blood on the TV?"

"What message?" Ray asked, shaking his head.

The detective proceeded to tell his friend, the coroner, showing him a snapshot of the message on his phone screen that led to the inevitable question: "Who are the chosen ones?"

"Beats the shit out of me." Dexter said as he looked around the room. Twelve bodies were hanging from the ceiling on hooks. Each one was symmetrically placed in a semi-circle around the room. In the bathroom, the tub was filled with blood. It seemed as though each person's body had been drained of its entire blood supply. Something odd occurred to Dexter while he was leaning over, looking into the tub. "What does it smell like in here to you?" he asked.

"Dead people!" Ray answered, repositioning himself just before snapping another picture.

"Not like normal dead people though, right?" He asked. "I would describe it as more of a sweet vinegar smell, similar to the smell of formaldehyde." Ray didn't respond, but he was certain there was a different smell than normal, the peculiarity of this fact made Dexter raise an eyebrow.

"Make sure we get tox screens on everyone." he insisted, making sure Ray acknowledged him.

The detective moved into a suitable position to start inspecting the bodies. Nothing seemed abnormal, except the lack of blood and the scratches and abrasions on the arms and legs of the deceased. He assumed that this had been from being dragged into this room that had become their final resting place, as noted into his recorder as the lights overhead flickered.

"Must be the wiring in this old house." Ray said with a nervous look on his face. The same two police officers that Dexter had spoken to downstairs appeared at the master bedroom door opening with body bags. From his bag, the coroner produced yellow gowns and handed one to each of the police officers and he put one on himself. Together, the three removed all the bodies from the hooks and onto the floor into body bags that they stacked against the wall as best they could in two rows. An hour passed between the time it took to get all the bodies off the hooks, into body bags and into the Coroner's van to be taken to the station for inspection. Ray came back upstairs and looked around to see if he had forgotten anything as picked up his equipment bag.

"I hope you will be able to solve this one, Dex." He said. "Folks around town are starting to get scared, especially with nothing being said yet. I'll be honest, I'm not feeling too hot about it either. This isn't something new and you know it. Things like this have been happening to people for over 50 years. I don't think we can rule out anyone as a suspect."

"I don't know what to tell anyone." The detective replied, sliding his hand down his face. "Aside from getting to see the mess, they know about as much as we do right now, Ray. I'll tell you what, though; this place is giving me the creeps!"

"Do what you have to do and get out of here. Part of me is starting to think this house is cursed." Ray said with a straight face before turning around and walking away. Dexter could hear his footsteps going down the stairs and then the front door opened and shut. Dexter closed the bedroom door and focused his mind. A faint whisper rang through Dexter's ears, and he suddenly had a horrible vision of a woman screaming as she was being dragged into the room. The vision changed to one of the woman being thrown against the wall, her neck snapping like a twig upon impact.

Dexter moved across the room to see the spot that his vision showed him to find a dent in the wall. Looking down at his hands, he perceived they were covered with the victims' blood and the blood inside his own veins felt as cold as ice. It felt to him as if the wind was blowing inside the room, cold and dark. There were no windows, just a dresser and a blood-stained mattress. The sheets and blanket had been removed by the coroner for evidence processing. It was impossible that the wind could be blowing inside this room. Turning around 180 degrees, the world became red in a crimson sea of blood as it poured down from the crack between the ceiling and the walls. He felt almost as if he were going to drown in this pool of death.

The rhythmic hum of the whispering that he heard earlier began again and it grew louder and louder. The lights overhead flickered until there was no light in the entire room. There was not even any light from the crack under the door. Absolute darkness filled the room as Dexter reached for his own flashlight from underneath his trench coat. Pushing the button to turn it on, it refused to shine. 'Impossible', he thought, knowing he had just changed the batteries two days ago.

"Son of a bitch!" He cursed.

Dexter kept butting the flashlight against his palm in the attempt to illuminate this darkness, but the lack of light made him grow increasingly more aggravated and nervous. That was magnified by the fact that the whispering noise was so intense now that it seemed to be coming from inside the room. A deafening roar of animosity and hatred engulfed him. If the goal had been to intimidate him and cause fear, then it definitely worked. Suddenly the room became silent. A silence that may have lasted an eternity. As his eyes adjusted to the darkness, Dexter could see that glowing green eyes encircled him. He quickly counted eight sets. Silence filled the room now to the extent that he could hear his own heart thumping rapidly against the sternum in his chest as it beat louder and louder. Dexter attempted to talk to the strangers in the dark.

"Who are you? What is it you want?"

His heart almost stopped at that moment, for it seemed that in response to his inquiry, the whispering resumed again, but this time much louder than before. Dexter clutched his hands over his ears as his eardrums felt like they could burst. The roar of the infernal whispering began affecting his mind, making him feel as if he were going insane. Dexter had to cover his mouth to keep himself from vomiting as a wave of nausea came over him. Inside he could feel the acids in his stomach churning in his gut trying to purge from his system. Countless thoughts swarmed through his mind. Suddenly, as if he had been hit in the back of the head by a hard object, he fell to the floor, unconsciousness tearing at his soul.

"We should have killed him." A voice said out of the darkness.

Blinking, Dexter lay face down on a concrete floor. Not too far away, he could hear two peoplearguing.

"Why kill him when scaring him will do the job just as well?" Another voice asked the first. "We don't always have to kill to get our point across, is all I'm saying. He's gonna shit a brick when he finds out that we staged the entire display at Reynold's house, per the request of Kane."

"We're changing the world." Another voice chimed in. "Never forget that!"

"Wait." The first voice spoke again, pausing. "I think he's listening to us. If he screws this up for us, I will kill him myself." Dexter heard some voices but never saw any of their faces as he felt someone grab him and a towel was placed over his face, the world slipping away again.

Meanwhile, in room 115 of the nearby motel, Kathleen O'Brian stared at the glowing white expanse of her laptop screen, her writing software loaded and ready to transcribe her thoughts into words. She felt like it was mocking her now, the blankness of this new chapter page reflecting the frustration churning inside her. She ran a hand through her dark curls, pulling at the strands in a futile attempt to summon inspiration. Nothing came. No words, no ideas—just an overwhelming void where her creativity should have been. Something had been blocking her mind, her ability to think clearly and objectively about this story. Maybe that was it? Maybe that was the entire point. She had been attempting to think about it like an object rather than what it truly was: the book and therefore the characters, were extensions of herself.

"Shit," she muttered, lightly kicking the wall beneath the desk. The dull thud did nothing to ease her irritation as another minute ticked by. Kathleen sat motionless, her fingers hovering over the keyboard like birds reluctant to take flight. Finally, she shoved the chair back and stood abruptly. "I need real coffee," she declared to the empty room, grabbing her coat.

The brisk air nipped at her cheeks as she stepped onto the second-floor walkway. Kathleen paused at the railing, leaning against the cool metal as her gaze drifted downward. A strange sensation tugged at her—a pull, faint but insistent, like an unseen thread drawing her attention to the shadowy parking lot below. She squinted, searching for anything out of the ordinary, but the dim lighting revealed only a few scattered cars and a rustling breeze.

"What is wrong with me?" she muttered, shaking her head to dispel the lingering unease.

With a sigh, Kathleen grabbed her coat, passing right by Marcus and the others on her way out. The small diner came into view, its glowing "Open" sign casting a warm red hue across the sidewalk and into the parking lot. Pushing open the glass door, she was greeted by the mingling scents of fried food, brewing coffee, and the faint tang of disinfectant. The place was cozy, if a bit worn. Red vinyl booths and a long counter lined with spinning stools, behind a waitress stood with an enthusiastic grin and uneven teeth bounded over, her apron slightly askew.

"Hey, you're the writer staying in room 115!" the waitress exclaimed like a fan-girl, her voice a little too loud for the quiet diner.

Kathleen blinked, caught off guard by the burst of energy. "I... yes, I am," she replied cautiously, her hands instinctively clutching the strap of her bag.

The waitress's grin widened. "I'm Nicole Davis. My brother Miles runs the motel with his wife, Karen. Wow! I'm a huge fan of your work. Read all your books. Hard to believe someone like you would come all the way out here to do what you do."

"I just write stories," Kathleen said, trying to temper the woman's enthusiasm. "Nothing more."

Nicole waved a hand dismissively, her words tumbling out in a rapid stream. "Don't be modest! You're amazing! I've reread Blood in the Snow like ten times. Oh, my God, are you working on something new?"

Kathleen hesitated, glancing at the laminated menu on the counter to dodge the question. "Something like that," she said vaguely. Her eyes scanned the options quickly. "Just coffee, please."

Nicole nodded eagerly and bustled off to fetch the drink, leaving Kathleen momentarily alone at the counter. She exhaled, her fingers drumming absently on the Formica surface. The diner's hum—the murmur of a small television, the clatter of dishes from the kitchen—was oddly soothing, grounding her in the here and now, but that strange pull still lingered, faint and persistent, stirring something deep within her. She couldn't shake the sense that there was a reason she was here, in this quiet little corner of nowhere. It wasn't just the motel or the diner—it was as though the universe itself had nudged her in this direction, aligning unseen threads to bring her here at this exact moment. Somehow it was new. Somehow it felt repeated and familiar. Nicole returned with the coffee, placing the mug down with a flourish. "Here you go, fresh and hot!" she chirped.

"Thanks," Kathleen replied, offering a faint smile. She wrapped her hands around the mug, the warmth seeping into her skin as she stared into the dark liquid. The faint pull in her chest grew stronger, though she still couldn't explain why. Whatever it was, she had a feeling she wouldn't be leaving Wellville anytime soon.

-Chapter 29-

Marcus!" Clarice said loudly, jostling his shoulder. "Wake up, Marcus."

Marcus blinked groggily, his senses slowly returning as the hum of the airplane cabin filled his ears. "What's the matter?" He muttered.

"We've landed," Clarice replied with her usual cheerful tone. "How did you not feel that?"

Rubbing his face, Marcus sat up, noticing a small line of drool on his chin. He wiped it away quickly, casting a glance at the window beside him. The runway stretched out beneath them, the airplane taxiing toward the terminal. Several planes were queued on the tarmac, their blinking lights dotting the dusky sky.

Clarice gave him a teasing smile. "You must have been dreaming about something good. You were out cold."

Marcus managed a weak chuckle. "Yeah, something like that." The irony of having slept soundly on this flight wasn't lost on him. It wasn't long ago that his last experience in the air ended with him parachuting out of a smoking wreck over the Peruvian mountains on the way to the Hollow Earth. Falling asleep during this trip felt surreal—almost reckless, given how much had happened in the past two weeks. He, like many others, had been changed by his up close and personal experience with the Pulse and the nexus consciousness.

His body ached with the memories of recent events. The burns on the left side of his face still stung, a vivid reminder of the explosion he'd caused while destroying Kane's machine. He reached up, brushing his fingers across the healing skin, the faintest trace of the Vril energy still humming deep within him.

Clarice leaned closer, lowering her voice as if sharing a secret. "Rose overheard some rumors back at Witchaven," she said. "People are already talking about Tamil and Atlan. Disputes over the land. Who's going to control it. Who's going to exploit it."

Marcus sighed, resting his head against the seat. "Of course they are. Humanity can't resist the allure of something new and powerful, even if it means ruining it."

Rose chimed in from the aisle seat, her voice tinged with frustration. "They're not just talking about exploiting it—they're talking about carving it up. Like it's a prize to be won instead of something sacred. We heard people arguing about who has the right to claim the land—governments, corporations, even a few eccentric billionaires."

Marcus's jaw tightened. The thought of Tamil—or Lemuria, as Kiara had called it—falling into the wrong hands sent a chill down his spine. "They have no idea what they're dealing with."

"That's putting it mildly," Rose said, her tone dark. "And don't even get me started on Ivyg's lot."

Clarice placed a reassuring hand on Marcus's arm. "We'll get back there. Right now, though, this is important too."

Marcus nodded, his thoughts lingering on the weight of the folder sitting in his lap. Tamil, Kiara, and the rising landmasses weren't the only upheavals drawing his focus. The file Kane had passed along before the meeting held fragments of something deeper—something tied to the Pulse, Whisperers, and a secretive military program with implications Marcus was still trying to grasp.

He opened the folder again, scanning the neatly typed pages for what felt like the hundredth time. Diagrams, incident reports, and redacted memos, each piece was tantalizing but incomplete. One report mentioned anomalies in small towns like Wellville: whispers of missing time, unexplainable phenomena, and mysterious disappearances. It was no coincidence their destination aligned with the data, yet he couldn't shake the feeling that this was only the beginning of something much larger.

His gaze flicked up briefly to Cesaro, seated a few rows ahead. The former football star was effortlessly charming a small crowd of passengers, signing autographs and cracking jokes as if the late-night flight were a fan meet-and-greet. Rose and Clarice were nearby, their soft laughter suggesting they were just as entertained by Cesaro's antics as his new admirers.

Marcus, however, felt none of their lightheartedness. Closing the folder, he leaned back in his seat and shut his eyes, letting the hum of the plane's engines drown out his thoughts. Images flickered in the darkness—golden threads weaving through dense jungles, a glowing beacon in the distance, the faint echo of whispers that weren't quite his own. He couldn't tell if they were warnings, memories, or something else entirely. But the pull of the Vril energy had been growing stronger since they boarded the plane, as if fate itself was steering him toward Wellville.

The plane jolted gently as it began its descent, breaking his reverie. Clarice's voice came from the seat next to him. "You okay over there, boss? You've been staring at that folder like it's a bomb."

Marcus gave her a faint smile. "Feels like one."

Clarice arched a brow. "Care to share with the class, or is this one of those 'need-to-know' situations?"

He hesitated. "Let's just say it's connected to the Whisperers and the Pulse. There's too much to unpack right now, but I'll fill you in when we're all together."

Clarice's expression softened. "Fair enough. Just don't keep it bottled up too long. Secrets have a way of biting back."

The plane touched down smoothly on the Denver runway, the city lights stretching out like a shimmering grid against the dark sky. Marcus stretched as they taxied to the gate, his muscles stiff from hours of sitting. Cesaro was already up and moving, his energetic wave to the crew earning more than a few chuckles.

As the group disembarked and moved through the terminal, Marcus felt the tug of the Vril again, sharper now, as if urging him forward. They retrieved their rental car, packed their bags, and began the drive toward Wellville under the cover of night.

Clarice broke the silence as they cruised along the dark highway. "So, what's the plan when we get there?"

Marcus sighed, glancing at the folder resting on the dashboard. "We dig in. Figure out why Wellville keeps showing up in everything I'm reading. And hope Kane was right about what we'll find."

Once on the ground, they hurried to rental car and headed straight on to Wellville. The rental car was a sleek, dark QX80, its polished exterior gleaming under the fluorescent lights of the garage. As Marcus handed over his ID at the counter, the tug in the Vril became almost overwhelming, like an invisible thread pulling him forward. A chill ran down his spine, silent confirmation that they were heading exactly where they needed to be.

Clarice lingered close by, her gaze sharp as she watched him. "You're quiet," she said softly once they reached the car.

Marcus managed a small smile, though his mind was elsewhere.

"Just... thinking. About what's waiting for us."

"You think it's bad?"

"I think it's bigger than us," Marcus replied, his voice low, thoughtful. "And I think it's time we find out just how big."

Cesaro, seemingly eager to shake off his earlier melancholy, stepped forward, jingling the keys in his hand. "Well, if we're walking into something big, we'd better look good doing it. And what's cooler than a Latino pimp pulling up in this bad boy?" He gave the QX80 a theatrical flourish.

Clarice rolled her eyes but laughed despite herself. "I hope you drive better than you dress."

"I'll have you know," Cesaro shot back with a playful grin, "I drive like a dream. Rose, you're my copilot. Let's show these two how to roll in style."

Marcus smirked but didn't argue, tossing his bag into the trunk as Cesaro slid behind the wheel with exaggerated flair. Rose hesitated for a moment before climbing into the passenger seat, a mixture of amusement and apprehension on her face. Clarice and Marcus took their seats in the back, settling in as Cesaro started the engine, its low purr filling the garage.

"That's fine." Clarice told them only half-jokingly. "Marcus and I can just sit back here and make out."

As they pulled out onto the highway, the lights of Denver faded into the rearview mirror, leaving the sprawling cityscape behind. The air in the car buzzed with a strange energy, a tension that none of them could quite put into words. Even Cesaro, usually the loudest in the group, seemed subdued as the road stretched endlessly before them.

After nearly an hour of driving, the silence became too much for Cesaro to bear. He reached over to nudge the stereo, flipping through stations until he landed on a classic rock channel. "Nothing like some tunes to set the mood," he quipped, though his tone lacked its usual bravado.

Clarice shot him a sidelong glance. "What mood, exactly? The one where we all get pulled over because you're going ten over the limit?"

Cesaro grinned mischievously, his foot easing off the gas. "Relax, querida. I've got this under control."

Rose smirked, shaking her head. "If you say so."

The conversation flowed more easily after that, the weight in the car lifting slightly. But as the miles ticked by and the faint glow of Wellville appeared on the horizon, the reality of their destination crept back in, settling over them like a heavy fog. The closer they got, the stronger the pull in the Vril became, a silent beacon guiding them toward something they couldn't yet see but felt in their bones.

The late afternoon sun hung low over the sleepy streets of Wellville, casting an eerie stillness over the small town. Gravel crunched under the SUV's tires as Cesaro pulled into the lot of the Mountain View Motel. The place had seen better days, with peeling paint and a flickering neon sign. Still, the windows glowed faintly warm—a quiet invitation for weary travelers.

When they finally reached the motel, the fluorescent sign buzzed faintly in the night, casting a cold, artificial glow over the cracked pavement. Cesaro parked the QX80 with a flourish, turning to Rose with a gleam in his eye. "After we settle in, how about I show you what this baby can really do?"

Rose arched an eyebrow but didn't dismiss him outright. "We'll see," she said lightly, stepping out of the car.

Marcus practically leaped from the backseat as soon as the SUV rolled to a stop, stretching dramatically. "Sweet freedom! Another hour in that car, and I'd have chewed off my own leg just to escape."

Clarice climbed out next, smirking as she tossed her duffel bag straight into Marcus's chest. "Should've volunteered to drive, honey."

"Yeah, you're right." He conceded.

Cesaro slid out of the driver's seat with a weary sigh, rubbing the tension from his shoulders. "If I let Marcus drive, we'd be halfway to Vegas by now."

Rose grabbed her suitcase, shaking her head. "Better than ending up in a ditch somewhere after he fell asleep at the wheel."

Unfazed, Cesaro shot her a grin. "Not fair. I only fell asleep once. Maybe twice."

The banter carried them into the motel's small check-in office. The faded wallpaper gave off an air of forgotten charm, and the clerk at the front desk—Miles, according to his name tag—looked half-asleep until the group approached. Marcus handled the check-in while the others collected their keys. Across the street, the neon glow of the Sunrise Diner caught Cesaro's eye.

"A diner straight out of a movie set," he said, pointing out the window. "Pie, coffee, and small-town charm. Who's in?"

Marcus shrugged. "I could eat."

"We ate twice on the way here," Clarice replied without looking up, already slinging her bag over her shoulder. "Go by them if you want. Let's get checked in, first."

Clarice looked back at Marcus, her expression serious. "Ready?"

Marcus nodded, gripping the handle of his bag. "As ready as I'll ever be."

The group moved toward the motel, their footsteps echoing faintly in the stillness. Whatever awaited them in Wellville, it was closer now than ever, and none of them could shake the feeling that their lives were about to change forever.

Inside, the Mountain View Motel lobby was a cozy, timeworn space that smelled faintly of wood polish and old coffee. Miles, the manager, looked up from the counter as they entered. An older man with silver hair and a kind face, he greeted them with a warm smile and a tip of his hat. In the background, the faint hum of a football game buzzed from a small TV perched on a shelf.

"Afternoon'. You must be the folks who've already got rooms reserved," he said, flipping open the ledger. "These newfangled systems tell me you're all set, but I'll be honest—I don't trust 'em entirely. Never hurts to get a good ol' signature in the book."

He slid the large, worn guest book across the counter, handing Marcus a pen. Marcus picked it up with a small smile, signing their names while Clarice leaned over his shoulder to peek.

"Who made the reservations?" Miles asked conversationally, his eyes crinkling with curiosity. "Some fancy assistant?"

Marcus didn't miss a beat. "Something like that," he replied smoothly, handing the book back.

"Well, everything's paid for," Miles said, glancing back at the computer like it might suddenly grow legs and walk off. "Got no idea how all this tech works, but it does the job. Y'all should be set with three rooms, all next to each other."

Marcus nodded. "Appreciate it. I was also wondering if Linda Williams or Katherine O'Brian might be staying here?"

Miles tilted his head, giving Marcus a scrutinizing look. "We're not supposed to give out guest information, but, uh... you're a friend, right?"

Marcus nodded smoothly. "Yeah, we've been trying to catch up."

"Well, you're in luck," Miles replied, flipping through the ledger. "Katherine O'Brian just got back from dinner a little while ago. Left instructions not to be disturbed, so I can't tell you much more than that. But if you're looking to bump into her, I'd recommend the diner up the road. Most of our guests eat there—it's practically part of the package." He winked conspiratorially. "Family-owned, just like the motel. Discounts, group rates, the whole shebang."

Cesaro muttered something under his breath, and Rose elbowed him gently, stifling a laugh. Marcus managed a polite smile, but Miles wasn't done yet.

"She usually heads out around 8 a.m. sharp. Early riser, that one," Miles continued, tucking the pen behind his ear. "If you're trying to catch her, breakfast at the diner's your best bet. My sister Nicole runs it—she'll take good care of you."

Marcus nodded, already filing the information away. "Thanks, we'll check it out."

Before they could step away, Miles' expression brightened as his gaze zeroed in on Cesaro.

"Wait a second— are you Juan Cesaro? From New Orleans?" His voice lifted with excitement. "Holy shit! You're that guy! The one with the legendary college plays!"

Cesaro's earlier weariness vanished, replaced by his signature grin. "The one and only. I played college ball with my friend Marcus here."

"No kidding? Ain't it a small world?" Miles fumbled for a notepad from behind the counter, practically glowing. "Man, I used to watch all your highlights. Unreal stuff! You got time for an autograph?"

Rose rolled her eyes, her laughter barely contained as Cesaro accepted the pen with a flourish. "What can I say? Greatness follows me wherever I go."

Miles launched into an enthusiastic recollection of Cesaro's football days, gesturing animatedly as he recounted memorable plays. "I watched you in college! That deep pass—the one Kid Dynamite caught? Still one of the greatest plays I've ever seen!"

"Feels like a lifetime ago," Cesaro said with a chuckle, clearly enjoying the attention.

As they wrapped up, Miles handed over the keys, and the group headed toward their rooms. Outside, the air was crisp, the quiet hum of the night punctuated by distant crickets. The weight of what they were walking into pressed on them, but Marcus kept his thoughts focused as he pocketed the key. Clarice fell into step beside him, nudging his arm.

"You're quiet again," she said, her voice soft.

"Just... thinking," Marcus replied. "It was nice talking about playing football. It was a break from all this."

"Are you worried about what's waiting for us?" Clarice wondered. "You think it's bad?"

"I think it's bigger than us," Marcus said. "And I think it's time we find out just how big. We're not here to sightsee." Marcus added, handing his friend one of the room keys. "Settle in. I don't want anyone drawing attention yet."

Cesaro threw up his hands in mock surrender. "You're killing me, boss. This town looks like it hasn't seen excitement in years. I'll grab a bite, scout the place, and make a few friends. You'll thank me later."

"Just don't get arrested," Marcus muttered, tossing him a sidelong look.

"Five bucks says we hear about him before the night's over," Clarice murmured to Rose as they headed toward their rooms.

"I'm not betting against that," Rose replied dryly before walking off with Juan, Marcus and Clarice's door shutting behind her.

"Wait up!" She yelled down the stairs after him, struggling to catch up with the much larger man.

By the time Cesaro made his way across the street, Rose finally caught up to him, but the diner was nearly empty. The bell above the door chimed softly as they stepped inside, the hum of an old jukebox playing something slow and sad. A couple sat huddled in a booth near the window, whispering over their coffee. The waitress—early thirties, blond ponytail, name tag reading Nicole—was wiping down the counter when she looked up.

Her eyes widened in recognition. "Hold up... aren't you Juan Cesaro? The football player?"

Cesaro flashed his trademark grin, leaning casually against the counter. "The one and only."

Nicole practically beamed as she grabbed a menu and slid it toward him. "Well, ain't that a surprise. Not a lot of big names come through here."

"Small towns have their charm," Cesaro said, taking a seat at the counter. "Though this place looks pretty quiet."

Nicole leaned in slightly, dropping her voice. "Quiet? Honey, you must've missed the memo. Things have been anything but quiet lately. The Pulse stirred up all kinds of weirdness—lights in the woods, strange shadows, people talking about creatures they've never seen before. UFO sightings reported in the skies. And the murders…" She hesitated, glancing toward the couple at the booth before lowering her voice further. "It's been bad. Business is suffering. Everyone's scared."

Cesaro frowned, suddenly more alert. "Murders?"

"People die every day." Rose added, though it wasn't much help.

Nicole wiped at an invisible spot on the counter. "Yeah. We had a body show up just this morning. Here. Right in Wellville. The cops don't say much, but folks are talking. Gruesome stuff. They think it's connected to whatever started after that light show last year."

Cesaro tapped his fingers against the counter, mind already racing. "Where exactly did this happen?"

"Over on Washington Street," she answered reluctantly. "Whole area's roped off. Cops are probably still there."

Cesaro glanced out the diner window, his instincts kicking in. "Thanks for the heads-up, Nicole. I owe you."

Nicole tilted her head, amused. "You owe me a signed napkin for my brother. He's a fan."

"Done," Cesaro said with a grin, scribbling his autograph and sliding it back to her. As he stood up to leave, Nicole added, "Oh, and you might want to tell your friends to stick together. Folks disappearing ain't unheard of around here lately."

Back at the motel, Clarice had just settled onto the bed when a sharp knock rattled the door. She shot Marcus a questioning look before getting up to answer.

Cesaro stood on the other side, already buzzing with energy. "Rose and I are going to check out the town. Do you two want to come with me?"

She frowned. "What?"

"Look, I just heard something in town—murders, strange lights, all kinds of creepy shit." He hesitated, for once deadly serious. "I don't like the idea of poking around alone."

"Take Rose with you. She'll be a good backup for you."

Rose stared at him for a beat. "Me? Why me?"

"Because you're not afraid to bust out those powers if something comes at you."

"Unbelievable," she muttered, even though she was already out with her coat on. "You're usually the one who needs calming down. If we get arrested, it's on you."

"You'll thank me later," Cesaro said, grinning as he led her toward the SUV.

The sun had dipped below the tree line by the time Cesaro and Rose arrived at the taped-off house. The structure loomed dark and still against the faint twilight glow, its windows black and lifeless. Cesaro parked a block away, killing the engine.

"This feels like a bad idea," Rose murmured, eyeing the house warily.

Cesaro shrugged. "Most good ideas do."

The street was easy to find in a town as small as Wellville, but the house stood out—a sagging silhouette cordoned off by fluttering yellow police tape and bathed in the eerie glow of twilight. Cesaro parked a block away, cutting the engine.

As they approached, Rose nudged Cesaro and gestured across the street. A car sat parked in the shadows, its presence oddly out of place in the otherwise empty neighborhood. "Someone's here," she murmured.

Cesaro squinted at the car, noting its foggy windows and the faint glint of moisture on its hood. He looked back at the house, and that's when he saw it—the front door. It was mostly closed, but not quite. It rested ajar, as though someone had left in a hurry and hadn't expected to be the last one out.

"That's not ominous at all," Cesaro muttered, rolling his shoulders before stepping under the yellow tape.

The gravel crunched beneath their shoes as they crept forward. Cesaro pushed the door open, the hinges letting out a long, drawn-out groan that cut through the quiet like a blade.

Inside, the air was heavy—thick and suffocating with a coppery tang that hit them both immediately. Rose faltered on the threshold, her face contorting as the smell turned her stomach. "Smells like blood," she said under her breath, the words barely audible.

Cesaro's jaw tightened as he scanned the dim interior. "Stay close," he murmured, his voice low but steady.

The unsettling silence swallowed their words as the two of them stepped inside, the door creaking shut behind them.

They were only a few steps in when Rose froze, her breath hitching. The living room unfolded before them in all its grotesque horror. Blood smeared the walls in chaotic streaks, like someone—or something—had been flung repeatedly against them. Furniture lay shattered, jagged pieces splintered across the floor. The TV, still glowing faintly with static, had toppled onto its side, leaving faint shadows of bloody fingerprints across the cracked screen.

"Holy—" Cesaro cut himself off, his voice low and strangled as he took it in. "What the hell happened here?"

Rose's hand shot to her mouth, her face pale. "I don't—this is bad. Really bad."

The coppery tang in the air clung to their lungs, thick and suffocating. Cesaro glanced down at the floor where faint trails of blood led toward the staircase. Rose's gaze darted nervously around the room before landing on the hallway.

"Stay close," Cesaro whispered again, forcing calm into his voice.

They followed the crimson trail into the hall, shoes sticking slightly with each step. Rose's hands trembled at her sides before glowing faintly, streaks of energy rippling over her fingers. "Something's here," she muttered, barely audible.

They barely made it to the base of the stairs when Rose suddenly froze again, her powers flaring brighter this time. "Wait. Did you hear that?"

Cesaro turned sharply, his body tensed. A faint groan echoed from upstairs—a low, guttural sound that sent chills crawling down his spine. He jerked his head toward the staircase. "Someone's here."

Rose's flickering energy didn't fade this time. Together, they climbed the stairs, each step creaking ominously beneath their weight. The smell of blood was stronger up here, clinging to the walls, and an unnatural stillness blanketed the air. The groan came again, clearer now. It led them to the master bedroom.

Cesaro eased the door open carefully, the hinges groaning in protest. The first thing they noticed was the bed—stripped bare, its stained mattress darkened with ominous blotches. The air was stifling, the coppery tang of blood almost suffocating. And then they saw him.

A man slumped against the wall, half-collapsed on the floor, his head tilted awkwardly as if he'd just slid down into that position. His face was bruised, a split lip crusted with dried blood, and smears of crimson streaked his collar.

Cesaro took a cautious step forward, his sharp gaze catching a glint of metal nearby. Lying just to the right of the man's limp hand was a police badge—partially open, its edges stained. He knelt to pick it up, flicking it open just enough to confirm the name etched on the gleaming surface.

"Dexter Simmons," Cesaro read aloud, his voice low and edged with surprise. "Detective."

The man groaned faintly at the sound of his name, shifting slightly as if dragged back to consciousness. Cesaro dropped to his knee, tucking the badge into Dexter's coat pocket as he gripped the detective's shoulder.

"Hey! You with us?" Cesaro asked firmly, giving him a gentle shake.

Dexter blinked slowly, his eyes struggling to focus. His voice came out as a cracked whisper. "Lights… whispers… they were everywhere..."

Rose hovered near the doorway, her hands still flickering faintly with energy. Her wide eyes darted around the room as if expecting the walls to start closing in on them. "We need to get him out of here," she said, her voice barely above a whisper.

Cesaro slipped Dexter's arm over his shoulder, pulling him up into a wobbly stance. "C'mon, big guy. Let's move before whatever did this decides to come back."

As they half-dragged, half-carried Dexter down the stairs, Cesaro shot Rose a pointed look. "You were about to go nuclear up there."

"Can you blame me?" Rose hissed back, her voice tight. "We walked into a literal nightmare."

"Yeah," Cesaro muttered darkly, glancing over his shoulder toward the house they were leaving behind. "And something tells me this nightmare's just getting started."

"Dexter!" Cesaro was at his side in seconds, kneeling down and gripping his shoulder. "Hey, you okay? What happened?"

Dexter's head lolled slightly as his eyes fluttered open. His gaze was distant, unfocused. "I don't know… the lights… whispers… they were everywhere…"

Rose hovered just behind Cesaro, her glowing hands slowly dimming. "Let's get him out of here. Now."

Cesaro slipped Dexter's arm over his shoulder, helping haul him upright as Rose stayed close. The man's legs were weak beneath him, but he managed to stumble forward with their support. As they moved down the stairs, the oppressive silence seemed heavier now, like something unseen was watching them leave. Once they crossed the threshold and stepped back into the open air, Cesaro exhaled deeply, his grip on Dexter still firm.

Rose shot him a sharp look, though her tone wavered. "How can you hear whispers in the dark and not freak out?"

Cesaro didn't argue or really even have a good answer. His gaze flicked back toward the house, its dark windows staring blankly back at him like empty eyes. Whatever had happened inside wasn't done with them yet—that much he knew. By the time they reached the car, Dexter had regained enough sense to mumble, "Police station. I have to report this."

"You're damn right you do," Cesaro muttered, starting the engine. "And we're coming with you."

-Chapter 30-

Command and Delirium

Deep inside the Wind Valley military installation, located just outside of Wellville, General Donovan Ashgrove sat at his desk, brooding over the notes scrawled across his yellow legal pad. His thoughts were a turbulent storm, much like the world outside his tightly controlled facility.

"I know there's a connection between the Whisperers and all these people suddenly converging in Wellville," he muttered under his breath. "Damn it. How could we not have seen this coming? Our security must be compromised. There's a leak somewhere... and if they expose us, it'll be a disaster."

The general rubbed his temples, his head throbbing with frustration. Being stuck in this underground facility for so long was taking a toll on his nerves. His voice grew harsher as he spoke to the empty room. "We have to keep 'the gate' and the other projects under wraps. If this gets out, we're finished. But with this staff of half-witted monkeys, how long can we maintain the cover?"

A knock at the door interrupted his thoughts. Reflexively, his hand went to the gun strapped to the inside of his thigh. "Come in," he barked, his sharp tone betraying his irritation.

Colonel Lucy O'Connor entered, her posture crisp and professional. The general glanced at his watch. At least she was punctual, a rare trait in this facility. He motioned for her to sit, simultaneously downing a handful of ibuprofen with a swig of water.

"You've been with us here at Wind Valley for almost three years, Colonel," he began, his tone measured but intense. "You're a brilliant scientist, and I'm proud to have you on this team. We were lucky to get you from the Aurora Initiative, I've been told. A far cry from a research base in the Caribbean, I'm sure."

"Indeed, sir, but there is no regret. I volunteered to be part of this program overseeing the Gate and the production of the Hades virus." "Let's not mince words: our situation is dire. We've mastered time travel and developed defenses against foreign threats, but with the Department of Defense cutting our funding, we've had to shift our priorities. Now, everything depends on keeping our work secret—from the Whisperers and from these people in Wellville."

Lucy's expression remained neutral, though internally she braced herself. She'd heard rants like this from him before.

"The average citizen," he continued, "is a simple creature. They can't handle knowledge like this. Give them too much, and they'll turn on us. Our job is to protect them from themselves, to keep them fat, stupid, living in fear and compliant, while we safeguard the tools and weapons that could save them. The Whisperers... they threaten all of that."

He paused, watching her for a reaction, but Lucy said nothing. She knew better than to interrupt when he was in full lecture mode.

"You remember the Mountain View Motel incident?" he asked suddenly.

"Yes, sir," she replied cautiously. "We had to erase their memories—of us, the virus, the gate, the Whisperers, and the entire facility."

"Now," Donovan said, his voice dropping to a dangerous whisper. "History is repeating itself. Another group is gathering at the same motel. Some of the same individuals we dealt with the last time around. They're sniffing around where they shouldn't be. We barely contained the situation last time. This time, we have to be proactive." "What would you have me do that has not already been done, sir?" She wondered.

He leaned forward, his eyes narrowing. "We're not just dealing with nosy civilians. There's a leak. Someone on the inside is feeding information to the outside world. If we don't shut this down, we'll lose control—not just of the Whisperers but of everything we've built here. And the Whisperers... they'll kill us all if they get the chance."

Lucy shifted uncomfortably in her chair, her unease evident despite her best efforts to mask it. "What are your orders, sir?"

"No one leaves this mountain," Donovan said firmly. "Recall all personnel. Seal the base. If anyone in Wellville gets too close, we'll handle them. And if that means erasing more memories—or worse—then so be it."

His tone softened slightly as he added, "Colonel, I don't enjoy giving these orders, but our survival depends on it. Do you understand?"

"Yes, sir," she replied, rising from her chair. She hesitated for a moment, then added, "If I may, sir, acting too quickly could tip our hand. It might be better to watch and wait for now."

Donovan scoffed. "Wait and see? That's exactly what those bureaucrats in Washington would do. And where has that gotten us?" He waved her off dismissively. "Just follow my orders, Colonel."

Lucy left the room, the door clicking shut behind her, muttering 'Asshole' under her breath.. Alone again, Donovan swiveled his chair to face the wall, muttering to himself. "They'll see I'm right. The Whisperers, the leak, these people in Wellville... they're all connected. And if no one else can stop this, then I will. Whatever it takes."

He reached into his top desk drawer and picked up a pistol, cocked and loaded the chamber. "They want a fight; they'll get a fight out of me."

Back at the police station, The fluorescent lights flickered faintly overhead as Cesaro and Rose burst through the front doors of the Wellville Police Station, supporting Dexter Simmons between them. Dexter, still groggy, staggered on his feet as Cesaro hauled him toward the nearest empty chair. The handful of officers on duty sprang up in alarm.

Officer Nadine Flores quickly made her way toward them: "What the hell happened?!"

"Your detective was napping in a haunted house. You're welcome." Cesaro said with deadpan humor, adjusting his grip.

Dexter, mumbled weakly. "Don't... touch me."

Cesaro and Rose exchanged glances as they eased him into the chair. Dexter's face was pale beneath the bruises, his disheveled trench coat and badge still visible—a man who clearly wasn't expecting to wake up on the floor of a blood-soaked crime scene.

Officer Philip Hurst eyed them suspiciously "Who are you two, again?"

"Good Samaritans, officer." Cesaro flashed his most charming grin before turning back to Dexter. "You're welcome, by the way."

Dexter blinked groggily, his sharp eyes narrowing as he regained focus. He gestured weakly toward Cesaro with one bruised hand. "Why... were you there?"

"Call it curiosity." Cesaro said, straightening up, yet still casual as ever. "I'm not a fan of leaving people to die in creepy houses. You're welcome again, by the way."

"We were supposed to be grabbing food." Rose said sharply, glaring at Cesaro. Cesaro grins shamelessly. "I did! And a detective. Two-for-one deal."

Dexter groaned, clutching his head as the officers hovered nervously nearby. He waved them off with a gruff motion.

"I'm fine. I'm fine. Just—give me a minute."

The officers hesitated before retreating back to their desks, leaving Cesaro and Rose alone with the detective, Dexter. He rubbed his temples, still looking rattled, before shooting them both a pointed look. Once they were in Dexter's cluttered office, he settled behind his desk, still pale but visibly more alert. He gestured for Rose and Cesaro to sit, though Cesaro chose to lean casually against the wall.

Dexter rubbed his temples. "All right. I'm awake, I'm alive, and I need answers. Why were you there? And don't give me that 'good Samaritan' crap."

Cesaro sighed dramatically, pulling his wallet from his pocket. He flipped it open and held out his driver's license. "My name is Juan Cesaro. Yeah, that Juan Cesaro. Football legend, rescuer of detectives, eater of midnight snacks. I'm sure you've seen my commercials on television or the internet."

Dexter snatched the ID, staring at it with narrowed eyes. His gaze flicked to Cesaro, then back to the card. Dexter looked flatly back at him, clearly surprised. "Unbelievable. You're the guy with the Hail Mary play from the Fiesta Bowl to Kid Dynamite."

"Guilty. Autographs later." Cesaro said grinning, never getting tired of his fans.

Dexter shook his head, clearly unimpressed, and handed the ID back. This was unusual for Juan who was usually showered with attention in moments like this. The detective's attention shifted to Rose, who sat with her arms folded, watching him carefully.

"And you? What's your story?" Dexter asked, looking over at Cesaro's female companion.

"Saoirse Rose O'Keenan, but everyone just calls me Rose." She replied calmly. "We're here on business. Let's leave it at that."

"Do you have any ID?"

"Not from this country." She giggled, producing her Irish passport.

"Business, huh?" Dexter frowned, his suspicion flaring again as he handed her documents back. "What kind of business leads a retired football player and a stranger from Ireland to break into an active crime scene?"

Cesaro hesitated for a beat, clearly debating how much to say. Finally, he gave in, gesturing vaguely. "Fine, fine. We're looking into some… classified stuff. One of our associates received a file about this place. Military experiments, accidents—stuff people probably don't want us digging up."

"Cesaro!" Rose sharply interrupted.

Dexter's expression darkened, his suspicion replaced with something closer to dread. He leaned back in his chair, running a hand over his face before muttering quietly. "Military experiments. Dammit…"

He glanced back at them, his tone turning weary but resigned. "The old man—he's been ranting about strange shit for years. Creatures in the woods, people going missing… I thought he was losing it. But after what I saw at that house today…" He trailed off, clearly haunted by the memory.

Rose seized the opening, leaning forward with confidence. "Here's the deal, Detective. We're here because something dangerous is happening in this town. We think it's connected to a bigger problem that started ever since the Pulse—one that's going to get worse unless we work together. You share what you know, and we'll do the same. We're on the same side here."

Dexter stared at her for a long moment, weighing her words. Finally, he exhaled, pulling two business cards from his desk and sliding them toward Rose and Cesaro.

"I will think about it. You need me, you call. But keep me in the loop, and for God's sake, don't tell any residents what you saw and do not let me catch you poking around any more houses otherwise you'll see yourselves inside a jail cell next time it happens."

Cesaro grabbed the card and twirled it between his fingers with a grin. "Deal. And hey, Detective—if you start hearing whispers again, call me. I'm a great listener."

"Call me Dexter. I'm getting too old for all the formalities."

"Okay, well then, thank you Dexter." As Rose and Cesaro turned to leave, Cesaro paused at the door, holding up Dexter's card like it was a badge of honor.

Dexter gave him a dry look, muttering to himself as the two walked away. "This town's gonna kill me."

Cesaro grinned in response. "I'll be in touch. Call me if you need backup—or, you know, company."

Dexter groaned, running a hand over his face as the door swung shut. Nadine and Philip hovered just outside, their expressions full of questions.

Philip, whispering to Nadine. "What just happened?"

"I don't know, but I'm guessing this shit is only going to keep getting weirder."

Dexter leaned back in his chair, staring at the ceiling, the weight of everything catching up to him. "We are so screwed."

-Chapter 31-

Into the Earth

The entrance to the Hollow Earth gaped like the maw of some ancient beast, the path ahead swallowed by shadow and an oppressive silence. The air was heavy with an almost electric charge, a sense that they were crossing into an entirely different realm. Pavel took the lead, his confident stride betraying his unease. Zen followed close behind, her voice echoing in the cavern as she called out directions, her tone sharp and precise.

"Keep to the left. Watch your footing," Zen instructed.

"Got it," Pavel replied, his voice clipped.

Behind them, Aron moved carefully, his eyes scanning the dim, shifting light of the cavern walls. Every now and then, he glanced back at Kiara, who trailed at the rear, her head tilted slightly as though listening to something only she could hear.

"You doing okay back there, Kiara?" Aron called out, his tone tinged with concern.

"I'm fine," she replied, her voice steady.

The path narrowed suddenly, forcing them to move in single file. Stalagmites and jagged rocks loomed on either side, and the ground became uneven, slick with an iridescent film that caught the dim glow of bioluminescent fungi clinging to the walls.

"Pavel, stop!" Zen's voice cut sharply through the air. "There's a drop-off ahead."

Pavel skidded to a halt, his boots sending a few loose rocks tumbling into the abyss below.

"Thanks for the warning," he muttered, peering cautiously over the edge.

"We'll have to go around," Zen said, pointing to a narrow ledge that hugged the cavern wall.

As they maneuvered along the ledge, the air grew thicker, the sound of dripping water and distant echoes amplifying the tension. Pavel moved deliberately, Zen close behind him, her hand resting lightly on his shoulder to guide him. Aron followed, his movements careful but awkward as he balanced on the slick surface.

Kiara was last, her cane tapping lightly against the ground as she felt her way forward. The group had just cleared the ledge when the cavern floor suddenly shifted beneath Aron's feet. He stumbled, his arms flailing as he fought for balance.

"Whoa, hang on!" Pavel shouted, turning back, but it was Kiara who moved first.

With a sharp intake of breath, she lunged forward, her free hand shooting out to grab Aron's arm just as he began to slip. Her grip was surprisingly firm, her movements precise and deliberate as she pulled him back onto solid ground.

"You okay?" she asked, her voice calm despite the adrenaline coursing through her.

"Yeah," Aron said, still catching his breath. "How the hell did you do that?"

Kiara tilted her head, her expression unreadable. "Did you know that everything makes noise?" she asked, her tone matter-of-fact.

Pavel frowned. "Noise?"

"Everything," Kiara repeated. "The air, the rocks, even the way the ground moves. It all makes a sound. Subtle, sure, but it's there. I could hear the ledge shift before it happened."

Zen raised an eyebrow, glancing at Kiara with newfound curiosity.

"I'm still getting the hang of focusing and filtering," Kiara continued, brushing her hands against her pants as though dusting off the moment. "But I'm not a frail child. I can take care of myself. And apparently, you." She smirked in Aron's direction.

For a moment, the group was silent, their previous assumptions hanging heavily in the air. Then Zen chuckled, a low, throaty sound that echoed off the cavern walls.

"Well," she said, turning back to Pavel, "I guess our frail child just schooled us."

The cavern was vast, its walls glowing faintly with the bioluminescence of fungi that clung to jagged stone. The air was damp and thick, amplifying the sound of the slow-moving river that cut through the heart of the passage. The group moved carefully, each step echoing softly as they traversed the uneven terrain.

Pavel led the way, his sharp eyes scanning the path ahead. Zen followed close behind, her movements fluid and deliberate. Aron stayed near the back, keeping a watchful eye on Kiara, who trailed last, her cane tapping rhythmically against the ground.

"Careful," Zen called softly to Pavel. "The path narrows up ahead."

"I see it," Pavel replied, adjusting his footing.

Behind them, Kiara paused. Her fingers brushed the cool stone of the cavern wall, and a sudden wave of dizziness washed over her. The sound of the river grew louder, rushing in her ears until it drowned out the voices of her companions. Her vision blurred, and she swayed slightly.

"Kiara?" Aron turned to her, his voice tinged with concern, "What's wrong?"

"I…" Kiara started, then clutched at her head as a flood of images filled her mind. She barely managed to whisper, "I see her."

Kiara opened her eyes, but she wasn't herself. She was Saywa, standing on the deck of a canoe as it glided upriver through dense jungle. Around her were companions, their paddles moving in synchronized silence. In her hand, Saywa held a talisman, its intricate design glinting in the sunlight that filtered through the canopy.

The jungle was alive with the sounds of insects and birds, but Saywa's heart was heavy with dread. The Spaniards were close, their greed insatiable. The talisman was meant as a peace offering, but she knew better. Peace was not what they sought.

The vision shifted abruptly. Saywa now stood before the Conquistadors. Their leader, Pizarro, demanded the talisman as proof of submission. Her father, Atahualpa, urged her to comply, though Saywa knew it would only whet their appetite for more. When cannon fire erupted, chaos consumed the meeting. Saywa fled, leading survivors to a hidden passage—the entrance to El Dorado.

Inside the mountain, Saywa triggered the ancient mechanism to seal the path, saving the sacred city but sacrificing her freedom. Captured by the Spaniards, she was haunted by the presence of the man she now knew to be Ivyg. He was no ordinary man, his glowing red eyes and twisted smile burning an image into her mind that she would not soon forget.

Kiara gasped, her knees hitting the damp ground. The rush of the river faded as she blinked, disoriented, and found herself back in the Hollow Earth. Aron was kneeling beside her, his hand lightly on her shoulder.

"Kiara?" he said, his voice urgent. "What did you see?"

She took a shaky breath, her fingers gripping the ground for stability. "Saywa," she whispered. "I saw myself as a woman named Saywa."

Zen knelt nearby, her sharp gaze fixed on Kiara. "What did she show you?"

Kiara hesitated, her mind racing to piece together the fragments of the vision. "She... just that she sealed the outside entrance to protect the amulet and that we are on the right path."

Pavel frowned, crossing his arms. "Are you sure? How can you know?"

"I just do," Kiara said, her voice steadying. "The vision showed me how to get there. The river, the path through the rocks—it's all here. She's guiding us."

Mallah's voice echoed softly in her mind. Trust the visions, Kiara. They will lead you to where you need to be.

That night, the group set up camp along the riverbank. The soft glow of bioluminescent fungi reflected off the still water, casting faint, eerie shadows that danced with the movement of the current. The damp, earthy smell of the cave mixed with the faint metallic tang of the nearby river.

Pavel took charge of making the fire, boasting that his Boy Scout skills were "second to none" after coming over from Pakistan to the United States as a boy. Aron watched him struggle for a solid ten minutes before stepping in, his patience worn thin by the cold.

"Let me help," Aron said, crouching beside the pile of kindling Pavel had meticulously arranged.

"I've got this!" Pavel replied, determined. "I might be rusty, but I still remember the scout master's training."

Aron shook his head with a wry smile and extended his hand toward the wood. A small arc of sparks leapt from his fingers to the kindling, and seconds later, flames flickered to life, warming the chilly cavern air.

"Cheater!" Pavel laughed, pulling a bottle from his bag. "I could've had that—eventually. You didn't have to show off."

"Sure," Aron teased, his voice dry.

Pavel offered the bottle to Zen, who took it with a raised eyebrow. "You're insufferable," she said with a smirk, taking a swig before handing it back. "Tell you what, genius—if you finish setting up my tent, I won't tell anyone you needed my help with your knots."

"Deal," Pavel replied, saluting her with the bottle before taking another pull.

Meanwhile, Aron, ever the practical survivalist, had already finished setting up both his and Kiara's tents. He brushed his hands off, satisfied, and sat down beside the crackling fire. Kiara joined him, the flickering flames casting warm highlights on her face.

"Is that why Clarice called you 'Sparky' the other day?" Kiara asked, her curiosity getting the better of her.

Aron chuckled softly, rubbing the back of his neck. "Not exactly," he admitted. "The nickname came from back in college. Me, Marcus, and Cesaro were pretty close. Anywhere Marcus went, Clarice was close behind. While we played football, Marcus and I shared a dorm briefly. It's fun when you get to spend so much time with your best friend from high school. That's how we became like brothers. Clarice, though, she was always trying to set me up with someone—probably thought I needed to loosen up."

Kiara tilted her head, listening intently while Aron continued, his voice tinged with both nostalgia and nervousness. "She managed to convince me to give it a shot a couple of times, but… let's just say things got awkward. I didn't have great control over my powers back then. Imagine trying to explain to a date why the lights in the room are flickering like a horror movie. I'd have to pretend there was some electrical malfunction—make a big show of being 'shocked'—just to play it off. It was… a mess."

From across the fire, Zen's laugh rang out, loud and unapologetic. "Please tell me you're not a virgin," she said, her tone dripping with mock disbelief.

Aron flushed, clearly flustered. "Not… exactly," he stammered. "It's complicated."

Beside him, Kiara's lips quirked into a knowing smile, though she said nothing.

"It's a little fuzzy," Aron added, his voice trailing off.

Kiara chuckled softly, her expression turning slightly sheepish. "Yeah, same," she murmured, her cheeks tinged pink.

Zen rolled her eyes, clearly unimpressed by their shared awkwardness. "Ugh, you two are nauseatingly cute," she said, leaning back against a rock. "Anyway. Sparky here isn't just playing with electricity. What's really going on with your powers, Aron? Channeling? Transmutation? Both?"

Aron shrugged. "I don't really think about it like that," he admitted. "I just... feel it. It's like I can tap into the energy around me and direct it where it needs to go. But it's not perfect—I'm still figuring things out."

"And what about you, Kiara?" Zen asked, her golden eyes narrowing thoughtfully. "I've seen glimpses of what you can do, but there's got to be more. You're not just hearing the world differently—you're interacting with it."

Kiara hesitated, her fingers fidgeting with the edge of her jacket. "Maybe. I don't know. It's not like I have a manual for this stuff."

Zen smirked. "No manuals, no mentors… just vibes."

Kiara laughed, her tension easing slightly. "Pretty much."

As the conversation shifted to lighter topics, the fire crackled merrily, its warmth chasing away the damp chill of the cavern. For the first time in what felt like days, the group allowed themselves to relax, the bond between them growing stronger with every shared laugh and story.

Aron hesitated before speaking, his voice softer than usual. "Now that we're all sharing awkward truths... how did you lose your sight? And how does that all work now? Seems like you don't just rely on sound or touch—you seem to perceive things in a way that's… different. Like when you hear something, it transforms into something you can 'see.' How does that work for you? And… if you're comfortable sharing, how did you lose your sight?"

Kiara's hand instinctively went to the coin she wore around her neck, her fingers tracing its smooth edges as she processed the question. It wasn't one she got often, especially in the context Aron had framed it. Most people were either too polite or too uncomfortable to bring up her blindness at all. But Aron's tone carried no pity, only genuine curiosity.

"I honestly have no idea how it works…I guess my brain just hears everything and, I dunno, it just started turning into pictures, it's hard to explain." She began, now herself shifting uncomfortably. "But it happened a long time ago," she began again, her voice distant as she turned her thoughts inward. "I was sixteen, rushing home after spending the evening with Robyn out at Fort Stevens. We'd gone stargazing—something we did a lot back then. Being out in nature always felt… freeing. I loved the quiet, the way the trees and the stars made the world feel bigger, like there was something more out there."

She paused, a faint smile touching her lips. "But I stayed too long. My parents were strict about curfews, and I didn't want to hear another lecture about responsibility. So, I pushed it, driving too fast on those back roads, trying to make it back before they noticed I was gone."

Kiara's fingers tightened around the coin as she continued. "We were crossing through the last stretch of the woods before town. The road was empty, or so I thought. And then… he was there. A man, standing in the middle of the road. He came out of nowhere."

Aron leaned forward slightly, his expression tense. "What did you do?"

"I panicked," Kiara admitted. "I slammed on the brakes and swerved hard to avoid him. The truck skidded off the road and into a ditch. I remember the airbag hitting me—hard. My ears were ringing, and everything was blurry. I thought I was okay, but then Robyn screamed. She was looking out the passenger window at an intersection up ahead. A truck sped through, right where we would've been if we hadn't crashed."

She swallowed hard, her voice dropping. "It would have killed us. There's no way we would have survived. And when I looked back to the road, he was gone. The man, I mean. But I could still feel… something. Like he had been there for a reason."

"What happened next?" Aron asked, his voice steady.

Kiara's hand went to her temple as if the memory still brought a dull ache. "I tried to get out of the truck, but my head was spinning. My vision was fading in and out—like looking through a foggy window. Then I felt someone grab me. A man pulled me out of the wreckage and carried me to a safe distance. Robyn got out on her own, coughing but okay. But the man was gone again before I could say a word."

Her fingers traced the coin again. "That's when I noticed this, in my hand. A coin, like an ancient artifact. I didn't understand it at the time, but I've carried it with me ever since. Later, I realized… it was Kane. He saved us."

Aron's eyes widened. "Kane? Are you sure?"

Kiara nodded slowly. "I didn't know who he was back then, but I've seen his face since. I know it was him. But saving us came at a cost. My vision didn't come back. The doctors said the force of the airbag and the trauma of the crash caused swelling in my brain. It damaged my optic nerves beyond repair."

She paused, letting the weight of her words settle. "It wasn't immediate. For a while, I could see light and color. Swirls and shapes, like everything was underwater. But even that faded over time. Now, when I open my eyes, it's just… nothing. And yet somehow something at the same time. I can't explain it."

Aron hesitated, searching for something meaningful to say. "I'm sorry you had to go through all of that."

"Don't be," Kiara replied, a faint smile tugging at her lips. "Losing my sight changed everything, but it also made me who I am. I stopped looking outward for answers and started listening—to people, to nature, to my own intuition. And then there's… her."

"Her?" Aron asked, his brow furrowing.

"Saywa," Kiara explained. "A part of me, from a past life, or so Mallah said. I've felt her guiding me, especially lately. She doesn't show me the way in the same sense as sight, but she points me toward what I need to know. It's like a whisper in the back of my mind."

Aron nodded, his gaze thoughtful. "And when you 'see' things now, like you did back at the cave, is that her?"

"Maybe," Kiara said softly. "Or maybe it's just me, learning to see the world differently."

For a long moment, they sat in silence, the firelight flickering between them. Aron finally spoke, his voice steady. "If Kane saved you, there was a reason. And if Saywa is guiding you, it's because you're meant for something greater."

Kiara tilted her head toward him, a wry smile crossing her lips. "You sure you're not just buttering me up to make me feel better?"

"Not at all," Aron replied, grinning. "Though it doesn't hurt if it works."

They both laughed softly, the moment of levity breaking the heaviness of the memory. Yet even as they laughed, the weight of her story lingered, a reminder of the purpose that had brought them all together.

Kiara's hand tightened around the coin, her voice lowering as she continued. "There's something else… something that doesn't make sense but feels too real to ignore."

Aron's brow furrowed. "What do you mean?"

Kiara hesitated, glancing down at the coin she always carried. "That night, after the accident… I could swear the man who pulled us from the truck was the same one who saved me and my mom when I was a little girl."

Kiara lifted her gaze to Aron, her expression a mix of awe and confusion. "When I saw him again that night, after the accident… I knew it was him. I'm almost certain it was Kane."

Aron's jaw tightened as he processed her words. "If that's true, then he's been watching over you for a long time."

She nodded slowly, her grip on the coin tightening. "But why? Why me?"

Aron placed a hand on her shoulder, his touch grounding her. "Maybe you're more important to all of this than you realize. Maybe he's trying to protect something only you can do."

Kiara glanced at the fire, the flickering flames reflecting in her eyes. "There's one more thing I haven't told anyone," she whispered, leaning in closer. "I don't completely trust Zen."

Aron blinked, startled. "Zen? Why?"

"I can't explain it," Kiara murmured. "She's helped us, and she seems sincere, but there's something about her… something I can't shake. I feel like she's hiding something."

Aron leaned back slightly, processing her words. "You think she has her own agenda?"

Kiara nodded, her voice barely audible. "I do."

Before Aron could respond, a familiar, honeyed voice interrupted. "Talking about me, are we?"

Both turned to see Zen standing just outside the firelight, her golden eyes gleaming with amusement. She held a small smile, but the sharpness in her gaze suggested she wasn't entirely pleased.

Kiara straightened, her expression calm. "Just saying how grateful we are for your help."

Zen's smile widened, though her eyes never left Kiara's. "Of course you were, darling. I'd hate to think I'd done something to lose your trust."

Her tone was playful, but the undertone was clear. Aron cleared his throat, deflecting. "We were just talking about everything that's happened. A lot to process."

Zen stepped closer, the firelight catching on her golden gown. "I'm sure it is," she said smoothly. Her gaze lingered on Kiara for a beat longer before shifting to Aron. "You both should get some rest. Tomorrow will be grueling, and you'll need all the energy you can muster."

She turned gracefully, her steps light as she headed back to her tent. Aron watched her go, then leaned closer to Kiara. "She definitely has her own agenda."

Kiara nodded, her fingers once again tracing the coin. "The question is, how does it involve us?"

The fire crackled softly, the sound of the jungle night enveloping them as they sat in thoughtful silence, the weight of the unknown pressing down on them both.

-Chapter 32-

Knock at the Door

The sunlight cut through the flimsy curtains of the Mountain View Motel, spilling across the bed where Marcus and Clarice lay, briefly enjoying the rare calm. Clarice smiled lazily, still curled against him.

"I could get used to this," she murmured.

Marcus kissed her forehead, a smirk tugging at his lips. "We might actually have a few minutes of peace—" He was immediately proven wrong.

Marcus sighed, dragging himself out of bed as the knocking continued—insistent but oddly polite. He swung open the door to find a woman standing there, dossier tucked under her arm.

"Linda, I presume?" Marcus asked.

"Miles called me last night—said some guests were asking questions about me and Katherine."

Marcus frowned, motioning her inside. "We might've brought your name up. What did Miles say?"

"Nothing specific, but enough to make me want answers," Linda replied, holding up the thick folder she carried. "I thought this was mine alone. Now I'm starting to think I'm just one piece of a bigger puzzle."

Before Marcus could respond, another knock sounded at the door—far less patient this time.

"Oh, for the love of—" Marcus muttered, pulling it open to find Cesaro, grinning like he'd just won the lottery.

"Morning!" Cesaro said brightly, hands shoved in his pockets as he leaned against the doorframe. "Thought I'd wait and let you two sleep in a bit, but then I saw you had a guest and figured it was fair game."

Clarice groaned audibly from the bed. "Of course you did."

Linda raised an eyebrow at Cesaro. "What do you want?"

"Me?" Cesaro feigned innocence. "Just here to offer breakfast. And to check in. You know, team bonding." His grin widened as he stepped into the room uninvited. "Besides, it looks like I came at the perfect time. What's this?" He gestured toward the folder in Linda's hands. Marcus shot him a look, then pointed for Linda to see his folder sitting on the table next to their bed. Her eyes widened slightly. "You have one too? That confirms it—either all the cool kids are getting them or something bigger is at play here."

Clarice, finally sitting up, rubbed her temples. Linda shook her head, a mix of frustration and urgency in her tone. "Someone left it for me—no note, no explanation."

"Someone wants us digging," Marcus added grimly. "They're spreading the breadcrumbs, but not enough for anyone to see the whole picture."

Cesaro plopped himself into a chair, arms crossed. "So, what now? I'm starving, and I'll bet Kathleen's already at the diner waiting to drop her own bombshells. We're not going to figure this out standing around in a motel room."

Linda nodded in agreement. "He's right. Kathleen usually heads to the diner first thing. I was supposed to meet her there anyway."

Clarice shot Cesaro a suspicious look. "You're unusually eager to help."

Cesaro held up his hands, grinning. "Hey, I have news too…not that you asked! Plus, I'm starving. Besides, you'll want me there to help charm the locals."

Marcus ignored him, turning back to Linda. "We'll head to the diner and regroup. But you're right about one thing—this is bigger than us."

Linda hesitated as they gathered their things, lowering her voice. "Just one more thing: one of my sources said the diner and the motel are being watched. We shouldn't all walk in together. No point painting a target on ourselves."

Clarice shot Marcus a look, her brow furrowed. "She's not wrong. Groups of five tend to stand out in places like this."

Marcus nodded. "We'll split up. Cesaro, you take Rose. Linda, you go first and let Kathleen know we're coming. Clarice and I will follow after."

Cesaro saluted sarcastically as he headed for the door. "You got it, boss. But don't expect us to wait to order coffee."

Clarice rolled her eyes, grabbing her coat. "You'd better not spill any of it, either."

As instructed, Cesaro and Rose had arrived first, with Linda and Katherine arriving moments later, spotting the pair already tucked into a corner booth near the window with coffee cups in hand. Cesaro waved dramatically. Marcus and Clarice arrived just behind them, slipping in as everyone was making their introductions.

"Told you we'd get the good seats," Cesaro said with a grin.

Clarice smirked. "Save it, hotshot. You didn't even wait to order."

Cesaro lifted his hands in mock surrender. "Guilty. You snooze, you lose."

Plates clattered, coffee pots hissed, and the low hum of conversation wove through the air. In their corner booth, Marcus, Clarice, Cesaro, Rose, Linda, and Katherine huddled over mugs and folders, the weight of their conversation setting them apart from the more relaxed diners. Marcus sipped his black coffee, watching Katherine as she sat across from him, flipping through her well-worn notebook. Linda sat beside her, scanning the room nervously.

"Alright," Clarice began, breaking the silence. "So, what's your story? How did you two get wrapped up in all of this?"

Kathleen looked up, exchanging a glance with Linda. She adjusted her glasses and leaned forward, her voice quiet but steady.

"I came to Wellville last August," Kathleen started. "I was working on a book, something unrelated. At least, I thought it was. One night, I went to bed as usual. When I woke up, twelve hours were missing. Just… gone. My phone, my watch, everything was perfectly synced. But to me, it felt like no time passed at all."

Clarice frowned. "And no one noticed?"

"No one." Kathleen's tone turned sharp with frustration. "It was like it hadn't happened—except to me. I started asking questions, trying to find anyone else who might have experienced something similar. That's when Linda found me."

Linda nodded, offering a tight smile. "I'd been looking into the strange stuff happening around here since spring. Apparently, Kathleen had since August…but neither of us got far, until these files just showed up a couple weeks ago. Each one included information about the other too, with pictures and everything…so I tracked her down and we started working together."

Marcus glanced over at Clarice. "What did they say about me?"

Both women shook their heads, insisting nothing about him had been included.

"What made you think it was connected to the Pulse?" Rose asked, studying Katherine intently.

Katherine hesitated. "The timing. Getting them right before that Pulse happened. That changed everything. People reported seeing strange lights, creatures in the woods… reality itself has just…felt off. I thought maybe whatever happened to me was part of that."

Before anyone else could speak, Marcus raised a hand, silencing them.

"It's not directly connected," he said firmly, his gaze locking onto Katherine. "The Pulse and what happened to you are separate events—at least on the surface. But I believe they are linked. Not by some supernatural accident, but by people. People working with—or within—the military. Likely in coordination with members of the secret society, the OAS."

"The OAS?" Katherine blinked, surprised at his confidence. "How can you be sure?"

Marcus leaned back slightly. "Let's just say I've been looking at the same puzzle from a different angle."

Linda leaned forward then, dropping her voice to a near-whisper. "It's the JUNE program."

The table fell silent. Clarice furrowed her brows, while Rose tilted her head.

"The what?" Cesaro asked.

Linda scanned the diner cautiously, her eyes flickering toward the counter where Nicole hovered, wiping down menus but clearly trying to eavesdrop.

"I just got this last night, it's something I learned from my contact," Linda murmured. "The Joint Committee for the Understanding of Non-Terrestrial Entities. JUNE. Back in the 1930s, the government reopened a mine outside Wellville after a… horrific incident."

Clarice crossed her arms, guarded but intrigued. "What kind of incident?"

Linda hesitated, her voice dropping even lower. "Miners disappeared. A survivor claimed he heard whispers—something humming in the dark. When they found the site, the walls were covered in blood. The government shut it down, covered it up, and launched the JUNE program to investigate. It's been running ever since."

Before anyone could react, Nicole appeared beside their table, her pot of coffee in hand and an overly curious gleam in her eyes.

"You all need a refill?" she asked sweetly, clearly fishing for details.

Marcus forced a polite smile. "I'm fine, thanks."

"Anyone else need a touchup?"

"No thank you." Cesaro told her.

Nicole ignored him, looking straight at Linda. "So, what's all this about mines and whispers? Sounds like something out of a ghost story. I really like watching those paranormal investigations shows on TV."

Linda froze, her expression carefully blank. "Just some research."

Nicole wasn't buying it. She set the coffee pot down, lowering her voice conspiratorially.

"Well, if you're looking into weird stuff around here, you've come to the right place. People have been talking about that mine for years. Lights in the woods, strange noises at night…" She glanced around theatrically. "Some folks even think there's something alive out there in those woods."

Cesaro leaned back, his grin lopsided. "Oh, this just keeps getting better."

"There are lots of creatures alive in the woods." Rose pointed out the obvious.

Nicole puffed up, pleased to be the center of attention. "Not just the woods or the mine, either. Ever since that Pulse, people have been seeing… things. Big, dark shapes in the trees. Animals acting strange. And those murders? Happened right near where the old mine entrance is. You ask me, it's all connected."

The words hung in the air, heavy with implication. Kathleen shot Marcus a pointed look, as if to say I told you so.

Linda leaned in, her voice low but urgent. "What did you mean, murders? Plural?"

Nicole glanced nervously at the counter, then lowered her voice. "Two in the last week. The last one happened just the other night…" She trailed off, her eyes widening as she realized who was sitting at the table. "Wait, didn't you say you were heading over to that house?"

Cesaro's smirk disappeared as he sat up straighter. "No!" He smirked.

"But we did last night…Me and Rose found a detective passed out there, named Dexter Simmons…in the middle of the worst crime scene I've ever seen."

Everyone turned toward him, their expressions a mix of curiosity and horror.

"What happened? And just how many crime scenes have you been to?" Marcus asked.

Cesaro ran a hand through his hair, his usual bravado giving way to a rare moment of vulnerability. "It was bad, amigo." He began, his voice quieter than usual. "The house... it looked like something out of a horror movie. It was gruesome. Blood everywhere—splattered on the walls, pooling on the floor. The furniture was torn to shreds, like some wild animal went through it."

He paused, swallowing hard before continuing. "And on the wall above the mantle…" His voice faltered, and he glanced at Rose as if seeking reassurance. "It said, 'Help us.' Written in blood."

Rose, sitting beside him, added quietly, "Whatever happened there wasn't human. I could feel it. The energy in that place… it was wrong."

Kathleen shivered. "And you think this is connected to the JUNE program?"

"Help Us! Is what was written on the walls of the mining tunnel in the 1930s. It can't be a coincidence." Linda reminded them.

"I don't know," Cesaro admitted. "But whatever's going on, it's not random. That house was set up almost like some fucked up ritual."

Marcus exchanged a glance with Clarice, then looked back at Cesaro. "And this detective, Dexter? What's his take?"

Cesaro shook his head. "He's spooked, but he's willing to talk. Said he'd meet us after he got cleaned up."

Marcus nodded grimly. "Then that's our next stop. If Dexter's in, we're going to need everything he knows."

Nearby, Dexter had just eased into his chair, feeling the weight of the prior day settle into his bones. He rubbed his temples, the events of the past 24 hours swirling in his mind like a bad dream. He glanced at the clock—8:05 a.m. He had reports to file, prisoners to check on, and questions without answers. The hum of the station's fluorescent lights felt oppressive in the eerie quiet.

First, he needed to question the man in holding—again. The same man who'd been ranting for years about shadows in the dark, whispers that no one else seemed to hear. Dexter grabbed the keys from the desk attendant, who barely stirred as he walked by.

As he entered the holding area, his gaze landed on Max Coburn. The young man lay on the cot, staring blankly at the ceiling, his fingers twitching as if caught in a memory he couldn't escape. The old man was in the next cell, rocking back and forth, muttering to himself.

Dexter turned to the old man first. "Hey, got a minute?"

The old man looked up, his cloudy eyes locking onto Dexter's. "Finally ready to listen, are you?" he said, his voice hoarse but steady.

"Yeah," Dexter replied, unlocking the cell door. "Let's talk."

The man didn't move, only gestured for Dexter to sit. "They've been here for years, Detective. Watching, waiting. You think what's happening now is new? It's not. The Whisperers don't just appear—they're called."

Dexter frowned. "Called? By whom?"

The old man gave a wry smile. "By those who think they can control them. The military tried first. Experiments, they called it. Thought they could harness the shadows. But you can't control what you don't understand. And now they're back."

Dexter leaned forward, his voice low. "Why now? What's changed?"

The old man shook his head. "You think I've got all the answers? I just know what I've seen. They come where and when the veil is thin, the Pulse has weakened the barriers. And someone—someone here—is making sure they stay."

Dexter's mind raced. The old man's words aligned with whispers he'd dismissed for years. He stood, locking the cell behind him. "Stay put. I'll be back."

Dexter turned to Max's cell, unlocking it and stepping inside. The young man sat up, his face pale and gaunt. "What do you want now, Detective? Come to call me crazy again?"

"No," Dexter said simply, pulling a chair closer. "I want you to tell me everything. No filters, no interruptions."

Max hesitated, his fingers tightening around the edge of the cot. "You mean it?"

"I mean it."

Max took a shaky breath. "It started five nights ago. Mary and I were at my place. Just hanging out, watching movies. Everything was fine until it got dark. That's when I heard them. Whispering."

Dexter leaned in. "What did they sound like?"

"Like... like the wind, but with words. I couldn't make them out at first, but they got louder. And then they came." Max's voice broke, his hands trembling. "Green eyes, no teeth—just claws. They took Mary. Tore her apart and I couldn't do anything to stop…so I just ran."

Max lifted his shirt, revealing two long, jagged scars across his chest. "They slashed me, but they didn't kill me."

Dexter's stomach turned as he examined the wounds. "Max, you said they only left her eyes. What did you mean by that?"

Max's face crumpled. "Her body was gone. Blood everywhere, but nobody. Just her eyes on the floor, staring at me."

Dexter felt a chill creep down his spine as Max's story settled heavily in the room. He stood, his voice firm but laced with a hint of compassion. "You're not crazy, Max. I believe you. But the house is still an active crime scene. I'm going to release you but can't let you go back there."

Max's eyes darted to Dexter's, desperate and pleading. "Then where am I supposed to go? I don't have anyone else. I can't leave—not until we figure this out. Not until they're gone."

Dexter hesitated, weighing his options. "You can't stay here in holding. Let's see about getting you a room at the Mountain View Motel. It's not far, and I can make sure someone checks in on you."

Max shook his head, his hands balling into fists. "No. I don't want to leave yet. What if they come for me again? What if…" He trailed off, his voice breaking.

Dexter placed a steadying hand on his shoulder. "Listen to me. You'll be safer out of here. The station doesn't have the resources to house you indefinitely, and you'll need a proper place to stay while we figure this out. The motel's close, I'll make sure the owners know to look out for you."

Dexter grabbed his coffee thermos, gesturing for Max to follow. "Come on. I'll walk you over to the Mountain View Motel. They've always got vacancies, and it'll give me a chance to clear my head."

Max, clutching his duffel bag, nodded silently. He was still in a mood for being put in that cell in the first place as a suspect in this ongoing murder investigation. He had no corroborated alibi for the time the crime took place, but without evidence, he was to be let go, kept under surveillance.

The early morning air carried a slight chill, and the streets of Wellville were eerily quiet except for the occasional chirp of a bird. The sun's golden rays cast long shadows, giving the small town an unsettling stillness. There was a storm coming on the horizon. For now, they were happy to enjoy a moment in the sun, rare for this time of year. As they neared the motel, Dexter noticed the diner across the street was already bustling. Through the large windows, he spotted Cesaro, Rose, Marcus, and Clarice seated in a corner booth. Cesaro was gesturing animatedly, his enthusiasm palpable even from across the street.

Dexter paused mid-step. "Looks like some of your neighbors are up early."

Max followed his gaze and frowned. "Who are they?"

"Let's just call them associates of mine." Dexter replied vaguely. "Wait here by the motel entrance. I need to check something."

Dexter pushed open the door, the scent of coffee and frying bacon wafting over him. Nicole, the ever-curious waitress, noticed him immediately and gave a bright smile and a wave. It was a small town and nearly everyone knew everyone else in some manner or other.

"Well, if it isn't Detective Simmons," she teased, wiping her hands on her apron. "Coffee's fresh if you need a pick-me-up. And we have those sticky buns this morning that I know you like so much."

"I could smell them before I even came in the door. Always delightful." Dexter told her politely. "I'm going to talk to this lot in the corner. Bring me some coffee and one of those rolls, please."

"Sure thing, darling." Nicole said as the detective's focus locked on the corner booth. Cesaro spotted him first and raised a hand.

"Detective!" Cesaro called out, standing to greet him. "What took you so long?"

Dexter crossed his arms, his tone dry. "Didn't think you'd still be in town. What's keeping you here?"

Cesaro grinned. "The ambiance, obviously."

Clarice shot Cesaro a look, then turned to Dexter. "What brings you in?"

Dexter nodded toward the windows. "I'm walking a guest from the station over to the motel. But since you're here, I need to talk to you all."

Nicole brought the detective his coffee, intimately knowing his order. Afterwards, she hovered around a nearby table, pretending to rearrange the sugar packets. Dexter glanced at her sharply. "Nicole, don't you have other tables?"

She huffed but walked away, though her curiosity was far from sated.

Dexter turned back to the group. "I'm serious. If you want to talk, it's not happening here. The walls in this place have ears."

Marcus nodded, closing the folder in front of him. "He's right. We need somewhere private."

"Where is private when half of the town works for the government?" Rose wondered.

"Back to the station then?" Cesaro suggested, leaning back with a grin. "Always dreamed of a police station debrief."

Dexter sighed, glancing toward the motel entrance where Max waited, his duffel bag slung over one shoulder. "Fine, but I've got someone to set up at the motel first."

Marcus raised an eyebrow. "Someone?"

"Kid from last night," Dexter explained vaguely. "Witnessed something he shouldn't have. I'm keeping an eye on him as a suspect. Let me take care of him, and we'll meet back at the station."

Rose tilted her head. "Why not bring him along? If he's involved, he might know something useful."

Dexter hesitated, his gaze flickering between the group and Max. "He's been through hell. I don't want to spook him."

"Or" Marcus interjected, "he might feel safer with more people around. Could help him open up."

Dexter's jaw tightened, considering it. "Alright. Let me ask him."

He stepped outside and waved Max over. The younger man approached cautiously, his gaze darting between Dexter and the diner. "What's going on?"

"We're heading to the station," Dexter said. "You're coming with us. There's a group inside I think you should meet."

Max hesitated. "They're not… Whisperers, are they?"

Dexter gave a small, reassuring smirk. "No. Just people trying to figure out the same things you and I are. Let's go."

Inside the diner, Marcus and Clarice were already settling the check, while Cesaro took the opportunity to charm Nicole with a well-timed compliment.

By the time they left the diner, Max was trailing close to Dexter, his shoulders hunched but his steps steady. The group walked briskly toward the station, the morning sun climbing higher as tension hung in the air.

The group filed into the conference room, Dexter leading Max inside before pouring himself a fresh cup of coffee. Max hovered near the door, his discomfort obvious as he took in the unfamiliar faces.

"This is Max," Dexter announced, gesturing toward the younger man. "He's staying at the motel for now, but he's got some firsthand experience we should all hear."

Max glanced nervously at the others, his fingers gripping the strap of his duffel bag. "Uh… hi."

Cesaro leaned back in his chair, giving Max an easy smile. "Don't worry, kid. We're on your side."

Rose nodded, her tone calm. "You've been through a lot, haven't you?"

Max shrugged, his gaze dropping to the floor. "Yeah. More than I ever wanted to."

Dexter clapped a hand on his shoulder, steering him toward a seat. "Start at the beginning, Max. Tell them what you told me…if you want to, you don't have to though"

Max agreed, hoping to help, recounting his harrowing experience. The room fell silent, the weight of his words filling the air. Dexter leaned against the wall, his expression grim. "Alright," he said, ending his story, setting the mug down. "You flagged me down. Now, let's hear it. What's going on?"

Marcus and Clarice exchanged a look before Marcus spoke. "We've been investigating strange events connected to the Pulse and some military programs. We think it's tied to the murders here in Wellville."

Dexter raised an eyebrow. "You think the military is involved? That's a bold claim."

"It's not a claim," Marcus said firmly. "It's a pattern. And from what we've gathered, this town is at the center of something bigger."

Rose leaned forward, her voice steady. "Detective, you've seen things. You know this town isn't normal. We're here to figure out why—and who's behind it."

Dexter hesitated, then nodded toward Max, who sat quietly in a corner. "Max here claims to have seen something—something that aligns with what you're saying. But I'm not ready to write off the possibility that he's just a traumatized kid."

Max's voice trembled, but he spoke up. "They're real. The Whisperers. I saw them. And they took Mary."

"They don't take people, son." Dexter told him sadly. "They kill them."

The room fell silent as his words hung heavy in the air.

Marcus broke the silence, his tone calm but firm. "Then we need to piece this together. Every detail matters. If we're going to figure this out, we have to work together."

Dexter's expression softened slightly as he leaned back in his chair. "Fine. But if we're doing this, we're doing it right. And if anyone else gets hurt, it's on all of us."

Dexter hesitated, his eyes narrowing as he stared down at his coffee mug, lost in thought. Finally, he looked up, his voice low but steady. "Alright. Here's what I've got so far. What you saw at the crime scene is consistent with others we've had—brutal, grotesque, and leaving more questions than answers."

He leaned forward, his elbows resting on the table. "The blood patterns? They weren't random. Someone—or something—made sure every drop served a purpose. It's like they're sending a message, but damned if I know what it is yet."

Rose's brow furrowed. "You said it's consistent. How many of these are we talking about?"

Dexter's jaw tightened. "Thirty-seven. That's the count of unexplained deaths or disappearances in this town that I can confirm in the past ten years. More if you go back further. But…" He glanced toward the door, as if expecting someone to be eavesdropping. "If what the old man told me this morning is true, this has been going on for much longer—decades, maybe even close to a century."

Cesaro folded his arms, his bravado momentarily subdued. "And no one's caught onto this? Thirty-seven people is a lot, man."

Dexter nodded grimly. "It's not for lack of trying. A lot of it gets written off—missing persons cases, animal attacks, suicides…and now, with the Pulse. But when you put it all together, the patterns start to emerge. The wounds? Always precise. Like someone knew exactly how to avoid making mistakes. And then there are the… other things."

"Other things?" Marcus pressed, leaning forward.

Dexter sighed, running a hand over his face. "You didn't see it, but the last crime scene? There was this smell—sweet, like vinegar, but sharp, almost like formaldehyde. I've only smelled it a couple of times before, and always at scenes like this. Forensics doesn't have an answer yet, but to me it doesn't seem human. That much I can tell you."

Rose shivered, wrapping her arms around herself. "And the old man? What did he say?"

Dexter's expression darkened. "He called them Whisperers. Said they've been around long before any of us. According to him, they come out at night, always whispering, always watching. He claimed they're not human—said they're from… somewhere else."

The room fell silent, tension thick in the air. Finally, Marcus spoke, his voice measured. "Do you believe him?"

Dexter's lips pressed into a thin line. "A few days ago, I laughed him off like everyone else. But now? After what I've seen, what I've heard…" He shook his head. "I don't know. But there's one thing I'm sure of—this isn't random. And it's not done."

Cesaro leaned forward, his tone serious for once. "You think the murders are connected to the Pulse?"

Dexter hesitated, then shook his head. "Not directly. The Pulse might've stirred the pot, but these killings? They were happening long before that. If anything, it feels like the Pulse gave them… permission. Like something that was sleeping finally woke up."

Rose exchanged a glance with Marcus, her voice trembling slightly. "If they've been around for that long, why now? Why so many murders all at once?"

Dexter shrugged, his frustration evident. "That's the million-dollar question, isn't it? I've got pieces of the puzzle, but none of them fit together. And every time I get close, it's like the trail goes cold. Someone—or something—is keeping this buried. I'm not a gambling man, but if I were, I'd put everything on the source of this madness coming from the Wind Valley Military Installation a few miles from here. There's been rumors coming out of that place for decades now. Hell, I even heard a story about intelligent mice they were experimenting on up there. Viral research too."

The weight of Dexter's words hung over the group, the enormity of the mystery pressing down like an invisible weight. Silence stretched as they absorbed the implications, each turning over fragments of what they knew.

Finally, Marcus spoke, his tone resolute. "Then we dig. Whatever's happening here, we're not leaving until we get answers."

Dexter nodded, his sharp gaze sweeping over the group. "Good. Because if we don't figure this out soon, it's not a question of if there'll be another murder—it's when."

Linda leaned forward, her voice cutting through the tension. "My contact said something about the installation being created after a horrible accident. Or maybe for the experiments that caused it. The timing seems to check out."

Marcus turned toward her, his brow furrowed. "It does. The dates line up with the early JUNE file reports. The Whisperers, the mine, all of it. But how do these events line up with the Pulse and the increase in attacks since then?"

Kathleen, who had been quietly flipping through her notes, looked up. "So, what are we saying here? That the installation was built to cover up the accident, or to keep experimenting with whatever caused it?"

"It's not one or the other," Marcus replied, his voice steady. "It's both. Accidents like these don't just happen. Someone was pushing boundaries—and kept pushing them even after it went horribly wrong."

Dexter exhaled sharply, leaning back in his chair. "That tracks. The kind of funding, resources, and secrecy we're talking about here? This wasn't some rogue operation. This was sanctioned by people high up, and they're still keeping it quiet."

"That is even more reason to believe that the OAS is involved." Clarice added. "They have many fronts for the face of their legitimate businesses that act as a front for their more nefarious plans, many of which contract with the government."

"That makes sense. I've seen several different black vans driving through town this week, marked with the logo for Obsidian Allied Sciences."

"Again with the OAS." Rose tapped her fingers on the table, her expression grim. "Then the question isn't just why this is happening—it's why now? What changed to bring all of this to the surface?"

Linda nodded. "It's like my contact said. The installation wasn't just about covering up the past. They were actively experimenting—on the phenomenon, on people, who knows what else."

Katherine's face paled slightly. "And if it's still active…"

Dexter cut in, his voice firm. "Then we're dealing with more than just the fallout of past mistakes. We're dealing with something ongoing—something they never stopped."

A heavy silence followed, broken only by the faint hum of the station's fluorescent lights. Marcus rubbed his temples, his mind racing. "If we're going to figure this out, we'll need to work together. No more holding back."

Dexter crossed his arms, his jaw tightening. "Fine. But if we're doing this, we're doing it my way. No heroics, no going rogue. If anyone else gets hurt because of this, it's on all of us."

Cesaro raised a hand, his usual smirk returning faintly. "Just to be clear, by 'your way,' you mean sticking to the law, right?"

Dexter shot him a look. "Don't push it."

Rose glanced at the others, her tone measured. "So, what's the next step? We have fragments of the puzzle, but we're missing the big picture."

Dexter leaned forward, his gaze intense. "We start by gathering everything we know—maps, records, anything tying this town to the installation. And we figure out who's still pulling the strings."

Marcus nodded. "Agreed. But we need to be smart about this. If they've kept this quiet for decades, they won't hesitate to shut us down if we get too close."

"Then we don't give them the chance," Dexter replied, his voice cold and determined. "We find the truth—and we expose it before they can stop us."

"Fuck yeah!" Marcus threw in for good measure, but it was the wrong timing for that kind of enthusiasm.

The group exchanged tense but resolute glances, a silent agreement passing between them. The stakes were higher than ever, but none of them were willing to back down. It wasn't just about solving a mystery anymore—it was about stopping whatever nightmare had been unleashed on Wellville before it could consume them all. Dexter broke the silence. "If this really is tied to the military, we need an inside line. Someone who knows how deep this runs."

Linda's eyes widened slightly. "You're not thinking what I think you are."

Marcus turned toward her, his expression calm but firm. "We are. Your contact—they've already shared some details with you. Do you think they'd be willing to talk?"

Linda shook her head immediately, leaning back in her chair. "Not a chance. They're already taking a massive risk by sharing what they have. If they so much as sniff out I'm even considering pushing for more, I'm cut off. Worse, they could be exposed."

Cesaro leaned forward, his tone casual but edged with curiosity. "What kind of person are we talking about here? Desk jockey? Field operative? Colonel Mustard in the library with a candlestick?"

Linda shot him a sharp look. "Not funny. They're... someone who knows things. Let's leave it at that."

Rose chimed in, her voice soft but insistent. "We're not asking them to put themselves in danger, Linda. Just to point us in the right direction. Right now, we're flying blind. Even a breadcrumb could mean the difference between stopping this or being one of the 'unexplained deaths.'"

Linda hesitated, glancing at Marcus, then back at Dexter. "Look, I get it. But you don't understand. They're already walking a fine line. If I push too hard, I could lose them."

Dexter folded his arms, his eyes narrowing. "And if you don't push, we could lose someone else. You think the people pulling the strings care how long we take? Every minute we sit on our hands, they're erasing evidence and covering tracks. We need leverage, Linda."

Linda exhaled slowly, her gaze dropping to the table. For a moment, she seemed to wrestle with herself, the weight of the group's expectations pressing heavily on her shoulders. Finally, she nodded, her voice quiet but resolute. "I'll ask. But I'm making no promises. If they say no, that's it; we find another way."

Marcus inclined his head slightly, his expression one of understanding. "That's all we're asking. Just the chance."

"Great," Cesaro added, leaning back with a smirk. "Now that we've got our inside agent, what's next? Do we storm the secret installation, or do we wait for them to come to us with cake and a confession?"

Dexter shot him a withering look. "We wait for Linda to get her answer. In the meantime, we focus on what we can do."

Rose nodded. "Which is?"

Dexter rubbed his temples, his mind working fast. "Recon. We need eyes on that installation and every connected location in this town. If there's activity, I want to know about it."

Marcus folded his arms. "Then we split up. Cesaro and Rose can check out the town's perimeter. Katherine and I will dig through historical records and see what else we can connect to the JUNE project. Linda..."

Linda nodded. "I'll make the call."

-Chapter 33-

The Minotaur

In ancient times, Minos, King of Crete, prayed to Poseidon for a white bull as a divine sign of his birthright to rule over all others, including his brothers. Poseidon granted his wish, sending the bull from the sea. However, instead of sacrificing the bull in the god's name as he had promised, Minos kept it for himself. Enraged by this disobedience, Poseidon cursed Minos by making his wife, Queen Pasiphae, fall in love with the bull. The offspring of this unnatural union was the Minotaur—a creature with the head of a bull, black horns, and the body of a man. The Minotaur was consumed by insatiable rage and a thirst for human blood. Unable to bear the shame and horror, Minos commissioned Daedalus to construct a labyrinth outside his palace in Knossos. At its center, the Minotaur dwelled, feeding on the lost and condemned, victims of Minos' punishments. Hidden away due to its grotesque form, the creature grew bitter and savage, its hunger never satisfied.

In the dystopian future ruled by Ivyg, humanity's darker instincts were exploited for his amusement, lust and anger primarily, taking joy in watching people fight and fornicate for his pleasure. With mastery over time travel, Ivyg devised a grim form of entertainment—sending people to die in brutal, historical settings, their deaths broadcast to legions of his worshippers. Bread and circuses, he reasoned, much like the Romans, but with himself as the ultimate God-King. In this twisted future, distraction and spectacle ruled over despairing lives, much like the kingdom of Rome with its bread and circuses. Based on their spins on the Wheel of Fate and judgment by the Titan Judge, Clovis Krott, and the artificial humanoid Murrin, Patel, Nova, and Kane were sentenced to compete in the ancient Cretan Labyrinth. Stepping through the portal, the three men found themselves in another time and place, the faint chime of their bracelets signaling their arrival in the heart of one of history's deadliest mazes with a cruel and vengeful foe at its center.

The armbands they wore glowed a foreboding red, signaling the activation of their explosive devices. Murrin had explained the rules in chilling detail: refusal to play the game meant death. Attempting to remove or tamper with the bracelets meant death. And failure to win? Death. There was no room for error or rebellion. Only survival.

Their starting point within the labyrinth was deceptively serene—a lush, well-manicured garden filled with fruit-laden trees and vibrant, fragrant flowers. It was a paradise that invited the unprepared to linger, though its beauty belied the horrors waiting below. Above, from the grand palace, King Minos and his advisors watched with anticipation. The labyrinth, open from above, was a theater for spectacle and cruelty, allowing the King and his court to relish the unfolding drama. High-stakes gambling fueled the revelry as Minos eagerly took wagers, confident in the deadly prowess of the Minotaur.

The labyrinth itself was a marvel of both nature and craftsmanship. Towering hedges interwoven with intricate stone masonry, the maze extending deep into the earth. The design was inspired by the legendary Egyptian labyrinths of Khem, a tribute from Daedalus to the God-King Pharaohs of old, Seth. This creation was his masterpiece, meant to imprison the abomination that stalked its halls and serve as a grim stage for punishing those who defied Crete.

Far below, Kane led Patel and Nova down a spiraling flight of stone stairs, descending from the vibrant garden into the oppressive confines of the labyrinth. The dim lighting at ground level cast flickering shadows, amplifying the sense of foreboding. None of the men had been here before, and while Kane and Patel recalled the myth of Theseus, it felt worlds away from the brutal reality they now faced. The Minotaur was no legend—it was alive, waiting somewhere within this maze of horrors, its cries could be heard even from the start of the labyrinth.

Unlike Theseus, they had no golden string to guide their way back or keep them from getting lost. The immaculately kept garden above sharply contrasted with the overgrowth below. Vines twisted and crawled along the walls, their dense patterns offering no clear path or assistance. The walls were too high to climb, and the labyrinth's design seemed determined to keep its victims trapped within.

At first, there was only one way forward. With no other choice, they moved cautiously. Patel, the smallest and most agile of the three, tested the strength of the vines, hoping to climb and gain some advantage. He managed only a few yards before the brittle vines snapped under his weight. He tumbled backward, but Nova was quick to catch him, breaking his fall and sparing him from serious injury.

Dusting himself off, Patel shook his head. "Well, that's not an option."

"No shortcuts here," Kane muttered grimly, his eyes scanning their surroundings. "We stick together. Keep moving."

The trio pressed forward into the labyrinth, the oppressive silence broken only by their breathing and the faint rustling of unseen movement in the distance. Somewhere in the depths, the Minotaur waited. And it was hungry.

"So, it looks like the only way out of here is to reach the end of the maze," Kane said, his tone steady despite the weight of their predicament.

"That means we have to face the Minotaur—and defeat it," Nova added, his voice calm but laced with unease as he pieced together their grim reality.

"It is of flesh and blood," Patel chimed in, his analytical mind taking over. "Which means it can be killed. But our challenge is complicated by the fact that you, Master Kane, are injured... and still missing your right arm."

Kane nodded, his expression hardened. "It's an inconvenience for sure. I won't pretend I'm operating at full strength. Maybe 75 percent, at best. But pain or no pain, the goal doesn't change. You've heard it a thousand times in the Order, but I truly believe this time—this time—we can save the world from this godforsaken fate."

"It won't be easy," Nova said, his tone pragmatic but unwavering. "But I made a pledge to help you along this journey, and that hasn't changed."

Patel stepped forward, his voice brimming with conviction. "I have served you for a long time, Master Kane. I will continue to serve you for all of my days."

"Good," Kane replied, his confidence bolstered by their loyalty. "If the three of us work together, we'll not only survive this labyrinth, but we'll kill this so-called God King, then we'll use his technology to change the past and rewrite this apocalyptic timeline."

Nova raised an eyebrow, a hint of skepticism creeping into his tone. "When you say it like that, it sounds... well, impossible. Or insane. I'm still in, but I can't say I'm sold on the part where everything magically works out."

"Crazy or not, it'll be fun, right?" Patel said with a wry grin, his excitement breaking through the tension.

Kane allowed himself a faint smile, giving Patel a thumbs-up without breaking his stride. He didn't voice his own doubts, but the idea of facing—and slaying—a literal monster, the Minotaur, weighed heavily on him. This creature wasn't just a hybrid of man and beast; it was a grotesque perversion of nature, a gluttonous embodiment of rage and wrath. That's why it had been imprisoned in this labyrinth—to contain its fury, its insatiable hunger for destruction. Still, Kane and company pressed on. The path ahead was uncertain, the stakes impossibly high, but their resolve was clear. Together, they would navigate this maze, confront the nightmare at its heart, and forge a future free from the horrors of their present.

They walked straight for what felt like an eternity before reaching a T-shaped intersection.

"Left or right?" Patel asked, glancing between the two options.

Unbeknownst to them, only visible from above, the labyrinth formed the intricate shape of the Tree of Life. Its many branches wove together with sacred geometric patterns—ratios designed to resonate with the forms of nature and long-held spiritual principles. These structures, imbued with the wisdom and magic of the ancients, served purposes long forgotten by most. Even Kane, with all his knowledge, could not claim to understand everything about such artifacts. Only one being he was aware of wielded that kind of omniscience. Something he hadn't seen for quite some time, a person of interest as part of a research study funded by Ivyg, the Aurora Initiative. A young Chinese woman named Zhilin Wei.

They didn't have her or anyone else to help them, making the debate over which direction to take a less-than-easy one. Both options seemed equally plausible, with no clear indication of what lay ahead. What they couldn't know was that the right path, while shorter, would still lead to the same destination: the lair of the Minotaur. Yet, the twists and turns along the way carried their own challenges and opportunities, depending on the route they chose.

"I say we go right," Kane offered, his tone resolute.

Nova and Patel, however, had other ideas. "Left feels better," Nova argued. "It's instinct, but I trust it."

"I agree," Patel added. "Sometimes the long way around is the safest."

Kane paused as the two turned toward their chosen path, hesitating as he weighed their decision. The instinct to go right tugged at him, a quiet voice in the back of his mind urging him to trust his own judgment. For a brief moment, he considered going his own way, leaving Patel and Nova to their choice, but as the Titan Judge had told them, they came in as a trio and they would too be leaving as a trio.

His thoughts drifted to Marcus Kydd, his former protégé, and the lessons Marcus had inadvertently taught him. After millennia of existence, Kane had thought he'd learned everything there was to know. Then came a new generation of Vril-enhanced individuals (VEI's) through the OAS recruitment process, challenging his views on humanity and its potential. His missing right forearm, a painful reminder of his confrontation with Marcus, symbolized the harsh realities of this new age—a future unlike any he had ever encountered in his countless attempts to alter the timeline. And yet, this future offered something different: a glimmer of hope. If they could survive this labyrinth, defeat the Minotaur, and claim the God King's technology, they might have a chance to rewrite history and prevent the catastrophic fate that had befallen their world.

Kane glanced down at his stump, his jaw tightening as he contemplated his next move. Patel, noticing his master's hesitation, paused and turned back.

"You're angry with him aren't you?" Patel asked, his voice soft with concern.

"Who do you mean?"

"Marcus. He always was your favorite. I can understand why you would be mad at him for turning on you back there in the Hollow Earth."

Kane exhaled deeply, his eyes still fixed on his missing limb. "In some ways, yes," he admitted. "But in others, no. It's... complicated."

Patel waited, sensing there was more Kane needed to say.

"I can't fault him for thinking he was doing what was right," Kane continued. "In his mind, his actions were justified. For that, I don't hold a grudge. But where he faltered—where he truly disappointed me—was in forgetting what I taught him. He made it personal, and in doing so, he lost sight of the bigger picture. That's where I couldn't help him."

Patel nodded thoughtfully, the weight of Kane's words sinking in. "It sounds like you still believe in him," he said after a pause.

Kane's gaze lifted, meeting Patel's. "Belief is a dangerous thing," he said quietly. "But maybe... maybe there's still hope for him yet."

"Hope." Nova repeated. Something about that word made him appear happier for that brief moment hanging heavy in the air before Kane finally stepped forward, following Patel and Nova begrudgingly down the left path. The maze loomed around them, its ancient walls bearing witness to their journey, each step bringing them closer to the heart of the labyrinth—echoes of the beast that awaited them.

"You don't have to go through that pain alone, is all I'm saying, master," Patel said a few minutes later, his tone earnest and unwavering.

Kane glanced at him, a rare softness in his expression. "I'm grateful for you having my back, my friend," he replied, his voice kind but weighted with sincerity. "I don't think I'd be able to accomplish this feat without you—and without our new ally here. Believe it or not, this whole experience has humbled me. I'm not used to relying on others for my protection, for my safety. It's... difficult, but I want you to know how much it means to me. Don't ever think I'm ungrateful, even if I have a rough demeanor these days."

He lifted his stump to make his point. Before Patel could respond, Nova's impatient voice echoed from several yards ahead. "Come on, you two! We don't have time for a heart-to-heart! We have to kill the beast. Save the world."

The moment ended abruptly. Kane exhaled a short laugh, shaking his head at Nova's lack of tact. Emotions weren't something he shared often, and even then, only with a very select few—Patel, Marcus, Clarice, Cesaro, and Dr. Moses chief among them. To open up, even briefly, felt unnatural, yet strangely freeing, not normal to his Draconian upbringing all those thousands of years ago.

The trio resumed their trek through the labyrinth, the air between them quiet but no longer heavy with unspoken tension. Each step took them deeper into the maze, its walls a tapestry of ancient overgrowth and haunting shadows. For a time, the silence became suffocating, their collective frustration threatening to bubble over as they navigated the seemingly endless corridors. Finally, Nova took charge, asserting himself as the group's navigator. Kane, unaccustomed to relinquishing control, found the experience awkward at first. But as they pressed forward, he began to accept the dynamic shift, seeing it as almost liberating. Allowing others to lead—even in a small way—was a novel concept for someone who had spent lifetimes carrying the weight of his decisions alone. Surprisingly, the tension eased, and the group's morale lifted as they fell into an easy rhythm. Conversation picked up again, their voices a quiet counterpoint to the oppressive silence of the maze.

That tentative peace didn't last long. As they turned another corner, their footsteps faltered. Ahead, the skeletal remains of a fallen warrior lay crumpled on the ground, armor rusted and weapons scattered. The eerie sight sent a chill through the group.

Patel's stomach twisted as Kane studied the remains, the stark evidence of the labyrinth's deadly purpose forcing the grim reality of their situation to the forefront of their minds. Patel's face hardened, while Nova let out a low whistle, his bravado faltering in the face of what awaited them.

"Looks like we know what's at the end of this maze," He muttered, his voice low and tight. "A fight to the death."

"His? Or ours?" Patel wondered.

Kane stepped forward, his gaze locked on the remnants of the unfortunate soul. "Not just a fight," he said quietly, his voice carrying the weight of centuries of understanding. "A warning. This isn't just about survival. It's a test—of our resolve, our strength, and our ability to trust each other."

Patel and Nova exchanged uneasy glances but nodded.

Without another word, the trio pressed on, the chilling specter of death now their silent companion. Each step forward carried a new weight, their earlier camaraderie replaced by a sobering awareness of the stakes. The Minotaur awaited, and their only choice was to face it—or meet the same fate as the warrior who had fallen before them.

Chapter 34

Saywa's Legacy

Later that night, the fire had dwindled to soft embers, casting long shadows across the cave walls. The others slept nearby, their breathing slow and steady, but Kiara's rest was anything but peaceful.

She twitched beneath her blanket; her face contorted in pain as the dream took hold.

She was no longer herself.

She was Saywa—bound at the wrists, kneeling in the center of a bloodstained stone chamber. The air reeked of smoke and death. Across from her stood Ivyg—no, Tezcatlipoca—his red eyes glowing like embers as he circled her slowly, his boots echoing off the damp floor. His voice slithered through the space like poison.

"You think you can defy me? You're nothing but a vessel. A puppet. All your resistance does is entertain me."

Saywa spat at his feet.

The strike came fast—a blur of motion and agony. Then his mouth was at her throat, teeth sinking in, and the world exploded into pain. The scream that tore from her lips shattered the vision and jolted Kiara awake.

She gasped, sitting upright in a cold sweat, clutching the blanket to her chest. Her body trembled as phantom pain tingled across her neck. It felt too real, too visceral—like the memory had been branded into her soul.

A hand touched her shoulder.

"Kiara?" Aron's voice was gentle, thick with concern. "It's okay. You're safe."

She nodded weakly, unable to speak at first. He sat beside her, offering his presence without pressing. The fire's embers gave just enough light to catch the sheen of sweat on her brow, the shadows under her eyes.

"It was Saywa again," she whispered at last. "Her final moments. Ivyg... he enjoyed it. It wasn't just about power—it was cruelty. Control. And she fought him. Right to the end."

Aron's jaw tensed, but his voice remained soft. "He'll never touch you like that."

Kiara turned to face him, her voice thick with emotion. "It's like her memories are trying to prepare me. Like I have to remember what he did, so I don't underestimate him. So I don't freeze if I ever stand in front of him."

He didn't respond right away. Instead, he wrapped an arm around her and pulled her against him. She let him, resting her head on his shoulder, letting the sound of his heartbeat ease her breathing.

They stayed like that for a long moment. Kiara stirred, her voice soft in the low light. "Hey… earlier, with Clarice—she called you 'Sparky.' I never asked... why's that?"

Aron chuckled under his breath, rubbing the back of his neck. "Ah, that. Stupid fucking nickname. Back in uni, any time I got nervous round a girl—especially one I fancied—I'd let off a bit of a zap. Nothing major, just... y'know, enough to light up the moment. Burned a few fingers. Fried a dorm alarm once."

Kiara laughed. "Seriously?"

"Swear on me Nan. Clarice copped one when we first met—Marcus brought me by her lab, I reached out all polite-like, and next thing I know she's yelpin' and callin' me bloody 'Sparky.' Name stuck."

"So, your charm is... literally electric?"

"Comes with a few sparks, yeah. Always has. Back then, I was still learning my limits. Turns out, it's what I do—energy builds up when I'm bottlin' things. Emotions, pressure... it's like I carry a charge till I've got no choice but to let it loose."

Kiara's hand found his, grounding. "So, you've been holding back."

His smile faded into something steadier. "That I have, love. But not much longer."

Then Aron asked quietly, "Are you still you?"

She nodded against his chest. "I am. I just... finally understand what I'm fighting for. Who I'm fighting with. And why I'm not allowed to fall apart anymore."

He kissed the top of her head. "Good. 'Cause I'd rather not carry you the whole way."

She chuckled softly, her fingers tracing lazy patterns on his arm. "You're good at this, you know. Holding the line. Grounding people."

"Yeah, well..." He smirked. "Someone's gotta be the stone in the river."

Kiara pulled back slightly to look at him. "Do you remember the story I told you about the accident? The one with Robyn and the coin?"

He nodded. "I never told anyone this, but I saw him. Kane. He was standing in the middle of the road, just... watching. Calm. Like he was supposed to be there. And after I crashed, after he pulled me out of the car, he left me that coin. It was him all along. I think he saved me, so I'd make it here. So I could do this."

Aron looked at her with newfound gravity. "You think he changed the timeline?"

"I think... I wasn't supposed to die that day. And someone made damn sure I didn't."

Before Aron could respond, footsteps approached. Zen's voice broke the silence.

"You alright?" she asked, her tone quiet but laced with genuine concern.

Kiara straightened up, brushing her hair behind her ear. "Yeah. Just... needed to get out of my own head for a second."

Pavel yawned, appearing from the other side of the firepit. "We all need to move out soon anyway. The air's getting thinner the longer we stay in this part of the Hollow."

Zen nodded. "Agreed. Whatever Saywa needed you to see, you've seen it. We keep moving."

Kiara stood, squaring her shoulders. "Let's go. El Dorado isn't going to find itself."

Aron gave her hand a final squeeze. "Back to work then."

Zen raised an eyebrow. "You two gonna keep making goo-goo eyes the whole way or are we getting moving?"

Kiara smirked. "Only if we're walking in the back."

"Ugh," Pavel groaned, grabbing his pack. "I take it back. Let's stay here forever."

The mood lifted just slightly as they gathered their gear, the fire now cold behind them. But as they turned toward the next leg of their journey, the weight of what they'd seen—and what Kiara now carried—was not lost on any of them.

His voice echoed faintly, swallowed by the vastness of the cavern.

Kiara remained silent, her focus unwavering. Saywa's memories tugged at her like a beacon, guiding her steps. Hours had passed since they had last rested, the monotonous yet surreal surroundings warping their sense of time. Each turn seemed to blend into the next, marked only by the subtle shifts in the terrain.

"This is it," Zen said, gesturing toward an alcove partially hidden by thick vines and crystalline growths.

"Saywa told me about this place. I never thought I'd see it for myself." Kiara tilted her head, intrigued.

"Saywa told you? I thought you'd never been here." Zen shrugged, brushing a hand over the vines to reveal more of the rock face. "I haven't, but how do you think I knew so much about her story? It wasn't just a legend for me; she was my friend." Zen's voice softened. "She trusted me with this knowledge, just in case someone like you ever came along."

Aron raised an eyebrow. "Someone like her?"

"A Champion," Zen said simply, her gaze flicking toward Kiara. "Saywa always believed someone would return to retrieve her amulet. Someone worthy of the secret that I kept for her in hopes she was right. That's why Ivyg can never know I was here"

Kiara stepped forward, letting her hands skim the rough stone. Saywa's memories surged within her, guiding her movements as her fingers found a deep groove etched into the surface. "This is it," Kiara said, her voice steady. "The entrance is here, behind this."

Zen crouched beside her, studying the wall with a critical eye.

"Saywa mentioned a symbol—something to mark the way." Kiara nodded, her brow furrowing as she rifled through Saywa's fragmented memories. "A sun with jagged rays," she murmured.

"It's the key." Zen gestured for Aron to help as she began pulling away vines and moss. After several minutes, her hand stilled. "Here," she said, brushing away more debris to reveal the intricate carving of a sunburst. Kiara stepped closer, her fingers hovering over the carving. "This feels right," she said, her voice tinged with awe. "It's not just a key—it's a puzzle."

Zen smirked, stepping back to let Kiara work. "Saywa always had a knack for making things difficult.

She must have designed this herself." Aron chuckled softly.

"Sounds like someone I know." Zen shot him a sharp look, but the corners of her lips twitched in amusement.

Kiara ran her hands over the carving, her fingers finding small indentations. "It's a sequence," she realized aloud. "The pieces need to align in a specific order."

Zen nodded, folding her arms as she watched. "Saywa told me the mechanism was designed to respond to touch—to ensure only someone with her memories could open it."

"Convenient," Aron muttered, earning another sharp glance from Zen.

Kiara ignored them both, her focus entirely on the puzzle, their words becoming mere background noise. Her fingers pressed and twisted parts of the carving, the grooves aligning with a faint grinding sound. Each click resonated through the stone, the energy in the air growing stronger.

"This place feels alive," Aron said, his gaze darting around the chamber. "Like it's watching us."

"It probably is," Zen said lightly, though her tone carried an edge of seriousness. Her fingers pressed and twisted parts of the carving, the grooves aligning with a faint grinding sound. Each click resonated through the stone, the energy in the air growing stronger.

As Kiara pressed the final piece into place, the carving began to glow softly. A low rumble reverberated through the ground, and the seam in the stone split wider, revealing a narrow passage bathed in faint, otherworldly light.

Zen's smirk widened. "And you doubted me."

"I never doubted you," Kiara replied, a faint smile tugging at her lips. "I just didn't expect Saywa to leave breadcrumbs for both of us."

The group stepped into the narrow tunnel, the bioluminescent moss casting eerie shadows along the walls. The air grew cooler, and the faint hum of energy seemed to pulse with their footsteps. The passage twisted and turned, gradually widening into a larger chamber.

As they walked, Zen spoke softly, her voice carrying a note of reverence. "Saywa knew this place like the back of her hand. She said it was a sanctuary—a place where the energy of the Vril could be harnessed."

Kiara glanced over her shoulder. "Did she tell you what's at the end of this path?"

Zen hesitated, her gaze fixed ahead. "I honestly just thought it would open up to a cave on the other side, maybe a cellar, or a room inside a palace!"

Aron snorted softly. "Cryptic. Very helpful. Guess they didn't want it to be too easy."

After what felt like hours of walking, the passage opened into a larger chamber. In the center stood a weathered mechanism, partially hidden by crystalline growths. Its design was ancient, a blend of natural and crafted elements.

Zen approached it first, brushing away debris with a practiced hand. "Saywa mentioned this too," she said, her voice filled with quiet awe. "A gatekeeper. It responds to the energy of the Vril."

Kiara stepped forward, her hands hovering over the intricate carvings and levers. "It's not just about energy," she said thoughtfully. "It's about intent. Saywa's memories... they're showing me how to activate it."

"Then lead the way," Zen said, stepping back.

Kiara's fingers moved over the mechanism, her movements deliberate. Each turn and press sent a pulse of energy through the chamber, the carvings glowing brighter with each step. Finally, with a deep groan, the gate began to shift, revealing another tunnel bathed in brilliant, iridescent light.

Zen rested a hand on Kiara's shoulder. Her voice was soft. "Saywa would be proud."Kiara nodded, her blind eyes fixed on the glowing path ahead. "Let's finish what she started."The air shifted as Kiara, Zen, and Aron stepped into the hidden passage. The faint hum of the Hollow Earth's energy receded, replaced by a palpable stillness. The narrow tunnel gradually widened, and as they emerged into the open, the sight before them stole their breath.

Lush, fertile gardens stretched out in every direction, vibrant and alive, as if untouched by time. Towering trees with shimmering leaves stood sentinel over winding pathways lined with golden flowers. Streams of crystalline water flowed into small, sparkling ponds, their surfaces rippling with energy. The entire valley seemed to hum with life, the Vril's presence unmistakable.

"It's just as I remember it," Zen whispered, her voice tinged with awe.

Kiara stepped forward, her golden hair catching the ethereal light that seemed to emanate from the valley itself. "Saywa showed me glimpses of this place in her memories, but even those didn't do it justice."Kiara's chest tightened as memories rolled through her mind like a rushing river. Saywa's voice echoed faintly, overlapping with her own thoughts. Protect them. Protect this place.

The trio moved further into the valley, their boots crunching softly against the smooth stone paths. The faint murmur of voices reached their ears, and as they rounded a bend, a small, vibrant town came into view.

Instead of ruins overtaken by jungle or crystal growths, they found a thriving settlement. Small, elegant structures made of stone and wood were arranged in a circular pattern, their walls adorned with intricate carvings. Families worked together, tending gardens, weaving fabrics, and preparing meals. Children played in the streets, their laughter mingling with the sounds of the valley.

"They've been here all this time," Aron said, his voice low. "Living, thriving. How?"

Zen tilted her head, her expression contemplative. "Did not see that coming!"

The moment they were spotted, the townspeople froze. Whispers rippled through the crowd as dozens of eyes turned toward them. Then, as if a dam had broken, the villagers rushed forward. They surrounded the group, their faces alight with curiosity and reverence.

Kiara heard it all and instinctively stiffened as hands reached out to touch her. But instead of fear, she felt warmth. The villagers murmured words in a language she didn't recognize, yet somehow, Saywa's memories translated for her. They saw her as a reincarnated deity; the Champion returned to them at last.

Zen and Aron stood back, allowing Kiara to take the lead.

A regal man stepped through the crowd, his colorful golden headdress catching the light. His face was painted with vibrant patterns, and his long braids hung over his shoulders. He raised a hand, and the villagers fell silent.

"I am Cusi," he said, his voice rich and commanding. Though his dialect was ancient, Kiara understood every word. "We have awaited your return, Saywa."Kiara did not know how to speak the language yet understood him with perfect clarity.

"Will you translate for me?" she asked of Zen.

Kiara blinked, caught off guard by the weight of his words. She shook her head slightly.

"I'm not Saywa," she said carefully, though her heart swelled with the truth she couldn't deny. "I carry her memories, but I'm here as myself—Kiara."

Cusi nodded, his expression unreadable. "Then you honor her by your presence. And these—" he gestured to Zen and Aron, "are your allies?"

"They are," Kiara confirmed, her voice steadying. "We've come to find what Saywa protected. A talisman, an amulet. It's the key to something much greater, and we need it."

The mention of the talisman caused a ripple of tension among the villagers. Cusi's gaze flickered to Zen, then back to Kiara.

"The Holy Relic is not easily given. It rests within the sacred chamber, beyond the Gates of the Sky."

Zen frowned. "And the gates? How do we access them?"

Cusi hesitated, his hands trembling slightly as he reached into his robes. From within, he drew a large, intricately carved key.

"The gates have not been opened in generations," he admitted, his voice barely above a whisper. "The path is sacred, and dangerous. Only the chosen may proceed." Cusi extended the key to Kiara, bowing deeply as he placed it in her hands. "You must prove yourselves worthy."

The villagers stepped back, creating a wide circle around Kiara, Zen, and Aron. Cusi raised his hand again, addressing the crowd in their ancient tongue. His words carried weight, resonating with authority.

"He says we must show them who we are," Kiara translated softly, her blind eyes glinting in the soft light. "They won't let us pass unless we prove our intentions."

Zen smirked, exchanging a glance with Aron. "Then let's give them a show." Zen stepped forward, her form shifting with a fluid grace. Her skin shimmered, golden scales rippling down her arms as her true Draconian nature revealed itself. She extended her hands, summoning a small display of light and energy that danced like flames above her palms.

The villagers gasped, their awe palpable.

Kiara followed suit, laughing nervously at what Saywa was showing her to do. "I have no idea what I'm doing right now," she admitted, straightening as the energy of the Vril coursed through her.

Though blind, her eyes began to glow faintly, and a subtle aura shimmered around her. Without a single word, her presence commanded the attention of the villagers, who watched in awe. A few gasps and murmurs of reverence rippled through the crowd.

Finally, Aron stepped forward, his usual quiet confidence hardening into something more resolute. He raised his hand, and a faint crackle of electricity arced between his fingers—a hint of the power he carried but rarely displayed.

The villagers erupted into cheers. The reverence in their eyes shifted into joyful celebration.

Cusi, standing nearby, smiled. His earlier hesitation had melted into conviction. "You are the ones Saywa foretold," he said. "I believe the gates will open for you, but it is not up to me. The gates themselves will decide if you are worthy of the secrets within."

He led them up a winding path toward the towering gates, where armored guardians stood watch. The air grew heavier as they climbed, charged with the latent energy of the sacred valley. The gates loomed before them, massive and ornate, etched with ancient symbols and adorned with glowing crystalline inlays.

Kiara stepped forward. The key in her hand pulsed with warmth, responding to her touch. With deliberate care, she inserted it into the central mechanism and turned it.

The ancient hinges groaned, and the gates began to creak open.

Beyond them lay a narrow passage, descending into shadow. A deep hum of energy rose up from within, resonating through the stone.

Kiara glanced back at Zen and Aron, her expression resolute. "This is it. The next step."Zen nodded, smirking. "Let's finish what Saywa started."Together, the trio stepped into the passage. The gates closed behind them with a final, echoing thud.

The tunnel grew colder as they moved deeper into the mountain. Faint veins of crystal illuminated the walls, casting rippling patterns of light across their faces. The air was thick with ancient power.

Zen looked to Kiara. "How do you know where to go?"Kiara ran her fingers along the stone. "I just... feel it. Saywa's memories aren't always clear, but they guide me. Sometimes I can almost hear her."Aron followed closely, his eyes scanning their surroundings. "Let's hope her guidance doesn't walk us into a trap."Zen smirked. "If it does, at least we'll know it's a very old one."The corridor widened into a vast, circular chamber.

351

At its center stood a pedestal of stone, softly glowing from within. Above it hovered the amulet—a large, pinkish-purple gem, suspended in midair by unseen forces. It pulsed like a heartbeat, casting a hypnotic light.

Kiara moved forward, but Zen threw out a hand. "Wait. These things are never simple. Saywa wouldn't have left it unprotected."Kiara paused, focusing. Saywa's memories stirred in her mind—images of rituals, of ancient mechanisms meant to test more than just courage.

"It's a trial," she murmured. "A test of intention."Zen's gaze swept the chamber. "What kind of test?"Before Kiara could answer, the air shifted. The light from the amulet intensified, and the hum of energy deepened into a resonant vibration. Shadows along the walls writhed, coalescing into humanoid forms with glowing red eyes.

Aron's arm snapped up, electricity crackling between his fingers. "Well, that answers that."Kiara inhaled slowly and stepped forward. The shadows didn't strike—they encircled her, their presence heavy and cold.

Saywa's voice whispered in her mind: Only one who acts with a pure heart can claim it.

She extended her hand. "I'm not here for power or glory. I'm here to protect what you entrusted to me, to finish what you started."The shadows hesitated. Then, one by one, they faded.

Silence returned. The light around the amulet softened, then intensified as Kiara's hand closed around it.

The instant her fingers touched the gem, a surge of energy exploded outward. Zen and Aron stumbled back as a visible wave of power radiated from Kiara. Her knees buckled.

The amulet's glow consumed her, merging with her own energy. Memories poured into her—Saywa's life, her death, her defiance across countless lifetimes. Pain. Sacrifice. Love. Hope.

Kiara collapsed to her knees, clutching the amulet.

Aron rushed forward, reaching for her. But as his hand met her shoulder, he froze.

Kiara's body glowed with a silver light. Her hair lifted as if caught in a breeze, shifting in hue until it shimmered a soft silver-white.

"Kiara!" Aron cried, panic rising in his voice. "Kiara!"Zen laid a hand on his arm. "Wait. Let it happen. This is what the amulet was meant to do."The glow faded as suddenly as it had come. Kiara slumped forward.

Aron caught her, holding her close. "She's unconscious. What the hell just happened to her?"

Zen crouched beside them. "The amulet... bonded with her. It never gives more than what's needed. But maybe she needed more than most. Everything Saywa protected—all that knowledge, all that power—it's part of her now."

Aron held her tighter. "Then we need to get her out of here. Now."

Zen turned toward the entrance. "Let's find Cusi. He may know a faster way out."As they exited the chamber, Cusi was already waiting, flanked by a small group of villagers. His eyes widened at the sight of Kiara, her now-silver hair glowing faintly.

Zen muttered, "We're not in the Hollow Earth anymore... Look up. It's the sky."

Aron looked up, stunned. "Then where the hell are we? And how do we get her to safety?"

Zen gestured to Pavel, who stood nearby, pale with worry."This is where you come in," she said.

Pavel stepped forward, placing a steadying hand on Aron's shoulder. "I can get us back to the entrance. Just hold her. Give me a moment."

Zen faced Cusi one last time. "Your people will be safe. But we must go now."Cusi bowed. "Thank you, divine ones. We will protect this valley. And remember."

Aron returned the bow as best he could with Kiara in his arms. "We will return."

Pavel closed his eyes. The air shimmered. In the blink of an eye, they were back at the cave entrance, hidden from sight.

Aron shifted Kiara in his arms. Her silver hair caught the faint light, her face peaceful in unconsciousness.

"She needs care," he said quietly.

Zen nodded. "Witchaven. Pavel, you can jump there now, right?"Pavel nodded. "Now that I've been, I can go again. It'll be chaotic, but she'll be safe."Aron shook his head. "I'm not letting her out of my sight. Wherever she goes, I go."Zen met his gaze. "Then come with us."

Chapter 35

The Tipping Point

The overhead lights in the east corridor of the Wind Valley operations wing flickered faintly as Lucy approached the secure wing. Her boots clicked against the polished tile, each step echoing too loudly in the sterile silence of the base's interior. It was late—past midnight but Donovan never kept regular hours. Not when the whole operation was teetering on a knife's edge.

A pair of guards posted outside the command suite barely glanced her way. She flashed her ID anyway, out of habit more than necessity. Everyone here knew her face. Knew who she reported to. And who she'd betray if she took one wrong step.

The hallway stretched ahead, humming with fluorescent light and tension. As she neared Donovan's door, Lucy slowed. Her fingers brushed the inside of her pocket, curling briefly around the edge of a worn photograph she kept hidden in her wallet—a younger version of herself and Linda, arms draped around each other at a protest, grinning like idiots before the world had gotten complicated.

Now she was about to walk into the office of the man responsible for making that silence necessary. Lucy stopped just short of the door. She could feel her pulse in her neck, her wrist, her temples. She wanted to believe this was still about duty. About protecting the country from truths it wasn't ready to bear. But lately... it felt like something else entirely.

She raised her hand to knock—then hesitated outside General Donovan's office, her hand hovering inches from the door. The corridor was quiet—too quiet—save for the distant hum of fluorescent lights and the occasional murmur of voices behind closed doors. Every sound felt amplified, like the base itself was holding its breath.

She closed her eyes for a moment and inhaled slowly, steadying herself. The hallway smelled faintly of disinfectant and burnt circuits. The scent reminded her of the labs below—places where truths were hidden behind lead-lined walls and sterilized steel. Places she wasn't cleared to access. A shadow of movement in the reflection of a framed photograph caught her attention. She turned just in time to see a figure disappear around the corner. Paranoia, or surveillance? On this base, it was hard to tell the difference. Finally, she knocked—firm, controlled.

"Come in," Donovan barked.

The door clicked open. She stepped inside and closed it behind her. His office was cold and utilitarian, all sharp lines and colorless tones. A coffee cup rested beside a stack of folders, its contents long forgotten and acrid. On the wall, a black-and-white photo of a shuttle launch hung like a relic from a more optimistic era.

"General," she said, standing at attention. "The local authorities have taken Max into custody."

Donovan looked up, his face a mask of skepticism. "That kid? In jail?"

"Yes, sir," Lucy replied. "But it won't last. If what we've heard about the Whisperers and the incident at the Mountain View Motel is true, then we've got a limited window. If we act now, we can contain it."

Donovan leaned back in his chair, tapping his fingers together. "Containment isn't the goal. Not yet. We wait. Let them scramble. The more noise they make, the easier it'll be to isolate the leak."

Lucy's jaw tightened. "With respect, sir, waiting might cost us more than time. The locals are already talking. People are disappearing. This isn't just a cover-up anymore. It's a crisis."

"Which is precisely why precision matters," he replied, his tone even but firm. "Loose ends are best identified when the rope starts to fray. You should know that by now."

She bit the inside of her cheek, resisting the urge to challenge him. "I've followed every order, sir. Every protocol. What else do I need to do to prove I'm loyal to the mission?"

Donovan rose from his chair and walked around the desk, standing close enough that she could smell the stale coffee on his breath. He studied her, head tilted, eyes sharp.

"Our job is to maintain order," he said quietly. "And to do that, we tell stories. Not lies—stories. Palatable versions of the truth, tailored for an overstimulated public. UFO sightings? Weather balloons. Mass disappearances? Cults. The Whisperers? Just another myth to entertain the masses between cat videos and political outrage. That's how the system survives."

He stepped back, voice hardening. "You think the public is ready to understand what really walks this Earth? What crawls beneath it? What's already crossed the veil? You think they can handle knowing we've failed to contain it?"

Lucy's hands clenched at her sides. "Maybe not. But some of us can."

"That's why you're still here," Donovan said. "But this isn't your decision to make. You're dismissed."

She saluted stiffly and turned to leave. The door clicked shut behind her, but the weight of his words followed her down the hall.

Back at her workstation, she stared blankly at the console screen. She couldn't shake the nausea rising in her gut. All the language— "containment," "narrative," "survival"—it was just a cleaner way of saying: keep the truth buried.

Her eyes drifted to the corner of her desk, where a worn photograph of her and Linda sat tucked beneath a plastic nameplate. The two of them, arms slung around each other, grinning like they had the world figured out. Before the mission. Before the silence. Before the lines blurred.

Her phone buzzed. She froze, heart stuttering as she tried maintain composure at the sight of the caller ID, Linda. As if summoned by thought, the name glowed from her personal phone screen. She stared at it, mind racing. If she answered, she would be stepping beyond the chain of command. Risking everything she'd built. But if she didn't… With a shaky hand, she picked up the phone.

"Hello?"

"Lucy," came the familiar voice—older, wearier, but still Linda. "We need to talk. In person."

"I can't—"

"Please," Linda said, soft but resolute. "I wouldn't be asking if it wasn't serious."

Lucy glanced toward Donovan's door, pulse thundering in her ears. Every protocol screamed at her to hang up. But something deeper—older—whispered that this was the moment that mattered.

"Alright," she said at last. "But not here."

"I'll send a location," Linda said.

The line went dead.

Lucy set the phone down slowly, her hand trembling. The flicker of doubt that had lived quietly in her chest now roared into something undeniable. This wasn't just a mission anymore. It was a reckoning.

357

-Chapter 36-

Maze of Madness

The labyrinth stretched endlessly before the trio, its walls carved from ancient stone, darkened with time and coated in creeping vines. The air was oppressive, heavy with the stench of decay and rot, making every breath a labor. Despite the faint shafts of sunlight breaking through gaps above, the place felt unnaturally dark, as if the light itself was reluctant to linger.

"Who even designed this death trap?" Patel wiped sweat from his brow, muttering nervously. "I swear this place was made to mess with your head."

"Not just your head." Nova, ever the pragmatist said as he scanned their surroundings. "Whoever built this wanted people to suffer before they died."

Kane, walking slightly ahead, paused to study the narrow corridor before them. His calm demeanor stood in stark contrast to the rising unease in the group. The faint sound of distant growls reverberated through the labyrinth's twisted passages, an ominous reminder of the predator that awaited them.

Rounding a corner, the trio came upon a grisly sight—a skeletal figure, half-buried in the dirt, its armor rusted and broken, and its bones picked clean. The remains told a grim story of struggle and inevitable death.

Nova crouched beside the corpse, prying a sword from its skeletal grip. The blade, though dulled, still held enough edge to be useful. "Better than nothing," he muttered, testing its weight and balance with a few swings in a direction away from his compatriots. Kane silently approached another body, this one pinned to the wall by a long, jagged spear. He wrenched it free with a sharp tug, examining the weapon as if it held answers to their predicament. Patel lingered, eyeing the shield lying near another fallen warrior. As he lifted it, he spoke, his voice tinged with a mix of humor and resolve. "Guess I'll be the shield guy. That's fitting, right? The thinker who hides behind the big strong types?" He laughed nervously, but then his tone shifted as he stared at the skeletal remains. "This could've been me."

Kane glanced over, his expression unreadable. "It's not. You're here now. Focus on that."

Patel hesitated, his grip tightening on the shield. Finally, he spoke with more determination. "You know what? I've been thinking about something. 'Alibi' doesn't feel like me anymore. I was given that name because I was part of Sanjay—his literal alibi—before the Nexus. Back then, I didn't even have my own identity. I was just…an extension of him, always together, but now apart. Now?" He looked up at Kane, his voice steady. "Now I have my own body to myself, for me to make my own choices. Experience my own successes or failures. I'm not just someone's excuse anymore. I want to create an identity for myself. A real one."

Kane nodded, understanding the weight of those words. "You remind me of someone I once knew named Rajneel. He was a wise and thoughtful man. I think that name suits you."

Nova raised an eyebrow. "Rajneel, huh? Got a nice ring to it. But let's see if Rajneel can survive this labyrinth before we start printing name tags."

Kane smirked faintly. "If you survive, it'll suit you well. Let's move."

"All right." Patel confirmed. "I guess from henceforth I'll be known as Rajneel Patel."

"Here, here." Kane agreed.

As they continued deeper into the labyrinth, Patel—or Rajneel, as he now identified—spotted something glinting in the dim light ahead. "Hold on," he said, pointing toward a recessed alcove in the stone wall.

They approached cautiously, their footsteps echoing against the cold stone. Inside the alcove was a cache of weapons, likely left behind by those who had entered the maze long before them. It was a grim discovery—evidence of others who had failed—but it also offered hope.

"Looks like someone didn't make it far," Nova remarked grimly as he picked up a sturdy crossbow and a quiver of bolts. "This might even the odds."

Kane inspected the collection, picking up a pair of short daggers. He handed one to Rajneel. "Keep this close. If the shield fails, this could be your last line of defense."

Rajneel took the blade, nodding solemnly. "Thanks. I'll make sure it doesn't come to that. If only Sanjay and Brad could see me now."

Kane chose a heavier weapon for himself—a broad, double-edged blade that had likely belonged to a seasoned fighter. He tested its weight and balance before nodding in approval. "This will do."

Among the discarded items, they also found a small pouch containing flint and a strip of dried meat—barely enough for a meal, but a welcome find, nonetheless.

"These people didn't stand a chance," Nova said, his voice low. "But maybe we do."

Kane looked at them both, his expression firm. "They didn't have us. Let's keep moving."

As the trio moved deeper into the labyrinth, the oppressive silence began to play tricks on Rajneel's mind. He clutched the shield close to his chest; the blade Kane had handed him trembling slightly in his grip. "You know," he started, his voice wavering, "I'm not exactly built for this kind of thing. I've read books about survival, sure, but theory and practice are two very different things. Sanjay and I were always more comfortable in the academic setting."

Nova chuckled, glancing over his shoulder. "Yeah, well, books don't prepare you for a labyrinth of death. You're doing fine—just don't drop the shield. That's kind of your whole thing now."

Rajneel forced a nervous laugh, his voice breaking slightly. "Good to know my defining trait is hiding behind metal."

Kane, walking a few paces ahead, turned back briefly. "Courage doesn't mean you're not afraid, Rajneel. It means you act despite the fear. The world needs thinkers as much as it needs fighters."

Rajneel sighed, nodding. "I appreciate that, but I'm still not thrilled about being stuck in a man-eating maze. Just saying."

Nova's dry wit served as a lifeline amidst the tension. "You know," he said, his tone light but edged with unease, "I'm not exactly thrilled either. This 'adventure' isn't how I pictured spending my day. A cold drink on a beach? Sure. But risking my neck against a pissed-off monster? Hard pass."

Rajneel snorted, some of his fear melting in the face of Nova's sarcasm. "I'd kill for a piña colada or margarita right now."

Nova raised his sword, eyeing it critically. "We'll add it to the list. Right after surviving this mess, killing the Minotaur, and, oh yeah, saving the world."

"Casual." Rajneel smirked, his tension easing slightly.

Kane's low voice cut through their banter. "Stay focused. Humor's fine, but don't let it dull your instincts."

Nova sighed. "Noted, fearless leader. But if we're not laughing, we're crying, right?"

Kane paused briefly, his eyes scanning the corridor ahead. The glow of the Vril energy around his missing arm faintly illuminated the path, unseen by the others but deeply felt by him. "This place was designed to test us," he said quietly, almost to himself.

"What's that supposed to mean?" Nova asked, his voice tinged with suspicion.

"It means that nothing here is random," Kane replied, turning back to face them. "Every step we take, every choice we make—it's all part of something bigger. You may not see it yet, but I do. I've felt it. Ever since coming into the dystopian future."

Rajneel frowned. "Are you saying this is fate? Because fate isn't exactly comforting right now."

Kane's gaze softened. "Fate isn't comforting, Rajneel. It's a guide. It doesn't promise safety, but it offers purpose. And our purpose here is clear: we survive this, not just for ourselves, but for what comes next."

Nova crossed his arms. "You've got a lot of faith in something none of us can see but I like the optimism, so let's just go with that."

Kane's lips twitched into a faint smile. "I've been around long enough to recognize patterns, Nova. And one pattern I've seen time and again is that when people like us come together, we can move mountains. Or… slay Minotaurs."

The trio's banter underscores their growing camaraderie while emphasizing their distinct personalities. Rajneel's self-deprecating humor and vulnerability make him relatable, while Nova's sarcasm offers levity. Kane's steady wisdom ties their dynamic together, offering reassurance and direction as they prepare for the challenges ahead. These dynamics create a balance of tension and humor, making the characters' bonds feel genuine and setting the stage for their growth throughout the journey. The dialogue showcases their individual perspectives while reinforcing their shared purpose.

As the trio pushed deeper into the labyrinth, the once lush and overgrown walls became more sinister. Vines twitched as if alive, and the faint rustling in the foliage hinted at unseen predators. A sickly-sweet scent filled the air, emanating from clusters of vibrant flowers that dripped with viscous sap.

Nova stopped abruptly, his blade raised. "Anyone else think those plants are... watching us?"

Rajneel frowned, his grip tightening on the shield. "Plants don't watch. They photosynthesize."

"Then explain why that one just moved." Nova gestured toward a cluster of vine-like tendrils slowly unfurling toward them.

Before they could react, a vine lashed out, narrowly missing Kane's arm. Another tendril snaked toward Rajneel, wrapping around his leg. He yelped, slashing at it wildly with his blade as the vine tried to drag him toward the carnivorous plant's gaping maw.

Kane acted quickly, channeling the Vril energy into his remaining hand. The glowing green light intensified, forcing the vines to recoil, their sensitive tendrils seemingly overwhelmed by the energy's power. "Keep moving," he ordered. "They won't stay back for long."

"Great." Rajneel stumbled to his feet, panting. "Even the plants are trying to eat us."

The air grew heavier as they moved, a faint hum growing louder. Rajneel noticed it first, his eyes darting upward. "What's that sound?"

A swarm of large, glowing insects emerged from the shadows, their iridescent bodies pulsating with light. They were about the size of small birds, and their wings emitted a faint, otherworldly hum. The insects seemed drawn to Kane, buzzing closer to the faint glow of his Vril energy.

"They're attracted to Vril!" Rajneel shouted, swatting at one of the insects that landed on his shield. Its pincers clamped down, leaving a deep scratch in the metal.

Kane quickly removed his shirt, wrapping it around his glowing arm to dampen the energy. "That should reduce the glow, but it won't keep them away for long."

Nova swung his sword in wide arcs, managing to slice a few insects in half. "I'm starting to think the Minotaur might not be the worst thing in here."

The trio moved quickly, swatting and dodging the persistent swarm.

Kane used his Vril-enhanced telekinesis to hurl loose stones at the insects, scattering them long enough for the group to escape down a narrow corridor.

As they left the swarm behind, the air became heavier with a metallic tang. Blood splatters stained the stone walls, fresh enough to glisten under the dim light filtering through the maze's cracks. Nova knelt to examine the marks. "This is recent," he muttered. "Whatever made these scratches dragged something—or someone—this way."

Kane nodded, his expression grim. "We're close."

The distant roars of the Minotaur echoed through the labyrinth, sending a shiver down Rajneel's spine. He tightened his grip on the shield. "I don't suppose we can talk it out with the beast?"

Nova smirked. "Sure. You go first."

Rajneel held back his urge to give Nova the middle finger, one winged bird salute. He kept his composure as they continued cautiously, their movements synchronized now, each watching for signs of danger. The sound of scavenger birds overhead signaled their proximity to the lair, and the oppressive silence around them amplified every footstep.

Kane raised his hand, signaling them to stop. Ahead, the maze opened into a small clearing. Piles of bones littered the ground, a stark reminder of the labyrinth's purpose. The trio exchanged glances, their unspoken understanding clear: the Minotaur was close, and there was no turning back. The air grew heavier as the trio advanced, the oppressive silence pressing against their ears like a tangible force. The labyrinth's dark walls opened into an expansive clearing, revealing an eerie scene that was equal parts grotesque and beautiful. Overgrown gardens sprawled chaotically around them, their vibrant flowers blooming alongside piles of bones— human and animal remains alike, bleached white by time and stained red in some places by fresh blood. The stench was unbearable, a foul mixture of decay and death that forced Kane, Nova, and Patel to cover their faces with scraps of cloth, tied around their faces like a bandana.

In the center of the clearing stood a crumbling stone structure, its temple-like design hinting at a former grandeur now marred by claw marks and dried blood. Vines climbed its walls, draping the entrance in an ominous green curtain. From within, the deep, guttural snores of the Minotaur echoed, a sound that vibrated through the ground beneath their feet.

Nova peered into the shadows of the doorway, his eyes narrowing at the sight of the slumbering beast. "That thing's even bigger than I imagined," he whispered.

Patel gripped the small axe he had scavenged earlier, his hands trembling. "How are we supposed to fight that?" he muttered, his voice tinged with panic.

Kane raised a hand to silence them, his voice calm but firm. "We don't fight unless we have to. Follow my lead and step lightly. We might be able to get through without waking it."

The three moved cautiously across the chamber, each step calculated and deliberate. Kane led the way, his keen eyes scanning the area for traps or hazards. Patel followed closely, his focus locked on the hulking form of the Minotaur sprawled on the temple floor. The beast's massive chest rose and fell with each breath, its glowing red eyes mercifully closed.

Patel's fear got the better of him. Distracted by his nerves, he misjudged his footing and accidentally knocked over a metal candelabra. The clanging sound echoed through the chamber like a gunshot, slicing through the tense silence.

The trio froze in place; their breaths caught in their throats. The Minotaur's snoring stopped abruptly. Its glowing eyes snapped open, and its head swiveled toward the noise. Slowly, it rose to its full height, towering over them with muscles rippling beneath its matted fur. The beast snorted, releasing a cloud of hot, foul-smelling breath that only added to the oppressive atmosphere.

"Oh no... oh no, no, no…" Patel stammered, his voice barely audible.

The Minotaur's deep growl escalated into a deafening roar, shaking the temple walls. It reached for a massive weapon resting nearby—a jagged hybrid of an axe and a club, its edges caked with dried blood.

Kane stepped forward, his expression calm and resolute. "Stay behind me," he ordered, his voice cutting through the tension like a blade. "If we fight together, we stand a chance."

Nova drew his sword with a grimace, muttering under his breath, "This is gonna suck." Patel raised his shield, his fear momentarily overshadowed by determination.

The Minotaur took its first thunderous step toward them, each footfall reverberating through the stone floor. Its glowing eyes locked onto Patel, the smallest and seemingly weakest of the group. It bared its jagged teeth in a feral snarl, its intent clear. Kane shifted his weight, readying his spear. "Stay focused," he said, his voice steady. "This is where we prove our worth."

The Minotaur lunged, its massive axe-club swinging with deadly force. Patel dove to the side, barely avoiding the weapon as it smashed into the ground, sending a shockwave through the air, followed by the stone floor. Nova rolled backward, his sword drawn, ready to counter. Kane stood his ground, analyzing the creature's movements with calm precision.

"Keep moving! Don't let it corner you!" Kane shouted, his voice cutting through the chaos.

The beast roared, spinning to face Rajneel, who had instinctively taken cover behind his shield. With terrifying speed, the Minotaur swung its weapon again, forcing Patel to scramble away. Nova seized the opportunity, rushing forward to strike at the creature's exposed side. His blade bit into the Minotaur's thigh, drawing a deep growl of pain and fury.

Enraged, the beast lashed out, backhanding Nova with a massive fist. The force sent him crashing into a nearby wall, where he slumped to the ground, momentarily stunned, unmoving.

"Nova!" Patel shouted, his fear replaced by concern for his companion.

Kane took advantage of the distraction, charging forward with his spear. He struck with precision, jabbing at the Minotaur's legs and arms to weaken its mobility. The beast bellowed, swiping at Kane with its free hand, but he ducked and rolled, avoiding the blow.

"Patel, circle around!" Kane ordered. "Strike where it can't see you!"

Patel hesitated, his hands trembling on the grip of his axe. But the determination in Kane's voice spurred him into action. He moved stealthily around the perimeter of the chamber; his eyes locked on the Minotaur's exposed back. The beast, focused on Kane, didn't notice Patel until it was too late.

With a surge of courage, Patel raised his axe and slashed across the Minotaur's lower back. The creature roared in pain, staggering forward and giving Kane an opening to strike its chest with the tip of his spear. The weapon pierced its hide, but the beast's strength was unrelenting.

The Minotaur lashed out wildly, its movements growing increasingly erratic as the battle wore on. Kane's sharp mind assessed the situation, his eyes darting around the lair for anything that could be used to their advantage. He spotted a pile of loose stones near the edge of the room, their jagged shapes hinting at potential.

With his innate understanding of how things worked, Kane quickly devised a plan. He grabbed one of the broken candleholders Patel had knocked over earlier, inspecting its weight and balance. The grooves in its base sparked an idea.

"Kane, what are you doing?" Nova shouted, scrambling to his feet after being knocked down by the Minotaur's sweeping arm.

"Buying us time," Kane replied, his tone calm despite the chaos.

Using the candle holder as a makeshift sling, Kane scooped up several stones from the pile and hurled them at the Minotaur with precision. The first stone struck its shoulder, and the second glanced off its head. The beast roared in frustration, momentarily distracted from its relentless assault.

The glowing green energy radiating faintly from Kane's missing arm drew the Minotaur's attention. As it turned toward him, Kane used the moment to lob a particularly sharp stone that hit its temple with a dull thud. The beast stumbled, disoriented.

"Now, Nova!" Kane shouted.

Nova seized the opportunity, rushing forward with the sword he'd scavenged. He slashed at the Minotaur's side, forcing it to pivot away from Kane. Meanwhile, Patel, emboldened by the shift in momentum, darted in with his axe, delivering a sharp blow to the beast's thigh.

Kane's ingenuity and quick thinking gave them the upper hand, turning the tide of the battle. The trio's combined efforts finally began to wear down the Minotaur, its movements growing slower and more labored with each passing second. The beast was powerful, but against their cunning and teamwork, even it was beginning to falter.

"Let's finish this!" Nova shouted, gripping his sword tightly. He charged forward, slashing at the Minotaur's arm, forcing it to drop its weapon. The creature howled, clutching its injured limb.

Kane seized the moment, stepping forward with the broken handle of his spear in hand. The jagged end glinted in the dim light as he drove it into the Minotaur's heart with all his strength. He took a dying rage punch to the chest knocking him backwards, but not out of a fight if it were to continue, but the damage done by the broken spear handle. The beast let out one final, guttural roar before collapsing to the ground, its massive body shaking the floor beneath them.

The trio stood in the aftermath, their breaths heavy and their bodies battered. Kane leaned on his broken spear handle, his calm exterior masking the exhaustion and pain he felt.

"Is it… is it dead?" Patel asked, his voice shy.

Kane nodded, his gaze fixed on the fallen beast. "It's over."

Nova wiped blood from his face, shaking his head in disbelief. "I can't believe we just killed that thing."

Patel dropped to his knees, his axe clattering to the floor. "We're alive. Somehow, we're alive."

Kane placed a hand on Rajneel's shoulder, offering a rare smile. "You did well. Both of you."

As they caught their breath, the devices on their wrists began to beep. Murrin's robotic voice crackled to life, breaking the tense silence with a flair of song bravado.

"You've survived the Minotaur's lair and did not die. Congratulations! Please proceed to the portal for your audience with the God King."

The trio exchanged weary glances, knowing their challenges were far from over.

The chamber was silent except for the trio's ragged breaths. The Minotaur's lifeless body sprawled across the stone floor, its once-mighty presence reduced to a grotesque heap. The oppressive energy that had filled the lair began to dissipate, leaving behind an eerie calm.

Kane leaned heavily on his broken spear handle, his face calm but pale. Patel sat cross-legged on the floor, clutching his axe, his eyes wide with disbelief. Nova leaned against the wall, nursing the deep bruises on his arm.

"We actually did it," Patel finally said, breaking the silence. His voice was a mix of awe and exhaustion. "We killed a freaking Minotaur."

Nova chuckled dryly, shaking his head. "I'm not sure if that makes us heroes or just crazy."

Rajneel looked down at his trembling hands. "I mean, I thought I was going to die back there. Multiple times. And I think I might've aged five years in the last ten minutes."

"You handled yourself well," Kane said, his tone steady despite the weariness in his eyes. "Both of you did."

Patel gave a weak laugh. "Well, I didn't wet myself, so that's something. But seriously, can we take a second to talk about how insane this is? We just fought a mythological creature in a labyrinth that looks like something out of a nightmare."

Nova smirked. "You wanted adventure, didn't you?"

"I wanted to exist, not end up on the menu!" Patel shot back, though his grin betrayed his relief. "But hey, I guess if we're going to die horribly, we might as well do it with style."

Kane allowed a faint smile to cross his lips. "We're not dying here. Not today."

Patel tilted his head, curiosity flickering in his eyes. "You seem awfully sure about that. Is that the Vril talking, or are you just really good at pretending you've got this all figured out?"

Kane straightened, his expression growing serious. "I told you before—we're here for a reason. Surviving this fight is proof of that. But this victory is only the beginning. There are greater challenges ahead, and they'll make this feel like child's play."

Nova frowned. "Great. Something to look forward to."

Rajneel Patel groaned, flopping onto his back dramatically. "Can't we have, like, five minutes to bask in our awesomeness before you start talking about the next nightmare?"

Kane chuckled softly. "Bask all you want, but don't lose focus. The God King isn't going to wait forever."

Patel sat up, his expression sobering. "Speaking of the God King, why exactly does he want to see us? I mean, what's his endgame here?"

"That's what we're going to find out." Kane's gaze darkened. As if on cue, the wrist devices beeped again, and Murrin's robotic voice echoed through the chamber.

"Congratulations, again, on your survival. The portal is now active. Please proceed at your earliest convenience."

Rajneel groaned again, scrambling to his feet. "Guess our five minutes are up."

Nova stretched, wincing at the movement. "Let's get this over with."

Kane led the way, his steps steady despite the battle's toll. As they approached the shimmering portal, Patel hesitated, looking back at the Minotaur's corpse one last time.

"Hey," he said, his voice lighter. "At least we've got one hell of a story to tell."

Nova smirked. "If we live to tell it."

With a deep breath, the trio stepped through the portal, the light swallowing them whole.

-Chapter 37-

Kings and Pawns

The sun dipped low over Atlantis, casting long, shimmering shadows across the sprawling settlement. The air crackled with tension, but Stan Wheeler moved through it like a man on top of the world. With Ivyg's attention elsewhere—or so he thought—Stan had spent the day carefully crafting alliances. Each handshake, every nod of agreement, layered another brick in the foundation of what he saw as his eventual rise to true power.

He stood at the head of a long conference table now, gesturing confidently to a glowing projection of charts and logistical plans. "We're ahead of schedule in Sectors 2 and 4," he declared, his voice full of smooth assurance. "Once we solidify control over the supply chain, we'll be able to extend our reach further inland without relying on Ivyg's personal resources."

A few chuckles of agreement rippled around the table. Even Landis, seated to Stan's right, seemed to tolerate the display—watchful, but silent.

"We've built something strong here," Stan continued, his tone slick. "And once our friends here"—he nodded to the gathered scientists and military brass. "see the results, they'll know it's better to answer to me than wait for... divine intervention."

Laughter followed, though it was the kind of uneasy laughter men shared when they weren't sure if the joke was safe. Then, the door hissed open as if someone had just let all the air out of the room. The laughter died instantly.

Ivyg entered like a storm front, silent and absolute. His steps were measured, the kind that didn't need to hurry because the world bent to him regardless. The room's temperature seemed to drop as he approached. Stan straightened, his heart skipping, but he pasted on a smile. "Grand Emissary, what a—"

Ivyg didn't break stride before he reached the table and placed a hand on its surface, silencing everything with a look. Without a word, he took Stan's place at the head. The air thickened.

"Gentlemen," Ivyg said, his voice smooth but with an edge sharp enough to bleed. "I trust the discussions have been... productive?"

The attendees barely dared to nod.

Ivyg's gaze scanned the room, cutting through them like a scalpel. "I overheard your concerns. Allow me to simplify."

He gestured toward the projected map. "Sector 4 will receive additional resources. Sector 6's personnel issues will be resolved within the week. Sector 2's equipment—" his eyes locked on a sweating scientist, "—will be fully operational, or I'll find someone else to oversee it."

No one spoke. Heads nodded like puppets on strings. Then his gaze returned to Stan. The amusement in his eyes was gone, replaced by cool disinterest.

"Mr. Wheeler, you'll compile this plan and distribute it with no further delays."

Stan cleared his throat, voice smaller now. "Of course, sir."

Ivyg stood. "Good. This meeting is over."

Chairs scraped, papers shuffled, and the room emptied like it was on fire—except for Stan.

"Mr. Wheeler, stay behind."

Stan froze, his heart pounding. He forced a polite smile and waited until the others had filed out, the door closing with a soft click.

Ivyg remained standing, his posture as unyielding as stone. "Tell me, Mr. Wheeler," he began, his voice devoid of warmth, "what progress have you made on the task I assigned to you personally?" He smiled, a grin that Stan knew all too well never led anywhere he enjoyed, as if expecting an answer that was going to be wrong.

Stan's mind raced. Task? "I, uh… I've been focused on solidifying alliances and addressing the operational concerns we've discussed," he stammered. "The mission is progressing well, sir."

Ivyg's smile vanished, replaced by an expression of thinly veiled contempt. "You misunderstand your role, Wheeler. You are not here to address operational concerns or play diplomat. You are here to execute my will. And yet, you stand before me empty-handed, with neither updates nor results."

Stan's throat went dry. "Grand Emissary, I—"

"Enough." Ivyg's voice was quiet but carried the weight of finality. "You are not indispensable, Mr. Wheeler. You are a public figure and pawn—a useful one, but a pawn, nonetheless. Do not confuse your proximity to power with actual power. I will not remind you of this again."

Stan swallowed hard, his mouth opening and closing as he struggled to respond. Before he could, Ivyg turned and walked out of the room, his movements fluid and purposeful, leaving Stan alone with the suffocating realization of how precarious his position truly was.

Ivyg strode into the command center nearby, the hum of machinery and quiet voices creating a backdrop of controlled chaos. Holographic displays flickered with maps, reports, and surveillance feeds from across the region. A group of reconnaissance officers snapped to attention as he approached.

"Status report," Ivyg ordered, his voice crisp.

One of the officers stepped forward, his tablet in hand. "Reconnaissance teams have reached their assigned locations and have begun sending preliminary reports. So far, none have provided actionable intelligence on the location of Witchaven. However, we have identified several anomalies in the surrounding areas—unusual energy signatures, increased civilian activity, and potential disruptions to local communications."

Ivyg's gaze sharpened. "None of this is sufficient. Increase surveillance in the areas with energy anomalies. Deploy additional teams if necessary. I want definitive intelligence, and I want it now."

The officer nodded. "Understood, Sir. I'll have updates for you within the hour."

Ivyg turned to a tactical display showing a map of the region, his mind already calculating the next move. He didn't trust chance or coincidence, and he certainly didn't trust the humans he'd aligned with to get it right. But he didn't need to. Everything was moving according to his design, and soon, the location of Witchaven—and the power it guarded—would be his.

-Chapter 38-

From Dreams to Ashes

The room was still, the faint glow of moonlight filtering through the curtains, casting soft, fragmented patterns across the walls. Kiara lay motionless on the bed, her breathing steady and deep as she rested. Aron sat in the chair beside her, his body slack with exhaustion but his heart strangely restless. He'd insisted on staying close, unwilling to leave her side after everything they had been through. As the night deepened, sleep finally claimed him. His head tilted back against the chair, his arms crossed over his chest, but even in sleep, his hand remained close to the amulet resting on his chest. It had been quiet for weeks, unless he removed it—but tonight, it stirred.

A faint hum vibrated through the metal, followed by a soft golden glow that pulsed in time with his heartbeat. Aron's features relaxed further as his dreams shifted. At first, the images were fleeting, like light scattered across rippling water. A woman's silhouette appeared against an endless sky; her figure bathed in sunlight. Her hair whipped in the wind, but it was her laughter that struck him—light, melodic, familiar. She turned, her eyes alight with warmth, and in that instant, he knew her. It was Kiara.

The scene shifted. A marketplace, bustling with life. She stood there again, a different version of herself—her hair braided intricately, her clothing regal yet practical. She smiled at him, this time with a spark of mischief in her eyes. He realized he wasn't just observing her. He was there, with her, his hand reaching out to hers.

Another shift. A battlefield. The air was thick with the clash of steel and the cries of men. She stood defiant, a warrior with her blindfold wrapped tightly over her eyes, her blade flashing as she moved with precision and grace. He was beside her again, protecting her back as they fought together, perfectly in sync.

The scenes came faster now—each a different time, a different place. Yet, in all of them, there was a connection between them, unspoken but undeniable. He felt the pull of her soul to his, the way their energies entwined effortlessly, no matter the life, no matter the circumstances.

Finally, the dream settled. They stood together in a serene garden bathed in twilight, a version of themselves from an age he could not name. Her face was turned up toward his, radiant and full of love. He felt the weight of the lives they had shared, the sacrifices, the triumphs. And then, as if the dream itself spoke to him, he understood: She had always been with him. Always.

The amulet grew brighter, warming against his skin. It seemed to hum with the resonance of this realization, as if affirming what he now knew deep within himself. His lips moved, whispering her name: "Kiara."

The glow of the amulet pulsed brighter one final time before fading. Aron stirred in the chair, his breathing deep and measured. His eyes fluttered open, heavy with the remnants of the dream, just as Kiara shifted on the bed. The faint rustle of fabric and her soft sigh pulled him fully from sleep.

She stretched slightly, her hand brushing against the edge of the blanket. Aron leaned forward instinctively, his heart thundering in his chest as he watched her. She opened her eyes, those deep, knowing eyes that seemed to see right into him, even without sight.

"Aron?" Her voice was soft, still tinged with sleep, but it carried a weight that made his chest tighten. She moved to sit up, her movements slow and deliberate.

"You're awake," he said, his voice rough from sleep. He sat back, trying to steady himself, but the dream lingered in his mind, vivid and unyielding.

Kiara tilted her head slightly, as if sensing the shift in him. "Did something happen?" she asked gently.

He hesitated, his hand brushing against the amulet. "I think…" He paused, searching for the right words. "I think I saw us—before. In other lives."

She blinked, her lips parting slightly in surprise. "You saw…us?"

"Not just saw," he corrected, his voice softening. "I felt it. Every lifetime, every moment. It was like…I remembered what I didn't even know I'd forgotten. And it was always you."

Her hand reached out, finding his. She laced her fingers with his, her touch steadying him. "Then it's true," she murmured, her voice barely above a whisper. "We've always found each other."

The intimacy of her words, combined with the weight of what he had experienced, left him breathless. In that moment, everything felt clear, as if the amulet had bridged a gap that neither time nor circumstance could sever.

"Kiara leaned back against the headboard, her fingers still loosely intertwined with Aron's as she processed the lingering warmth of his words. The room was quiet except for the faint sound of the wind outside and the occasional crackle from a lantern near the window.

After a moment, she broke the silence, her voice soft yet curious. "What happened after I passed out?"

Aron shifted in his chair, his hand tightening slightly around hers as if grounding himself in the present. "Zen made sure you were okay. She said the amulet's activation was overwhelming but not harmful. Something about it syncing with you, unlocking what you were ready to receive."

Kiara raised an eyebrow, her lips curving into a faint smile. "Sounds like her."

He chuckled, nodding. "Yeah, she's not the most... comforting presence, but she knew what she was doing. She had you checked out by someone here at Elysium. Meanwhile, Pavel went back to help the others finish the transition to Lemuria. He didn't want to push himself too hard with teleportation, so he's been making shorter trips."

Kiara tilted her head, her curiosity deepening. "And what about you? Were you just waiting here the whole time?"

"Damn straight, I wouldn't trust Zen with my own life, I'm sure as hell not trusting her with yours.." Aron admitted, leaning forward, resting his elbows on his knees. "So, after Zen made sure you were stable, she agreed to leave me here to keep an eye on you while she handled... something. Before she left, Pavel gave me his number. Said to call him whenever we're ready to head back."

Kiara's smile widened, and a mischievous glint appeared in her eyes. "Whenever we're ready, huh?"

He nodded, his brow furrowing slightly as he studied her expression. "What are you thinking?"

Her smile turned coy, and she shifted to sit cross-legged on the bed, her posture relaxed yet purposeful. "I'm thinking... maybe we won't rush back just yet."

Aron blinked, caught off guard by her suggestion. "You don't want to go back?"

"Not immediately," she clarified, hesitating a bit, her voice carrying a hint of playfulness. "Think about it, Aron. We've been through so much in such a short time—running, fighting, saving the world, apparently remembering past lives. Maybe we deserve one night to just... exist."

His gaze softened, and the corners of his mouth twitched as if fighting a smile. "You're not wrong, but I didn't expect that from you."

Kiara shrugged, her fingers absently tracing the edge of the blanket. "I didn't expect a lot of things—like learning you were Zeus in a past life—but here we are." She looked up at him, her expression more serious now. "I just think... If we're going to keep fighting, we need moments like this. To breathe, to connect, to remember why we're doing it all."

Aron considered her words, the weight of them settling in his chest. "And you think staying here a little longer will help with that?"

"I do," she said firmly, pulling him toward her with a teasing grin. Aron didn't hesitate, climbing atop her and capturing her lips in a gentle yet fervent kiss. His hand caressed her skin, trailing down the curve of her waist with a touch that sent shivers through her.

Kiara giggled, leaning back into the pillows as she tugged the covers down just enough to give him more access. "You're still wearing too much," she murmured playfully, her fingers brushing the hem of his shirt.

"I could say the same about you," Aron retorted, his voice low and warm as he leaned in to kiss her neck, his hand exploring her waistline.

Just as the tension between them built, a sudden knock at the door startled them both. Kiara froze, her eyes widening in surprise. Aron groaned, his forehead dropping against her shoulder.

"Of course," he muttered under his breath. "Perfect timing."

Kiara bit her lip to stifle a laugh, nudging him playfully. "Better see who it is. Could be important."

Aron sighed, sitting up and running a hand through his hair as he adjusted his shirt. "If it's Zen, I'm going to kill her."

He moved to open the door, only to find a bubbly young woman with a clipboard and a headset standing there. She looked barely older than her early twenties, her bright smile radiating a mix of eagerness and nervous energy.

"Hi! Sorry to interrupt," she began, her voice chipper and professional. "I'm part of Elysium's guest engagement team, and I noticed you haven't checked in with our concierge yet. I just wanted to personally invite you to tonight's festivities!"

Aron blinked, caught off guard. "Festivities?"

"Oh, yes!" she said, her enthusiasm unwavering. "We have an incredible lineup downstairs tonight—one of the best bands around is performing for some of our most exclusive guests. It's a celebration of resilience and community during these... turbulent times." She lowered her voice conspiratorially. "I even heard some really high-profile clients are attending. Super secret, of course, but you didn't hear it from me."

Kiara, who had propped herself up on her elbows to listen, smirked at Aron's baffled expression. "Sounds like quite the party," she called out. "Don't you think, Aron?"

The young woman noticed Kiara and brightened even further. "Oh, it'll be amazing! You won't want to miss it. Food, drinks, dancing—it's the perfect way to unwind. And the band's lead singer is just... wow. You'll see." The girl's bubbly energy hadn't dimmed as she reached into the folds of her apron, producing an intricately designed flyer. "Here you go!" she chirped, holding it out toward Kiara with a grin.

Kiara's gaze remained fixed, unchanging, as though she were staring straight through the girl. The flyer hovered awkwardly in the space between them, the girl's hand bobbing a little as she waited for Kiara to take it. A few seconds of silence stretched, the grin on her face faltering slightly as the realization dawned.

"Oh..." she muttered, looking mildly flustered.

Before she could say more, Aron, standing just off to the side, swooped in and snatched the flyer from her hand. "I'll take that, thanks," he said with a crooked smile, giving Kiara a sidelong glance.

The girl blinked, then laughed nervously. "Oh! Of course. Sorry about that." She shifted her weight, brushing a stray curl from her face. "Um, so... you were asking about Zen, right?"

"Yeah," Aron replied, glancing briefly at the flyer in his hand before tucking it into his jacket. "We need to speak with her."

"Well, you're in luck! She's hosting the event. It's happening right now, actually. Downstairs," the girl explained with an enthusiastic nod. "She's expecting all the guests to be there."

Kiara arched an eyebrow, her lips curving into a faint, amused smile. "Let me guess. This is your way of saying we don't have a choice but to go."

The girl grinned, unabashed. "You got it! But don't worry, it's going to be amazing! We've got drinks, music, and everyone dressed to the nines. Speaking of which…" She glanced at Aron, her enthusiasm bubbling over again. "Do you guys need something to wear? I can help with that."

"Do you have something comfortable for her?" Aron asked, tilting his head toward Kiara. "Something that works for…" He let the sentence trail off delicately, knowing she'd catch the meaning.

"Oh, absolutely! Leave it to me," the girl said, bouncing slightly on her toes. "She'll look stunning. And I'll make sure you're taken care of too." She gave them both an excited wave before darting off, presumably to make arrangements.

As she disappeared, Aron turned back to Kiara, his expression somewhere between amused and concerned. "You're sure about this?"

Kiara smiled faintly, tilting her head toward him. "I have to be. Besides, I've faced worse than a fancy dress party, right?"

Aron smirked, adjusting his jacket. "Guess I'll just have to make sure you don't have to face it alone."

Aron closed the door, turning back to Kiara with an exasperated look. "Guess the universe has other plans for us."

Kiara shrugged, her smile turning mischievous. "Maybe it's a sign."

"A sign for what?" he asked, raising an eyebrow.

"To get out of this room and have a little fun," she replied, swinging her legs over the side of the bed. "Come on, Aron. We've been through hell and back—don't you think we deserve one night to just let go?"

He hesitated, studying her with a mix of amusement and resignation. "You're really serious about this?"

"Oh, I'm very serious," she said, standing and grabbing the card from his hand. "Besides, who knows what we'll find out there? Sometimes the best discoveries happen when you least expect them."

Her tone carried a weight of meaning he couldn't ignore. Aron exhaled, a faint smile tugging at his lips. "All right, fine. But if this band's terrible, you owe me."

Kiara laughed, already pulling him toward the small wardrobe to find something suitable for the event. "Deal. Now, let's see if the formerly 'great Zeus' knows how to dance."

Aron and Kiara descended the grand staircase of Elysium, the sound of music and laughter growing louder with each step. The main ballroom was a spectacle of extravagance, filled with shimmering lights, an impressive band on stage, and a crowd of guests dressed to the nines. The air buzzed with excitement, yet there was an undercurrent of something else—something unspoken.

As they entered the room, Kiara's arm looped through Aron's, her keen senses picking up on the subtle shifts in the atmosphere. Aron scanned the crowd, his eyes catching a familiar figure at the far end of the room. Zenobia.

Before he could direct her in the direction of Zen, whose piercing gaze locked onto them instantly, Kiara had already locked onto her, appearing like an energetic magnet from her perspective. Aron gave her a wave and nodded with a polite smile, noting she seemed busy, but they would catch up with her to thank her later. To their surprise, Zen's expression didn't change, her lips pressed into a thin line as if contemplating something.

"That look," Aron said, his voice low. "She's hiding something."

"No kidding," Kiara whispered. "Think she knows about the amulet?"

"Probably. But I don't think that's what's on her mind right now." Aron's tone was cautious, but his body remained relaxed. "Let's keep moving. If she's going to make a move, it won't be here."

Zen began weaving through the crowd, her eyes never leaving them. But Aron subtly steered Kiara deeper into the throng of dancing guests, their path obscured by the swirling bodies around them.

As Zen tried to track them, Kiara leaned into Aron, her lips near his ear. "She'll lose us in the crowd. Let's blend in."

Aron smirked. "You're enjoying this, aren't you?"

"Oh, immensely," she teased, pulling him onto the dance floor just as the band transitioned into a sultry, rhythmic number. "Let's give her something to really talk about."

The music swelled, and Kiara moved against Aron with a fluid grace that surprised even her. She wasn't typically one to dance but tonight felt different—liberating. Aron caught on quickly, his movements confident yet measured as he matched her rhythm. For a moment, the tension faded, replaced by an intoxicating mix of adrenaline and attraction.

"You're full of surprises," Aron murmured, his hands lightly resting on her hips as they moved together.

"Maybe I'm just remembering a little more of who I am," she replied, her voice laced with playful mystery. "Don't tell me the mighty Zeus can't keep up."

He laughed softly, leaning closer. "Oh, I can keep up. But don't think I'll make it easy for you."

The two spun and swayed, lost in the music and the moment, until Aron's focus shifted. His eyes scanned the crowd, catching a glimpse of a man he'd seen upon their arrival at Elysium. At the time, the man had been gray-haired and frail-looking. Now, under the ballroom lights, he looked decades younger, vibrant and full of life.

"That's... odd," Aron said, his dancing slowing. "That guy—over by the bar. I swear he looked at least 70 when we got here."

Kiara tilted her head, her heightened senses picking up on something unusual. "You're right. He's not the only one. A lot of people here look... unnaturally young." She closed her eyes briefly, focusing on the hum of conversation. Kiara let her senses take over. The air was thick with the hum of conversation, the clink of glasses, and the occasional burst of laughter. For her, it was less about the words and more about the tones, the undercurrent of energy threading through the crowd. It buzzed, sharp and chaotic, like static against her skin.

Then she made a face—one Aron immediately recognized as her something's not right expression, mixed with a bit of disgust.

"What's wrong?" he asked, leaning in close so only she could hear.

She tilted her head slightly, her nose scrunching. "I'm... listening," she muttered under her breath.

"Listening?" he repeated, his tone bordering on a teasing challenge. "To what?"

Kiara turned her head toward him, her voice low and flat. "Ewww. These people are gross."

Aron blinked, caught somewhere between amusement and concern. "Gross?" His voice dropped further, almost inaudible against the noise of the party. "What are they saying?"

Kiara's expression darkened as she leaned toward him. "It's not just what they're saying. It's the vibe. We're standing in the middle of a hornet's nest." She paused, lowering her voice even more. "A lot of these people are in Ivyg's inner circle. They're celebrating—the chaos he created, the promises he's made. It's like… they think he's some kind of savior."

Aron stiffened, his easy demeanor slipping for just a moment. His eyes flicked discreetly across the room, scanning the crowd. "Don't react," he murmured firmly. "You can't let them know you've figured it out."

Kiara arched a brow, her lips twitching into a wry smile. "What do you think I'm going to do, yell boo and make them scatter?"

"Wouldn't put it past you," Aron muttered, his voice tinged with humor as he straightened up, feigning nonchalance.

"Please. I'd do something way more dramatic than that," she quipped, her tone lightening despite the tension simmering beneath the surface. She allowed herself a quick smirk before adding, "But seriously, we need to find Zen. This place makes my skin crawl."

"Agreed," Aron said, placing a steadying hand on her elbow as they wove further into the room. "Just… keep listening. Maybe we'll pick up something useful."

Her eyes snapped open, and she turned to Aron. "Casual…" He reminded her, brushing his lips across her earlobe while looking up to see if anyone had noticed her expression. "What did you hear?"

"What's 'fairy dust'?" She asked in his ear as she wrapped her arms tightly around his neck. "Tell me that's not what I think it is…"

Aron sighed, his expression darkening. "It's not good, I'm afraid. Clarice told me about it—it's rare and insanely valuable. The dust is supposedly harvested from fairies, and when consumed or used topically, it has rejuvenating effects because of something in fairies that keeps them looking young.. People pay fortunes for it, but the process to extract it... it's cruel, you don't want to know…"

"All that to look younger?"

"Would you have guessed that Clarice is like 63?" he chuckled.

"Wow, she is spunky for 63!" Kiara's jaw tightened. "Then we need to find out what's going on here."

Spotting Zen at the edge of the room, Kiara and Aron approached her with purpose. Zen turned to them, her expression guarded.

"Enjoying yourselves?" she asked, her voice calm but wary.

"Not as much as you seem to be," Aron replied coolly. "Want to explain why half the people here look like they just walked out of a skincare commercial?"

Zen's eyes narrowed. "I don't know what you're talking about."

"Don't play dumb," Kiara interjected. "We overheard people talking about fairy dust. You know exactly what that means."

Before Zen could respond, a petite woman with delicate features and glimmering, almost translucent skin appeared beside them. Her ethereal presence immediately marked her as a fairy. She looked nervous but resolute.

"I can show you where it's coming from," the fairy said quietly, her voice trembling. "Please—you have to stop it."

Zen shot the fairy a glare. "This is not your concern. Go back to your duties."

But Aron stepped closer, his presence towering. "Let her talk, Zen. Or I'll make sure this entire place lights up like a storm."

Zen hesitated, frustration flickering across her face. "Fine," she snapped. "But don't think for a second I had anything to do with this. If you want someone to blame, look no further than Ivyg. He's the one pulling the strings."

"Convenient," Kiara said, her voice dripping with skepticism. "You always have someone else to point to, don't you?"

Zen's expression softened, a hint of genuine sorrow breaking through. "You think I enjoy being his pawn? I hate it, more than you could imagine. But if I don't play along, it's not just me who suffers."

Kiara and Aron exchanged a glance. While Zen's words held a ring of truth, neither fully trusted her.

"We'll pretend to believe you," Aron said firmly. "But we're taking her with us." He gestured to the fairy. "For her safety—and to get the answers we need."

Zen clenched her jaw but relented. "Do what you want. Just don't come crying to me when this all goes south."

After escorting the fairy out of the ballroom, Aron pulled out his phone and dialed Pavel. The line connected almost instantly.

"Pavel here," his voice crackled through the receiver.

"We've got a situation," Aron said into the phone. "Fairy dust is being trafficked through a dark market near Elysium. It's worse than we thought."

"Of course it is," Pavel replied. "Where are you now?"

"At Zen's. South wing."

"Perfect," Pavel said. "Meet me in the garden downstairs. Give me two minutes."

Aron ended the call and turned to the fairy. "Can you show me where it is exactly?"

She fluttered over to the old map sprawled across a low table, her fingers tracing the faded lines until she pointed to a narrow pass just beyond the southern ridge.

"Take a picture of that," Kiara said, her voice firm.

Aron did, snapping a quick photo before tucking the device away. "Let's go."

By the time they reached the garden, Pavel was already there, arms crossed, face grim.

"Show me," he said.

Aron held out the phone. Pavel studied the image for a breath, then gave a tight nod. A pulse of light enveloped them, and in the next instant, they stood on damp, uneven stone at the outskirts of the market, cloaked by jungle. This wasn't just black-market territory—this was something older, deeper. A strange fusion of trade, secrecy, and survival that had drawn every kind of trafficker, drifter, and desperate soul into its tangled veins. Since the Veil had fallen after the Pulse, the place was thriving. What was once scarce was now hunted openly. Beings, artifacts, and parts long believed to be mythical were now visible, real, and terrifyingly easy to acquire—if you had the right currency.

Kiara inhaled slowly, ears tuned to the rhythmic clang of machinery mixed with the dull roar of muffled voices and the occasional burst of laughter that never sounded quite human. Her cane tapped once against uneven stone, steadying her. She didn't need to see to feel the wrongness in the air—or the sharp spike of tension that preceded danger.

"We're close," she whispered, her voice barely audible over the hum.

Aron came to a halt beside her, his hand resting lightly on her back. Pavel flanked the other side, eyes scanning every shadow.

"I see it," Pavel murmured, voice low and thick with his Russian accent. "Open gate. Two guards up ahead. Looks like it leads straight into madness."

"How big are they?" Aron asked.

Pavel narrowed his eyes. "Big enough to make me miss my quiet flat and instant noodles."

Kiara tilted her head. "I can feel them. The air gets itchy around them."

Aron cracked his neck. "Right then. Keep it clean. I'll sneak in and take the one on the right if you want to..." he offered Kiara to hold Pavel's arm. "Of course…" Pavel obliged.

She raised a hand. "I'm good! I'll just stay—"

"You sure?" Pavel offered his arm.

"I'm blind, not five," she snapped.

Aron chuckled. "Fair enough."

What followed was fast and brutal. Kiara heard every impact—the dull thuds, a wet crunch, then a heavy body hitting the ground. Silence.

"You good?" Pavel called, breath ragged.

"Aye," Aron grunted. "That one had bloody scales. Hissed at me like a busted kettle."

"I think mine had tiny feathers, was actually very soft" Pavel muttered. "But I don't want to know what it was."

"Same," Aron replied, grabbing Kiara's arm once again. "Let's move."

They stepped through the gate into the dark market. It pulsed with life—most of which was human, particularly the merchandise. Rows of mismatched stalls, lit by flickering lanterns and glowing moss, stretched like a fever dream. Vendors barked in languages that tripped over each other.

Fluids and limbs of unknown species in jars sat alongside stones that throbbed like hearts. Spices that shimmered like oil slicks. Weapons that hummed softly, like they were whispering.

Cages haphazardly tucked behind curtains, others proudly displayed. Creatures inside them ranged from humanoid to wholly unrecognizable. Some stared back with blank eyes. Others trembled in fear.

"Don't look too long," Pavel murmured. "They think you want to buy."

A vendor grinned, teeth shaped like spikes. "Memory extractions? Quick and mostly clean."

Aron scowled. "Jog on. We're not here for party tricks."

Another hawker gestured with charred fingers. "Portable portals—single use."

Pavel snorted. "You sell garbage, da? Move along."

A vendor reached toward Kiara with a crooked grin.

Aron's voice cut through the air like a blade. "I wouldn't."

His hand lifted—barely—and a dense, volatile spark flared to life at his fingertips, crackling with barely leashed power. The nearest lantern guttered, shadows lurching across the vendor's face.

Kiara's fingers tightened on Aron's arm—subtle, grounding. The man recoiled instantly, hands raised. "Smart," Aron muttered. "Now walk away, quietly."

The vendor backed off fast as they moved deeper, past bone-setters, rune-etchers, and a woman promising to remove ancestral curses for "a drop of true blood."

"Over my dead body," Pavel muttered, stepping wide.

A vendor polishing strange charms looked up. "Looking for someone?" he asked.

"Where are they holding the fresh merchandise?" Aron asked, voice low.

The vendor paused. Eyes flicked to Kiara, then to Pavel. "You don't want that path."

"We didn't ask what we wanted," Pavel replied coldly. "Just where to walk."

The vendor hesitated, his eyes darting once more to Kiara as if weighing whether to speak. Then he exhaled slowly, resigning himself. "Inside the cave," he said, jerking his chin toward the far edge of the market where the torches burned lower and the crowd thinned. "You'll see a hollow cut into the stone near the end of the strip. There's a staircase behind it—half buried, looks like it leads nowhere."

He leaned in slightly, lowering his voice. "That's the entrance to the basement. That's where they keep the fresh ones—new catches, rare stock, anything that still breathes."

Another pause. This one heavier.

"It's guarded. Heavily. Not just by brutes, either. The kind of guards that don't ask questions and don't leave marks. And if by some miracle you get past them…"

He trailed off, shaking his head with a bitter chuckle. "You'll still have to get through the Warden. And no one gets through the Warden."

The vendor's mouth tightened, but he stepped back, muttering something under his breath in a language none of them recognized.

Aron gave a short nod. "Cheers, mate."

They turned as one and made their way toward the far end of the strip, where the torches flickered against jagged stone and the air felt colder, denser. The sounds of haggling and distant growls gave way to something else—something heavier. A silence not born of peace, but pressure.

As they neared the steps, a shape peeled from the shadows—slim, hooded, and unthreatening. A woman with copper-toned skin and eyes too pale to be human stepped cautiously into their path.

"You're looking for the cages," she said softly, her voice laced with something old. "You're not like the others."

Aron's stance shifted, his body angling protectively. "We're not here to shop."

"You're here to free someone," she said, her gaze flicking briefly to Kiara.

"Everyone," Aron snapped.

Kiara stepped forward, hesitant. "How do you—"

"I feel things," the woman replied. "And she's not meant to be seen in a place like this."

Aron exchanged a look with Pavel, then back to her. "Can you keep her safe?"

The woman dipped her head. "If you start with the back cells, I'll wait with her. I have a friend there—I'll know when to move. If you don't make it out… I'll get her out. That's all I can promise."

Aron turned to Kiara, his voice low and steady. "Stay with her. If people come running—free, terrified—help them. But don't come down those stairs, no matter what you hear."

Kiara's jaw clenched, but she nodded, reaching for him as he turned away. Her fingers found the edge of his jacket and tugged gently.

She kissed him—quick, fierce, all tension and unspoken promises. "Please don't die."

Aron paused, the weight of her touch anchoring him. He leaned in close, his voice dark and sharp. "After the week we've had? I'm so juiced up, it'll be hard not to cause an explosion."

Kiara smirked, fingers lingering. "Save some of that for me…"

"Neit!" Pavel interrupted. "No juice-talking now… you'll break his focus!" Pavel hissed, clapping a hand on Aron's shoulder and pushing him toward the path ahead.

The two men moved quickly now, every step dragging them deeper into something that felt ancient and wrong. The market behind them buzzed and churned, but here… silence reigned. The air grew colder, damper, and smelled of rust, rot, and something worse—fear.

They reached the edge of the hollow and found the steps just as the vendor had said—partially buried in loose gravel and shadow, steep and narrow, leading down into the bowels of the mountain. Two guards flanked the entrance. One blinked out of sync, his eyes didn't seem to land right, like the body wearing them didn't know how it worked.

"Who the hell are you?," one croaked.

Aron took one, striking him hard several times before quickly wrapping one arm around his neck and the other around his side, releasing an electric bolt straight through the side of his chest. Pavel took the other, taking a few hits before striking him down with a heavy-handed haymaker. It wasn't subtle, and it wasn't clean—but it was fast. Both guards hit the ground with sickening thuds, unconscious or worse.

"Creepy bastard," Pavel muttered, shaking out his hand. "Eyes like broken dolls."

"Keep moving," Aron growled, stepping over the bodies and into the dark.

The steps groaned beneath their weight. The gate at the bottom of the steps opened into a wide chamber, dimly lit with greenish lights that cast long, warped shadows on every surface. It smelled like piss and scorched metal. The prisoners—men, women, children—huddled in corners or pressed against the bars of their cells, their faces hollowed by time and torment.

The deeper he pushed into the compound, the worse the air became. It stank of blood, burnt metal, and something far more unsettling—sweet rot, like fruit left to die in the heat.

Without a word, Pavel reached the back as promised, where he began his work. Shimmering bursts of light flared around him as he teleported small groups outside the gate, instructing them to wait there until he returned. Each time he reappeared, the toll showed deeper—etched into the lines of his face, burning behind his eyes. And still, he pressed on.

Aron lingered near the edge of the chamber, cracking open locks and ushering people toward the stairs, his expression tight, coiled. All the while, his eyes swept the area.

Halfway through, he muttered, "So much for some scary warden…" but the words died the moment he heard boots pounding from a side corridor—heavy, fast, and not alone.

A prisoner, older and hunched in the corner, grabbed his arm on her way out of her cage. "You're looking in the wrong place," she rasped. "The worst ones? They're not kept down here. They keep them upstairs, in the back."

Aron's posture snapped straight. As Pavel teleported the last group, Aron gave a nod. "Get them out. I'll be right behind you."

Aron didn't wait for a response before he tore up the stairs, then veered hard away from the main entrance, deeper into the mountain's spine. The corridor opened into a containment space—too clean, too quiet.

Two guards charged him, their movements too clean, too synced. One swung wide, the other darted in low. Aron ducked under the arc of a blade, kicked out hard, and caught one square in the chest with an elbow to the spine. It shrieked—definitely not human. The second slashed across his shoulder with a jagged blade. Aron hissed, rolled with the strike, and slammed both fists into the first until it crumpled.

The other took one look at its fallen partner and ran. Aron let it. He didn't have time for cleanup. He needed the warden. A corridor to the left opened into something colder. Quieter. A room too clean for a prison—too sterile. It buzzed with a faint electromagnetic hum. That's when he saw her. A child—no older than ten—stood behind reinforced glass. Pale skin, patchy hair. Arms darkened with thin black veins, temple sensors pulsing faintly. She wasn't shackled. She didn't need to be. Her lips moved in some dull, broken chant—like she'd been programmed to recite her own surrender.

Aron's gut clenched as he took in the sight behind the reinforced glass. This wasn't just a prisoner. This was a test subject.

A young girl—maybe ten—stood motionless, lips twitching in a silent chant. Her hair was patchy, her skin sickly pale, and black veins webbed across her arms. Blinking sensors clung to her temples like parasites. The room buzzed with faint electromagnetic pulses—designed to hold her still, to break her slowly.

His breath shortened. The rage came in a low hum beneath his skin, building like a storm in the marrow of his bones. Then—movement.

Three more shadows entered the corridor. Mercs, or whatever was left of them. One had bone-etched blades fused to his arms. Another wore a glyph-etched breather mask pulsing with dim light. The third flickered oddly with every step, like his body couldn't decide on a stable form. Aron didn't wait.

The hallway exploded with sound and light. He spun on the first, catching his throat with a jolt that lit the air in a flash of searing blue. The man spasmed, convulsed, and dropped smoking to the floor. Pavel surged into the fray beside him, taking the second down with a crunching tackle that shattered ribs. The third lunged—until Aron's palm met his chest in a thunderous crack. Electricity surged from his fingertips, arcing down the man's spine and frying his nervous system in a violent shudder. The merc collapsed, twitching once, then lay still.

The pressure dropped, the temperature shifted. A buzz ran through the floor like the mountain itself was bracing. Aron didn't turn. Just cracked his neck once more, breath steady now as the storm settled into place.

From the far corridor, slow, heavy, certain, footsteps could be heard as the warden emerged from the shadows. Tall, armored, his skin gleamed with some kind of black ceremonial resin, as if slicked in ritual. Plating wrapped his chest like a badge of importance—like this was a throne room, not a prison.

Aron's jaw flexed. Sparks flickered beneath his skin, trailing up his arms like veins made of wire.

"Get them out of here, and don't come back this time." He said to Pavel, never breaking eye contact with the newcomer.

Pavel hesitated, then moved fast—herding the freed experiments down the corridor as the warden's eyes tracked Aron with cold disdain.

"So," he said, voice low and gravelly, "you're the one making all the noise."

Electricity crackled between Aron's fingers as his fists clenched. He didn't respond. His boots echoed as he stepped forward, body humming with restrained power. He was done talking.

The warden struck first—fast, a brutal arc of shadowy energy slamming into Aron's ribs. It hurled him back across the stone, crashing him into a support pillar. He hit hard, groaning as pain tore through him. A trickle of blood ran down his chin from debris.

His fingers curled slowly against the floor. And then... he got up. Aron let go of his rage, directing his power toward the beast now running toward him. The blast sent him right through the glass.

The warden groaned, trying to push himself up, but Aron was faster. With a final burst of power, he sent the man sprawling, his weapon clattering uselessly to the ground.

Aron loomed over him, his voice low and sharp. "This place—your power, your control—it's done. You'll never hurt anyone again."

The warden coughed, blood speckling his lips as he glared up at Aron. "You think they'll thank you for this?" He spat. "The world doesn't care about your kind—or theirs."

Aron's eyes narrowed, the glow around him intensifying. "Maybe not," he said, his voice steady, "But I do."

With a final, blinding surge of energy, the warden's sneer was swallowed by light—his body swallowed by the surge of power that followed. The chamber pulsed once... then went still.

Aron turned, breath sharp, power still crackling along his arms. He emerged victoriously into the market, and the few vendors and guards still lingering froze. Some were armed. Some were preparing to run. One made the mistake of reaching for a cage latch.

Aron's voice boomed like thunder. "Anyone still holding prisoners—open the cages. Now."

Lightning danced up his arms, forming arcs that curled and snapped like they had minds of their own. No one moved. Aron's eyes sparked. "Fine." He raised a hand.

The nearest cage door snapped open with a concussive burst, the lock twisted inward like it had been crushed by invisible hands. Another door shattered open, then another and another, as screams echoed and chains rattled. Vendors dropped their wares and fled.

A few still tried to stand their ground—until Aron stepped toward them, energy flaring in his wake. No words. Just presence. And that was enough. Cages flew open as prisoners bolted for the exits. The entire market seemed to tremble, as if unsure whether to collapse or bow.

Kiara's lips parted. "Is it done?"

Aron didn't answer at first. He turned back toward the market, sparks coiling up his arm, humming louder and louder until—the air cracked, and the entire backside of the mountain ignited in a blast of white-hot energy. The stalls, the tunnels, the remnants of the warden's empire—gone in a flash of wrath and fire.

Only then did Aron let the storm go. His shoulders dropped, the light dimming around him as he stepped into the open night.

"It's done," he said simply.

Kiara let out a slow breath, coughing as the heat and ash brushed past her like the final breath of something dead. "Good." Her voice was quiet but resolute.

Pavel cracked his knuckles. "Time to go, then." He extended a hand toward them both. "Better we go before someone comes to see what all the boom was about, eh?"

A pulse of energy enveloped them, and in the blink of an eye, the burning market vanished, replaced by the cool stillness of Witchaven's sanctuary.

-Chapter 39-

Brother Against Brother

Stepping through the portal into Atla was like stepping into another world—one where the passage of time seemed a cruel joke. Kane's first impression was not awe but disdain. The kingdom before him was a combination of a twisted reflection of what could have been and the last memories he had of fighting with his brother and destroying Atlantis. For all its technological splendor, the place reeked of unchecked power and hollow grandeur. Golden spires pierced the hazy sky, glinting in the light like daggers pointed toward the heavens. Streets thrummed with activity, yet there was an eerie sense of control, a rigidness that left no room for spontaneity or true joy.

Kane's gaze swept over the carefully orchestrated scene, his sharp mind cataloging the signs of a society molded by fear and domination. This was Ivyg's vision—a vision Kane had spent centuries trying to prevent. He could almost hear his brother's smug laughter echoing in the air, as though the very atmosphere was saturated with Ivyg's presence.

The ostentatious displays of wealth were everywhere: shimmering fountains flowing with liquid that looked like molten gold, market stalls laden with goods that only the elite could afford, and courtiers adorned in garments finer than anything Kane had seen in decades. But beneath the glittering surface, there was a darkness—a rigid order enforced by a subtle but pervasive fear.

Kane inhaled deeply, the air thick with the scent of control and suppression. His thoughts drifted to Marcus Kydd, his protégé, who had inherited much of his ideals but none of his brother's brutality. Marcus had been meant to carry on Kane's work, but there was still so much left undone. He also was unsure if the fracture in his relationship with Marcus could ever be fully mended.

Kane's chest tightened as he thought of his own son, Horus during the time when humans called him Osiris. He had pushed the boy through a portal to safety in Khem centuries ago, during another moment of chaos. The memory of his son's anger and betrayal lingered. Horus had believed his father had abandoned him, siding with the enemy Seth. How similar, Kane thought bitterly, was his relationship with Ivyg—a rivalry steeped in resentment and misunderstanding, an eternal struggle that seemed to stretch beyond lifetimes.

As Kane took in the sheer scale of Ivyg's kingdom, a question gnawed at him: Had the council truly allowed this? The balance they'd fought to maintain for eons now seemed shattered. Either they had acquiesced to Ivyg's control, or, more likely, Ivyg had eliminated them entirely. The grotesque violence of his brother's past made the latter far more plausible. And yet, there was something undeniably clever about Ivyg's methods. He hadn't merely subjugated a planet; he had built a twisted kind of utopia—a meticulously crafted society that functioned like clockwork under his iron fist. Kane's lip curled. It was a mockery of everything they had once stood for, a perversion of their shared heritage.

The familiar sensation of old wounds reopened as Kane turned his thoughts to his brother. How many times had he tried to show Ivyg another path? A path that was not paved with cruelty and pain? But Ivyg had rejected every effort, consumed by a vision of power and prophecy that left no room for mercy or humanity, who he always saw as being lesser, there to serve and nothing else, in his mind.

Kane's boots clicked against the polished stone walkway as he moved forward, his face set in grim determination. He was here now, in this moment, with a singular purpose: to end this nightmare. Whatever it took, he would ensure that Ivyg's reign of terror would not stand.

Ahead, a cadre of guards awaited him, their polished armor gleaming like mirrors. They stood stiffly, weapons at the ready, their faces expressionless. They were not men, Kane realized, but constructs—automatons imbued with just enough intelligence to carry out their tasks without question. A fitting representation of Ivyg's kingdom, where free will had no place.

Beyond the guards, Kane caught sight of the palace gates, adorned with intricate carvings that depicted Ivyg's many conquests. Each panel was a story of domination, a reminder of the lives crushed under his brother's ambition. Kane's stomach churned, but he forced the emotion down. This was no time for sentimentality.

As he approached the gates, the guards stepped aside in perfect unison, a silent acknowledgment of his arrival. Kane squared his shoulders and strode forward, his heart a storm of conflicting emotions. Whatever lay ahead, he would face it with the resolve of someone who had nothing left to lose.

Ivyg's voice echoed in his memory, a taunt from centuries past: "You always thought you were better than me, little brother. But in the end, I will prove that I am the one destined to rule."

Kane's jaw tightened, his fists clenched at his sides. Not if he had anything to say about it. The stakes had never been higher, and this time, there would be no compromise.

The harsh glare of artificial light reflected off the polished floors of the preparation chamber, where Kane, Nova, and Patel were being processed for their audience with Ivyg. The scent of chemical disinfectants mingled with the faint hum of unseen machinery, creating an atmosphere of sterility and unease. Kane was lost in thought, replaying the history that had led him here, when a soft voice broke through his reverie.

"Excuse me, sir."

Kane turned to see a man of unassuming stature, his face worn but intelligent, standing near a console. His name tag read Oliver Kross. Something about the man tugged at the edges of Kane's memory, but he couldn't quite place it.

"You're Kane," Oliver said, his voice low and measured. It wasn't a question. "I remember you."

Kane's gaze sharpened. "Do you now? And how is that?"

"I worked for the government, long ago," Oliver explained. "Research division. Artificial limbs and biomechanical enhancements were my specialty." His eyes flicked to Kane's bandaged arm. "I see you're in need of one."

Kane raised an eyebrow. "Astute observation."

Oliver stepped closer, lowering his voice. "If you survive this meeting, I can help you. I know where to get the materials for a replacement—better than anything Ivyg's cronies could provide. There's a facility in Colorado, a place called Wellville. I was stationed there once, years ago."

The mention of Wellville struck a chord, but Kane filed it away for later. "Why are you telling me this?"

Oliver hesitated, glancing toward the ever-watchful Murrin, who loitered nearby. He stepped closer to Kane, his voice barely above a whisper. "Because I need your help. They've been using a program—something I helped develop—to predict and manipulate outcomes. It's called the Temporal Analysis System. It's paired with their time-travel devices to simulate timeline changes based on variables. That's how they've been able to achieve such precision."

Kane's brow furrowed. "Precision? You're saying they're not guessing when they interfere with time?"

Oliver nodded. "They input scenarios—cause and effect—and the program predicts outcomes with startling accuracy. It's not perfect; variables can still shift unexpectedly. But it's good enough that they've managed to stay several steps ahead. You've seen it yourself, haven't you? Their uncanny ability to anticipate resistance."

Kane's jaw tightened. He had seen it. Too many times. "And you're telling me this because?"

"Because it doesn't account for everything," Oliver said urgently. "They've made mistakes. Ivyg thinks he's infallible, but his arrogance blinds him. The system relies on the data it's given, and even the smallest miscalculation can throw everything off. That's where you come in. You can disrupt the system, but only if you act decisively."

Kane's mind raced. He thought of his own error—his slight miscalculation when arriving in Witchaven. It had seemed inconsequential at the time, but he now realized it had been enough to alter events subtly. If Ivyg's system was as fragile as Oliver claimed, there was hope.

Oliver's expression darkened. "I wouldn't be telling you this if I didn't believe you were the only one who could stop him. But I need something in return."

Kane crossed his arms. "And what's that?"

"My daughter," Oliver said, his voice breaking. "She… she was taken. Killed in one of his purges. She was special—different. I don't think he realized what he destroyed when he ordered her death."

Kane's gaze narrowed. "Special how?"

"She had this… presence," Oliver said, struggling to find the words. "An energy. She could connect with people, inspire them, make them see things differently. And she had dreams—vivid, prophetic dreams. She would wake up talking about places she'd never been, people she'd never met. I didn't understand it at the time, but now I think… I think she was one of the Champions Ivyg was trying to eliminate. She had the potential to change everything."

Kane felt a chill run down his spine. The Champions—those chosen to protect the Veil and its secrets. If Oliver's daughter had been one of them, her death was more than a tragedy; it was a calculated move to weaken the resistance.

"I know this sounds crazy," Oliver continued, his desperation mounting. "But if there's even a chance to undo what's been done, to give her a second chance, I'll do whatever it takes. Just… Please, help me."

Kane's mind churned as he considered the implications. He didn't know Oliver's daughter, but her description sounded eerily familiar—too familiar. Could she have been connected to the amulet, the key to unlocking the truth about Lemuria? The thought gnawed at him, but he pushed it aside for now.

"I can't promise miracles," Kane said finally. "But I'll do what I can."

Oliver's shoulders sagged with relief. "Thank you. That's all I can ask."

"I know it's fun to catch up on the good old days but now is not the time." Murrin's cheerful voice interrupted the moment. "Hurry up and get dressed, please. The God-King doesn't like to be kept waiting."

Oliver's expression hardened as he pressed something into Kane's hand—a small, unassuming data chip. "This is what you need to know about the program. Study it. Use it. And don't let him win."

Kane nodded, slipping the chip into his pocket. As he followed Murrin toward the next chamber, his resolve hardened. This wasn't just about defeating Ivyg; it was about dismantling the system that allowed him to thrive. And somewhere, in the tangled threads of time, was the key to unraveling it all.

The gilded doors of the throne room swung open with a theatrical flourish, revealing an ostentatious chamber bathed in gold and crimson. Pillars adorned with serpentine carvings coiled toward a vaulted ceiling, where a massive chandelier crafted of crystal and bone cast an eerie glow. Kane stepped forward, his allies, Nova and Rajneel, flanking him. Their footsteps echoed ominously against the polished marble floor.

At the far end of the hall, perched atop a throne fashioned from jagged obsidian and inlaid with glowing runes, sat Ivyg. Draped in golden regalia, his presence radiated arrogance and command. His piercing eyes, sharp as a predator's, scanned the group with a mixture of amusement and disdain.

"Well, well," Ivyg drawled, his voice carrying an unnerving combination of charm and menace. "If it isn't my little brother, Enki. You've aged, though not gracefully. Time has not been kind."

Kane's jaw tightened, but he held his tongue. He would not give Ivyg the satisfaction of a reaction.

"I must say, your arrival is… unexpected," Ivyg continued, a sly grin spreading across his face. "The Oracle twins foretold your return, but even they couldn't pinpoint when. And here you are, as if plucked from the ether. How poetic."

He rose from the throne, his movements fluid and deliberate. "Tell me, brother, did you enjoy my labyrinth? I crafted it myself—a little test of wit and survival. And yet, here you stand, victorious. Impressive, if not entirely surprising. You always were resourceful."

Kane met Ivyg's gaze, his expression calm but resolute. "No thanks to you, but I've faced worse."

Ivyg chuckled darkly. "Spoken like a true underdog. But let's not dwell on past triumphs, brother. You're here now, in my domain. Surely you've come seeking something. Redemption for your failure in the Hollow Earth, perhaps?"

Before Kane could respond, Ivyg turned his attention to Nova and Rajneel, his smile widening. "Ah, and who are these companions of yours? Survivors of my Wheel of Fate, no less. Truly remarkable. Tell me, gentlemen, what do you desire? Wealth? Power? Or perhaps a reunion with loved ones lost?"

Nova stepped forward hesitantly, his voice unsteady. "I just want to see my family again. That's all."

Ivyg tilted his head, feigning sympathy. "Family, you say? How touching." He waved his scepter, and a shimmering portal materialized beside Nova. "There you go. Step through, and you'll find them waiting. But be warned—reunions are seldom as sweet as we imagine."

Nova glanced back at Kane and Rajneel, his expression conflicted. Kane gave him a subtle nod. "Go," he said softly. "You've earned it."

With a deep breath, Nova stepped through the portal, which closed behind him with a faint hum.

"And you?" Ivyg turned to Rajneel, his tone more mocking now. "What grand desire does the ever-curious Dr. Patel harbor? Knowledge? Redemption? Or perhaps a second chance at life?"

Rajneel hesitated, his composure faltering. "I want to be whole," he said at last. "To reconcile with the parts of myself I've lost."

Ivyg's grin widened, a predatory gleam in his eyes. "Ah, the fractured man seeks unity. How poetic." He waved his scepter again, opening a second portal. "Go, then. But remember, the past has a way of clinging to us, no matter how far we run."

As Rajneel approached the portal, Ivyg leaned in close, his voice a sinister whisper. "You shouldn't exist, you know. Your presence here is an anomaly—a blip in the grand design. Enjoy your fleeting moment of grace. Just know that you WILL be back before me soon."

Rajneel disappeared through the portal, leaving Kane and Ivyg alone in the cavernous room.

Ivyg turned to Kane, his smile fading. "And now we come to you, little brother. What is it that you seek? A truce? A favor? Or perhaps vengeance for all the slights you've suffered at my hands?"

Kane took a step forward, his voice steady. "I seek an end to this madness. To your tyranny. To the suffering you've inflicted on this world."

Ivyg laughed, a harsh, grating sound that echoed through the chamber. "Oh, Kane, always the idealist. Always dreaming of a better world. But you see, brother, this is the better world. My world. And there's no place in it for your quaint notions of justice and compassion."

He leaned closer, his expression darkening. "But I'm feeling generous. Kneel before me, swear your loyalty, and I'll grant you a place by my side. Together, we could rule over this wretched planet, shaping it in our image."

Kane's eyes burned with quiet defiance. "Never."

Ivyg straightened, his grin returning. "So be it. But know this, little brother—no matter what you do, no matter how hard you fight, I will always win. I am the God-King, and my will is absolute."

As the tension between them reached its peak, a guard entered the room and whispered something to Ivyg. His expression soured, but he quickly regained his composure.

"It seems our time is up for now," Ivyg said, turning back to Kane. "But don't worry—we'll meet again soon enough. After all, fate has a way of bringing us together, doesn't it?"

With a final, mocking bow, Ivyg swept out of the throne room, leaving Kane standing alone amidst the splendor and shadows of his brother's empire.

Ivyg's scepter shimmered as he waved it, opening a swirling portal beside them. "Come, brother," he said with a smirk. "There's something I'd like to show you—a little piece of history I think you'll find... enlightening."

Without waiting for a response, Ivyg stepped through the portal, his golden regalia gleaming in the dim light. Kane hesitated briefly, his instincts screaming to tread carefully, but he followed, his resolve unshaken.

The portal deposited them on a misty hillside under a leaden sky. The air was heavy, carrying the scent of damp earth and decay. Before them stretched a vast graveyard, row upon row of headstones rising from the fog like silent sentinels. Each stone bore a name, meticulously engraved, accompanied by a brief epitaph.

"This," Ivyg declared grandly, spreading his arms wide, "is my monument to your failures."

Kane's gaze swept over the graves, his breath catching as familiar names leapt out at him: Dr. "Brad" Moses. Mallah. Ogma. Marcus Kydd. Clarice Murphy. Juan Cesaro. Esme Edwards.

Each name struck like a physical blow. He stumbled forward, unable to look away from the grim testament to Ivyg's cruelty. The epitaphs were brief but cutting, each one a twisted reminder of the lives lost in their struggle to protect the world from Ivyg's dominion.

"They all fought bravely, I'll give them that," Ivyg continued, his tone mockingly reverent. "But bravery only takes you so far when you're up against destiny—my destiny."

Kane clenched his fists, his nails digging into his palms as he fought to keep his emotions in check. "You call this destiny?" he growled, his voice low but seething. "This isn't greatness, Ivyg. It's genocide. It's madness."

"Call it what you will," Ivyg replied, unbothered. "History will remember it as victory. My victory."

He gestured toward a larger, ornately carved monument at the center of the graveyard. "Ah, and here we have the pièce de résistance," he said, his voice dripping with mockery. "A collective tribute to those who dared to stand against me—and failed."

Kane's gaze fell on the monument, and his breath hitched. The intricate carvings depicted scenes of battle, moments frozen in stone: Mallah wielding her staff in defiance, Ogma standing against impossible odds, and Marcus Kydd leading a charge, his determination immortalized in granite. At the base of the monument was a chilling inscription: "Here lie the remnants of rebellion. Let their folly serve as a lesson."

"You did this," Kane said, his voice barely above a whisper. "All of them… they trusted me. They believed in the fight. And you slaughtered them."

"Slaughter is such an ugly word," Ivyg replied casually. "I prefer to think of it as... pruning. Removing the weeds to let the garden flourish."

Kane turned to face his brother, his eyes blazing with fury. "You call yourself a god, but you're nothing more than a monster."

Ivyg chuckled, unfazed by the accusation. "Oh, brother, always so self-righteous. But tell me this—what has your morality ever won you? This graveyard is proof of your failure. Proof that your way doesn't work."

For a long moment, Kane stood in silence, the weight of loss pressing down on him. But as he looked over the graves, his grief began to transform into something else—something stronger. A quiet, unyielding determination took root in his heart.

"They may have fallen," Kane said, his voice steady, "but their sacrifice wasn't in vain. They fought for something greater than themselves— something you'll never understand. And I will honor their memory by one day ending your reign."

Ivyg's smile faltered for the briefest of moments, but he quickly recovered, clapping his hands in mock applause. "Such conviction. It's almost endearing. But conviction alone won't save you, brother. You're alone. Powerless. Broken. And soon, you'll join them."

He gestured with his scepter, opening another portal. "But enough sentimentality. We have more pressing matters to attend to. Come, let's return to the castle. I'm growing weary of this little trip down memory lane."

Kane cast one last, lingering look at the graves, silently vowing to avenge each name etched into the stone. Then, with a deep breath, he stepped through the portal, his resolve stronger than ever.

In the brief reprieve afforded by Ivyg's orchestrated cleansing ritual, Kane found himself alone with Oliver Kross in the preparation chambers.

The atmosphere was tense, the air thick with the weight of shared desperation. Oliver, trembling slightly, glanced toward the door to ensure no one was watching before pulling a small, intricately crafted knife from within his tunic.

"This," Oliver whispered, his voice barely audible, "is your chance."

Kane's eyes narrowed as he took the blade, running his thumb along its edge. "A knife against a tyrant wielding a scepter capable of reshaping time? Seems like a long shot."

Oliver leaned in, his face lined with desperation. "It's not just about the knife. It's about disrupting his timeline—his control. That scepter isn't just a weapon; it's the lynchpin of his entire operation. Without it, his ability to manipulate events collapses."

Kane raised an eyebrow. "And this knife is supposed to help me do that?"

"There's more to it," Oliver continued, his voice shaking slightly. "Ivyg's forces have been using a program—something that analyzes outcomes based on variables changed in the timeline. It's how they've stayed one step ahead of everyone, how they've known exactly where and when to strike. But the system isn't perfect. If you destroy the scepter and eliminate Ivyg, the program loses its foundation."

Kane considered this, his mind racing. He'd been wary of time manipulation ever since arriving in this fragmented timeline, but this revelation added a new layer of complexity. "And you're sure this will work?"

"It has to," Oliver insisted. "If it doesn't, we're finished. All of us."

For the first time since their encounter, Kane allowed himself a faint smile. He placed a reassuring hand on Oliver's shoulder. "You've done well, Oliver. And if there's one thing I've learned, it's that even the smallest actions can ripple into something far greater. Your daughter… her death won't be meaningless. I swear it."

Oliver's eyes welled with tears, but he quickly wiped them away. "Thank you, Kane. For giving me hope."

With that, they returned to their duties, each carrying the weight of their mission in silence.

The opportunity came during an audience with Ivyg in the throne room, where the self-proclaimed God-King held court with his usual arrogance. Kane, standing with forced deference, approached Ivyg and requested a private word.

Ivyg raised an eyebrow, amused. "What could you possibly have to say that my court cannot hear, little brother?"

"It concerns a favor," Kane replied, his tone measured. "Something I can only entrust to you."

Intrigued, Ivyg waved a hand, dismissing the guards and courtiers. The room emptied, leaving the two brothers alone.

"Speak," Ivyg commanded, leaning back on his golden throne. "What is it you desire?"

Kane stepped closer, his voice dropping to a near-whisper. "Come closer, and I'll tell you."

Ivyg hesitated, then rose from his throne, approaching with a smirk. "You've always been one for theatrics, haven't you?"

As Ivyg leaned in, Kane's hand shot out, the knife slicing through the air in a blur. The blade sank deep into Ivyg's chest, piercing his heart. Ivyg's eyes widened in shock, blood bubbling at his lips.

"I can't believe you actually fell for that!" Kane cackled indignantly. "This is for everyone you've killed," Kane said, whispering coldly into his ear, twisting the blade and repeating. "Your reign ends now."

Ivyg staggered back, clutching at the wound as his scepter slipped from his grasp. It hit the floor and shattered into pieces, a cascade of glowing fragments scattering across the room.

The once-imposing figure of the God-King crumpled to the ground, his final words barely audible. "You'll never… win…"

Kane stood over the lifeless body, his breath ragged but steady. "Watch me."

Ivyg stumbled back, blood pooling around his ornate golden robes, his face contorted in shock. Kane stood over him, breathing heavily, the bloodied knife still clenched in his hand. For a moment, there was silence—stifling, oppressive silence.

Then chaos erupted.

Guards surged into the throne room, weapons drawn. Clovis Krott barked orders, his voice cutting through the clamor like a whip. "Seize him! Alive, if possible!"

Kane dropped the knife and raised his hands, offering no resistance as the guards swarmed him. His gaze never left Ivyg, who crumpled to the floor with a guttural gasp. The self-proclaimed God-King clawed weakly at the air, his eyes meeting Kane's with a mixture of fury and fear.

"You… do you think this changes anything?" Ivyg gasped, his voice faint but laced with venom. "You think you've won?"

Kane's expression was cold, resolute. "You won't live to see it, brother, but your empire will crumble. Watch me."

The guards shoved Kane to his knees, binding his wrists with harsh, unyielding restraints. One of them struck him across the face, but Kane didn't flinch, his focus locked on Ivyg as the so-called God-King's movements stilled.

Ivyg's scepter fell from his grasp, clattering to the floor and shattering into jagged pieces. The room seemed to hold its breath, as if the very fabric of Ivyg's rule had cracked alongside it.

Kane felt the weight of dozens of eyes on him—guards, advisors, even Clovis Krott—all teetering on the edge of disbelief and rage. But Kane didn't care. He had done what needed to be done. A low growl broke the tension as Clovis stepped forward, his predatory gaze narrowing on Kane, his voice cutting through the chaos. "You'll pay for this," he hissed. "I'll make sure of it. Take him and bring the traitor Kross too. I want them both alive."

The guards yanked Kane to his feet, dragging him out of the throne room with brutal efficiency. As they passed Oliver, who had been cowering in the shadows, Clovis barked another command. "Bring him with us."

Oliver's protests fell on deaf ears as the guards hauled him off alongside Kane. The corridors blurred into a haze of cold stone and harsh lights, the echoes of their footfalls ringing hollow in the oppressive silence. When they finally reached the prison wing, Kane was unceremoniously thrown into a dim, damp cell. Oliver was shoved into the same cell moments later, collapsing onto the cold floor with a pained grunt.

The heavy door slammed shut, the metallic clang reverberating through the narrow space. Outside, Clovis's mocking laughter echoed faintly down the corridor.

Kane leaned against the wall, his expression impassive despite the blood trickling from the corner of his mouth. Oliver sat hunched in the corner, his hands trembling as he clutched at his knees.

For a long moment, neither spoke, the weight of their situation settling over them like a suffocating shroud. Then, Kane broke the silence, his voice low but steady.

"It's not over," he said, his tone resolute. "And once my arm is repaired, I'm hoping to be able to use my Vril powers once again."

Oliver looked up, his eyes shadowed with despair. "You don't think he'll kill us? He wipes out anyone who opposes him."

Kane met his gaze with unwavering determination. "Maybe. But we have to make this right."

And with that, the seed of a plan began to take root, fragile but alive in the darkness.

The cell was cold and dimly lit, the only sounds the distant drip of water and the faint shuffle of guards outside. Kane sat on the hard bench, his face battered and bruised but his spirit unbroken. Across the cell, Oliver Kross huddled in the corner, staring blankly at the floor. His shoulders sagged under the weight of despair, his hands gripping the edges of his tattered sleeves.

"She was all I had left," Oliver muttered, his voice thick with grief. "First my wife, now my daughter. Everything I ever loved—gone. And for what?"

Kane studied him silently, the knife wound on his brother's chest still vivid in his mind. His own betrayal, murdering one of his own kind. The old teachings still brought guilt into his mind, even though he knew he had done the world a favor by killing Ivyg, the self-proclaimed god-king. His thoughts then turned to the words Oliver had spoken before the confrontation, about the timelines, the scepter, and the program. He was trying to get his mind off his brother and onto something else when it just clicked in his mind, like the grooves of a key fitting into the tumblers of a lock, perfectly.

"She wasn't just your daughter, Oliver," Kane said at last, his voice steady but laced with intent. "She was special. You said so yourself."

Oliver looked up, his face lined with sorrow and confusion. "Of course she was special. To me. But to the world? She was just a girl. A brilliant, kind, wonderful girl… who didn't deserve to die."

Kane leaned forward, his expression firm. "No. She wasn't just a girl. Ivyg doesn't do anything without a reason. He's methodical, calculating. If he killed her, it wasn't just cruelty—it was strategy. He saw her as a threat to his Order."

Oliver's brow furrowed. "What are you saying?"

"I'm saying that I don't believe she was a random casualty," Kane continued. "She was a threat to him. A Champion—one of the few who could stand against him, maybe even lead others to do the same."

Oliver shook his head, his eyes filling with tears. "She was brilliant, yes, but a Champion? That's… that's not possible, and even if it were, you saw his shrine of all the ones he DID kill."

"Think about it," Kane urged. "Ivyg's greatest fear has always been losing his grip on power. If your daughter held the potential to disrupt his plans—to be something more than even you realized—he would have seen her as a danger. That's why she's gone. He saw her for what she could become, and he acted to eliminate her before she had the chance."

Oliver's breath hitched as Kane's words sank in. "If that's true… if she really was that important…" His voice broke. "Then it's my fault. I should have done more to protect her."

Kane reached out, placing a steady hand on Oliver's shoulder. "Listen to me. What's done is done. But if she was a Champion—if she had that potential—then her death might not be permanent. You said it yourself: the timelines can be altered. If we can change the variables, if we can pinpoint where things went wrong, we might be able to bring her back. And not just her. We could fix everything."

Oliver's eyes widened, a flicker of hope piercing the cloud of despair. "You… you really believe that?"

"I do," Kane said, his tone resolute. "I've seen enough to know that fate isn't as fixed as we like to think. With the right tools, the right actions, we can rewrite the story. Your daughter's death doesn't have to be the end. It can be the beginning."

For the first time in days, Oliver sat up straighter, his gaze meeting Kane's with a mixture of doubt and longing. "But how? How do we even begin to change something like that?"

Kane's mind churned with possibilities. "It starts with understanding. The program Ivyg used—the one that calculates outcomes based on timeline changes. If we can get access to it, if we can learn how it works, we can use it to our advantage. And then… we act."

Oliver nodded slowly, the spark of determination returning to his eyes. "She always believed in me. She said I was capable of anything." His voice steadied. "If there's a chance to save her, to stop all of this, I'll do whatever it takes."

Kane gave him a small, encouraging smile. "Good. Because we're going to need every bit of that brilliance if we're going to pull this off. Ivyg may have thought he'd won, but he underestimated us. And that was his first mistake."

As the two men sat in the gloom of their cell, a shared resolve began to take shape. The path ahead was uncertain, fraught with danger and complexity, but for the first time, there was something neither had felt in a long time. Hope.

-Chapter 40-

Caught In the Middle

The sunlight poured through the car's windshield as Cesaro navigated the narrow backroads of Wellville. Rose sat in the passenger seat, absently fiddling with the hem of her jacket. The quiet hum of the car engine filled the air, broken only by the occasional rustle of leaves blowing across the pavement.

"You've been quiet," Cesaro remarked, glancing at her. "Not like you."

Rose sighed, staring out the window. "Just thinking."

"About?" he prompted, though his tone was light.

"Everything." She gestured vaguely at the world beyond the glass. "This town, the murders, the Pulse. You ever feel like you're caught in the middle of something way bigger than you?"

Cesaro chuckled. "All the time. It's basically my brand. But that's why we're here, isn't it? To figure out our piece of the puzzle?"

Rose nodded, but her expression remained distant. "What about the Hollow Earth? You really think it's connected to all of this?"

He hesitated before answering, his usual bravado giving way to sincerity. "If there's one thing I've learned, it's that the world is stranger than we give it credit for. The Hollow Earth? Zen? Everything we've seen so far? It's all part of the same web. We're just trying to find the threads."

As they rounded a bend in the road, Rose's breath caught. A sense of familiarity washed over her, though she couldn't place its source. "Pull over," she said suddenly.

"What?" Cesaro asked, startled.

"Just pull over," she insisted, her voice tinged with urgency.

He obliged, guiding the car onto the shoulder and cutting the engine. "What is it?"

Rose stepped out of the car, her boots crunching on the gravel. She walked a few steps into the grassy field by the roadside, her brow furrowed. The air felt heavy, electric, like the moments before a thunderstorm.

Then it hit her.

The vision swept through her mind like a tidal wave. She was no longer in Wellville but standing in a field bathed in an eerie twilight. Around her, figures stood frozen, their faces indistinct but their fear palpable. The whispering began—soft at first, like leaves rustling in the wind, but quickly growing louder, more insistent.

Thunder rumbled overhead, though the sky showed no sign of rain. Movement in the grass caught her eye—shadows slithering just beneath the surface. And then, those eyes. Glowing green, malevolent, and countless, they emerged from the darkness, surrounding the figures in the field.

A blazing fire drew her attention—a jeep overturned, its tires still spinning. She saw a man screaming, his voice drowned out by the whispers. Another man, whose name she inexplicably knew to be Conrad, stood frozen as one of the creatures loomed over him.

Rose felt her legs buckle. She was back in the car, gasping for air as the vision released her.

"Rose!" Cesaro was by her side in an instant, steadying her as she swayed. "What happened?"

She shook her head, her breaths ragged. "I—I saw something. Something terrible."

He frowned, his grip on her tightening. "Talk to me."

"I think…" Her voice faltered, her eyes wide with residual fear. "I think it's happening here. Across the highway, near the motel. There's something in the field."

Cesaro glanced toward the stretch of grass across the road, his usual swagger replaced by genuine concern. "We're checking it out. Now."

Once back at the diner, the atmosphere was warm and bustling, a stark contrast to Rose's inner turmoil. Cesaro led her to a booth, ordering coffee for them both as she stared blankly at the table.

Nicole hovered nearby, clearly intrigued. "You two okay? You look like you've seen a ghost."

"We're fine," Cesaro said curtly, though his tone lacked its usual charm.

Nicole hesitated, her curiosity evident, but eventually moved on. Cesaro leaned closer to Rose, his voice low. "What did you see?"

She shook her head. "It's hard to explain. There were whispers, green eyes… people in the field, dying. It felt like the Pulse, but worse."

Before Cesaro could respond, the diner door swung open, and Dexter walked in with Max trailing behind him. Dexter's sharp gaze landed on them immediately, and he approached their table.

"We need to talk," Dexter said without preamble. "Somewhere private."

Nicole, pretending to rearrange sugar packets, perked up at the conversation. Dexter shot her a pointed look. "Nicole, other tables."

With a huff, she walked away, though her curiosity was far from sated.

"The station," Cesaro suggested, rising from the booth. "Let's go."

As they filed out of the diner, Rose glanced back at the field across the highway, her stomach churning with unease. Whatever was happening in Wellville, she knew they were running out of time.

The group was mid-discussion in the station's conference room when the door creaked open, and Linda and Katherine entered, their faces pale with urgency.

"Did you meet with your contact?" Cesaro asked, his brow furrowing as he leaned back in his chair.

Linda shook her head. "No. She couldn't make it."

"But she did call," Katherine added quickly, stepping forward. "She said we need to get out of town. Now."

The room fell silent.

"What do you mean 'get out of town'?" Rose asked, her voice wary.

Linda's tone was steady but tense. "She warned me that something bad is about to happen. She called it a 'cleanup.' Said if we stay here, we'll be caught in it."

"A cleanup?" Cesaro echoed. "What the hell does that mean?"

"It means the military is getting ready to sweep through," Katherine explained. "And if what she says is true, they'll erase anything and anyone that might compromise whatever operation they've got going on."

"That's insane," Max muttered, pacing the room. "We can't just leave—there are people here who don't know what's happening."

Before anyone could respond, Dexter entered the room, holding a folder in one hand and a steaming cup of coffee in the other. He looked around at the group, his face a mix of determination and exhaustion.

"I've been putting pieces together," he said without preamble, setting the folder on the table. "And I think we've been looking at this all wrong."

Katherine's eyes narrowed. "What do you mean?"

Dexter gestured for everyone to sit. "Last summer, you had an experience, right? Losing time, the whispers, the green eyes. It all started after you left the Mountain View Motel, correct?"

Katherine nodded slowly, her jaw tightening.

Dexter continued, flipping open the folder to reveal reports, photos, and scribbled notes. "There was an incident a few miles outside of town. A supposed hazardous materials spill. The Army blocked off the highway and detained everyone at the motel for a week. Officially, there were no severe injuries, but the people who were there… well, let's just say their accounts don't line up with the government's version of events."

Cesaro leaned forward, his expression dark. "So, they detained people to cover something up?"

"Exactly," Dexter replied. "But it wasn't just about containment. I think they were studying them. Trying to understand how they survived whatever happened."

Katherine's face paled. "You think they were exposed to the Whisperers?"

"Or something else up there at the Wind Valley Army Base." Cesaro added.

Dexter nodded grimly. "It's the only thing that makes sense. They've gone to extreme lengths to keep this quiet, and now, with you all snooping around, I think they're ready to cut their losses. That 'cleanup' your contact mentioned? It's their way of tying up loose ends."

Linda crossed her arms, her voice sharp. "If that's true, then we need to warn everyone at the motel."

"No," Dexter said firmly. "We can't tip them off. If they know we're onto them, it'll only escalate things."

Rose, still shaken from her earlier vision, spoke up. "Then what do we do?"

Dexter took a deep breath, glancing around the room. "We regroup. Marcus and Clarice are still out there gathering intel. When they're back, we'll pool everything we've got and figure out our next move. But for now, we stay low. No one leaves town without letting me know first."

"And if the military moves in before we're ready?" Linda asked pointedly.

Dexter's jaw tightened. "Then we figure it out. Together."

The room fell into a tense silence as each person absorbed the weight of the situation. Outside, the late afternoon sun cast long shadows across the station's parking lot, a stark reminder that time was running out.

The cave loomed before Marcus and Clarice, its entrance an inky void nestled at the base of a jagged cliffside. The surrounding earth bore scars of upheaval—cracks spiderwebbed through the dirt, and the faint smell of scorched rock lingered in the air. Stone and wood lay everywhere around the mine entrance. The eerie stillness made Marcus tighten his grip on the crowbar slung over his shoulder, though he doubted it would be much use if trouble arose.

Clarice adjusted the strap of her equipment pack, glancing at Marcus as they approached the cave. "Remind me again why we're chasing ghost stories into an abandoned military site that's behind a trespassing sign that says 'DO NOT ENTER'?"

Marcus smirked but didn't take his eyes off the terrain. "Because someone," he teased, emphasizing the word, "decided Dexter's lead about Whisperers being linked to an old JUNE program experiment wasn't compelling enough on its own."

Clarice rolled her eyes. "Oh, yeah. I wanted specifics, Marcus. It's called 'being thorough.' A vague note about dimensional breaches at a site near this cave isn't exactly a smoking gun."

"Right, because the last time we ignored vague leads, everything worked out fine," Marcus quipped, raising a brow.

Clarice couldn't help a wry smile. "Touché. Just don't say I didn't warn you when something explodes or tries to eat us."

"Noted." Marcus slowed as they neared the cave's entrance, his expression growing serious. "Still, there's something about this place. Feels... wrong."

She nodded, feeling the heavy, electric energy that seemed to hang in the air. It made the hairs on her arms stand up, and her phone beeped faintly before giving a high-pitched whine and powering down.

"Dammit," she muttered, shaking the device. "Piece of shit!"

Marcus chuckled. "Looks like instincts win again."

Clarice shot him a look. "I really hate how often you get to say that."

He grinned but didn't reply, crouching near the cave entrance instead. His eyes narrowed as he spotted a glint of metal half-buried in the dirt. "Looks like we're not the first ones here."

"What is it?" Clarice asked, kneeling beside him.

"Some kind of panel or hatch." He brushed away the dirt, revealing a corroded metal surface that seemed to hum faintly under his fingertips. "Definitely not natural."

Clarice tilted her head, studying it. "Think it's connected to the old base Dexter mentioned?"

"Only one way to find out," Marcus said, standing and flexing his fingers. "Let's see what's behind door number one."

As they prepared to investigate further, the weight of the cave and its secrets pressed against them, urging them forward with equal parts curiosity and trepidation. Whatever was inside, Marcus and Clarice were determined to uncover it.

The passage descended into darkness, the stale air growing colder as they ventured deeper. At the end of the tunnel, a reinforced door stood firmly in their way, its steel surface marred by rust and scorch marks. Clarice inspected the control panel on the wall beside it, wires exposed and sparking faintly.

"No way this thing still works," she said, shaking her head.

Marcus grinned and flexed his hands. "Good thing we don't need it to."

Heat radiated from his palms as flames flickered to life. He focused the fire on the hinges, the intense heat cutting through the metal like a blowtorch. After a few minutes, the door groaned and fell inward, revealing a dimly lit chamber filled with old filing cabinets, shelves of prototype devices, and maps pinned to the walls.

Clarice's jaw dropped. "This… this is a treasure trove."

Marcus stepped cautiously inside, the soft glow from his hands illuminating the dusty space. "Or a graveyard. Let's grab what we can and get out of here."

Clarice pulled out her camera, only for the screen to glitch and go black. She groaned. "Figures. This field is scrambling everything."

"Then we go old school," Marcus said, grabbing a stack of yellowed documents from a nearby table. He handed them to Clarice, who scanned the titles, her eyes widening.

"JUNE program," she read aloud. "Experimentation on dimensional crossings. Enhanced entities… Marcus, they were trying to weaponize the Veil."

He rifled through another folder, his expression darkening. "Containment breaches. One at the Mountain View Motel… this one says decades ago. But that doesn't make sense. The Pulse just happened."

"Exactly," Clarice said, flipping through more pages. "Look here. These breaches predate the Pulse. They were experimenting long before any of this started."

Clarice's hand trembled as she pulled a red-marked file from the bottom of a cabinet. The title read, Dimensional Energy Conduits: The Champion Initiative. She opened it slowly, her heart racing as she scanned the contents.

Clarice's gaze darkened as her fingers hovered over another entry. "Different abilities... conduits, amplifiers, suppressors. They cataloged every type they could find. It wasn't enough to have the Vril—they needed people who could manipulate it with precision. And Kiara…" She hesitated, her voice catching. "She fits the profile, doesn't she? She's the perfect balance of power and control."

Marcus exhaled sharply, his expression grim. "No wonder she's so important. If she really can stabilize the Vril…"

Clarice finished the thought, her voice barely above a whisper. "Then she's the key to everything—the Veil, the Vril, maybe even undoing what the Pulse has done."

Marcus's jaw tightened, his hand curling into a fist. "That's why Ivyg went after her," he muttered. "He must have known. He tried to take her out before she could reach her full potential."

"But he underestimated her," Clarice said fiercely, her eyes flashing with defiance. "Leaving her blind wasn't enough to stop her. If anything, it made her stronger."

They exchanged a heavy glance, the weight of their discovery pressing on them. The realization that Kiara—and others like her—might hold the answers to saving the Veil only deepened the mystery of what lay ahead.

"And now?" Marcus asked, his voice low.

Clarice straightened, determination hardening her features. "Now, we figure out how to protect her. And we finish what they started—on our terms."

Marcus leaned over her shoulder, his brow furrowing as he read the notes. "References to enhanced sensory perception, energy manipulation, precognition… They've been tracking us."

Clarice's voice was barely audible. "Tracking… or targeting?"

Before Marcus could respond, a distant hum filled the chamber. It grew louder, reverberating through the walls. Clarice's flashlight flickered violently before going out, plunging them into near darkness.

"We need to move," Marcus said, his tone sharp. "Now."

The pair emerged from the bunker, the cool night air a stark contrast to the oppressive atmosphere inside. Marcus glanced toward the cave and spotted another path leading away from it. "There's more," he said. "Look."

They followed the path to a clearing on the other side of the hill. The ground here was scorched, the earth melted and twisted in unnatural patterns. Burned-out vehicles lay scattered across the site, their metal frames warped beyond recognition.

Clarice crouched beside a patch of soil, pulling out a fragment of strange material embedded in the ground. It pulsed faintly in her hand, emitting a low hum.

"This isn't from here," she said. "Whatever it is, it's… alive."

Clarice stared at the scattered documents, her fingers tightening around a faded report. "It doesn't make sense," she murmured. "All these breaches, the containment failures, predate the Pulse by decades."

Marcus leaned against the edge of the desk, his arms crossed as he surveyed the blueprints and fragmented data. "That's because the Pulse wasn't the catalyst," he said quietly. "We caused the Pulse—unintentionally—but this... this was already happening. The experiments, the breaches, the Whisperers... they were all in motion long before we ever set foot in the Hollow Earth."

Clarice glanced up at him, her expression conflicted. "Then maybe the Pulse wasn't just a disaster—it was a trigger. A ripple that brought all of this back into focus."

Marcus frowned, his gaze falling to a detailed schematic of what appeared to be an energy field generator. "Or a magnifier. But look at this," he said, tapping the file. "They were studying people connected to the Vril. People who could stabilize or manipulate it. That's why they were so focused on the Whisperers—they weren't just accidents. They were failed attempts at creating tools to control dimensional energy."

Clarice's breath caught as she scanned the notes. "They weren't just looking for power," she said, her voice trembling with realization. "They were looking for people who could repair the damage. Stabilize the Veil. People like Kiara."

Marcus nodded slowly. "It explains a lot. Her connection to the Vril, the way she... adapts. We always knew she was special, but this research—it suggests she's more than that. If the Veil really is as fractured as it seems, she might be the one who can repair it."

"But why her?" Clarice asked, her voice a mix of awe and frustration. "Why would Ivyg go after her if she could help fix everything?"

Marcus's expression hardened, a shadow crossing his face. "Because he didn't want it fixed. He wanted control. If Kiara could stabilize the Veil, she'd be a threat to everything he's built."

Clarice exhaled sharply, the weight of their discovery pressing on her. "This changes everything. If Kiara really can repair the Veil... if this research is right... then we have a responsibility to help her figure it out."

Marcus stepped closer, his voice low but steady. "We also have to protect her. If they find out what she's capable of, they'll come for her again. We've seen what they'll do to keep control."

Clarice nodded, determination sparking in her eyes. "Then we don't give them the chance. We get this information to the others and figure out how to help Kiara. If she really is the key, we can't afford to let her down."

Marcus placed a hand on her shoulder, his grip firm but reassuring. "We won't. Let's get out of here and make sure the others see this. If anyone can figure out what to do next, it's Kiara."

Together, they gathered the most critical pieces of the research, their resolve strengthened. They knew the stakes had just been raised—and that the fight to protect Kiara, the Veil, and their world was only beginning.

Marcus and Clarice moved quickly across the uneven terrain, the weight of their discovery urging them forward as the sun dipped low on the horizon. Marcus glanced over his shoulder at the cave they had just left, its shadow stretching like a reminder of what they'd uncovered.

"Do you think they'll even believe us?" Clarice asked, breathless as she matched his pace.

Marcus frowned, his mind racing. "I think they'll believe something happened. But explaining it without... explaining it?" He shook his head. "That's going to be tricky."

Clarice smirked despite the tension. "So, we're just supposed to say, 'Hey, there's a secret military project involving Vril and the Veil, but don't ask us how we know it's not the Pulse because, uh... reasons?' Yeah, that'll go over well."

Marcus chuckled dryly, unlocking the car with a quick swipe of his hand. "Exactly. And while we're at it, let's not forget to remind them that we're not exactly unbiased sources, given, you know... fire hands and clairvoyance."

Clarice slid into the passenger seat, tossing the collected files onto her lap. "We could spin it," she offered. "Keep it focused on the Whisperers, the experiments. Frame it like the Pulse just exposed something that was already broken."

Marcus started the car, the engine sputtering to life as he pulled onto the dirt road. "That works, but we need to be careful. If we try too hard to avoid the Pulse angle, they'll start asking questions we don't want to answer."

"Which means we'll have to walk the line between honesty and omission," Clarice said, flipping through the files. "Great. I hate that line."

Marcus grinned. "You and I both. Maybe we should've had that chat with Cesaro before coming out here. He'd probably have some... colorful advice on how to handle this."

Clarice rolled her eyes but couldn't help but laugh. "Oh, you know exactly what he'd say: 'Just tell them the truth but make it sound cooler.'" She imitated Cesaro's swagger with exaggerated gestures.

Marcus laughed, the tension easing just slightly. The car bounced along the road, their laughter fading as the weight of their task settled back in. "Alright," Marcus said, his tone turning serious. "We'll keep it simple. Focus on the experiments, the Whisperers, and we will talk to the others about this stuff related to Kiara once we're back in Witchaven. Leave the Pulse out of it unless we absolutely have to."

Clarice nodded, her resolve matching his. "Deal. But you know Cesaro's going to want the whole story. We'd better be ready when he starts asking."

Marcus sighed, his eyes fixed on the road ahead. "We'll cross that bridge when we get to it. First, let's get back and make sure everyone else knows what we've found. Whatever's coming, they're going to need to be ready."

Clarice tightened her grip on the files. "Let's hope this doesn't just raise more questions than it answers."

Marcus didn't reply. Deep down, he suspected it would—but that was a problem for later. For now, they had a story to tell, and a world to save.

Chapter 41

No Rest for the Reborn

Kiara and Aron barely had time to catch their breath after Pavel dropped them back in Witchaven. The air was cooler here, but it didn't make the grime clinging to them any less suffocating. Aron took one look at her in the foyer's light and felt his stomach twist—her clothes were scorched and soaked through with something dark and half-dried, an unholy mix of ooze, soot, and ash. Whatever blast radius she'd been caught in, it had left its mark.

She said nothing, didn't even flinch, but he saw the tension in her jaw, the way her hands twitched slightly as if ready to move again at a moment's notice. He reached for her instinctively, arms wrapping around her despite the stench. She melted into the embrace, and for a heartbeat, it felt perfect—grounding.

Then the castle rumbled beneath them, a deep BOOM reverberating up through the stone. Dust rained from the beams above, and smoke curled in from the direction of the main hall.

Still filthy, still breathless, they took off running.

By the time they reached the central lobby, the damage was clear— blackened scorch marks, scattered debris, and three unexpected figures waiting in the haze, standing just a little too calmly in the aftermath.

"CHET!" Pavel barked, his voice sharp as he pointed toward one of the men across the scorched entryway.

Aron stepped forward cautiously, eyes narrowing. "Wait a sec… I know your faces." He squinted. "Had this weird dream—one of you was Hercules… the other was Perseus."

Kiara turned toward his voice. "Wait…" Her tone dropped. "So, these were your sons…?"

Aron blinked. "Huh?"

She tilted her head. "Zeus was their father."

The taller one glanced around, confused. "What?"

The shorter one turned toward Pavel. "Hello, Father."

"Well, this is awkward…" Aron muttered.

Pavel stepped in coolly, arms folded. "In this life, I'm his father." He nodded toward the shorter one. "Archie is my son."

Aron gave a sheepish chuckle. "Right. Makes sense. But still… I had no idea Perseus and Hercules were my kids. That's a new one."

Kiara's voice turned dry. "So, if you're their father… and one of them's Hercules… that would make me—"

Aron groaned. "Oh gods."

Pavel smirked. "I would've preferred you as his mother, to be honest."

Aron pinched the bridge of his nose. "This is a therapy session waitin' to happen."

Kiara laughed. "And just to really mess with you? I'm pretty sure Zen was Persephone… which would've made her your daughter."

Aron stiffened. "Bloody hell. I need a drink."

Kiara added sweetly, "Didn't she date your sister?"

Pavel exhaled. "Zeus had many children. We could chase bloodlines all night—but right now, we have bigger problems."

Aron was still recovering from the mental tangle of bloodlines and ancient gods when the shorter man—the one Pavel had called Archie— took a sudden step forward. His expression was blank, unnervingly so, like a machine running on orders.

The taller one beside him shifted, fists clenched at his sides. Pavel's eyes darkened.

"Trydan," he said cautiously, his voice edged with regret. "What are you doing?"

Trydan didn't answer. Neither did Archie. Behind them, a third man emerged from the smoke—Chet, broad-shouldered, pale-eyed, and pulsing with barely-contained power. Where the others looked conflicted or blank, Chet radiated confidence. Malice.

"You've got your memories," Pavel said, voice low. "But not your minds."

Chet grinned. "And yet you still stand there talking."

Without warning, the trio lunged.

They phased into a decrepit barn in the middle of nowhere, hay and dust flying as blows landed. From there, they shifted to the arid heat of a desert, sand whipping at their faces as they grappled. The fight spilled into a jungle, their movements tangling with vines and dense undergrowth, then into a museum, where a startled tour group screamed as the men crashed through a priceless exhibit, their brawl lasting barely ten seconds before they blinked out again.

The next stop—a bullfighting ring. Archie, using his immense strength, managed to fend off a charging bull, though not without a gash to his ribs. Enraged, he knocked the beast to the ground and, with a roar, hurled it toward Pavel. Pavel teleported to safety at the last moment, dragging Aron with him.

They reappeared in the chaos of a Texas Waffle House during the breakfast rush. Tables overturned, dishes shattered, and terrified customers scrambled for the exits as the battle raged on.

Aron, his Irish resilience kicking in, tapped into his powers, sending bolts of lightning toward Archie. The larger man, despite his size, proved surprisingly fast, dodging the strikes with brute agility. But Aron had a backup plan: years of Krav Maga training. In the tight quarters of the diner, Aron's sharp knees and elbows struck the soft spots on Archie's hulking frame—knees, throat, and kidneys—exploiting the man's focus on strength while lacking technique or finesse.

Meanwhile, Pavel landed a clean shot to Archie's jaw, stunning him momentarily. But his follow-up punch was caught mid-air, and with a grunt of effort, Archie hurled Pavel over the counter into a pile of fleeing customers.

Chet, desperate to regain control, swung a plate at Pavel's head, but a flying coffee pot intercepted him, shattering against his skull with a satisfying crack.

Archie's raw strength was both his greatest asset and his weakness. He swung wildly, connecting a few powerful punches on Aron, who staggered but refused to go down. The Irishman, known for his grit, took the blows with a defiant glare and kept fighting, matching Archie's brute force with calculated precision. He dodged a few of the wild haymaker punches and picked up an egg frying pan from off the floor and swung upward, catching the big Herculean man in the chin, knocking him off of his feet.

He was still conscious, but not for long as Aron picked his burly ass up off the floor up into the fireman's carry position. Like a professional wrestler, he dumped the bigger man over and slammed him down onto the counter where people had been eating their food mere minutes ago, enjoying their breakfast before their lives were going to be changed forever. Seeking the fight to be over and this massive man wouldn't stop trying to get back up, unwilling to give up or concede that he had been beaten, Aron used his powers to act like a stun gun and knock out his opponent. He picked up the smaller Chet off the floor, even graciously removing pieces of the broken glass from his head like a good human would do for another while several of the breakfast diners watched on, holding up their smartphones to record the mayhem they had just witnessed, before magically being gone in an instant.

Pavel teleported them back to where they came from, the main lobby within the Witchaven castle, and they were surprised when they returned to see Kiara holding her own against the speedy and agile Trydan Holmes, aka Perseus, beating his ass with her blind walking stick. Throwing Archie back to his brother, Aron joined Kiara to face off in a two-on-two situation.

He rose up in the air and summoned the lightning of Zeus and rained down thunder on his enemies, who took some damage but kept coming back into the fight. Trydan zoomed around the room and made a difficult target for Aron to attack. Pavel decided to join back in the fight and grabbed the speedy man and portalled him up high into the air before dropping him, landing himself to safety. Archie dove to catch his brother and when they landed, Aron lit them up with lightning. They were dazed by the attack. Kiara used the fight training that she remembered from training with Marcus and her life as Malie, enhanced by the teachings undertaken by her master Marcus Kydd in his mind palace as his apprentice, during their shared experience within the Nexus Consciousness. Now she had become the master and as the two opponents simultaneously tried to attack her, she paused.

The moment stretched—longer than it should have. Kiara stood still, every sound sharpening around her: the shift of boots against stone, the rush of breath, the rapid cadence of hearts beating. She listened, not just with her ears, but with something deeper. Their rhythm was off—not fierce, not driven by intent. It was hollow. Like someone else was pulling the strings, puppets in a fight they didn't choose. The lights were on, but no one was home.

But Chet? Chet was different. His malice was real, his intent sharp and cruel. Pavel saw it too, and with each strike of his fists, he made sure Chet felt it—over and over, until his own knuckles bled.

Something stirred inside her—a rising force, ancient and unyielding, like a deep well of truth pressing against her chest. It wasn't just hers. It never had been. It was something older, something infinite.

"Stop!" The word burst from her, not just a command but a wave of Vril-born power. Her voice rang out, echoing through the chamber, reverberating in every corner.

The two men froze, their confusion painted across their faces, as if waking mid-dream. But it wasn't just them. The whole room went still, suspended in the gravity of her voice. Kiara stepped forward, steady, sure. She raised her hands, fingers brushing the sweat-damp foreheads of both men.

"Remember," she whispered, her voice now soft, but no less powerful. As her hands withdrew, the spell broke.

The two men shook their heads and looked at one another. It was as if they had awoken from a dream. The spell that Ivyg had them under was now broken and the look of relief on their faces said it all as the two men both broke down in tears from the memory of the horrors they unleashed while in Ivyg's trance of mind control.

"I don't know what you did but the name's Archie, me and my brother Trydan thank you." Archie told her. "That was like a nightmare. And I remember it all. I remember all the horrible things he made us do in his name. I don't understand how he was able to make us do that."

"Knew something was wrong the second after ya called yourself 'Archibald'!" Pavel quipped.

"It is his power to manipulate people." Mallah stepped in to explain. "Some use the Vril for the construct of good and some use it to create chaos and disorder. Ivyg is in the latter. In joining his Order of the Ancient Serpent, you consented to this, knowingly or unknowingly. So have so many that have inadvertently been sucked into the cult that is the OAS. The ability to change the world has such an alluring potential, an alluring power."

"Marcus Kydd is in great danger." Trydan told Mallah. "Ivyg set up the entire thing in Colorado to try to take out his greatest threats."

"Something tells me he assumed something like that was afoot and still went because he thought he could handle himself." She told him.

"Good thing he has some help there with him. I have a feeling that I already know how this is going to turn out."

At that moment, Ivyg himself stood motionless in his expansive command chamber, the flickering light of holographic displays casting long shadows across his face. His icy gaze was fixed on the data streaming before him—a series of vitals, coordinates, and erratic fluctuations tied to his scouts, among them Trydan and Archie. Despite their failure to maintain contact, their tracking devices painted a compelling picture: Witchaven had been infiltrated.

"Two pawns played, two pawns lost," he murmured to himself, his tone a blend of contempt and satisfaction. "Yet even pawns serve their purpose."

The patterns were clear. Though Trydan and Archie's movements suggested forced relocations, their vitals had stabilized after an earlier, violent spike—likely the moment of conflict. This alone was confirmation enough. Not only had the stronghold been found, but it had resisted the assault, proving its inhabitants were not the vulnerable mystics many believed them to be.

Ivyg clenched his jaw, a flicker of disappointment crossing his face. They had survived. Worse, they seemed to have broken free of his control. Still, their survival served another purpose: their erratic trail had traced the outline of what could only be Witchaven's precise location.

"Send the word to the Council," Ivyg commanded, his voice sharp and cold. "Prepare every available fleet. I want Witchaven decimated; burned to the ground, its people scattered to the winds." His lips curled into a faint smile, equal parts malevolent and amused. "They think they can defy me. Let them witness the futility of resistance."

One of his advisors, a cautious officer named Verit, stepped forward. "My Lord, are you certain we should divert resources from—"

Ivyg silenced him with a single glare. "I did not ask for your counsel, Verit. This is not a war of logistics; it is a war of survival. Witchaven's continued existence is an affront to my reign and a threat to my legacy."

His tone softened, though his expression remained deadly. "This is not just about conquest, Verit. This is about sending a message. They will learn that no one escapes my grasp, no matter how far they flee or how deeply they hide."

As Ivyg turned to the holographic display once more, his pale hand hovered over the console, his fingers lingering on the image of the stronghold's faint outline. "Send the order. Begin the assault. And ensure that when the dust settles, no one remembers a place called Witchaven."

Chapter 42

Rising Tide

As the group in Wellville prepared to leave the diner, the distant rumble of an engine grew louder, cutting through the tense atmosphere. Moments later, an SUV rolled into the parking lot, its exterior dusted with snow and its headlights flickering like a warning signal. The vehicle screeched to a halt, and Marcus and Clarice stepped out, looking rattled but resolute.

Dexter was the first to approach, his expression a mix of relief and frustration. "Took you long enough. What did you find?"

Clarice stepped forward, brushing snow off her jacket. "Something we weren't expecting—a hidden archive near the caves. Military experiments, the Whisperers, and mentions of… us."

The group exchanged glances, and Rose pressed, "What do you mean 'us'?"

Marcus slung a satchel off his shoulder, revealing a collection of old folders and maps. "This. It's all connected to the Veil, experiments with dimensional crossings, and Vril energy. They were looking for people who could stabilize the energy—conduits like us. We think that's part of why this whole mess started."

"Conduits like… Kiara?" Linda asked cautiously.

"Maybe," Clarice admitted, her tone grave. "But we're still piecing it together. We were going to bring this back for all of us to analyze."

Dexter held up a hand to stop her. "You can explain it later. Right now, we have a bigger problem."

Clarice frowned. "What problem?"

"The military's coming for us," Rose said bluntly, her gaze darting nervously toward the sound of approaching helicopters.

Marcus and Clarice froze, their shock evident. "What?" Marcus said, his voice low but sharp. "How do you know that?"

"We connected some dots while you were gone," Dexter replied. "They've been cleaning up their mess since last August, and we're next on their list."

Clarice's face darkened. "Damn it. We didn't see this coming."

"Well, now you know," Dexter said curtly. "And if you want to stay out of their hands, you better move."

Marcus glanced at Clarice, then back to the group. "We'll explain what we found once we're clear of this."

"Yeah, no kidding," Rose muttered. "That would've been nice before now."

"Enough," Dexter snapped. "Get in the cars. We're leaving."

Without further delay, the group scrambled to their vehicles, Marcus and Linda climbing into the Bronco. As the convoy roared out of the lot, the sound of helicopters grew louder, their spotlight sweeping the snow-covered ground in pursuit.

The convoy sped out of the Mountain View Motel parking lot, tires screeching against the icy pavement. In the lead, Dexter gripped the wheel of the Explorer, his jaw tight as the military helicopters' spotlight swept over them. With him was Clarice in the passenger seat and Max in the back driver's side seat.

Behind him, the Bronco, driven by Marcus, fishtailed slightly as it hit the snow-covered road with Linda and Kathleen. Cesaro followed in the rear, his rented Hummer roaring as he tried to cover the group's retreat, Rose having his back.

"They're gaining on us!" Clarice shouted from the passenger seat of the Explorer, her voice barely audible over the cacophony of the pursuit.

Dexter glanced in the rearview mirror, catching sight of two black military vans and a pair of armored Humvees closing in fast. "Everyone, hang on," he warned, his hands tightening on the wheel.

In the Bronco, Marcus glanced at Linda, who was holding a map she had grabbed from the diner. "What's our best bet?" he called out.

"Head toward Wind Valley," Linda replied, flipping pages with urgency. "There's a perimeter fence near the installation. It's our only shot to lose them."

"Noted," Marcus muttered, his grip on the steering wheel firm. "Everyone, brace yourselves. This is going to get messy."

Gunfire erupted behind them, sharp pops breaking through the cold night air. Max leaned out of the passenger window of the Explorer, his arm trembling as he fired back at their pursuers. The crack of returning shots shattered the vehicle's side mirror, and Max ducked back inside.

"Damn it!" he hissed, clutching his shoulder where a bullet had grazed him.

Clarice leaned forward, placing her hands on his shoulder. "Hold still," she ordered, her voice steely as frost began to form around her fingertips. In a moment, the ice spread over Max's wound, stopping the bleeding. That didn't stop him from yelling out from the excruciating pain.

Behind them, Marcus saw one of the black vans creeping closer, its engine roaring as it prepared to ram the Bronco. "Not today," he growled, focusing on his Vril energy. Heat radiated from his hands, and with a sharp flick of his wrist, a burst of fire arced toward the van. The flames hit the front tires, sending the vehicle careening into a snowbank, where it flipped onto its side.

"Good shot!" Linda yelled, her adrenaline spiking.

"Don't celebrate yet," Marcus replied, his gaze fixed on the remaining vehicles.

In the Hummer, Cesaro saw another Humvee pulling alongside him, its mounted turret swiveling into position. "Rose, hold on!" he yelled as he veered sharply, slamming the Hummer into the military vehicle's side. The impact caused the turret to miss its mark, firing into the night sky instead of down into their vehicle.

Rose let out a blast of red Vril energy that was enough to gain some separation between them. Rose steadied herself, her face pale but determined. "Cesaro, watch out for the fence!"

The Bronco reached the perimeter fence first, its headlights catching the glint of barbed wire stretched across the top. Marcus didn't hesitate, flooring the gas pedal. The Bronco smashed through the steel barrier, the impact jarring everyone inside. Smoke poured from under the hood as the vehicle sputtered to a crawl.

"Marcus, it's not going to hold!" Linda yelled, clutching her bleeding arm where a shard of wire had grazed her.

Kathleen tore a piece of fabric from the bottom of her shirt and wrapped it around Linda's arm.

"It just has to get us a little further!" Marcus shot back, his knuckles white on the wheel.

The Explorer followed close behind, Dexter swerving to avoid the wreckage left by the Bronco. Clarice glanced back at the remaining vehicles and narrowed her eyes. Focusing her energy, she unleashed a wave of ice that coated one of the pursuing hummers, causing it to skid out of control and slam into a tree.

"Nice work," Dexter muttered, his relief short-lived as bullets ricocheted off the Explorer's rear bumper.

The Hummer brought up the rear, its reinforced body allowing it to barrel through the remnants of the fence with minimal damage. Cesaro gritted his teeth as he followed the others into the installation's perimeter, the darkened landscape of the base sprawling out ahead.

Inside the Bronco, Linda winced as Marcus pulled the vehicle to a stop behind a row of abandoned barracks. Smoke continued to pour from the engine, and Marcus cursed under his breath. "We're not going anywhere in this," he said grimly.

In the Explorer, Clarice checked on Max, who was pale but conscious. "We can't stay here," she said, her voice urgent. "They'll catch up any minute."

Dexter nodded, grabbing a shotgun from the backseat. "We'll regroup on foot if we have to. Everyone grab what you can carry."

As they climbed out of their vehicles, the group worked together to assess injuries and plan their next move. Linda's arm was hastily bandaged, while Marcus and Clarice exchanged a look of silent determination.

"We're not done yet," Marcus said, his tone resolute.

"Not by a long shot," Cesaro agreed, stepping out of the Hummer and slinging a rifle over his shoulder.

The sound of approaching engines spurred them into action. With no time to waste, the group got back into their vehicles, disappearing into the shadows of the installation, leaving behind the wreckage of their escape and the faint glow of the Whisperers in the distance.

The chase stretched into a blur of chaos and adrenaline. Snow whipped past the vehicles as they careened through the rocky terrain. The Bronco led the charge, its engine screaming in protest as Marcus pushed it to its limits.

"Hold on!" Marcus yelled, slamming the steering wheel hard to the left as the Bronco narrowly avoided a boulder jutting out from the snowy field. Linda, clutching the makeshift bandage to her bleeding arm, grimaced in pain.

Behind them, the Explorer swerved to avoid the same obstacle. Dexter's jaw was set, his knuckles white as he gripped the wheel. "Keep your head down!" he shouted to Max, who was leaning out the shattered window, firing at the pursuing vehicles.

A Humvee surged forward, its heavy frame forcing its way through the rugged terrain. Gunfire erupted from its mounted turret, the rounds striking dangerously close to the Bronco's rear. "We need to do something about that!" Linda shouted.

"I'm on it," Marcus replied, summoning his fire/demolition-based Vril energy. He released a controlled burst toward the hummer, the heat curling into an explosion that engulfed its front tires. The vehicle swerved violently before flipping onto its side, smoke billowing from the wreckage.

"Nice shot!" Linda called out, though her voice was strained from the pain in her arm.

The Bronco's battered engine groaned as Marcus spotted the steel perimeter fence of the Wind Valley Military Installation looming ahead. "We're out of options," he said grimly, gripping the wheel tighter. "This is going to hurt."

With a final surge of power, the Bronco plowed into the fence, metal screeching as the vehicle tore through. Sparks flew, and shards of barbed wire lashed through the open window, slicing into Linda's arm. She cried out, clutching the fresh wound as blood soaked through the bandage.

The Bronco sputtered and rolled to a halt, smoke pouring from the hood. "We're done here," Marcus said, his voice heavy with frustration. "Everyone out. Now."

Behind them, the Explorer skidded to a stop just short of the wrecked fence. Clarice leapt out, her ice-based powers crackling at her fingertips. She turned toward the remaining hummer, which was bearing down on them. With a sharp motion, she unleashed a freezing wave that encased the vehicle's tires, sending it skidding off-course and into a tree.

In the rear, Cesaro's rented Hummer plowed through the gap left by the Bronco. He hit the brakes hard, the vehicle skidding to a halt beside the others. "Everyone okay?" he shouted as Rose helped Linda out of the Bronco.

"Define okay," Linda replied, wincing as she pressed her uninjured hand against her bleeding arm. "I'll live, but this hurts like hell."

The group huddled near the Bronco, the cold air biting at their exposed skin. The sound of engines in the distance reminded them that they weren't safe yet. "We've slowed them down, but they're not stopping," Dexter said, his eyes scanning the perimeter.

"We'll have to move on foot," Marcus said, adjusting his coat and grabbing a weapon from the Explorer. "Stick together. We're not out of this yet."

Despite their growing injuries and the loss of one vehicle, the group pressed on, their determination unshaken. The snow continued to fall, covering their tracks as they disappeared into the shadows of the installation, leaving the burning wreckage behind. The tension was palpable as they pressed forward, unsure of where the chase would lead.

Above them, the steady thrum of helicopter blades grew louder, and a powerful spotlight cut through the darkness, sweeping across the snowy fields. "They're herding us," Dexter said, his eyes flicking between the road ahead and the hovering light above. "They're driving us straight into their trap."

"We don't have a choice!" Marcus called from the back seat. "We either run or we're sitting ducks!"

They crested a hill, and suddenly, the sprawling Wind Valley Military Installation came into view. Towering fences lined with barbed wire surrounded the base, and distant lights illuminated rows of buildings and vehicles. Clarice's sharp intake of breath broke the tense silence. "The source," she murmured, her voice laced with dread. "We're heading straight for the source of all this."

"What's the plan, Detective?" Cesaro asked. "We've run out of road!"

Dexter tightened his grip on his gun, his expression grim. "We don't stop. If they want us here, we'll give them hell before they take us."

The sound of gunfire erupted again as one of the remaining military vehicles pulled closer. Marcus turned and unleashed another blast of his fire-based Vril energy. The fireball struck the pursuing hummer squarely, forcing it off the road and into a snowbank, imploding its engine with a loud pop.

"That'll buy us a little time!" Marcus shouted, but the group's relief was short-lived as the helicopter above descended lower, its spotlight now locked onto them. The high-pitched whine of a loudspeaker crackled through the air. "This is a restricted area. Surrender immediately or face lethal force."

"Yeah, like that's happening," Clarice muttered, her ice-based powers sparking faintly in her hands. She turned to Marcus. "I hope you've got more of that fire left in you."

The vehicles skidded onto the snow-covered access road leading to the installation's main gate. Cesaro took the lead. "Follow me!" he shouted. "We're not walking into the front door of this place."

Kathleen used her Vril powers to create ice spears that she volleyed at the attacking soldiers, from the OAS vans. Dexter was trying to avoid bullets hailing down from a circling helicopter. "Come on!" he yelled as he led them under the chain-link perimeter fence loomed larger with each passing second.

"We're not stopping, are we?" Clarice asked, her voice tense.

"Nope," Dexter replied flatly. "Brace yourselves for the fight that's yet to come, but don't forget about the here and now.."

"Is everyone alright!" Marcus shouted out as the group scrambled into the shadowy expanse of the installation, their breaths visible in the freezing air.

"They're coming," Cesaro said, glancing back at the gate, where the remaining military vehicles were closing in fast. "We've got minutes, maybe less."

"Then we use them," Dexter said, loading his weapon. "We're here for answers, so let's get them."

Clarice looked at the massive complex ahead, her eyes narrowing. "If this place is the source of everything, it's time we find out what they're hiding."

Together, the group darted into the shadows of the Wind Valley Military Installation, determined to uncover the truth before it was too late. The roar of engines and the thrum of helicopters followed close behind, a relentless reminder that their fight was far from over.

As the group pressed deeper into the installation, the sheer scale of the base began to reveal itself. They had entered through a crumpled section of the outer perimeter, the mangled fence behind them now barely visible through the dense snowfall. Beyond it, faint plumes of smoke from their wrecked vehicles rose into the icy night air—a stark reminder that retreat was no longer an option.

Ahead, the base stretched in every direction, a maze of towering hangars, stark concrete bunkers, and imposing guard towers that loomed over the landscape like silent sentinels. To their left, an abandoned motor pool lay in disarray, rows of trucks and armored vehicles coated in frost. On the right, a series of low, flat buildings emitted an eerie glow, their frosted windows hinting at the activity within. The faint thrum of drones patrolling above added an almost mechanical heartbeat to the tension, their blinking lights a chilling counterpoint to the encroaching darkness.

"We need to head for the command center," Dexter whispered, motioning toward the tallest structure in the distance. Its spire pierced the night sky, crowned with a rotating array of antennas. "If there are answers, that's where we'll find them."

"And if it's where they're waiting for us?" Rose countered, her eyes darting nervously between the shadows.

"Then we face them head-on," Marcus said, though even he sounded uncertain.

Behind them, the faint crunch of boots on snow sent a jolt of urgency through the group. Soldiers. Close. Too close. They darted between two warehouses, the narrow passageway offering a momentary reprieve from the searchlights sweeping the compound. The temperature seemed to drop even further as they crouched in the icy shadows, their breaths clouding the air.

From the depths of the base, a low, resonant hum began to rise—a sound that seemed to come from the very ground beneath their feet. It pulsed faintly, like a heartbeat, growing louder with each passing second. Linda pressed a hand to the wall of the nearest building, her face pale. "Do you feel that? It's... alive."

The group exchanged uneasy glances, their instincts screaming at them to keep moving. But as they edged closer to the command center, the layout of the base seemed to shift around them. Pathways that had appeared clear moments ago now led to dead ends. Doors that should have opened were sealed shut, their control panels flashing red. It was as though the base itself were alive, anticipating their movements, herding them.

"They're driving us into a trap," Clarice whispered, the frost forming on her fingertips betraying her rising fear. "This whole place is designed to keep us in."

The whispers began then—soft, insidious, like wind through cracked glass. At first, they seemed distant, but soon they grew louder, more distinct. They came not from outside, but from within, winding through their thoughts like a dark thread. Words of doubt, fear, and despair.

"This isn't just a base," Marcus said, his voice low and grim. "It's something else. Something... wrong."

The hum beneath their feet intensified, and from the direction of the command center, a faint green glow began to spill out into the night, casting long, flickering shadows. The glow wasn't steady; it pulsed in time with the whispers, as though the very air was alive with some malevolent force.

"What's that?" Rose asked, her voice trembling.

"The source," Marcus replied. "Whatever's powering this place."

The sound of boots grew louder, echoing against the walls of the towering structures around them. The group darted into another alleyway, only to find themselves staring at a massive wall of barbed wire blocking their path. The realization hit them all at once: they were being funneled.

"No way out," Dexter muttered, his voice heavy with frustration. "They've got us boxed in."

Ahead, the green glow seemed to beckon, growing brighter with every step they took. Whatever lay at the heart of this place, it wasn't salvation—it was something darker, something ancient. And as the whispers swirled louder in their minds, the base seemed to mock their every move, its labyrinthine layout a testament to the futility of resistance.

For the first time, a chilling thought crept into Marcus's mind: What if they hadn't stumbled into this place by chance? What if they'd been led here—drawn by something far beyond their understanding?

The oppressive glow painted their faces in sickly green as they turned a final corner, the command center looming before them. The doors slid open with an almost mocking hiss, and the whispers stopped abruptly, leaving an unnatural silence in their wake.

-Chapter 43-

Future Shocks

Ivyg's death sent shockwaves across the planet, leaving a power vacuum that ignited a fierce war among the Titans in Atla and Lemuria. No longer held in check by Ivyg's brutal reign, the Titans turned on one another, each vying for supremacy. Their infighting created chaos, destabilizing the few remaining societies that had endured Ivyg's apocalyptic vision.

In North America, the departure of the Titan Judges plunged the continent into further disarray. Territories were carved out and ruled by violent warlords, individuals who had risen to power through cruelty, deception, and unrelenting violence. These self-proclaimed rulers controlled the land with iron fists, exploiting the weakened population for resources and labor.

Amid this chaos, nature began its slow reclamation of the scarred landscape. Abandoned cities and once-thriving metropolises were overtaken by creeping vines, broken concrete shattered by resilient plant life. Forests expanded, rivers widened, and animals reclaimed territories that humans could no longer defend. This juxtaposition of rebirth and destruction painted a vivid picture of the planet's potential for renewal even as humanity struggled to survive.

The exodus of the Titans and the collapse of centralized power left the remaining inhabitants to fend for themselves in a harsh, fragmented world. Many clung to the hope of rebuilding, but for most, survival became the only guiding principle. As Kane emerged from his five-year imprisonment, he found a world fractured beyond recognition, a grim testament to Ivyg's enduring legacy of destruction.

The years Kane spent imprisoned after Ivyg's death were both a punishment and a crucible. Five long years passed in the shadow of his brother's shattered reign, his mind unable to escape the weight of the world outside his cell. With Ivyg gone, the planet's descent into chaos accelerated. The power vacuum left behind had consumed what little order remained, and Kane could feel the echoes of the devastation even from his confinement.

During those years, Kane replayed the events leading to his imprisonment and Ivyg's death over and over in his mind. Though in the cell next to him, Kanee couldn't shake the memory of Oliver Kross's desperate plea he had made to save his daughter, Kiara, in the past. The man's words had lingered, their weight growing heavier with time: "If you can save her, you can save everything."

At first, Kane dismissed the idea as a fleeting notion born from desperation. Yet, as the desolation of his incarceration dragged on, Oliver's plea began to crystallize into something more—an anchor to a purpose greater than himself. He started to see Kiara as the key to undoing not just Ivyg's dystopian legacy, but the countless tragedies and horrors that had led to it.

Kane's determination to change the timeline became his singular focus. He resolved to find a way to travel back, to reach the pivotal moments that had shaped the future and prevent them from unfolding as they had. His time in the cell became less about endurance and more about preparation. Each moment of solitude sharpened his resolve and deepened his understanding of what was at stake.

By the time Clovis Krott came to free him, seeking Kane's reluctant aid in the aftermath of his own failed attempt to seize power, Kane's mission had already solidified in his heart. The dystopian world outside was a stark reminder of what needed to be undone, and Kane knew the path forward would demand everything of him.

Ivyg's death had far-reaching consequences, not only for the crumbling world he left behind but also for the tools that had once held it together. Much of Ivyg's advanced technology, biometrically linked to him, became immediately useless. Devices that had powered entire regions of his empire shut down without warning. Others, including key pieces of experimental equipment, self-destructed in elaborate fail-safes to prevent their use by anyone else. Among these was the time-control scepter, which shattered the moment Kane struck the fatal blow.

This loss was a devastating blow to Kane's plans. The scepter had been Ivyg's most powerful tool—able to manipulate time and space with precision—and without it, the possibility of returning to the past seemed to evaporate. The shards of the once-mighty device were scattered, their intricate circuitry fried beyond repair.

As Kane surveyed the wreckage of Ivyg's technological empire, the magnitude of the challenge before him became clear. To undo the future's horrors, he would need to find another way to breach the timeline. But with the destruction of Ivyg's network, many resources had either vanished or become irretrievable, leaving Kane to grapple with the daunting question of how to proceed.

The loss of the scepter was particularly painful, as it represented the most direct path to rewriting history. Without it, Kane would have to rely on fractured remnants of the past—buried technologies, forgotten prototypes, and the ingenuity of those who had once served under Ivyg. It was a grim realization, but Kane's resolve only hardened. He knew the answers were still out there, hidden in the ruins of Ivyg's fallen reign, waiting to be uncovered.

Clovis Krott, once a loyal follower of Ivyg, attempted to fill the power vacuum left by the fallen God-King. His ambitions, however, were doomed from the start. Lacking Ivyg's cunning and charisma, Clovis's reign was short-lived. His inability to control the chaos of the Titans' wars or the fractured territories of Earth left him desperate for a solution. Reluctantly, he released Kane from his five-year imprisonment, knowing that the younger brother of the God-King might hold the answers he needed.

Kane, though bitter and scarred from his time in prison, saw an opportunity in Clovis's desperation. The two, joined by Oliver Kross, formed an unlikely alliance to piece together what remained of Ivyg's shattered time-control device. While the scepter itself was beyond repair, its technology had roots in earlier prototypes, scattered in the ruins of Ivyg's empire. Clovis's knowledge of Ivyg's operations, combined with Oliver's technical expertise, made progress possible, albeit painstakingly slow.

For years, the trio scoured abandoned installations, recovered scraps of machinery, and reverse-engineered what they could salvage. Clovis's role, while often relegated to grunt work, proved invaluable; his familiarity with Ivyg's network of hidden facilities led them to critical components that had escaped the initial wave of destruction. Meanwhile, Oliver's genius as a scientist shone, turning fragments of ancient technology into functional systems. Kane, ever the strategist, kept them focused on the mission, channeling their shared frustrations into progress.

Finally, after years of relentless effort, they managed to rebuild a rudimentary version of the device, capable of a one-way trip. It lacked the elegance and versatility of Ivyg's original scepter, but it was enough to set their plan in motion. They calibrated the device for Denver, Colorado—a city that, according to Oliver's recollections and Clovis's records, held critical ties to Ivyg's early experiments and the JUNE program.

Amid the ruins of Ivyg's shattered empire, Kane stumbled across a set of schematics tucked inside a weathered file labeled Atmospheric Stabilization Unit—Prototype Quantum Regenerator. At first glance, it seemed like another of Ivyg's failed ambitions, discarded in his relentless pursuit of control. But as Kane studied the details, something sparked.

This wasn't just about stabilizing weather systems or cleaning irradiated zones. The technology was reactive—alive in the way it interfaced with energy fields. It pulsed with the same dimensional frequency he'd come to recognize in Vril-powered tech.

"This could work," Oliver murmured, reading over Kane's shoulder. "Not for time travel—but for life. It could heal the land, the air... even us."

Kane's mind raced. If they failed to stop the timeline, this could be their second chance—not to change the past, but to rebuild the future. Maybe both.

As they prepared for the leap, Clovis couldn't help but look to Kane for guidance, his earlier arrogance tempered by years of hardship. Kane, who had spent countless nights envisioning this moment, stood resolute. He knew the stakes, not just for himself but for the countless lives that depended on rewriting the past. It was important for him to know that Kane forgave him for siding with his brother. What was more important was the help he was rendering now in this time of need.

When the moment came, the device activated with a guttural hum, tearing open a swirling portal of light and energy. The three stepped through, uncertain of what awaited them on the other side but united in their determination to reclaim the future. As they emerged in the outskirts of Denver, the cold air hit them like a slap, a stark reminder of the unforgiving world they were fighting to save.

Arriving in the ruins of Denver, Kane, Oliver, and Clovis found themselves in an unforgiving wasteland. The city bore the scars of war, with crumbling buildings, frozen streets, and a barren atmosphere permeated by a haunting silence. What little life remained was tenacious, eking out an existence amidst the wreckage. For Kane and his group, survival became their immediate priority.

The trio scavenged for food, clothing, and supplies, trading labor for meals with small groups of survivors they encountered. It was during one of these exchanges that they learned of a thriving farm on the outskirts of the city. Curious and desperate, they followed the lead and were eventually welcomed into a self-sustaining community led by a man named Rico.

Rico was a man of principles, hardened by the apocalypse but unwavering in his commitment to protect his people. His farm, fed by an underground aquifer, stood as an oasis of life amidst the desolation. Crops grew in the fertile soil, and livestock roamed the fenced pastures. The farm was fortified against the marauding gangs that prowled the region, and its people were armed, vigilant, and disciplined.

Intrigued by the newcomers, Rico took a particular interest in Kane's story. Over nights spent around a fire, Kane recounted his experiences, sparing no detail about Ivyg's reign, the Pulse, and the events that led him to this dystopian future. Rico listened intently, his sharp mind piecing together the implications of what Kane shared. Two aspects of the story captivated him most: Nova and Kiara.

Rico revealed that Nova, a skilled hunter and occasional trader, lived as a recluse in the nearby wilderness. He promised to send scouts to locate him, knowing Nova's knowledge and abilities could prove invaluable. However, it was Kiara's story that truly resonated with Rico. The idea of changing the past to save the future appealed deeply to his sense of duty and hope. Rico believed in the possibility of redemption, both for humanity and for himself.

One evening, he brought Kane to meet an elderly woman named Lucy, a shaman who had once worked for the OAS as a contractor. Lucy's knowledge of the region's history and its ties to Ivyg's experiments was unmatched. She remembered Oliver Kross by reputation, speaking with reverence about his work and regret about her own complicity in the horrors that took place.

Lucy confirmed the existence of a hidden military base deep within the Wind Valley mountains, near a place called Wellville. She described the facility as a hub of experimentation, including the development of the Hades virus and prototypes of Ivyg's time-control technology. Though the base had been abandoned after the fall, she believed its secrets still lay buried within.

For Kane, this revelation was a breakthrough. With Rico's resources and Lucy's guidance, the path forward became clearer. The trio, now strengthened by the farm's support, prepared to embark on a journey to the Wind Valley base. Kane's resolve deepened, fueled by the possibility of finding the tools to change the past and a growing understanding of Kiara's importance.

Though the road ahead was perilous, they knew it was their only chance to reclaim what was lost and to prevent the future they now endured from ever coming to pass.

While discussing their next steps, Clovis suddenly recalled a detail buried deep in his memory—a project he had overseen decades earlier while working for the OAS. He had commissioned miners to excavate a tunnel leading into a vast hollow cavern near a town called Wellville, Colorado. The purpose of the project had been shrouded in secrecy even to him, but he suspected it had been connected to the experimental work conducted at the Wind Valley military base.

Now, he was certain that whatever lay hidden in that cavern could hold critical information. "It's there," Clovis insisted, his voice tinged with both conviction and urgency. "I might not remember every detail, but if we find that tunnel, we'll find answers."

Rico, ever the curious leader, suggested they consult Lucy, an elderly shaman whose knowledge of the area's history was unparalleled. Lucy had once worked as a contractor for the OAS and had since dedicated her post-apocalyptic life to guiding those seeking redemption or enlightenment. Her wisdom came not only from her experiences but also from her spiritual insight.

When Kane and Clovis met Lucy, she greeted them with wary curiosity. Upon hearing Oliver Kross's name, her demeanor shifted. Though they had never met, she knew of him and his work and expressed sorrow over the tragedies that had stemmed from their shared employer's ambitions. "You carry the weight of the past," Lucy said, her voice heavy with regret, "but you also carry the hope to make things right."

She confirmed the existence of the Wind Valley military base near Wellville, describing it as a place of horrors. Her voice quivered as she recounted the experiments conducted there: the creation of the Hades virus that triggered the apocalypse, the enhancement of Whisperers as cross-dimensional weapons, and the prototype beta unit of Ivyg's time-travel device. "The device you seek is likely still there," Lucy revealed, "but it is guarded by the ghosts of its dark past. What was hidden will resist being uncovered."

Lucy's knowledge came at a price—she was haunted by her role in the base's operations. "I followed orders," she confessed, tears streaming down her face. "I watched the atrocities and said nothing. This place, this Wind Valley base… it is cursed. But perhaps, through you, it can serve a greater purpose."

Offering her help, Lucy pledged to guide Kane and his group to the base, ensuring they could navigate the treacherous terrain and find the remnants of the beta time-travel machine. Her warnings were dire, but her hope was resolute: "Hidden things always rise to the surface. It is the way of the world. And sometimes, what rises can bring healing."

In the years leading to the apocalypse, it had been easier to believe the lies propagated by those in power than to face the horrifying truth—that the devastation had come not from a foreign adversary but from within. The narrative of an external threat had been carefully constructed, a false flag operation designed to consolidate control. The Hades virus, engineered in secret, was unleashed under the guise of national defense. As the death toll rose, the world fractured. Sides were drawn, and the collapse of society began, plunging humanity into chaos.

Rico had lived through that chaos. As a young man, he witnessed the destruction of his home and the near extinction of his family. Yet, somehow, he had emerged on the other side, not hardened but transformed. The horrors he had seen left him with an unshakable conviction to lead differently. Violence, he believed, was a last resort—but when necessary, it had to be swift and decisive. His commune was a testament to his vision: a refuge for those who had grown disillusioned with the old ways, seeking instead to build a better, more compassionate society.

Rico's principles were simple yet profound, rooted in a balance of strength and compassion. He shared them freely with those who joined his community:1.   Do no harm but take no shit.

2.   If you have to fight, win.

3.   No one is a lonely island in this world.

4.   It takes a village.

5.   Do your part. Everyone contributes.

6.   Life is hard; don't be hard on yourself. You get out of life what you put in.

7.   Don't take life too seriously; you'll never get out alive.

At first, Kane dismissed the code as overly simplistic. But as days turned into weeks, and weeks into months, he began to appreciate its wisdom. In a world as broken as this, simple truths were often the most enduring.

During his time at the commune, Kane recounted his story to Rico and the others. It took countless nights to tell, each tale more unbelievable than the last. Rico listened intently, fascinated by two parts of Kane's story above all else.

The first was about Nova, a man Rico immediately recognized. "I know this man," Rico said, his face lighting up with recognition. "He's a hunter, a loner. We only see him when he brings in a big catch to trade for supplies. If he's still out there, I'll have him found and brought to you."

The second was the story of Oliver Kross and his daughter, Kiara. The idea that saving these two people in the past could alter the future resonated deeply with Rico. For years, he had dreamed of undoing the pain and destruction he had witnessed. If helping Kane could achieve that, he was all in.

Rico introduced Kane and his group to Lucy, an elderly woman who had once worked for the Office of Advanced Science (OAS). Now living as a shaman among a tribe of survivors, Lucy carried the weight of her past like a stone around her neck. She listened quietly as Kane explained their mission, her expression unreadable until she heard Oliver Kross's name. "I know of him," she said, her voice tinged with sorrow. "Though we never met, his reputation was well known."

Lucy confirmed the existence of the Wind Valley military base near Wellville, Colorado, and its connection to the Hades virus. She spoke of the horrors conducted in the name of national defense: the creation of the virus, the manipulation of the Whisperers, and the development of a prototype time-travel device. "The beta unit," she said, her voice cracking, "should still be there. It's likely the only thing that survived."

As Lucy recounted her time at Wind Valley, her composure began to falter. "We did things," she admitted, tears streaming down her face. "Things I can't even speak of. We were told it was for the greater good, that it was necessary to protect our nation. But it was a lie. We were the ones who brought destruction."

Her voice broke as she continued. "I was too afraid to speak out, too afraid to do anything but follow orders. And when the bombs fell, I thought I could leave it all behind. But you can't leave behind something like that. It stays with you."

As Lucy prepared to guide them to the Wind Valley base, she drew a crude map in the dirt. Her trembling hand traced the contours of the mountain range, marking key landmarks with deliberate precision. "The entrance lies here," she said, pointing to a notch in the range near Wellville. "A tunnel carved into the rock, leading to what was once a bustling hub of experimentation. Now, it's just a graveyard for Ivyg's ambitions."The group studied the map, their expressions heavy with a mixture of anticipation and dread. Rico, crouched beside Kane, ran a calloused hand over the drawn lines. "This cavern," he murmured, tracing the path with his finger. "How deep does it go?"Lucy hesitated, her gaze distant. "Deeper than most would dare to venture. The miners spoke of strange sounds coming from the lower chambers—whispers, even when no one was there. They said the air grew colder the further they descended, as if the earth itself were warning them to turn back."Her words hung in the air, heavy and oppressive. Kane clenched his fists, his resolve hardening. "Whatever's down there, it's our only shot. We can't afford to turn back now."Lucy nodded solemnly. "The base sprawls across levels. The upper tiers housed administrative offices and living quarters for the staff. But the real horrors were buried deeper—labs, holding cells, the testing chambers. That's where you'll find what you're looking for, but it won't come easily."Rico stood, his gaze fixed on the horizon. "We'll prepare for the worst. My people know these lands—if there's a way to approach without drawing attention, we'll find it."As the group finalized their plans, Lucy's warning echoed in Kane's mind. The Wind Valley base was more than a physical place; it was a symbol of humanity's darkest impulses. And as the sun dipped below the horizon, casting long shadows over the commune, he couldn't shake the feeling that their journey was only beginning.

With Lucy's guidance, Rico's resources, and Clovis's rediscovered memory of the hollow cavern, Kane's mission gained new momentum. For the first time in years, he felt the stirrings of hope. The path ahead would be treacherous, but the goal—a chance to rewrite humanity's story—was worth any risk.

-Chapter 44-

Convergence

"General Ashgrove! We have a problem!" Lucy's voice rang out, urgent and firm, as she stepped briskly into the room.

Donovan Ashgrove's face hardened at those four words, words he had grown to despise. They were a harbinger of everything going wrong, and he could already feel his anger rising. He took a deep breath, forcing himself to stay calm. "Go on," he said, gesturing for her to continue.

"The group from the Mountain View Motel has escaped," Lucy said, her voice trembling slightly, though she tried to maintain her composure. "It seems they're heading this way, and—" she hesitated, then pushed forward, "they appear to be regaining total recall of last year's events."

Donovan sat back in his chair, his expression unreadable. For a moment, he didn't say anything. Then, with a bitter laugh, he muttered, "They remember everything?"

"Yes, sir," Lucy confirmed, her words quick and precise. "We weren't sure how to handle it, but... I want you to know that you made the right decision, sir."

"Did I?" Donovan's voice dropped, his tone laden with doubt. His gaze drifted, as though he was staring at something only he could see. "Because from where I'm sitting, it feels like we've sold our souls to the devil."

Lucy stiffened, surprised by the shift in his demeanor. She had known Donovan as an unshakable leader, unwavering in his decisions. But now, he looked almost... vulnerable.

"What we're doing here," Donovan continued, his voice quieter now but no less intense, "it's unnatural. It's perverse. We're tampering with things we have no right to tamper with. Disturbing the balance of power across the entire planet—for what? To prove we can? To play God? What the fuck are we doing here?"

Lucy remained silent, unsure how to respond to her superior's mental breakdown. She had never seen him like this before. He wasn't just questioning the mission—he was questioning everything.

Donovan leaned forward, running his hands over his face. "Ivyg's experiments, the Order, these Champions—it's all spiraling out of control.

These people, Lucy... they were pawns, sure, but they weren't meant to be destroyed like this. And now, here we are, cleaning up his mess while the world crumbles around us."

Lucy hesitated for only a moment before doing the unthinkable: she slapped him hard across the face. The sharp sound of her hand meeting his cheek echoed in the room, breaking the heavy silence. Donovan's head snapped to the side, and for a moment, he was stunned. Slowly, he turned back to face her, his expression shifting from disbelief to clarity. "Thanks," he muttered gruffly. "I needed that."

Lucy, though still shaken herself, nodded and pressed on. "What do you want us to do about Conrad?" she asked. "With the base in chaos, he could easily escape. We've only got one guard watching him, and we both know he's crafty. If he gets out—"

"Tell the guard to kill him," Donovan interrupted, his tone heavy but resolute. "We don't have the time or resources to deal with him anymore. This whole operation is falling apart—it's karma, Lucy. For him, for us, for all of this. Handle it."

Lucy's stomach churned, but she forced herself to nod. "Yes, sir."

Donovan stormed out of the office, slamming his fist against the doorframe as he left. Lucy remained for a moment, frozen by the weight of his order. She repeated the command in her mind: Conrad must die.

Her steps were slow and heavy as she made her way to the makeshift holding cell. The guard stationed outside stood at attention when she arrived, but Lucy didn't acknowledge him. She stepped past him without a word, her hand already resting on her holster.

Inside, Conrad looked up, his expression a mixture of resignation and defiance. Lucy's hand trembled as she drew her weapon. Two shots echoed in the confined space: one to the chest, one to the head. Conrad slumped to the floor, lifeless.

A single tear slipped down Lucy's cheek as she dropped to her knees. "I didn't want to kill anyone," she whispered, her voice cracking.

The guard stepped inside, placing a hand on her shoulder. "You did what you had to do, ma'am. You followed orders. When this is all over, we'll go home. But not yet. We're soldiers—we have to see this through."

Lucy inhaled shakily, nodding as she forced herself to her feet. Together, she and the guard left the holding area, the sound of her boots echoing in the empty corridor.

The group had managed to make it to the base, they crouched among the shadows, catching their breath after the chaotic confrontation.

Dexter, ever the detective, couldn't hold his tongue. He gestured wildly at Marcus, his voice laced with incredulity. "Did I just see you blow up a military vehicle with your bare hands? What the hell was that?!"

Before Marcus could respond, Clarice, still fuming from the firefight, snapped back.

"It was survival. You're welcome, by the way."

Rose's wide eyes darted between Marcus and Clarice. Her voice was soft but trembling with wonder.

"You… you didn't just destroy that van… I mean, you melted it, didn't you? The energy—it wasn't just fire. It looked like it was alive."

Marcus exhaled heavily, his glow fading. He avoided Rose's gaze, brushing off her observation.

"Call it what you want. It got us out of there."

Max, the youngest among them, was practically bouncing on his feet.

"That was insane! You guys are like some next-level X-Men! Do I get powers too? Or is that, like, a family secret? Or something I have to go to school for?"

"Max," Cesaro cut in, his voice low and steady, "maybe we should focus on staying alive before we talk about superhero clubs and shit that ain't real."

The group fell quiet as they moved deeper into the base. Kathleen, who had been quietly observing from the back, finally spoke, her voice filled with unease.

"So… this whole time, you've been hiding this from us? What else aren't you telling us? Are you even on our side?"

Clarice stopped in her tracks and turned to face the group, her icy tone as sharp as the air around them.

"We've been using these powers to keep people safe. To keep you safe. If you think for a second we'd ever use them against you, then maybe we shouldn't have bothered."

Kathleen flinched, and Rose stepped forward, raising her hands in a calming gesture.

"Hey, nobody's saying that. This is just… a lot. For all of us."

Dexter crossed his arms, his brow furrowed.

"I've seen some weird things in my line of work, but glowing hands and conjured fire aren't exactly in the manual. What are we dealing with here?"

Marcus finally looked up, his gaze firm.

"Something we didn't ask for. Something we've been trying to understand ourselves. But right now, all you need to know is that we're here to fight the same fight as you."

Cesaro, who had been quietly listening, broke the tension.

"We don't have time to argue. Whatever you two can do, we're going to need it. Those soldiers back there? They'll regroup. If we don't move now, none of us will live long enough to have this conversation again. You're going to have to trust us."

Kathleen reluctantly nodded, though the tension in her shoulders remained. Dexter, still skeptical, gestured for the group to move forward. "Fine. But this isn't over. You owe us an explanation when we're safe."

As they continued toward their vehicles, Rose lingered behind to walk beside Marcus. She looked up at him with a quiet, searching expression.

"It's not just fire, is it? It's something more. Something... ancient."

Marcus hesitated but gave her a slight nod.

"Yeah. It's more than fire. But don't ask me to explain it. Half the time, I don't understand it myself."

Rose smiled softly, her initial fear replaced by a sense of wonder.

"Well, whatever it is, I think it saved all of us tonight. Thank you."

Max, still buzzing with excitement, leaned over to Dexter and said. "I mean, come on. Fire powers? Ice blasts? How cool is that?"

Dexter gave him a pointed look but couldn't completely hide the smirk tugging at the corner of his mouth.

"Let's hope 'cool' is enough to keep us alive."

Marcus and Clarice sat in silence for a moment before Clarice spoke.

"They're scared of us."

Marcus shrugged.

"Maybe. But they're still here. That counts for something."

Clarice's voice softened.

"They're going to find out what we are sooner or later. The truth about why we're here."

Marcus didn't answer right away.

"When that time comes, we'll tell them. But not yet. Not while everything's still this fragile."

Clarice nodded, and the two fell silent, their shared resolve unspoken but understood.

Elsewhere, Marcus, Clarice, and their companions faced an ambush. OAS mercenaries disguised as soldiers opened fire. That left Max dead and Dexter wounded. Amid the chaos, Rose used her Vril powers to shield the group, creating dazzling barriers and launching projectiles at their attackers. Clarice, digging through a bag of salvaged weapons, surprised the group with her strength, delivering a knockout punch to a soldier attempting to flank her.

Marcus used his Vril energy to blow open another set of steel doors of the Wind Valley base, allowing the group to slip inside, going deeper into the installation. As they navigated the rubble, their resolve hardened. Together, they prepared to uncover the secrets hidden within the base, knowing the answers they sought could change everything.

"Ridiculous. This whole damn incident is ridiculous!" General Donovan Ashgrove muttered furiously as he strode down the corridor. His ranting echoed around him, half-intended for anyone who might overhear. Moments earlier, the sound of an explosion at the main steel door had set his resolve. This was the last straw. He would put an end to this entire operation himself. Ashgrove moved toward the red level, where "the Gate" was housed. The sound of gunfire and the shouts of his soldiers signaled the intruders' progress, their intent clear—they were heading for the Gate. But the General had different plans. He would use the Gate to travel back to last August, erase the problem at its root, and eliminate these nuisances once and for all. Forget the Order's directives; he worked for the United States government, not for some secretive cabal. Today, he would be judge, jury, and executioner.

Smiling darkly at the thought of wielding the Gate's power, Ashgrove felt invincible. In his hands, the Gate wasn't just a machine—it was control over time itself. The rush of power emboldened him, and his grin took on an unsettling, devilish quality.

Marcus, Cesaro, Clarice, and Rose led the charge, with Dexter and

Max providing cover. As the lights in the corridor surged to an almost blinding brightness, Marcus's stomach dropped.

"Oh no," he muttered, glancing at the others. "It's started! We have to stop this now!"

The group moved swiftly, weapons ready. Rose, trembling slightly, clutched her pistol as Cesaro stayed close, a steadying presence. Clarice's icy determination matched Marcus's fiery resolve as they pressed forward into the blue corridor.

Ahead, they found two doors. Marcus blasted open the second one with a controlled burst of Vril energy, revealing an elevator that led to the red level. The cramped service elevator descended, carrying the group toward their destination.

Inside the Gate room, Ashgrove worked frantically to calibrate the machinery. Normally, a team of scientists would have handled the intricate process, but the current crisis left him to manage alone. Two soldiers stood by, guarding the door, but their utility was minimal in the General's eyes.

As the banging on the door grew louder, Ashgrove's focus shifted between the controls and the armed soldiers. He set the Gate's date to August 13th, 2023, aiming to strike when his enemies least expected it. Just as he locked in the coordinates, gunfire erupted at the door's locking mechanism. Startled, he dove behind a steel pillar, scrambling for the duffle bag of weapons he'd stashed earlier.

The door burst open. Marcus and Clarice stepped through first, their Vril powers radiating energy. Marcus's fiery aura illuminated the room as Clarice's icy calm chilled the air around them. Rose and Cesaro followed closely, weapons raised, while Dexter and Max took defensive positions near the doorway.

Ashgrove's two soldiers opened fire, but Marcus countered with a wave of flame, disarming them instantly. Clarice froze one soldier's weapon mid-fire, rendering it useless. The soldiers, realizing they were outmatched, surrendered and moved to the side.

"Ashgrove!" Marcus called, his voice echoing in the chamber. "You've lost. Step away from the Gate."

From his hiding spot, Donovan snarled. "You think you can just waltz in here and take control? You have no idea what you're dealing with!"

Marcus's gaze swept the room, landing on the Gate's controls. The realization hit him—Ashgrove had already set the machine to transport.

"You're trying to reset everything," Clarice said, stepping forward. "But you've lost control."

"Control?" Ashgrove sneered, emerging from behind the pillar with his weapon drawn. "I am control!"

Before he could fire, Marcus unleashed a concentrated burst of flame at the weapon, forcing Ashgrove to drop it. Cesaro surged forward, tackling the General to the ground and pinning him.

"You're done," Cesaro growled, his tone resolute.

As Clarice moved to secure the controls, a warning light began flashing on the Gate. The machine emitted a low hum, growing in intensity.

"It's too late," Ashgrove laughed maniacally from the floor. "You can't stop it now."

Marcus exchanged a worried glance with Clarice. "What's it set to?"

Clarice's expression hardened as she examined the display. "He's targeting August 13th, 2023—before the Pulse."

Realizing the danger, Marcus nodded. "We'll deal with it," he said firmly. "But first, let's shut this down."

Together, the group worked to disable the Gate, determined to end Ashgrove's twisted plans before they spiraled further out of control.

Soldiers armed only with batons surged toward the intruders in desperation, their faces determined yet grim. Marcus, reluctantly unleashing his restrained power, sent controlled bursts of fire toward their feet, forcing them back without causing fatal harm. Clarice, staying close to Linda and Kathleen, used her ice-based Vril abilities to create a slippery barrier, slowing the soldiers' advance.

The group pressed forward, pushing through the chaos and into the brightly lit main chamber. The overhead lights were blinding, and the incessant whirring of the machines created an overwhelming din. Everyone instinctively squinted, their senses heightened as they searched for any sign of General Ashgrove.

"Where is he?" Cesaro growled, scanning the room with his weapon drawn.

"You can't hide forever!" Kathleen shouted, clutching her gun tightly, her voice defiant despite the fear creeping in.

Suddenly, from the shadows, a figure lunged forward. Donovan Ashgrove grabbed Clarice, twisting her arm behind her back in a brutal hold, the muzzle of his gun pressed against the back of her skull. She froze, the glow of her powers flickering out in her panic.

"Stay back!" Ashgrove barked, dragging her further into the room. His voice was steady, but there was an unmistakable edge of desperation. "I'll put a bullet in her brain if you come any closer."

The group froze. Guns were raised, but hesitation gripped them. The room pulsed with tension, each second stretching impossibly long.

"Let her go!" Marcus shouted, his hands glowing faintly as his control wavered.

Donovan sneered.

"Don't even think about it, hotshot. One wrong move, and your girlfriend here's done for."

"You don't have to do this," Cesaro said, his voice calm and steady. "Whatever you think you've accomplished, it's over. You're outnumbered, and you've lost control."

Donovan laughed darkly, pressing the gun harder against Clarice's head.

"Lost control? You think I've lost control? Look around, you fools! I've already won! I have 'The Gate.' I hold your lives in my hands. As far as I'm concerned, you're already dead."

"You don't even know what you're dealing with," Cesaro replied, stepping forward cautiously. "Whatever you're trying to do with that machine will only backfire. You can't rewrite history without consequences."

Ashgrove's eyes darted between Cesaro and the others, his confidence faltering for just a moment. Then, his gaze fixed on Dexter. A slow, sinister grin spread across his face.

"Ah, Detective Simmons," he said, his tone mocking. "You look like you've had a rough night. Did you think I wouldn't recognize you? I've been keeping tabs on all of you for a long time."

Dexter's eyes narrowed, and his grip on his weapon tightened.

"How do you know who I am?"

Donovan chuckled, his voice dripping with derision.

"Oh, I know all of you better than you think. You and your little band of misfits. Did you really think you could waltz in here and stop me? You're nothing but pawns, and I'm the one who moves the pieces."

"You talk too much," Marcus said through clenched teeth, his fists glowing brighter.

"Careful, Marcus," Clarice said through gritted teeth, her voice low and steady despite the gun to her head. "If you lose control, we all lose."

Marcus took a deep breath, forcing himself to calm down. He couldn't risk Clarice's life—not now, not when they'd come so far.

"You don't have to do this," Rose said, her voice cutting through the tension like a knife. "You think you're in control but look around you. You're alone. You're scared. Whatever you're planning—it won't save you."

Ashgrove faltered for the briefest moment, his eyes darting toward the machine behind him. The group seized the opportunity.

Cesaro moved first, his hand steady as he aimed at Ashgrove's shoulder. He fired, the shot ringing out in the confined space. Ashgrove cried out, his grip on Clarice loosening just enough for her to wrench herself free. She turned, a wave of frost emanating from her hands, freezing Ashgrove's weapon before he could aim again.

Marcus followed, his fire surging toward the remaining soldiers who had regrouped at the door. He didn't burn them, but the heat was enough to force them back, disarming and incapacitating them.

Clarice, breathing heavily, turned to Ashgrove, who was now clutching his injured shoulder.

"It's over," she said coldly, her hands glowing faintly.

Ashgrove glared at her, defiance still burning in his eyes.

"Fools. You have no idea what you're meddling with. The Gate will open, and you'll all wish you had stayed dead."

The group exchanged uneasy glances as the machine behind them began to hum louder, the lights on its console flickering ominously.

"Don't look so shocked. It's really heartbreaking to see this," Donovan said mockingly, his tone dripping with sarcasm. He let out a cold, menacing laugh that echoed through the room. "We've been watching you for some time now. We knew you'd all show up here eventually. Sooner than we anticipated, but here we are. And now… here you are."

Clarice squirmed in his grip, the muzzle of the gun pressing harder against the back of her head.

"Let go of me, you son of a bitch!" she snapped, her voice filled with defiance despite the precariousness of her situation.

"Shut up, Clarice," Donovan replied, his tone suddenly flat and impatient. The audible click of the hammer being pulled back made everyone freeze. "One more word, and I'll end this for you now. Understand?"

Clarice stilled, her breathing heavy, her glare as sharp as the blade she wished she had in her hand.

Donovan's lips curled into a cruel smirk as his eyes swept across the room, meeting the gaze of each person in turn.

"Let's see who else we have here. Linda Baker, Kathleen O'Brian, Marcus Kydd, Rose O'Keenan, Juan Cesaro, Detective Dexter Simmons…" His voice lingered on each name with mock familiarity, dripping disdain. "And Max? Ah, I take it he's dead since he isn't gracing us with his presence tonight. Just like your other dear friends, Billy and Conrad. A shame we couldn't clean up this mess properly the first time."

"What are you talking about?" Linda demanded, her voice wavering between confusion and anger.

Donovan ignored her, shifting his attention back to the group as a whole.

"None of you are soldiers. None of you have the training or resolve to kill me. You're just weak, pathetic civilians stumbling in the dark, thinking you understand the forces you're meddling with. Newsflash: you don't. You don't have a damned clue what you've been exposed to."

"Oh, really?" Kathleen shot back, her voice laced with venom. "And what exactly are we supposed to have been exposed to?"

Donovan's expression darkened, his voice dropping to a harsh growl.

"The Whisperers," he spat. "Those creatures aren't from here. They're not human. They're killing machines—soulless, relentless, and unstoppable. They've caused nothing but destruction, chaos, and death. And if it hadn't been for that little slip-up causing the accident last August, we wouldn't have been able to contain them. We had a chance to put things back in order… until you stuck your noses where they didn't belong and interfered with my plans."

The group exchanged uneasy glances, the weight of his words sinking in.

Donovan's grip on Clarice tightened as he barked, "Do you have any idea the lengths we went to, to save your miserable lives? My men and I erased your pathetic memories to protect you—and to protect the operation. And yet here you are, hell-bent on remembering things that should've stayed buried. You should be thanking me. Kissing my ass, even. Without me, you wouldn't have survived."

Linda stepped forward, her fists clenched, trembling with righteous fury.

"You didn't have to brainwash us!" she shouted, her voice breaking. "That's a violation of our civil liberties!"

Donovan's laugh was sharp and humorless.

"Civil liberties? Are you serious? The world was falling apart, and you want to talk about civil liberties? This is an issue of national security, lady. You're only alive because I made hard decisions. Decisions that spared your lives and kept you from descending into madness. But no, that wasn't good enough for you. You just had to dig deeper. Had to remember the truth. And look where that's gotten you."

Dexter stepped forward, gun still trained on the General.

"And what exactly is the truth, Donovan? What aren't you telling us?"

Donovan hesitated for a fraction of a second, but his arrogance wouldn't allow him to admit defeat.

"The truth?" he repeated, his voice dripping with condescension. "The truth is, you're all just pawns in a much bigger game. A game you'll never understand."

"You're the one who doesn't understand," Marcus said, his voice low and steady, his hands glowing faintly with restrained energy. "We're not pawns, and we're not going to let you win."

The tension in the room reached its breaking point as the group tightened their circle around Donovan, who realized his grip on the situation—and Clarice—was slipping.

"You don't have the right to lecture me about a damned thing!" Donovan bellowed, his voice echoing through the chamber. "I've been doing my country's work for decades while you people go about your lives, taking everything for granted. The world you live in is nothing like mine. The real world is where I live. The one filled with threats you can't even comprehend. And you? You're just parasites, leeching off the system I protect. It makes me sick to my stomach to clean up after you, to keep the horrors of this world from tearing apart your happy little delusions."

Clarice winced as Donovan jerked her arm further behind her back, his other hand gripping the gun pointed at her head. Her sharp glare burned into him, but the discomfort in her arm was growing unbearable. Donovan smirked at her defiance, reveling in her silent struggle.

"The Gate is the answer!" Donovan declared, gesturing toward the vortex with the gun still in hand. "A few more adjustments and I'll make things right. I'll erase every mistake, every failure—including all of you."

The blinding light of the vortex intensified as Donovan reached the edge of the ramp, dragging Clarice closer. His laugh was hollow and grating.

"In a moment, I'll step through, and all of this will be nothing more than a bad memory. Get it? History! Come on, seriously? No laughs? Ah, screw you all."

The group was frozen in a tense standoff. Marcus stepped forward, his hands glowing faintly with suppressed Vril energy, his expression tight with anger and desperation.

"You can't do this!" Kathleen shouted, her voice cracking under the strain of the moment.

"Come back here and fight like a man, you coward!" Cesaro growled, his gun trained on Donovan.

"You're not going to get away with this, you slimy piece of shit!" Marcus spat, his voice trembling with emotion. His eyes locked on Clarice, her fear unmistakable even as she tried to hide it. Memories of the Hollow Earth and the Nexus Consciousness surged through his mind. He could feel the weight of those moments again—the helplessness, the grief, and the unrelenting will to keep fighting for the one person who mattered more than anything.

Clarice turned her head slightly, just enough to meet Marcus's gaze. There was no need for words; he could see the plea in her eyes. She was terrified in a way he'd never seen before, and it broke something inside him.

"No," Marcus whispered to himself. The faint glow of his hands intensified as his resolve hardened.

"MARCUS!" Clarice cried out, her voice cracking with fear. "HELP

ME!"

Marcus froze, his mind racing through memories of destruction he'd caused before. The explosion that had blasted his former friends and colleagues within the Order, into another realm. Kane, Patel, Val Batticus, Norman Greene—he had scattered them all to who knows where. Could he risk it again? Could he wield his powers without losing everything? His hesitation wasn't out of fear for himself but for Clarice. He couldn't bear the thought of losing her, of destroying the very life they'd fought so hard to build together.

Marcus clenched his fists, his hands faintly glowing with Vril energy. His resolve was torn. If need be, he would fight through any obstacle, face hell itself, to keep her safe. Yet, he longed for the simplicity of their quiet moments, watching old shows like Downton Abbey, laughing together, sharing a life beyond all this chaos. He couldn't let that future slip away.

Their eyes met, and Marcus felt the pain of her fear like a dagger in his chest. He couldn't let her down. He wouldn't.

"Well then, I guess I'll see you all in hell!" Donovan yelled, shoving Clarice to the ground. The sound of her body hitting the floor reverberated in Marcus's ears as time seemed to slow. The General raised his pistol, firing twice in quick succession.

The first shot went wide, slamming into the wall behind the group. The second struck true, hitting Marcus in the abdomen. He staggered, the glowing light of his powers dimming as pain coursed through him.

"NO!" Clarice screamed, scrambling toward Marcus.

The room erupted into chaos. Cesaro and Kathleen raised their weapons, ready to fire back, but before anyone could act, the air was filled with a chilling sound—a low, guttural whispering that seemed to seep into their very bones.

Green eyes began to appear, one set after another, glowing eerily in the dimly lit room. The Whisperers had arrived.

"What the hell…?" Dexter muttered, his voice trembling as the inhuman figures materialized around them.

Donovan's eyes widened in terror as he realized his only escape lay through the vortex. Without hesitation, he turned and sprinted toward "the Gate," abandoning the group as he disappeared into its blinding light.

The Whisperers, however, seemed uninterested in the humans huddled on the floor. Instead, several of them moved purposefully toward the control station. Their long, clawed hands manipulated knobs and buttons with unsettling precision. It was as if they knew exactly what they were doing, their goal clear: shutting down the vortex.

Clarice knelt beside Marcus, her hands trembling as she pressed against the wound to stop the bleeding. "Stay with me," she pleaded, tears streaming down her face. "You're not leaving me, do you hear me?"

"I'm… not going anywhere," Marcus gasped, his voice strained but steady. His eyes flicked toward the Whisperers, their strange presence a surreal backdrop to the chaos unfolding around them. "They're… not here for us."

"They're shutting it down," Cesaro observed, his voice low with awe and confusion. "Why would they—?"

"We don't have time to figure that out," Dexter interrupted, his voice sharp. "We need to get out of here, now."

Clarice nodded, determination hardening her features as she helped Marcus to his feet. Around them, the Whisperers worked with eerie efficiency, their green eyes glowing brighter as the vortex began to flicker and fade.

"Let's move," Cesaro urged, covering the group as they made their way to the door of the room but then stopped to look back. The Whisperers didn't follow, their focus entirely on the machinery as the blinding light of the Gate dimmed, then disappeared entirely.

Marcus managed a weak smile despite the pain. "Guess… we're not the only ones trying to stop the end of the world."

Clarice tightened her grip on him, her voice firm. "Let's make sure we're around to see it saved."

As Donovan turned to face the vortex, a pair of glowing green eyes emerged from the blinding light, locking onto his own. For a moment, time seemed to stand still. He froze, unable to look away, his breath caught in his throat.

"Oh, my God," Donovan muttered, taking a hesitant step back.

The Whisperer stood silently, its presence overwhelming. In a burst of defiance, Donovan clenched his fists and swung with all his strength, landing a solid punch to the creature's face. It staggered slightly but quickly regained its balance, its expressionless demeanor somehow exuding fury.

"Come on, you piece of shit!" Donovan roared, his voice trembling with both rage and desperation. He followed up with a swift roundhouse kick to the chest, sending the Whisperer into the side of the machine with a metallic thud.

For a moment, Donovan felt victorious, a grin spreading across his face. "Not so tough now, are you?"

But his confidence was short-lived. As he aimed another punch at the creature's head, it shifted just enough to avoid the blow. His fist connected with the cold, unyielding metal wall, and he cried out in pain, clutching his now-broken hand. Gritting his teeth, he swung with his left, but the Whisperer blocked the attack effortlessly with its forearm and countered with a powerful strike to his sternum, knocking the wind out of him.

Donovan stumbled back, gasping for air as the Whisperer loomed closer. Desperation flared in his eyes. With a guttural growl, he launched a last-ditch attack, driving his injured right arm upward into the creature's midsection. The unexpected low blow caused the Whisperer to stagger and drop momentarily to the floor.

"Ha!" Donovan shouted triumphantly, raising his arms as if he'd won a championship fight. "That's right! I'm still the alpha here!"

His victory celebration was cut short as the Whisperer rose with eerie calm, two gleaming, metallic blades emerging from its arm. In one fluid motion, the blades sliced into Donovan's knee, sending him crashing to the concrete floor with a scream of agony. Blood pooled around him as the creature towered above, its glowing green eyes fixed on his trembling form.

Donovan writhed in pain, clutching his shattered knee. "No! Stay back! Please don't kill me!" he pleaded, his bravado replaced with raw terror. "What have I done to make you angry?"

The Whisperer said nothing. Instead, it extended its glowing, metallic hand and pressed it against Donovan's forehead. The General's panicked cries abruptly ceased as his body went limp, his arms falling lifelessly to his sides.

Through the touch, a telepathic link was established. Donovan's eyes widened in shock as unspoken words, images, and emotions flooded his mind. He saw glimpses of destruction, suffering, and the consequences of his actions—not just the Whisperers' creation, but the countless lives he had destroyed in his blind pursuit of power and control.

The General's lips moved silently as if trying to respond, but no words came out. His defiance, his arrogance, his sense of control—all were stripped away, leaving only fear and regret. As the Whisperer removed its hand, Donovan slumped to the floor, his eyes vacant, his once-indomitable will shattered.

The other Whisperers stood motionless, watching as their comrade turned back toward the vortex. The glow of "the Gate" intensified for a moment before dimming, leaving Donovan's broken body lying in the center of the room, silent and still.

"You want to know what you've done?" The Whisperer's voice echoed in Donovan's mind, calm yet piercing, its tone fluent in English yet alien in its clarity. "Let me show you…"

A torrent of images and sensations flooded Donovan's consciousness. He saw humanity's future: the release of the Hades virus, the devastation of World War III, billions of lives lost, and the creation of "the Gate." The atrocities played out before him as though he were standing amid the ruins, witnessing firsthand the consequences of his actions. His body trembled, his breath came in shallow gasps, and a single tear rolled down his cheek.

Meanwhile, Marcus, Clarice, and the rest of the group stood frozen, watching the scene unfold in stunned silence. The glowing green eyes of the Whisperer were fixed on the General, its imposing form radiating an aura of finality. Then, to everyone's astonishment, the Whisperer reached up and removed its helmet.

Gasps filled the room as the face beneath the mask was revealed: Morton Kane. Their former mentor, thought lost to time, stood before them, his face a mixture of sorrow and wrath. One by one, the other Whisperers began to remove their helmets as well, unveiling their own human faces—each one bearing the haunted expressions of those who had endured unimaginable suffering.

"Now that you have seen the pain you have caused in the name of my brother, Ivyg." Kane said, his voice heavy with emotion, "Now you will feel the pain."

Kane's glowing right prosthetic hand remained pressed to Donovan's forehead, keeping the telepathic connection alive. With his left arm, metallic blades extended menacingly, he raised them to the General's throat. The room seemed to hold its breath as Kane prepared to exact retribution, his intent clear: to make Donovan experience the agony of the billions whose deaths he had orchestrated.

"Stop!" Clarice's voice rang out, desperate and firm. She stepped forward, her hands trembling yet outstretched in a gesture of peace. "Please, don't kill him. No one else needs to die today. Please."

For a moment, silence filled the room. Kane's eyes met Clarice's, and something flickered in his expression—an internal struggle between his thirst for justice and the appeal for mercy. The tension was palpable, the weight of the moment pressing down on everyone present.

But the decision was taken out of his hands.

Unbeknownst to the group, Donovan had managed to retrieve a concealed pistol from a hidden pocket. In a final act of defiance, he raised the weapon—not to attack, but to end his own life. The gunshot rang out, deafening in the confined space.

"Nooooooo!" Clarice screamed, rushing forward, but it was too late. The General's lifeless body crumpled to the floor, blood pooling beneath him.

Donovan had seen himself as the captain of a sinking ship, unwilling to let anyone else dictate his end. To him, this was his penance, his way of taking responsibility—or perhaps escaping it entirely. The light from "the Gate" dimmed and then went out completely, leaving only the flickering overhead lights to cast eerie shadows across the room.

Behind the group, Marcus lay near the door, clutching his abdomen as blood seeped through his fingers. Clarice was at his side in an instant, her face etched with fear.

"I'm not afraid, Clarice," Marcus said weakly, his voice trembling. "But I don't want to die. Not today, at least."

Around them, the room seemed to shift. The remaining Whisperers—revealed as men bearing Kane's mark—moved silently, forming a circle around the group. Their expressions were unreadable, their intentions unclear.

The group huddled together, their attention split between Marcus's injury and the ominous presence surrounding them. In that moment, they realized they were not just witnesses to history but pivotal players in a battle far greater than they had imagined. The stakes had never been higher, and the lines between ally and enemy had never been blurrier.

"No, man, you're not going to die." Cesaro said firmly, placing his hands on top of Marcus's wound. The group stepped back, giving him space, their faces pale with worry. Slowly, Cesaro's hands began to emit a soft, golden glow, spreading warmth across Marcus's abdomen.

Kathleen's gaze darted around the room, her breath catching as she noticed the glowing hands of the Whisperers. Their previously indistinct forms were now illuminated, the golden light revealing outlines of their bodies. What had once seemed like shadowy figures now took on a distinctly human appearance, with faces that bore deep, knowing expressions.

"Is he dead?" Clarice asked desperately, tears streaming down her face as she looked down at Marcus.

"No, look." Dexter pointed, his voice steady despite the tension. "He's still breathing."

Marcus stirred slightly, his breaths growing stronger. Relief flooded through the group as Clarice clutched his hand tightly. Meanwhile, Dexter turned away from the group, standing tall as he faced the Whisperers directly.

"Who are you?" Dexter demanded, his voice firm.

One of the Whisperers stepped forward, the light from his hands intensifying as he moved. The others followed suit, their forms shimmering and transforming until their true appearances became visible. The group gasped as they realized they were looking at ordinary people—men with faces full of wisdom and determination.

"We mean you no harm," the leading figure said, his voice calm and reassuring. "We never intended to frighten you."

"Then who are you?" Clarice asked, her voice tinged with suspicion and awe.

"I am Nova," the man replied. He gestured toward Kane, who stood silently, his gaze fixed on Marcus. "You already know Kane. The rest of us… we are the children of your future."

"The future?" Linda asked, her brow furrowing in confusion. "Our future? What do you mean?"

"Last August, we reached out to you," Nova explained, his tone solemn. "We hoped that your group would help us. We had no other choice but to risk contacting you through the Veil."

"Help you with what?" Kathleen asked, her voice soft but insistent.

Nova glanced at Kane, who stepped forward to answer. "To save us from extinction," Kane said. "And to stop what began here, in this very base."

Kane gestured toward the vortex of "the Gate," its machinery now silent. "Within this base, the deadliest virus humanity has ever known was created under Ivyg's orders. It is not just a weapon—it is the catalyst for a war that would tear your world apart. A false flag attack designed to justify global devastation."

The group exchanged uneasy glances, the gravity of the situation sinking in. Clarice stepped forward, still holding Marcus's hand, her voice shaking but determined. "And you're saying this… this 'Gate' is the only way to stop it?"

"Yes," Nova said, his voice resolute. "It is not only a weapon of destruction but also a tool of salvation. If used correctly, it can undo the damage, prevent the outbreak, and restore what has been lost."

"But why us?" Cesaro asked, his skepticism evident. "Why reach out to us of all people?"

Kane's gaze softened as he looked at each member of the group in turn. "Because you are not just ordinary people. You are connected to the Vril, to the very energy that powers the Veil and everything tied to it. Each of you carries a piece of the puzzle needed to fix what has been broken. You had to spend time serving the Order to be the ones to bring it down. There was no other way."

The room fell silent, the weight of Kane's words pressing down on them. Their entire lives were orchestrated by this man to prepare them for this moment. Marcus stirred again, his voice weak but determined. "If it's broken, then let's stop it," he said, his eyes locked with Clarice's. "Together."

Clarice nodded, squeezing his hand. "We'll figure this out."

The group stood united, their resolve strengthening in the face of the revelations. The path ahead was uncertain, but for the first time, they began to see themselves as more than bystanders. They were part of something much larger—a fight not just for survival, but for the future of humanity itself.

-Chapter 45-

Resolution

The light of the setting sun bathed Witchaven in hues of gold and crimson, casting its sprawling terraces and spiraling towers in an otherworldly glow. The city, nestled atop a cliff overlooking the restless sea, resembled a jewel of another era—a sanctuary of crystalline spires and alabaster walls reminiscent of the grandeur of Atlantis itself. But it wasn't just the breathtaking beauty that made this place sacred; it was the history, the memories, and the legacy etched into its very stones.

Mallah stood at the edge of the cliff, the wind catching her silver hair and billowing her cloak like the wings of an ancient guardian. Below her, the remaining inhabitants of Witchaven scurried toward the portal Ogma had opened. The shimmering gateway pulsed with radiant light, a final beacon of hope for those fleeing the inevitable.

Behind her, Skyler followed silently, his camera capturing every moment. He recorded the weight of her farewell, the grief etched into her face, and the rare vulnerability in her voice as she spoke aloud to the city she had called home for centuries.

"This land has cradled us, sheltered us," Mallah began, her voice steady despite the storm of emotions swirling within her. "Once, it was the northernmost part of Atlantis, a place of learning and unity. It stood as a beacon for peace—before the fall, before the wars."

She paused, her gaze sweeping across the architecture, from the polished marble walkways to the intricate carvings of ancient symbols on every column. "And now, it is the last remnant of a dream we could not hold. How fitting that this place, too, should be given back to the stars, a fragment of the cosmos it always belonged to."

Skyler shifted, lowering his camera for a moment. "Mallah," he ventured, "if this place meant so much, why must we leave it now?"

Mallah turned to him, her eyes soft but resolute. "Because Witchaven has given all that it can. That is never easy, nor is it ever meant to be. But the time has come to usher Lemuria from the shadows, to bring forth the truths that have been hidden for far too long. Witchaven's purpose was to protect those truths, and now it must pass the torch to what lies ahead."

As if to underscore her point, the air around them was pierced by an ear-splitting cry—a shriek so harrowing it reverberated through their very bones. Skyler instinctively covered his ears, grimacing at the sound.

"That," Mallah said grimly, "is Kihleen. The banshee cries not out of malice, but as a favor to me. Her screams are a warning, one that cannot be ignored." She placed a hand on Skyler's shoulder. "It is her way of giving me the time I need to say goodbye."

Ogma's voice boomed from below, cutting through the wails. "Mallah! We cannot linger any longer! The enemy is closer than you think!"

Mallah turned back toward the city one final time, her heart breaking as she took in the sight. This sanctuary had been her refuge, her purpose, her solace. But now it was time to leave it behind.

"I will carry you with me," she whispered, as much to herself as to the city. "Not as a place, but as a memory. A promise."

The cries grew louder, closer, their haunting resonance shaking the very air. Ogma's frantic voice called out again. "MALLAH! NOW!"

With a deep breath, Mallah turned and began descending the winding stairs toward the portal. Her steps were slow at first, as if every moment spent leaving was a betrayal. But as she neared the light of the gateway, her pace quickened.

She paused briefly at the threshold, her hand brushing Ogma's shoulder. "It is done," she said simply. "Let us go."

As the last creatures fled through the portal, Mallah stepped through with Ogma, the light swallowing them whole just as the first sign of Ivyg's assault burst over the horizon.

On the other side, the air was different—warmer, brighter, alive with a vitality that was both foreign and familiar. Lemuria stretched out before them, its landscape a harmonious blend of untamed wilderness and advanced architecture. Towering crystalline structures rose from verdant hills, their shapes reflecting the natural world around them. Streams of iridescent water wove through the city like veins of light, and the air itself seemed to hum with energy.

Surrounded by towering tents and hurriedly assembled shelters. The chaos of the camp was palpable—people darting back and forth, organizing supplies, calming frightened children, and tending to the injured. Despite the confusion, the breathtaking beauty of Lemuria loomed just beyond the camp, tantalizingly out of reach. Hints of its grandeur—a cascade of crystal-clear waterfalls, golden sunlight filtering through massive ancient trees, and distant glowing structures—were visible, but the urgency of the moment demanded focus.

Mallah took a deep breath, the weight of responsibility etched on her face as she surveyed the temporary sanctuary. She turned to Ogma. "What of the others?"

Before Ogma could respond, Pavel appeared, his face lined with exhaustion. "They're still back in Witchaven," he said grimly, motioning toward a nearby tent where his sons lay. "I've done what I can here, but I can't take that many. They're holding out until you can bring them through."

Mallah's gaze hardened. "We mustn't delay."

Kiara stumbled, clutching the wall of the sanctuary as the first distant explosions sent vibrations through the ancient stone. The banshee's screams pierced the air, loud enough to make her teeth ache and her head spin. Disoriented, she pressed her hands over her ears, but the cries seemed to reverberate in her very bones. Aron steadied her, his strong arm around her shoulder, while Scarlett and Robyn crouched nearby, guiding a group of frightened children toward the safest area they could find.

"We have to keep moving!" Aron urged, his voice barely audible over the shrieks and distant detonations.

"I'm trying!" Kiara snapped, struggling to focus through the cacophony. Her heightened senses, normally her strength, were overwhelmed by the chaos. Every sound, every vibration, every distant cry for help crashed into her like a tidal wave.

Robyn looked up sharply, her eyes narrowing. "They'll come back. They have to."

The ground shook again as another blast echoed through the sanctuary. Kiara instinctively reached out, grabbing a fleeing child by the arm and pulling them to safety. Around them, the crumbling sanctuary was alive with activity—survivors scrambled to gather what they could carry, Ogma's previous portals slowly closing as others disappeared into them. But even as the sanctuary emptied, their group remained, waiting for the final portal.

The air in WItchaven grew thick with smoke as fires began to spread, consuming the sanctuary's outer edges. Just as it seemed all hope was lost, another portal shimmered into existence. Mallah and Ogma stepped through, their expressions grim and determined.

"Mallah!" Kiara called, her voice breaking as another wave of sound battered her. She stumbled forward, nearly collapsing as Aron and Rose rushed to support her.

Mallah's eyes scanned the room, taking in the chaos. "Quickly!" she commanded, motioning for the group to move toward the portal.

As the survivors began funneling through, the banshee's cries grew louder, almost unbearable. Kiara winced, her body trembling as the sounds pushed her to the edge of consciousness.

Ogma barked out directions, ensuring the last stragglers crossed safely. Mallah reached for Kiara, pulling her close and whispering urgently, "Stay with me. You're almost there."

Aron and Teddy helped the last stragglers through the portal, their steps hurried as flames began licking at the edges of the room. Mallah cast one final glance at Witchaven—her beloved sanctuary, now engulfed in chaos. A wave of grief passed over her face, but she turned back resolutely, stepping through the portal.

Ogma lingered just long enough to seal the gateway, his hands weaving intricate patterns in the air. The flames surged, the sanctuary collapsing behind him as the portal snapped shut with a flash of light.

On the other side, the chaos of Witchaven was replaced by the relative calm of Lemuria. The group stumbled into the camp, surrounded by the vibrant hues and strange serenity of their new home. Kiara collapsed to her knees, gasping for air as the world slowly settled into focus.

Mallah knelt beside her, her voice low but steady. "You made it. You're safe now."

Kiara's chest rose and fell heavily as she tried to ground herself amidst the overwhelming symphony of energy flooding her senses. Lemuria was unlike anything she had ever experienced. She couldn't see it in the conventional sense, but the vivid pulses of energy were almost tangible to her, resonating like harmonious vibrations through her body. She reached out hesitantly, feeling the invisible threads of life intertwining around her. The air was alive, shimmering with warmth and a rhythm that felt older than time itself.

"It's so… bright," Kiara whispered, though the light wasn't visible to her. "It hums. Everything hums."

Mallah stood beside her, her gaze sweeping over the land she hadn't seen in millennia. "Yes," she said, her voice tinged with reverence. "This is Lemuria—the cradle of ancient wisdom, a place where the earth itself sings. Every stone, every tree, every breath carries the memories of a time before division. Before fear."

Kiara tilted her head, absorbing Mallah's words as the energy around her seemed to respond, enveloping her like a gentle embrace. "It feels alive," she murmured.

"Because it is," Mallah replied, her eyes moist as she gazed upon the crystalline towers that rose gracefully from the earth, their surfaces shimmering like liquid light. "Lemuria was never truly gone. It hid, waiting for its moment to rise again, for its purpose to be fulfilled. Its truths, buried and forgotten, will guide us now."

Mallah paused, a faint smile curling her lips. She glanced at Skyler, who was diligently recording every word, every gesture. "Chapter 42," he said softly, to which Kiara understood the reference. Confused, Mallah furrowed her eyes, tilting her head slightly toward him.

"Ya know…the answer to life, the universe, and everything." He answered, smiling.

Kiara turned her head slightly, her brows furrowing. "Chapter 42!" she agreed with a giggle.

Mallah chuckled, the sound light despite the weight of their journey. "A reminder that even amidst chaos, the universe has its humor. Its meaning." Her gaze swept the luminous horizon. "And here, at last, we step into the heart of it."

Skyler lowered his camera for a moment, his voice filled with quiet wonder. "The heart of everything?"

"Perhaps," Mallah said with a knowing glint in her eyes. "Or perhaps just the beginning of truly understanding it."

Aron and Teddy approached, staring in awe as she extended a hand toward the distant structures. "This," Mallah began, her voice steady, "was a sanctuary of unity, where nature and creation worked as one. Those towers you see are not simply buildings—they are living crystals, grown and nurtured by the energy of this land. They store knowledge, power, and the hopes of an era lost to history. The water you hear rushing in the distance flows from the Lifespring, a source of pure energy that feeds this place, sustaining all who walk here."

Mallah turned to Kiara, her voice softening. "This is what Witchaven protected for so long—a place of balance, untouched by the wars and destruction of the surface world. It is a promise of what can be, should we have the strength to reclaim it."

Kiara's breath caught as she reached out again, feeling the currents of life swirling around her fingers. "It's… overwhelming."

Mallah nodded, her own composure breaking for a moment as she looked back toward where the portal had sealed. "I know. Saying goodbye to Witchaven wasn't easy, but it has fulfilled its purpose. Lemuria has waited in the shadows for this moment, just as we have. Now, it is time for it to rise, and for us to ensure its truth is never hidden again."

A familiar presence approached, and Kiara turned her head as Aron knelt beside her. His hand rested lightly on her arm, grounding her. "Are you okay?" he asked softly, his concern evident.

Kiara nodded, though her voice wavered. "I think so. It's just… so much."

Aron smiled faintly, squeezing her arm. "You did great back there. We all did."

Before she could reply, Aron stood, his expression shifting to something more resolute as he turned to Ogma. "I'm going with you," Aron said firmly. "Rose, Marcus and the others are still out there, I need to check on them and maybe help them get here safely. They need to know we are here and that this place really exists."

Ogma gave a single nod, his demeanor as calm and steady as always. "You'll need to move quickly. The longer they stay where they are, the greater the risk."

Aron turned back to Kiara, his voice gentle but determined. "Stay here, Kiara. Rest. You're safe now, and this is where you need to be. I'll make sure they get here."

Kiara frowned, her hand instinctively reaching for him. "Aron, wait—"

But he stepped back, shaking his head. "I'll be back. I promise."

He looked to Mallah, who placed a hand over her heart in acknowledgment. "Go with Ogma," Mallah said softly. "We'll be ready to receive them when the time comes."

With that, Aron turned, following Ogma as they prepared to open the next portal. Mallah lingered, watching them depart before turning back to Kiara. "Come," she said gently. "There is much to show you, and much to prepare."

-Chapter 46-

The Sanctuary of the First Flame

As the ten walked out of the now-deserted Wind Valley ARMY base, Marcus paused, turning back toward the entrance. He raised his hands, golden Vril energy sparking to life, and unleashed a controlled explosion. The mountainside groaned, debris collapsing and sealing off the entrance in a cascade of rubble. Kane, standing nearby, chuckled as he surveyed the now-hidden base.

"It's ironic," Kane muttered with a dry smile. "This is exactly how I found it years later."

The group continued walking, the first rays of dawn creeping over the eastern horizon. The snow glistened under the growing light, and for a moment, the world seemed calm—like a promise of something better.

Dexter, still nursing his injured shoulder, broke the silence. "Before we leave, we need to talk about what comes next. If this gets out, it could cause chaos."

Kane nodded, his usual smugness tempered by an air of gravity. "Agreed. The truth must come out, but it needs to be framed correctly. People need to know about the experiments, the military's collaboration with the OAS, and Ivyg's manipulation. But they also need to understand that many of those involved—on both sides—were victims themselves."

Marcus stepped forward, his voice resolute despite the weight he carried. "I'll take responsibility for the Pulse. It wasn't intentional, but that doesn't change the harm it caused. People deserve to know the truth, even if it's messy."

Kane placed a hand on Marcus's shoulder, a rare gesture of camaraderie. "We all bear the weight of what's happened, Marcus. None of this was done alone. We've all played a part in this long war—some knowingly, others not."

Kathleen and Linda exchanged glances. Kathleen spoke first. "We'll tell the story. The real one. Not just about what went wrong, but about the people caught in it—the ones who didn't know, who didn't have a choice."

Linda nodded, her voice softer but equally determined. "People need to see the humanity in this. It wasn't all monsters and villains. It never is."

Dexter sighed, his tone pragmatic. "I'll handle the authorities. Someone has to keep the lid on this long enough for you all to do…whatever it is you need to do. But let's get our stories straight. This is bigger than all of us."

The group stood in a solemn circle, a shared understanding binding them together. Each carried their burdens, but for the first time, it felt like they were walking toward a future they could shape.

As they approached the base's perimeter, a small car rolled up the driveway, stopping abruptly in front of them. A man stepped out, looking both cautious and intrigued.

"Morton Kane?" the man called out, to which Kane responded by raising his arm up.

"Yeah, that's me."

"Oliver Kross," the man introduced himself. "I got your message to be here at this exact location at this exact time. That was a lot of money you spent to make sure I showed."

Kane stepped forward, his demeanor calm and commanding. "Just Kane," he corrected. "And I appreciate your punctuality, Mr. Kross."

Oliver reached into his coat pocket and pulled out a weathered leather-bound journal. The edges were frayed, and the cover bore an emblem that none of them recognized—a striking symbol of intertwined serpents encircling a starburst.

"This journal," Oliver began, his voice tinged with disbelief, "you gave this to me over twenty years ago. At the time, I thought you were insane. But now…" He hesitated, flipping it open to reveal meticulously written entries in Kane's unmistakable handwriting. "It predicted everything. Dates, locations, even people I would meet. And it all came true."

Linda leaned closer, her eyes wide as she caught a glimpse of the pages. "These entries… they reference us," she murmured, pointing to a line that read: Linda Baker will arrive at Wellville on August 10th, carrying the energy needed to reignite the path.

Kathleen's eyes scanned the pages, landing on a passage that read: Kathleen O'Brian will pen the truths that reshape the narrative, helping the world understand the burden shared by the innocent.

Marcus stepped forward, his jaw tight as he studied the journal. "This isn't just foresight. You've been orchestrating this for decades," he accused, though his voice carried more awe than anger.

Kane allowed himself a small, satisfied smile. "Not orchestrating, Marcus. I like to think of it more like guiding; planting seeds in the right places at the right times. Ensuring that when the moment came, all of you were ready."

"But how could you know?" Linda pressed. "How could you possibly predict all this?"

Kane tapped the side of his head. "The Nexus Consciousness isn't just a place, Linda. It's a map of infinite possibilities. I've spent lifetimes learning to navigate its currents. What you see as predictions, I see as the inevitable paths converging."

Oliver flipped to the last page of the journal and held it up. "This was the part that convinced me to come today." The entry read: On this day, at this location, Oliver Kross will arrive with the answers they need to build what's next.

Marcus stared at Kane, his expression conflicted. "You went back in time. You made sure everything happened exactly as it needed to."

Kane met his gaze, his voice calm but resolute. "I didn't just go back in time. I went back to ensure you would all have the tools and knowledge to change the future." He paused, his smile fading as he grew serious. "And now it's up to us to use them wisely."

Kane smirked, but there was no malice in it. "I prefer to think of it as strategic preparation. Oliver, your expertise will be invaluable. We're bringing technology from the future to rebuild something critical. Are you in?"

Marcus stood near the remnants of the Wellville base, his gaze lost in the distant horizon. The crisp morning air was still heavy with the aftermath of their chaotic escape. His cell phone buzzed in his hand, snapping him out of his thoughts.

"Aron?" Marcus answered, his voice steady but cautious.

"Yeah, it's me," Aron replied, his voice carrying an edge of exhaustion. "I'm calling from Ogma's place in Oregon."

Marcus straightened, immediately alert. "What's going on? Are you okay? The others watched with intrigue.

"Is everyone safe now?" Marcus pressed, his heart pounding.

Marcus felt a wave of relief wash over him. "Thank God," he muttered, then added, "Thank you for letting me know. How are you holding up?"

"Got it," Marcus replied. Marcus turned back to the group, who had been anxiously waiting. His expression was a mix of relief and urgency as he addressed them. "I just heard from Aron. Witchaven was attacked, but Ogma and Mallah got everyone out safely to Lemuria—including Kiara."

A ripple of relief spread through the group, though Oliver Kross looked visibly stunned. "Kiara? My daughter?" Oliver asked, his voice almost a whisper. "I haven't been able to reach her in days!"

Marcus nodded. "Yes. She's safe."

Kane, who had been standing silently, stepped forward. "There's much to discuss," he said smoothly, his tone almost casual. "But not here. Ogma is on his way, and when he arrives, he'll take us where we need to go. Let's go see your daughter, shall we?"

Seconds later, the air shimmered near the group, and a swirling portal began to take shape. From within, a tall, cloaked figure with curved horns stepped through—Ogma. His imposing presence was both awe-inspiring and otherworldly. He gave the group a slight wave, his hand moved elegantly, before turning back to the portal.

"Time to go," Kane said, his voice commanding yet calm. He gestured for Marcus, Clarice, Cesaro, Rose, and Oliver to step forward.

Linda and Kathleen watched in awe, unable to hide their excitement as the group began walking toward the portal. Ogma stood on the other side, holding it open with an air of effortless power.

Kane turned back to Linda and Kathleen, his expression composed. "I'll be in touch," he said with a faint smile. "When the time is right, you'll have the interview of a lifetime."

Both women exchanged thrilled glances, their faces lighting up at the promise.

Kane gave them a slight nod, then turned and walked through the portal. The swirling energy rippled once, twice, and then vanished completely, leaving only silence in its wake.

Just as the portal disappeared, the sound of approaching sirens echoed in the distance. Federal and state troopers arrived on the scene, their vehicles pulling up to the base's gate. Linda and Kathleen exchanged knowing looks before stepping forward to meet the officers, their expressions calm yet resolute.

They had a story to tell—and a promise to keep.

Back in Lemuria, Kane and the group stepped through the shimmering portal, a wave of warmth and light washed over them. Emerging into a place where nature and ancient technology harmonized seamlessly. Crystalline towers rose from the ground, shimmering with iridescent light, and lush greenery intertwined with gleaming pathways of polished stone. The air hummed with energy, vibrant and alive.

Kane glanced around, his composed demeanor softening as he saw the others waiting for them. Kiara stood near Mallah, her energy vibrant despite the recent chaos. Oliver Kross, wide-eyed and breathless, looked as though he were seeing a dream made real.

Without hesitation, Kane strode forward, his usually stoic demeanor softening as he embraced Kiara briefly. "You're safe," he murmured, his voice unusually tender.

Kiara nodded, her energy steady yet quietly reverent. She sensed the weight of his words, the layered emotions behind them—relief, determination, and something deeper that only he fully understood. "Thanks to all of you," she replied softly, her gratitude genuine.

Kane then turned to Oliver Kross, his sharp eyes meeting the scientist's gaze as he clasped his shoulder. "And here we are, Doctor Kross. Welcome to Lemuria."

Oliver stared in awe, his breath catching as he took in the surreal landscape around them. "This is… beyond anything I imagined," he whispered, his voice trembling with disbelief and wonder. For a moment, his analytical mind faltered, unable to process the magnificence before him.

Kiara stepped toward her father, her presence grounding him. "Dad?!?" she cried out, to which he nodded as he embraced his daughter.

"It's real, Dad," she said gently, reaching out to him. "I have so much to tell you."

Overwhelmed, his arms wrapping tightly around his daughter. "I thought I'd lost you," he said, his voice breaking. "I didn't think I'd get another chance to tell you how proud I am of you, Kiara."

Aron, standing nearby, watched the emotional reunion with a small, proud smile. As the two parted, Kiara, already knowing he was there, reached for him next, her expression both grateful and curious. Oliver followed her gaze, his eyes narrowing slightly as he assessed the young man.

"Dad," Kiara said, gesturing toward him, "this is Aron. He's been helping me... a lot."

Aron stepped forward, extending his hand. "Dr. Kross, it's an honor. Your daughter is... extraordinary. She's already helped more people than she realizes."

Oliver shook Aron's hand, his grip firm but his gaze softening. "She gets it from her mother," he said with a faint smile. Then, looking back at Kiara, he added, "But it sounds like you and I have a lot to talk about—especially about these newfound abilities of yours, huh?"

Kiara nodded, her expression a mix of anticipation and understanding. Before she could say anything, Oliver's eyes squinted, and he leaned back slightly, taking in the sight of his daughter and Aron, both streaked with soot and glistening patches of unidentifiable goo that clung to their clothes and skin.

"What on God's green earth is all over you two?" Oliver asked, his tone equal parts concerned and incredulous. "Is that... ash? And... is that green slime?"

Aron glanced down at himself, grimacing as he flicked a glob of sticky, iridescent goo off his sleeve. "Yeah, uh, about that..." he started, rubbing the back of his neck sheepishly. "There was... an incident."

Kiara tilted her head toward him with a smirk. "He means he ran face-first into the remains of the Dark Market. Literally."

"Ran?" Oliver raised an eyebrow, his voice dripping with disbelief. "Were you trying to negotiate with it?"

"Not exactly," Aron muttered, shooting Kiara a playful glare. "More like... dismantle it. With style."

Kiara rolled her eyes, brushing a streak of ash off her arm. "It was less 'style' and more 'Aron vs. a very sticky explosion.'"

Oliver groaned, pinching the bridge of his nose before looking between the two of them. "You're telling me my daughter is not only surviving explosions but apparently accessorizing with the aftermath?"

Aron shrugged, his lips twitching into a grin. "Hey, it's not just slime. It's premium-grade otherworldly goo."

Kiara snorted. "You're not helping."

Oliver sighed, shaking his head as a smile tugged at his lips despite himself. "You two are going to give me an aneurysm," he muttered, rubbing his temples before wrapping an arm around Kiara and pulling her close.

From a distance, Kane smirked faintly, the momentary levity not lost on him. Even in the midst of monumental change, some things—like family dynamics—remained endearingly human. Only he seemed to grasp the full significance of this moment—the delicate interplay of destinies now converging in Lemuria, goo and all.

Kane's gaze shifted, and his expression softened further as he locked eyes with Mallah. She stepped forward, regal and composed, but her smile betrayed deep emotion.

"Mallah," Kane said, his voice quieter now, friendly, almost lovingly. They hold centuries of history between them.

"Kane," she replied, opening her arms. The two embraced, their connection unspoken but palpable to everyone present. It wasn't just a reunion—but clearly a mending of old wounds.

As they stepped back, Marcus approached Kane. For a moment, there was hesitation, but then Marcus extended his hand. Kane accepted it, and Marcus gripped it firmly.

"I forgive you," Marcus said, his voice steady but laden with emotion. "And… Thank you. For everything."

Kane nodded, his expression unreadable, but a flicker of something genuine crossed his face. "It's good to see you've grown into the leader I knew you could be."

Meanwhile, Skyler and Teddy caught Mallah's attention. They spoke briefly, their words lost in the hum of activity around them, before Mallah raised her voice to address the group. "Everyone," she began, her tone firm yet kind, "it has been suggested—and I agree—that we share what happened in Witchaven, as well as our arrival here in Lemuria. The world needs to know."

There was a murmur of agreement from the group. Marcus, standing beside Clarice, stepped forward. "If it's alright, I'd like to say a few words after the stream."

Mallah nodded. "Of course."

After the video of Witchaven's destruction finished playing, Skyler signaled the live stream had begun, Skyler directed the camera toward Marcus, who stood at the forefront of the group. His posture was steady, his voice calm but resolute.

"Hello, my name is Marcus Kydd," he began. "I was recruited into the Order of the Ancient Serpent at a very young age—an organization that operates in the shadows under many names. I was taught to use my special abilities, trained alongside others like me. Before the Pulse, we were few. After the Pulse, it appears there are many more out there among us now. Which is why so many are seeing beyond the veil that has been weakened in recent days. And they need better guidance than most of us ever had."

He paused, looking directly into the camera. "I was tricked into causing the Pulse from within the Hollow Earth. I live with that every day. But I've also learned to see it for what it really was—a catalyst of change. The world is in chaos right now, but chaos is often where true change begins. I've come to realize that maybe the Pulse was meant to happen... so we could finally see the truth. So we could remember who we are, where we come from, and what truly matters."

He gestured behind him, the camera panning to reveal the breath-taking expanse of Lemuria. "Look at this place. A harmony of beauty, ancient technology, and wisdom. A place like this should inspire us to want more than the lives we've been conditioned to accept. We don't have to live under oppression or work just to survive."

Turning back to the camera, Marcus's voice grew stronger. "That's not living, that's just surviving. I don't know how yet, but I will help burn the old systems to the ground. And I'm coming for the man behind it all. Some know him as Enlil. Some as Set. Some know him as Hades. I know him as Ivyg Semagial Wistroc, Grand Emissary of the OAS, first and foremost, and I assure you he is the mastermind behind all these crimes. We will bring him to justice and end his reign of terror. We are the Champions of Lemuria!"

The group around him erupted in agreement. Kane stepped forward, lifting his newly enhanced prosthetic hand, the technology gleaming. "You have my support," he said firmly.

One by one, others raised their hands or voices in agreement, affirming their commitment to the fight ahead, including Mallah, who stepped into view, her voice calm yet resolute. "This is what Lemuria stands for—renewal, hope, and unity. Let it remind us that a better world is possible."

Marcus stepped forward, the intensity of his earlier speech giving way to a softer, more vulnerable tone. "Before I burn anything else to the ground, I have one thing I need to do," he said, turning to Clarice.

She blinked, confused, until Marcus dropped to one knee and reached for her hand. "Clarice Murphy, you've stood by me through everything—the chaos, the uncertainty, the danger. If we're building a new world, I can't imagine it without you by my side. Will you marry me?"

Clarice's hands flew to her mouth as tears streamed down her cheeks. She nodded fervently, choking out a teary, "Yes!"

Cheers erupted from the crowd, and for a moment, the tension of their journey was replaced by unfiltered joy. Marcus stood and pulled Clarice into a tight embrace as those around them clapped and shouted their congratulations.

As the live stream ended, the camera lingered on the group standing together, united against the challenges ahead. Lemuria shimmered in the background, a beacon of what could be, and the scene faded into the promise of a new chapter for humanity.

Meanwhile, on the other side of the world, Ivyg sat in his private chamber, his steely gaze fixed on the live stream playing on a massive monitor. Watching as Skyler's camera panned across the stunning landscape of Lemuria, punctuated by Marcus's triumphant declaration of rebellion.

Just as Skyler wrapped up the stream, he queued up an unexpected touch: Good Thing by the Fine Young Cannibals began to play in the background, its upbeat tempo adding a cheeky final note to the broadcast. The stream cut out, leaving Ivyg seething in his seat.

For a moment, his face remained eerily calm, but then his hand shot out, sending a crystal tumbler of whiskey flying into the wall, shattering it into pieces. "How dare they!" he roared, his composed demeanor cracking wide open. "How dare they humiliate me like this?!"

A knock sounded at the door, and one of his aides stepped in, his expression anxious. "Sir, stock prices in several of our key holdings are plummeting. Investors are calling—they're demanding answers."

Ivyg's jaw clenched so tightly it looked as though it might snap. He turned slowly, his eyes blazing with fury. "Shut them all up," he growled. "I don't care what it takes. Spin whatever story you have to—this is a temporary setback, nothing more."

"Yes, sir," the aide stammered, retreating quickly as Ivyg paced the room like a caged animal, his mind churning with rage and the need for retribution.

As the music's echo faded in his mind, Ivyg's focus sharpened. This affront would not go unanswered. "Let them bask in their moment," he hissed to himself. "Because I'll burn their precious Lemuria to ash before they ever see their revolution take hold. I will take my revenge by killing each and every one of these… Champions."

"Oh, my God!" Kiara kind of shouted out. "You guys are going to get MARRIED?!?

I got so caught up in jumping around the globe trying to save the world, I forgot that you guys were a long-term couple. I have barely had the chance to get to know you, Clarice. I spent so much time with Marcus in his mind that I am just now realizing how much I've missed out on with you guys."

"Good Thing" by the Fine Young Cannibals played on the Marcus Kydd soundtrack.

Kiara's two best friends Robyn and Scarlett caught back up with them.

"We've been told that the Champions have returned to Earth once again." Robyn said to her friend.

"Mallah says that we are the Champions." Scarlett added in for good measure. "Nobody starts singing that Queen song, though, please. Aron started out like he was going to sing the song anyways. Scarlett gave him a gentle swat and the evil eye for a second. "You are meant to lead us." Robyn told Kiara in a more serious tone of voice.

"I don't know about that or what's going to happen." Kiara confessed. "I do know that we are all going to have to work together if we are ever going to stop Ivyg and his forces of evil."

"One triumph does not mean we have won the war." Aron interjected. "We still have a long way to go before we are done."

"We seem to have won today, however so I say we work hard and celebrate equally hard, but first… it seems we have a wedding to plan!" Kiara shouted out, jumping up and down with Clarice, Scarlett, and Robyn. Even her own friends had never seen her get this giddy before, downright excited even.

"I feel like we're missing the party." The group heard as Cesaro and

Rose rejoined them after spending some time looking around at the base camp that had been set up within some old ruins that still held their test of time, even underwater for many millennia. Cesaro and Marcus and Aron all bro-hugged it out.

"So…?" Rose joined in with the women. "Let's talk about this wedding, huh? He likes it so he wants to put a ring on it."

"I want to have our wedding here, on this island of Lemuria, here with all of our friends." Clarice turned around and told her soon-to-be husband.

"Let's do it right now, how about right here?" Marcus asked, smiling, knowing that they had been talking about this moment for some time now and one of the biggest hang-ups was always the venue. He loved her and had since the moment he met her back in college, but it was difficult how picky she had become about where she wanted the most important day of her life to be. He felt a huge sense of relief that this had been decided now after talking about it for so long.

"Okay, we can go find a spot together…The only question left is Rivendell or the Shire?" Marcus smiled big.

"Ooh, I love when you talk nerdy to me." She said, giving him a light kiss. "We're only doing this once, so I'm going to say: BOTH!"

Cesaro wasn't into all the fantasy nerd stuff that his friends Marcus and Clarice were, but this wasn't about him, it was about them. If this is what they wanted, then he himself was going to do everything he could to make it happen. Clarice danced around with the other women, elated. It was finally going to happen, her dream wedding to the man of her dreams was coming true.

The guys stood back and watched. Cesaro pulled out a joint from his pocket and sparked it up, pulling in a big drag of the smoke into his lungs. Now normally for celebrations, Juan Cesaro liked to ball out and go big. Right now, at this moment, they didn't have any champagne for a celebration toast. No booze at all. That just wasn't right, and he only now just remembered about this hidden hooch he had been keeping inside his jacket's inner pocket all this time. He knew that Marcus wasn't smoking as much, but now was the time to forget all the rest of the world for just a few moments. After all, they were on an untamed island. Cesaro passed the doobie to Marcus, who passed it to Aron. Neither had smoked with him since college. Now in Tamil that felt like so long ago, almost in another life, it seemed. Every one of them had grown and matured so much in the last couple of weeks. The world had changed. Yet somehow, they were all hopeful, because that's what the world needed most in this moment: HOPE.

That hope keeps us alive, revitalized, and human. The marriage of Marcus Kydd and Clarice Murphy held a prime example of how folks needed to hold onto that hope, hold onto those friendships, and hold onto love. Nothing would be easy. They all knew that.

Upon noticing Rajneel Patel, Brad Moses, and Sanjay Patel, Marcus rushed over and hugged his former professors from SWSU, also members of the order, who had accompanied him to the Hollow Earth and were recovered by Mallah and her team, before requiring their assistance in the migration of Witchaven. By technicality they were not done with the Order. None of them were. Soon it would be time to officially resign from the OAS, and when it happened, it would be explosive. Marcus had done his best to make Rajneel feel welcome among them, also giving him a hug, but there was a sort of resistance. He could not put his finger on what was going on, but he also did not know what this man had gone through in the future. Trauma plagued this tormented man from his life, his time spent in the future dystopian timeline with Kane, who was now off with Mallah playing brave new world explorers of a land they only remembered from their childhood long, long ago.

As the women came over, done with their dancing, the doob continued to be passed around. Cesaro excused himself from the others and went over to have a nice little chat with Ogma. He put his arm around the big magical fella and as the two were walking away from the others, it seemed they were having a nice chat. No one was sure about what those two would be talking about. The last time Ogma saw Cesaro he got the middle finger bird on his way out of the pocket dimension and into Mexico just before their descent into the Hollow Earth. He did, after all, go into his Chupacabra form and try to attack both Ogma and DJ Yeti, and would have if not for Marcus' intervention. He had hated his friend for doing that but now understood. Cesaro couldn't stop thinking about the wedding. Marcus and Clarice deserved something spectacular, something that honored their love and the journey they'd endured together. He couldn't shake the feeling that this was his chance to give his best friend a moment of pure happiness, free from the chaos of their lives.

Lost in thought, he didn't notice Rose approaching until she was standing beside him. "You look deep in thought," she said, her tone teasing as she leaned casually against the table.

"Just thinking about the wedding," Cesaro replied, glancing at her with a small smile. "Marcus and Clarice deserve something amazing, and I'm going to make sure they get it."

Rose's eyebrow quirked. "You're taking this pretty seriously."

"Of course, I am," Cesaro said earnestly. "Marcus is like a brother to me. This wedding isn't just about them; it's about all of us. After everything we've been through, we could use a reminder of what we're fighting for. I'm grateful he has been willing to forgive me for trying to kill him in the name of the Order."

Rose nodded, her expression softening. "That's actually really sweet that you two have made up and decided to be friends again."

Cesaro chuckled. "Don't tell anyone. I have a reputation to maintain."

"Big pro-football athlete image." Rose smirked. "I get it. You're famous. Don't worry, your secret's safe with me. But, if you're planning to pull off the wedding of the century, you're going to need some help."

Cesaro tilted his head, intrigued. "Are you offering?"

"Why not?" Rose shrugged. "I'm not much of a planner, but I'm good with details. And hey, I'm great at bossing people around."

"I'll take all the help I can get," Cesaro admitted. "You sure you want to spend your time on this and not be somewhere else doing something different?"

"I've had a time with you so far…" Rose leaned in slightly, her voice lowering. "I think spending time with you could be… interesting."

Cesaro's lips twitched into a smirk. "Interesting, huh? That what you looking for?"

"Maybe," Rose said, her gaze locking with his, meeting him with a little wink. "Or maybe I just want to see if you're as charming as you think you are."

Without thinking, Cesaro leaned closer, the tension between them thick enough to cut. "Guess there's only one way to find out."

Rose didn't move away. Instead, she grinned and said, "You better be ready to work if I'm helping you. No slacking."

"Don't worry," Cesaro replied, his voice softening. "I'm all in."

The moment lingered, and before either of them could think twice, Rose closed the gap, pressing her lips to his in a kiss that was equal parts bold and slightly unexpected. Cesaro responded immediately, his hand gently brushing her cheek. When they finally pulled apart, Rose smirked, her cheeks slightly flushed. "Well, that's one way to seal the deal."

Cesaro laughed, feeling lighter than he had in months. "Guess I should be thanking Marcus and Clarice for giving us an excuse to spend some time together."

Rose chuckled. "You better not mess this wedding up, Juan Cesaro. We've got a reputation to uphold now."

"Trust me," Cesaro said, his voice filled with warmth and confidence. "It's going to be perfect."

As they walked off together, Rose wrapped her hand around his and Cesaro couldn't help but feel that this was the start of something unexpected—but maybe exactly what he needed.

-Chapter 47-

The Fire We Chose

The dim lights of the generators offered a soft glow over the Lemurian settlement, perfectly harmonizing with the mingling chatter of voices and the soft clinking of dishes as camps began to settle for the night. String lights cast a warm, golden shimmer across the gathering, lending the scene an almost festive ambiance.

It was a rare moment of peace amidst the chaos of their journey, and the Champions stood in a loose semicircle near one of the central tents to bid farewell to Oliver Kross.

Oliver's coat bore the signs of travel, his sleeves dusted, and face lined with the weariness of a man who'd seen too much in a single day. Yet his eyes were fixed on Kiara, shining with pride.

"I hate to say goodbye again so soon," he said, voice steady despite the lump in his throat. "But I've got to get back to your mother and fill her in on… well, on all of this."

He gestured vaguely around him, encompassing the surreal atmosphere of Lemuria.

Kiara stepped forward, her throat tight as she hugged him. "Thank you for coming, Dad. It means more than I can say."

"I'm so proud of the woman you've become," Oliver said, hugging her tightly before pulling back, his hand resting on her shoulder. "You don't need to thank me. Just take care of yourself. And don't worry about us—we'll be okay."

Oliver pulled back from Kiara, studying her face one last time before shifting his gaze to the man just a few steps behind her.

Aron stood quietly, hands in his pockets, his posture respectful but not stiff. Just… present. Solid. Oliver gave him a long look—the kind that weighed more than it seemed—before reaching out and clasping his hand in a firm shake.

Oliver's eyes dropped to the smears of dried sludge caked along Kiara's sleeves, then followed the trail up into her hair and over to Aron—his neck and jacket streaked with the same charred green and purple goo, cracked and flaking at the edges like it had been cooked into the fibers.

He squinted. "Please tell me that was a paintball match and not something that used to be alive."

Aron managed a tired grin.

Oliver gave a slow, dubious nod. "Let me guess—protecting my daughter?"

Aron hesitated, then said quietly, "Not just her. A lot of people's daughters."

That gave Oliver pause. He held Aron's gaze a few seconds longer, then exhaled and nodded. "Then on behalf of all of us fathers… thank you."

Aron's face turned red as he nodded. Oliver patted him on the shoulder, then turned back to Kiara. "I was gonna ask him to take care of you," he said, glancing back at Aron with a lopsided smile. "But after hearing that? Poor guy looks like he might need you to take care of him."

Kiara smiled, pleasantly surprised, and then gave a solemn little nod. "I will," she promised.

Satisfied, Oliver straightened up, already shifting into dad-mode escape velocity. "Alright. I'm out of here before I start crying or lecturing. Or both."

Kiara reached for one more hug. "Safe travels, Dad."

As Oliver turned and disappeared into the darkness, escorted by Ogma, a voice floated in from the side.

"He's not wrong, you know."

Scarlett stepped into view, arms crossed, her expression somewhere between amused and approving. "You both look like you crawled out of a swamp, rolled through a fire, and then got sneezed on by a radioactive jellyfish."

Kiara blinked. "That's… disturbingly accurate."

"That's because it's true," Scarlett said, jerking a thumb over her shoulder. "We found a set of geothermal tubs earlier. Natural pools carved into the cliffside—cascade down like hot waterfalls, but you still get your own little pod. Lemurians really nailed the sacred spa thing." She reached into her satchel and pressed a glowing stone into Aron's palm. "This'll light your way."

"Thank you," Kiara said gratefully.

"Oh! And swing by the yellow canvas tent," Scarlett added, already backing away. "Junel's got soap that smells like citrus and lavender—and don't forget fresh clothes. You'll thank me later."

Kiara furrowed her brow. "Shit!" She groaned. "I forgot I'm still in the dress from Elysium and totally forgot to grab my bag. I was expecting to go back to our room!"

Aron glanced her way. "You want to swing by your tent?"

She hesitated. "Do I have one?"

"There weren't enough for everyone to have one, so men got their own, but women and children are sharing…so I put a cot for you in with us!" Scarlett explained.

Aron's brow lifted. "Oh. Someone told me earlier they brought my stuff from Witchaven—I've gotta grab some clothes anyway. I'm sure I have something that would fit you…"

Kiara smiled softly. "Thanks. That would help."

Then, without a word, they nodded and headed off to get cleaned up, following the glowing path into the darkness. As they walked, the faint hum of the camp faded behind them, replaced by the soothing sound of bubbling water and the gentle warmth of steam rising from the pools ahead.

It was a brief respite—a moment of calm in a world that offered precious little of it—and one they both desperately needed. Above their heads, the heavens opened in quiet splendor, the Milky Way galaxy stretching across the sky like a whispered promise.

Back at camp, Marcus and Clarice sat across from Morton Kane in a quieter corner of Lemuria's newly formed dining pavilion. The remnants of a surprisingly hearty meal lingered on their plates, thanks to Chef Cheung Wei—another former OAS member who had awakened in Witchaven after venturing with Kane and his team into Agartha, deep within the Hollow Earth.

He had since been welcomed by Nan, the unofficial culinary head of Witchaven, a woman with no title—just a deep love for feeding people. Together, with the help of the children and the Hokuten, they had managed to scavenge a bounty of vegetables to complement what had been brought in over the last two days.

Under the warm glow of bioluminescent lanterns that lined the soft curves of the village, the settlement was beginning to wind down, basking in a rare, intimate sense of peace.

Clarice folded her arms and leaned forward, her voice edged with curiosity. "So, Kane. How exactly did you manage to coordinate all of this? I mean, not just your arrival here, but the years of planning, saving Kiara—everything."

Marcus nodded, resting his elbows on the table. "Yeah, I'd love to hear the full story. You've been pulling strings for decades, haven't you?"

Kane smiled faintly, swirling the wine in his glass before taking a measured sip. "You could say that," he replied. "But the truth is far more complicated."

Clarice arched her brow. "Try us."

Kane chuckled and set the glass down. "Very well. Let's start with the part you'll find most unbelievable. I've had the advantage of speaking with… myself."

Clarice blinked. "Excuse me?"

Marcus tilted his head. "Like… a version of you from the future?"

"Exactly," Kane replied. "Many years ago, in the timeline we were trying to correct, I received a visitor—an older, more weathered version of myself. He explained everything: the whisperers, the pandemic, the Hades Virus, the nuclear holocaust, and the eventual rise of Ivyg's tyranny."

Marcus leaned back, letting out a low whistle. "That's… a lot to process."

"It was," Kane admitted. "But he—or rather, I—came with a clear message. There were three individuals who would be key to preventing that future: Clarice Murphy, Marcus Kydd, and Kiara Kross. He made me repeat those names until they were etched into my mind."

Clarice exchanged a glance with Marcus. "So, you knew about us… before we ever met."

Kane nodded. "Indeed, but it wasn't just about knowing who you were. I was given instructions on how to guide specific events subtly, without revealing too much. That's why I planted clues—things like the notes and seemingly coincidental encounters."

Clarice frowned. "But why all the secrecy? Why not just come out and tell us everything?"

"Because Ivyg has been manipulating this timeline for his own ends as well," Kane explained. "If he suspected even for a moment that I had this knowledge, he'd alter events to counter me. My advantage was in staying one step ahead while keeping my true intentions hidden."

Marcus rubbed his chin thoughtfully. "And what about the Hollow Earth? You mentioned needing to rebuild your machine there."

Kane's smile grew slightly wistful. "Ah, the machine. Yes, it was a key component of our fight against Ivyg, but it wasn't my machine… it was a nexus hub that I didn't have access to be Ogma did. But I couldn't approach Ogma myself to retrieve the necessary information to get there—my presence would have been too conspicuous. That's why I needed you, Marcus. You're the only one I trusted who could earned his trust too, that wouldn't have raised alarms."

"Ogma," Marcus muttered. "That guy's… interesting, to say the least."

Kane chuckled. "He has his quirks, but his knowledge is invaluable. Without him, the prophecies foretold by the Oracles could not be fulfilled."

Clarice tilted her head. "The Oracles? What do they have to do with this?"

Kane's expression grew serious. "The Oracles hold the most ancient knowledge of our shared histories—of Lemuria, Atlantis, the Veil, and the Nexus itself, and beyond into the stars. They are the keepers of truth, and their guidance is essential if we're to succeed."

Marcus leaned forward, intrigued. "So, you've spoken to them?"

Kane's gaze turned reflective, his usually sharp eyes softening. "The Oracles, yes" he said simply. "They didn't just tell me everything I needed to know—they helped me create the conditions to bring it all together."

Marcus frowned. "Wait—you're saying you didn't just receive a prophecy. You engineered it?"

Kane leaned back, his mechanical arm resting on his knee. "Precisely. The Oracles and I devised the vision that my younger self in this time-line was meant to receive. Without their help, none of this would have aligned as it did."

Clarice tilted her head, incredulous. "You got the Oracles—these ancient, all-seeing beings—to go along with your plan? How?"

Kane allowed himself a small, proud smile. "With a great deal of effort and humility, not that it was easy, but it helps that we go way back and that I have done some favors for them. I had to earn their trust and convince them that the threads of destiny needed to be rewoven. That the only way to prevent the annihilation of everything was to guide myself—this version of myself—toward the right path.”

Marcus leaned forward, intrigued. “So, you didn’t just ask for their help. You gave them the exact message to deliver?”

Kane nodded. “Yes and no. They know more than I do—always. But when we’re in alignment and I offer something that improves the probability of success, they listen. I told them what my past self needed to see, what he needed to believe: a vision of destruction, of volcanic eruptions claiming Heraklion and Pompeii, all tied to the prophecy of three individuals—a man with fire, a woman with ice, and a blind seer who could bridge worlds. That vision was enough to set everything into motion.”

Clarice narrowed her eyes. “And they just went along with it? They didn’t question your motives?”

Kane’s expression darkened slightly. “Oh, they questioned everything—or rather, they made me question everything. They don’t deal in blind trust. I had to place my hand in theirs, allow them to see my intentions—the good, the bad, and the ugly. Let’s just say they saw enough to believe that my cause was worth their cooperation.”

Marcus tilted his head, intrigued. “So, what happened? What did they say?”

Kane leaned forward, his voice steady but tinged with gravity. “They warned me that rewriting destiny is not without consequence. That even if we succeed, the forces we awaken will be beyond our control.”

Clarice folded her arms. “And what exact forces are we awakening?”

“The grid from which we accessed in the Hollow Earth,” Kane replied, his tone heavy. “...which, unbeknownst to us at the time, served as both a central hub and a cloaking mechanism. It maintained the Veil over Earth—something Mallah and a few others understood better than I ever did, though there were reasons for that we won’t unpack right now.” Point is, this Veil concealed the true nature of reality, shielding the multiversal connection point known as the Nexus.”

He paused, swirling the wine in his glass before continuing. “The Nexus isn’t a place, exactly. It’s more like a universal conduit—an energetic circulatory system linking timelines, densities, even galaxies. Everything flows through it.

When we planned that mission into Hollow Earth, none of us fully understood what we were walking into. The Nexus was cloaked—hidden behind a dimensional blind spot. And because each of us came with our own beliefs, our own motives… things got messy.

The explosion was the catalyst—sending me, or most of me anyway, through the nexus to the dystopian timeline while creating enough of a shift in Earth's axis to force a recalibration of the entire field. And that's when the Veil fell, because 'The Nexus' always gives those who access it what they need."

Marcus leaned forward, his brow furrowed. "So, we exposed the Nexus without realizing it?"

Kane nodded solemnly. "And that changed everything. Now, with the Veil gone, Kiara is the only one who can safely activate the grid. She can align it from Telos. But who knows where that is, and there's more at stake. Tapping into the Nexus stirs more than just energy—if done incorrectly, it disrupts balance. The Oracles warned that the fall of the Veil, the awakening of the Nexus, and the eventual collapse of Ivyg's regime would draw attention. Power abhors a vacuum. Whatever force steps in next... may not be better."

Clarice's voice was quiet. "But Ivyg is still alive in this timeline... And you still went through with it?"

Kane exhaled, his gaze distant. "Not in the timeline I came from. There, he was already gone. But here? I was never told if he would fall, or when, or by whose hand. Maybe that's the point. All I know is, my role was to set the stage—to ensure the right people came together at the right time. And something tells me... that's where Aron and Kiara come in."

Clarice's expression softened. "So, we are all the key to this?"

Kane nodded. "The Oracles said the two of you would initiate the fall of the Veil from within the Hollow Earth. And she—Kiara—would awaken the Nexus from Telos. Aron's role? They were vague, but I knew there was something about him when I tried to recruit him. I've learned to pay attention to energetic patterns. Beyond the fact that I recognize his amulet as my brother's, the deeper he's drawn in, the clearer it becomes that he's not just meant to protect her. He's here to evolve with her. Possibly even to face what's coming."

Marcus leaned back, a mix of awe and apprehension on his face. "Well, I'm glad you had faith in us and all, but don't count us out yet...

Aron and Kiara won't be doing it alone."

Kane smirked. "Faith? More like calculated trust. You've clearly earned your places in this story, Marcus. Clarice. Each of you has. But don't mistake my confidence for certainty. This is a gamble—one I hope we all survive…and I'm confident having you two there when they need you will help ensure that."

Kiara and Aron walked in comfortable silence through the glowing paths of Lemuria, the light from bioluminescent flora illuminating their way. After a while, she turned to him, her curiosity breaking through.

"What happened back there?" she asked softly. "At the dark market?"

Aron hesitated, his jaw tightening. He stared ahead for a moment before answering. "It was… a lot," he said finally. "I could feel the weight of everything—what they were doing, the fear in the air. And then, when it all went south, it was like something inside me just snapped."

Kiara waited patiently, sensing there was more he needed to say.

"I was angry," Aron continued, his voice rough with emotion. "I didn't just use my power—I let it take over. I didn't hold back, and for a moment, I… I liked it. The destruction, the way they couldn't stop me."

He shifted beside her, silent for a long beat. The air between them grew heavier, weighed down by guilt he hadn't spoken aloud but that she felt — thick as fog.

She stopped walking and turned toward him, reaching out until her fingertips found his chest. She let them rest there, right over his heart, feeling the faint crackle of static beneath his skin.

"Aron," she said softly, "whatever you're feeling right now… you're not hiding it as well as you think."

He let out a heavy breath as her hand found his.

"And I noticed something else back there," she continued, her voice steady. "Something I didn't know how or when to tell you. But now seems like the right time."

Before he could ask, Kiara closed her eyes, focusing on the rhythm of his electricity. A moment later, tiny sparks danced along her arm, the faint pulses of his power flowing through her. She let out a soft gasp, her lips parting just slightly.

She let out a soft gasp, her lips parting just slightly.

"It doesn't hurt me," she said, opening her eyes. "If anything… it feels exhilarating."

The sparks danced across her arm — and then, to Aron's amazement, they didn't vanish. They sank into her skin, one by one, until nothing was left but a faint shimmer and the steady thrum of peace in the air.

His jaw dropped. "How are you doing that?"

"Anytime I stand close to you, it does this. Usually just a few sparks here and there, like I draw them in or something," she explained, her voice calm but firm. "But back there, I realized... it doesn't matter how much power you release — I can handle it."

He stared at her, dumbfounded. "But... how? And why didn't you say anything earlier?"

"I wasn't sure at first," Kiara admitted. "And it wasn't the right time. But now you see — you can't hurt me. Not like you were worried about."

The tension in his shoulders eased slightly, though his expression remained conflicted. "I don't know, Kiara. What if there's a limit? What if—"

She cut him off with a teasing smile, grabbing his hand and tugging him forward. "No 'what ifs.' I don't want you treating me like I'm made of glass. I don't need you to hold back, Aron. I want you to be yourself — really yourself — with me. You've done nothing wrong, you have nothing to be ashamed of, and you can't hurt me."

He hesitated for a moment, then let out a soft chuckle, shaking his head in disbelief. "You're something else, you know that?"

"Yup. And so are you... we should team up or something," she replied, her grin widening as they approached the baths.

She smiled, soft and steady. "See? Even in water, you can't hurt me."

Before he could respond, she let go of his hand and turned, stepping onto the warm stone at the pool's edge. Steam curled around her like a veil.

Then, without hesitation, she lifted her shirt over her head and let it fall.

Aron froze, struck silent as the soft light from the cascading pools touched her skin — radiant, unfiltered, fearless. She undressed with simple, fluid movements, completely unselfconscious. Not putting on a show — just being.

And somehow that was even more powerful.

She wasn't flaunting anything. She was letting him see the truth of her. She was telling him without words: This is me. I trust you. I'm not afraid.

By the time she stepped into the water, his throat was dry and his heart was hammering. He didn't move at first — not because he was unsure, but because he was in awe.

She turned toward the sound of his breath, her voice soft but sure.

"You coming, or are you just going to stand there and worship me from a distance?"

He laughed — breathless, wrecked — and began to undress.

Aron exhaled, his shoulders finally relaxing as the weight he'd been carrying slowly began to lift, as if each piece of clothing he removed peeled back a layer of the fear he'd clung to for lifetimes.

By the time he stepped into the water, Kiara was already waist-deep, her arms gliding across the surface like she was part of it — fluid, elemental, at home.

He laughed again, the sound lighter than before. "You're not wasting any time, are you?"

"Never again, not a second," she replied, the heat enveloping them as they sank into the soothing water. Kiara teased him, kissing his neck and chest as he leaned back, melting into the tub, the water hot enough to soothe his aching muscles. She climbed atop his lap, reaching her hands around his neck, gently massaging him with her fingers. Using her fingernails to gently massage his scalp before running them through his hair, she pulled her hands back and ran them gently down her own. He watched as she continued on, running them down her breasts and beneath the water. She grabbed his now throbbing cock and asked him to help her piece the fateful night they had shared together, firmly stroking him as he tried to speak.

"I honestly can't recall it all..." he answered as best he could.

She smiled as he pulled her as close as he could. He wrapped his arms around her waist, hugging and kissing her as he reached down to grab her ass. Aron could feel her tremble as he began stroking her thighs. He rocked her hips a few times along with her, before reaching between her legs from behind and causing her to clench as he moved into a better position.

"Not yet!" She giggled as she pulled away. She pulled him to a standing position before going down. He grabbed the edges of the pool and watched in delight. Groaning and giggling with delight, he wrapped one hand around the back of her head as he continued to watch. The moment was perfect, yet all he wanted to do was hold her in his arms. After waiting another moment, he took his turn pulling away and lifting her back to a standing position.

Surprised, she wiped her face of excess water. "But I wasn't finished yet…" she giggled, feeling herself being tugged back toward him.

He kissed her gently as he sat back down. With one of his hands wrapped around the back of her head and jaw and the other around her waist, he sat back down. In one swift motion, he reached for her ass once again, this time seating her right into position. She tilted her hips as she smiled and wrapped her arms around him, clenching him tightly as they both felt him slide into her. After a few thrusts, he was able to make his way deep inside, causing them both to cry out to one another as the pace quickened.

"Come to think of it, I do think I remember this…" he whispered into her ear. "I was starting to wonder there for a bit." She could feel his lips curl into a smile.

She pulled her head back so he could see her grin. "I always knew. I couldn't sit right for two days!" she informed him, causing Aron to groan again as he pulled her back into what he felt was the perfect position.

As he moved deeper inside her, he trembled as energy began to surge through him.

There it was again. He'd seen it before — that first night, when everything had felt too fast and too electric to process. When he'd lit up with more power than he meant to, and she'd taken it without flinching. Back then, he hadn't questioned it. He'd been too high, too wrapped in the rush of her. But now…He saw it clearly.

The sparks — his energy — flickered along her shoulders and spine. And instead of arcing away or crackling into the air, they sank into her skin, like she was drinking it in. Each wave of pleasure fed the glow — shimmering and pulsing — before it gently dissolved. She didn't even seem to notice.

To her, this was normal. As if her body was made to do this. To hold his charge. To calm it. To transform it. Aron froze, hand on her hip, eyes locked on the place where the last of the sparks melted into her back.

"Oh my god," he whispered.

Kiara tilted her head, breath catching from the shift. "What is it?"

"You're not just 'handling' me," he murmured. "You're transmuting me. I can see it. I saw it that first night too, but I thought I was imagining it."

She blinked, confused but curious. "Transmuting?"

He rested his forehead against hers, his voice low, reverent.

"Some people short-circuit around energy like mine. Others try to contain it, and it fries them. But you… you're a conduit. You don't just take it in — you move it. You channel it like it's meant to pass through you."

She stilled, her lips parting slightly as she absorbed his words.

"You don't just balance me," he said, his voice cracking with awe. "You alchemize me."

She smiled softly, resting her forehead to his.

"What if we really did pick this life to be together?" she whispered. "What if we wanted to make sure we waited for each other? Maybe this is how…?"

A soft flickering light caused children in their makeshift village to glance nervously toward the lights stretching across their encampment, their eyes wide. It wasn't the first time the lights had behaved erratically, and it didn't take a genius to guess the source.

"Why do the lights keep doing that?" one child whispered, clutching a blanket.

Clarice glanced over toward Robyn and Scarlett before leaning over to Marcus, her lips making a teasing smile as she whispered, "I think we know exactly why."

Marcus stifled a laugh, his ears reddening as he murmured back, "They're still figuring things out."

The flickering intensified briefly, prompting one particularly curious child to pipe up, "Can we have a story? Something to keep us from thinking the lights are haunted?"

Mallah, seated nearby with her usual poise, tilted her head thoughtfully. "A story? Very well. Let me tell you a tale of love, courage, and a bond that defied even the gods."

The children quickly gathered closer, settling around her as the flickering subsided into a soft, rhythmic glow. Behind them, the Champions—many of whom had been deep in conversation—turned their attention to Mallah's voice. Even Marcus and Clarice quieted, curious about what she might say.

Mallah's voice carried a timeless cadence, each word deliberate and laden with emotion.

"Long ago, before humanity had risen to its current state, there were Titans—beings of great power and purpose. Among them was one who dared to defy the order of things. Prometheus was her name, and she sought to give humanity fire—not just the flame to warm their homes, but the spark of knowledge, creativity, and independence."

The children gasped, several of them whispering, "Her?"

"Yes, her," Mallah confirmed with a soft smile. "Prometheus risked everything for humanity. But the Titans, fearing what such knowledge might bring, punished her cruelly. She was stripped of her immortality, her power, and cast out into the mortal realm—wounded, weak, and left for dead."

Several of the Champions exchanged glances, their expressions growing solemn. The weight of Mallah's words resonated deeply, reminding them of the sacrifices they had made and would continue to make.

"Enter Zeus," Mallah continued, her voice growing softer, more wistful. "A powerful figure, full of wrath and righteousness, who hunted Prometheus to his conquest to defeat the Titans. Yet when he found her—beaten but unbroken, proud of her choice despite the cost—he saw something in her that stayed his head."

Her gaze swept across the room, pausing briefly on Marcus and Clarice, then Aron and Kiara.

"Zeus, against his better judgment, fell in love with her. For a fleeting moment, the god and the rebel stood as equals, united by something greater than themselves."

The children, wide-eyed and captivated, leaned forward as Mallah added with a dramatic flourish, "But their love could not last. Zeus, bound by duty and his own struggles, could not abandon his place among the gods. And Prometheus, proud and unyielding, would not forsake her cause. Yet from their union came a child—a bridge between their worlds, destined to reshape the future."

Mallah smiled wistfully, her voice growing playful. "Of course, this is where I must admit that I was once called Hera—Zeus's wife— I was frequently annoyed by his… let's call them shenanigans."

The adults chuckled knowingly, while the children furrowed their brows in confusion. One finally asked, "Why was she annoyed? Wasn't she supposed to be a goddess too?"

"Oh, she was," Mallah said with a sly grin. "And quite an impressive one at that. But let's just say Zeus had a habit of complicating things for her. Then again so did his brothers Poseidon and Hades. Of course, the stories you've heard about Hera and Zeus aren't entirely accurate. Time has a funny way of twisting the truth. What you think of as sibling rivalries or… other such things… often came from misunderstandings about soul families."

The children murmured curiously, and Mallah continued, "Soul families are different from physical families. They're groups of beings who return to each other across lifetimes, not bound by blood but by purpose. The Champions, for instance, are part of such a soul family. We've lived many lives, taken on many roles, and learned many lessons. Sometimes as friends, sometimes as adversaries, and yes, sometimes as family."

By now, even the Champions were fully immersed in the story. When Mallah described the bond between Prometheus and Zeus—how their love had endured across lifetimes, though never allowing them to actually be together—a few of them discreetly wiped their eyes. Marcus, in particular, tightened his grip on Clarice's hand, whispering, "Remind me to thank her for this later."

"What happened next?" The children asked.

Mallah continued, her tone growing reverent. "What happened next, you ask? Their love didn't end—it transformed. Prometheus became a guardian of humanity, watching over the very fire she had given them. And Zeus, though he could not stand beside her, never forgot her courage. Every flicker of light, every spark of hope, was a reminder of what they had shared."

Mallah gestured around them, her gaze sweeping across the landscape. "And now, here we are. The dawn of a new age, where the fire of humanity burns brighter than ever. It has taken us lifetimes to reach this point—to remember who we are and why we are here. And just as Prometheus and Zeus fought for the future, so must we."

The Champions nodded solemnly, their resolve deepening. The children, though less aware of the weight of Mallah's words, felt the warmth of her voice and the comfort it carried.

As Mallah leaned back, her story complete, one of the children whispered, "But what happened to the Titans?"

Mallah smiled enigmatically. "Ah, that is a story for another time."

The flickering lights brightened momentarily, as though in agreement, before settling into a steady glow.

Aron and Kiara strolled back toward the group moments later, Kiara wearing his oversized linen shirt, the sleeves dangling comically past her hands, while he walked beside her shirtless—skin still flushed from heat and exertion. The mix of the lanterns and soft Lemurian glow played off the lean muscle carved along his arms and chest, casting him in an unintentional spotlight. More than one glance lingered as they approached.

"See?" Kiara said, nudging him playfully. "Told you the baths weren't haunted."

Aron chuckled; the sound low in his chest. "Didn't say they were haunted, love—just... suspiciously steamy."

But his smile faded as he looked up and caught sight of the others.

Nearly everyone had teary eyes, some redder than others. Mallah, seated with her usual poise, still had a soft sheen of emotion behind her calm. Even Cesaro and Marcus looked like they'd been through something.

Aron leaned in, dropping his voice. "Uh... who bloody died?"

Kiara tilted her head, concerned. "Why, what happened?"

Before either of them could speculate, Cesaro spotted them and waved them over. His grin returned, though his eyes were still a bit glassy.

"Don't worry—you didn't miss the apocalypse. Just a damn good story."

Marcus nodded, wiping his eyes with exaggerated flair. "Come on, man. Sit down. Mallah gave us a proper emotional beating. You two missed the group cry."

Aron frowned slightly. "So... why's everyone still starin' at us?"

"They're probably thinkin' what I was," Teddy said, eyes wide. "That's what's under the flannel?"

Skyler leaned forward, blinking like he was recalibrating. "I thought you were wiry. You know, scrappy woodsman chic. Not… forged-in-a-volcano hot."

Robyn gasped, clutching her bowl. "Bozhe moi. Kiara, you are missing out."

"You remember I told you blind people are super sensory-oriented, right?"

Robyn nodded slowly. "Da?"

Kiara smirked. "Well, I haven't missed shit, enjoy the view."

Laughter rippled through the group as Aron rubbed the back of his neck, clearly flustered. "Feelin' a little vulnerable, here…" he muttered, half-laughing.

Teddy elbowed him. "So… are all you OAS built like that under your shirts?"

Skyler shook his head. "Aron wasn't with the OAS. And no, at least I'm not…"

Teddy raised his eyebrows. "Don't feel bad. I'm more grizzly bear than lumberjack. Let's be real."

Skyler's voice dropped with a teasing lilt. "Perfect. I like Teddy bears."

Robyn clapped her hands together. "Ooooh! Is this a thing now? Because I am very here for it."

Cesaro leaned in with a grin. "Well, that escalated quickly. Should we leave you two alone, or…?"

Scarlett sipped her drink without missing a beat. "And here I thought tonight couldn't get any more entertaining."

Teddy, realizing how hot his face just became, muttered, "I need a reset button."

Skyler's smile lingered just a few seconds longer, his eyes flicking back to Teddy.

Aron groaned. "Right. That's it. I'm never takin' my shirt off around you lot again."

As Kiara was swept into the girls' circle—eager hands pulling her down into whispered recaps and giggled theories about flickering lights and fated lovers—Aron hesitated near the edge of the gathering.

He caught Marcus watching him—less amused now, more thoughtful. Around them, heads nodded. Smiles lingered. Even the quiet ones looked at him like they knew more than he did.

He sat down slowly, still catching up, as Marcus clapped him on the shoulder.

"Welcome back," Marcus said quietly. "You two missed a very interesting story."

-Chapter 48-

The Thread That Pulls

Kiara stirred in her sleep that night. She shifted slightly, her head twitching as if trying to block out an invisible force tugging at her awareness. It wasn't a sound, not exactly—more like a low vibration that resonated through her chest, pulling her consciousness awake.

Her eyes fluttered open, seeing not the tent's fabric walls but the intricate, colorful threads of energy that outlined everything around her. In the darkness, they pulsed faintly, as if beckoning her. The pull was undeniable, like a gentle hand urging her to follow.

She sat up slowly, mindful not to disturb Aron beside her, his breaths deep and even. For a moment, she hesitated. The camp was full of activity during the day, and it wasn't uncommon for everyone to encourage her to rest whenever possible. Aron, especially, had a knack for overprotecting her in moments like this, not that she blamed him or anything like that.

Kiara swung her legs over the edge of the cot and felt around for the shirt she had been wearing. She tried to keep her movements subtle, knowing Aron would wake at the faintest noise if she wasn't careful.

Her fingers brushed against the rough fabric of his bag. Realizing her clothes were scattered about, she frowned as she realized she couldn't distinguish which piece was which. Every object in her view was a cascade of shimmering energy—beautiful, yes, but utterly impractical when trying to tell some of his garments from hers…especially since they are all actually his.

While she was adept at telling the different feelings of various types of fabric, similar and less familiar ones made it a challenge. She pursed her lips and began pulling random pieces into her arms.

"Okay, this has sleeves… I think," she murmured under her breath.

Kiara tried to dress as quietly as possible, struggling with her movements awkward in the confined space of the tent. She winced as a rustling sound broke the stillness, and she glanced toward Aron's nude silhouette, holding her breath.

She listened intently as he shifted slightly but didn't wake. She exhaled in relief, clutching her shirt and slipping out of the tent before her clumsiness could betray her further.

The air outside was cool against her skin and quickly finished pulling the shirt over her head then turned toward the source of the pull and began walking, her feet tentative on the uneven ground. Kiara moved cautiously through the darkened camp, the shimmering threads of energy guiding her steps. Each pulse of the unseen force tugged at her chest, urging her forward despite her incomplete understanding of what it was or where it led. Her bare feet brushed against soft grass as she adjusted the ill-fitting cloak draped over her shoulders. She was determined not to wake Aron or anyone else—this was her journey to follow.

She had only made it a few steps when a soft voice startled her. As she rounded a cluster of tents, a familiar voice broke the stillness, startling her.

"Kiara? What are you doing out here?" Scarlett's sharp whisper carried a mix of concern and curiosity.

Relieved, Kiara stepped closer. "I could ask you the same thing. I thought I was the only one awake."

Scarlett studied her in the faint moonlight, her sharp eyes catching every detail, including Kiara's hastily assembled attire. "You're practically naked," she smiled, crossing her arms. "Going for a midnight stroll in your birthday suit?"

Kiara flushed, clutching her clothes tighter. "I'm wearing a shirt!" She insisted. "Something's pulling me—calling me. I couldn't ignore it."

Scarlett raised an eyebrow, then scanned the quiet space between tents. "Funny… I've been feeling the same thing. Thought I was imagining it until I saw you. My guides have been mostly silent."

Kiara turned slightly toward her voice, pausing as the pull inside her swelled again. It wasn't sound, exactly—but it resonated through her chest like a tuning fork. "You're feeling it too?"

"Not hearing, exactly," Scarlett replied, lowering her voice. "It's more like… a whisper at the edge of my thoughts. Like someone's trying to show me something important."

Kiara shifted her weight, her fingers twitching at her sides. The vibration pulsed again—deep and rhythmic. Not loud, but certain. It wasn't just external—it moved through her, like she was wired to receive it.

"I don't think I'm supposed to ignore this," Kiara said softly. "It's in my bones. Like a thread pulling me forward from the inside."

Scarlett hesitated, watching her. "Do you know where it's coming from?"

Kiara shook her head. "No. But I can feel when I'm getting closer. It's… inside me and ahead of me at the same time."

She reached a hand slightly out, not toward Scarlett directly, but into the space between them—testing. Scarlett noticed and stepped closer.

"Want me to walk with you?" she asked gently. "I'll follow your lead."

Kiara nodded slowly. "That would help. Just… let me stay in front. I can feel the direction through the energy lines—like a current."

"Got it," Scarlett murmured. "I'll be your shadow."

Without another word, they began walking together, their steps quiet as they left the camp behind. The pull grew stronger with each step, the faint hum of unseen energy threading through the air around them, the Spirit Talker and Kiara.

They began moving together—Scarlett just behind and to the side, careful not to interfere with Kiara's pace. With each step, the pull intensified, not as a noise but as a resonance—a frequency threading through the soles of Kiara's feet, up through her spine, humming just beneath her skin.

The terrain changed subtly as they walked, the soft grass giving way to rocky outcroppings and patches of wild vegetation. The whispers grew louder in Kiara's mind, a symphony of voices weaving together in a language she couldn't fully understand, strange and foreign to her ears, yet somehow familiar. Scarlett seemed equally transfixed, her gaze darting between shadows and shapes in the distance.

Suddenly, the air shifted—a faint glow appeared ahead, emanating from behind a cluster of massive, moss-covered stones. Kiara hesitated, her hand instinctively brushing Scarlett's arm.

She moved steadily now, certain of her steps, even on unfamiliar ground.

Scarlett followed, more curious with each passing moment.

Neither of them spoke. There was no need. Whatever called them was doing so with a language deeper than words.

"Do you hear that?" she asked, her voice barely above a whisper.

Scarlett nodded. "Let's check it out."

They moved closer, weaving through the stone pillars that seemed to grow taller as they approached. The glow intensified, revealing an ancient structure nestled in the heart of a natural hollow. It was unlike anything either of them had seen before—part sanctuary, part workshop, with intricate carvings that pulsed faintly with energy. Vines and moss clung to the stone, but the space felt alive, as if it had been waiting for someone to find it.

Scarlett let out a low whistle. "Well, this definitely isn't on the map we've been working on."

Kiara stepped forward, her fingers brushing the smooth surface of the nearest pillar. The energy within the stone hummed in response, sending a tingling sensation up her arm. "It's beautiful," she murmured. "And powerful."

Scarlett knelt by a nearby spring bubbling up from the earth. She scooped a handful of water and sniffed it cautiously. "It's fresh," she said, glancing back at Kiara. "This could be a game-changer."

Kiara nodded, her gaze sweeping over the sanctuary. She could feel the potential in this place—a haven for their people, a resource waiting to be tapped. The voices in her mind grew clearer, their whispers taking on a note of urgency.

"This isn't just a sanctuary," Kiara said, her voice trembling with realization. "It's a key. To what, I don't know yet, but… we're meant to find it."

Scarlett rose to her feet, brushing dirt from her hands. "Then we'd better tell Mallah. She'll know what to do."

As the two women turned to leave, Kiara paused, glancing back at the glowing structure. The energy pulsed once more, a quiet acknowledgment of their discovery. Whatever this place was, it had chosen them—and it held secrets they had yet to uncover.

She slipped back into bed beside Aron, who wrapped his warm arms back around her, pulling her close to him. As the sun rose higher over the encampment, the two joined the others for breakfast. Kiara couldn't shake the pull she felt, a mix of instinct and memory tugging at her. It wasn't just the energy she sensed beneath her feet; it was something more—a deep recognition of this place.

While everyone else was discussing their plans for the day, Kiara asked Robyn and Scarlett to go scouting with her. "There's something about this land. I don't know how I know, but I need to explore. Will you come with me?" she asked, intriguing both of them.

Scarlett, always intrigued by Kiara's uncanny instincts, nodded. "You lead, and I'll follow. Just don't get too far ahead." Together, the three women navigated the rugged terrain, Kiara moving with a surprising sense of purpose despite her lack of sight.

As they wandered, Kiara began describing sensations and flashes of knowledge that seemed to bubble up unbidden.

"There's something here," she said, pausing near a rocky outcrop. "I remember… a garden. Not just any garden—it was a place of healing."

Scarlett raised a brow, glancing at Robyn. "You mean here? On this island?"

Kiara nodded. "Yes. The people of Lemuria cultivated plants for medicine, food, and energy. They designed the gardens to be self-sustaining, almost symbiotic with the land."

Guided by Kiara's intuition, they stumbled upon a hidden grove, lush and overgrown with greenery. The air was rich with the scent of herbs and flowers. Scarlett crouched to inspect the plants.

"These are incredible," Scarlett said, picking a sprig of something aromatic. "Some of these look like ancient varieties of herbs we still use today. Others… I've never seen before."

Kiara laughed, the sound light and playful. "There's more! I know it! Follow me!"

Kiara dashed ahead, her hands brushing over plants and trees as if she were reacquainting herself with old friends. Scarlett and Robyn struggled to keep up, shouting for her to slow down.

"Kiara!" Robyn called, laughing as she dodged a low-hanging branch. "You're like a kid in a candy store!"

Kiara turned, her silver hair catching the light as she grinned. "It's like I can feel where everything is meant to be. Over here—this was a water source!"

Sure enough, they found a small spring trickling into a series of shallow pools. The water was crystal clear, the kind that seemed to hum with purity. Scarlett knelt by the edge, running her fingers through it.

"This is amazing," she said. "We could use this for drinking water—and maybe more."

Kiara pointed further ahead. "And there—there should be a grove of fruit trees."

When they reached the grove, it was even more bountiful than Kiara had described. Trees heavy with a variety of vibrant, colorful fruits stretched off into the distance, their branches bending under the weight. The women stared in awe.

As they explored, Kiara began recalling the uses for various plants, describing their medicinal and nutritional properties. Scarlett and Robyn started gathering samples, impressed by her knowledge.

"This one," Kiara said, gesturing toward a cluster of tall, spindly plants. "Its leaves were used to make a tea that boosts energy and focus."

"And this?" Scarlett asked, holding up a bright red berry.

"A natural antiseptic," Kiara replied. "Crush it into a paste to treat wounds."

Robyn looked at her, wide-eyed. "How do you know all this?"

Kiara hesitated, then smiled. "It's like the memories are part of me. This place… it's waking them up within me."

By the time they returned to the encampment, their arms were full of herbs, fruit, and other discoveries. The group marveled at the abundance they had found, and Mallah herself came over to inspect the treasures.

"This knowledge will save lives," Mallah said, placing a hand on Kiara's shoulder. "You've done more than you know."

Kiara beamed, feeling a deep sense of purpose. For the first time since arriving, she felt like she was truly contributing—truly connected to the legacy she had inherited.

As the day wound down and the camp prepared for the night's festivities, Kiara felt a newfound confidence. Scarlett and Robyn teased her playfully about her enthusiasm during the day, and she laughed, promising there was more to discover tomorrow.

The encampment buzzed with energy, and the group came together, their spirits lifted by the day's success. The bonds between them felt stronger than ever, setting the stage for the celebrations to come.

As she stumbled with an armful of supplies, Aron quickly appeared at her side, his voice soft but firm. "Let me help." Together, they managed the load, his strength effortlessly complementing her determination.

Rose kept spirits high, cracking jokes with Cesaro and her brother, her fiery hair bouncing as she waved her hands dramatically. "You think lifting that is hard, Cesaro? Try dealing with Kiara's sass all day," she teased, earning a chuckle from the group.

Scarlett, ever the mentor, was guiding a young refugee through basic self-defense techniques. Her calm voice and steady demeanor reassured the nervous teen, reminding him that they were safe here. Nearby, Robyn skillfully tied supplies together, her precision and efficiency with knots left the others quite impressed.

Teddy and Skyler, perhaps the most unlikely pair, were deep in conversation, bonding over their shared sense of humor. Skyler animatedly recounted a tale of past mischief, and Teddy's deep laughter rumbled through the camp, a rare sound that drew smiles from Archibald and Trydan who were sitting together nearby, coming to terms with their own roles in all of this after Kiara had awakened them from Ivyg's mind control. Over it all, Mallah stood quietly, her watchful gaze taking in the scene. Her posture was calm, her eyes sharp, as though measuring the weight of the moment and savoring the unity they had forged in the face of chaos.

As the sun dipped below the horizon, painting fiery orange and deep purple hues across the sky, the camp took on an almost magical quality. Fires flickered to life, lighting the ancient architecture that encircled the settlement. Two distinct gatherings began to form—one for the men, another for the women—each carving out their own space amidst the shadows.

The men gathered by a large bonfire near the water, the flames casting long shadows on the crumbling stone pathways. Kane, with his usual air of authority, oversaw the cooking, reciting an ancient recipe like a priest performing a sacred rite. The aroma of charred herbs and freshly caught fish wafted through the air as the group shared stories and laughter, periodically sending heaping plates back to camp for others to enjoy.

Marcus took center stage, holding up a bottle of wine. "So there we were, freshmen at SWSU—me, the loudmouth hotshot, and Aron, the golden boy."

Aron groaned, shaking his head. "I didn't even think I'd survive freshman year."

"And we probably wouldn't have without help from Cesaro and Clarice." Marcus continued, grinning. "I'm out there showing off, and this guy decides he's going to outshine me. Long story short—he did. Who knew we'd end up here, saving the world instead of fighting over the same football?"

Aron's expression softened, his voice turning reflective. "Standing here now, with all of you...I think this is what I was always meant to do."

Cesaro, never one to let a sentimental moment linger, clapped Aron on the shoulder. "Alright, save the emotional speeches for the wedding, Kydd. We've got Lemurian brews to finish!"

Aron looked at his bottle with mock seriousness, furrowing his brow. "Mine says Deschutes Black Butte Porter. I don't think it counts as Lemurian unless it was actually made in Lemuria. But you know what we should do? Brew our own beer right here. Imagine it—Lemurian Ale. "We could make a fortune!" Cesaro laughed in agreement.

Marcus laughed, shaking his head. "Or," he countered, "we could just keep it to our community. Think about it—our own secret brew, only for us."

Aron raised an eyebrow. "Sure, but if you're in charge, I'm guessing it'll taste like one of those spiced or fruity things you like so much."

Marcus grinned, unbothered. "Hey, what's wrong with a crisp Belgian witbier? A little citrus, maybe some coriander—it's refreshing!"

Aron groaned dramatically. "Man, your tastes are all wrong. A proper beer is dark, rich, and heavy. None of this 'hint of orange peel' nonsense."

Before Marcus could retort, Kane cleared his throat, stepping into the fray with a knowing smirk. "Gentlemen, if you want to discuss 'proper beer,' I suggest you listen to someone who's been around long enough to witness its invention."

The group fell silent, their attention fully on Kane. He adjusted his collar, his voice smooth with authority. "The finest brew," he declared, "comes not from some overly complex recipe or gimmicky flavoring. It's about balance—bitterness, malt, and just enough strength to remind you why you're drinking it in the first place."

"And what would you recommend?" Marcus asked, raising an eyebrow.

Kane raised his glass with a touch of flair. "A true ale—something akin to Fuller's ESB or Guinness Extra Stout, though I doubt even they match the craftsmanship of an original recipe from the ancient isles of Lemuria." He took a slow sip, savoring the moment before adding, "Perhaps one day, I'll teach you all what real brewing looks like. Until then, this will do quite nicely.'"

Aron grinned and leaned back, lifting his bottle. "To Lemurian brews, whenever we finally figure it out."

"To Lemurian brews," the others echoed, laughing as they clinked their bottles together.

The women's gathering unfolded deeper within the ruins, beneath stone arches adorned with vines that shimmered faintly in the firelight. Braziers and torch sconces lit the space with a warm glow, their flames reflecting on the intricate carvings that adorned the walls. The ruins didn't feel abandoned so much as dormant, as if waiting for this moment of renewal.

Clarice stood at the center, her rainbow-colored hair glinting as she concentrated on shaping ice. Frost curled around her fingers, taking form as she attempted to sculpt an archway. Each attempt brought murmurs of encouragement or playful teasing from the others.

"You know," Rose said, smirking as she poured more wine into Clarice's glass, "if we're drinking every time you chisel something off-center, we're going to be drunk before this thing looks halfway decent."

Clarice sighed, laughing despite herself. "It's harder than it looks!"

Kiara, sitting nearby, offered a soft smile. "Take your time. Try visualizing exactly what you want before you create it. That's what Marcus always said when he taught me to focus."

Clarice paused, knowing her future husband's advice to be sound. Her hands stilled. She closed her eyes, took a breath, and then began again. This time, the ice formed more smoothly, shaping itself into a graceful arch. She stepped back, admiring her work. "Huh. That actually worked."

"Marcus will love it," Kiara said warmly. Clarice beamed at the thought, her cheeks tinged with a blush. "Thanks, Kiara." Teddy, who had wandered over to the women's gathering, grinned. "You're not the only one who's grown, Kiara. I saw you today, running around like you own this place, helping everyone. You're not the same woman I bought a haunted house with back in Oregon. You or Robyn for that matter. I'm downright impressed, I have to say."

Rose, ever the pragmatic one, nodded. "You've stepped into something bigger than yourself, and it suits you."

Kiara hesitated, then decided to share the thought that had been gnawing at her. "When I was in the Nexus, Marcus told me I'm destined to be the Queen of Lemuria. But... 'Queen' feels so cheesy. I hate it."

Scarlett raised an eyebrow. "Why? What's wrong with being a queen?"

"It just doesn't feel like me," Kiara admitted. "I'd rather be called an ambassador or something. 'Queen' sounds...I dunno, vain."

Rose crossed her arms, her fiery hair catching the light. "Cheesy or not, if the powers that be chose that title for you, who are you to question it? Maybe the problem isn't the title—it's how you see yourself."

The women murmured their agreement, and Scarlett added with a teasing grin, "Besides, that amulet looks pretty queenly on you, silver hair and all."

Kiara laughed, relaxing into the moment as they clinked their cups together. "Fine. Here's to the Queen of Lemuria—though I'm still not calling myself that..."

The group erupted into laughter, their cheers echoing through the ruins.

As the night deepened over the next couple of hours, a chill settled over the island. Clarice rubbed her hands together, her breath visible in the cool air. "Okay, enough ice. I'm freezing, and that's saying a lot coming from a Welsh fairy with power over ice."

Scarlett pointed toward the nearest cluster of geothermal pools, steam curling into the night. "Then let's warm up. The hot springs are calling."

With a whoop of agreement, the women gathered their things and extra bottles of wine, then headed toward the springs. As they arrived, they saw the men had the same idea, their laughter mingling with the hiss of steam.

"What took you so long?" Aron teased, reaching for Kiara as she stepped into the steaming water.

She rolled her eyes, splashing him as she waded in. "Don't get cocky, Sparky."

Clarice smirked from her spot nearby, swirling her fingers in the water. Her eyes glinted with mischief. "Must be serious if you told her about our little nickname."

Aron gave her a sheepish grin, the faintest blush coloring his cheeks. "She's special," he admitted, his voice soft but sincere.

The teasing was good-natured, and the group chuckled as they settled into the warm, inviting waters. The camaraderie of the moment erased the exhaustion of the day. Beneath the vast, star-strewn sky and amidst the remnants of ancient architecture, they shared laughter, stories, and the simple joy of being together—a rare moment of peace in a world on the brink of transformation.

-Chapter 49-

The Wedding

The first rays of sunlight filtered through the dense canopy, casting golden light across the ancient city now alive with purpose. The camp stirred with energy as preparations for Marcus and Clarice's wedding began. The scent of freshly baked bread and roasted coffee wafted through the air, mingling with the sound of laughter and the occasional bark of instructions.

Kiara sat near the edge of camp, weaving a simple floral crown from wildflowers she'd found earlier. Scarlett and Robyn bustled nearby, tying colorful ribbons to the makeshift archway Clarice had perfected the night before.

Mallah, ever the overseer, moved efficiently through the encampment, offering suggestions and nodding approval. She paused briefly by Aron, who was carrying a large bundle wrapped in cloth. "You're sure he won't notice?" she asked, her tone low.

Aron shook his head. "Marcus thinks I'm helping set up a lookout post. He's too distracted with the day to question it." He glanced toward the tree line, where Pavel was waiting. "We'll be back before anyone realizes we're gone."

Mallah placed a hand on his arm. "This means a lot to him. Thank you."

With a small nod, Aron hefted the bundle and disappeared into the forest with Pavel, leaving Mallah to resume her tasks. She turned toward the center of camp, where Marcus stood near the ceremonial area, inspecting the decorations with an expression caught between nervousness and awe.

Clarice's rainbow-colored hair shimmered in the sunlight as she carefully arranged the last touches on the ice sculptures. A cool mist lingered around her, accentuating the crystalline beauty of her creations. Kiara approached, her floral crown complete, and handed it to Clarice.

"For you," Kiara said softly, her pale blue eyes bright with excitement.

Clarice smiled, taking the crown. "Thank you, Kiara. This means a lot." She paused, then added with a mischievous grin, "But don't think this gets you out of the dance later."

"Dance?" Kiara raised an eyebrow, feigning confusion. "You must have confused me with someone who's coordinated."

The two women laughed, the sound drawing Marcus's attention. He watched them with a mixture of affection and gratitude, his nerves momentarily forgotten.

Nearby, Rose and Cesaro were with Robyn organizing chairs, with Cesaro cracking jokes to keep the mood light. "I don't know, Marcus," Cesaro called out. "Are you sure you're ready for this? Marriage is a big step."

Marcus grinned. "Coming from the guy who can't keep a date past the appetizers?"

Laughter rippled through the group as Cesaro mockingly clutched his chest. "Low blow, Kydd. Low blow."

The soft hum of voices and rustling fabric filled the air as the wedding preparations neared their conclusion. Guests were finding their seats, the vibrant decorations glinting in the sunlight. Marcus, however, stood near the edge of the ceremonial area, scanning the crowd with a growing sense of frustration.

"Where is he?" he muttered, his hands on his hips.

"Where's who?" Clarice asked, stepping up beside him, her rainbow-colored hair pinned back elegantly. Her eyes sparkled with a mix of excitement and teasing suspicion.

"Aron," Marcus replied, glancing toward the tree line. "He's been missing all morning. He's supposed to be helping me keep things on track, and now he's gone MIA."

Clarice smiled softly, placing a calming hand on his shoulder. "Relax. He's probably just..."

Marcus turned abruptly and nearly caught sight of Clarice's gown. "You're not supposed to be here yet!" he exclaimed, averting his gaze and waving her off. "Go hide or something! My Nana always told me it was bad luck to see a bride before she walks down the aisle."

Clarice laughed, stepping back. "Fine, fine! But he'll show up. He wouldn't miss this for anything."

As Marcus paced the perimeter of the ceremonial space, muttering about how he was going to wring Aron's neck, a ripple of movement caught his eye. He turned just in time to see Aron emerging from the tree line, a figure walking beside him.

Marcus squinted, his confusion melting into astonishment as he recognized the woman at Aron's side. His breath caught in his throat. "Mom?"

Akiro Kydd stood there, her petite Japanese frame dwarfed by the taller men on either side of her—Aron and Kane. She wore a serene smile, her eyes glistening with emotion. Behind her, Mallah watched quietly, her expression one of satisfaction and warmth.

Marcus didn't hesitate. He sprinted forward, his emotions surging to the surface as he threw his arms around his mother. "Mom," he repeated, his voice cracking as he held her tightly.

The small Japanese woman wrapped her arms around him, tears spilling freely down her cheeks. "My little dragon," she whispered, using the nickname she'd called him when he was a child.

Marcus laughed through his tears, pulling back slightly to look at her. "How—how are you here? When did this happen...?"

His gaze shifted to Aron and then to Mallah, realization dawning. "You two were in on this?"

Aron grinned, scratching the back of his head. "Hey, it was Kane and Mallah's idea. I just did the heavy lifting."

Mallah crossed her arms, her expression sly. "He needed a little help making it happen, but it was worth it, don't you think?"

Marcus nodded, his gratitude evident. "Thank you, all of you. This means...everything."

Akiro touched his face gently, her smile warm. "You've grown into such an incredible man. I'm so proud of you."

As the crowd began to notice the scene unfolding, Kane stepped forward, offering his arm to Akiro. "Shall we escort you to your seat?" he asked, his voice calm but touched with kindness.

Akiro nodded, her hand trembling slightly as she took his arm. Mallah flanked her on the other side, and the three walked together to a seat near the front, where Akiro could have a perfect view of her son's moment.

Marcus stood watching them for a moment, his heart full as he wiped his eyes. Clarice appeared beside him again, smiling brightly. "See? I told you he wouldn't miss it."

Marcus chuckled, taking a steadying breath. "Guess I owe him an apology later."

With a final glance at his mother, now seated and beaming with pride, Marcus turned and walked to the center of the ceremonial area. The murmurs of the crowd quieted, and all eyes fell on him as he prepared to take his place in one of the most important moments of his life.

The ceremonial space was transformed into a breathtaking scene. Clarice's ice arch stood resplendent at the center, shimmering like a portal to another world beneath the soft glow of the sun. Flowers and vines native to the island adorned the edges, a tribute to the land they now called home. The wedding party, dressed in their best given the circumstances, flanked the bride and groom. The blend of ancient architecture and makeshift charm made the setting feel both timeless and uniquely theirs.

Mallah, draped in her flowing ceremonial robes, exuded an air of calm command. Her presence was both grounding and inspiring, as if she embodied the history of the land itself. As she stood before them, the gathered audience quieted, captivated by her aura.

"We stand here," Mallah began, her voice resonant and warm, "on sacred ground—land that has witnessed the rise and fall of ages. And yet, today, it bears witness to something eternal: love. The bond that transcends time, space, and even lifetimes. Today, we gather not just to celebrate the union of Clarice and Marcus, but to honor the love that has guided them here."

Mallah turned to Clarice, her green eyes kind and knowing. "Clarice, speak your heart."

Clarice took a deep breath, her hands trembling slightly as she grasped Marcus's. Her voice, though soft, was steady with emotion.

"Marcus," she began, her eyes glistening. "From the moment I met you, I knew you were different. Not just because of your fiery personality—though that is part of it—but because you saw me, all of me, in a way no one else ever has, past the pink hair and punk rock clothes. You've been my partner in every sense of the word, through every battle, every heartbreak, every impossible challenge. And somehow, through it all, you've managed to make me laugh, even when I didn't think I could."

A tear slipped down her cheek, but she smiled as she continued. "I promise to stand by your side, no matter what comes our way. To protect you as fiercely as you've protected me. To love you in the light of day and the darkest of nights. You're my fire, my strength, my heart—and I'm so grateful to walk this path with you from the Hollow Earth to other planets in the sky. I will follow you wherever you may go."

Mallah smiled softly and turned to Marcus. "Marcus, it's your turn. Speak your heart."

Marcus sniffled, wiping at his eyes. He took Clarice's hands in his own, his voice thick with emotion.

"Clarice," he said, his tone trembling slightly. "I used to think love was something other people found. That it wasn't in the cards for someone like me—someone who's messed up, who's made mistakes, who's been through...a lot."

He paused, glancing at the audience. His eyes landed on his mother, who smiled encouragingly, and then on Aron, Kane, and Kiara. "But then you came into my life, and you showed me what love really is. It's not about perfection. It's about finding someone who sees you for who you are, flaws and all, and still chooses you every single day. Love is a choice, and I choose you."

Tears were now streaming freely down his face, though he didn't seem to care. "You've been my rock, my reason, my light in every dark moment. And standing here, surrounded by the people we love most, I realize I'm the luckiest man alive. Not just because I get to marry you, but because I get to call you my partner, my teammate, my best friend."

He squeezed her hands tightly, his voice breaking. "I promise to love you with everything I have, for every moment we have, for as long as we're given. You're my home, Clarice. And I'll never stop being grateful for you."

Mallah let the silence settle, allowing the weight of their words to resonate. Then, she smiled and gestured for the rings.

"Let these rings serve as a symbol of your bond," Mallah said. "A circle unbroken, eternal as the love you share. Marcus, place the ring on Clarice's hand, and repeat after me."

Marcus followed her words, his hands steady despite his emotion. "With this ring, I give you my heart, my soul, and my promise to walk beside you always."

Clarice mirrored his actions, her voice clear and sure. "With this ring, I give you my heart, my soul, and my promise to walk beside you always."

Mallah's expression softened, and for a moment, she looked at them as though she were seeing every version of their souls across time. "By the ancient and unyielding powers of love, I now pronounce you husband and wife. Marcus, you may kiss your bride."

Marcus didn't hesitate. He pulled Clarice close and kissed her with all the love and passion he felt, the audience erupting into cheers and applause.

As they turned to face the crowd, Marcus took a moment to soak it all in. The faces of everyone he loved—his mother, his brothers, his friends, his allies—were filled with joy. The backdrop of ancient Lemuria seemed almost to glow, as if the island itself were blessing their union.

Marcus squeezed Clarice's hand and leaned toward her. "We made it," he whispered, his voice full of wonder, kissing her again.

Clarice smiled back at him, her eyes shining before she turned back toward the crowd. "We sure did." Together, they stepped forward, ready to greet their loved ones and embrace whatever came next.

As the Kydd's turned to face their family and friends, the applause erupted like a wave, washing over the couple in a tidal surge of love and celebration. "Let's party!!" Clarice shouted with jubilance.

The sun, now dipping lower on the horizon, bathed the scene in a golden glow, making everything feel suspended in time. For that fleeting moment, the weight of their responsibilities seemed far away.

Mallah stepped forward, gesturing toward the tables that had been arranged just beyond the ceremony site, adorned with garlands of wildflowers and glowing lanterns.

The guests cheered as music began to play, the lively tune weaving through the warm evening air. People started making their way to the reception area, where long tables of simple but delicious fare awaited them. Clarice and Marcus lingered, stealing a few moments together as they whispered quietly and shared another kiss.

Kane approached them, his polished demeanor momentarily softened. "Don't linger too long," he said with a sly smile. "You wouldn't want to miss Cesaro's attempts at public speaking."

Clarice laughed, her nerves easing. "I wouldn't miss it for the world."

With one final kiss, Marcus took her hand, and they walked toward the reception arm in arm, their path lit by flickering lanterns and the faces of the people they held most dear.

After getting the traditional formalities out of the way, full of toasts, cake cutting, and some themed photos of the wedding party, the reception was in full swing. The Lemurian moon bathed the celebration in a silvery glow, casting the ancient architecture in a surreal light. Lanterns swayed gently in the warm breeze, and the tables were laden with simple yet beautifully presented foods from the island. Music filled the air, laughter rang out, and the sounds of people dancing reverberated through the space. For the first time in what felt like years, they allowed themselves to relax.

Marcus and Clarice were catching up with Marcus's mother, Akiro, at a quieter table near the edge of the festivities. She was sharing a memory about Marcus's childhood, one that had Clarice laughing so hard she nearly spilled her drink. Nearby, Kane, Mallah, and Pavel kept a watchful but relaxed eye on the crowd, blending into the jovial atmosphere.

Out of the crowd, Zen appeared, her movements deliberate yet understated. She approached Kiara and Aron, who were near the dance floor. Her face was uncharacteristically soft, her eyes betraying a trace of vulnerability.

"I owe you both an apology," Zen began, her voice quieter than usual. "That dark market… I hated it. Always did. But I had to make a scene, had to play the part for Ivyg's elite friends, his colleagues, his investors. If they suspected anything less, it would've been… worse."

Kiara tilted her head, sensing more beneath Zen's words. "Why tell us this now?"

Zen glanced around, her eyes briefly landing on Marcus and Clarice's table, then Pavel and Kane. "Because I need you to know I'm not your enemy. I never was. Everything I've done… it's all been for survival. For my son."

Aron's brow furrowed. "You could've told us that before," he said, his voice edged with caution.

Zen smiled faintly, a bittersweet expression that didn't quite reach her eyes. "I didn't think you'd believe me. Maybe you still don't. But for what it's worth, I am sorry."

The evening continued on, while Cesaro had everyone in stitches with a heartfelt yet hilariously embellished recount of Marcus's college days when his shoes nearly caught on fire from running so fast. Aron raised his glass to Clarice, saying he had never seen his brother happier. Mallah, ever the commanding presence, offered a toast of her own, blending humor and wisdom in a way that brought tears and laughter in equal measure.

As the music swelled, people began to dance in earnest. Scarlett led a group of younger guests in a spirited jig, while Robyn spun through the crowd, her laughter infectious. Kiara and Aron danced closely, savoring the rare moment of peace.

Zen stood on the outskirts, her presence almost forgotten in the revelry.

As Kiara and Aron danced, they caught sight of Ogma and DJ Yeti in the distance, orchestrating the event with the effortless synergy of long-time partners. The two were in their element, DJ Yeti pumping out beats that vibrated through the crowd while Ogma moved with his signature flair, ensuring everything ran smoothly. Watching them work together, Kiara couldn't help but be reminded of the night she and Aron first met, their connection sparked amid the chaos of one of Ogma's infamous gatherings. When Aron noticed her wistful smile, he nudged her playfully. "Hard to believe those two do weddings," he teased, drawing a laugh from Kiara. "Seriously," she replied, shaking her head, "who knew they could switch from raves to rings?" They weren't the only ones who found it amusing—others in their group chimed in with quips about Ogma officiating ceremonies with glowing crystals and DJ Yeti remixing the wedding march.

The day had gone exactly to plan. Nothing had come up to derail the wedding, and everyone had stepped up to make it magical. Yet, just as Kiara thought everything was perfect, a familiar tingle swept through her. Earlier, she had dismissed it, unable to pinpoint its source, but now, in closer quarters, she could sense the tension radiating from Rajneel. His eyes darted around, his unease palpable, as though he were expecting someone to appear out of thin air. How ironic that would be.

The atmosphere shifted as the faint ringing of a glass drew attention. Dr. Badr al Din Moses, Brad to his former students, stood and cleared his throat to deliver a toast. Silence fell as the crowd turned their focus to him.

"I cannot speak for everyone here," Brad began, their former professor and Pavel's husband, his voice steady, "but I am overjoyed in this union between you and Clarice." He directed a warm smile at Marcus. "I cannot help but think this marriage is far overdue, and I'm sure many share my sentiments."

There were murmurs of agreement and soft laughter among the guests.

"Ever since I first met Marcus, I could tell he would go on to great things," Brad continued. "And so far, he has not disappointed me. Both he and Clarice have exceeded expectations, and I have no doubt they will continue to do so for long into their lives together."

He raised his glass, his face illuminated by the glow of the moment—then froze. Blood trickled from his lips, the vibrant stain spreading across his crisp shirt as the room plunged into chaos.

Brad collapsed to the floor, revealing a knife's hilt protruding from his back. The collective shock of the crowd erupted into a flurry of motion as Zenobia appeared, dagger in hand, her expression sharp with resolve. She moved swiftly toward Rajneel, who stood paralyzed, his eyes wide with fear. Before anyone could react, Zen pressed the bloodied blade against his throat.

The dance floor, which moments ago had been alive with people swaying to DJ Yeti's rhythms, emptied in a flurry of movement. The music halted abruptly, the festival's celebratory energy vanishing in an instant. From near the altar-turned-dance-floor, the horizon's edge glinted ominously as Chet emerged, his smirk as infuriating as ever.

Zen's voice, cold and sharp, sliced through the clamor. "You thought you could hide from us, Rajneel?" Her grip on the knife tightened as she began backing toward the platform's edge, Rajneel trembling under her grasp. Sanjay's furious voice rang out, grief contorting his words into raw accusations.

"You murdered him! Zen, how could you?"

Kiara pushed her way through the crowd, her own voice cutting through the chaos. "Zen, what are you doing?"

Tears streamed down Zen's face as she turned to face them all.

The platform's edge loomed behind her, the abyss a silent reminder of how precariously they all balanced. Rajneel's trembling frame mirrored the tension within the group as the implications of Zen's actions began to sink in. Above it all, the echoes of DJ Yeti's earlier beats seemed to mock the now-broken harmony of the gathering. The wedding, a union meant to symbolize hope and new beginnings, had become the stage for chaos and tragedy.

Sanjay came forward and pleaded with Zen to stop this and to not hurt his brother. She held out her arm, away from Rajneel, letting him go and then handing him the blade, as if she was going to surrender and give up then and there. But that's not what happened at all. A moment later, Sanjay found himself with the knife in his own chest, pierced through the heart by his own brother, who chanted an incantation while slaying his other half, pledging his allegiance to the future god-king. Rajneel's body twisted and contorted, losing all semblance of humanity, mutated into a demonic form, cackling with laughter, his new wings spread, flapping.

Zen didn't wait for the group's judgment. She stepped back, then disappeared into a portal with Chet before anyone could stop her. Moments later, followed by Rajneel.

The reception was left in chaos. Marcus and Clarice's table sat abandoned as Marcus rushed over, his mother close behind. Mallah moved to restore calm, but the damage had been done.

Kiara stood frozen, her hands trembling as the Champions quickly wrapped up both Sanjay and Brad's still-warm bodies lying on the ground. "She was forced to do it," she said quietly, as if convincing herself as much as the others. "Ivyg wanted to remind us that he believes he's still in control, always lingering nearby, always a threat."

Mallah placed a hand on Kiara's shoulder, her presence a grounding force amidst the chaos. "The shadows grow darkest before the dawn," Mallah said softly, her voice steady. "But we must not let this break us. We have seen what we are capable of—together."

As the group began to pick up the pieces of their shattered celebration, the joyous evening gave way to the sobering reality of their fight for survival. The ancient city loomed in the distance, dark and foreboding, a reminder of the challenges still to come.

Kiara's breath steadied as she turned toward the horizon, her sightless eyes fixed with an intensity that seemed to pierce through the darkness itself. "Ivyg wanted us to fear him," she said, her voice firmer now. "But he's the one who should be afraid. We'll rise stronger from this. He'll never see us coming."

Mallah's gaze lingered on Kiara, seeing not just a young woman shaped by loss, but a leader stepping into her own power. As the stars emerged one by one, illuminating the ancient land around them, the Champions stood united, their resolve rekindled.

The night carried on, their grief tempered by determination. They were no longer just survivors. They were the vanguard of something greater—a legacy poised to reclaim the light.